EVERYMAN'S LIBRARY

EVERYMAN,
I WILL GO WITH THEE,
AND BE THY GUIDE,
IN THY MOST NEED
TO GO BY THY SIDE

IVAN TURGENEV

NEST OF THE GENTRY

VIRGIN SOIL

TRANSLATED FROM THE RUSSIAN
BY CONSTANCE GARNETT

WITH AN INTRODUCTION
BY ANDREW KAHN

EVERYMAN'S LIBRARY
Alfred A. Knopf   New York   London

THIS IS A BORZOI BOOK
PUBLISHED BY ALFRED A. KNOPF

First included in Everyman's Library, 1911 (*Virgin Soil*),
1914 (*Nest of the Gentry*)
This translation first published in Everyman's Library, 2026
Introduction copyright © 2026 by Andrew Kahn
Bibliography and Chronology copyright © 2026 by Everyman's Library

Penguin Random House values and supports copyright. Copyright fuels creativity, encourages diverse voices, promotes free speech, and creates a vibrant culture. Thank you for buying an authorized edition of this book and for complying with copyright laws by not reproducing, scanning, or distributing any part of it in any form without permission. You are supporting writers and allowing Penguin Random House to continue to publish books for every reader. Please note that no part of this book may be used or reproduced in any manner for the purpose of training artificial intelligence technologies or systems.

Published in the United States by Alfred A. Knopf, a division of Penguin Random House LLC, 1745 Broadway, New York, NY 10019. Published in the United Kingdom by Everyman's Library, 50 Albemarle Street, London W1S 4BD and distributed by Penguin Random House UK, One Embassy Gardens, 8 Viaduct Gardens, London SW11 7BW.

everymanslibrary.com   penguinrandomhouse.com
www.penguin.co.uk/about/publishing-houses/everyman

ISBN: 979-8-217-00827-8 (US)
978-1-84159-437-8 (UK)

A CIP catalogue reference for this book is available from the British Library

Typography by Peter B. Willberg and James Sutton

Book design by Barbara de Wilde and Carol Devine Carson

Typeset in the UK by Input Data Services Ltd, Bridgwater, Somerset

Printed and bound in Germany by GGP Media GmbH, Pössneck

The authorized representative in the EU for product safety and compliance is Penguin Random House Ireland, Morrison Chambers, 32 Nassau Street, Dublin D02 YH68, Ireland, https://eu-contact.penguin.ie

CONTENTS

Introduction	vii
Note on the Translation	xxxvii
Select Bibliography	xxxix
Chronology	xlii
Names of Characters	lxx
NEST OF THE GENTRY	1
VIRGIN SOIL	187

INTRODUCTION

Ivan Turgenev's mature novels breathe the passions of the day. All eight of his major fictions fold the lives of their characters into the struggle to create a different Russia as the country modernized economically and socially. In the 1850s his subject was the decline of the gentry, the landowning class to which he belonged. *Nest of the Gentry* (1859) glows with a nostalgia for a pastoral Russia. Increasingly from the late 1860s, the prospect of reforms to the tsarist state overtook the question of the land. *Virgin Soil* (1877), his last and longest fiction, understands that in politics idealists may struggle to enact change. From the 1860s literature closely engaged with the increasing discontent that bred new generations of activists. From the soft approaches of populist students who went to the people to the radical actions of militant individuals and groups, all can be found on the pages of fiction of the period. Turgenev, perhaps most and best of all, saw this as an opportunity to capture new character types as new social and historical forces brought them into being. Most of the revolutionaries he portrays lack action plans, but all feel dissatisfaction with tsarism. The question they address repeatedly is: what must they do?

The classic nineteenth-century novel excelled in representing to its immediate readership the fractious spirit of their age. For all Turgenev's satisfyingly detailed grasp of the world he depicts, Henry James esteemed his attentiveness to character even more than to reality. James chose his words carefully when he called Turgenev a 'social' novelist rather than a realist. Turgenev is interested in what his heroes and heroes are like, and no less in what they stand for. In the memorial essay he wrote for the *Atlantic* in 1884, James shared a remark Turgenev made to him: namely, that 'the germ of a story, with him, was never an affair of plot . . . it was the representation of certain persons . . . whom he wished to see in action, being sure that such people must do something very special and interesting'. The remark draws attention to the special quality of the greatest literary characters who embody and transcend types. Turgenev's imagination came to life in fashioning characters who reflected national characteristics – and the nineteenth century loved to categorize this way – and then endowing them with something more universally human. The vision of the relationship between type and subject, or model and hero, is the focus of his celebrated essay 'Hamlet and Don Quixote' (1860). Classic dreamers and vacillators were timeless figures in the history of societies no less than in literature. It took the novelist to select and rework these types to capture their re-emergence in specific historical circumstances.

Turgenev was far too subtle a student of human nature to believe that characters in real life or in literature could ever conform entirely to categorical definitions or plot their lives successfully according to a plan. For one thing, his most poignant and powerful protagonists are usually in a state of becoming and not just being. His power to trace their moral growth through trials and passions, of a personal and social and political kind, is at its finest in *Nest of the Gentry* and *Virgin Soil*. That human capacity his characters display was not a uniform expectation of Russian literary fiction of the time. More tendentious writers such as Nikolai Chernyshevsky believed that the purpose of art was to create models that would transform readers into rational subjects capable of achieving, and living in, utopia. Peter Tkachev, a violence-oriented populist, regarded Chernyshevsky's *What is to be Done?* as the 'gospel of the movement'. Convinced, as was Dostoevsky, that this conceptualization of human nature was grossly reductive, Turgenev attacked it head on in the figure of Bazarov, the hero of *Fathers and Children* (1862), whose attempt to be purely scientific fails when he falls calamitously in love; other novels, including *Nest of the Gentry* and *Virgin Soil*, continue to study the fallibility of emotions and illusions.

A man of liberal mind, Turgenev as a writer had a strong feeling for the value of art as its own creative reality. The French critic Emile Hennequin put it nicely in 1889 when he wrote that Turgenev knew the 'particular individual and not man in general'. His method was to base characters on people he studied. In other words, for all that they serve as representatives of types they can also be remarkably individual and most compelling when struggling to reconcile their commitment to ideals with their personal choices. The all-important larger national

INTRODUCTION

context, its class divisions and inter-generational tensions about serfdom and emancipation, women and education, autocracy and freedom, literature and ideology, is the stuff of their lives and conversations. The roundedness that exceeds type is also an effect of how Turgenev handles individual and group interaction in the prosaic settings of daily life.

Nest of the Gentry

A sketchy idea for a 'long tale' came to Turgenev in 1856, soon set aside because of bouts of illness and work on two of his finest short stories ('Faust' and 'Asya'). In the winter of 1857–8, prompted during a stay in Rome by news that the Russian government intended to promulgate an Emancipation Manifesto to free the serfs, Turgenev resumed work on *Nest of the Gentry*. The novel was published in 1859 in the progressive literary journal, the *Contemporary*. Turgenev had maintained a close working relationship with the *Contemporary* ever since its relaunch in 1847 by the poet Nikolai Nekrasov in close collaboration with the great critic and socialist Vissarion Belinsky (1811–48); this would continue until the journal was closed in 1866 on the personal order of Tsar Alexander II after an assassination attempt on his life. While Turgenev later claimed that the title was imposed on him by Nekrasov, the phrase 'nest of the gentry' in fact first occurs in *A Sportsman's Notebook* (also known as *Sketches from a Hunter's Album*, 1852). From this debut collection of tales, the Russian countryside would remain a constant setting and theme. The son of a landowning mother, notorious for her cruelty to her sons and her serfs, Turgenev knew country life first-hand. Even after he moved abroad for the sake of greater freedom and to live in Paris and Baden-Baden with the opera singer Pauline Viardot and her husband Louis, Turgenev would retreat for long periods at Spasskoe, the estate he inherited in Orel Province in central Russia.

The sympathetic portrayals of peasant types and folk customs brought his first important work, *A Sportsman's Notebook*, popular acclaim. Its unpolitical but poignant treatment of serfdom annoyed critics on the left, outraged conservatives on the right, and earned him a spell of house arrest from the government. The same critical response was destined to be repeated at the end of his career with *Virgin Soil*. From *A Sportsman's Notebook* to his very late 'Portraits of Old' (1881) with its marvellous evocations of the tattered remains of an eighteenth-century period of ascendancy, his fiction dismantled an illusion of the countryside as a timeless agrarian paradise. The literariness of Turgenev's style and his avoidance of the most brutal realism appealed to a middle-class readership both in Russia and abroad in English, French, and German translations. The radical literary press, by contrast, considered that he had forfeited a chance to advocate reform.

Nest of the Gentry deliberately retreated from the present. The action takes place in 1842, more than a decade earlier than the year of its composition. The date suited Turgenev for two reasons. First, it created distance between the current uncertainty about the Emancipation, made the plot contemporary with the Slavophile movement at its height, and captured the countryside at a moment that seemed timeless. Second, when the hero Lavretsky retreats from Europe after the collapse of his marriage, he is also retreating from the burgeoning of liberalism and European progress that would conclude in the failed revolutions of 1848. At a distance, then, from contemporary history and spiritually closer to the world of the landed gentry in the previous century, *Nest of the Gentry* shifts the focus away from the life of the peasantry to the life of the manor house. Both dislocations, that is, the shift from 1858 to 1842 and from the serfs to masters, offer a more detached perspective on the key question of the day: could changes to Russia's serf economy and estates culture bring about renewal, and for whom?

In moving the spotlight onto the masters from the serfs, Turgenev also bucked a trend in the fiction surrounding the Emancipation. In 1854, the literary journalist Pavel Annenkov, author of the first biography of Alexander Pushkin, a highly readable *Literary Reminiscences* and a defender of quality fiction, hoped that the peasant question had run its course in literature. His diagnosis that novels and stories about simple peasant life 'were not destined to develop and make progress' after Dmitry Grigorovich's *The Village* (1846), a landmark of brutal depiction, was

INTRODUCTION

wide of the mark. The work of so-called 'plebeian' novelists like Nikolai Pomyalovsky and Fedor Reshetnikov enjoyed a substantial readership. The latter's *Where is Better?*, published in 1868, four years after the founding of the First International, seemed a harbinger of the agrarian socialism that would soon gain traction and bring the urban intelligentsia to the people. Works of this kind focused relentlessly on the squalor of the village. To the dismay of leading socialist thinkers like Chernyshevsky and Alexander Herzen, they also illustrated the deep-rooted aversion of the peasantry to reform.

One question posed by *Nest of the Gentry* concerns incentive and motivation. Why would the owner of a country estate return to dwell on the land rather than collect rent and live in the city (like Ivan Goncharov's Oblomov, a byword for the superannuated landowner)? In *Nest of the Gentry*, answers are wrapped up in a plot about the search for love. Here, as in *Fathers and Children* and *Virgin Soil*, alongside the public energy for reform there is a private desire for lasting relationships. It is characteristic of Turgenev to use an emotional plot to humanize the quest for each ideal and to ennoble the private dimension with a vision for national renewal. These dreams of renewal are juxtaposed with a conservative reality dominated by a claustrophobic interiority captured in the description (Chapter XVII) of Marfa Timofeyevna's rooms, and a religious devotion. For her, even drinking tea is an indulgence. Nonetheless, Lavretsky succeeds at working the land more productively, hailed at the end as 'an excellent farmer' who had improved the welfare of the peasants. Spiritually, however, he is old before his time, and while Marfa Timofeyevna only means to chide him when she claims he has come back to Russia not to farm but to chase women, the quest for love is part of his vision of a country idyll. He suffers two setbacks when the report of his wife's sudden death abroad turns out to be false and his new love Lisa, recoiling from the situation, decides on a spiritual life. No one is lightly let off in Turgenev's novels. The failures of the heart must be paid for here. Having a bad time romantically cannot be cured by taking refuge in an outdated Slavophile rural idyll; and we see this again in *Virgin Soil*, when Nezhdanov's high-flown thoughts of freedom end in chaos and ruin. The characters who survive best spiritually, including Lisa, Marianna and Solomin, follow their moral imperatives and find redemption through religion and revolution.

To see what forces condition these predicaments is a matter of understanding how character develops from a kernel of personality, background, and family history set out early on. The whole book could be compared to a symphony with a perfect development over four movements and an epilogue (as a coda). Chapters I to VII present the Kalitin household and the arrival of Lavretsky. Chapters VIII to XIII digress onto Lavretsky's ancestors and his biography. Rolled into one consecutive set of stories is a historical chronicle of distant forebears, a picaresque history of Lavretsky's father, and a *bildungsroman* about the growth of the hero's sensibility. This section takes the still innocent Lavretsky, a naïf, to the theatre in St Petersburg and the *coup de foudre* when he lays eyes on the glamorous Varvara. Chapters XIV to XXXV extend and wrap up the marriage plot, leading to Lavretsky's return to Russia and search for rebirth, a reintroduction of the Kalitin household, the hero's journey into the countryside and the re-encounter with his homeland and with Lisa, culminating with Lisa's brief biography and their embrace in the garden, after which an unravelling ensues from a turning point in Chapter XXXVI until the final Chapter XLV. Inevitably, the development of the emotional plot and personal stories requires these longer parts, which unwind conclusively in much swifter moments concentrated at the end. With a symmetry that looks like fate, the final three chapters circle back to these longer movements. In Chapter XLIII, Marya Dmitrievna, a force for propriety over love, announces to Lavretsky that his estranged 'wife has come'. This is in effect old news since the unexpected return of his adulterous wife Varvara – from the dead as much as from Europe – was announced earlier in Chapter XXXVI. However, it takes the ensuing period for the full effect of the calamity to sink in. The epilogue brings the novel and Lavretsky and Lisa's love to a point of closure on a note of *smirenie*, that classic state in Turgenev of resignation and renunciation. At the same time, Panshin re-emerges, this time as Varvara's admirer. The pairing off of these two frivolous and heartless characters only ennobles the bitter sacrifice of Lisa, over which for the one

INTRODUCTION

and only time in the novel the imperturbable Marfa Timofyevna weeps bitterly (Chapter XLV).

Both novels published in this edition establish the primacy of character in the way they make use of their initial chapters. *Nest of the Gentry* perhaps best of all his major fictions uses the early chapters to set up characters and the fundamental dilemmas that will be worked out, or left unresolved, in the rest of the novel. Turgenev loved amateur theatricals and while his own plays only ever achieved lukewarm critical success, his craft is evident in the first seven chapters of *Nest of the Gentry*. They choreograph introductions and back stories with great skill, establishing family groups and friendships and anticipating appearances. By establishing personalities, professions, and vocations, the process makes characters free to touch on themes that are part of the world of the novel such as poetry and music, to drop into their exchanges information about estate management and marriage that will help drive the plot. This is the nest out of which will emerge Lavretsky's search for personal redemption from the flawed marriage to Varvara by loving Lisa. The present plot is framed, however, in a narrative that involves events from history, writing the story of the landed gentry through the account of the changing sensibilities and attitudes to education of generations of Lavretsky's family, with excursions into the tension between European travel and Russian inwardness, modern life as consumption and patriarchal life as subsistence, renewal and decay. Lavretsky's quest for personal happiness is bound up in his attempt to restore his estates.

As the novel begins, Marya Dmitrievna, the mother of Lisa, and the elderly Marfa Timofyevna, Marya Dmitrievna's aunt, are shown seated at an open window, a typical framing device. As they chat, they mention Fedor Ivanich Lavretsky and his disastrous marriage. New characters are introduced chapter by chapter. By Chapter IV, Panshin and Lemm have made their entrances, the first as a lightweight poet and careerist civil servant, the second as a music teacher and lofty Romantic. When Lisa arrives at the end of Chapter III, she becomes embroiled in conversation with Panshin. The contrast between her reticence and his bumptiousness is important in establishing their characters; it also sets up Panshin as a foil to the music master

IVAN TURGENEV

Lemm, a genuine artist unlike this sham poet, and as a potential love rival to Lavretsky. Readers of classic Russian literature would be right to find in this scene echoes of Pushkin's *Eugene Onegin*, the initial appearance in Chapter 2 of the arch-Romantic poet Lensky and the bashful, bookish heroine Tatyana. While Panshin proves too worldly to be a new Lensky, the comparison between Tatyana and Lisa turns out to be sustainable. By the second half of the nineteenth century Pushkin's heroine had become a model for the representation of Russian womanhood, revered as pure of heart and noble of intention, qualities that Lisa will acquire over the course of the novel.

Once Lavretsky finally makes his appearance in Chapter VII, the next chapters expand on the history of his marriage, foreshadowed by the scandalous gossip Marya and Sergei Gedeonovsky (the first guest to arrive) have exchanged earlier. In the fiction of his middle period, of which *Nest of the Gentry* is a prime example, the disenchantments of love shape Turgenev's plots, and his heroes – examples of the legendary 'superfluous man' of Russian literature, to which Turgenev had given a name in a story of 1852 – suffer from a failure of nerve. Lavretsky is a near neighbour to Lisa – as was the Byronic Onegin to Tatyana – and while he exudes disenchantment, he is a more positive character than his avatar. For one thing, Lavretsky is a man of action, and his strapping appearance juxtaposes him with Panshin as a man of action; he also turns out to be sensitive and musical. The story of Lavretsky's childhood and education place the development of his sensibility in the context of a family chronicle that is also a short history of the culture of the gentry from the eighteenth century. The history of the gentry as a class was very much on Turgenev's radar during these years. The teaching of academic history had finally become established in the two major universities. Amateur historical societies published a massive amount of family papers and archival holdings in the pages of journals like *Russian Antiquity* and the *Russian Archive*. For the older elites, the history of the nation was inseparable from the history of gentry families. The reign of Catherine the Great was viewed nostalgically as a golden age. In 1785, the monarch freed the gentry from their service role within the civil bureaucracy, enabling them to live on their estates, cultivate the land and

INTRODUCTION

continue their path towards Europeanization culturally. The account *Nest of the Gentry* gives of the assimilation of Western manners rings true. At their most provincial, attempts were half-baked and scions of the gentry were always prone to trying eccentric educational experiments on their young, inspired by love of the Ancients and their moral code, or a patchy grasp of the French *philosophes*.

By the time we reach Lavretsky's generation, torpor and underinvestment had already contributed to the economic decline of the landowning class, a trajectory that was only exacerbated after 1861. While estate owners might try to implement economic reforms, what use could their reading of Plutarch and their admiration of Sparta be in the vast, sprawling Russian countryside? Lavretsky as a product of this cultural synthesis, or confusion, is the answer. Underlying his evident polish, the Lavretsky we meet has the appearance of a Russian folk hero, the *bogatyr*.

Lavretsky certainly did not look like the victim of fate. His rosy-cheeked typical Russian face, with its large white brow, rather thick nose, and wide straight lips seemed breathing with the wild health of the steppes, with vigorous primaeval energy. He was splendidly well-built, and his fair curly hair stood up on his head like a boy's. It was only in his blue eyes, with their overhanging brows and somewhat fixed look, that one could trace an expression, not exactly of melancholy, nor exactly of weariness, and his voice had almost too measured a cadence.

Whether his Spartan outlook or a Russian temperament define his character, his directness of manner and sense of moral rightness are attributed by others to his peasant mother (emphasizing spiritual kinship with Marfa Timofyevna, a distant cousin on his father's side, who, we are told, 'for ten whole years lived in a smoky peasants' hut'). Lavretsky himself recalls that his maternal grandfather was a 'peasant man' (*muzhik*). A figure of fierce gypsy power, his aunt Glafira, who raises him and for many years manages the property on his behalf, provides a further contrast to the imperfectly Europeanized males. When he returns after her death, he chooses to live at her smaller estate of Vassilyevskoe rather than his main estate at Lavriky, perhaps a way psychologically of embedding himself again in the nest of the gentry. Her example of domestic control, vested in Christian charity to mendicants and the routines of serf ownership, is salient as an example of the powers that defy modernizing. Capable of restraint and resignation, Lavretsky is temperamentally not built to push forward. In *Nest of the Gentry*, Russian history, as Jane Costlow eloquently observes, remains cyclical rather than progressive and all 'apparent movement forward' masks a return.* Lavretsky's name derives from the word 'laurel', Turgenev thus associating him with the natural world and growth, consistent with the pastoral vision he shares with Slavophile thinkers. Yet the plot hardly rewards him with a crown of laurels.

If Lavretsky is one of nature's Hamlets (as well as being, as noted, a man of action), the novel brings him into contact with Quixotes like Mihalevitch and the German music master Christopher Lemm (himself sometimes a Hamlet), each of whom speaks for ideals. An old university friend, Mihalevitch is both a genuine poet and an intellectual. When seen from the perspective of Turgenev's first readers on publication, the stormy debates in Chapter XXV would have given some distance on an 1840s preoccupation with Russia's identity that looked dated even a decade later. Even within a single generation, a gap had opened up between progressive intellectual ideals, voiced by Mihalevitch, and the Slavophile view that informs Lavretsky's attitudes. A figure like Mihalevitch as a believer that progress is inherent in History anticipates the more radical socialist and Marxist beliefs of the 1870s, ideals that reappear in *Virgin Soil*. In the passage below he takes issue with the romantic Slavophile belief dominant from the 1820s to the 1840s that Russia was on its own separate path away from industrialization and inspired by peasant institutions. A typical figure of the post-Decembrist generation, as a university student in the 1830s Mihalevitch absorbed the ideals of the Young Hegelians, and he speaks in the phraseology of his educated class.

---

* Jane Costlow, *Worlds Within Worlds: The Novels of Ivan Turgenev* (Princeton, NJ: Princeton University Press, 1990), p.64.

INTRODUCTION

'But what is all this abuse about?' Lavretsky clamoured in his turn. 'Work – doing – you'd better say what is to be done, instead of abusing me, Desmosthenes of Poltava!'

'There, what a thing to ask! I can't tell you that, brother; that, every one ought to know for himself,' retorted the Desmosthenes ironically. 'A landowner, a nobleman, and not know what to do? You have no faith, or else you would know; no faith – and no intuition.'

'Let me at least have time to breathe; you don't let me have time to look round,' Lavretsky besought him.

'Not a minute, nor a second!' retorted Mihalevitch with an imperious wave of the hand. 'Not one second: death does not delay, and life ought not to delay.'

'And what a time, what a place for men to think of loafing!' he cried at four o'clock, in a voice, however, which showed signs of sleepiness; 'among us! now! in Russia where every separate individuality has a duty resting upon him, a solemn responsibility to God, to the people, to himself. We are sleeping, and the time is slipping away; we are sleeping.' . . .

'Permit me to observe,' remarked Lavretsky, 'that we are not sleeping at present, but rather preventing others from sleeping. We are straining our throats like the cocks – listen! there is one crowing for the third time.'

This sally made Mihalevitch laugh, and calmed him down. 'Goodbye till to-morrow,' he said with a smile, and thrust his pipe into his pouch.

'Till to-morrow,' repeated Lavretsky. But the friends talked for more than an hour longer. Their voices were no longer raised, however, and their talk was quiet, sad, friendly talk.

Lavretsky does look wrong-footed here. His reasons may well be admirable, but he is out of step with his generation. Unlike Mihalevitch, he sees no reason to trust abstract laws of history as guarantees of the progress that will eliminate serfdom; nor does he succumb to the despair that drives reformers: ' "Are pessimists usually like this?" replied Lavretsky. "They are usually all pale and sickly – would you like me to lift you with one hand?" ' But the attitude comes with the risk of passivity. As he departs, proclaiming a holy trinity to his friend of 'religion, progress, humanity', Mihalevitch admonishes him to be more vigorous in 'sowing the seeds of future prosperity'.

As a returning native, Lavretsky expects to reconstitute his nest and finds himself no less alienated than Lemm, an émigré. In fact, Lavretsky and Lemm are both dreamers: Russia represents for Lavretsky's soul what musical harmony means to Lemm. Yet the reader will note how often shades of sadness characterize his state of mind: when returning briefly to Vassilyevskoe from his house in town (Chapter XXXVI) he is beset by a 'melancholy mood' (in the original the word is simply 'sadness'), and even at the end, he achieves a stoic poise about age and lost youth: 'his heart was sad, but not weighed down, nor bitter; much there was to regret, nothing to be ashamed of'. Lisa and Lemm can find harmony and escape in religion and music. That realm of the 'pure stars' is only partly open to Lavretsky. Inertia proves a dogged obstacle, something to which other Russian protagonists like Oblomov succumb. Figures like Levin in *Anna Karenina* who actually manage to change agrarian practices are unusual. The counter-example of Tolstoy is germane here, since it has even been suggested that in writing Lavretsky's biography, Turgenev borrowed from Tolstoy's life, aware that from around 1857, Tolstoy, with whom his friendship was always strained, began his own efforts to reform his estate. In the fiction of his middle period, of which *Nest of the Gentry* is a prime example, the disenchantments of love are symptomatic of a superfluousness that crystallized as a type. While Lavretsky is left with a ruined marriage, Lisa can dedicate herself to a selfless devotion to a love that cannot be realized. Yet a common element they now share is precisely that feeling of bitterness:

Marfa Timofyevna went off, and Lisa sat down in a corner and began to cry. There was bitterness in her soul. She had not deserved such humiliation. Love had proved no happiness to her: she was weeping for a second time since yesterday evening. This new unexpected feeling had only just arisen in her heart, and already what a heavy price she had paid for it, how coarsely had strange hands touched her sacred secret. She felt ashamed, and bitter, and sick; but she had no doubt and no dread – and Lavretsky was dearer to her than ever. She had hesitated while she did not understand herself; but after that meeting, after that kiss – she could hesitate no more: she knew that she loved, and now she loved honestly and seriously, she was bound firmly for all her life, and she did not fear reproaches. She felt that by no violence could they break that bond.

INTRODUCTION

If renewal will not come from love, can Lavretsky find solace in his agricultural project? Insofar as the novel departs strikingly from *A Sportsman's Notebook* by underplaying attention to the rural serf economy, this is consistent with its purpose as an obliquely affectionate critique of the dream that landowners could bring about national renewal. The idea that both the peasant population and the gentry inhabited an unchanging pastoral realm was central to Slavophile beliefs, one of the main trends in Russian thought often juxtaposed with or plainly opposed to a more Europeanizing outlook. Slavophile thought was a form of Romantic nationalism that mythologized the connection between landowners, the peasantry, and the land. It assumed that a balance could be achieved between man and nature, idealizing a conservative vision of subsistence for the peasantry and landowners, and painted a life made up of hunting, fishing, shooting, and less exploitative agricultural labour. Turgenev's nests of the gentry, however, hardly contains the seeds of future renewal and they lead to Chekhov's *Cherry Orchard* (1904) almost fifty years later.

Yet even when read as a deconstruction of a certain myth of Russia, it is impossible to dismiss the beauty of the landscape descriptions, close studies of the ecology of the countryside and its wildlife that have rightly been praised for their lyricism and sometimes pantheistic sense of nature as full of divine mystery. The Russian satirist M. E. Saltykov-Schedrin, who hardly ever saw the brighter side of human nature, much less the Russian character, responded rapturously when he first read *Nest of the Gentry*: 'It has been a long time since I have been so astonished by the luminous poetry suffusing every sound in this novel [. . .] and in general what can one say about Turgenev's works? Perhaps that after reading them one breathes more readily, one has greater faith, one feels more warmly?' That sense of a mind able to encompass feeling, belief, and moral states at a higher level, and doing so in 'transparent images seemingly woven from air' is one source of the spell Turgenev continues to cast on readers. This is close to what Flaubert experienced as 'a charming sadness that penetrates my soul to the depth'.

Nest of the Gentry belongs to a generation of fiction conceived in the transition from serfdom to a new economy. The question of what changes to Russia's land economy portended for the nation's renewal had been deferred for generations from the 1780s. When it finally came to a head nearly a century later the economic model was not fit for purpose. The gentry were left poorer and the new tenancy arrangements provided little more than subsistence for the peasantry. Even as he kept one eye on the gentry class, Turgenev maintained his gaze on movements spearheaded by populist and radical political action. He represented them in *Virgin Soil*. It would be misleading to think the title promises another book about working the actual land. The virgin soil is the country of the future to be achieved through more drastic action, if the conspirators of Turgenev's final novel are to be trusted.

Virgin Soil

In *Virgin Soil* (1877), Turgenev arguably fulfilled his promise as the foremost Russian political novelist of the nineteenth century, an influence on Henry James in *The Princess Casamassima* (1885–6) and the equal of Dostoevsky in *The Demons* (1871–2) and Conrad as the author of *Under Western Eyes* (1911). *Virgin Soil* is a study of a generation in political ferment, examining from the inside how a small group of well-educated young men and women conspire to cause unrest. *Nest of the Gentry* takes up the gradualist, reformist trajectory launched by *A Sportsman's Notebook*. Other novels, extending from *Rudin* (1856) to *Virgin Soil*, engaged with Russian radical thought and movements as they became increasingly volatile and, by the 1870s, violent. *Rudin* fared poorly with the critics. Even a death on the barricades in Paris in 1848 could not redeem the uncharismatic title character. Much more successful with readers was *Fathers and Children*, whose hero, the physician Yevgeny Bazarov, a man of the people, attained a level of tragic pathos not granted to Rudin. To the chagrin of his critics, Turgenev still refused to provide a positive hero fit for their political requirements. Over a decade later, and at a time when peasant rebellions were rife, *Virgin Soil* suggests that the seeds of revolution are finally taking root. It is a timely stroke on Turgenev's part that the novel creates its

INTRODUCTION

drama around the uncertainty about the means for revolutionary ends.

He claimed that the idea for the new novel first came to him in 1870 when he jotted down the phrase 'Romantics of realism: the Russian revolutionary'. Turgenev's detractors regularly and wrongly accused him of being out of touch because he lived abroad. In fact, he paid lengthy visits to St Petersburg and Moscow, still networking with prominent editors such as Mikhail Stasyulevich, who ran *The Herald of Europe*, the liberal journal in which he serialized *Virgin Soil* over two issues in 1877 before its publication in book form later in the year. He spent extended periods on his estate Spasskoe in Orel Province in the 1870s. On these trips, and after publishing *Spring Torrents* (1872), that work being a return to the theme of ill-starred love, he gathered materials. Thinking about the new idea, he confided to a friend that he still had 'something to say' but had not yet 'worked out all the dance moves'. An avid reader of the foreign and Russian press, Turgenev knew about the peasant uprisings that were widespread in certain regions in the 1860s. By the 1870s, especially in the south, rebels (made up of intellectuals and revolutionaries), even with scant resources, explored the possibility of orchestrating more local regional peasant uprisings, following the Bakuninist idea that even small revolts that were quickly crushed nonetheless provided a way to educate the peasants. Turgenev was especially well informed about the inevitable prosecutions and trials, since he counted leading defence lawyers among his acquaintance. In addition, he was well versed in the various radical ideologies, material that directly informs the different revolutionary tactics the conspirators of *Virgin Soil* adopt. Foremost among these figures, and most relevant to this novel, were Peter Tkachev and his antagonist Peter Lavrov, the latter a correspondent when Turgenev was drafting the novel.

Superfluous men (rarely women) came in different degrees of futility and included the disenchanted (Pushkin's Eugene Onegin), the fallen angel (Lermontov's Demon), sometimes the merely passive (Oblomov) or deeply alienated (Dostoevsky's Underground Man), or the idealistic (Rudin), and all were generally paralysed by pessimism. Turgenev's third novel was the political story *On the Eve* (1860). It followed a Bulgarian (rather than Russian) revolutionary and his Russian lover into the misfortunes of war in the Balkans. In a review that became a landmark in the history of Russian literature, Nikolai Dobrolyubov asked 'When Will the Real Day Come?' He was only one of a vociferous band of journalists on the left whose vision of literature was programmatic, assigning to the novel as a genre a didactic role in educating a new readership in modern values that were essentially anti-authoritarian, anti-serfdom, anti-clerical – and to a large degree anti-art. For Dobrolyubov, *On the Eve* failed because the protagonists were not worthy role models; and its lamentation of Insarov as a latter-day Tristan, another important archetypal hero for Turgenev, was defeatist. Love was simply the wrong transcendent ideal.

By the late 1860s, a different chapter on superfluousness had begun. The new emphasis shifted away from passivity to active resistance even at the cost of failure. The question critics aimed at Turgenev was when would his protagonists flip from pathetic to admirable. The question clearly haunted Turgenev. Readers of *Virgin Soil* may note appreciatively that in response to Dobrulyubov Turgenev claimed the last word here in a way that mixes pragmatism and irony. With ostensible affection, Marianna shows her interest in Nezhdanov by reading his manuscript book. She turns out to be 'a severe critic' and does not spare him. Insofar as she likes his verse, she feels approval only for the non-didactic and therefore unpolitical work. Her taste turns out to be an intuition about his suitability as a radical. She asks whether he knows a poem of Dobrolyubov that she particularly likes – 'Let me die – small call for grief', commenting that Dobrolyubov's verse is 'not poetry . . . though it's something as good'. While she acknowledges that 'one ought to write poems like Pushkin's' there is another kind of poetry that suits their times because it will provide the clichés by which radicals will mourn fallen comrades like Markelov and indeed Nezhdanov – and these sentiments are to be found in Dobrolyubov rather than in Nezhdanov's poetry. In the debate between art and politics (much discussed earlier in *Fathers and Children*), Turgenev hands Marianna the right to commit to political art whose emotional value is defined by a cause. But whereas *On the Eve* and *Fathers and Children* intimated that the answer to Dobrolyubov's question was far off, *Virgin Soil* captures a transition in progress from a social welfare style of populism to radicalism.

The novel's first critics regarded the ambivalent ending as a sign of Turgenev's defeatism. Among detractors, Nikolai Mikhailovsky a prominent critic of nationalist views, felt that Turgenev had lost his earlier and unique capacity to 'quickly catch and wrap in artistic form trends as they came into being'; while even more hostile critics lamented the work's 'false ideas, useless heroes and Russian types' who are 'so trivial, small scale, too stupid to have any political character and unworthy of consideration as social phenomena' – or, in the words of another journal, 'children playing at revolution'. Among his defenders was Annenkov, once again. Writing in the *Russian Herald*, a liberal journal, he hailed the novel as a return to form after the failure of *Smoke*:

It has been a long time since I've experienced what I felt when reading *Virgin Soil*. It's not just a matter of the burning interest, the broad picture of manners that it unfolds, the endless mastery with which the author approaches each figure in the novel. But rather when you read *Virgin Soil* on every page it's as though the words kindle into flame [. . .] Indeed, our public has practically forgotten the times when a novel constituted an event, compelled everyone to talk about it, to clash and to swear to themselves: *Virgin Soil* is destined to bring back these times.

Abroad, Flaubert was bowled over by the French translation of *Virgin Soil*. Aware that Turgenev's reception in Russia was always a politically charged affair, he aimed a salvo at any ungrateful Russians who failed to appreciate the book as 'a marvel', claiming hyperbolically that it had purged his brain of everything else he had read: 'What a painter, and what a moralist you are, my dear, my dear friend!' In Russia, the critics were soon overtaken by events – and made to eat their words. In February 1877 the government brought to public trial a large number of young subversives. The Trial of the Fifty seemed to come straight off the pages of *Virgin Soil*. The similarities were not lost on the public. For instance, Vsevolod Garshin, acclaimed later in the same year as the author of psychologically penetrating short fictions, spoke for many in a letter to his mother: 'Ivan Sergeevich [Turgenev] in his dotage has completely shaken off his old age. What a wonder! I only fail to understand how he managed while living outside Russia so brilliantly to divine this entire situation.' The conclusion that life was imitating art even inspired some critics to say that the novel would have been regarded as a rip-off had it appeared after the judicial proceedings. Now the consensus was that Turgenev had brilliantly portrayed a generation of Hamlet-types, resolved to act but confused about quite what to do (and it has to be noted that late in *Virgin Soil* Nezhdanov in a long letter to a friend dismisses Hamlets and superfluous people as relics of the previous generation). In a piece published in the *Athenaeum*, no less an expert than the radical activist Lavrov commented that the 'Mashurinas, Ostrodumovs, and Nezhdanovs' and 'Solomins, Markelovs and Mariannas' represented a 'new higher morality immune to egoism and personal gain and ready to sacrifice themselves for others'.

Conservative readers accused Turgenev of overt bias by stacking the ranks of the progressives with the novel's most attractive characters in *Virgin Soil*. The Sipyagins, husband and wife, are perhaps more postures than people, and even among their own family members (Anna Zaharovna and Kolya seem innocent of these faults) they stand out as arriviste by inclination and constitutionally hypocritical. Their hypocritical attitudes do give them some life; but what are we to say of the intemperate and reactionary Kallomyetsev whose class-solidarity looks like hysterical cowardice? Yet the dissidents hardly redeem themselves. Whereas *Nest of the Gentry* marginalizes other characters to focus on Lisa and Lavretsky (the 'nesting' plot overshadowing the 'gentry' plot), in *Virgin Soil* the revolutionaries drop out of sight for long periods while the Sipyagins are highly visible for as long as the action is set in their house. When they do appear, the conspirators are a motley group and typically inept. This is the reality we find depicted satirically when Markelov and Nezhdanov attempt to muster support in countryside in decline from the time of *Nest of the Gentry*. The wealthy businessman Golushkin, whose name may derive from the word meaning 'naked', is straight off the pages of Gogol's *Dead Souls*, a gluttonous, avaricious, and loquacious figure. Hardly more promising in revolutionary terms are the comically bizarre

INTRODUCTION

elderly couple, the Subotchevs. As Paklin says, 'We have been in the eighteenth century!' This, too, is the world of Gogolian impoverished small landowners, highly reminiscent of characters like Dobchinsky and Bobchinsky (whose comic names are a model for Fomushka and Fimushka) in *The Inspector General* for whom the world outside their home, village, and province seems impossibly remote and modern. Marianna and Solomin pull away from these types as they strive toward new political consciousness.

Much of the novel charts the growing gap between characters who discover their true revolutionary mettle (Markelov, Marianna, Solomin) and laggards (Paklin, Nezhdanov). Political energy does not necessarily belong to the most obvious participants. Here Turgenev's technique of foregrounding the characters at the start is very much to the point. Consider the first glimpse we have of Paklin, an ineffectual conspirator who is always just too late and unimposing:

It was a little round head with rough black hair, a broad, wrinkled forehead, very keen, little brown eyes under bushy eyebrows, a nose pointing in the air like a duck's, and a tiny, rosy, comical mouth. This head took a look round, nodded, smiled – showing a number of tiny white teeth – and came into the room, accompanied by its rickety little body, short arms, and somewhat bandy and lame little legs. Directly Mashurina and Ostrodumov caught sight of this head, the faces of both expressed a sort of condescending contempt, as though each of them were inwardly saying, 'Oh! It's only he!' and they did not utter a single word, did not stir a muscle. However, the reception accorded him not only failed to embarrass the visitor, but apparently afforded him positive gratification.

'What's the meaning of this? 'he said in a squeaky voice. 'A duet?' Why not a trio?' And where's the first tenor?'

'Do you mean to inquire after Nezhdanov, Mr Paklin?' replied Ostrodumov with a serious face.

In his sporadic appearances, Paklin is the voice of caution and in that respect has an advantage in encouraging the hesitant Solomin. Like Mihalevitch and Lemm in *Nest of the Gentry*, his role is to connect characters, prompting comment and triggering action, such as the arrival of Nezhdanov. That name has been devised to convey disappointment, since it derives from the Russian meaning 'unexpected' and 'unreliable'. While his arrival is certainly expected, the question of whether he is unreliable in terms of the revolutionary plot remains to be answered. None of this at the start, however, gives much confidence that any of these figures are doing more than playing a part. The collapse of Nezhdanov's mission seems predictable based on the interpersonal and group dynamic which gives the novel's opening pages a bohemian atmosphere. Mashurina and Ostrodumov ('Sharpthinker') come across like pantomime conspirators in love with the cloak-and-dagger aspect of their clandestine lives. If the precise goals of the conspiracy remain unclear – and Turgenev well knew the factional differences that separated anarchists, socialists, terrorists – perhaps it is because activity for its own sake matters most to this initial group. From the start subversion looks more about behaving conspiratorially – it is entirely performative. In the absence of a precise common goal, bravado quickly gives way to backbiting. Turgenev exposes the visceral dislike Mashurina and Ostrodumov feel for Paklin, which bodes ill for their effectiveness as a group. When she departs for Geneva, a hub for radicals across Europe, it is questionable whether Mashurina genuinely carries with her the potential for future action. Eighteen months later we find her back in Russia in the last chapter, still masquerading as an Italian countess. The farcical, even operatic element robs her group of the kind of menace to be found in the conspirators treated brilliantly in Conrad's *Under Western Eyes*. Do any of the conspirators actually know what they want to achieve?

Still, where there are conspirators there must be a conspiracy. The early chapters do what is required to plant Nezhdanov with a landed family. The home of the Sipyagins will provide their base to form a revolutionary cell with the purpose of stirring unrest in the countryside. It is a proof of Turgenev's undiminished talent as a social novelist that this environment becomes the setting for a domestic drama filled with political and family tensions, eventually determining how the characters act on their personal feelings and on their political convictions. When Paklin and Mashurina return at the end, the effect is more than a circling back to the opening chapter, since Marianna and Solomin

INTRODUCTION

are now in the vanguard, meant to lead them into a radiant future envisaged beyond the end of the novel.

Virgin Soil engineers turning points through group scenes, consistent with the way the plot works through the family and radicals as collective units. A key example is at the beginning of Part II (Chapters XXIII and XXIV) when Solomin is introduced to the Sipyagins, first visiting their factory, then joining them for dinner. The question is whether Sipyagin will succeed in enlisting Solomin to work for him. Turgenev is habitually drawn to intra- and inter-generational contrasting pairs. In *Fathers and Children* he juxtaposes the young student friends Arkady and Bazarov with Arkady's uncle and father – the men of the 1860s with the men of the 1840s, resonant historical categories at the time. But within the younger generation the contrast between the two students, also juxtaposing heart and mind, looks similar to the opposition of Lavretsky and Panshin. Further along, Sipyagin and Solomin demonstrate the widening gulf between a member of the gentry representing the owners of capital (with social pretensions based on his land ownership) and a factory manager, standing for the educated progeny of the clergy whose upward mobility into the ranks of government, university education, and commerce had an effect on the social structure of the country. Who will be the new man of the future? Sipyagin is shown wanting because he is aloof from both peasants and workers; more egregiously, his social prejudices blind him to Solomin's ability to mediate between the owners of capital and their employees, and to act as a force of moderation. These character flaws in fact are the basis of a resemblance between him and Nezhdanov who proves no less inept as a revolutionary than Sipyagin is as a manager. Just as Solomin will come to overshadow Sipyagin and gain in stature, Marianna will also develop by shedding her pretensions and become more secure in her own identity as a class warrior rather than a pretend peasant.

The portrait of Solomin shows a man of routine ('his life began to turn round again, like a huge fly-wheel'), capturing him on his morning rounds in the factory, amidst factory workers who show him deference out of genuine respect for his ability, noting his 'unusually good' relations with these employees, his knowledge of English and familiarity with English manufacturing (British and Russian trade relations grew hugely in the period), and his mateyness with Pavel, a clever, literate, peasant type embodying native wit. If Solomin is upwardly mobile, he owes his advancement not to his work for the government (like Panshin) but rather to his technical ability. He is the Russian heir to the figure of the dynamic German regularly contrasted with disorderly Russians (readers of Goncharov and Leskov will remember the contrast between Stoltz and the hero in *Oblomov*, and Hugo Pectoralis in the story 'An Iron Will'). As a nationalist, Sipyagin is happy to abuse 'Germans in general', and in his snobbery he fails to recognize that even he needs to get the workers on side. The basis of the mutual antagonism between Sipyagin and the workers, including Solomin, has an element of class critique. No fool, Sipyagin has a grasp of the real problems of cost and productivity that landowners, capitalists, and manufacturers faced as a result of the unsatisfactory conditions of the Emancipation. Solomin gives no quarter because nothing in Sipyagin's factory persuades him that the gentry have the qualifications, either technical or personal, to run industry. Their discord is cemented by Kallomyetsev, a loudmouth and far worse version of the Panshin type, who is always the first to react from a reflexive class hostility. He speaks for both Sipyagin and his wife when he calls Solomin a nihilist in private to Madame Sipyagin. While this is completely inaccurate it is the sort of comment that nudges Solomin off the fence.

Despite the setback at the inspection of the factory, Sipyagin persists in his wooing of Solomin over dinner. So much of the social tension and comedy resides in the handling of details including forms of address, what people smoke, what they say or their silences. Even before the scene itself, Turgenev anticipates awkwardness. In the brief interlude between the factory tour and dinner, Sipyagin and his wife Valentina Mihalovna have a chat. When she questions whether Solomin's engineering skills in managing a textile plant are transferrable to a paper factory, he replies derogatorily, 'There's machinery in the one and machinery in the other – and he's a mechanician.' Earlier the same day his introductory letter to Solomin with its armorial crest had been delivered by a lackey driven in a smart open carriage, and received by Solomin at his factory wearing a modest, stained workers' jacket. Dangling the privilege of the social occasion, Sipyagin comes off as high-handed despite trying to sound casual (' "I hope you will not refuse to dine with me quite simply – not evening dress." (The words "quite simply" were underlined.') Cast as an invitation, it seems more like a summons and exudes literally 'some sort of English stench' while reeking, metaphorically, of pomposity. When Solomin arrives at their house the Sipyagins mangle his actual name (the patronymic is 'Fedotitch' from the name 'Fedoty' and not 'Fedosyevitch' from the name 'Feodosy'). He corrects them immediately. In both locations he remains self-possessed. Sipyagin's liberal affectations and genialness are only skin deep. Always attentive to looks and gestures, Turgenev follows Sipyagin's body language closely; it is the key to his character. For instance, while he allows an 'half-blind old nurse' to kiss his hand when he retires for the evening, he kisses the hands of his wife when he is fresh from his toilette. On his estate his lord-of-the-manor attitudinizing is caricatured, and he appears in a critical light in comparison with the favourable characterization of Solomin and his easy-going manner with his workpeople.

The dinner scene sizzles with social satire and simmers with hatreds. Overtly, all is *comme il faut* at a table featuring a printed menu, linen napkins, and household staff. The seating plan seems devised by the hosts to minimize conflict but also is cleverly arranged to afford the right sightlines. Marianna's meaningful glances convey encouragement to Solomin. As hosts, Valentina Mihalovna and Sipyagin are seated on opposite sides of the table, diagonally across from one another, as are Kallomyetsev and Nezhdanov (who can be left to chat with the innocuous Anna Zaharovna). Solomin and Marianna are at opposite ends of the table, facing one another. There is a strategy in this *placement* since the hosts, who have asked Kallomyetsev to keep his opinions to himself, box him in; and he is a buffer between Madame Sipyagin and Marianna whose mutual antipathy increases. As Marianna and Solomin exchange glances across the table and conceive their mutual attraction, the family and conspiratorial plots intersect. It is not accidental that Solomin's name and moderation carry the name of the biblical king. But the personal genuinely is the political, and the attraction to Marianna will open his mind to political action.

It is from this moment that Solomin and Marianna begin to emerge as combative characters. He is more overt and baits Sipyagin ironically. Marianna keeps her own counsel, but her ironic glances and asides show that she is spoiling for a fight. (In the confrontation between her and Valentina Mihalovna on the day after the dinner she will rise to dramatic heights, liberating herself from her stifling bourgeois confines.) There is open debate about the role of the people. Irony is key here because the scene raises awareness about miscommunication and mistrust on both sides. Central is the connotation of the word 'liberal'. The term trips off Sipyagin's lips and is part of his self-image from the start when this 'pillar of society' and 'future minister' is also cast as 'a man of liberal, progressive ideas'. By the 1870s, the public had concluded that Alexander II's Reforms were a veneer used to distract liberals and screen a new authoritarian era (of which Kallomyetsev is a defender). Harsh censorship, reprisals, and growing poverty, something that Turgenev noted during his trips to Russia in the late 1860s, widened the gap between the people and the government, motivating a sense of mission among the younger generation. The exchanges before, after, and during the meal make a mockery of the term 'liberal'. Sipyagin nonetheless remains committed to his narrative of progress:

'... But nowadays, after all the beneficial reforms ... in our industrial age, why cannot the nobility turn their energies and abilities into such enterprises? Why should they be unable to understand what is understood by the simple, often unlettered, merchant? They don't suffer from lack of education, and one may even claim with confidence that they are in some sense the representatives of enlightenment and progress.'

Boris Andreevitch spoke well; his fluency would have had great effect in Petersburg – in his department – or even in higher quarters, but on Solomin it produced no impression whatever.

Solomin's indifference outrages Kallomyetsev, who challenges him again at dinner, only to find class warfare and revolution are on the table. Solomin, whose politics give priority to realism based on economic assessments, begins to budge from his earlier

INTRODUCTION

caution and considers the possibility of a gradualist reversal of ownership, still far short of the classic Marxist prediction that revolution would be led by the workers in an advanced manufacturing economy. While the managerial class inspires no admiration, and he does, after all, call them 'brigands', he accepts that they will in effect drive change by displacing the landowners. The differing attitudes of Solomin and Marianna to political action will have a mutual effect. He finds her inspirational but is able to temper her romantic approach, and that moderation aids her as she converts him to the conspiracy later in Chapter XXIX. It is perhaps no wonder that when she and Nezhdanov run away together their relations are purely comradely (she locks the door on him every night). Solomin's concept of the marginal role of the people ('the people . . . are asleep') may set him apart from both Marxists and from future terrorist organizations (such as *The People's Will*). In terms of plot, this also distances him from Nezhdanov's reckless approach. Desperate to put this debacle to an end, Sipyagin attempts to reassert control by giving a long speech and then pronounces a toast to 'Religion, Agriculture and Industry,' which looks like a motto aimed at moving on from the state doctrine of 'Orthodoxy, Autocracy, and the People' that was the slogan of the reign of Nicholas I.

The effect of the meal has been to take the lid off personal hatreds inflamed by political antagonisms. The decisive fight comes quickly and spectacularly in the confrontation between Marianna and her aunt Valentina Mihalovna in Chapter XXVI. This is the turning point in Marianna's characterization. Valentina Mihalovna objects to Marianna's relationship with Nezhdanov, unaware that a much more sexual spark has been kindled between her and Solomin. Based on her moral growth, there will be a great transformation from the initial portrait of Marianna in Chapter VI:

These two women did not like each other. In comparison with her aunt, Marianna might almost have been called 'a plain little thing.' She had a round face, a large hawk nose, grey eyes, also large and very clear, thin eyebrows, thin lips. She had cropped her thick dark-brown hair, and she looked unsociable. But about her whole personality there was something vigorous and bold, something stirring and passionate. Her feet and hands were tiny; her strongly knit, supple little body recalled the Florentine statuettes of the sixteenth century; she moved lightly and gracefully.

These two characters then play their parts histrionically. When the reader first meets Valentina she is reading the French *La Revue des Deux Mondes*, a sign of literary taste and also progressive, albeit monarchist, politics. Now, drawing herself up like a classical tragédienne, she orders Marianna to leave the room, quoting a famous line in Racine's tragedy *Bajazet*. Not to be outdone for stage effect, Marianna fights fire with fire and opposes her own dignity to what she considers Valentina's bad taste. Even a great actress like Rachel could not make Racine's famous injunction, perhaps more a stage direction than a command, work aloud:

'I will rid you of my presence directly; but do you know what, Valentina Mihalovna? They say that even in Rachel's mouth in Racine's *Bajazet* that '*Sortez!*' was not effective, and you are far behind her! And something more, what was it you said? "*Je suis une honnête femme, je l'ai été, et le serai toujours.*" Only fancy, I am convinced I'm a great deal honester than you! Good-bye!'

Earlier, Marianna had been more silent than verbal, her ability to communicate through eye contact one of Turgenev's more theatrical stylistic touches. This controlled fury is also an aspect of her character although life under Valentina's auspices has certainly inhibited her, and perhaps also honed her conspiratorial instincts. Here, finally, she bursts into speech and also bursts the constraints of family. Having rejected one family, she now seeks to gain the trust of the common folk or people in the sense of the Russian *narod*. When Solomin remains as a guest overnight, the house party becomes a hothouse of radical talk. In Chapter XXV Nezhdanov recalls Paklin's Juggernaut metaphor, originally mentioned in Chapter IV, as the force that crushes a restive population. Nonetheless, the chapter maintains faith with the revolutionaries and stages something like a secular political marriage between Nezhdanov and Marianna over which Solomin (who is her real love interest) presides:

INTRODUCTION

Marianna and Nezhdanov both went up to him on the right and the left, and each clasped one of his hands.

'Only tell us what to do,' said Marianna. 'Supposing the revolution is still far off . . . there are preparatory steps to be taken, work to be done, impossible in this house, in these surroundings, to which we should go so eagerly together . . . you point them out to us, you only tell us where we are to go . . . Send us! You will send us, won't you?'

'Where?'

'To the peasants . . . Where should we go, if not to the people?'

'Into the forest,' thought Nezhdanov . . . Paklin's saying recurred to his mind. Solomin looked intently at Marianna.

'You want to get to know the people?'

'Yes; that is, we don't only want to get to know the people, but to influence . . . to work for them.'

'Very good; I promise you, you shall get to know them. I will give you a chance of influencing them and working for them. And you, Nezhdanov, are ready to go . . . for her . . . and for them?'

'Of course I am ready,' he declared, hurriedly. 'Juggernaut,' another saying of Paklin's recurred to him; 'here it comes rolling along, the huge chariot . . . and I hear the crash and rumble of its wheels. . . .'

The culmination of the conspiracy, and the realignment of love interests, engender her courage and bring out her true beauty. As Paklin exclaims, 'You're a Roman woman of the time of Cato! Cato of Utica!' Given how often Turgenev invents names for the sake of symbolic connotations, the name Marianna may be understood through the lens of French political culture. As she becomes more of a true revolutionary, dissuaded from rabble-rousing only by Solomin, the republican symbolism of her name becomes more inescapable. The initial description of her head gave her the appearance of a bust. We will come to see that she may be the bust of Marianna brought to life. Her politics come through trial and error and a genuine engagement with the people, a world apart from Nezhdanov's untested, politically correct sympathies. Russian Populism, whose first phase unfolded between the 1820s and the Emancipation in 1861, was a broad church in its first decades, with a variety of political visions of how to achieve social reform whether through rebellion (the Decembrists in 1825) or utopian ideologies (Alexander Herzen and Socialism). The fundamental populist idea was the obligation the upper classes owed the 'people' (*narod*), to be enacted in the liberation of the peasantry. However, when that goal was attained, it failed to solve widespread economic problems. In its second phase, questions of a revolution from below or radical reform from above galvanized political thinkers and activists, who had lost hope in a dictatorship of the Tsar. Populism now ranged from the activism of going to the people as teachers and doctors to the more radical spreading of propaganda and fomenting revolt. Russian literature of the last quarter of the nineteenth century returns repeatedly to types, adjusting and updating them to include a terrorist figure like Markelov, an anarchist like Paklin, a reformer like Solomin, alongside the more 'superfluous' Nezhdanov. Turgenev's vision of politics is here at its most inclusive and least defeatist. He does not exclude workers, a new class of managers, university students, and would-be aristocrats, as Tolstoy excluded them.

Marianna's encounters are a reflection on both attitudes to the peasantry and to the intelligentsia. She receives an entire education at the hands of the peasant woman Tatyana on what the intelligentsia can do for the people in Chapter XXVII. A conversation of this kind typically distances Turgenev from both the brutal realism of more populist writers, and also the idealism of Tolstoy. Marianna emerges as the kind of figure who might develop in one of two directions, either taking the path of a social activist like the teacher Lydia in Chekhov's 'The House with the Mezzanine' (1896), or possibly following the more radical path of Vera Zasulich, who in the mid-1870s after her release from prison went to the people by joining the populist revolutionary group, 'Land and Liberty'. The final chapters of *Virgin Soil* juxtapose Nezhdanov's naïve attempts as a rabble-rouser and his growing despair as he learns first-hand of the enormous difficulty of effective action, a frustration that is justified when he is manhandled by a peasant mob. His story will be one of failure, but Marianna's budding relationship with Solomin holds promise for revolutionary action of the future. This sets her more firmly on her radical path. Through restraint and curiosity, Marianna acquires genuine republican credentials: the reader of Racine, steeped in the culture of the *ancien régime*, has acquired the stature to become a revolutionary heroine or Marianne in her own right.

INTRODUCTION

As the novel that enjoyed the greatest popularity with his readers, *Nest of the Gentry* saw its characters in the round, their identities defined no less by the psychology of love than other conditions such as nationality, class, and family values. It may be that *Virgin Soil* shows no lessening of that skill at human depiction. Yet as a story of personal relations and politics, the narrative sustains a more complex double motion. If *Nest of the Gentry* moves slowly away from the issues of the land to focus on its love plot, *Virgin Soil* subjects the question of love to the pressures of generational change. As Marianna develops, Nezhdanov falters, and as Nezhdanov fades, Solomin grows in stature. Out of that shared commitment to the cause their new love develops. Whereas love is not sufficient to sustain radicalism, a conclusion that *On the Eve* reached earlier, it is a necessary condition for the pragmatism and courage Solomin and Marianna cultivate.

Turgenev's earlier novels created typical characters like the intelligentsia figure, the martyred tutor, the progressive landowner, the man of science, the conspirator, the terrorist, the exile, the superfluous man, the Romantic heroine – all of them doomed. In *Virgin Soil* he sought to invent the type that needed to come next. He uses Paklin, who is often quoted by others in *Virgin Soil*, to bring types into focus. Himself unheroic, he is, nonetheless, astute enough to conclude that change will be driven by 'sturdy, rough, dull men of the people' and this means someone like Solomin, whose 'heart aches at what makes ours ache' and who 'hates the same things we hate [. . .] a man with no nonsense about him; educated – and from the people'. To end a prediction, as he does, on a rhetorical question ('What more do you ask?') is to admit no other response.

*

For Turgenev, historical information lacking 'invention, power, fiction, imagination' was lifeless. Turgenev, contemporaries noted, seemed to anticipate changes in character even before they appeared in real life. However closely they embody the universal types of a Don Quixote or Hamlet, Turgenev's heroes and heroines are also representative men and women of their generation. Abstractions can only go so far. Types distil patterns of human behaviour that are describable, while history is partly the result of actions that can be plotted and brought to life in the novel. Without predicting when the 'day would come', they capture history as it is being made.

In two earlier masterpieces central to the Russian tradition, Alexander Pushkin and Nikolai Gogol took a more abstract and vatic approach to their country's future. At the end of *The Bronze Horseman* (1833), Pushkin's great narrative poem about Russian history, the hero, a classic little man of Russian literature, challenges the equestrian statue of Peter the Great when it comes to life supernaturally. He asks, 'In which direction are you heading, proud horse?' The line has usually been understood as a question about the direction of the country and its position straddling East and West. A decade or so later, at the end of part I of *Dead Souls*, Russia's greatest comic novel, Gogol evokes the figure of the troika, the three-horse carriage flying into the future, again a symbol of the country's headlong flight toward an unknown destiny. Turgenev lacked this prophetic streak. He kept his focus on a human scale, seeing destiny in terms of class and individual agency. In an early sketch of *Virgin Soil*, he jotted down his intention to create characters who 'seek within the real . . . something great and significant, but this is nonsense: real life is prosaic and must be so'. That was in 1870, the same year in which he wrote 'King Lear of the Steppes', one of his finest stories. It was a last tribute to Shakespeare from a creator of many a Russian Hamlet. But if one looks more broadly at his debt to the Bard one might well conclude that his fiction remains imprinted with nothing less than the 'body and pressure of time'.

Andrew Kahn

ANDREW KAHN is Professor of Russian Literature at the University of Oxford and a Fellow of St Edmund Hall, Oxford. His books include *Pushkin's Lyric Intelligence* (2008), *Mandelstam's Worlds* (2020), and he is co-author with Mark Lipovetsky of *All the World on a Page. A Critical Anthology of Modern Russian Poetry* (2025).

NOTE ON THE TRANSLATION

This edition in Everyman Classics brings back into print translations by Constance Garnett (1861–1946), who single-handedly brought more classic Russian authors into English than anyone before and after in versions that remain indelible for the beauty of the English prose. Her list of translations (to be found in the lively biography by her grandson Richard Garnett, 1991) features eighteen volumes of Turgenev (including his plays), Tolstoy (whom she met in Russia), Dostoevsky's major novels and short fiction, and much by Chekhov. *Virgin Soil* was the last of Turgenev's novels she translated (1896) before tackling the shorter works. Acclaimed in her lifetime, on the centenary of her birth a letter to the *Times Literary Supplement* referred to Garnett as the 'empress of Russian translators', and more recently distinguished scholars and writers such as S. S. Prawer, the Germanist, and Craig Raine, the critic and poet, credit her with revealing Chekhov's 'full range and flavour to an English-speaking public' and, in the estimation of the latter, with being 'everything a good translator should be'. Newer versions of individual authors, most notably Dostoevsky, have modernized by adopting a less smooth approach and replicated forcefully in English his more tortuous Russian syntax and idioms with the aim of bringing the English reader closer to the experience of the original. In the case of Turgenev, whose perfection of style Flaubert and James greatly admired, the match between Garnett and the original is highly felicitous in all respects, leading to readability that is entirely comparable. Among features that one might analyse one could draw attention to the challenge of rendering Turgenev's choice of adjectives and noun adjuncts. They not only enhance his famous landscape descriptions but are essential in adding with quick strokes key elements of character and psychology; and Garnett also understood the tendency in Russian to imply causal connections in phrases strung together by commas whereas in English these may need to be stated. In *Nest of the Gentry*, these techniques are captured in the initial description of Marfa Timofeyevna. The Russian says that she 'was known to be an eccentric lady, had an independent character [. . .] and with the most impoverished means maintained herself as though she had thousands'. Garnett's correct and stylish version, rather than the literal meaning, is what's needed: 'She had a reputation for eccentricity as she was a woman of independent character [. . .] and even in the most straitened circumstances behaved just as if she had a fortune at her disposal.'

This edition retains her transliterated spelling of Russian names but uses the now more standard and accurate title *Nest of the Gentry* for her original *A House of Gentlefolk* – Garnett herself regretted not using 'Nest' but thought readers at the time would find it odd. The text of that novel includes corrections Garnett made for the 1906 edition.

SELECT BIBLIOGRAPHY

JANE COSTLOW, *Worlds Within Worlds: The Novels of Ivan Turgenev* (Princeton, NJ: Princeton University Press, 1990).
ORLANDO FIGES, *The Europeans: Three Lives and the Making of a Cosmopolitan Culture* (London: Penguin Books, 2019).
RICHARD FREEBORN, 'Turgenev and Revolution', *Slavonic and East European Review* 61:4 (1983), 518–27.
RICHARD FREEBORN, *Turgenev: The Novelist's Novelist* (Oxford: Oxford University Press, 1960).
RICHARD GARNETT, *Constance Garnett: A Heroic Life* (London: Faber and Faber, 1991).
ROYDEN J. HARRISON, 'Turgenev's Later Political Commitments: Six Letters to Beesly, 1880', *Slavic and East European Journal* 9:4 (1965), 400–419.
THOMAS P. HODGE, *Hunting Nature: Ivan Turgenev and the Organic World* (Boston: Academic Studies Press, 2022).
IRVING HOWE, 'The Virtues of Hesitation', *The Hudson Review* 8:4 (1956), 533–51.
HENRY JAMES's essays on Turgenev in *French Poets and Novelists* (London: Macmillan, 1878), *Partial Portraits* (London: Macmillan, 1888) and *The Critical Muse*, ed. Roger Gard (Harmondsworth: Penguin Books, 1987).
CHRISTINE JOHANSON, 'Turgenev's Heroines: A Historical Assessment', *Canadian Slavonic Papers* (1 March 1984), 15–23.
EVA KAGAN-KANS, *Hamlet and Don Quixote: Turgenev's Ambivalent Vision* (Berlin: De Gruyter, 2015).
HARRY KIRSHKOWITZ, *Democratic Ideas in Turgenev's Novels* (New York: AMS Press, 1932).
A. V. KNOWLES (ed. and tr.), *Turgenev's Letters* (London: Athlone Press and New York: Charles Scribner's, 1983).
ANNE LOUNSBERY, *Life is Elsewhere: Symbolic Geography in the Russian Provinces, 1800–1917* (Ithaca: Cornell University Press, 2019).
MARTIN A. MILLER, *The Russian Revolutionary Emigrés, 1825–1870* (Baltimore: Johns Hopkins University Press, 2019).
D. S. MIRSKY, *A History of Russian Literature* (New York: Alfred A. Knopf and London: Routledge, 1927, 1949).
ORWIN, DONNA TUSSING, *Consequences of Consciousness: Turgenev, Dostoevsky, and Tolstoy* (Stanford, CA: Stanford University Press, 2007).
V. S. PRITCHETT, *The Gentle Barbarian: The Life and Work of Turgenev* (London: Chatto & Windus, 1977).

IVAN TURGENEV

ROBERT REID and JOE ANDREW (eds), *Turgenev: Art, Ideology and Legacy* (Amsterdam and New York: Rodopi, 2010).

CHRISTINE RICHARDS, 'Occasional Criticism: Henry James on Ivan Turgenev', *Slavonic and East European Review* 78:3 (2000), 463–86.

LEONARD SCHAPIRO, *Turgenev: His Life and Times* (New York: Random House and Oxford: Oxford University Press, 1978).

VICTOR TERRAS, 'Turgenev's Aesthetic and Western Realism', *Comparative Literature* 22:1 (1970), 19–35.

FRANCO VENTURI, *Roots of Revolution: A History of the Populist and Socialist Movements in Nineteenth-Century Russia*, trans. Francis Haskell with introduction by Isaiah Berlin (London: Weidenfeld and Nicolson, 1960).

PATRICK WADDINGTON, 'Turgenev and the Translator of *Virgin Soil*', *New Zealand Slavonic Journal* 1 (1977), 35–76.

EDMUND WILSON, 'Turgenev and the Life-Giving Drop' in *Turgenev's Literary Reminiscences*, ed. David Magarshack (London: Faber and Faber, 1959).

AVRAHM YARMOLINSKY, *Turgenev, The Man, His Art and His Age* (New York: Orion Press, 1959; London: André Deutsch, 1960).

CHRONOLOGY

DATE	AUTHOR'S LIFE	LITERARY CONTEXT
1815		
1816	Marriage of Turgenev's parents, Sergei Turgenev, army officer (decorated at the Battle of Borodino) and minor aristocrat, and Varvara Lutovinova, a rich landowner. Birth of their first child, Nikolai.	Constant: *Adolphe*. Byron: *Childe Harold*, Canto III.
1817		Batyushkov: *Essays in Verse and Prose*.
1818	Ivan Turgenev born in Orel, central Russia (28 October).	Karamzin: 12-vol. *History of the Russian State* (to 1824). Byron: *Beppo*. Scott: *Heart of Midlothian*.
1819		Byron: *Don Juan* (to 1824).
1820		Pushkin: *Ruslan and Ludmila*. Hegel: *The Philosophy of Right*.
1821	Father retires from army. Family moves to Spasskoe in Orel Province, the large estate owned by his mother, who rules both her sons and her serfs despotically.	Birth of Dostoevsky and Flaubert.
1822	Family embarks on an extended European tour (to 1823).	De Quincey: *Confessions of an English Opium Eater*.
1825		Pushkin: *Yevgeny Onegin* (to 1832). Saint-Simon: *The New Christianity*.
1826		Pushkin: *Stanzas*. Scott: *Woodstock*.

HISTORICAL EVENTS

End of Napoleonic Wars. Congress of Vienna. Russia emerges as significant European power, and gains control over Poland and Finland. Monarchical rule restored in France (Louis XVIII). Tsar Alexander I forms Holy Alliance with Austria and Prussia, seen as heralding era of conservatism. In Russia, the Union of Salvation, the first of several secret societies of army officers and other noblemen, is formed. All societies support the abolition of serfdom and agrarian reform but their political aims diverge.

Construction begins of Russia's first hard-surface road, between St Petersburg and Moscow (finished 1834).
Congress of Aix-la-Chapelle: France readmitted to 'Concert of Europe'. Occupying Allied troops withdrawn from France.

Metternich's repressive Karlsbad Decrees in Austria. Peterloo Massacre in Britain, followed by repressive Six Acts.
Congress of Troppau: Great Powers agree to check revolutionary movements in Spain, Portugal and the Two Sicilies. Purging of Russian universities by Golitsyn and Magnitsky. Russian expedition led by Bellingshausen and Lazarev discovers Antarctica.
Death of Napoleon in exile on St Helena. Greek War of Independence: Alexander I refuses to support his co-religionists against the Ottoman Empire.

Death of Alexander I. Decembrist revolt: disaffected army officers organize demonstration in favour of constitutional reform, swiftly suppressed by new Tsar, Nicholas I. Five Decembrists are hanged on a bastion of Peter and Paul Fortress, their martyrdom to provide a source of inspiration for future revolutionaries, and more than a hundred are exiled to Siberia.
Nicholas I develops system of autocratic government based on militarism and bureaucracy. To his personal Chancery he adds two departments, the Second Section under M. M. Speransky, to deal with legal reform, the notorious Third Section under A. K. Benckendorff, to act against subversion and revolution. Censorship tightened and a widespread network of spies employed.

IVAN TURGENEV

DATE	AUTHOR'S LIFE	LITERARY CONTEXT
1826 cont.		
1827	Family moves to Moscow. The boys continue to be educated by private tutors at home. During childhood Turgenev becomes fluent in French, German and English.	Heine: *Book of Songs*. Manzoni: *The Betrothed*.
1828		Birth of Tolstoy. Baratynsky: *The Ball*. Pogorelsky: *The Double*. Bulwer-Lytton: *Pelham: or the Adventures of a Gentleman*.
1829	Spends a few months at the Armenian Institute in Moscow.	Zagoskin: *Yury Miloslavsky*, first Russian historical novel, in style of Scott, becomes a bestseller. Lermontov writing *The Demon* (to 1841).
1830	Attends the Weidenhammer boarding school in Moscow (to 1831).	Pushkin: *Boris Godunov*. Stendhal: *Scarlet and Black*.
1831	Birth of his brother Sergei.	Gogol: *Evenings on a Farm near Dikanka*. Griboedov: *Woe from Wit*. Hugo: *The Hunchback of Notre-Dame*. Goethe: *Faust* (Part II). Death of Hegel.
1832		Bestuzhev-Marlinsky: *Ammalak-Bek*. Death of Goethe and Scott.
1833	Attends Moscow University. His mother adopts a baby girl, Varvara, probably the natural daughter of Andrei Behrs, the family's physician, and possibly also her own child.	Katenin: *Princess Milusha*. Balzac: *Eugénie Grandet*. Sand: *Jacques*.

CHRONOLOGY

HISTORICAL EVENTS

Increase in peasant unrest. Official statistics record over 700 peasant uprisings 1826–54.
In Britain the Aliens Act (1793) is allowed to lapse, making the country a haven for political refugees throughout the 19th century, including many Russians.

Russo-Turkish War (to 1829) in which Russia gains control of Black Sea coast up to the Danube.

Major cholera epidemic in Russia (to 1831). First All-Russia Industrial and Art Exhibition opens in St Petersburg. Caucasian Imamate, an Islamic state, established in eastern Caucasus, to resist Russian advances.

Polish nationalist uprising against Russia. July Revolution in France; Louis Philippe becomes King of the French under new constitutional charter. Belgian revolt against the Dutch. Greece recognized by Great Powers as an independent state.
1830s: Proliferation of discussion groups influenced by German idealistic philosophy, particularly in and around Moscow University. Later in the decade, Hegel becomes the chief focus of their interest.
Russian troops crush Polish rebellion: Poles lose their constitution and most of the autonomy granted them in 1815. Cholera riots in Russia.
Belgian independence.

Parliamentary Reform Act in Britain.

Doctrine of 'Official Nationality' – Orthodoxy, autocracy and nationality – proclaimed by Nicholas I's Minister of Education, S. S. Uvarov. Treaty of Unkiar Skelessi marks period of rapprochement between Russia and Ottoman Empire.
Abolition of slavery in British Empire.

IVAN TURGENEV

DATE	AUTHOR'S LIFE	LITERARY CONTEXT
1834	His mother is absent in Europe. His father moves to St Petersburg to be near Nikolai (who is in the army). Turgenev transfers to St Petersburg University. His first literary effort, a dramatic poem, *Steno*. Death of his father.	Pushkin: 'The Queen of Spades'.
1835		Balzac: *Old Goriot*. Strauss: *Life of Jesus*.
1836		Chaadayev: *Philosophical Letters*; government has Chaadayev declared insane. Gogol: *The Inspector General*. Pushkin founds the *Contemporary*.
1837	Graduates. Spends summer and autumn at Spasskoe and is appalled by his mother's tyrannical treatment of her serfs. Death of his younger brother Sergei.	Pushkin dies following a duel. Mérimée: 'The Venus of Ille'. Sand: *Mauprat*. Bulwer-Lytton: *Ernest Maltravers*. Dickens: *Oliver Twist* (to 1839).
1838	Begins studies at Berlin University (history, classics, philosophy, notably Hegel) until 1841. Meets Bakunin, Stankevich and Granovsky, Russian liberal and radical political thinkers.	
1839	Manor house at Spasskoe burns down; returns there (a single wing remains) for summer and autumn.	Blanc: *The Organization of Labour*. Stendhal: *The Charterhouse of Parma*.
1840	Travels in Italy and Germany.	Fet: *A Lyrical Pantheon*. Lermontov: *A Hero of Our Time*. Proudhon: *What is Property?*
1841	Returns to Russia (June). Spends time at Spasskoe and in Moscow. Inclines to the side of the Westerners in the Slavophile–Westerner debate though remains on friendly terms with many conservative Slavophiles, including the Aksakov brothers. Begins to publish poetry in periodicals.	Lermontov killed in a duel. Feuerbach: *The Essence of Christianity*. Carlyle: *On Heroes, Hero-Worship and the Heroic in History*.

CHRONOLOGY

HISTORICAL EVENTS

Iman Shamil becomes Iman of the Caucasian Imamate; successfully conducts guerrilla war against Russian troops until 1859.

Michael Pogodin becomes first professor of Russian history at University of Moscow.
Nicholas I appoints P. D. Kiselyov to reform and improve the position of the c. 20 million peasants owned by the state (to 1841). Emergence of Slavophile–Westernizer debate, in part triggered by Chaadayev, much exercising intellectuals in mid-19th-century Russia.

First Russian railway line constructed, between St Petersburg and imperial palace at Tsarkoe Selo.
Accession of Queen Victoria.

Grand Kremlin Palace built (to 1849) to design by K. A. Ton.

Construction (to 1883) of Ton's Cathedral of Christ the Saviour in Moscow (to commemorate victory over the invading French army in 1812).

Straits Convention signed by Great Powers and Ottoman Empire: Dardanelles and Bosphorus closed to all non-Ottoman warships (except Ottoman allies in wartime), thus denying Russia the preferential treatment it had enjoyed since 1833.
Robert Peel British prime minister (to 1846).

DATE	AUTHOR'S LIFE	LITERARY CONTEXT
1842	Birth of a daughter following an affair with a serf girl, Avdotia Ivanova. Abandons his intention of pursuing an academic career.	Baratynsky: *Twilight*. Gogol: *Dead Souls*; 'The Overcoat'. Sand: *Consuelo*. Schiller: *Foundation of the Positive Philosophy* (to 1843). Tennyson: *Poems*.
1843	Works in the Ministry of the Interior (to 1845). *Parasha*, a verse romance, is his first literary work to attract attention. Friendship with the critic Belinsky. Falls in love with the French opera singer Pauline Viardot, who is performing in St Petersburg (Oct), accompanied by her husband Louis, critic and theatre director. Turgenev will devote his life to her.	Krylov: *Fables* (9-vol. edition). Carlyle: *Past and Present*. Dickens: *Martin Chuzzlewit*; *A Christmas Carol*.
1844	Writing poetry, publishes first story. Pauline Viardot returns for another season in St Petersburg in the autumn.	Dumas: *The Count of Monte Cristo* (to 1846); *The Three Musketeers*. Schopenhauer: *The World as Will and Representation* (expanded edition).
1845	Travels to France; spends the summer ('the happiest time of all my life') with the Viardots in their house at Courtavenel, some 40 miles south-east of Paris. Meets George Sand. Travels in France. Returns with the Viardots to St Petersburg for the opera season. Meets Dostoevsky (Nov).	Herzen: *Who is to Blame?* (to 1846). Mérimée: *Carmen*.
1846	Visit to Spasskoe for five months, spent writing and shooting (a favourite pastime). Relations with his mother deteriorating.	Dostoevsky: *Poor Folk*; *The Double*. Grigorovich: *The Village*. Balzac: *Cousin Bette*. Sand: *The Devil's Pool*. Dickens: *Dombey and Son* (to 1848).
1847	Writing for the relaunched *Contemporary*. The sketches later included in *A Sportsman's Notebook* are published in the journal	Belinsky: 'Letter to Gogol'. Druzhinin: *Polinka Saks*. Goncharov: *An Ordinary Story*. Grigorovich: *Anton the Hapless*.

CHRONOLOGY

HISTORICAL EVENTS

St Petersburg–Moscow railway built (to 1851). Première of Glinka's opera *Ruslan and Ludmila* in St Petersburg.

Nicholas I visits England.

Penal code of 1845 prescribes exile and *katorga* (hard labour in factory, fortress or mines) as punishment for a greatly expanded range of crimes. 635,319 offenders sent to Siberia 1807–81, the highest numbers in the reign of Nicholas I (1825–55) and in the 1860s and 1870s. The knout is abolished.

Repeal of Corn Laws in Britain. Peasant revolt in Galicia.

Pushkin's *Contemporary* revived under Nekrasov; publishes early works by Turgenev, Tolstoy, Herzen and Goncharov; with the involvement of Chernyshevsky and Dobrolyubov in the 1850s, it becomes an important voice in radical politics. Herzen leaves Russia.

IVAN TURGENEV

DATE	AUTHOR'S LIFE	LITERARY CONTEXT
1847 cont.	(to 1851) and play a role in influencing public opinion against serfdom. Leaves Russia (to 1850): following the Viardots, travels to Germany (Jan), London (July) and back to Paris (Aug) where he sees Belinsky for the last time.	Michelet: *History of the French Revolution* (to 1853). Tennyson: *The Princess*. Thackeray: *Vanity Fair* (to 1848).
1848	In Paris during the revolution. Witnesses the workers' demonstration on 15 May and the June Days uprising. Sees much of the Herzens. Suffering, as he often does, from ill health.	Death of Belinsky. Druzhinin: *The Story of Alexei Dmitrich*. Comte: *A General View of Positivism*. Dumas *fils*: *The Lady of the Camellias* (later adapted for stage). Thackeray: *Pendennis* (to 1850).
1849	*The Bachelor* performed in Russia (the only one of his plays of this period not to fall foul of the censor). Contracts cholera.	Dostoevsky sentenced to hard labour and exile in Siberia (10 years). Storm: *Immensee*. Dickens: *David Copperfield* (to 1850).
1850	'Diary of a Superfluous Man' published in *Annals of the Fatherland* (April). Returns to Russia (June). Sends his daughter Pelageia, now 8, to join the Viardot household, providing for her support. Death of his mother (Nov).	Herzen: *From the Other Shore*. Ostrovsky: *A Family Affair* causes a furore; it is banned from performance (to 1861) and he loses his civil service job.
1851	Two more plays staged – *The Provincial Lady* and *Lunch with the Marshal of the Nobility*. Affair with serf girl at Spasskoe.	Solovyov: *History of Russia from the Earliest Times* (29 vols, to 1879). Proudhon: *The General Idea of Revolution in the Nineteenth Century* Ruskin: *The Stones of Venice* (to 1853). Melville: *Moby-Dick*.
1852	*A Sportsman's Notebook* published in volume form to great acclaim. Arrested (April) and confined to Spasskoe under police	Death of Gogol. Tolstoy: *Childhood*. Dickens: *Bleak House* (to 1853). Stowe: *Uncle Tom's Cabin*.

CHRONOLOGY

HISTORICAL EVENTS

Liberal revolutions across Europe affecting France, Germany, Italy and the Austrian Empire. Second Republic in France; Louis Napoleon elected president. Chartist Petition presented in London. *Communist Manifesto* published. First Pan-Slav Congress held in Prague.
In Russia, the Buturlin Committee set up, expanding censorship to unprecedented levels ('Buturlin takes the stage with hatred for word, thought and freedom, preaching boundless obedience, silence and discipline', writes the critic Annenkov).

Nicholas I moves against radical Petrashevsky circle in St Petersburg. Hungarian Diet proclaims independence from Austria, with Kossuth as governor-president; Russia sends troops to help Austria put down the revolutionary government.
First performance of Meyerbeer's *Le Prophète* at the Paris Opéra attended by Louis-Napoleon and other European dignitaries is a huge commercial success, and a triumph for Pauline Viardot, making her Paris Opéra debut (Turgenev in the audience).
European revolutions end in defeat and period of reaction ensues.

Louis Napoleon's coup d'état (Dec) keeps him in office, with dictatorial powers. A year later the Second Empire is proclaimed. Great Exhibition in London.

Dispute over Christian sites in the Holy Land; the Sultan grants France the guardianship, formerly a Russian prerogative. Work starts on rail link between St Petersburg and Warsaw (finished in 1863 in time to transport troops to crush the Polish rebellion).

IVAN TURGENEV

DATE	AUTHOR'S LIFE	LITERARY CONTEXT
1852 cont.	surveillance after publishing eulogistic obituary of Gogol (to Nov 1853).	
1853	Frees his domestic servants and takes measures to improve the lot of his serfs (he has 2,000). Travels secretly to Moscow to meet Pauline (March).	Ostrovsky's first play to pass the censors is performed in Moscow. Tolstoy: *The Raid*.
1854	Lives in St Petersburg (to 1856), one of the *Contemporary*'s literary circle, which includes Nekrasov, Annenkov, Botkin, Grigorovich, Druzhinin and Goncharov. Friend and literary adviser of the poet Fet. Romance with a distant cousin, 18-year-old Olga Turgeneva, but hesitates to commit to marriage. Short stories include 'A Quiet Spot' and 'The Two Friends'.	Herzen: *My Past and Thoughts* (to 1870). Tolstoy: *Boyhood*. Tyutchev's first poetry collection published. Dickens: *Hard Times*. Thoreau: *Walden*.
1855	*A Month in the Country* (play written 1849–50) is published. Writes the novel *Rudin*. Short stories include 'A Correspondence' and 'Yakov Pasynkov'. Writes to Tolstoy (admiring his work), who arrives in St Petersburg from service in Crimea and stays with Turgenev for some weeks (Nov).	Annenkov publishes first biography of Pushkin. Tolstoy: *Sevastapol Sketches*. Dickens: *Little Dorrit* (to 1857). Lewes: *Life of Goethe*.
1856	*Rudin* and 'Faust' published. With the Crimean War at an end, he is able to travel to France again. After a brief visit to London (Sept) he stays with the Viardots and their children at Courtavenel, then in Paris, though here he takes his own apartment in the rue de Rivoli.	S. T. Aksakov: *A Family Chronicle*. Fet: *Poems by A. A. Fet*. Nekrasov: *Poems*. Tolstoy: *Two Hussars*. Tocqueville: *The Ancien Régime and the Revolution*.
1857	Estrangement from Pauline, much travelling (to 1863). Sees his daughter (now known as Paulinette), who is at boarding school in Paris. Lifelong friendship with exiled	Chicherin: 'Contemporary Tasks of Russian Life'. Tolstoy: *Youth*. Baudelaire: *Les Fleurs du mal*. Flaubert: *Madame Bovary*. Trollope: *Barchester Towers*.

CHRONOLOGY

HISTORICAL EVENTS

The new Hermitage Museum in St Petersburg housing the royal collection is first opened to the public in a building designed by neoclassical German architect Leo von Klenze.
Russian troops occupy Danubian principalities of Moldavia and Wallachia (current Romania, then vassal states of Ottoman Empire); Turks declare war on Russia. Russian naval victory at Sinope.
Marriage of Napoleon III and Eugénie de Montijo. Haussmann made Prefect of the Seine (to 1870): embarks on reconstruction of Paris.
Herzen founds Free Russian Press in London.
Britain and France enter war against Russia. Crimean campaign: battle of Alma; year-long siege of Sevastopol by allied armies; battle of Balaclava (and charge of the Light Brigade); battle of Inkerman.

Death of Nicholas I and accession of Alexander II. Palmerston swept to premiership in Britain on a tide of public anger against the mismanagement of the Crimean War. Russia brought to terms after fall of Sevastopol (Sept). Relaxation of restrictions on student enrolment; at St Petersburg University numbers increase from 476 to 1026 in 1858. Uniforms and drill abolished. During these years first libraries and Friendly Societies, administrative bodies and newspapers set up by students.
Russian expansion in Far East.

Peace of Paris: the Black Sea is completely demilitarized; the integrity of the Ottoman Empire is upheld; Russia surrenders Bessarabia on the Danube. The Crimea, however, is returned to Russia (to Palmerston's chagrin). Alexander II announces to an assembly of nobles in Moscow his intention to end serfdom on private land in Russia and invites them to consider how this might be done. After a relaxation in censorship, the number of journals doubles by 1860.

In Paris, inauguration of Napoleon III's iconic Louvre expansion. Millet paints *The Gleaners*. The landscape artists' (and photographers') colony at Barbizon, in the forest near Fontainebleau, is flourishing, with Millet, Rousseau, Corot, Dupré, Daubigny, Troyon and Jacque all painting there. Excursion trains to Fontainebleau run from 1850; in 1857, 135,000 tourists visit, including Turgenev with Tolstoy on a day-trip. Turgenev will later

IVAN TURGENEV

DATE	AUTHOR'S LIFE	LITERARY CONTEXT
1857 cont.	Decembrist N. I. Turgenev. Friendship with writers Ducamp and Mérimée. Stays in London (May–June), welcomed in political and intellectual circles. Visits Salisbury and Manchester. Introduced to the Carlyles, Thackeray and Macaulay. Attends Parliament, briefly meets Disraeli. Proposed as member of the Athenaeum Club. Visits Herzen, now based in London. Travels in Germany. Spends winter in Rome.	
1858	'Asya' (Jan). Returns to Russia (June). In advance of Emancipation, makes his own arrangements with his peasants at Spasskoe, estimating that he will lose a quarter of his income. Working on *Nest of the Gentry*.	S. T. Aksakov: *Years of Childhood*. Pisemsky: *A Thousand Souls*.
1859	*Nest of the Gentry* published in the *Contemporary*, proving enormously popular. Living mainly in Russia but in Europe May–Sept, including two months at Courtavenel.	Goncharov: *Oblomov*. Ostrovsky: *The Storm*. Tolstoy: *Family Happiness*. Eliot: *Adam Bede*. Darwin: *The Origin of Species*. Mill: *On Liberty*.
1860	'Hamlet and Don Quixote' published. Along with other liberals, breaks with the *Contemporary*, becoming uncompromisingly radical under Chernyshevsky. Severs relations with Nekrasov. *On the Eve* published (to mixed critical reception) in the *Russian Messenger*. 'First Love' published. With Annenkov joins the colony	Chekhov born. Dobrolyubov: 'When Will the Real Day Come?' Dickens: *Great Expectations* (to 1861). Eliot: *The Mill on the Floss*.

CHRONOLOGY

HISTORICAL EVENTS

collect many Barbizon landscapes (but has no taste for the Impressionists). Turgenev also attends the Art Treasures Exhibition in Manchester, one of the biggest ever held, with 16,000 artworks on display. British Museum Reading Room and South Kensington (later the V&A) open.
Herzen and Ogaryov's periodical *The Bell* launched in London (to 1867).
First gymnasium for girls opens in Russia. There are 343 girls' gymnasia with some 80,000 pupils by 1898.

Orsini bomb plot: Italian nationalists, backed by British radicals, attempt to assassinate Napoleon III as an obstacle to Italian unification; execution of Orsini. Fall of Palmerston's government. Napoleon III and Cavour meet at Plombières and form alliance against Austria.
First of Offenbach's phenomenally popular operettas, *Orpheus in the Underworld*, opens in Paris. St Isaac's Cathedral, St Petersburg completed (begun 1818).
Defeat and capture of Shamil gives Russia victory in eastern Caucasus.
Huge range of voluntary societies emerge in late 1850s – agricultural, economic, technical, professional, educational and literary. Litfond (Society for Aid to Needy Writers and Scholars) founded, with *c.* 600 members by 1861 including many leading writers, its events attracting a wide audience; from it springs the Sunday school movement to increase literacy which establishes hundreds of schools across Russia by 1862.
Franco-Austrian War (Second War of Italian Independence) begins (April); French-Piedmontese armies win battles of Magenta and Solferino; Peace of Villafranca (July). Napoleon III offers amnesty to political exiles.
Two long-running operatic successes at the Théâtre Lyrique, Paris: Gounod's *Faust*, which goes on to achieve international renown, and a revival of Gluck's *Orfée* with Pauline Viardot, at the height of her career, in the title role.
Vladivostok founded.
Central Italian states annexed by Piedmont; Savoy and Nice ceded to France. Garibaldi and 'the Thousand' conquer Sicily and Naples.
First constitutional changes in France: Senate and Legislative Body permitted annual debates on the speech from the throne. (By 1869 it achieves the power to initiate and amend legislation.)

IVAN TURGENEV

DATE	AUTHOR'S LIFE	LITERARY CONTEXT
1860 cont.	of Russian reformers (including the Herzens) holidaying in Ventnor on the Isle of Wight (Aug). Back in Paris in the autumn, in an apartment on the rue de Rivoli with his daughter.	
1861	Unlike radicals, he is not critical of the terms of the Emancipation. Returns to Spasskoe in the spring. Quarrel with Tolstoy ends their friendship for 17 years. His literary earnings are by now substantial and his work is appearing in French, English and German translation. (Under his uncle's mismanagement, his estates, however, do not prosper.) Elected to Imperial Academy of Sciences.	Dostoevsky: *The House of the Dead*.
1862	*Fathers and Children* (in which he popularizes the term 'Nihilists' to describe the young generation of materialists opposed to all established authority) begins serialization in the *Russian Herald* (March), incurring criticism from both left and right. Sees St Petersburg shortly after the fire (May). With the Viardots (Aug–Oct) in Baden-Baden, Germany, where they plan to move (Pauline, whose voice is past its best, intends to give up singing in opera; Louis, a convinced republican, is keen to escape the regime of Napoleon III.)	Hugo: *Les Misérables*. Trollope: *The Small House at Allington*.
1863	First meeting in Paris with Flaubert, who will become a close friend. Takes an apartment in Baden-Baden (May). Spends some happy years there, enjoying unusually good health.	Chernyshevsky: *What is to be Done?* Ostrovsky: *A Profitable Position* (1st perf.) Tolstoy: *The Cossacks*. Renan: *The Life of Jesus*.

CHRONOLOGY

HISTORICAL EVENTS

Tsar's Proclamation (19 Feb) initiates emancipation of serfs. Increase in peasant revolts (1,100 cases 1861–3 officially recorded), violently suppressed. Herzen's *Bell* calls intelligentsia to 'go to the people'. Political activists in Litfond including Lavrov and Chernyshevsky form 'Chess Club'. One member, poet M. L. Mikhailov, co-author of Populist manifesto 'To the Young Generation', sentenced to hard labour and permanent exile in Siberia (where he dies in 1865).
Y. V. Putyatin, Minister of Education, introduces repressive measures including restricting university access and banning of student meetings, resulting in demonstrations and violent clashes; in December St Petersburg university closed (to 1863). Putyatin dismissed and replaced by liberal A. V. Golovnin (to 1866).
D. A. Milyutin appointed Minister for War and instigates programme of military reform over next 20 years.
American Civil War (to 1865). Victor Emmanuel first king of a united Italy. Litfond tries to establish a Free University by organizing public lectures; Professor P. V. Pavlov's lecture (March) on Russia's 1000th anniversary leads to his arrest and exile. Zaichnevsky's 'Young Russia' pamphlet advocates violent overthrow of the state. Fire in St Petersburg lasting several weeks dubiously linked to Nihilists (May). Government crackdown (June–July) on intelligentsia activism, many organizations banned and Sunday schools closed; hundreds arrested, including Chernyshevsky (sentenced to penal servitude and Siberian exile until 1883) and Nihilist journalist Pisarev (probably the only radical to approve of *Fathers and Children*, imprisoned until 1886). Their journals *The Contemporary* and *Russian Word* suspended (to 1863). Political dissent moves underground: Land and Freedom founded, a revolutionary organization of students and officers inspired by the ideas of Herzen and Chernyshevsky (to 1864).
Third Section initiates investigation (to 1864) of connections between Russian revolutionaries and London radicals headed by Herzen (this will involve Turgenev).
First Russian Conservatory founded by Anton Rubinstein in St Petersburg. Bismarck becomes prime minister of Prussia.
First performance (in Baden Baden) of Berlioz's *Beatrice and Benedict*.
Polish Revolt followed by severe reprisals and large-scale deportations to Siberia. Golovnin's University Regulations grant autonomy to universities but severely restrict students' corporate life.
Rouher, enemy of liberalism, becomes Napoleon's chief minister (dubbed 'vice-emperor'). Salon des Refusés: founding of French Impressionist school. Manet's *Le Déjeuner sur l'herbe*.

IVAN TURGENEV

DATE	AUTHOR'S LIFE	LITERARY CONTEXT
1863 cont.	The Viardots' new villa and concert hall nearby are centres of musical and social activity.	
1864	Appears before committee of inquiry in St Petersburg (Jan) concerning his relations with Herzen and London radicals. His exoneration is regarded by Herzen as evidence of 'base appeasement' and their friendship is seriously damaged. Buys land to build a grand villa for himself in Baden-Baden.	Dostoevsky: *Notes from Underground*. Nekrasov: *Who Can Live Happy and Free in Russia?* (to 1877). Reshetnikov: *Podlipovtsy*. Dickens: *Our Mutual Friend* (to 1865). Trollope: *Can You Forgive Her?*
1865	Marriage of Paulinette to a French factory owner. Brief visit to Spasskoe in summer.	Leskov: *Lady Macbeth of Mtensk*. Tolstoy publishes *1805*, the first two volumes of *War and Peace*, in the *Russian Herald* (to 1866). Quinet: *The Revolution*.
1866	Writing songs and operettas with Pauline (to 1869).	Dostoevsky: *Crime and Punishment*. Eliot: *Felix Holt, the Radical*.
1867	*Smoke* published, again causing controversy. Reconciled with Herzen. He and Dostoevsky (in Baden) quarrel. Dostoevsky later satirizes him in *Demons*. Visit to Russia but not to Spasskoe. Pays his uncle off at great expense and instals a new young manager (who embezzles him). In Paris for the Exposition Universelle.	Gautier's *Travels in Russia* is a bestseller. Marx: *Das Kapital* (to 1894). Trollope: *Phineas Finn*.

CHRONOLOGY

HISTORICAL EVENTS

Abraham Lincoln's Emancipation Proclamation frees slaves in the United States.

Alexander II's Great Reforms continue: Zemstva (elected local councils) set up, followed by Duma (elected town councils) in 1870.
Judicial reforms on Western model: judicial and executive power separated; judges to be unimpeachable and irremoveable; new court system established. Trial by jury introduced (1866) – though not for all cases, and not for political crimes; public hearings become more common. Inquisitorial replaced with adversarial system; an Office of Public Prosecution set up and a bar established. Justices of the Peace introduced to try minor offences, to be elected locally by new local councils.
Golovnin's statutes on primary and secondary education.
Serfdom abolished in Poland. Following their military defeat, mass deportation of Circassian population from the western Caucasus begins, with huge loss of life.
Geneva Convention signed. Inaugural meeting of First International in London.
Minister of the Interior, the conservative P. A. Valuyev, introduces a Press Law, a more restrictive measure than liberals had hoped.
Russian expansion into Central Asia with capture of Tashkent; by 1876 the whole of Turkestan has been annexed.

Emancipation of state-owned serfs. Revolutionary Dmitry Karakozov tries to shoot Alexander II outside the Summer Garden in St Petersburg (4 April), the first of a number of assassination attempts. He is hanged, and fellow members of the Ishutin circle are imprisoned and exiled. Government policies become increasingly conservative. Education Minister Golovnin replaced by the reactionary D. A. Tolstoy (also Chief Procurator of the Holy Synod to 1880). *The Contemporary* and *Russian Word* closed down by imperial decree.
In France, growing opposition to Napoleon III from both right and left wing. Austro-Prussian War; Prussian victory at Sadowa.
Membership of any secret society deemed illegal (most *narodniki* convicted on this basis). Russian Industrial Society founded. Sale of Alaska to the United States.
Letter of Napoleon III announcing constitutional changes. Republicans and monarchists alike resist proposals for rearmament. Second Exposition Universelle in Paris, a chance for Napoleon III to show off his newly designed capital.

IVAN TURGENEV

DATE	AUTHOR'S LIFE	LITERARY CONTEXT
1868	Moves into his new villa in Baden-Baden (April). In Russia in early summer, from Spasskoe writing, 'The impression that Russia now makes on me is a very sad one . . . I have never seen dwellings so pitiable so decrepit, or faces so emaciated or so sad . . .' 'The Brigadier' published.	Dostoevsky: *The Idiot* (to 1869). Reshetnikov: *Where is Better?* Goncourt brothers: *Charles Démailly*. Gorky born.
1869	'The Unhappy Girl'. Based in Karlsruhe (for Viardot children's education) and Baden. The liberal *European Herald*, newly founded by Stasyulevich, becomes his new Russian publisher. *Literary and Social Memoirs*.	Flerovsky: *The Condition of the Working Class in Russia*. Goncharov: *The Precipice*. Tolstoy: The completed *War and Peace* published as a 6-volume edition. Flaubert: *Sentimental Education*. Auerbach: *The Villa on the Rhine*. Mill: 'The Subjection of Women'.
1870	'A Strange Story' and 'King Lear of the Steppes' published. Ducamp persuades him to attend a public guillotining in Paris, an experience he much regrets and describes graphically in 'Execution of Tropman'. In Weimar (Feb–March). Visits Russia (May–June). In Berlin when Franco-Prussian War breaks out (15 July). Unhappy about 'hideous, disgusting war' but hopes it will put an end to Napoleon III's regime. He later comes to deplore Prussian imperialist ambitions. His reports on the war published in the *St. Petersburg Chronicle*. The Viardots remove to London where he follows them (Nov).	Death of Herzen, Dickens and Mérimée. Lavrov: *Historical Letters*. Saltykov-Schedrin: *The History of a Town*. Blanc: *History of the Revolution of 1848* (2 vols, 1870–80).
1871	Six-week visit to Russia in spring, involving some early research for *Virgin Soil*. Takes	Dostoevsky: *Demons* (to 1872). Ostrovsky: *The Forest*. Eliot: *Middlemarch* (to 1872).

CHRONOLOGY

HISTORICAL EVENTS

French press laws relaxed. A watered-down Army Law passed.
Public executions banned in Britain. First Gladstone ministry (to 1874).

Nechayev's influential *Catechism of a Revolutionary* calls for 'merciless destruction' of the existing order, defining the revolutionary as an immoralist for whom the end justifies the means. Nechayev flees Russia after murdering a fellow-conspirator. Bakunin's Russian translation of the *Communist Manifesto*. D. I. Mendeleyev presents his formulation of the periodic table to the Russian Chemical Society in St Petersburg. Development of Sakhalin penal colony.
Suez Canal opens.
Das Rheingold, first opera of Wagner's *Ring* cycle, premiered in Munich (Turgenev finds it 'unbearable'.)
In France, Gambetta's Belleville Manifesto defines republican agenda (May); government wins elections with a much reduced majority. Resignation of Rouher.
Burgeoning of student Populist groups in St Petersburg (the Tchaikovsky circle) and other cities, who prepare themselves to take socialist and anarchist ideas directly to the peasants and workers. Lenin born in Simbirsk.
Women allowed to attend an abbreviated from of university course at St Petersburg University with no degree at the end; 740 women attend the lectures.
Government of Ollivier in France (Jan). Liberal reforms to constitution (April) supported by plebiscite (May). Franco-Prussian War begins (July). French defeats; fall of Ollivier (Aug). Surrender of Napoleon III at Sedan; Third Republic declared and Government of National Defence set up; Gambetta Minister of Interior and of War; siege of Paris begins (September).

Bombardment and surrender of Paris (Jan). Election of Assembly; government of Thiers (Feb). Paris Commune set up (March); brutally suppressed by regular French army under General MacMahon in

IVAN TURGENEV

DATE	AUTHOR'S LIFE	LITERARY CONTEXT
1871 cont.	measures to improve the school he had set up at Spasskoe. While in England, meets Tennyson, Swinburne, George Lewes and George Eliot. Attends Walter Scott centenary celebration in Edinburgh and goes grouse shooting at Pitlochrie. Browning and Jowett also of the company (Aug). Viardots re-establish themselves in republican Paris; Turgenev lives with them there permanently until his death; summers are spent at their new house at Bougival, on the Seine.	Zola: *The Fortune of the Rougons*.
1872	*Spring Torrents* published (Jan). Years of his closest social contact with French writers – Flaubert, Zola, Daudet, Maupassant, Edmond de Goncourt. Friendship with George Sand. During the 70s he is busy promoting French writers' work in Russia, and Russian writers in Europe (including Tolstoy, in spite of their quarrel). Begins an art collection. Six-week trip to Russia. With his brother, sets up an almshouse at Spasskoe. *A Month in the Country* staged in Moscow, but is not a success.	Engelgardt: *Letters from the Country* (to 1887). Leskov: *Cathedral Folk*. Tolstoy: *A Prisoner in the Caucasus*. Verne: *Around the World in Eighty Days*. Darwin: *The Descent of Man*.
1873		Bakunin: *Statism and Anarchy*. Leskov: *The Enchanted Wanderer*.
1874	Two-and-a-half months in Russia, partly to research *Virgin Soil*. Follows the trial in St Petersburg of the Dolgushin group, Bakuninists who had tried to stir up a peasant revolt. Pleased to find himself more popular – 'the young generation	Daudet: *Fromont and Risler*. Flaubert: *The Temptation of St Anthony*. Hardy: *Far from the Madding Crowd*.

CHRONOLOGY

HISTORICAL EVENTS

'la semaine sanglante' (May). Treaty of Frankfurt (May): France cedes Alsace-Lorraine to Germany. William I of Prussia becomes emperor of a united Germany.
84 of Nechayev's followers prosecuted in Russia's first public political trial in St Petersburg, causing a sensation (the murder, the extreme methods Nechayev espoused) as the government intended.
D. A. Tolstoy's proposal that university entrance should be restricted to those who had studied Greek and Latin at the gymnasia, is adopted (Turgenev is much opposed to this).
Trade Unions Act legalizes trade unions in Britain.

Government becomes alarmed at number of women studying at universities abroad (over 100 in Zurich alone) and, fearing their radicalization, issues a circular summoning them to return. D. A Tolstoy permits Professor V. I. Guerrier to open a private higher education institution for women in Moscow; 1,232 students attend between 1872 and 1888.
Russian translation of Marx's *Das Kapital* published.
Meeting of the three emperors in Berlin leads to an entente between Russia, Austria-Hungary and Germany.

Trial of Nechayev (arrested in Zurich and extradited in 1872) who is sentenced to 20 years' imprisonment in the Peter and Paul Fortress, where he dies in 1882. Arrests of members of the Tchaikovsky circle begin.
In France, Thiers resigns and right-wing monarchist MacMahon is elected president. Last German troops leave France. Death of Napoleon III in England.
'Mad summer of 74'; several thousand student *narodniki* head for the countryside to share the life and work of the people. According to Stepnyak, 'Nothing like it had ever been seen before or after . . . It was a powerful cry . . . that called living souls to the great work of redeeming the Fatherland and the human race . . . Overflowing with grief and indignation for their past . . . they gave up their homes, their riches, honours and families . . . It was not yet a poltical movement. Rather it was like a religious movement . . .' The peasants are often suspicious of the revolutionaries;

IVAN TURGENEV

DATE	AUTHOR'S LIFE	LITERARY CONTEXT
1874 cont.	has now more goodwill towards me than it showed on my last visit'. Falls out with Fet.	
1875	Henry James comes to Paris to meet him.	Tolstoy: *Anna Karenina* begins publication in the *Russian Herald* (to 1877). Taine: *The Ancien Régime*. Trollope: *The Way We Live Now*.
1876	Writing *Virgin Soil*. Two months in Russia. Financial problems: dismisses dishonest manager and leases Spasskoe to a Shchepkin, a neighbour, for 12 years; it is lived in and managed efficiently by Shchepkin's son.	Daudet: *Jack*. Zola: *L'Assommoir* (to 1877). Eliot: *Daniel Deronda*. Trollope: *The Prime Minister*. Twain: *Tom Sawyer*.
1877	*Virgin Soil* published in the first two issues of the *European Herald*. Criticism initially hostile but the Populist trials help to swing public opinion in Turgenev's favour. By the end of the year it has been widely translated. 'The Dream' and 'The Story of Father Alexis' published. Suffering increasingly from gout. Reconciliation with Nekrasov, who will die not long afterwards.	Garshin: *Four Days*. Storm: *Aquis submersus*.

CHRONOLOGY

HISTORICAL EVENTS

a huge clamp-down by the authorities follows – of the hundreds arrested many are not brought to trial until 1877.
New conscription law makes all males over 21 liable for military service of 18 years (with exemptions including 'only sons'), beginning in standing army, then moving to reserve.
First performance of Mussorgsky's opera *Boris Godunov* in St Petersburg.
First Impressionist exhibition in Paris.
Disraeli prime minister in Britain (to 1880).
Republican constitution passed by one vote: Third Republic declared in France; the following year the National Assembly replaced by a new (conservative) Senate and (republican) Chamber of Deputies.
Unsuccessful première of *Carmen* at the Opéra Comique, Paris. Turgenev, who had recommended Mérimée's novella to Bizet's librettists, is in the audience. Death of Bizet.
Revolt of Bosnia and Herzegovina against Ottoman rule, triggering Serbo-Turkish war the following year.
Engineer and inventor F. A. Pirotsky demonstrates his electric tram on Miller line in St Petersburg.
Land and Freedom relaunched as a party organized from St Petersburg by Natanson and others; work amongst peasants and workers resumes with the founding of Populist 'colonies' (to 1877). Demonstration of workers and students outside Kazan Cathedral in St Petersburg, regarded as the birth of the public socialist movement in Russia; amongst those arrested, intellectuals treated with particular brutality. Anarchist Peter Kropotkin escapes from prison and spends the rest of his life in exile. Death of Bakunin in Switzerland.
Serbia and Montenegro declare war on Ottoman Empire. Revolt against Ottoman rule in Bulgaria; Ottoman massacres of civilians. In Russia much support for their fellow Slavs and discussion of Russian involvement. Turgenev deplores continued British support of Turks; as does public opinion in Britain, stirred up by Gladstone's 'Bulgarian Horrors' pamphlet.
Disraeli proclaims Queen Victoria Empress of India.
Bell patents the telephone (his company opens the first telephone exchanges in Russia in 1882).
Russia declares war on Ottoman Empire (Britain in the event denies support to the Turks).
Public 'trial of the 50' (Feb–March), including 16 women Populists, in Moscow with spirited speeches in defence given by Sofia Bardina and radical worker Peter Alexyev; heavy sentences imposed. 'Trial of the 193' (to 1878), government successfully eliminates the 'going to the people' movement. In France, constitutional crisis when President MacMahon dismisses moderate republican prime minister Simon, and dissolves parliament. Republicans win majority in ensuing election and MacMahon resigns in 1879, a pleasing outcome for Turgenev.
Première of *Swan Lake*, Tchaikovsky's first ballet, in Moscow.
Edison invents the phonograph.

IVAN TURGENEV

DATE	AUTHOR'S LIFE	LITERARY CONTEXT
1878	Continues with annual visits to Russia. Financial difficulties oblige him to sell his art collection (at a loss). Makes up quarrel with Tolstoy and visits him at Yasnaya Polyana.	Hardy: *The Return of the Native*. James: *Daisy Miller*; *The Europeans*.
1879	Death of his brother Nikolai. Surprised by his rapturous reception by students at Moscow and St Petersburg Universities where he is hailed both as a writer and as a potential leader of progressive political opinion. Consequently comes under suspicion of the authorities who also object to his association with revolutionaries such as Lavrov and Kropotkin. Receives honorary DCL at Oxford. *A Month in the Country* revived, this time successfully, starring the actress Maria Savina, with whom he conducts the last of his romantic friendships.	Dostoevsky: *The Brothers Karamazov* (to 1880). Ibsen: *A Doll's House*.
1880	Deeply grieved at death of Flaubert. Socially active visit to St Petersburg and a longer stay with his friend the poet Polonsky at Spasskoe. Involved with running a festival in honour of Pushkin in Moscow.	Annenkov: *The Extraordinary Decade* (literary memoir of the 1840s). Saltykov-Shchedrin: *The Golovlyov Family*. Maupassant: 'Boule de Suif'. Zola: *Nana*. James: *The Portrait of a Lady* (to 1881).

CHRONOLOGY

HISTORICAL EVENTS

Assassination attempt on General Trepov, governor of St Petersburg, by revolutionary Vera Zasulich, in retaliation for his ordering the unlawful flogging of a comrade in prison. Zasulich is acquitted in a trial presided over by the liberal jurist A. F. Koni, the verdict receiving wide public support. This is the first political case to be tried by jury; government announces that in future crimes involving violence against officials will be tried in military courts; the Tsar sacks the Minister of Justice, K. I. Pahlen.

Terrorist tactics increasingly adopted by revolutionaries: Stepnyak assassinates General Mezentsov, head of the Third Section for his role in the 'Trial of the 193', and escapes to London (where he will later become the mentor of Constance Garnett, Turgenev's future translator).

'Bestuzhev' Higher Education courses for women open at St Petersburg. By 1881 some 2,000 women are studying at universities in Russia.

Russian forces threaten Constantinople. Treaty of San Stefano (Russia and Ottoman Empire) rejected by other European powers and superseded by Treaty of Berlin (less favourable to Russia); Bosnia and Herzegovina are occupied by Austria-Hungary; Serbia, Romania and Montenegro gain independence; Bulgaria returned to Ottoman rule.

Stalin born in Gori, Georgia.

Attempted assassination of Tsar by Solovyev (April), who is publicly hanged. Split in Land and Freedom party: The People's Will breaks away to follow the route of political terrorism (its executive committee condemns the Tsar to death;) the short-lived Populist group led by Plekhanov takes the name 'Black Partition' (supporting peasants' desire for a fairer distribution of land).

Prison reform: Main Prison Administration set up, addressing management rather than conditions.

Première in Moscow of Tchaikovsky's opera *Yevgeny Onegin*. (Turgenev, who loves the opera – though disapproving of the libretto – attends a general rehearsal in February.)

In France, Grévy elected president. Amnesty granted to Communards.

A bomb is planted in the Winter Palace by The People's Will but fails to kill the Tsar. State security tightened and fight against terror concentrated on the State Police Department within Loris-Melikov's Ministry of the Interior: many revolutionary leaders are tracked down, including A. D. Mikhailov, co-founder of Land and Freedom and The People's Will (dies in Peter and Paul Fortress, 1884).

K. P. Pobedonostsev becomes Procurator of the Holy Synod (to 1905); moves against religious sectaries.

Trans-Caspian railway begins construction (to 1898).

IVAN TURGENEV

DATE	AUTHOR'S LIFE	LITERARY CONTEXT
1880 cont.		Death of Eliot and Flaubert. Birth of Blok and Bely.
1881	Last trip to Russia and to Spasskoe (where Tolstoy visits on return from a retreat at Optyna Pustyn). Supports the attempts of Alexander II and Loris-Melikov to seek some kind of political compromise; deplores the assassination. Writes unsigned article on Alexander III, hoping he will continue his father's policies of constitutional reform. 'Old Portraits' and 'Song of Triumphant Love' published. Last trip to England.	Death of Dostoevsky. Flaubert: *Bouvard and Pécuchet*. Maupassant: *The House of Madame Tellier*.
1882	*Prose Poems* published. Health deteriorating. (Though never correctly diagnosed, he was probably suffering from spinal cancer.) Summer, as usual, spent at the Viardots' summer house at Bougival. Violent collapse of Paulinette's marriage; he settles her and her children in Switzerland.	Bakunin: *God and the State*. Chicherin: *Property and the State*. Tolstoy: *A Confession*. Fontaine: *The Woman Taken in Adultery*.
1883	'Clara Milic' published. Undergoes an unsuccessful operation. Louis Viardot dies (May). Turgenev dies at Bougival on 3 September. His body is transported to Russia for burial at the Volkovo cemetery in St Petersburg near Belinsky, as he had wished. The government places many restrictions on the ceremony which nonetheless is very well attended.	Fet: *Evening Lights* (to 1891). Garshin: 'The Scarlet Flower'. Maupassant: *A Life*. Nietzsche: *Thus Spoke Zarathustra*.

CHRONOLOGY

HISTORICAL EVENTS

Loris-Melikov seeks to isolate revolutionaries from liberal reformists by proposing modest constitutional changes. The People's Will carries out planned assassination of Alexander II by bombing his carriage in St Petersburg (1 March). Conspirators are executed. In manifesto of 29 April, drafted by Pobedonostsev, his former tutor, Alexander III announces his intention to preserve autocracy. Loris-Melikov resigns. Pobedonostsev becomes chief adviser, largely controlling ministerial appointments.
'Measures for the protection of state order and social tranquillity' (14 August): Minister of the Interior enabled to declare any region in a state of emergency, suspend regular legal procedures and give extra powers of arrest to police – a temporary measure which remains in effect until 1914. New secret police division (the Okhrana) set up. Alexander III and family move out of central St Petersburg to Gatchina Palace.
Pogroms in Ukraine and Poland (to 1882).
D. A. Tolstoy Minister of the Interior (to 1889); stricter 'temporary' press laws restore censorship (remain in place until 1905). I. D. Delyanov Minister of Education (to 1897), aims to transform universities from 'hotbeds of political agitation to hotbeds of science'. N. K. Bunge, Minister of Finance, founds the Peasants' Land Bank.
Between 1882 and 1898 148,032 people are exiled to Siberia, 6% of them for political crimes (*c.* one third after 1905). Over half are banished for civil offences by 'administrative order' (not by court sentence) of local authorities (a practice abolished in 1900). Central government also uses this method, especially for those it deems politically unreliable (rather than guilty of a specific crime): 12,479 political suspects banished by this means, 4,794 of them to Siberia (1881–1900).
Discriminatory laws against Jews (to 1917); beginning of large-scale emigration (1.9 million by 1912).
Anarchist protest in Paris (March). Coronation of Alexander III in Moscow (May).
Death of Wagner and Marx.

NAMES OF CHARACTERS

(Marked to show on which syllable the accent falls)

NEST OF THE GENTRY

Márya Dmítrievna Kalítin
Márfa Timof-yévna Péstov
Sergéi Petróvitch Gedeónovsky
Fédor (*pr. Fyódor*) Ivánitch Lavrétsky
Elisavéta Mihálovna (Lisa)
Lénotchka
Shúrotchka
Nastásya Kárpovna
Vladímir Nikoláitch Pánshin
Christopher Fédoritch Lemm
Piótr Andréitch Lavrétsky
Anna Pávlovna
Iván Petróvitch
Glafíra Petróvna
Malánya Sergyévna
Mihalévitch
Pável Petróvitch Korobýin
Kalliópa Kárlovna
Varvára Pávlovna
Antón
Apráxya
Agáfya Vlásyevna

In transcribing the Russian names into English –
    a has the sound of *a* in *father*
    e   "   "   *a* in *pane*
    i   "   "   *ee*
    u   "   "   *oo*
    y is always consonantal except when it is
        the last letter of the word
    g is always hard

VIRGIN SOIL

Alexéy (Al-yósha) Dmítritch Nezhdánov
Síla Samsónitch Páklin
Borís André-itch Sip-yágin
Sem-yón Petróvitch Kallom-yétsev
Valentína Mihálovna
Mariánna Viként-yevna Sinétsky
Ánna Zahárovna
Sergéi Mihálitch Markélov
Vassíly Fedótitch Solómin
Mashúrina
Ostrodúmov
Golúshkin
Vladímir Sílin
Tat-yána Ósipovna
Pável Yegóritch
Fímushka
Fómushka
Snandúliya (Snapótchka)

NEST OF
THE GENTRY

I

A BRIGHT SPRING day was fading into evening. High overhead in the clear heavens small rosy clouds seemed hardly to move across the sky but to be sinking into its depths of blue.

In a handsome house in one of the outlying streets of the government town of O———— (it was in the year 1842) two women were sitting at an open window; one was about fifty, the other an old lady of seventy.

The name of the former was Marya Dmitrievna Kalitin. Her husband, a shrewd determined man of obstinate bilious temperament, had been dead for ten years. He had been a provincial public prosecutor, noted in his own day as a successful man of business. He had received a fair education and had been to the university; but having been born in narrow circumstances he realised early in life the necessity of pushing his own way in the world and making money. It had been a love-match on Marya Dmitrievna's side. He was not bad-looking, was clever and could be very agreeable when he chose. Marya Dmitrievna Pestov – that was her maiden name – had lost her parents in childhood. She spent some years in a boarding-school in Moscow, and after leaving school, lived on the family estate of Pokrovskoe, about forty miles from O————, with her aunt and her elder brother. This brother soon after obtained a post in Petersburg, and made them a scanty allowance. He treated his aunt and sister very shabbily till his sudden death cut short his career. Marya Dmitrievna inherited Pokrovskoe, but she did not live there long. Two years after her marriage with Kalitin, who succeeded in winning her heart in a few days, Pokrovskoe was exchanged for another estate, which yielded a much larger income, but was utterly unattractive and had no house. At the same time Kalitin took a house in the town of O————, in which he and his wife took up their permanent abode. There was a large garden round the house, which on one side looked out upon the open country away from the town.

'And so,' decided Kalitin, who had a great distaste for the quiet of country life, 'there would be no need for them to be dragging themselves off into the country.' In her heart Marya Dmitrievna more than once regretted her pretty Pokrovskoe, with its babbling brook, its wide meadows, and green copses; but she never opposed her husband in anything and had the greatest veneration for his wisdom and knowledge of the world. When after fifteen years of married life he died leaving her with a son and two daughters, Marya Dmitrievna had grown so accustomed to her house and to town life that she had no inclination to leave O———.

In her youth Marya Dmitrievna had always been spoken of as a pretty blonde; and at fifty her features had not lost all charm, though they were somewhat coarser and less delicate in outline. She was more sentimental than kind-hearted; and even at her mature age, she retained the manners of the boarding-school. She was self-indulgent and easily put out, even moved to tears when she was crossed in any of her habits. She was, however, very sweet and agreeable when all her wishes were carried out and none opposed her. Her house was among the pleasantest in the town. She had a considerable fortune, not so much from her own property as from her husband's savings. Her two daughters were living with her; her son was being educated in one of the best government schools in Petersburg.

The old lady sitting with Marya Dmitrievna at the window was her father's sister, the same aunt with whom she had once spent some solitary years in Pokrovskoe. Her name was Marfa Timofyevna Pestov. She had a reputation for eccentricity as she was a woman of an independent character, told every one the truth to his face, and even in the most straitened circumstances behaved just as if she had a fortune at her disposal. She could not endure Kalitin, and directly her niece married him, she removed to her little property, where for ten whole years she lived in a smoky peasants' hut. Marya Dmitrievna was a little afraid of her. A little sharp-nosed woman with black hair and keen eyes even in her old age, Marfa Timofyevna walked briskly, held herself upright and spoke quickly and clearly in a sharp ringing voice. She always wore a white cap and a white dressing-jacket.

'What's the matter with you?' she asked Marya Dmitrievna suddenly. 'What are you sighing about, pray?'

'Nothing,' answered the latter. 'What exquisite clouds!'

'You feel sorry for them, eh?'

Marya Dmitrievna made no reply.

'Why is it Gedeonovsky does not come?' observed Marfa Timofyevna, moving her knitting needles quickly. (She was knitting a large woollen scarf.) 'He would have sighed with you – or at least he'd have had some fib to tell you.'

'How hard you always are on him! Sergei Petrovitch is a worthy man.'

'Worthy!' repeated the old lady scornfully.

'And how devoted he was to my poor husband!' observed Marya Dmitrievna; 'even now he cannot speak of him without emotion.'

'And no wonder! it was he who picked him out of the gutter,' muttered Marfa Timofyevna, and her knitting needles moved faster than ever.

'He looks so meek and mild,' she began again, 'with his grey head, but he no sooner opens his mouth than out comes a lie or a slander. And to think of his having the rank of a councillor! To be sure, though, he's only a village priest's son.'

'Every one has faults, auntie; that is his weak point, no doubt. Sergei Petrovitch has had no education: of course he does not speak French, still, say what you like, he is an agreeable man.'

'Yes, he is always ready to kiss your hands. He does not speak French – that's no great loss. I am not over strong in the French lingo myself. It would be better if he could not speak at all; he would not tell lies then. But here he is – speak of the devil,' added Marfa Timofyevna looking into the street. 'Here comes your agreeable man striding along. What a lanky creature he is, just like a stork!'

Marya Dmitrievna began to arrange her curls. Marfa Timofyevna looked at her ironically.

'What's that, not a grey hair surely? You must speak to your Palashka, what can she be thinking about?'

'Really, auntie, you are always so ...' muttered Marya Dmitrievna in a tone of vexation, drumming on the arm of her chair with her finger-tips.

'Sergei Petrovitch Gedeonovsky!' was announced in a shrill piping voice, by a rosy-cheeked little page who made his appearance at the door.

II

A TALL MAN entered, wearing a tidy overcoat, rather short trousers, grey doeskin gloves, and two neckties – a black one outside, and a white one below it. There was an air of decorum and propriety in everything about him, from his prosperous countenance and smoothly brushed hair, to his low-heeled, noiseless boots. He bowed first to the lady of the house, then to Marfa Timofyevna, and slowly drawing off his gloves, he advanced to take Marya Dmitrievna's hand. After kissing it respectfully twice he seated himself with deliberation in an arm-chair, and rubbing the very tips of his fingers together, he observed with a smile –

'And is Elisaveta Mihalovna quite well?'

'Yes,' replied Marya Dmitrievna, 'she's in the garden.'

'And Elena Mihalovna?'

'Lenotchka's in the garden too. Is there no news?'

'There is indeed!' replied the visitor, slowly wrinkling his brows and pursing up his mouth. 'Hm! ... yes, indeed, there is a piece of news, and very surprising news too. Lavretsky – Fedor Ivanitch is here.'

'Fedya?' cried Marfa Timofyevna. 'Are you sure you are not romancing, my good man?'

'No, indeed, I saw him myself.'

'Well, that does not prove it.'

'Fedor Ivanitch looked much more robust,' continued Gedeonovsky, affecting not to have heard Marfa Timofyevna's last remark. 'Fedor Ivanitch is broader and has quite a colour.'

'He looked more robust,' said Marya Dmitrievna, dwelling on each syllable. 'I should have thought he had little enough to make him look robust.'

'Yes, indeed,' observed Gedeonovsky; 'any other man in Fedor Ivanitch's position would have hesitated to appear in society.'

'Why so, pray?' interposed Marfa Timofyevna. 'What nonsense are you talking! The man's come back to his home – where would you have him go? And has he been to blame, I should like to know!'

'The husband is always to blame, madam, I venture to assure you, when a wife misconducts herself.'

'You say that, my good sir, because you have never been married yourself.' Gedeonovsky listened with a forced smile.

'If I may be so inquisitive,' he asked, after a short pause, 'for whom is that pretty scarf intended?'

Marfa Timofyevna gave him a sharp look.

'It's intended,' she replied, 'for a man who does not talk scandal, nor play the hypocrite, nor tell lies, if there's such a man to be found in the world. I know Fedya well; he was only to blame in being too good to his wife. To be sure, he married for love, and no good ever comes of those love-matches,' added the old lady, with a sidelong glance at Marya Dmitrievna, as she got up from her place. 'And now, my good sir, you may attack any one you like, even me if you choose; I'm going, I will not hinder you.' And Marfa Timofyevna walked away.

'That's always how she is,' said Marya Dmitrievna, following her aunt with her eyes.

'We must remember your aunt's age . . . there's no help for it,' replied Gedeonovsky. 'She spoke of a man not playing the hypocrite. But who is not hypocritical nowadays? It's the age we live in. One of my friends, a most worthy man, and, I assure you, a man of no mean position, used to say, that nowadays the very hens can't pick up a grain of corn without hypocrisy – they always approach it from one side. But when I look at you, dear lady – your character is so truly angelic; let me kiss your little snow-white hand!'

Marya Dmitrievna with a faint smile held out her plump hand to him with the little finger held apart from the rest. He pressed his lips to it, and she drew her chair nearer to him, and bending a little towards him, asked in an undertone –

'So you saw him? Was he really – all right – quite well and cheerful?'

'Yes, he was well and cheerful,' replied Gedeonovsky in a whisper.

'You haven't heard where his wife is now?'

'She was lately in Paris; now, they say, she has gone away to Italy.'

'It is terrible, indeed – Fedya's position; I wonder how he can bear it. Every one, of course, has trouble; but he, one may say, has been made the talk of all Europe.'

Gedeonovsky sighed.

'Yes, indeed, yes, indeed. They do say, you know that she associates with artists and musicians, and as the saying is, with strange creatures of all kinds. She has lost all sense of shame completely.'

'I am deeply, deeply grieved,' said Marya Dmitrievna. 'On account of our relationship; you know, Sergei Petrovitch, he's my cousin many times removed.'

'Of course, of course. Don't I know everything that concerns your family? I should hope so, indeed.'

'Will he come to see us – what do you think?'

'One would suppose so; though, they say, he is intending to go home to his country place.'

Marya Dmitrievna lifted her eyes to heaven.

'Ah, Sergei Petrovitch, Sergei Petrovitch, when I think how careful we women ought to be in our conduct!'

'There are women and women, Marya Dmitrievna. There are unhappily such . . . of flighty character . . . and at a certain age too, and then they are not brought up in good principles.' (Sergei Petrovitch drew a blue checked handkerchief out of his pocket and began to unfold it.) 'There are such women, no doubt.' (Sergei Petrovitch applied a corner of the handkerchief first to one and then to the other eye.) 'But speaking generally, if one takes into consideration, I mean . . . the dust in the town is really extraordinary to-day,' he wound up.

'*Maman, maman,*' cried a pretty little girl of eleven running into the room, 'Vladimir Nikolaitch is coming on horseback!'

Marya Dmitrievna got up; Sergei Petrovitch also rose and made a bow. 'Our humble respects to Elena Mihalovna,' he said, and turning aside into a corner for good manners, he began blowing his long straight nose.

'What a splendid horse he has!' continued the little girl. 'He was at the gate just now, he told Lisa and me he would dismount at the steps.'

The sound of hoofs was heard; and a graceful young man, riding a beautiful bay horse, was seen in the street, and stopped at the open window.

III

'HOW DO YOU DO, Marya Dmitrievna?' cried the young man in a pleasant, ringing voice. 'How do you like my new purchase?'

Marya Dmitrievna went up to the window.

'How do you do, *Woldemar*! Ah, what a splendid horse! Where did you buy it?'

'I bought it from the army contractor. . . . He made me pay for it too, the brigand!'

'What's its name?'

'Orlando. . . . But it's a stupid name; I want to change it . . . *Eh bien, eh bien, mon garçon.* . . . What a restless beast it is!'

The horse snorted, stamped, pawed the ground, and shook the foam off the bit.

'Lenotchka, stroke him, don't be afraid.'

The little girl stretched her hand out of the window, but Orlando suddenly reared and started. The rider with perfect self-possession gave it a cut with the whip across the neck, and keeping a tight grip with his legs forced it, in spite of its opposition, to stand still again at the window.

'*Prenez garde, prenez garde,*' Marya Dmitrievna kept repeating.

'Lenotchka, pat him,' said the young man, 'I won't let him be perverse.'

The little girl again stretched out her hand and timidly patted the quivering nostrils of the horse, who kept fidgeting and champing the bit.

'Bravo!' cried Marya Dmitrievna, 'but now get off and come in to us.'

The rider adroitly turned his horse, gave him a touch of the spur, and galloping down the street soon reached the courtyard. A minute later he ran into the drawing-room by the door from the hall, flourishing his whip; at the same moment there appeared in the other doorway a tall, slender dark-haired girl of nineteen, Marya Dmitrievna's eldest daughter, Lisa.

IV

THE NAME OF the young man whom we have just introduced to the reader was Vladimir Nikolaitch Panshin. He served in Petersburg on special commissions in the department of internal affairs. He had come to the town of O——— to carry out some temporary government commissions, and was in attendance on the Governor-General Zonnenberg, to whom he happened to be distantly related. Panshin's father, a retired cavalry officer and a notorious gambler, was a man with insinuating eyes, a battered countenance, and a nervous twitch about the mouth. He spent his whole life hanging about the aristocratic world; frequented the English clubs of both capitals, and had the reputation of a smart, not very trustworthy, but jolly good-natured fellow. In spite of his smartness, he was almost always on the brink of ruin, and the property he left his son was small and heavily encumbered. To make up for that, however, he did exert himself, after his own fashion, over his son's education. Vladimir Nikolaitch spoke French very well, English well, and German badly; that is the proper thing: fashionable people would be ashamed to speak German well; but to utter an occasional – generally a humorous – phrase in German is quite correct, *c'est même très chic*, as the Parisians of Petersburg express themselves. By the time he was fifteen, Vladimir knew how to enter any drawing-room without embarrassment, how to move about in it gracefully and to leave it at the appropriate moment. Panshin's father gained many connections for his son. He never lost an opportunity, while shuffling the cards between two rubbers, or playing a successful trump, of dropping a hint about his Volodka to any personage of importance who was a devotee of cards. And Vladimir, too, during his residence at the university, which he left without a very brilliant degree, formed an acquaintance with several young men of quality, and gained an entry into the best houses. He was received cordially everywhere: he was very good-looking, easy in his manners, amusing, always in good health, and ready for everything; respectful, when he ought to be; insolent, when he dared to be; excellent company, *un charmant garçon*. The promised land lay before him. Panshin quickly learnt the secret of getting on in the world; he knew how to yield with genuine respect to its decrees; he knew how to take up trifles with half ironical seriousness, and to appear to regard everything serious as trifling; he was a capital dancer; and dressed in the English style. In a short time he gained the reputation of being one of the smartest and most attractive young men in Petersburg. Panshin was indeed very smart, not less so than his father; but he was also very talented. He did everything well; he sang charmingly, sketched with spirit, wrote verses, and was a very fair actor. He was only twenty-eight, and he was already a *kammerjunker*, and had a very good position. Panshin had complete confidence in himself, in his own intelligence, and his own penetration; he made his way with light-hearted assurance, everything went smoothly with him. He was used to being liked by every one, old and young, and imagined that he understood people, especially women: he certainly understood their ordinary weaknesses. As a man of artistic leanings, he was conscious of a capacity for passion, for being carried away, even for enthusiasm, and, consequently, he permitted himself various irregularities; he was dissipated, associated with persons not belonging to good society, and, in general, conducted himself in a free and easy manner; but at heart he was cold and false, and at the moment of the most boisterous revelry his sharp brown eye was always alert, taking everything in. This bold, independent young man could never forget himself and be completely carried away. To his credit it must be said, that he never boasted of his conquests. He had found his way into Marya Dmitrievna's house immediately he arrived in O———, and was soon perfectly at home there. Marya Dmitrievna absolutely adored him. Panshin exchanged cordial greetings with every one in the room; he shook hands with Marya Dmitrievna and Lisaveta Mihalovna, clapped Gedeonovsky lightly on the shoulder, and turning round on his heels, put his hand on Lenotchka's head and kissed her on the forehead.

'Aren't you afraid to ride such a vicious horse?' Marya Dmitrievna questioned him.

'I assure you he's very quiet, but I will tell you what I am afraid of: I'm afraid to play preference with Sergei Petrovitch; yesterday he cleaned me out of everything at Madame Byelenitsin's.'

Gedeonovsky gave a thin, sympathetic little laugh; he was anxious to be in favour with the brilliant young official from Petersburg – the governor's favourite. In conversation with Marya Dmitrievna, he often alluded to Panshin's remarkable abilities. Indeed, he used to argue how can one help admiring him? The young man is making his way in the highest spheres, he is an exemplary official, and not a bit of pride about him. And, in fact, even in Petersburg Panshin was reckoned a capable official; he got through a great deal of work; he spoke of it lightly as befits a man of the world who does not attach any special importance to his labours, but he never hesitated in carrying out orders. The authorities like such subordinates; he himself had no doubt, that if he chose, he could be a minister in time.

'You are pleased to say that I cleaned you out,' replied Gedeonovsky; 'but who was it won twelve roubles of me last week and more?' . . .

'You're a malicious fellow,' Panshin interrupted, with genial but somewhat contemptuous carelessness, and, paying him no further attention, he went up to Lisa.

'I cannot get the overture of Oberon here,' he began. 'Madame Byelenitsin was boasting when she said she had all the classical music: in reality she has nothing but polkas and waltzes, but I have already written to Moscow, and within a week you will have the overture. By the way,' he went on, 'I wrote a new song yesterday, the words too are mine, would you care for me to sing it? I don't know how far it is successful. Madame Byelenitsin thought it very pretty, but her words mean nothing. I should like to know what you think of it. But I think, though, that had better be later on.'

'Why later on?' interposed Marya Dmitrievna, 'why not now?'

'I obey,' replied Panshin, with a peculiar bright and sweet smile, which came and went suddenly on his face. He drew up a chair with his knee, sat down to the piano, and striking a few chords began to sing, articulating the words clearly, the following song –

>   Above the earth the moon floats high
>   Amid pale clouds;
>   Its magic light in that far sky
>   Yet stirs the floods.
>
>   My heart has found a moon to rule
>   Its stormy sea;
>   To joy and sorrow it is moved
>   Only by thee.
>
>   My soul is full of love's cruel smart,
>   And longing vain;
>   But thou art calm, as that cold moon,
>   That knows not pain.

The second couplet was sung by Panshin with special power and expression, the sound of waves was heard in the stormy accompaniment. After the words 'and longing vain,' he sighed softly, dropped his eyes and let his voice gradually die away, *morendo*. When he had finished, Lisa praised the motive, Marya Dmitrievna cried, 'Charming!' but Gedeonovsky went so far as to exclaim, 'Ravishing poetry, and music equally ravishing!' Lenotchka looked with childish reverence at the singer. In short, every one present was delighted with the young dilettante's composition; but at the door leading into the drawing-room from the hall stood an old man, who had only just come in, and who, to judge by the expression of his downcast face and the shrug of his shoulders, was by no means pleased with Panshin's song, pretty though it was. After waiting a moment and flicking the dust off his boots with a coarse pocket-handkerchief, this man suddenly raised his eyes, compressed his lips with a morose expression, and his stooping figure bent forward, he entered the drawing-room.

'Ah! Christopher Fedoritch, how are you?' exclaimed Panshin before any of the others could speak, and he jumped up quickly from his seat. 'I had no suspicion that you were here, – nothing would have induced me to sing my song before you. I know you are no lover of light music.'

'I did not hear it,' declared the new-comer, in very bad Russian, and exchanging greetings with every one, he stood awkwardly in the middle of the room.

'Have you come, Monsieur Lemm,' said Marya Dmitrievna, 'to give Lisa her music lesson?'

'No, not Lisaveta Mihalovna but Elena Mihalovna.'

'Oh! very well. Lenotchka, go up-stairs with Mr. Lemm.'

The old man was about to follow the little girl, but Panshin stopped him.

'Don't go after the lesson, Christopher Fedoritch,' he said. 'Lisaveta Mihalovna and I are going to play a duet of Beethoven's sonata.'

The old man muttered some reply, and Panshin continued in German, mispronouncing the words –

'Lisaveta Mihalovna showed me the religious cantata you dedicated to her – a beautiful thing! Pray, do not suppose that I cannot appreciate serious music – quite the contrary: it is tedious sometimes, but then it is very elevating.'

The old man crimsoned to his ears, and with a sidelong look at Lisa, he hurriedly went out of the room.

Marya Dmitrievna asked Panshin to sing his song again; but he protested that he did not wish to torture the ears of the musical German, and suggested to Lisa that they should attack Beethoven's sonata. Then Marya Dmitrievna heaved a sigh, and in her turn suggested to Gedeonovsky a walk in the garden. 'I should like,' she said, 'to have a little more talk, and to consult you about our poor Fedya.' Gedeonovsky bowed with a smirk, and with two fingers picked up his hat, on the brim of which his gloves had been tidily laid, and went away with Marya Dmitrievna. Panshin and Lisa remained alone in the room; she fetched the sonata, and opened it; both seated themselves at the piano in silence. Overhead were heard the faint sounds of scales, played by the uncertain fingers of Lenotchka.

V

CHRISTOPHER THEODOR GOTTLIEB LEMM was born in 1786 in the town of Chemnitz in Saxony. His parents were poor musicians. His father played the French horn, his mother the harp; he himself was practising on three different instruments by the time he was five. At eight years old he was left an orphan, and from his tenth year he began to earn his bread by his art. He led a wandering life for many years, and performed everywhere in restaurants, at fairs, at peasants' weddings, and at balls. At last he got into an orchestra, and constantly rising in it, he obtained the position of director. He was rather a poor performer; but he understood music thoroughly. At twenty-eight he migrated into Russia, on the invitation of a great nobleman, who did not care for music himself, but kept an orchestra for show. Lemm lived with him seven years in the capacity of orchestra conductor, and left him empty-handed.

The nobleman was ruined, he intended to give him a promissory note, but in the sequel refused him even that – in short, did not pay him a farthing. He was advised to go away; but he was unwilling to return home in poverty from Russia, that great Russia which is a mine of gold for artists; he decided to remain and try his luck. For twenty years the poor German had been trying his luck; he had lived in various gentlemen's houses, had suffered and put up with much, had faced privation, had struggled like a fish on the ice; but the idea of returning to his own country never left him among all the hardships he endured; it was this dream alone that sustained him. But fate did not see fit to grant him this last and first happiness: at fifty, broken-down in health and prematurely aged, he drifted to the town of O———, and remained there for good, having now lost once for all every hope of leaving Russia, which he detested. He gained his poor livelihood somehow by lessons. Lemm's exterior was not prepossessing. He was short and bent, with crooked shoulders, and a contracted chest, with large flat feet, and bluish white nails on the gnarled bony fingers of his sinewy red hands. He had a scowl on his face, sunken cheeks, and compressed lips, which he was for ever twitching and biting; and this, together with his habitual taciturnity, produced an impression almost sinister. His grey hair hung in tufts on his low brow; like smouldering embers, his little set eyes glowed with dull fire. He moved painfully, at every step swinging his ungainly body forward. Some of his movements recalled the clumsy actions of an owl in a cage when it feels that it is being looked at, but itself can hardly see out of its great yellow eyes timorously and drowsily blinking. Pitiless, prolonged sorrow had laid its indelible stamp on the poor musician; it had disfigured and deformed his person, by no means attractive to begin with. But any one who was able to get over the first impression would have discerned something good, and honest, and out of the common in this half-shattered creature. A devoted admirer of Bach and Handel, a master of his art, gifted with a lively imagination and that boldness of conception which is only vouchsafed to the German race, Lemm might, in time – who knows? – have taken rank with the great composers of his fatherland, had his life been different; but he was born under an unlucky star! He had written much in his life, and it had not been granted to him to see one of his compositions produced; he did not know how to set about things in the right way, to gain favour in the right place, and to make a push at the right moment. A long, long time ago, his one friend and admirer, also a German and also poor, had published two of Lemm's sonatas at his own expense – the whole edition remained on the shelves of the music-shops; they disappeared without a trace, as though they had been thrown into a river by night. At last Lemm had renounced everything; the years too did their work; his mind had grown hard and stiff, as his fingers had stiffened. He lived alone in a little cottage not far from the Kalitins' house, with an old cook he had taken out of the poorhouse (he had never married). He took long walks, and read the Bible and the Protestant version of the Psalms, and Shakespeare in Schlegel's translation. He had composed nothing for a long time; but apparently, Lisa, his best pupil, had been able to inspire him; he had written for her the cantata to which Panshin had made allusion. The words of this cantata he had borrowed from his collection of hymns. He had added a few verses of his own. It was sung by two choruses – a chorus of the happy and a chorus of the unhappy. The two were brought into harmony at the end, and sang together, 'Merciful God, have pity on us sinners, and deliver us from all evil thoughts and earthly hopes.' On the title-page was the inscription, most carefully written and even illuminated, 'Only the righteous are justified. A religious cantata. Composed and dedicated to Miss Elisaveta Kalitin, his dear pupil, by her teacher C. T. G. Lemm.' The words, 'Only the righteous are justified' and 'Elisaveta Kalitin,' were encircled by rays. Below was written: 'For you alone, *für Sie allein.*' This was why Lemm had grown red, and looked reproachfully at Lisa; he was deeply wounded when Panshin spoke of his cantata before him.

VI

PANSHIN, WHO WAS playing bass, struck the first chords of the sonata loudly and decisively, but Lisa did not begin her part. He stopped and looked at her. Lisa's eyes were fixed directly on him, and expressed displeasure. There was no smile on her lips, her whole face looked stern and even mournful.

'What's the matter?' he asked.

'Why did you not keep your word?' she said. 'I showed you Christopher Fedoritch's cantata on the express condition that you said nothing about it to him.'

'I beg your pardon, Lisaveta Mihalovna, the words slipped out unawares.'

'You have hurt his feelings and mine too. Now he will not trust even me.'

'How could I help it, Lisaveta Mihalovna? Ever since I was a little boy I could never see a German without wanting to tease him.'

'How can you say that, Vladimir Nikolaitch? This German is poor, lonely, and broken-down – have you no pity for him? Can you wish to tease him?'

Panshin was a little taken aback.

'You are right, Lisaveta Mihalovna,' he declared. 'It's my everlasting thoughtlessness that's to blame. No, don't contradict me; I know myself. So much harm has come to me from my want of thought. It's owing to that failing that I am thought to be an egoist.'

Panshin paused. With whatever subject he began a conversation, he generally ended by talking of himself, and the subject was changed by him so easily, so smoothly and genially, that it seemed unconscious.

'In your own household, for instance,' he went on, 'your mother certainly wishes me well, she is so kind; you – well, I don't know your opinion of me; but on the other hand your aunt simply can't bear me. I must have offended her too by some thoughtless, stupid speech. You know I'm not a favourite of hers, am I?'

'No,' Lisa admitted with some reluctance, 'she doesn't like you.'

Panshin ran his fingers quickly over the keys, and a scarcely perceptible smile glided over his lips.

'Well, and you?' he said, 'do you too think me an egoist?'

'I know you very little,' replied Lisa, 'but I don't consider you an egoist; on the contrary, I can't help feeling grateful to you.'

'I know, I know what you mean to say,' Panshin interrupted, and again he ran his fingers over the keys: 'for the music and the books I bring you, for the wretched sketches with which I adorn your album, and so forth. I might do all that – and be an egoist all the same. I venture to think that you don't find me a bore, and don't think me a bad fellow, but still you suppose that I – what's the saying? – would sacrifice friend or father for the sake of a witticism.'

'You are careless and forgetful, like all men of the world,' observed Lisa, 'that is all.'

Panshin frowned a little.

'Come,' he said, 'don't let us discuss me any more; let us play our sonata. There's only one thing I must beg of you,' he added, smoothing out the leaves of the book on the music stand, 'think what you like of me, call me an egoist even – so be it! but don't call me a man of the world; that name's insufferable to me. . . . *Anch'io sono pittore.* I too am an artist, though a poor one – and *that* – I mean that I'm a poor artist, I shall show directly. Let us begin.'

'Very well, let us begin,' said Lisa.

The first *adagio* went fairly successfully though Panshin

made more than one false note. His own compositions and what he had practised thoroughly he played very nicely, but he played at sight badly. So the second part of the sonata – a rather quick *allegro* – broke down completely; at the twentieth bar, Panshin, who was two bars behind, gave in, and pushed his chair back with a laugh.

'No!' he cried, 'I can't play to-day; it's a good thing Lemm did not hear us; he would have had a fit.'

Lisa got up, shut the piano, and turned round to Panshin.

'What are we going to do?' she asked.

'That's just like you, that question! You can never sit with your hands idle. Well, if you like let us sketch, since it's not quite dark. Perhaps the other muse, the muse of painting – what was her name? I have forgotten . . . will be more propitious to me. Where's your album? I remember, my landscape there is not finished.'

Lisa went into the other room to fetch the album, and Panshin, left alone, drew a cambric handkerchief out of his pocket, rubbed his nails and looked as it were critically at his hands. He had beautiful white hands; on the second finger of his left hand he wore a spiral gold ring. Lisa came back; Panshin sat down at the window, and opened the album.

'Ah!' he exclaimed: 'I see that you have begun to copy my landscape – and capitally too. Excellent! only just here – give me a pencil – the shadows are not put in strongly enough. Look.'

And Panshin with a flourish added a few long strokes. He was for ever drawing the same landscape: in the foreground large dishevelled trees, a stretch of meadow in the background, and jagged mountains on the horizon. Lisa looked over his shoulders at his work.

'In drawing, just as in life generally,' observed Panshin, holding his head to right and to left, 'lightness and boldness – are the great things.'

At that instant Lemm came into the room, and with a stiff bow was about to leave it; but Panshin, throwing aside album and pencils, placed himself in his way.

'Where are you going, dear Christopher Fedoritch? Aren't you going to stay and have tea with us?'

'I go home,' answered Lemm in a surly voice; 'my head aches.'

'Oh, what nonsense! – do stop. We'll have an argument about Shakespeare.'

'My head aches,' repeated the old man.

'We set to work on the sonata of Beethoven without you,' continued Panshin, taking hold of him affectionately and smiling brightly, 'but we couldn't get on at all. Fancy, I couldn't play two notes together correctly.'

'You'd better have sung your song again,' replied Lemm, removing Panshin's hands, and he walked away.

Lisa ran after him. She overtook him on the stairs.

'Christopher Fedoritch, I want to tell you,' she said to him in German, accompanying him over the short green grass of the yard to the gate, 'I did wrong – forgive me.'

Lemm made no answer.

'I showed Vladimir Nikolaitch your cantata; I felt sure he would appreciate it, – and he did like it very much, really.'

Lemm stopped.

'It's no matter,' he said in Russian, and then added in his own language, 'but he cannot understand anything; how is it you don't see that? He's a dilettante – and that's all!'

'You are unjust to him,' replied Lisa, 'he understands everything, and he can do almost everything himself.'

'Yes, everything second-rate, cheap, scamped work. That pleases, and he pleases, and he is glad it is so – and so much the better. I'm not angry; the cantata and I – we are a pair of old fools; I'm a little ashamed, but it's no matter.'

'Forgive me, Christopher Fedoritch,' Lisa said again.

'It's no matter,' he repeated again in Russian, 'you're a good girl . . . but here is some one coming to see you. Good-bye. You are a very good girl.'

And Lemm moved with hastened steps towards the gate, through which had entered some gentleman unknown to him in a grey coat and a wide straw hat. Bowing politely to him (he always saluted all new faces in the town of O———; from acquaintances he always turned aside in the street – that was the rule he had laid down for himself), Lemm passed by and disappeared behind the fence. The stranger looked after him in amazement, and after gazing attentively at Lisa, went straight up to her.

VII

'YOU DON'T RECOGNISE ME,' he said, taking off his hat, 'but I recognised you in spite of its being seven years since I saw you last. You were a child then. I am Lavretsky. Is your mother at home? Can I see her?'

'Mamma will be glad to see you,' replied Lisa; 'she had heard of your arrival.'

'Let me see, I think your name is Elisaveta?' said Lavretsky, as he went up the stairs.

'Yes.'

'I remember you very well; you had even then a face one doesn't forget. I used to bring you sweets in those days.'

Lisa blushed and thought what a queer man. Lavretsky stopped for an instant in the hall. Lisa went into the drawing-room, where Panshin's voice and laugh could be heard; he had been communicating some gossip of the town to Marya Dmitrievna, and Gedeonovsky, who by this time had come in from the garden, and he was himself laughing aloud at the story he was telling. At the name of Lavretsky, Marya Dmitrievna was all in a flutter. She turned pale and went up to meet him.

'How do you do, how do you do, my dear cousin?' she cried

in a plaintive and almost tearful voice, 'how glad I am to see you!'

'How are you, cousin?' replied Lavretsky, with a friendly pressure of her out-stretched hand; 'how has Providence been treating you?'

'Sit down, sit down, my dear Fedor Ivanitch. Ah, how glad I am! But let me present my daughter Lisa to you.'

'I have already introduced myself to Lisaveta Mihalovna,' interposed Lavretsky.

'Monsieur Panshin . . . Sergei Petrovitch Gedeonovsky . . . Please sit down. When I look at you, I can hardly believe my eyes. How are you?'

'As you see; I'm flourishing. And you, too, cousin – no ill-luck to you! – have grown no thinner in eight years.'

'To think how long it is since we met!' observed Marya Dmitrievna dreamily. 'Where have you come from now? Where did you leave . . . that is, I meant to say,' she put in hastily, 'I meant to say, are you going to be with us for long?'

'I have come now from Berlin,' replied Lavretsky, 'and to-morrow I shall go into the country – probably for a long time.'

'You will live at Lavriky, I suppose?'

'No, not at Lavriky; I have a little place, twenty miles from here: I am going there.'

'Is that the little estate that came to you from Glafira Petrovna?'

'Yes.'

'Really, Fedor Ivanitch! You have such a magnificent house at Lavriky.'

Lavretsky knitted his brows a little.

'Yes . . . but there's a small lodge in this little property, and I need nothing more for a time. That place is the most convenient for me now.'

Marya Dmitrievna was again thrown into such a state of agitation that she became quite stiff, and her hands hung lifeless by her sides. Panshin came to her support by entering into conversation with Lavretsky. Marya Dmitrievna regained her composure, she leaned back in her arm-chair and now and then put in a word. But she looked all the while with such sympathy at her guest, sighed so significantly, and shook her head so dejectedly, that the latter at last lost patience and asked her rather sharply if she was unwell.

'Thank God, no,' replied Marya Dmitrievna; 'why do you ask?'

'Oh, I fancied you didn't seem to be quite yourself.'

Marya Dmitrievna assumed a dignified and somewhat offended air. 'If that's how the land lies,' she thought, 'it's absolutely no matter to me; I see, my good fellow, it's all like water on a duck's back for you; any other man would have wasted away with grief, but you've grown fat on it.' Marya Dmitrievna did not mince matters in her own mind: she expressed herself with more elegance aloud.

Lavretsky certainly did not look like the victim of fate. His rosy-cheeked typical Russian face, with its large white brow, rather thick nose, and wide straight lips seemed breathing with the wild health of the steppes, with vigorous primæval energy. He was splendidly well-built, and his fair curly hair stood up on his head like a boy's. It was only in his blue eyes, with their over-hanging brows and somewhat fixed look, that one could trace an expression, not exactly of melancholy, nor exactly of weariness, and his voice had almost too measured a cadence.

Panshin meanwhile continued to keep up the conversation. He turned it upon the profits of sugar-boiling, on which he had lately read two French pamphlets, and with modest composure undertook to expound their contents, without mentioning, however, a single word about the source of his information.

'Good God, it is Fedya!' came through the half-opened door the voice of Marfa Timofyevna in the next room. 'Fedya himself!' and the old woman ran hurriedly into the room. Lavretsky had not time to get up from his seat before she had him in her arms. 'Let me have a look at you,' she said, holding his face off at arm's length. 'Ah! what a splendid fellow you are! You've grown older a little, but not a bit changed for the worse, upon my word! But why are you kissing my hands – kiss my face if you're not afraid of my wrinkled cheeks. You never asked after me – whether your aunt was alive – I warrant: and you were in my arms as soon as you were born, you great rascal! Well, that is nothing to you, I suppose; why should you remember me? But it was a good idea of yours to come back. And pray,' she added, turning to Marya Dmitrievna, 'have you offered him something to eat?'

'I don't want anything,' Lavretsky hastened to declare.

'Come, you must at least have some tea, my dear. Lord have mercy on us! He has come from I don't know where, and they don't even give him a cup of tea! Lisa, run and stir them up, and make haste. I remember he was dreadfully greedy when he was a little fellow, and he likes good things now, I daresay.'

'My respects, Marfa Timofyevna,' said Panshin, approaching the delighted old lady from one side with a low bow.

'Pardon me, sir,' replied Marfa Timofyevna, 'for not observing you in my delight. You have grown like your mother, the poor darling,' she went on, turning again to Lavretsky, 'but your nose was always your father's, and your father's it has remained. Well, and are you going to be with us for long?'

'I am going to-morrow, aunt.'

'Where?'

'Home to Vassilyevskoe.'

'To-morrow?'

'Yes, to-morrow.'

'Well, if to-morrow it must be. God bless you – you know best. Only mind you come and say good-bye to me.' The old woman patted his cheek. 'I did not think I should be here to see you; not that I have made up my mind to die yet a while – I shall last another ten years, I daresay: all we Pestovs live long; your late grandfather used to say we had two lives; but you see there was no telling how much longer you were going to dangle about abroad. Well, you're a fine lad, a fine lad; can you lift twenty stone with one hand as you used to do, eh? Your late papa was fantastical in some things, if I may say so; but he did well in having that Swiss to bring you up; do you remember you used to fight with your fists with him? – gymnastics, wasn't it they called it? But there, why I am gabbling away like this; I have only been hindering Mr. Panshín (she never pronounced his name Pánshin as was correct) from holding forth. Besides, we'd better go and have tea; yes, let's go on to the terrace, my boy, and drink it there; we have some real cream, not like what you get in your Londons and Parises. Come along, come along, and you, Fedusha, give me your arm. Oh! but what an arm it is! Upon my word, no fear of my stumbling with you!'

Every one got up and went out on to the terrace, except Gedeonovsky, who quietly took his departure. During the whole of Lavretsky's conversation with Marya Dmitrievna, Panshin, and Marfa Timofyevna, he sat in a corner, blinking attentively, with an open mouth of childish curiosity; now he was in haste to spread the news of the new arrival through the town.

At eleven o'clock on the evening of the same day, this is what was happening in Madame Kalitin's house. Down-stairs, Vladimir Nikolaitch, seizing a favourable moment, was taking leave of Lisa at the drawing-room door, and saying to her, as he held her hand, 'You know who it is draws me here; you know why I am constantly coming to your house; what need of words when all is clear as it is?' Lisa did not speak, and looked on the ground, without smiling, with her brows slightly contracted, and a flush on her cheek, but she did not draw away her hands. While up-stairs, in Marfa Timofyevna's room, by the light of a little lamp hanging before the tarnished old holy images, Lavretsky was sitting in a low chair, his elbows on his knees and his face buried in his hands; the old woman, standing before him, now and then silently stroked his hair. He spent more than an hour with her, after taking leave of his hostess; he had scarcely said anything to his kind old friend, and she did not question him. . . . Indeed, what need to speak, what was there to ask? Without that she understood all, and felt for everything of which his heart was full.

VIII

FEDOR IVANITCH LAVRETSKY — we must ask the reader's permission to break off the thread of our story for a time — came of an old noble family. The founder of the house of Lavretsky came over from Prussia in the reign of Vassili the Blind, and received a grant of two hundred *chetverts* of land in Byezhetsk. Many of his descendants filled various offices, and served under princes and persons of eminence in out-lying districts, but not one of them rose above the rank of an inspector of the Imperial table nor acquired any considerable fortune. The richest and most distinguished of all the Lavretskys was Fedor Ivanitch's great-grandfather, Andrei, a man cruel and daring, cunning and able. Even to this day stories still linger of his tyranny, his savage temper, his reckless munificence, and his insatiable avarice. He was very stout and tall, swarthy of countenance and beardless, he spoke in a thick voice and seemed half asleep; but the more quietly he spoke, the more those about him trembled. He had managed to get a wife who was a fit match for him. She was a gipsy by birth, goggle-eyed and hook-nosed, with a round yellow face. She was irascible and vindictive, and never gave way in anything to her husband, who almost killed her, and whose death she did not survive, though she had been for ever quarrelling with him. The son of Andrei, Piotr, Fedor's grandfather, did not take after his father; he was a typical landowner of the steppes, rather a simpleton, loud-voiced, but slow to move, coarse but not ill-natured, hospitable and very fond of coursing with dogs. He was over thirty when he inherited from his father a property of two thousand serfs in capital condition; but he had soon dissipated it, and had partly mortgaged his estate, and demoralised his servants. All sorts of people of low position, known and unknown, came crawling like cockroaches from all parts into his spacious, warm, ill-kept halls. All this mass of people ate what they could get, but always had their fill, drank till they were drunk, and carried off what they could, praising and blessing their genial host; and their host too, when he was out of humour, blessed his guests – for a pack of sponging toadies, but he was bored when he was without them. Piotr Andreitch's wife was a meek-spirited creature; he had taken her from a neighbouring family by his father's choice and command; her name was Anna Pavlovna. She never interfered in anything, welcomed guests cordially, and readily paid visits herself, though being powdered, she used to declare, would be the death of her. 'They put,' she used to say in her old age, 'a fox's brush on your head, comb all the hair up over it, smear it with grease, and dust it over with flour, and stick it up with iron pins, – there's no washing it off afterwards; but to pay visits without powder was quite impossible – people would be offended. Ah, it was a torture!'

She liked being driven with fast-trotting horses, and was ready to play cards from morning till evening, and would always keep the score of the pennies she had lost or won hidden under her hand when her husband came near the card-table; but all her dowry, her whole fortune, she had put absolutely at his disposal. She bore him two children, a son Ivan, the father of Fedor, and a daughter Glafira. Ivan was not brought up at home, but lived with a rich old maiden aunt, the Princess Kubensky; she had fixed on him for her heir (but for that his father would not have let him go). She dressed him up like a doll, engaged all kinds of teachers for him and put him in charge of a tutor, a Frenchman, who had been an abbé, a pupil of Jean-Jacques Rousseau, a certain M. Courtin de Vaucelles, a subtle and wily intriguer – the very, as she expressed it, *fine fleur* of emigration – and finished at almost seventy years old by marrying this '*fine fleur*,' and making over all her property to him. Soon afterwards, covered with rouge, and redolent of perfume *à la Richelieu*, surrounded by negro boys, delicate-shaped greyhounds and shrieking parrots, she died on a crooked silken divan of the time of Louis XV., with an enamelled snuff-box of Petitot's workmanship in her hand – and died, deserted by her husband; the insinuating M. Courtin had preferred to remove to Paris with her money. Ivan had only reached his twentieth year when this unexpected blow (we mean the princess's marriage, not her death) fell upon him; he did not care to stay in his aunt's house, where he found himself suddenly transformed from a wealthy heir to a poor relation; the society in Petersburg in which he had grown up was closed to him; he felt an aversion for entering the government service in the lower grades, with nothing but hard work and obscurity before him, – this was at the very beginning of the reign of the Emperor Alexander. He was obliged reluctantly to return to the country to his father. How squalid, poor, and wretched his parents' home seemed to him! The stagnation and sordidness of life in the country offended him at every step. He was consumed with *ennui*. Moreover, every one in the house, except his mother, looked at him with unfriendly eyes. His father did not like his town manners, his swallow-tail coats, his frilled shirt-front, his books, his flute, his fastidious ways, in which he detected – not incorrectly – a disgust for his surroundings; he was for ever complaining and grumbling at his son. 'Nothing here,' he used to say, 'is to his taste; at table he is all in a fret, and doesn't eat; he can't bear the heat and close smell of the room; the sight of folks drunk upsets him, one daren't beat any one before him; he doesn't want to go into the government service; he's weakly, as you see, in health; fie upon him, the milksop! And all this because he's got his head full of Voltaire.' The old man had a special dislike to Voltaire, and the 'fanatic' Diderot, though he had not read a word of their works; reading was not in his line. Piotr Andreitch was not mistaken; his son's head for that matter was indeed full of both Diderot and Voltaire, and not only of them alone, of Rousseau too, and Helvetius, and many other writers of the same kind – but they were in his head only. The retired abbé and encyclopédist who had been Ivan Petrovitch's tutor had taken pleasure in pouring all the wisdom of the eighteenth century into his pupil, and he was simply brimming over with it; it was there in him, but without mixing in his blood, nor penetrating to his soul, nor shaping itself in any firm convictions. . . . But, indeed, could one expect convictions from a young man of fifty years ago, when even at the present day we have not succeeded in attaining them? The guests, too, who frequented his father's house, were oppressed by Ivan Petrovitch's presence; he regarded them with loathing, they were afraid of him; and with his sister Glafira, who was twelve years older than he, he could not get on at all. This Glafira was a strange creature; she was ugly, crooked, and spare, with severe, wide-open eyes, and thin compressed lips. In her face, her voice, and her quick angular movements, she took after her grandmother, the gipsy, Andrei's wife. Obstinate and fond of power, she would not even hear of marriage. The return of Ivan Petrovitch did not fit in with her plans; while the Princess Kubensky kept him with her, she had hoped to receive at least half of her father's estate; in her avarice, too, she was like her grandmother. Besides, Glafira envied her brother, he was so well educated, spoke such good French with a Parisian accent, while she was scarcely able to pronounce '*bon jour*' or '*comment vous portez-vous*.' To be sure, her parents did not know any French, but that was no comfort to her. Ivan Petrovitch did not know what to do with himself for wretchedness and *ennui*; he had spent hardly a year in the country, but that year seemed to him as long as ten. The only consolation he could find was in talking to his mother, and he would sit for whole hours in her low-pitched rooms, listening to the good woman's simple-hearted prattle, and eating preserves. It so happened that among Anna Pavlovna's maids there was one very pretty girl with clear soft eyes and refined features, Malanya by name, a modest intelligent creature. She took his fancy at first sight, and he fell in love with her: he fell in love with her timid movements, her bashful answers, her gentle voice and gentle smile; every day she seemed sweeter to him. And she became devoted to Ivan Petrovitch with all the strength of her soul, as none but Russian girls can be devoted – and she gave herself to him. In the large household of a country squire nothing can long be kept a secret; soon every one knew of the love between the young master and Malanya; the gossip even reached the ears of Piotr Andreitch himself. Under other circumstances, he would probably have paid no attention to a matter of so little importance, but he had long had a grudge against his son, and was delighted at an opportunity of humiliating the town-bred wit and dandy. A storm of fuss and clamour was raised; Malanya was locked up in the pantry, Ivan Petrovitch was summoned into his father's presence. Anna Pavlovna too ran up at the hubbub. She began trying to pacify her husband, but Piotr Andreitch would hear nothing. He pounced down like a hawk on his son, reproached him with immorality, with godlessness, with hypocrisy; he took the opportunity to vent on him all the wrath against the Princess Kubensky that had been simmering within him, and lavished abusive epithets upon him. At first Ivan Petrovitch was silent and held himself in, but when his father thought fit to threaten him with a shameful punishment he could endure it no longer. 'Ah,' he thought, 'the fanatic Diderot is brought out again, then I will take the bull by the horns, I will astonish you all.' And thereupon with a calm and even voice, though quaking inwardly in every limb, Ivan Petrovitch declared to his father, that there was no need to reproach him with immorality; that though he did not intend to justify his fault he was ready to make amends for it, the more willingly as he felt himself to be superior to every kind of prejudice – and in fact – was ready to marry Malanya. In uttering these words Ivan Petrovitch did undoubtedly attain his object; he so astonished Piotr Andreitch that the latter stood open-eyed, and was struck dumb for a moment; but instantly he came to himself, and just as he was, in a dressing-gown bordered with squirrel fur and slippers on his bare feet, he flew at Ivan Petrovitch with his fists. The latter, as though by design, had that morning arranged his locks *à la Titus*, and put on a new English coat of a blue colour, high boots with little tassels and very tight modish buckskin breeches. Anna Pavlovna shrieked with all her might and covered her face with her hands; but her son ran over the whole house, dashed out into the courtyard, rushed into the kitchen-garden, into the pleasure-grounds, and flew across into the road, and kept running without looking round till at last he ceased to hear the heavy tramp of his father's steps behind him and his shouts, jerked out with effort, 'Stop you scoundrel!' he cried, 'stop! or I will curse you!' Ivan Petrovitch took refuge with a neighbour, a small landowner, and Piotr Andreitch returned home worn out and perspiring, and without taking breath, announced that he should deprive his son of his blessing and inheritance, gave orders that all his foolish books should be burnt, and that the girl Malanya should be sent to a distant village without loss of time. Some kind-hearted people found out Ivan Petrovitch and let him know everything. Humiliated and driven to fury, he vowed he would be revenged on his father, and the same night lay in wait for the peasant's cart in which Malanya was being driven away, carried her off by force, galloped off to the nearest town with her and married her. He was supplied with money by the neighbour, a good-natured retired marine officer, a confirmed tippler, who took an intense delight in every kind of – as he expressed it – romantic story. The next day Ivan Petrovitch wrote an ironically cold and polite letter to Piotr Andreitch, and set off to the village where lived his second cousin, Dmitri Pestov, with his sister, already known to the reader, Marfa Timofyevna. He told them all, announced his intention to go to Petersburg to try to obtain a post there, and besought them, at least for a time, to give his wife a home. At the word 'wife' he shed tears, and in spite of his city breeding and philosophy he bowed himself in humble, supplicating Russian fashion at his relations' feet, and even touched the ground with his forehead. The Pestovs, kind-hearted and compassionate people, readily agreed to his request. He stayed with them for three weeks, secretly expecting a reply from his father; but no reply came – and there was no chance of a reply coming. Piotr Andreitch, on hearing of his son's marriage, took to his bed, and forbade Ivan Petrovitch's name to be mentioned before him; but his mother, without her husband's knowledge, borrowed from the rector, and sent 500 roubles and a little image to his wife. She was afraid to write, but sent a message to Ivan Petrovitch by a lean peasant, who could walk fifty miles a day, that he was not to take it too much to heart; that, please God, all would be arranged, and his father's wrath would be turned to kindness; that she too would have preferred a different daughter-in-law, but that she sent Malanya Sergyevna her motherly blessing. The lean peasant received a rouble, asked permission to see the new young mistress, to whom he happened to be godfather, kissed her hand and ran off at his best speed.

And Ivan Petrovitch set off to Petersburg with a light heart. An unknown future awaited him; poverty perhaps menaced him, but he had broken away from the country life he detested, and above all, he had not been false to his teachers, he had actually put into practice the doctrines of Rousseau, Diderot, and *la Déclaration des droits de l'homme.* A sense of having done his duty, of triumph, and of pride filled his soul; and indeed the separation from his wife did not greatly afflict him; he would have been more perturbed by the necessity of being constantly with her. That deed was done, now he wanted to set about doing something fresh. In Petersburg, contrary to his own expectations, he met with success; the Princess Kubensky, whom

Monsieur Courtin had by that time deserted, but who was still living, in order to make up in some way to her nephew for having wronged him, gave him introductions to all her friends, and presented him with 5000 roubles – almost all that remained of her money – and a Lepikovsky watch with his monogram encircled by Cupids. Three months had not passed before he obtained a position in a Russian embassy to London, and in the first English vessel that sailed (steamers were not even talked of then) he crossed the sea. A few months later he received a letter from Pestov. The good-natured landowner congratulated Ivan Petrovitch on the birth of a son, who had been born into the world in the village of Pokrovskoe on the 20th of August 1807, and named Fedor, in honour of the holy martyr Fedor Stratilat. On account of her extreme weakness Malanya Sergyevna added only a few lines; but these few lines were a surprise, for Ivan Petrovitch had not known that Marfa Timofyevna had taught his wife to read and write. Ivan Petrovitch did not long abandon himself to the sweet emotion of parental feeling; he was dancing attendance on a notorious Phryne or Lais of the day (classical names were still in vogue at that date); the Peace of Tilsit had only just been concluded and all the world was hurrying after pleasure, in a giddy whirl of dissipation, and his head had been turned by the black eyes of a bold beauty. He had very little money, but he was lucky at cards, made many acquaintances, took part in all entertainments, in a word, he was in the swim.

IX

FOR A LONG time the old Lavretsky could not forgive his son for his marriage. If six months later Ivan Petrovitch had come to him with a penitent face and had thrown himself at his feet, he would, very likely, have pardoned him, after giving him a pretty severe scolding, and a tap with his stick by way of intimidating him, but Ivan Petrovitch went on living abroad and apparently did not care a straw. 'Be silent! I dare you to speak of it,' Piotr Andreitch said to his wife every time she ventured to try to incline him to mercy. 'The puppy, he ought to thank God for ever that I have not laid my curse upon him; my father would have killed him, the worthless scamp, with his own hands, and he would have done right too.' At such terrible speeches Anna Pavlovna could only cross herself secretly. As for Ivan Petrovitch's wife, Piotr Andreitch at first would not even hear her name, and in answer to a letter of Pestov's, in which he mentioned his daughter-in-law, he went so far as to send him word that he knew nothing of any daughter-in-law, and that it was forbidden by law to harbour run-away wenches, a fact which he thought it his duty to remind him of. But later on, he was softened by hearing of the birth of a grandson, and he gave orders secretly that inquiries should be made about the health of the mother, and sent her a little money, also as though it did not come from him. Fedya was not a year old before Anna Pavlovna fell ill with a fatal complaint. A few days before her end, when she could no longer leave her bed, with timid tears in her eyes, fast growing dim, she informed her husband in the presence of the priest that she wanted to see her daughter-in-law and bid her farewell, and to give her grandchild her blessing. The heart-broken old man soothed her, and at once sent off his own carriage for his daughter-in-law, for the first time giving her the title of Malanya Sergyevna. Malanya came with her son and Marfa Timofyevna, who would not on any consideration allow her to go alone, and was unwilling to expose her to any indignity. Half dead with fright, Malanya Sergyevna went into Piotr Andreitch's room. A nurse followed, carrying Fedya. Piotr Andreitch looked at her without speaking; she went up to kiss his hand; her trembling lips were only just able to touch it with a silent kiss.

'Well, my upstart lady,' he brought out at last, 'how do you do? let us go to the mistress.'

He got up and bent over Fedya; the baby smiled and held out his little white hands to him. This changed the old man's mood.

'Ah,' he said, 'poor little one, you were pleading for your father; I will not abandon you, little bird.'

Directly Malanya Sergyevna entered Anna Pavlovna's bedroom, she fell on her knees near the door. Anna Pavlovna persuaded her to come to her bedside, embraced her, and blessed her son; then turning a face contorted by cruel suffering to her husband she made an effort to speak.

'I know, I know, what you want to ask,' said Piotr Andreitch; 'don't fret yourself, she shall stay with us, and I will forgive Vanka for her sake.'

With an effort Anna Pavlovna took her husband's hand and pressed it to her lips. The same evening she breathed her last.

Piotr Andreitch kept his word. He informed his son that for the sake of his mother's dying hours, and for the sake of the little Fedor, he sent him his blessing and was keeping Malanya Sergyevna in his house. Two rooms on the ground floor were devoted to her; he presented her to his most honoured guests, the one-eyed brigadier Skurehin, and his wife, and bestowed on her two waiting-maids and a page for errands. Marfa Timofyevna took leave of her; she detested Glafira, and in the course of one day had fallen out with her three times.

It was a painful and embarrassing position at first for poor Malanya, but, after a while, she learnt to bear it, and grew used to her father-in-law. He, too, grew accustomed to her, and even fond of her, though he scarcely ever spoke to her, and a certain involuntary contempt was perceptible even in his signs of affection to her. Malanya Sergyevna had most to put up with from her sister-in-law. Even during her mother's lifetime, Glafira had succeeded by degrees in getting the whole household into her hands; every one, from her father downwards, submitted to her rule; not a piece of sugar was given out without her sanction; she would rather have died than shared her authority with another mistress – and with such a mistress! Her brother's marriage had incensed her even more than Piotr Andreitch; she set herself to give the upstart a lesson, and Malanya Sergyevna from the very first hour was her slave. And, indeed, how was she to contend against the masterful, haughty Glafira, submissive, constantly bewildered, timid, and weak in health as she was? Not a day passed without Glafira reminding her of her former position, and commending her for not forgetting herself. Malanya Sergyevna could have reconciled herself readily to these reminiscences and commendations, however bitter they might be – but Fedya was taken away from her, that was what crushed her. On the pretext that she was not capable of undertaking his education, she was scarcely allowed to see him; Glafira set herself to that task; the child was put absolutely under her control. Malanya Sergyevna began, in her distress, to beseech Ivan Petrovitch, in her letters, to return home soon. Piotr Andreitch himself wanted to see his son, but Ivan Petrovitch did nothing but write. He thanked his father on his wife's account, and for the money sent him, promised to return quickly – and did not come. The year 1812 at last summoned him home from abroad. When they met again, after six years' absence, the father embraced his son, and not by a single word made allusion to their former differences; it was not a time for that now, all Russia was rising up against the enemy, and both of them felt that they had Russian blood in their veins. Piotr Andreitch equipped a whole regiment of volunteers at his own expense. But the war came to an end, the danger was over; Ivan Petrovitch began to be bored again, and again he felt drawn away to the distance, to the world in which he had grown up, and where he felt himself at home. Malanya Sergyevna could not keep him; she meant too little to him. Even her fondest hopes came to nothing; her husband considered that it was much more suitable to intrust Fedya's education to Glafira. Ivan Petrovitch's poor wife could not bear this blow, she could not bear a second separation; in a few days, without a murmur, she quietly passed away.

All her life she had never been able to oppose anything, and she did not struggle against her illness. When she could no longer speak, when the shadows of death were already on her face, her features expressed, as of old, bewildered resignation and constant, uncomplaining meekness; with the same dumb submissiveness she looked at Glafira, and just as Anna Pavlovna kissed her husband's hand on her deathbed, she kissed Glafira's, commending to her, to Glafira, her only son. So ended the earthly existence of this good and gentle creature, torn, God knows why, like an uprooted tree from its natural soil and at once thrown down with its roots in the air; she had faded and passed away, leaving no trace, and no one mourned for her. Malanya Sergyevna's maids pitied her, and so did even Piotr Andreitch. The old man missed her silent presence. 'Forgive me . . . farewell, my meek one!' he whispered, as he took leave of her the last time in church. He wept as he threw a handful of earth in the grave.

He did not survive her long, not more than five years. In the winter of the year 1819, he died peacefully in Moscow, where he had moved with Glafira and his grandson, and left instructions that he should be buried beside Anna Pavlovna and 'Malasha.' Ivan Petrovitch was then in Paris amusing himself; he had retired from service soon after 1815. When he heard of his father's death he decided to return to Russia. It was necessary to make arrangements for the management of the property. Fedya, according to Glafira's letter, had reached his twelfth year, and the time had come to set about his education in earnest.

X

IVAN PETROVITCH RETURNED to Russia an Anglomaniac. His short-cropped hair, his starched shirt-front, his long-skirted pea-green overcoat with its multitude of capes, the sour expression of his face, something abrupt and at the same time indifferent in his behaviour, his way of speaking through his teeth, his sudden wooden laugh, the absence of smiles, his exclusively political or politico-economical conversation, his passion for roast beef and port wine – everything about him breathed, so to speak, of Great Britain. But, marvellous to relate, while he had been transformed into an Anglomaniac, Ivan Petrovitch had at the same time become a patriot, at least he called himself a patriot, though he knew Russia little, had not retained a single Russian habit, and expressed himself in Russian rather queerly; in ordinary conversation, his language was spiritless and inanimate and constantly interspersed with Gallicisms.

Ivan Petrovitch brought with him a few schemes in manuscript, relating to the administration and reform of the government; he was much displeased with everything he saw; the lack of system especially aroused his spleen. On his meeting with his sister, at the first word he announced to her that he was determined to introduce radical reforms, that henceforth everything to do with him would be on a different system. Glafira Petrovna made no reply to Ivan Petrovitch; she only ground her teeth and thought: 'Where am I to take refuge?' After she was back in the country, however, with her brother and nephew, her fears were soon set at rest. In the house, certainly, some changes were made; idlers and dependants met with summary dismissal; among them two old women were made to suffer, one blind, another broken down by paralysis; and also a decrepit major of the days of Catherine, who, on account of his really abnormal appetite, was fed on nothing but black bread and lentils. The order went forth not to admit the guests of former days; they were replaced by a distant neighbour, a certain fair-haired, scrofulous baron, a very well educated and very stupid man. New furniture was brought from Moscow; spittoons were introduced, and bells and washing-stands; and breakfast began to be served in a different way; foreign wines replaced vodka and syrups; the servants were put into new livery; a motto was added to the family arms: *in recto virtus*. . . . In reality, Glafira's power suffered no diminution; the giving out and buying of stores still depended on her. The Alsatian steward, brought from abroad, tried to fight it out with her and lost his place, in spite of the master's protection. As for the management of the house, and the administration of the estates, Glafira Petrovna had undertaken these duties also; in spite of Ivan Petrovitch's intention, – more than once expressed – to breathe new life into this chaos, everything remained as before; only the rent was in some places raised, the mistress was more strict, and the peasants were forbidden to apply direct to Ivan Petrovitch. The patriot had already a great contempt for his fellow-countrymen. Ivan Petrovitch's system was applied in its full force only to Fedya; his education really underwent a 'radical reformation'; his father devoted himself exclusively to it.

XI

UNTIL IVAN PETROVITCH'S return from abroad, Fedya was, as already related, in the hands of Glafira Petrovna. He was not eight years old when his mother died; he did not see her every day, and loved her passionately; the memory of her, of her pale and gentle face, of her dejected looks and timid caresses, were imprinted on his heart for ever; but he vaguely understood her position in the house; he felt that between him and her there existed a barrier which she dared not and could not break down. He was shy of his father, and, indeed, Ivan Petrovitch on his side never caressed him; his grandfather sometimes patted him on the head and gave him his hand to kiss, but he thought him and called him a little fool. After the death of Malanya Sergyevna, his aunt finally got him under her control. Fedya was afraid of her: he was afraid of her bright sharp eyes and her harsh voice; he dared not utter a sound in her presence; often, when he only moved a little in his chair, she would hiss out at once: 'What are you doing? sit still.' On Sundays, after mass, he was allowed to play, that is to say, he was given a thick book, a mysterious book, the work of a certain Maximovitch-Ambodik, entitled 'Symbols and Emblems.' This book was a medley of about a thousand mostly very enigmatical pictures, and as many enigmatical interpretations of them in five languages. Cupid – naked and very puffy in the body – played a leading part in these illustrations. In one of them, under the heading, 'Saffron and the Rainbow,' the interpretation appended was: 'Of this, the influence is vast'; opposite another, entitled 'A heron, flying with a violet in his beak,' stood the inscription: 'To thee they are all known.' 'Cupid and the bear licking his fur' was inscribed, 'Little by little.' Fedya used to ponder over these pictures; he knew them all to the minutest details; some of them, always the same ones, used to set him dreaming, and afforded him food for meditation; he knew no other amusements. When the time came to teach him languages and music, Glafira Petrovna engaged, for next to nothing, an old maid, a Swede, with eyes like a hare's, who spoke French and German with mistakes in every alternate word, played after a fashion on the piano, and above all, salted cucumbers to perfection. In the society of this governess, his aunt, and the old servant maid, Vassilyevna, Fedya spent four whole years. Often he would sit in the corner with his 'Emblems'; he sat there endlessly; there was a scent of geranium in the low pitched room, the solitary candle burnt dim, the cricket chirped monotonously, as though it were weary, the little clock ticked away hurriedly on the wall, a mouse scratched stealthily and gnawed at the wall-paper, and the three old women, like the Fates, swiftly and silently plied their knitting-needles, the shadows raced after their hands and quivered strangely in the half darkness, and strange, half dark ideas swarmed in the child's brain. No one would have called Fedya an interesting child; he was rather pale, but stout, clumsily built and awkward – a thorough peasant, as Glafira Petrovna said; the pallor would soon have vanished from his cheeks, if he had been allowed oftener to be in the open air. He learnt fairly quickly, though he was often lazy; he never cried, but at times he was overtaken by a fit of savage obstinacy; then no one could soften him. Fedya loved no one among those around him. . . . Woe to the heart that has not loved in youth!

Thus Ivan Petrovitch found him, and without loss of time he set to work to apply his system to him.

'I want above all to make a man, *un homme*, of him,' he said to Glafira Petrovna, 'and not only a man, but a Spartan.' Ivan Petrovitch began carrying out his intentions by putting his son in a Scotch kilt; the twelve-year-old boy had to go about with bare knees and a plume stuck in his Scotch cap. The Swedish lady was replaced by a young Swiss tutor, who was versed in gymnastics to perfection. Music, as a pursuit unworthy of a man, was discarded. The natural sciences, international law, mathematics, carpentry, after Jean-Jacques Rousseau's precept, and heraldry, to encourage chivalrous feelings, were what the future 'man' was to be occupied with. He was waked at four o'clock in the morning, splashed at once with cold water and set to running round a high pole with a cord; he had only one meal a day, consisting of a single dish; rode on horseback; shot with a cross-bow; at every convenient opportunity he was exercised in acquiring after his parent's example firmness of will, and every evening he inscribed in a special book an account of the day and his impressions; and Ivan Petrovitch on his side wrote him instructions in French in which he called him *mon fils*, and addressed him as *vous*. In Russian Fedya called his father *thou*, but did not dare to sit down in his presence. The 'system' dazed the boy, confused and cramped his intellect, but his health on the other hand was benefited by the new manner of life; at first he fell into a fever but soon recovered and began to grow stout and strong. His father was proud of him and called him in his strange jargon 'a child of nature, my creation.' When Fedya had reached his sixteenth year, Ivan Petrovitch thought it his duty in good time to instil into him a contempt for the female sex; and the young Spartan, with timidity in his heart and the first down on his lip, full of sap and strength and young blood, already tried to seem indifferent, cold, and rude.

Meanwhile time was passing. Ivan Petrovitch spent the greater part of the year in Lavriky (that was the name of the principal estate inherited from his ancestors). But in the winter he used to go to Moscow alone; there he stayed at a tavern, diligently visited the club, made speeches and developed his plans in drawing-rooms, and in his behaviour was more than ever Anglomaniac, grumbling and political. But the year 1825 came and brought much sorrow. Intimate friends and acquaintances of Ivan Petrovitch underwent painful experiences. Ivan Petrovitch made haste to withdraw into the country and shut himself up in his house. Another year passed by, and suddenly Ivan Petrovitch grew feeble, and ailing; his health began to break up. He, the free-thinker, began to go to church and have prayers put up for him; he, the European, began to sit in steam-baths, to dine at two o'clock, to go to bed at nine, and to doze off to the sound of the chatter of the old steward; he, the man of political ideas, burnt all his schemes, all his correspondence, trembled before the governor, and was uneasy at the sight of the police-captain; he, the man of iron will, whimpered and complained, when he had a gumboil or when they gave him a plate of cold soup. Glafira Petrovna again took control of everything in the house; once more the overseers, bailiffs and simple peasants began to come to the back stairs to speak to the 'old witch,' as the servants called her. The change in Ivan Petrovitch produced a powerful impression on his son. He had now reached his nineteenth year, and had begun to reflect and to emancipate himself from the hand that pressed like a weight upon him. Even before this time he had observed a little discrepancy between his father's words and deeds, between his wide liberal theories and his harsh petty despotism; but he had not expected such a complete breakdown. His confirmed egoism was patent now in everything. Young Lavretsky was getting ready to go to Moscow, to prepare for the university, when a new unexpected calamity overtook Ivan Petrovitch; he became blind, and hopelessly blind, in one day.

Having no confidence in the skill of Russian doctors, he began to make efforts to obtain permission to go abroad. It was refused. Then he took his son with him and for three whole years was wandering about Russia, from one doctor to another, incessantly moving from one town to another, and driving his physicians, his son, and his servants to despair by his cowardice and impatience. He returned to Lavriky a perfect wreck, no better than a capricious child. Bitter days followed, every one had much to put up with from him. Ivan Petrovitch was only quiet when he was dining; he had never been so greedy and eaten so much; all the rest of the time he gave himself and others no peace. He prayed, cursed his fate, abused himself, abused politics, his system, abused everything he had boasted of and prided himself upon, everything he had held up to his son as a model; he declared that he believed in nothing and then began to pray again; he could not put up with one instant of solitude, and expected his household to sit by his chair continually day and night, and entertain him with stories, which he constantly interrupted with exclamations, 'You are for ever lying, . . . a pack of nonsense!'

Glafira Petrovna was specially necessary to him; he absolutely could not get on without her – and to the end she always carried out every whim of the sick man, though sometimes she could not bring herself to answer at once, for fear the sound of her voice should betray her inward anger. Thus he lingered on for two years and died on the first day of May, when he had been brought out on to the balcony into the sun. 'Glasha, Glashka! soup, soup, old foo'— his halting tongue muttered and before he had articulated the last word, it was silent for ever. Glafira Petrovna, who had only just taken the cup of soup from the hands of the steward, stopped, looked at her brother's face, slowly made a large sign of the cross and turned away in silence; and his son, who happened to be there, also said nothing; he leaned on the railing of the balcony and gazed a long while into the garden, all fragrant and green, and shining in the rays of the golden sunshine of spring. He was twenty-three years old; how terribly, how imperceptibly quickly those twenty-three years had passed by! . . . Life was opening before him.

XII

AFTER BURYING HIS father and intrusting to the unchanged Glafira Petrovna the management of his estate and superintendence of his bailiffs, young Lavretsky went to Moscow, whither he felt drawn by a vague but strong attraction. He recognised the defects of his education, and formed the resolution, as far as possible, to regain lost ground. In the last five years he had read much and seen something; he had many stray ideas in his head; any professor might have envied some of his acquirements, but at the same time he did not know much that every schoolboy would have learnt long ago. Lavretsky was aware of his limitations; he was secretly conscious of being eccentric. The Anglomaniac had done his son an ill turn; his whimsical education had produced its fruits. For long years he had submitted unquestioningly to his father; when at last he began to see through him, the evil was already done, his habits were deeply-rooted. He could not get on with people; at twenty-three years old, with an unquenchable thirst for love in his shy heart, he had never yet dared to look one woman in the face. With his intellect, clear and sound, but somewhat heavy, with his tendencies to obstinacy, contemplation, and indolence he ought from his earliest years to have been thrown into the stream of life, and he had been kept instead in artificial seclusion. And now the magic circle was broken, but he continued to remain within it, prisoned and pent up within himself. It was ridiculous at his age to put on a student's dress, but he was not afraid of ridicule; his Spartan education had at least the good effect of developing in him a contempt for the opinion of others, and he put on, without embarrassment, the academical uniform. He entered the section of physics and mathematics. Robust, rosy-cheeked, bearded, and taciturn, he produced a strange impression on his companions; they did not suspect that this austere man, who came so punctually to the lectures in a wide village sledge with a pair of horses, was inwardly almost a child. He appeared to them to be a queer kind of pedant; they did not care for him, and made no overtures to him, and he avoided them. During the first two years he spent in the university, he only made acquaintance with one student, from whom he took lessons in Latin. This student, Mihalevitch by name, an enthusiast and a poet, who loved Lavretsky sincerely, by chance became the means of bringing about an important change in his destiny.

One day at the theatre – Motchalov was then at the height of his fame and Lavretsky did not miss a single performance – he saw in a box in the front tier a young girl, and though no woman ever came near his grim figure without setting his heart beating, it had never beaten so violently before. The young girl sat motionless, leaning with her elbows on the velvet of the box; the light of youth and life played in every feature of her dark, oval, lovely face; subtle intelligence was expressed in the splendid eyes which gazed softly and attentively from under her fine brows, in the swift smile on her expressive lips, in the very pose of her head, her hands, her neck. She was exquisitely dressed. Beside her sat a yellow and wrinkled woman of forty-five, with a low neck, in a black headdress, with a toothless smile on her intently-preoccupied and empty face, and in the inner recesses of the box was visible an elderly man in a wide frock-coat and high cravat, with an expression of dull dignity and a kind of ingratiating distrustfulness in his little eyes, with dyed moustache and whiskers, a large meaningless forehead and wrinkled cheeks, by every sign a retired general. Lavretsky did not take his eyes off the girl who had made such an impression on him; suddenly the door of the box opened and Mihalevitch went in. The appearance of this man, almost his one acquaintance in Moscow, in the society of the one girl who was absorbing his whole attention, struck him as curious and significant. Continuing to gaze into the box, he observed that all the persons in it treated Mihalevitch as an old friend. The performance on the stage ceased to interest Lavretsky, even Motchalov though he was that evening in his 'best form,' did not produce the usual impression on him. At one very pathetic part, Lavretsky involuntarily looked at his beauty: she was bending forward, her cheeks glowing, under the influence of his persistent gaze, her eyes, which were fixed on the stage, slowly turned and rested on him. All night he was haunted by those eyes. The skilfully constructed barriers were broken down at last; he was in a shiver and a fever, and the next day he went to Mihalevitch. From him he learnt that the name of the beauty was Varvara Pavlovna Korobyin; that the old people sitting with her in the box were her father and mother; and that he, Mihalevitch, had become acquainted with them a year before, while he was staying at Count N.'s, in the position of a tutor, near Moscow. The enthusiast spoke in rapturous praise of Varvara Pavlovna. 'My dear fellow,' he exclaimed with the impetuous ring in his voice peculiar to him, 'that girl is a marvellous creature, a genius, an artist in the true sense of the word, and she is very good too.' Noticing from Lavretsky's inquiries the impression Varvara Pavlovna had made on him, he himself proposed to introduce him to her, adding that he was like one of the family with them; that the general was not at all proud, and the mother was so stupid she could not say 'Bo' to a goose. Lavretsky blushed, muttered something unintelligible, and ran away. For five whole days he was struggling with his timidity; on the sixth day the young Spartan got into a new uniform and placed himself at Mihalevitch's disposal. The latter being his own valet, confined himself to combing his hair – and both betook themselves to the Korobyins.

XIII

VARVARA PAVLOVNA'S FATHER, Pavel Petrovitch Korobyin, a retired general-major, had spent his whole time on duty in Petersburg. He had had the reputation in his youth of a good dancer and driller. Through poverty, he had served as adjutant to two or three generals of no distinction, and had married the daughter of one of them with a dowry of twenty-five thousand roubles. He mastered all the science of military discipline and manœuvres to the minutest niceties, he went on in harness, till at last, after twenty-five years' service, he received the rank of a general and the command of a regiment. Then he might have relaxed his efforts and have quietly secured his pecuniary position. Indeed this was what he reckoned upon doing, but he managed things a little incautiously. He devised a new method of speculating with public funds – the method seemed an excellent one in itself – but he neglected to bribe in the right place, and was consequently informed against, and a more than unpleasant, a disgraceful scandal followed. The general got out of the affair somehow, but his career was ruined; he was advised to retire from active duty. For two years he lingered on in Petersburg, hoping to drop into some snug berth in the civil service, but no such snug berth came in his way. His daughter had left school, his expenses were increasing every day. Resigning himself to his fate, he decided to remove to Moscow for the sake of the greater cheapness of living, and took a tiny low-pitched house in the Old Stables Road, with a coat of arms seven feet long on the roof, and there began the life of a retired general at Moscow on an income of

2750 roubles a year. Moscow is a hospitable city, ready to welcome all stray comers, generals by preference. Pavel Petrovitch's heavy figure, which was not quite devoid of martial dignity, however, soon began to be seen in the best drawing-rooms in Moscow. His bald head with its tufts of dyed hair, and the soiled ribbon of the Order of St. Anne which he wore over a cravat of the colour of a raven's wing, began to be familiar to all the pale and listless young men who hang morosely about the card-tables while dancing is going on. Pavel Petrovitch knew how to gain a footing in society; he spoke little, but, from old habit, condescendingly – though, of course, not when he was talking to persons of a higher rank than his own. He played cards carefully; ate moderately at home, but consumed enough for six at parties. Of his wife there is scarcely anything to be said. Her name was Kalliopa Karlovna. There was always a tear in her left eye, on the strength of which Kalliopa Karlovna (she was, one must add, of German extraction) considered herself a woman of great sensibility. She was always in a state of nervous agitation, seemed as though she were ill-nourished, and wore a tight velvet dress, a cap, and tarnished hollow bracelets. The only daughter of Pavel Petrovitch and Kalliopa Karlovna, Varvara Pavlovna, was only just seventeen when she left the boarding-school, in which she had been reckoned, if not the prettiest, at least the cleverest pupil and the best musician, and where she had taken a decoration. She was not yet nineteen, when Lavretsky saw her for the first time.

XIV

THE YOUNG SPARTAN'S legs shook under him when Mihalevitch conducted him into the rather shabbily furnished drawing-room of the Korobyins, and presented him to them. But his overwhelming feeling of timidity soon disappeared. In the general the good-nature innate in all Russians was intensified by that special kind of geniality which is peculiar to all people who have done something disgraceful; the general's lady was as it were overlooked by every one; and as for Varvara Pavlovna, she was so self-possessed and easily cordial that every one at once felt at home in her presence; besides, about all her fascinating person, her smiling eyes, her faultlessly sloping shoulders and rosy-tinged white hands, her light and yet languid movements, the very sound of her voice, slow and sweet, there was an impalpable, subtle charm, like a faint perfume, voluptuous, tender, soft, though still modest, something which is hard to translate into words, but which moved and kindled – and timidity was not the feeling it kindled. Lavretsky turned the conversation on the theatre, on the performance of the previous day; she at once began herself to discuss Motchalov, and did not confine herself to sighs and interjections only, but uttered a few true observations full of genuine insight in regard to his acting. Mihalevitch spoke about music; she sat down without ceremony to the piano, and very correctly played some of Chopin's mazurkas, which were then just coming into fashion. Dinner-time came; Lavretsky would have gone away, but they made him stay: at dinner the general regaled him with excellent Lafitte, which the general's lackey hurried off in a street-sledge to Dupré's to fetch. Late in the evening Lavretsky returned home; for a long while he sat without undressing, covering his eyes with his hands in the stupefaction of enchantment. It seemed to him that now for the first time he understood what made life worth living; all his previous assumptions, all his plans, all that rubbish and nonsense had vanished into nothing at once; all his soul was absorbed in one feeling, in one desire – in the desire of happiness, of possession, of love, the sweet love of a woman. From that day he began to go often to the Korobyins. Six months later he spoke to Varvara Pavlovna, and offered her his hand. His offer was accepted; the general had long before, almost on the eve of Lavretsky's first visit, inquired of Mihalevitch how many serfs

Lavretsky owned; and indeed Varvara Pavlovna, who through the whole time of the young man's courtship, and even at the very moment of his declaration, had preserved her customary composure and clearness of mind – Varvara Pavlovna too was very well aware that her suitor was a wealthy man; and Kalliopa Karlovna thought '*meine Tochter macht eine schöne Partie*,' and bought herself a new cap.

XV

AND SO HIS OFFER was accepted, but on certain conditions. In the first place, Lavretsky was at once to leave the university; who would be married to a student, and what a strange idea too – how could a landowner, a rich man, at twenty-six, take lessons and be at school? Secondly, Varvara Pavlovna took upon herself the labour of ordering and purchasing her trousseau, and even choosing her present from the bridegroom. She had much practical sense, a great deal of taste, and a very great love of comfort, together with a great faculty for obtaining it for herself. Lavretsky was especially struck by this faculty when, immediately after their wedding, he travelled alone with his wife in the comfortable carriage, bought by her, to Lavriky. How carefully everything with which he was surrounded had been thought of, devised and provided beforehand by Varvara Pavlovna! What charming expensive knick-knacks appeared from various snug corners, what fascinating toilet-cases and coffee-pots, and how delightfully Varvara Pavlovna herself made the coffee in the morning! Lavretsky, however, was not at that time disposed to be observant; he was blissful, drunk with happiness; he gave himself up to it like a child. Indeed he was as innocent as a child, this young Hercules. Not in vain was the whole personality of his young wife breathing with fascination; not in vain was her promise to the senses of a mysterious luxury of untold bliss; her fulfilment was richer than her promise.

When she reached Lavriky in the very height of the summer, she found the house dark and dirty, the servants absurd and old-fashioned, but she did not think it necessary even to hint at this to her husband. If she had proposed to establish herself at Lavriky, she would have changed everything in it, beginning of course with the house; but the idea of staying in that out-of-the-way corner of the steppes never entered her head for an instant; she lived as in a tent, good-temperedly putting up with all its inconveniences, and indulgently making merry over them. Marfa Timofyevna came to pay a visit to her former charge; Varvara Pavlovna liked her very much, but she did not like Varvara Pavlovna. The new mistress did not get on with Glafira Petrovna either; she would have left her in peace, but old Korobyin wanted to have a hand in the management of his son-in-law's affairs; to superintend the property of such a near relative, he said, was not beneath the dignity even of a general. One must add that Pavel Petrovitch would not have been above managing the property even of a total stranger. Varvara Pavlovna conducted her attack very skilfully, without taking any step in advance, apparently completely absorbed in the bliss of the honeymoon, in the peaceful life of the country, in music and reading, she gradually worked Glafira up to such a point that she rushed one morning, like one possessed, into Lavretsky's study, and throwing a bunch of keys on the table, she declared that she was not equal to undertaking the management any longer, and did not want to stop in the place. Lavretsky, having been suitably prepared beforehand, at once agreed to her departure. This Glafira Petrovna had not anticipated. 'Very well,' she said, and her face darkened, 'I see that I am not wanted here! I know who is driving me out of the home of my fathers. Only you mark my words, nephew; you will never make a home anywhere, you will come to be a wanderer for ever. That is my last word to you.' The same day she went away to her own little property, and in a week General Korobyin was there, and with a pleasant melancholy in his looks and movements he took the superintendence of the whole property into his hands.

In the month of September, Varvara Pavlovna carried her husband off to Petersburg. She passed two winters in Petersburg (for the summer she went to stay at Tsarskoe Selo), in a splendid, light, artistically-furnished flat; they made many acquaintances among the middle and even higher ranks of society; went out and entertained a great deal, and gave the most charming dances and musical evenings. Varvara Pavlovna attracted guests as a fire attracts moths. Fedor Ivanitch did not altogether like such a frivolous life. His wife advised him to take some office under government; but from old association with his father, and also through his own ideas, he was unwilling to enter government service, still he remained in Petersburg for Varvara Pavlovna's pleasure. He soon discovered, however, that no one hindered him from being alone; that it was not for nothing that he had the quietest and most comfortable study in all Petersburg; that his tender wife was even ready to aid him to be alone; and from that time forth all went well. He again applied himself to his own, as he considered, unfinished education; he began again to read, and even began to learn English. It was a strange sight to see his powerful, broad-shouldered figure for ever bent over his writing-table, his full-bearded ruddy face half buried in the pages of a dictionary or notebook. Every morning he set to work, then had a capital dinner (Varvara Pavlovna was unrivalled as a housekeeper), and in the evenings he entered an enchanted world of light and perfume, peopled by gay young faces, and the centre of this world was also the careful housekeeper, his wife. She rejoiced his heart by the birth of a son, but the poor child did not live long; it died in the spring, and in the summer, by the advice of the doctor, Lavretsky took his wife abroad to a watering-place. Distraction was essential for her after such a trouble, and her health, too, required a warm climate. The summer and autumn they spent in Germany and Switzerland, and for the winter, as one would naturally expect, they went to Paris. In Paris, Varvara Pavlovna bloomed like a rose, and was able to make herself a little nest as quickly and cleverly as in Petersburg. She found very pretty apartments in one of the quiet but fashionable streets in Paris; she embroidered her husband such a dressing-gown as he had never worn before; engaged a coquettish waiting-maid, an excellent cook, and a smart footman, procured a fascinating carriage, and an exquisite piano. Before a week had passed, she crossed the street, wore her shawl, opened her parasol, and put on her gloves in a manner equal to the most true-born Parisian. And she soon drew round herself acquaintances. At first, only Russians visited her, afterwards Frenchmen too, very agreeable, polite, and unmarried, with excellent manners and well-sounding names; they all talked a great deal and very fast, bowed easily, grimaced agreeably; their white teeth flashed under their rosy lips – and how they could smile! All of them brought their friends, and *la belle Madame de Lavretsky* was soon known from Chaussée d'Antin to Rue de Lille. In those days – it was in 1836 – there had not yet arisen the tribe of journalists and reporters who now swarm on all sides like ants in an ant-hill; but even then there was seen in Varvara Pavlovna's salon a certain M. Jules, a gentleman of unprepossessing exterior, with a scandalous reputation, insolent and mean, like all duellists and men who have been beaten. Varvara Pavlovna felt a great aversion to this M. Jules, but she received him because he wrote for various journals, and was incessantly mentioning her, calling her at one time *Madame de L . . . tzki*, at another, *Madame de . . . , cette grande dame russe si distinguée, qui demeure rue de P. . . .* and telling all the world, that is, some hundreds of readers who had nothing to do with Madame de L . . . tzki, how charming and delightful this lady was; a true Frenchwoman in intelligence (*une vraie française par l'esprit*) – Frenchmen have no higher praise than this – what an extraordinary musician she was, and how marvellously she waltzed (Varvara Pavlovna did in fact waltz so that she drew all her hearts to the hem of her light flying skirts)— in a word, he spread her fame through the world, and, whatever one may say, that is pleasant. Mademoiselle Mars had already left the stage, and Mademoiselle Rachel had not yet made her appearance; nevertheless, Varvara Pavlovna was assiduous in visiting the theatres. She went into raptures over Italian music, yawned decorously at the Comédie Française, and wept at the acting of Madame Dorval in some ultra-romantic melodrama; and a great thing – Liszt played twice in her salon, and was so kind, so simple – it was charming! In such agreeable sensations was spent the winter, at the end of which Varvara Pavlovna was even presented at court. Fedor Ivanitch, for his part, was not bored, though his life, at times, weighed rather heavily on him – because it was empty. He read the papers, listened to the lectures at the Sorbonne and the Collège de France, followed the debates in the Chambers, and set to work on a translation of a well-known scientific treatise on irrigation. 'I am not wasting my time,' he thought, 'it is all of use; but next winter I must, without fail, return to Russia and set to work.' It is difficult to say whether he had any clear idea of precisely what this work would consist of; and there is no telling whether he would have succeeded in going to Russia in the winter; in the meantime, he was going with his wife to Baden . . . An unexpected incident broke up all his plans.

XVI

HAPPENING TO GO one day in Varvara Pavlovna's absence into her boudoir, Lavretsky saw on the floor a carefully folded little paper. He mechanically picked it up, unfolded it, and read the following note, written in French:

'Sweet angel Betsy! (I never can make up my mind to call you Barbe or Varvara), I waited in vain for you at the corner of the boulevard; come to our little room at half-past one to-morrow.

Your stout good-natured husband (*ton gros bonhomme de mari*) is usually buried in his books at that time; we will sing once more the song of your poet *Pouskine* (*de votre poète Pouskine*) that you taught me: "Old husband, cruel husband!" A thousand kisses on your little hands and feet. I await you.

'ERNEST.'

Lavretsky did not at once understand what he had read; he read it a second time, and his head began to swim, the ground began to sway under his feet like the deck of a ship in a rolling sea. He began to cry out and gasp and weep all at the same instant.

He was utterly overwhelmed. He had so blindly believed in his wife; the possibility of deception, of treason, had never presented itself to his mind. This Ernest, his wife's lover, was a fair-haired pretty boy of three-and-twenty, with a little turned-up nose and refined little moustaches, almost the most insignificant of all her acquaintances. A few minutes passed, half an hour passed, Lavretsky still stood, crushing the fatal note in his hands, and gazing senselessly at the floor; across a kind of tempest of darkness pale shapes hovered about him; his heart was numb with anguish; he seemed to be falling, falling – and a bottomless abyss was opening at his feet. A familiar light rustle of a silk dress roused him from his numbness; Varvara Pavlovna in her hat and shawl was returning in haste from her walk. Lavretsky trembled all over and rushed away; he felt that at that instant he was capable of tearing her to pieces, beating her to death, as a peasant might do, strangling her with his own hands. Varvara Pavlovna in amazement tried to stop him; he could only whisper, 'Betsy,' – and ran out of the house.

Lavretsky took a cab and ordered the man to drive him out of the town. All the rest of the day and the whole night he wandered about, constantly stopping short and wringing his hands, at one moment he was mad, and the next he was ready to laugh, was even merry after a fashion. By the morning he grew calm through exhaustion, and went into a wretched tavern in the outskirts, asked for a room and sat down on a chair before the window. He was overtaken by a fit of convulsive yawning. He could scarcely stand upright, his whole body was worn out, and he did not even feel fatigue, though fatigue began to do its work; he sat and gazed and comprehended nothing; he did not understand what had happened to him, why he found himself alone, with his limbs stiff, with a taste of bitterness in his mouth, with a load on his heart, in an empty unfamiliar room; he did not understand what had impelled her, his Varya, to give herself to this Frenchman, and how, knowing herself unfaithful, she could go on being just as calm, just as affectionate, as confidential with him as before! 'I cannot understand it!' his parched lips whispered. 'Who can guarantee now that even in Petersburg' . . . And he did not finish the question, and yawned again, shivering and shaking all over. Memories – bright and gloomy – fretted him alike; suddenly it crossed his mind how some days before she had sat down to the piano and sung before him and Ernest the song, 'Old husband, cruel husband!' He recalled the expression of her face, the strange light in her eyes, and the colour on her cheeks – and he got up from his seat, he would have liked to go to them, to tell them: 'You were wrong to play your tricks on me; my great-grandfather used to hang the peasants up by their ribs, and my grandfather was himself a peasant,' and to kill them both. Then all at once it seemed to him as if all that was happening was a dream, scarcely even a dream, but some kind of foolish joke; that he need only shake himself and look round. . . . He looked round, and like a hawk clutching its captured prey, anguish gnawed deeper and deeper into his heart. To complete it all, Lavretsky had been hoping in a few months to be a father. . . . The past, the future, his whole life was poisoned. He went back at last to Paris, stopped at an hotel and sent M. Ernest's note to Varvara Pavlovna with the following letter: –

'The enclosed scrap of paper will explain everything to you. Let me tell you by the way, that I was surprised at you; you, who are always so careful, to leave such valuable papers lying about.' (Poor Lavretsky had spent hours preparing and gloating over this phrase.) 'I cannot see you again; I imagine that you, too, would hardly desire an interview with me. I am assigning you 15,000 francs a year; I cannot give more. Send your address to the office of the estate. Do what you please; live where you please. I wish you happiness. No answer is needed.'

Lavretsky wrote to his wife that he needed no answer ... but he waited, he thirsted for a reply, for an explanation of this incredible, inconceivable thing. Varvara Pavlovna wrote him the same day a long letter in French. It put the finishing touch; his last doubts vanished, – and he began to feel ashamed that he had still had any doubt left. Varvara Pavlovna did not attempt to defend herself; her only desire was to see him, she besought him not to condemn her irrevocably. The letter was cold and constrained, though here and there traces of tears were visible. Lavretsky smiled bitterly, and sent word by the messenger that it was all right. Three days later he was no longer in Paris; but he did not go to Russia, but to Italy. He did not know himself why he fixed upon Italy; he did not really care where he went – so long as it was not home. He sent instructions to his steward on the subject of his wife's allowance, and at the same time told him to take all control of his property out of General Korobyin's hands at once, without waiting for him to draw up an account, and to make arrangements for his Excellency's departure from Lavriky; he could picture vividly the confusion, the vain airs of self-importance of the dispossessed general, and in the midst of all his sorrow, he felt a kind of spiteful satisfaction. At the same time he asked Glafira Petrovna by letter to return to Lavriky, and drew up a deed authorising her to take possession; Glafira Petrovna did not return to Lavriky, and printed in the newspapers that the deed was cancelled, which was perfectly unnecessary on her part. Lavretsky kept out of sight in a small Italian town, but for a long time he could not help following his wife's movements. From the newspapers he learned that she had gone from Paris to Baden as she had arranged; her name soon appeared in an article written by the same M. Jules. In this article there was a kind of sympathetic condolence apparent under the habitual playfulness; there was a deep sense of disgust in the soul of Fedor Ivanitch as he read this article. Afterwards he learned that a daughter had been born to him; two months later he received a notification from his steward that Varvara Pavlovna had asked for the first quarter's allowance. Then worse and worse rumours began to reach him; at last, a tragic-comic story was reported with acclamations in all the papers. His wife played an unenviable part in it. It was the finishing stroke; Varvara Pavlovna had become a 'notoriety.'

Lavretsky ceased to follow her movements; but he could not quickly gain mastery over himself. Sometimes he was overcome by such a longing for his wife that he would have given up everything, he thought, even, perhaps . . . could have forgiven her, only to hear her caressing voice again, to feel again her hand in his. Time, however, did not pass in vain. He was not born to be a victim; his healthy nature reasserted its rights. Much became clear to him; even the blow that had fallen on him no longer seemed to him to have been quite unforeseen; he understood his wife, – we can only fully understand those who are near to us, when we are separated from them. He could take up his interests, could work again, though with nothing like his former zeal; scepticism, half-formed already by the experiences of his life, and by his education, took complete possession of his heart. He became indifferent to everything. Four years passed by, and he felt himself strong enough to return to his country, to meet his own people. Without stopping at Petersburg or at Moscow he came to the town of O———, where we parted from him, and whither we will now ask the indulgent reader to return with us.

XVII

THE MORNING AFTER the day we have described, at ten o'clock, Lavretsky was mounting the steps of the Kalitins' house. He was met by Lisa coming out in her hat and gloves.

'Where are you going?' he asked her.

'To service. It is Sunday.'

'Why, do you go to church?'

Lisa looked at him in silent amazement.

'I beg your pardon,' said Lavretsky; 'I – I did not mean to say that; I have come to say good-bye to you, I am starting for my village in an hour.'

'Is it far from here?' asked Lisa.

'Twenty miles.'

Lenotchka made her appearance in the doorway, escorted by a maid.

'Mind you don't forget us,' observed Lisa, and went down the steps.

'And don't you forget me. And listen,' he added, 'you are going to church; while you are there, pray for me too.'

Lisa stopped short and turned round to him: 'Certainly,' she said, looking him straight in the face, 'I will pray for you too. Come, Lenotchka.'

In the drawing-room Lavretsky found Marya Dmitrievna alone. She was redolent of *eau de Cologne* and mint. She had, as she said, a headache, and had passed a restless night. She received him with her usual languid graciousness and gradually fell into conversation.

'Vladimir Nikolaitch is really a delightful young man, don't you think so?' she asked him.

'What Vladimir Nikolaitch?'

'Panshin to be sure, who was here yesterday. He took a tremendous fancy to you; I will tell you a secret, *mon cher cousin*, he is simply crazy about my Lisa. Well, he is of good family, has a capital position in the service, and a clever fellow, a *kammerjunker*, and if it is God's will, I for my part, as a mother, shall be well pleased. My responsibility of course is immense; the happiness of children depends, no doubt, on parents; still I may say, up till now, for better or for worse I have done everything, I alone have been everywhere with them, that is to say, I have educated my children and taught them everything myself. Now, indeed, I have written for a French governess from Madame Boluce.'

Marya Dmitrievna launched into a description of her cares and anxieties and maternal sentiments. Lavretsky listened in silence, turning his hat in his hands. His cold, weary glance embarrassed the gossiping lady.

'And do you like Lisa?' she asked.

'Lisaveta Mihalovna is an excellent girl,' replied Lavretsky, and he got up, took his leave, and went off to Marfa Timofyevna. Marya Dmitrievna looked after him in high displeasure, and thought, 'What a dolt, a regular peasant! Well, now I understand why his wife could not remain faithful to him.'

Marfa Timofyevna was sitting in her room, surrounded by her little court. It consisted of five creatures almost equally near her heart; a big-cropped, learned bullfinch, which she had taken a fancy to because he had lost his accomplishments of whistling and drawing water; a very timid and peaceable little dog, Roska; an ill-tempered cat, Matross; a dark-faced, agile little girl of nine years old, with big eyes and a sharp nose, called Shurotchka; and an elderly woman of fifty-five, in a white cap and a cinnamon-coloured abbreviated jacket, over a dark skirt, by name, Nastasya Karpovna Ogarkov. Shurotchka was an orphan of the tradesman class. Marfa Timofyevna had taken her to her heart like Roska, from compassion; she had found the little dog and the little girl too in the street; both were thin and hungry, both were being drenched by the autumn rain; no one came in search of Roska, and Shurotchka was given up to Marfa Timofyevna with positive eagerness by her uncle, a drunken shoemaker, who did not get enough to eat himself, and did not feed his niece, but beat her over the head with his last. With Nastasya Karpovna Marfa Timofyevna had made acquaintance on a pilgrimage at a monastery; she had gone up to her at the church (Marfa Timofyevna took a fancy to her because in her own words she said her prayers so prettily) and had addressed her and invited her to a cup of tea. From that day she never parted from her. Nastasya Karpovna was a woman of the most cheerful and gentle disposition, a widow without children, of poor noble family; she had a round grey head, soft white hands, a soft face with large mild features, and a rather absurd turned-up nose; she stood in awe of Marfa Timofyevna, and the latter was very fond of her, though she laughed at her susceptibility. She had a soft place in her heart for every young man, and could not help blushing like a girl at the most innocent joke. Her whole fortune consisted of only 1200 roubles; she lived at Marfa Timofyevna's expense, but on an equal footing with her: Marfa Timofyevna would not have put up with any servility.

'Ah! Fedya,' she began, directly she saw him, 'last night you did not see my family, you must admire them, we are all here together for tea; this is our second, holiday tea. You can make friends with them all; only Shurotchka won't let you, and the cat will scratch. Are you starting to-day?'

'Yes.' Lavretsky sat down on a low seat. 'I have just said good-bye to Marya Dmitrievna. I saw Lisaveta Mihalovna too.'

'Call her Lisa, my dear fellow. Mihalovna indeed to you! But sit still, or you will break Shurotchka's little chair.'

'She has gone to church,' continued Lavretsky. 'Is she religious?'

'Yes, Fedya, very much so. More than you and I, Fedya.'

'Aren't you religious then?' lisped Nastasya Karpovna. 'To-day, you have not been to the early service, but you are going to the late.'

'No, not at all; you will go alone; I have grown too lazy,

my dear,' replied Marfa Timofyevna. 'Already I am indulging myself with tea.' She addressed Nastasya Karpovna in the singular, though she treated her as an equal. She was not a Pestov for nothing: three Pestovs had been put on the death-list of Ivan the Terrible. Marfa Timofyevna was well aware of the fact.

'Tell me, please,' began Lavretsky again, 'Marya Dmitrievna has just been talking to me about this – what's his name? Panshin. What sort of a man is he?'

'What a chatterbox she is, Lord save us!' muttered Marfa Timofyevna. 'She told you, I suppose, as a secret that he has turned up as a suitor. She might have whispered it to her priest's son; no, he's not enough for her, it seems. And so far there's nothing to tell, thank God, but already she's gossiping about it.'

'Why thank God?' asked Lavretsky.

'Because I don't like the fine young gentleman; and so what is there to be glad of in it?'

'You don't like him?'

'No, he can't fascinate every one. He must be satisfied with Nastasya Karpovna's being in love with him.'

The poor widow was utterly dismayed.

'How can you, Marfa Timofyevna? you've no conscience!' she cried, and a crimson flush instantly overspread her face and neck.

'And he knows, to be sure, the rogue,' Marfa Timofyevna interrupted her, 'he knows how to captivate her; he made her a present of a snuff-box. Fedya, ask her for a pinch of snuff; you will see what a splendid snuff-box it is; on the lid a hussar on horseback. You'd better not try to defend yourself, my dear.'

Nastasya Karpovna could only wring her hands.

'Well, but Lisa,' inquired Lavretsky, 'is she indifferent to him?'

'She seems to like him, but there, God knows! The heart of another, you know, is a dark forest, and a girl's more than any. Shurotchka's heart, for instance – I defy you to understand it!

What makes her hide herself and not come out ever since you came in?'

Shurotchka choked with suppressed laughter and skipped out of the room. Lavretsky rose from his place.

'Yes,' he said in an uncertain voice, 'there is no deciphering a girl's heart.'

He began to say good-bye.

'Well, shall we see you again soon?' inquired Marfa Timofyevna.

'Very likely, auntie; it's not far off, you know.'

'Yes, to be sure you are going to Vassilyevskoe. You don't care to stay at Lavriky: well, that's your own affair, only mind you go and say a prayer at your mother's grave, and your grandmother's too while you are there. Out there in foreign parts you have picked up all kinds of ideas, but who knows? Perhaps even in their graves they will feel that you have come to them. And, Fedya, don't forget to have a service sung too for Glafira Petrovna; here's a silver rouble for you. Take it, take it, I want to pay for a service for her. I had no love for her in her lifetime, but all the same there's no denying she was a girl of character. She was a clever creature; and a good friend to you. And now go and God be with you, before I weary you.'

And Marfa Timofyevna embraced her nephew.

'And Lisa's not going to marry Panshin; don't you trouble yourself; that's not the sort of husband she deserves.'

'Oh, I'm not troubling myself,' answered Lavretsky, and went away.

XVIII

FOUR DAYS LATER, he set off for home. His coach rolled quickly along the soft cross-road. There had been no rain for a fortnight; a fine milky mist was diffused in the air and hung over the distant woods; a smell of burning came from it.

A multitude of darkish clouds with blurred edges were creeping across the pale blue sky; a fairly strong breeze blew a dry and steady gale, without dispelling the heat. Leaning back with his head on the cushion and his arms crossed on his breast, Lavretsky watched the furrowed fields unfolding like a fan before him, the willow bushes as they slowly came into sight, and the dull ravens and rooks, who looked sidelong with stupid suspicion at the approaching carriage, the long ditches, overgrown with mugwort, wormwood, and mountain ash; and as he watched the fresh fertile wilderness and solitude of this steppe country, the greenness, the long slopes, and valleys with stunted oak bushes, the grey villages, and scant birch-trees, – the whole Russian landscape, so long unseen by him, stirred emotion at once pleasant, sweet and almost painful in his heart, and he felt weighed down by a kind of pleasant oppression. Slowly his thoughts wandered; their outlines were as vague and indistinct as the outlines of the clouds which seemed to be wandering at random overhead. He remembered his childhood, his mother; he remembered her death, how they had carried him in to her, and how, clasping his head to her bosom, she had begun to wail over him, then had glanced at Glafira Petrovna – and checked herself. He remembered his father, at first vigorous, discontented with everything, with strident voice; and later, blind, tearful, with unkempt grey beard; he remembered how one day after drinking a glass too much at dinner, and spilling the gravy over his napkin, he began to relate his conquests, growing red in the face, and winking with his sightless eyes; he remembered Varvara Pavlovna, – and involuntarily shuddered, as a man shudders from a sudden internal pain, and shook his head. Then his thoughts came to a stop at Lisa.

'There,' he thought, 'is a new creature, only just entering on life. A nice girl, what will become of her? She is good-looking too. A pale, fresh face, mouth and eyes so serious, and an honest innocent expression. It is a pity she seems a little enthusiastic. A good figure, and she moves so lightly, and a soft voice. I like the way she stops suddenly, listens attentively, without a smile, then grows thoughtful and shakes back her hair. I fancy, too, that Panshin is not good enough for her. What's amiss with him, though? And besides, what business have I to wonder about it? She will go along the same road as all the rest. I had better go to sleep.' And Lavretsky closed his eyes.

He could not sleep, but he sank into the drowsy numbness of a journey. Images of the past rose slowly as before, floated in his soul, mixed and tangled up with other fancies. Lavretsky, for some unknown reason, began to think about Robert Peel, . . . about French history – of how he would gain a battle, if he were a general; he fancied the shots and the cries. . . . His head slipped on one side, he opened his eyes. The same fields, the same steppe scenery; the polished shoes of the trace-horses flashed alternately through the driving dust; the coachman's shirt, yellow with red gussets, was puffed out by the wind. . . . 'A nice home-coming!' glanced through Lavretsky's brain; and he cried, 'Get on!' wrapped himself in his cloak and pressed close into the cushion. The carriage jolted; Lavretsky sat up and opened his eyes wide. On the slope before him stretched a small hamlet; a little to the right could be seen an ancient manor-house of small size, with closed shutters and a winding flight of steps; nettles, green and thick as hemp, grew over the wide courtyard from the very gates; in it stood a store-house built of oak, still strong. This was Vassilyevskoe.

The coachman drove to the gates and drew up; Lavretsky's groom stood up on the box and as though in preparation for jumping down, shouted, 'Hey!' There was a sleepy, muffled sound of barking, but not even a dog made its appearance; the groom again made ready for a jump, and again shouted 'Hey!' The feeble barking was repeated, and an instant after a man from some unseen quarter ran into the courtyard, dressed in a nankeen coat, his head as white as snow; he stared at the coach, shading his eyes from the sun; all at once he slapped his thighs with both hands, ran to and fro a little, then rushed to open the gates. The coach drove into the yard, crushing the nettles with the wheels and drew up at the steps. The white-headed man, who seemed very alert, was already standing on the bottom step, his legs bent and wide apart. He unfastened the apron of the carriage, holding back the strap with a jerk and aiding his master to alight; then kissed his hand.

'How do you do, how do you do, brother?' began Lavretsky. 'Your name's Anton, I think? You are still alive, then?' The old man bowed without speaking, and ran off for the keys. While he went, the coachman sat motionless, sitting sideways and staring at the closed door, but Lavretsky's groom stood as he had leaped down in a picturesque pose with one arm thrown back on the box. The old man brought the keys, and, quite needlessly, twisting about like a snake, with his elbows raised high, he opened the door, stood on one side, and again bowed to the earth.

'So here I am at home, here I am back again,' thought Lavretsky, as he walked into the diminutive passage, while one after another the shutters were being opened with much creaking and knocking, and the light of day poured into the deserted rooms.

XIX

THE SMALL MANOR-HOUSE to which Lavretsky had come and in which two years before Glafira Petrovna had breathed her last, had been built in the preceding century of solid pine-wood; it looked ancient, but it was still strong enough to stand another fifty years or more. Lavretsky made the tour of all the rooms, and to the great discomfiture of the aged languid flies, settled under the lintels and covered with white dust, he ordered the windows to be opened everywhere; they had not been opened ever since the death of Glafira Petrovna. Everything in the house had remained as it was; the thin-legged white miniature couches in the drawing-room, covered with glossy grey stuff, threadbare and rickety, vividly suggested the days of Catherine; in the drawing-room, too, stood the mistress's favourite arm-chair, with high straight back, against which she never leaned even in her old age. On the principal wall hung a very old portrait of Fedor's great-grandfather, Andrey Lavretsky; the dark yellow face was scarcely distinguishable from the warped and blackened background; the small cruel eyes looked grimly out from beneath the eyelids, which drooped as if they were swollen; his black unpowdered hair rose bristling above his heavy indented brow. In the corner of the portrait hung a wreath of dusty immortelles. 'Glafira Petrovna herself was pleased to make it,' Anton announced. In the bedroom stood a narrow bedstead, under a canopy of old-fashioned and very good striped material; a heap of faded cushions and a thin quilted counterpane lay on the bed, and at the head hung a picture of the Presentation in the Temple of the Holy Mother of God; it was the very picture which the old maid, dying alone and forgotten by every one, had for the last time pressed to her chilling lips. A little toilet-table of inlaid wood, with brass fittings and a warped looking-glass in a tarnished frame stood in the window. Next to the bedroom was a picturesque little room with bare walls and a heavy case of holy images in the corner; on the floor lay a threadbare rug spotted with wax; Glafira Petrovna used to pray bowing to the ground upon it. Anton went away with Lavretsky's groom to unlock the stable and coach-house; to replace him appeared an old woman of about the same age, with a handkerchief tied round to her very eyebrows; her head shook, and her eyes were dim, but they expressed zeal, the habit of years of submissive service, and at the same time a kind of respectful commiseration. She kissed Lavretsky's hand and stood still in the doorway awaiting his orders. He positively could not recollect her name and did not even remember whether he had ever seen her. Her name, it appeared, was Apraxya; forty years before, Glafira Petrovna had put her out of the master's house and ordered that she should be poultry-woman. She said little, however; she seemed to have lost her senses from old age, and could only gaze at him obsequiously. Besides these two old creatures and three pot-bellied children in long smocks, Anton's great-grandchildren, there was also living in the manor-house a one-armed peasant, who was exempted from servitude; he muttered like a woodcock and was of no use for anything. Not much more useful was the decrepit dog who had saluted Lavretsky's return by its barking; he had been for ten years fastened up by a heavy chain, purchased at Glafira Petrovna's command, and was scarcely able to move and drag the weight of it. Having looked over the house, Lavretsky went into the garden and was very much pleased with it. It was all overgrown with high grass, and burdock, and gooseberry and raspberry bushes, but there was plenty of shade, and many old lime-trees, which were remarkable for their immense size and the peculiar growth of their branches; they had been planted too close and at some time or other – a hundred years before – they had been lopped. At the end of the garden was a small clear pool bordered with high reddish rushes. The traces of human life very quickly pass away; Glafira Petrovna's estate had not had time to become quite wild, but already it seemed plunged in that quiet slumber in which everything reposes on earth where there is not the infection of man's restlessness. Fedor Ivanitch walked also through the village; the peasant-women stared at him from the doorways of their huts, their cheeks resting on their hands; the peasants saluted him from a distance, the children ran out, and the dogs barked indifferently. At last he began to feel hungry; but he did not expect his servants and his cook till the evening; the waggons of provisions from Lavriky had not come yet, and he had to have recourse to Anton. Anton arranged matters at once; he caught, killed, and plucked an old hen; Apraxya gave it a long rubbing and cleaning, and washed it like linen before putting it into the stew-pan; when, at last, it was cooked,

Anton laid the cloth and set the table, placing beside the knife and fork a three-legged salt-cellar of tarnished plate and a cut decanter with a round glass stopper and a narrow neck; then he announced to Lavretsky in a sing-song voice that the meal was ready, and took his stand behind his chair, with a napkin twisted round his right fist, and diffusing about him a peculiar strong ancient odour, like the scent of a cypress-tree. Lavretsky tried the soup, and took out the hen; its skin was all covered with large blisters; a tough tendon ran up each leg; the meat had a flavour of wood and soda. When he had finished dinner, Lavretsky said that he would drink a cup of tea, if— 'I will bring it this minute,' the old man interrupted. And he kept his word. A pinch of tea was hunted up, twisted in a screw of red paper; a small but very fiery and loudly-hissing samovar was found, and sugar too in small lumps, which looked as if they were thawing. Lavretsky drank tea out of a large cup; he remembered this cup from childhood; there were playing-cards depicted upon it, only visitors used to drink out of it – and here was he drinking out of it like a visitor. In the evening his servants came; Lavretsky did not care to sleep in his aunt's bed; he directed them to put him up a bed in the dining-room. After extinguishing his candle he stared for a long time about him and fell into cheerless reflection; he experienced that feeling which every man knows whose lot it is to pass the night in a place long uninhabited; it seemed to him that the darkness surrounding him on all sides could not be accustomed to the new inhabitant, the very walls of the house seemed amazed. At last he sighed, drew up the counterpane round him and fell asleep. Anton remained up after all the rest of the household; he was whispering a long while with Apraxya, he sighed in an undertone, and twice he crossed himself; they had neither of them expected that their master would settle among them at Vassilyevskoe when he had not far off such a splendid estate with such a capitally built house; they did not suspect that the very house was hateful to Lavretsky; it stirred painful memories within him. Having gossiped to his heart's content, Anton took a stick and struck the night watchman's board, which had hung silent for so many years, and laid down to sleep in the courtyard with no covering on his white head. The May night was mild and soft, and the old man slept sweetly.

XX

THE NEXT DAY Lavretsky got up rather early, had a talk with the village bailiff, visited the threshing-floor, ordered the chain to be taken off the yard dog, who only barked a little, but did not even come out of his kennel, and, returning home, sank into a kind of peaceful torpor, which he did not shake off the whole day.

'Here I am at the very bottom of the river,' he said to himself more than once. He sat at the window without stirring, and, as it were, listened to the current of the quiet life surrounding him, to the few sounds of the country solitude. Something from behind the nettles chirps with a shrill, shrill little note; a gnat seems to answer it. Now it has ceased, but still the gnat keeps up its sharp whirr; across the pleasant, persistent, fretful buzz of the flies sounds the hum of a big bee, constantly knocking its head against the ceiling; a cock crows in the street, hoarsely prolonging the last note; there is the rattle of a cart; in the village a gate is creaking. Then the jarring voice of a peasant-woman, 'What?' 'Hey, you are my little sweetheart,' cries Anton to the little two-year-old girl he is dandling in his arms. 'Fetch the kvas,' repeats the same woman's voice, and all at once there follows a deathly silence; nothing rattles, nothing is moving; the wind is not stirring a leaf; without a sound the swallows fly one after another over the earth, and sadness weighs on the heart from their noiseless flight. 'Here I am at the very bottom of the river,' thought Lavretsky again. 'And always, at all times life here is quiet, unhasting,' he thought; 'whoever comes within its circle must submit; here there is nothing to agitate, nothing to harass; one can only get on here by making one's way slowly, as the ploughman cuts the furrow with his plough. And what vigour, what health abound in this inactive place! Here under the window the sturdy burdock creeps out of the thick grass; above it the lovage trails its juicy stalks, and the Virgin's tears fling still higher their pink tendrils; and yonder further in the fields is the silky rye, and the oats are already in ear, and every leaf on every tree, every grass on its stalk is spread to its fullest width. In the love of a woman my best years have gone by,' Lavretsky went on thinking, 'let me be sobered by the sameness of life here, let me be soothed and made ready, so that I may learn to do my duty without haste.' And again he fell to listening to the silence, expecting nothing – and at the same time constantly expecting something; the silence enfolded him on all sides, the sun moved calmly in the peaceful blue sky, and the clouds sailed calmly across it; they seemed to know why and whither they were sailing. At this same time in other places on the earth there is the seething, the bustle, the clash of life; life here slipped by noiseless, as water over marshy grass; and even till evening Lavretsky could not tear himself from the contemplation of this life as it passed and glided by; sorrow for the past was melting in his soul like snow in spring, and strange to say, never had the feeling of home been so deep and strong within him.

XXI

IN THE COURSE of a fortnight, Fedor Ivanitch had brought Glafira Petrovna's little house into order and had cleared the courtyard and the garden. From Lavriky comfortable furniture was sent him; from the town, wine, books, and papers; horses made their appearance in the stable; in brief Fedor Ivanitch provided himself with everything necessary and began to live – not precisely after the manner of a country landowner, nor precisely after the manner of a hermit. His days passed monotonously; but he was not bored though he saw no one; he set diligently and attentively to work at farming his estate, rode about the neighbourhood and did some reading. He read little, however; he found it pleasanter to listen to the tales of old Anton. Lavretsky usually sat at the window with a pipe and a cup of cold tea. Anton stood at the door, his hands crossed behind him, and began upon his slow, deliberate stories of old times, of those fabulous times when oats and rye were not sold by measure, but in great sacks, at two or three farthings a sack; when there were impassable forests, virgin steppes stretching on every side, even close to the town. 'And now,' complained the old man, whose eightieth year had passed, 'there has been so much clearing, so much ploughing everywhere, there's nowhere you may drive now.' Anton used to tell many stories, too, of his mistress, Glafira Petrovna; how prudent and saving she was; how a certain gentleman, a young neighbour, had paid her court, and used to ride over to see her, and how she was even pleased to put on her best cap, with ribbons of salmon colour, and her yellow gown of *tru-tru lévantine* for him; but how, later on, she had been angry with the gentleman neighbour for his unseemly inquiry, 'What, madam, pray, might be your fortune?' and had bade them refuse him the house; and how it was then that she had given directions that, after her decease, everything to the last rag should pass to Fedor Ivanitch. And, indeed, Lavretsky found all his aunt's household goods intact, not excepting the best cap with ribbons of salmon colour, and the yellow gown of *tru-tru lévantine*. Of old papers and interesting documents, upon which Lavretsky had reckoned, there seemed no trace, except one old book, in which his grandfather, Piotr Andreitch, had inscribed in one place, 'Celebration in the city of Saint Petersburg of the peace, concluded with the Turkish empire by his Excellency Prince Alexander Alexandrovitch Prozorovsky'; in another place a recipe for a pectoral decoction with the comment, 'This recipe was given to the general's lady, Prascovya Federovna Soltikov, by the chief priest of the Church of the Life-giving Trinity, Fedor Avksentyevitch'; in another, a piece of political news of this kind: 'Somewhat less talk of the French tigers'; and next this entry: 'In the *Moscow Gazette* an announcement of the death of Mr. Senior-Major Mihal Petrovitch Kolitchev. Is not this the son of Piotr Vassilyevitch Kolitchev?' Lavretsky found also some old calendars and dream-books, and the mysterious work of Ambodik; many were the memories stirred by the well-known, but long-forgotten *Symbols and Emblems.* In Glafira Petrovna's little dressing-table, Lavretsky found a small packet, tied up with black ribbon, sealed with black sealing wax, and thrust away in the very farthest corner of the drawer. In the parcel there lay face to face a portrait, in pastel, of his father in his youth, with effeminate curls straying over his brow, with almond-shaped languid eyes and parted lips, and a portrait, almost effaced, of a pale woman in a white dress with a white rose in her hand – his mother. Of herself, Glafira Petrovna had never allowed a portrait to be taken. 'I, myself, little father, Fedor Ivanitch,' Anton used to tell Lavretsky, 'though I did not then live in the master's house, still I can remember your great-grandfather, Andrey Afanasyevitch, seeing that I had come to my eighteenth year when he died. Once I met him in the garden, and my knees were knocking with fright indeed; however, he did nothing, only asked me my name, and sent me into his room for his pocket-handkerchief. He was a gentleman – how shall I tell you – he didn't look on any one as better than himself. For your great-grandfather had, I do assure you, a magic amulet; a monk from Mount Athos made him a present of this amulet. And he told him, this monk did, "It's for your kindness, Boyar, I give you this; wear it, and you need not fear judgment." Well, but there, little father, we know what those times were like; what the master fancied doing, that he did. Sometimes, if even some gentleman saw fit to cross him in anything, he would just stare at him and say, "You swim in shallow water"; that was his favourite saying. And he lived, your great-grandfather of blessed memory, in a small log-house; and what goods he left behind him, what silver, and stores of all kinds! All the store-houses were full and overflowing. He was a manager. That very decanter, that you were pleased to admire, was his; he used to drink brandy out of it. But there was your grandfather, Piotr Andreitch, built himself a palace of stone, but he never grew rich; everything with him went badly, and he lived worse than his father by far, and he got no pleasure from it for himself, but spent all his money, and now there is nothing to remember him by – not a silver spoon has come down from him, and we have Glafira Petrovna's management to thank for all that is saved.'

'But is it true,' Lavretsky interrupted him, 'they called her the old witch?'

'What sort of people called her so, I should like to know!' replied Anton with an air of displeasure.

'And, little father,' the old man one day found courage to ask, 'what about our mistress, where is she pleased to fix her residence?'

'I am separated from my wife,' Lavretsky answered with an effort, 'please do not ask questions about her.'

'Yes, sir,' replied the old man mournfully.

After three weeks had passed by, Lavretsky rode into O——— to the Kalitins', and spent an evening with them. Lemm was there; Lavretsky took a great liking to him. Although, thanks to his father, he played no instrument, he was passionately fond of music, real classical music. Panshin was not at the Kalitins' that evening. The governor had sent him off to some place out of the town. Lisa played alone and very correctly; Lemm woke up, got excited, twisted a piece of paper into a roll, and conducted. Marya Dmitrievna laughed at first, as she looked at him, later on she went off to bed; in her own words, Beethoven was too agitating for her nerves. At midnight

Lavretsky accompanied Lemm to his lodging and stopped there with him till three o'clock in the morning. Lemm talked a great deal; his bent figure grew erect, his eyes opened wide and flashed fire; his hair even stood up on his forehead. It was so long since any one had shown him any sympathy, and Lavretsky was obviously interested in him, he was plying him with sympathetic and attentive questions. This touched the old man; he ended by showing the visitor his music, played and even sang in a faded voice some extracts from his works, among others the whole of Schiller's ballad, *Fridolin*, set by him to music. Lavretsky admired it, made him repeat some passages, and at parting, invited him to stay a few days with him. Lemm, as he accompanied him as far as the street, agreed at once, and warmly pressed his hand; but, when he was left standing alone in the fresh, damp air, in the just dawning sunrise, he looked round him, shuddered, shrank into himself, and crept up to his little room, with a guilty air. '*Ich bin wohl night klug*' (I must be out of my senses), he muttered, as he lay down in his hard short bed. He tried to say that he was ill, a few days later, when Lavretsky drove over to fetch him in an open carriage; but Fedor Ivanitch went up into his room and managed to persuade him. What produced the most powerful effect upon Lemm was the circumstance that Lavretsky had ordered a piano from town to be sent into the country expressly for him. They set off together to the Kalitins' and spent the evening with them, but not so pleasantly as on the last occasion. Panshin was there, he talked a great deal about his expedition, and very amusingly mimicked and described the country gentry he had seen; Lavretsky laughed, but Lemm would not come out of his corner, and sat silent, slightly tremulous all over like a spider, looking dull and sullen, and he only revived when Lavretsky began to take leave. Even when he was sitting in the carriage, the old man was still shy and constrained; but the warm soft air, the light breeze, and the light shadows, the scent of the grass and the birch-buds, the peaceful light of the starlit, moonless night, the pleasant tramp and snort of the horses – all the witchery of the roadside, the spring and the night, sank into the poor German's soul, and he was himself the first to begin a conversation with Lavretsky.

XXII

HE BEGAN TALKING about music, about Lisa, then of music again. He seemed to enunciate his words more slowly when he spoke of Lisa. Lavretsky turned the conversation on his compositions, and half in jest, offered to write him a libretto.

'H'm, a libretto!' replied Lemm; 'no, that is not in my line; I have not now the liveliness, the play of the imagination, which is needed for an opera; I have lost too much of my power . . . But if I were still able to do something, – I should be contented with a song; of course I should like to have beautiful words . . .'

He ceased speaking, and sat a long while motionless, his eyes lifted to the heavens.

'For instance,' he said at last, 'something in this way: "Ye stars, ye pure stars!"'

Lavretsky turned his face slightly towards him and began to look at him.

'"Ye stars, pure stars,"' repeated Lemm. . . . '"You look down upon the righteous and the guilty alike . . . but only the pure in heart," – or something of that kind – "comprehend you" – that is, no – "love you." But I am not a poet. I'm not equal to it! Something of that kind, though, something lofty.'

Lemm pushed his hat on to the back of his head; in the dim twilight of the clear night his face looked paler and younger.

'"And you too,"' he continued, his voice gradually sinking, '"ye know who loves, who can love, because ye, pure ones, ye alone can comfort" . . . No, that's not it at all! I am not a poet,' he said, 'but something of that sort.'

'I am sorry I am not a poet,' observed Lavretsky.

'Vain dreams!' replied Lemm, and he buried himself in the corner of the carriage. He closed his eyes as though he were disposing himself to sleep.

A few instants passed ... Lavretsky listened ...' "Stars, pure stars, love," ' muttered the old man.

'Love,' Lavretsky repeated to himself. He sank into thought – and his heart grew heavy.

'That is beautiful music you have set to Fridolin, Christopher Fedoritch,' he said aloud, 'but what do you suppose, did that Fridolin do, after the Count had presented him to his wife ... became her lover, eh?'

'You think so,' replied Lemm, 'probably because experience,' – he stopped suddenly and turned away in confusion. Lavretsky laughed constrainedly, and also turned away and began gazing at the road.

The stars had begun to grow paler and the sky had turned grey when the carriage drove up to the steps of the little house in Vassilyevskoe. Lavretsky conducted his guest to the room prepared for him, returned to his study and sat down before the window. In the garden a nightingale was singing its last song before dawn, Lavretsky remembered that a nightingale had sung in the garden at the Kalitins'; he remembered, too, the soft stir in Lisa's eyes, as at its first notes, they turned towards the dark window. He began to think of her, and his heart was calm again. 'Pure maiden,' he murmured half-aloud: 'pure stars,' he added with a smile, and went peacefully to bed.

But Lemm sat a long while on his bed, a music-book on his knees. He felt as though sweet, unheard melody was haunting him; already he was all aglow and astir, already he felt the languor and sweetness of its presence ... but he could not reach it.

'Neither poet nor musician!' he muttered at last ... And his tired head sank wearily on to the pillows.

XXIII

THE NEXT MORNING the master of the house and his guest drank tea in the garden under an old lime-tree.

'Maestro!' said Lavretsky among other things, 'you will soon have to compose a triumphal cantata.'

'On what occasion?'

'For the nuptials of Mr. Panshin and Lisa. Did you notice what attention he paid her yesterday? It seems as though things were in a fair way with them already.'

'That will never be!' cried Lemm.

'Why?'

'Because it is impossible. Though, indeed,' he added after a short pause, 'everything is possible in this world. Especially here among you in Russia.'

'We will leave Russia out of the question for a time; but what do you find amiss in this match?'

'Everything is amiss, everything. Lisaveta Mihalovna is a girl of high principles, serious, of lofty feelings, and he . . . he is a dilettante, in a word.'

'But suppose she loves him?'

Lemm got up from the bench.

'No, she does not love him, that is to say, she is very pure in heart, and does not know herself what it means . . . love. Madame von Kalitin tells her that he is a fine young man, and she obeys Madame von Kalitin because she is still quite a child, though she is nineteen; she says her prayers in the morning and in the evening – and that is very well; but she does not love him. She can only love what is beautiful, and he is not, that is, his soul is not beautiful.'

Lemm uttered this whole speech coherently, and with fire, walking with little steps to and fro before the tea-table, and running his eyes over the ground.

'Dearest maestro!' cried Lavretsky suddenly, 'it strikes me you are in love with my cousin yourself.'

Lemm stopped short all at once.

'I beg you,' he began in an uncertain voice, 'do not make fun of me like that. I am not crazy; I look towards the dark grave, not towards a rosy future.'

Lavretsky felt sorry for the old man; he begged his pardon. After morning tea, Lemm played him his cantata, and after dinner, at Lavretsky's initiative, there was again talk of Lisa. Lavretsky listened to him with attention and curiosity.

'What do you say, Christopher Fedoritch,' he said at last, 'you see everything here seems in good order now, and the garden is in full bloom, couldn't we invite her over here for a day with her mother and my old aunt . . . eh? Would you like it?'

Lemm bent his head over his plate.

'Invite her,' he murmured, scarcely audibly.

'But Panshin isn't wanted?'

'No, he isn't wanted,' rejoined the old man with an almost child-like smile.

Two days later Fedor Ivanitch set off to the town to see the Kalitins.

XXIV

HE FOUND THEM all at home, but he did not at once disclose his plan to them; he wanted to discuss it first with Lisa alone. Fortune favoured him; they were left alone in the drawing-room. They had some talk; she had had time by now to grow used to him – and she was not shy as a rule with any one. He listened to her, watched her, and mentally repeated Lemm's words, and agreed with them. It sometimes happens that two people who are acquainted, but not on intimate terms with one another, all of a sudden grow rapidly more intimate in a few minutes, and the consciousness of this greater intimacy is at once expressed in their eyes, in their soft and affectionate smiles, and in their very gestures. This was exactly what came to pass with Lavretsky and Lisa. 'So he is like that,' was her thought, as she turned a friendly glance on him; 'so you are like that,' he too was thinking. And so he was not very much surprised when she informed him, not without a little faltering, however, that she had long wished to say something to him, but she was afraid of offending him.

'Don't be afraid; tell me,' he replied, and stood still before her.

Lisa raised her clear eyes to him.

'You are so good,' she began, and at the same time, she thought: 'Yes, I am sure he is good' ... 'you will forgive me, I ought not to dare to speak of it to you ... but – how could you ... why did you separate from your wife?'

Lavretsky shuddered: he looked at Lisa, and sat down near her.

'My child,' he began, 'I beg you, do not touch upon that wound; your hands are tender, but it will hurt me all the same.'

'I know,' Lisa went on, as though she did not hear him, 'she has been to blame towards you. I don't want to defend her; but what God has joined, how can you put asunder?'

'Our convictions on that subject are too different, Lisaveta Mihalovna,' Lavretsky observed, rather sharply; 'we cannot understand one another.'

Lisa grew paler: her whole frame was trembling slightly; but she was not silenced.

'You must forgive,' she murmured softly, 'if you wish to be forgiven.'

'Forgive!' broke in Lavretsky. 'Ought you not first to know whom you are interceding for? Forgive that woman, take her back into my home, that empty, heartless creature! And who told you she wants to return to me? She is perfectly contented with her position, I can assure you. ... But what a subject to discuss here! Her name ought never to be uttered by you. You are too pure, you are not capable of understanding such a creature.'

'Why abuse her?' Lisa articulated with an effort. The trembling of her hands was perceptible now. 'You left her yourself, Fedor Ivanitch.'

'But I tell you,' retorted Lavretsky with an involuntary outburst of impatience, 'you don't know what that woman is!'

'Then why did you marry her?' whispered Lisa, and her eyes fell.

Lavretsky got up quickly from his seat.

'Why did I marry her? I was young and inexperienced; I was deceived, I was carried away by a beautiful exterior. I knew no women. I knew nothing. God grant you may make a happier marriage! but let me tell you, you can be sure of nothing.'

'I too might be unhappy,' said Lisa (her voice had begun to be unsteady), 'but then I ought to submit, I don't know how to say it; but if we do not submit'—

Lavretsky clenched his hands and stamped with his foot.

'Don't be angry, forgive me,' Lisa faltered hurriedly.

At that instant Marya Dmitrievna came in. Lisa got up and was going way.

'Stop a minute,' Lavretsky cried after her unexpectedly. 'I have a great favour to beg of your mother and you; to pay me a visit in my new abode. You know, I have had a piano sent over; Lemm is staying with me; the lilac is in flower now; you will get a breath of country air, and you can return the same day – will you consent?' Lisa looked towards her mother; Marya Dmitrievna was assuming an expression of suffering; but Lavretsky did not give her time to open her mouth; he at once kissed both her hands. Marya Dmitrievna, who was always susceptible to demonstrations of feeling, and did not at all anticipate such effusiveness from the 'dolt,' was melted and gave her consent. While she was deliberating which day to fix, Lavretsky went up to Lisa, and, still greatly moved, whispered to her aside: 'Thank you, you are a good girl; I was to blame.' And her pale face glowed with a bright, shy smile; her eyes smiled too – up to that instant she had been afraid she had offended him.

'Vladimir Nikolaitch can come with us?' inquired Marya Dmitrievna.

'Yes,' replied Lavretsky, 'but would it not be better to be just a family party?'

'Well, you know, it seems,' began Marya Dmitrievna.

'But as you please,' she added.

It was decided to take Lenotchka and Shurotchka. Marfa Timofyevna refused to join in the expedition.

'It is hard for me, my darling,' she said, 'to give my old bones a shaking; and to be sure there's nowhere for me to sleep at your place: besides, I can't sleep in a strange bed. Let the young folks go frolicking.'

Lavretsky did not succeed in being alone again with Lisa; but he looked at her in such a way that she felt her heart at rest, and a little ashamed, and sorry for him. He pressed her hand warmly at parting; left alone, she fell to musing.

XXV

WHEN LAVRETSKY REACHED HOME, he was met at the door of the drawing-room by a tall, thin man, in a threadbare blue coat, with a wrinkled, but lively face, with dishevelled grey whiskers, a long straight nose, and small fiery eyes. This was Mihalevitch, who had been his friend at the university. Lavretsky did not at first recognise him, but embraced him warmly directly he told his name. They had not met since their Moscow days. Torrents of exclamations and questions followed; long-buried recollections were brought to light. Hurriedly smoking pipe after pipe, tossing off tea at a gulp, and gesticulating with his long hands, Mihalevitch related his adventures to Lavretsky; there was nothing very inspiring in them, he could not boast of success in his undertakings – but he was constantly laughing a hoarse, nervous laugh. A month previously he had received a position in the private counting-house of a spirit-tax contractor, two hundred and fifty miles from the town of O———, and hearing of Lavretsky's return from abroad he had turned out of his way so as to see his old friend. Mihalevitch talked as impetuously as in his youth; made as much noise, and was as effervescent as of old. Lavretsky was about to acquaint him with the position, but Mihalevitch interrupted him, muttering hurriedly, 'I have heard, my dear fellow, I have heard – who could have anticipated it?' and at once turned the conversation upon general subjects.

'I must set off to-morrow, my dear fellow,' he observed; 'to-day if you will excuse it, we will sit up late. I want above all to know what you are like, what are your views and convictions, what you have become, what life has taught you.' (Mihalevitch still preserved the phraseology of 1830.) 'As for me, I have changed in much; the waves of life have broken over my breast – who was it said that? – though in what is important, essential I have not changed; I believe as of old in the good, the true: but I do not only believe – I have faith now, yes, I have faith, faith. Listen, you know I write verses; there is no poetry in them, but there is truth. I will read you aloud my last poem; I have expressed my truest convictions in it. Listen.' Mihalevitch fell to reading his poem: it was rather long, and ended with the following lines:

> 'I gave myself to new feelings with all my heart,
> And my soul became as a child's!
> And I have burnt all I adored,
> And now adore all that I burnt.'

As he uttered the two last lines, Mihalevitch all but shed tears; a slight spasm – the sign of deep emotion – passed over his wide mouth, his ugly face lighted up. Lavretsky listened, and listened to him – and the spirit of antagonism was aroused in him; he was irritated by the ever-ready enthusiasm of the Moscow student, perpetually at boiling-point. Before a quarter of an hour had elapsed a heated argument had broken out between them, one of these endless arguments, of which only Russians are capable. After a separation of many years spent in two different worlds, with no clear understanding of the other's ideas or even of their own, catching at words and replying only in words, they disputed about the most abstract subjects, and they disputed as though it were a matter of life and death for both: they shouted and vociferated so that every one in the house was startled, and poor Lemm, who had locked himself up in his room directly after Mihalevitch arrived, was bewildered, and began even to feel vaguely alarmed.

'What are you after all? a pessimist?' cried Mihalevitch at one o'clock in the night.

'Are pessimists usually like this?' replied Lavretsky. 'They are usually all pale and sickly – would you like me to lift you with one hand?'

'Well, if you are not a pessimist you are a *scepteec*, that's still worse.' Mihalevitch's talk had a strong flavour of his mother-country, Little Russia. 'And what right have you to be a *scepteec*? You have had ill-luck in life, let us admit; that was not your fault; you were born with a passionate loving heart, and you were unnaturally kept out of the society of women: the first woman you came across was bound to deceive you.'

'She deceived you too,' observed Lavretsky grimly.

'Granted, granted; I was the tool of destiny in it – what nonsense I talk, though – there is no such thing as destiny; it is an old habit of expressing things inexactly. But what does that prove?'

'It proves this, that they distorted me from my childhood.'

'Well, it's for you to straighten yourself! What's the good of being a man, a male animal? And however that may be, is it possible, is it permissible, to reduce a personal, so to speak, fact to a general law, to an infallible principle?'

'How a principle?' interrupted Lavretsky; 'I don't admit—'

'No, it is your principle, your principle,' Mihalevitch interrupted in his turn.

'You are an egoist, that's what it is!' he was thundering an hour later: 'you wanted personal happiness, you wanted enjoyment in life, you wanted to live only for yourself.'

'What do you mean by personal happiness?'

'And everything deceived you; everything crumbled away under your feet.'

'What do you mean by personal happiness, I ask you?'

'And it was bound to crumble away. Either you sought support where it could not be found, or you built your house on shifting sands, or—'

'Speak more plainly, *or* I can't understand you.'

'Or – you may laugh if you like – or you had no faith, no warmth of heart; intellect, nothing but one farthing's worth of intellect . . . you are simply a pitiful, antiquated Voltairean, that's what you are!'

'I'm a Voltairean?'

'Yes, like your father, and you yourself do not suspect it.'

'After that,' exclaimed Lavretsky, 'I have the right to call you a fanatic.'

'Alas!' replied Mihalevitch with a contrite air, 'I have not so far deserved such an exalted title, unhappily.'

'I have found out now what to call you,' cried the same Mihalevitch, at three o'clock in the morning. 'You are not a sceptic, nor a pessimist, nor a Voltairean, you are a loafer, and you are a vicious loafer, a conscious loafer, not a simple loafer. Simple loafers lie on the stove and do nothing because they don't know how to do anything; they don't think about anything either, but you are a man of ideas – and yet you lie on the stove; you could do something – and you do nothing; you lie idle with a full stomach and look down from above and say, "It's best to lie idle like this, because whatever people do, is all rubbish, leading to nothing." '

'And from what do you infer that I lie idle?' Lavretsky protested stoutly. 'Why do you attribute such ideas to me?'

'And, besides that, you are all, all the tribe of you,' continued Mihalevitch, 'cultivated loafers. You know which leg the German limps on, you know what's amiss with the English and the French, and your pitiful culture goes to make it worse, your shameful idleness, your abominable inactivity is justified by it. Some are even proud of it: "I'm such a clever fellow," they say, "I do nothing, while these fools are in a fuss." Yes! and there are fine gentlemen among us – though I don't say this as to you – who reduce their whole life to a kind of stupor of boredom, get used to it, live in it, like – like a mushroom in white sauce,' Mihalevitch added hastily, and he laughed at his own comparison. 'Oh! this stupor of boredom is the ruin of Russians. Ours is the age for work, and the sickening loafer' . . .

'But what is all this abuse about?' Lavretsky clamoured in his turn. 'Work – doing – you'd better say what is to be done, instead of abusing me, Desmosthenes of Poltava!'

'There, what a thing to ask! I can't tell you that, brother; that, every one ought to know for himself,' retorted the Desmosthenes ironically. 'A landowner, a nobleman, and not know what to do? You have no faith, or else you would know; no faith – and no intuition.'

'Let me at least have time to breathe; you don't let me have time to look round,' Lavretsky besought him.

'Not a minute, not a second!' retorted Mihalevitch with an imperious wave of the hand. 'Not one second: death does not delay, and life ought not to delay.'

'And what a time, what a place for men to think of loafing!' he cried at four o'clock, in a voice, however, which showed signs of sleepiness; 'among us! now! in Russia! where every separate individuality has a duty resting upon him, a solemn responsibility to God, to the people, to himself. We are sleeping, and the time is slipping away; we are sleeping.' . . .

'Permit me to observe,' remarked Lavretsky, 'that we are not sleeping at present, but rather preventing others from sleeping. We are straining our throats like the cocks – listen! there is one crowing for the third time.'

This sally made Mihalevitch laugh, and calmed him down. 'Good-bye till to-morrow,' he said with a smile, and thrust his pipe into his pouch.

'Till to-morrow,' repeated Lavretsky. But the friends talked for more than an hour longer. Their voices were no longer raised, however, and their talk was quiet, sad, friendly talk.

Mihalevitch set off the next day, in spite of all Lavretsky's efforts to keep him. Fedor Ivanitch did not succeed in persuading him to remain; but he talked to him to his heart's content. Mihalevitch, it appeared, had not a penny to bless himself with. Lavretsky had noticed with pain the evening before all the tokens and habits of years of poverty: his boots were shabby, a button was off on the back of his coat, his hands were unused to gloves, his hair wanted brushing; on his arrival, he had not even thought of asking to wash, and at supper he ate like a shark, tearing his meat in his fingers, and crunching the bones with his strong black teeth. It appeared, too, that he had made nothing out of his employment, that he now rested all his hopes on the contractor who was taking him solely in order to have an 'educated man' in his office. For all that Mihalevitch was not discouraged, but as idealist or poet, lived on a crust of bread, singing, rejoicing or grieving over the destinies of humanity, and his own vocation, and troubling himself very little as to how to escape dying of hunger. Mihalevitch was not married: but had been in love times beyond number, and had written poems to all the objects of his adoration; he sang with especial fervour the praises of a mysterious black-tressed 'noble Polish lady.' There were rumours, it is true, that this 'noble Polish lady' was a simple Jewess, very well known to a good many cavalry officers – but, after all, what do you think – does it really make any difference?

With Lemm, Mihalevitch did not get on; his noisy talk

and brusque manners scared the German, who was unused to such behaviour. One poor devil detects another by instinct at once, but in old age he rarely gets on with him, and that is hardly astonishing, he has nothing to share with him, not even hopes.

Before setting off, Mihalevitch had another long discussion with Lavretsky, foretold his ruin, if he did not see the error of his ways, exhorted him to devote himself seriously to the welfare of his peasants, and pointed to himself as an example, saying that he had been purified in the furnace of suffering; and in the same breath called himself several times a happy man, comparing himself with the fowl of the air and the lily of the field.

'A black lily, any way,' observed Lavretsky.

'Ah, brother, don't be a snob!' retorted Mihalevitch, good-naturedly, 'but thank God rather that there is pure plebeian blood in your veins too. But I see you want some pure, heavenly creature to draw you out of your apathy.'

'Thanks, brother,' remarked Lavretsky. 'I have had quite enough of those heavenly creatures.'

'Silence, ceeneec!' cried Mihalevitch.

'Cynic,' Lavretsky corrected him.

'Ceeneec, just so,' repeated Mihalevitch unabashed.

Even when he had taken his seat in the carriage, to which his flat, yellow, strangely light trunk was carried, he still talked; muffled in a kind of Spanish cloak with a collar, brown with age, and a clasp of two lion's paws; he went on developing his views on the destiny of Russia, and waving his thick hand in the air, as though he were sowing the seeds of her future prosperity. The horses started at last.

'Remember my three last words,' he cried, thrusting his whole body out of the carriage and balancing so, 'Religion, progress, humanity! . . . Farewell.'

His head, with a foraging cap pulled down over his eyes, disappeared. Lavretsky was left standing alone on the steps, and he gazed steadily into the distance along the road till the carriage disappeared out of sight. 'Perhaps he is right, after all,' he thought as he went back into the house; 'perhaps I am a loafer.' Many of Mihalevitch's words had sunk irresistibly into his heart, though he had disputed and disagreed with him. If a man only has a good heart, no one can resist him.

XXVI

TWO DAYS LATER, Marya Dmitrievna visited Vassilyevskoe according to her promise, with all her young people. The little girls ran at once into the garden, while Marya Dmitrievna languidly walked through the rooms and languidly admired everything. She regarded her visit to Lavretsky as a sign of great condescension, almost as a deed of charity. She smiled graciously when Anton and Apraxya kissed her hand in the old-fashioned house-servants' style; and in a weak voice, speaking through her nose, asked for some tea. To the great vexation of Anton, who had put on knitted white gloves for the purpose, tea was not handed to the grand lady visitor by him, but by Lavretsky's hired valet, who in the old man's words, had not a notion of what was proper. To make up for this, Anton resumed his rights at dinner: he took up a firm position behind Marya Dmitrievna's chair, and would not surrender his post to any one. The appearance of guests after so long an interval at Vassilyevskoe fluttered and delighted the old man; it was a pleasure to him to see that his master was acquainted with such fine gentlefolk. He was not, however, the only one who was fluttered that day; Lemm, too, was in agitation. He had put on a rather short snuff-coloured coat with a swallow-tail, and tied his neckhandkerchief stiffly, and he kept incessantly coughing and making way for people with a cordial and affable air. Lavretsky noticed with pleasure that his relations with Lisa were becoming more intimate; she had held out her hand to him affectionately directly she came in. After dinner Lemm drew out of his coat-tail pocket, into which he had continually been fumbling, a small roll of music-paper and compressing his lips he laid it without speaking on the pianoforte. It was a song composed by him the evening before, to some old-fashioned German words, in which mention was made of the stars. Lisa sat down at once to the piano and played at sight the song. . . . Alas! the music turned out to be complicated and painfully strained; it was clear that the composer had striven to express something passionate and deep, but nothing had come of it; the effort had remained an effort. Lavretsky and Lisa both felt this, and Lemm understood it. Without uttering a single word, he put his song back into his pocket, and in reply to Lisa's proposal to play it again, he only shook his head and said significantly: 'Now – enough!' and shrinking into himself he turned away.

Towards evening the whole party went out to fish. In the pond behind the garden there were plenty of carp and groundlings. Marya Dmitrievna was put in an arm-chair near the bank, in the shade, with a rug under her feet and the best line was given to her. Anton as an old experienced angler offered her his services. He zealously put on the worms, and clapped his hand on them, spat on them and even threw in the line with a graceful forward swing of his whole body. Marya Dmitrievna spoke of him the same day to Fedor Ivanitch in the following phrase, in boarding-school French: '*Il n'y a plus maintenant de ces gens comme ça, comme autrefois.*' Lemm with the two little girls went off further to the dam of the pond; Lavretsky took up his position near Lisa. The fish were continually biting, the carp were constantly flashing in the air with golden and silvery sides as they were drawn in; the cries of pleasure of the little girls were incessant, even Marya Dmitrievna uttered a little feminine shriek on two occasions. The fewest fish were caught by Lavretsky and Lisa; probably this was because they paid less attention than the others to the angling, and allowed their floats to swim back right up to the bank. The high reddish reeds rustled quietly around, the still water shone quietly before them, and quietly too they talked together. Lisa was standing on a small raft; Lavretsky sat on the inclined trunk of a willow; Lisa wore a white gown, tied round the waist with a broad ribbon, also white; her straw hat was hanging on one hand, and in the other with some effort she held up the crooked rod. Lavretsky gazed at her pure, somewhat severe profile, at her hair drawn back behind her ears, at her soft cheeks, which glowed like a little child's, and thought, 'Oh, how sweet you are, bending over my pond!' Lisa did not turn to him, but looked at the water, half frowning, to keep the sun out of her eyes, half smiling. The shade of the lime-tree near fell upon both.

'Do you know,' began Lavretsky, 'I have been thinking over our last conversation a great deal, and have come to the conclusion that you are exceedingly good.'

'That was not at all my intention in—' Lisa was beginning to reply, and she was overcome with embarrassment.

'You are good,' repeated Lavretsky. 'I am a rough fellow, but I feel that every one must love you. There's Lemm for instance; he is simply in love with you.'

Lisa's brows did not exactly frown, they contracted slightly; it always happened with her when she heard something disagreeable to her.

'I was very sorry for him to-day,' Lavretsky added, 'with his unsuccessful song. To be young and to fail is bearable; but to be old and not be successful is hard to bear. And how mortifying it is to feel that one's forces are deserting one! It is hard for an old man to bear such blows! . . . Be careful, you have a bite. . . . They say,' added Lavretsky after a short pause, 'that Vladimir Nikolaitch has written a very pretty song.'

'Yes,' replied Lisa, 'it is only a trifle, but not bad.'

'And what do you think,' inquired Lavretsky; 'is he a good musician?'

'I think he has great talent for music; but so far he has not worked at it, as he should.'

'Ah! And is he a good sort of man?'

Lisa laughed and glanced quickly at Fedor Ivanitch.

'What a queer question!' she exclaimed, drawing up her line and throwing it in again further off.

'Why is it queer? I ask you about him, as one who has only lately come here, as a relation.'

'A relation?'

'Yes. I am, it seems, a sort of uncle of yours?'

'Vladimir Nikolaitch has a good heart,' said Lisa, 'and he is clever; *maman* likes him very much.'

'And do you like him?'

'He is nice; why should I not like him?'

'Ah!' Lavretsky uttered and ceased speaking. A half-mournful, half-ironical expression passed over his face. His steadfast gaze embarrassed Lisa, but she went on smiling. – 'Well God grant them happiness!' he muttered at last, as though to himself, and turned away his head.

Lisa flushed.

'You are mistaken, Fedor Ivanitch,' she said: 'you are wrong in thinking. . . . But don't you like Vladimir Nikolaitch?' she asked suddenly.

'No, I don't.'

'Why?'

'I think he has no heart.'

The smile left Lisa's face.

'It is your habit to judge people severely,' she observed after a long silence.

'I don't think it is. What right have I to judge others severely, do you suppose, when I must ask for indulgence myself? Or have you forgotten that I am a laughing stock to every one, who is not too indifferent even to scoff? . . . By the way,' he added, 'did you keep your promise?'

'What promise?'

'Did you pray for me?'

'Yes, I prayed for you, and I pray for you every day. But please do not speak lightly of that.'

Lavretsky began to assure Lisa that the idea of doing so had never entered his head, that he had the deepest reverence for every conviction; then he went off into a discourse upon religion, its significance in the history of mankind, the significance of Christianity.

'One must be a Christian,' observed Lisa, not without some effort, 'not so as to know the divine . . . and the . . . earthly, but because every man has to die.'

Lavretsky raised his eyes in involuntary astonishment upon Lisa and met her gaze.

'What a strange saying you have just uttered!' he said.

'It is not my saying,' she replied.

'Not yours. . . . But what made you speak of death?'

'I don't know. I often think of it.'

'Often?'

'Yes.'

'One would not suppose so, looking at you now; you have such a bright, happy face, you are smiling.'

'Yes, I am very happy just now,' replied Lisa simply.

Lavretsky would have liked to seize both her hands, and press them warmly.

'Lisa, Lisa!' cried Marya Dmitrievna, 'do come here, and look what a fine carp I have caught.'

'In a minute, *maman*,' replied Lisa, and went towards her, but Lavretsky remained sitting on his willow. 'I talk to her just as if life were not over for me,' he thought. As she went away, Lisa hung her hat on a twig; with strange, almost tender emotion, Lavretsky looked at the hat, and its long rather crumpled ribbons. Lisa soon came back to him, and again took her stand on the platform.

'What makes you think Vladimir Nikolaitch has no heart?' she asked a few minutes later.

'I have told you already that I may be mistaken; time will show, however.'

Lisa grew thoughtful. Lavretsky began to tell her about his daily life at Vassilyevskoe, about Mihalevitch, and about Anton; he felt a need to talk to Lisa, to share with her everything that was passing in his heart; she listened so sweetly, so attentively; her few replies and observations seemed to him so simple and so intelligent. He even told her so.

Lisa was surprised.

'Really?' she said; 'I thought that I was like my maid, Nastya, I had no words of my own. She said one day to her sweetheart, "You must be dull with me; you always talk so finely to me, and I have no words of my own." '

'And thank God for it!' thought Lavretsky.

XXVII

MEANWHILE THE EVENING had come on, Marya Dmitrievna expressed a desire to return home, and the little girls were with difficulty torn away from the pond, and made ready. Lavretsky declared that he would escort his guests half-way, and ordered his horse to be saddled. As he was handing Marya Dmitrievna into the coach, he bethought himself of Lemm; but the old man could nowhere be found. He had disappeared directly after the angling was over. Anton, with an energy remarkable for his years, slammed the doors, and called sharply, 'Go on, coachman!' The coach started. Marya Dmitrievna and Lisa were seated in the back seat; the children and their maid in the front. The evening was warm and still, and the windows were open on both sides. Lavretsky trotted near the coach on the side of Lisa, with his arm leaning on the door – he had thrown the reins on the neck of his smoothly-pacing horse – and now and then he exchanged a few words with the young girl. The glow of sunset was disappearing; night came on, but the air seemed to grow even warmer. Marya Dmitrievna was soon slumbering, the little girls and the maid fell asleep also. The coach rolled swiftly and smoothly along; Lisa was bending forward, she felt happy; the rising moon lighted up her face, the fragrant night breeze breathed on her eyes and cheeks. Her hand rested on the coach door near Lavretsky's hand. And he was happy; borne along in the still warmth of the night, never taking his eyes off the good young face, listening to the young voice that was melodious even in a whisper, as it spoke of simple, good things, he did not even notice that he had gone more than half-way. He did not want to wake Marya Dmitrievna, he lightly pressed Lisa's hand and said, 'I think we are friends now, aren't we?' She nodded, he stopped his horse, and the coach rolled away, lightly swaying and oscillating up and down; Lavretsky turned homeward at a walking pace. The witchery of the summer night enfolded him; all around him seemed suddenly so strange – and at the same time so long known, so sweetly familiar. Everywhere near and afar – and one could see into the far distance, though the eye could not make out clearly much of what was seen – all was at peace; youthful, blossoming life seemed expressed in this deep peace. Lavretsky's horse stepped out bravely, swaying evenly to right and left; its great black shadow moved along beside it. There was something strangely sweet in the tramp of its hoofs, a strange charm in the ringing cry of the quails. The stars were lost in a night mist; the moon, not yet at the full, shone with steady brilliance; its light was shed in an azure stream over the sky, and fell in patches of smoky gold on the thin clouds as they drifted near. The freshness of the air drew a slight moisture into the eyes, sweetly folded all the limbs, and flowed freely into the lungs. Lavretsky rejoiced in it, and was glad at his own rejoicing. 'Come, we are still alive,' he thought; 'we have not been altogether destroyed by' – he did not say – by whom or by what. Then he fell to thinking of Lisa, that she could hardly love Panshin, that if he had met her under different circumstances – God knows what might have come of it; that he understood Lisa, though she had no words of 'her own'; but that, he thought, was not true; she had words of her own. 'Don't speak lightly of that,' came back to Lavretsky's mind. He rode a long way with his head bent in thought, then drawing himself up, he slowly repeated aloud:

> 'And I have burnt all I adored,
> And now adore all that I burnt.'

Then he gave his horse a switch with the whip, and galloped all the way home.

Dismounting from his horse, he looked round for the last time with an involuntary smile of gratitude. Night, still, kindly night stretched over hills and valleys; from afar, out of its fragrant depths – God knows whence – whether from the heavens or the earth – rose a soft, gentle warmth. Lavretsky sent a last greeting to Lisa, and ran up the steps.

The next day passed rather dully. Rain was falling from early morning; Lemm wore a scowl, and kept more and more tightly compressing his lips, as though he had taken an oath never to open them again. When he went to his room, Lavretsky took up to bed with him a whole bundle of French newspapers, which had been lying for more than a fortnight on his table unopened. He began indifferently to tear open the wrappings, and glanced hastily over the columns of the newspapers – in which, however, there was nothing new. He was just about to throw them down – and all at once he leaped out of bed as if he had been stung. In an article in one of the papers, M. Jules, with whom we are already familiar, communicated to his readers a 'mournful intelligence, that charming, fascinating Moscow lady,' he wrote, 'one of the queens of fashion, who adorned Parisian salons, Madame de Lavretsky, had died almost suddenly, and this intelligence, unhappily only too well-founded, had only just reached him,

M. Jules. He was,' so he continued, 'he might say a friend of the deceased.'

Lavretsky dressed, went out into the garden, and till morning he walked up and down the same path.

XXVIII

THE NEXT MORNING, over their tea, Lemm asked Lavretsky to let him have the horses to return to town. 'It's time for me to set to work, that is, to my lessons,' observed the old man. 'Besides, I am only wasting time here.' Lavretsky did not reply at once; he seemed abstracted. 'Very good,' he said at last; 'I will come with you myself.' Unaided by the servants, Lemm, groaning and wrathful, packed his small box and tore up and burnt a few sheets of music-paper. The horses were harnessed. As he came out of his own room, Lavretsky put the paper he had read last night in his pocket. During the whole course of the journey both Lemm and Lavretsky spoke little to one another; each was occupied with his own thoughts, and each was glad not to be disturbed by the other; and they parted rather coolly, which is often the way, however, with friends in Russia. Lavretsky conducted the old man to his little house; the latter got out, took his trunk, and without holding out his hand to his friend (he was holding his trunk in both arms before his breast), without even looking at him, he said to him in Russian, 'good-bye!' 'Good-bye,' repeated Lavretsky, and bade the coachman drive to his lodging. He had taken rooms in the town of O———... After writing a few letters and hastily dining, Lavretsky went to the Kalitins'. In their drawing-room he found only Panshin, who informed him that Marya Dmitrievna would be in directly, and at once, with charming cordiality, entered into conversation with him. Until that day, Panshin had always treated Lavretsky, not exactly haughtily, but at least condescendingly; but Lisa, in describing her expedition of the previous day to Panshin, had spoken of Lavretsky as an excellent and clever man, that was enough; he felt bound to make a conquest of an 'excellent man.' Panshin began with compliments to Lavretsky, with a description of the rapture in which, according to him, the whole family of Marya Dmitrievna spoke of Vassilyevskoe; and then, according to his custom, passing neatly to himself, began to talk about his pursuits, and his views on life, the world and government service; uttered a sentence or two upon the future of Russia, and the duty of rulers to keep a strict hand over the country; and at this point laughed light-heartedly at his own expense, and added that among other things he had been intrusted in Petersburg with the duty *de populariser l'idée du cadastre*. He spoke somewhat at length, passing over all difficulties with careless self-confidence, and playing with the weightiest administrative and political questions, as a juggler plays with balls. The expressions: 'That's what I would do if I were in the government'; 'you as a man of intelligence, will agree with me at once,' were constantly on his lips. Lavretsky listened coldly to Panshin's chatter; he did not like this handsome, clever, easily-elegant young man, with his bright smile, affable voice, and inquisitive eyes. Panshin, with the quick insight into the feelings of others, which was peculiar to him, soon guessed that he was not giving his companion any special satisfaction, and made a plausible excuse to go away, inwardly deciding that Lavretsky might be an 'excellent man,' but he was unattractive, *aigri*, and, *en somme*, rather absurd. Marya Dmitrievna made her appearance escorted by Gedeonovsky; then Marfa Timofyevna and Lisa came in; and after them the other members of the household; and then the musical amateur, Madame Byelenitsin, arrived, a little thinnish lady, with a languid, pretty, almost childish little face, wearing a rustling dress, a striped fan, and heavy gold bracelets. Her husband was with her, a fat red-faced man, with large hands and feet, white eye-lashes, and an immovable smile on his thick lips; his wife never spoke to him in company, but at home, in moments of tenderness, she used to call him her little sucking-pig. Panshin returned; the rooms were very full of people and noise. Such a crowd was not to Lavretsky's taste; and he was particularly irritated by Madame Byelenitsin, who kept staring at him through her eye-glasses. He would have gone away at once but for Lisa; he wanted to say a few words to her alone, but for a long time he could not get a favourable opportunity, and had to content himself with following her in secret delight with his eyes; never had her face seemed sweeter and more noble to him. She gained much from being near Madame Byelenitsin. The latter was for ever fidgeting in her chair, shrugging her narrow little shoulders, giving little girlish giggles, and screwing up her eyes and then opening them wide; Lisa sat quietly, looked directly at every one and did not laugh at all. Madame Kalitin sat down to a game of cards with Marfa Timofyevna, Madame Byelenitsin, and Gedeonovsky, who played very slowly, and constantly made mistakes, frowning and wiping his face with his handkerchief. Panshin assumed a melancholy air, and expressed himself in brief, pregnant, and gloomy phrases, played the part, in fact, of the unappreciated genius, but in spite of the entreaties of Madame Byelenitsin, who was very coquettish with him, he would not consent to sing his song; he felt Lavretsky's presence a constraint. Fedor Ivanitch also spoke little; the peculiar expression of his face struck Lisa directly he came into the room; she felt at once that he had something to tell her, and though she could not herself have said why, she was afraid to question him. At last, as she was going into the next room to pour out tea, she involuntarily turned her head in his direction. He at once went after her.

'What is the matter?' she said, setting the teapot on the samovar.

'Why, have you noticed anything?' he asked.

'You are not the same to-day as I have always seen you before.'

Lavretsky bent over the table.

'I wanted,' he began, 'to tell you a piece of news, but now it is impossible. However, you can read what is marked with pencil in that article,' he added, handing her the paper he had brought with him. 'Let me ask you to keep it a secret; I will come to-morrow morning.'

Lisa was greatly bewildered. Panshin appeared in the doorway. She put the newspaper in her pocket.

'Have you read Obermann, Lisaveta Mihalovna?' Panshin asked her pensively.

Lisa made him some vague reply, and went out of the room and up-stairs. Lavretsky went back to the drawing-room and drew near the card-table. Marfa Timofyevna, flinging back the ribbons of her cap and flushing with annoyance, began to complain of her partner, Gedeonovsky, who in her words, could not play a bit.

'Card-playing, you see,' she said, 'is not so easy as talking scandal.'

The latter continued to blink and wipe his face. Lisa came into the drawing-room and sat down in a corner; Lavretsky looked at her, she looked at him, and both felt the position insufferable. He read perplexity and a kind of secret reproachfulness in her face. He could not talk to her as he would have liked to do; to remain in the same room with her, a guest among other guests, was too painful; he decided to go away. As he took leave of her, he managed to repeat that he would come to-morrow, and added that he trusted in her friendship.

'Come,' she answered with the same perplexity on her face.

Panshin brightened up at Lavretsky's departure; he began to give advice to Gedeonovsky, paid ironical attentions to Madame Byelenitsin, and at last sang his song. But with Lisa he still spoke and looked as before, impressively and rather mournfully.

Again Lavretsky did not sleep all night. He was not sad, he was not agitated, he was quite calm; but he could not sleep.

He did not even remember the past; he simply looked at his life; his heart beat slowly and evenly; the hours glided by; he did not even think of sleep. Only at times the thought flashed through his brain: 'But it is not true, it is all nonsense,' and he stood still, bowed his head and again began to ponder on the life before him.

XXIX

MARYA DMITRIEVNA DID not give Lavretsky an over-cordial welcome when he made his appearance the following day. 'Upon my word, he's always in and out,' she thought. She did not much care for him, and Panshin, under whose influence she was, had been very artful and disparaging in his praises of him the evening before. And as she did not regard him as a visitor, and did not consider it necessary to entertain a relation, almost one of the family, it came to pass that in less than half-an-hour's time he found himself walking in an avenue in the grounds with Lisa. Lenotchka and Shurotchka were running about a few paces from them in the flower-garden.

Lisa was as calm as usual but more than usually pale. She took out of her pocket and held out to Lavretsky the sheet of the newspaper folded up small.

'That is terrible!' she said.

Lavretsky made no reply.

'But perhaps it is not true, though,' added Lisa.

'That is why I asked you not to speak of it to any one.'

Lisa walked on a little.

'Tell me,' she began: 'you are not grieved? not at all?'

'I do not know myself what I feel,' replied Lavretsky.

'But you loved her once?'

'Yes.'

'Very much?'

'Yes.'

'So you are not grieved at her death?'

'She was dead to me long ago.'

'It is sinful to say that. Do not be angry with me. You call me your friend: a friend may say everything. To me it is really terrible. . . . Yesterday there was an evil look in your face. . . . Do you remember not long ago, how you abused her, and she, perhaps, at that very time was dead? It is terrible. It has been sent to you as a punishment.'

Lavretsky smiled bitterly.

'Do you think so? At least, I am now free.'

Lisa gave a slight shudder.

'Stop, do not talk like that. Of what use is your freedom to you? You ought not to be thinking of that now, but of forgiveness.'

'I forgave her long ago,' Lavretsky interposed with a gesture of the hand.

'No, that is not it,' replied Lisa, flushing. 'You did not understand me. You ought to be seeking to be forgiven.'

'To be forgiven by whom?'

'By whom? God. Who can forgive us, but God?'

Lavretsky seized her hand.

'Ah, Lisaveta Mihalovna, believe me,' he cried, 'I have been punished enough as it is. I have expiated everything already, believe me.'

'That you cannot know,' Lisa murmured in an undertone. 'You have forgotten – not long ago, when you were talking to me – you were not ready to forgive her.'

She walked in silence along the avenue.

'And what about your daughter?' Lisa asked, suddenly stopping short.

Lavretsky started.

'Oh, don't be uneasy! I have already sent letters in all directions. The future of my daughter, as you call – as you say – is assured. Do not be uneasy.'

Lisa smiled mournfully.

'But you are right,' continued Lavretsky, 'what can I do with my freedom? What good is it to me?'

'When did you get that paper?' said Lisa, without replying to his question.

'The day after your visit.'

'And is it possible you did not even shed tears?'

'No. I was thunderstruck; but where were tears to come from? Should I weep over the past? but it is utterly extinct for me! Her very fault did not destroy my happiness, but only showed me that it had never been at all. What is there to weep over now? Though indeed, who knows? I might, perhaps, have been more grieved if I had got this news a fortnight sooner.'

'A fortnight?' repeated Lisa. 'But what has happened then in the last fortnight?'

Lavretsky made no answer, and suddenly Lisa flushed even more than before.

'Yes, yes, you guess why,' Lavretsky cried suddenly, 'in the course of this fortnight I have come to know the value of a pure woman's heart, and my past seems further from me than ever.'

Lisa was confused, and she went gently into the flower-garden towards Lenotchka and Shurotchka.

'But I am glad I showed you that newspaper,' said Lavretsky, walking after her; 'already I have grown used to hiding nothing from you, and I hope you will repay me with the same confidence.'

'Do you expect it?' said Lisa, standing still. 'In that case I ought – but no! It is impossible.'

'What is it? Tell me, tell me.'

'Really, I believe I ought not – after all, though,' added Lisa, turning to Lavretsky with a smile, 'what's the good of half confidence? Do you know I received a letter to-day?'

'From Panshin?'

'Yes. How did you know?'

'He asks for your hand?'

'Yes,' replied Lisa, looking Lavretsky straight in the face with a serious expression.

Lavretsky on his side looked seriously at Lisa.

'Well, and what answer have you given him?' he managed to say at last.

'I don't know what answer to give,' replied Lisa, letting her clasped hands fall.

'How is that? Do you love him, then?'

'Yes, I like him; he seems a nice man.'

'You said the very same thing, and in the very same words, three days ago. I want to know do you love him with that intense passionate feeling which we usually call love?'

'As you understand it – no.'

'You're not in love with him?'

'No. But is that necessary?'

'What do you mean?'

'Mamma likes him,' continued Lisa, 'he is kind; I have nothing against him.'

'You hesitate, however.'

'Yes – and perhaps – you, your words are the cause of it. Do you remember what you said three days ago? But that is weakness.'

'O my child!' cried Lavretsky suddenly, and his voice was shaking, 'don't cheat yourself with sophistries, don't call weakness the cry of your heart, which is not ready to give itself without love. Do not take on yourself such a fearful responsibility to this man, whom you don't love, though you are ready to belong to him.'

'I'm obeying, I take nothing on myself,' Lisa was murmuring.

'Obey your heart; only that will tell you the truth,' Lavretsky interrupted her. 'Experience, prudence, all that is dust and ashes! Do not deprive yourself of the best, of the sole happiness on earth.'

'Do you say that, Fedor Ivanitch? You yourself married for love, and were you happy?'

Lavretsky threw up his arms.

'Ah, don't talk about me! You can't even understand all that a young, inexperienced, badly brought-up boy may mistake for love! Indeed though, after all, why should I be unfair to myself? I told you just now that I had not had happiness. No! I was happy!'

'It seems to me, Fedor Ivanitch,' Lisa murmured in a low voice – when she did not agree with the person who she was talking to, she always dropped her voice; and now too she was deeply moved – 'happiness on earth does not depend on ourselves.'

'On ourselves, ourselves, believe me' (he seized both her hands; Lisa grew pale and almost with terror but still steadfastly looked at him): 'if only we do not ruin our lives. For some people marriage for love may be unhappiness; but not for you, with your calm temperament, and your clear soul; I beseech you, do not marry without love, from a sense of duty, self-sacrifice, or anything. . . . That is infidelity, that is mercenary, and worse still. Believe me, – I have the right to say so; I have paid dearly for the right. And if your God—.'

At that instant Lavretsky noticed that Lenotchka and Shurotchka were standing near Lisa, and staring in dumb amazement at him. He dropped Lisa's hands, saying hurriedly, 'I beg your pardon,' and turned away towards the house.

'One thing only I beg of you,' he added, returning again to Lisa: 'don't decide at once, wait a little, think of what I have said to you. Even if you don't believe me, even if you did decide on a marriage of prudence – even in that case you mustn't marry Panshin. He can't be your husband. You will promise me not to be in a hurry, won't you?'

Lisa tried to answer Lavretsky, but she did not utter a word – not because she was resolved to 'be in a hurry,' but because her heart was beating too violently and a feeling, akin to terror, stopped her breath.

XXX

AS HE WAS coming away from the Kalitins', Lavretsky met Panshin; they bowed coldly to one another. Lavretsky went to his lodgings, and locked himself in. He was experiencing emotions such as he had hardly ever experienced before. How long ago was it since he had thought himself in a state of peaceful petrifaction? How long was it since he had felt as he had expressed himself, in the very bottom of the river? What had changed his position? What had brought him out of his solitude? The most ordinary, inevitable, though always unexpected event, death? Yes; but he was not thinking so much of his wife's death and his own freedom, as of this question – what answer would Lisa give Panshin? He felt that in the course of the last three days, he had come to look at her with different eyes; he remembered how after returning home when he thought of her in the silence of the night, he had said to himself, 'if only!' . . . That 'if only' – in which he had referred to the past, to the impossible, had come to pass, though not as he had imagined it, – but his freedom alone was little. 'She will obey her mother,' he thought, 'she will marry Panshin; but even if she refuses him, won't it be just the same as far as I am concerned?' Going up to the looking-glass he minutely scrutinised his own face and shrugged his shoulders.

The day passed quickly by in these meditations; and evening came. Lavretsky went to the Kalitins'. He walked quickly, but his pace slackened as he drew near the house. Before the steps was standing Panshin's light carriage. 'Come,' thought Lavretsky, 'I will not be an egoist' – and he went into the house. He met with no one within-doors, and there was no sound in the drawing-room; he opened the door and saw Marya Dmitrievna playing picquet with Panshin. Panshin bowed to him without speaking, but the lady of the house cried, 'Well, this is unexpected!' and slightly frowned.

Lavretsky sat down near her, and began to look at her cards.

'Do you know how to play picquet?' she asked him with a kind of hidden vexation, and then declared that she had thrown away a wrong card.

Panshin counted ninety, and began calmly and urbanely taking tricks with a severe and dignified expression of face. So it befits diplomatists to play; this was no doubt how he played in Petersburg with some influential dignitary, whom he wished to impress with a favourable opinion of his solidity and maturity. 'A hundred and one, a hundred and two, hearts, a hundred and three,' sounded his voice in measured tones, and Lavretsky could not decide whether it had a ring of reproach or of self-satisfaction.

'Can I see Marfa Timofyevna?' he inquired, observing that Panshin was setting to work to shuffle the cards with still more dignity. There was not a trace of the artist to be detected in him now.

'I think you can. She is at home, up-stairs,' replied Marya Dmitrievna; 'inquire for her.'

Lavretsky went up-stairs. He found Marfa Timofyevna also at cards; she was playing old maid with Nastasya Karpovna. Roska barked at him; but both the old ladies welcomed him cordially. Marfa Timofyevna especially seemed in excellent spirits.

'Ah! Fedya!' she began, 'pray sit down, my dear. We are just finishing our game. Would you like some preserve? Shurotchka, bring him a pot of strawberry. You don't want any? Well, sit there; only you mustn't smoke; I can't bear your tobacco, and it makes Matross sneeze.'

Lavretsky made haste to assure her that he had not the least desire to smoke.

'Have you been down-stairs?' the old lady continued. 'Whom did you see there? Is Panshin still on view? Did you see Lisa? No? She was meaning to come up here. And here she is: speak of angels—'

Lisa came into the room, and she flushed when she saw Lavretsky.

'I came in for a minute, Marfa Timofyevna,' she was beginning.

'Why for a minute?' interposed the old lady. 'Why are you always in such a hurry, you young people? You see I have a visitor; talk to him a little, and entertain him.'

Lisa sat down on the edge of a chair; she raised her eyes to Lavretsky – and felt that it was impossible not to let him know how her interview with Panshin had ended. But how was she to do it? She felt both awkward and ashamed. She had not long known him, this man who rarely went to church, and took his wife's death so calmly – and here was she, confiding all her secrets to him . . . It was true he took an interest in her; she herself trusted him and felt drawn to him; but all the same, she was ashamed, as though a stranger had been into her pure, maiden bower.

Marfa Timofyevna came to her assistance.

'Well, if you won't entertain him,' said Marfa Timofyevna, 'who will, poor fellow? I am too old for him, he is too clever for me, and for Nastasya Karpovna he's too old, it's only the quite young men she will look at.'

'How can I entertain Fedor Ivanitch?' said Lisa. 'If he likes, had I not better play him something on the piano?' she added irresolutely.

'Capital; you're my clever girl,' rejoined Marfa Timofyevna. 'Step down-stairs, my dears; when you have finished, come back: I have been made old maid, I don't like it, I want to have my revenge.'

Lisa got up. Lavretsky went after her. As she went down the staircase, Lisa stopped.

'They say truly,' she began, 'that people's hearts are full of contradictions. Your example ought to frighten me, to make me distrust marriage for love; but I—'

'You have refused him?' interrupted Lavretsky.

'No; but I have not consented either. I told him everything, everything I felt, and asked him to wait a little. Are you pleased with me?' she added with a swift smile – and with a light touch of her hand on the banister she ran down the stairs.

'What shall I play to you?' she asked, opening the piano.

'What you like,' answered Lavretsky as he sat down so that he could look at her.

Lisa began to play, and for a long while she did not lift her eyes from her fingers. She glanced at last at Lavretsky, and stopped short; his face seemed strange and beautiful to her.

'What is the matter with you?' she asked.

'Nothing,' he replied; 'I'm very happy; I'm glad of you, I'm glad to see you – go on.'

'It seems to me,' said Lisa a few moments later, 'that if he had really loved me, he would not have written that letter; he must have felt that I could not give him an answer now.'

'That is of no consequence,' observed Lavretsky, 'what is important is that you don't love him.'

'Stop, how can we talk like this? I keep thinking of your dead wife, and you frighten me.'

'Don't you think, Voldemar, that my Liseta plays charmingly?' Marya Dmitrievna was saying at that moment to Panshin.

'Yes,' answered Panshin, 'very charmingly.'

Marya Dmitrievna looked tenderly at her young partner, but the latter assumed a still more important and care-worn air and called fourteen kings.

XXXI

LAVRETSKY WAS NOT a young man; he could not long delude himself as to the nature of the feeling inspired in him by Lisa; he was brought on that day to the final conviction that he loved her. This conviction did not give him any great pleasure. 'Have

I really nothing better to do,' he thought, 'at thirty-five than to put my soul into a woman's keeping again? But Lisa is not like *her*; she would not demand degrading sacrifices from me: she would not tempt me away from my duties; she would herself incite me to hard honest work, and we would walk hand in hand towards a noble aim. Yes,' he concluded his reflections, 'that's all very fine, but the worst of it is that she does not in the least wish to walk hand in hand with me. She meant it when she said that I frightened her. But she doesn't love Panshin either – a poor consolation!'

Lavretsky went back to Vassilyevskoe, but he could not get through four days there – so dull it seemed to him. He was also in agonies of suspense; the news announced by M. Jules required confirmation, and he had received no letters of any kind. He returned to the town and spent an evening at the Kalitins'. He could easily see that Marya Dmitrievna had been set against him; but he succeeded in softening her a little, by losing fifteen roubles to her at picquet, and he spent nearly half an hour almost alone with Lisa in spite of the fact that her mother had advised her the previous evening not to be too intimate with a man *qui a un si grand ridicule*. He found a change in her; she had become, as it were, more thoughtful. She reproached him for his absence and asked him would he not go on the morrow to mass? (The next day was Sunday.)

'Do go,' she said before he had time to answer, 'we will pray together for the repose of her soul.' Then she added that she did not know how to act – she did not know whether she had the right to make Panshin wait any longer for her decision.

'Why so?' inquired Lavretsky.

'Because,' she said, 'I begin now to suspect what that decision will be.'

She declared that her head ached and went to her own room up-stairs, hesitatingly holding out the tips of her fingers to Lavretsky.

The next day Lavretsky went to mass. Lisa was already in the church when he came in. She noticed him though she did not turn round towards him. She prayed fervently, her eyes were full of a calm light, calmly she bowed her head and lifted it again. He felt that she was praying for him too, and his heart was filled with a marvellous tenderness. He was happy and a little ashamed. The people reverently standing, the homely faces, the harmonious singing, the scent of incense, the long slanting gleams of light from the windows, the very darkness of the walls and arched roofs, all went to his heart. For long he had not been to church, for long he had not turned to God: even now he uttered no words of prayer – he did not even pray without words – but, at least, for a moment in all his mind, if not in his body, he bowed down and meekly humbled himself to earth. He remembered how, in his childhood, he had always prayed in church until he had felt, as it were, a cool touch on his brow; that, he used to think then, is the guardian angel receiving me, laying on me the seal of grace. He glanced at Lisa. 'You brought me here,' he thought, 'touch me, touch my soul.' She was still praying calmly; her face seemed to him full of joy, and he was softened anew: he prayed for another soul, peace; for his own, forgiveness.

They met in the porch; she greeted him with glad and gracious seriousness. The sun brightly lighted up the young grass in the church-yard, and the striped dresses and kerchiefs of the women; the bells of the churches near were tinkling overhead; and the crows were cawing about the hedges. Lavretsky stood with uncovered head, a smile on his lips; the light breeze lifted his hair, and the ribbons of Lisa's hat. He put Lisa and Lenotchka who was with her into their carriage, divided all his money among the poor, and peacefully sauntered home.

XXXII

PAINFUL DAYS FOLLOWED for Fedor Ivanitch. He found himself in a continual fever. Every morning he made for the post, and tore open letters and papers in agitation, and nowhere did he find anything which could confirm or disprove the fateful rumour. Sometimes he was disgusting to himself. 'What am I about,' he thought, 'waiting, like a vulture for blood, for certain news of my wife's death?' He went to the Kalitins every day, but things had grown no easier for him there; the lady of the house was obviously sulky with him, and received him very condescendingly. Panshin treated him with exaggerated politeness; Lemm had entrenched himself in his misanthropy and hardly bowed to him, and, worst of all, Lisa seemed to avoid him. When she happened to be left alone with him, instead of her former candour there was visible embarrassment on her part, she did not know what to say to him, and he, too, felt confused. In the space of a few days Lisa had become quite different from what she was as he knew her: in her movements, her voice, her very laugh a secret tremor, an unevenness never there before was apparent. Marya Dmitrievna, like a true egoist, suspected nothing; but Marfa Timofyevna began to keep a watch over her favourite. Lavretsky more than once reproached himself for having shown Lisa the newspaper he had received; he could not but be conscious that in his spiritual condition there was something revolting to a pure nature. He imagined also that the change in Lisa was the result of her inward conflicts, her doubts as to what answer to give Panshin. One day she brought him a book, a novel of Walter Scott's, which she had herself asked him for.

'Have you read it?' he said.

'No; I can't bring myself to read just now,' she answered, and was about to go away.

'Stop a minute, it is so long since I have been alone with you. You seem to be afraid of me.'

'Yes.'

'Why so, pray?'

'I don't know.'

Lavretsky was silent.

'Tell me,' he began, 'you haven't yet decided?'

'What do you mean?' she said, not raising her eyes.

'You understand me.'

Lisa flushed crimson all at once.

'Don't ask me about anything!' she broke out hotly. 'I know nothing; I don't know myself.' And instantly she was gone.

The following day Lavretsky arrived at the Kalitins' after dinner and found there all the preparations for an evening service. In the corner of the dining-room on a square table covered with a clean cloth were already arranged, leaning up against the wall, the small holy pictures, in gold frames, set with tarnished jewels. The old servant in a grey coat and shoes was moving noiselessly and without haste all about the room; he set two wax-candles in the slim candlesticks before the holy pictures, crossed himself, bowed, and slowly went out. The unlighted drawing-room was empty. Lavretsky went into the dining-room and asked if it was some one's name-day.

In a whisper they told him no, but that the evening service had been arranged at the desire of Lisaveta Mihalovna and Marfa Timofyevna; that it had been intended to invite a wonder-working image, but that the latter had gone thirty versts away to visit a sick man. Soon the priest arrived with the deacons; he was a man no longer young, with a large bald head; he coughed loudly in the hall; the ladies at once filed slowly out of the boudoir, and went up to receive his blessing; Lavretsky bowed to them in silence; and in silence they bowed to him. The priest stood still for a little while, coughed once again, and asked in a bass undertone –

'You wish me to begin?'

'Pray begin, father,' replied Marya Dmitrievna.

He began to put on his robes; a deacon in a surplice asked obsequiously for a hot ember; there was a scent of incense. The maids and men-servants came out from the hall, and remained huddled close together before the door. Roska, who never came down from up-stairs, suddenly ran into the dining-room; they began to chase her out; she was scared, doubled back into the room and sat down; a footman picked her up and carried her away.

The evening service began. Lavretsky squeezed himself into a corner; his emotions were strange, almost sad; he could not himself make out clearly what he was feeling. Marya Dmitrievna stood in front of all, before the chairs; she crossed herself with languid carelessness, like a grand lady, and first looked about her, then suddenly lifted her eyes to the ceiling; she was bored. Marfa Timofyevna looked worried; Nastasya Karpovna bowed down to the ground and got up with a kind of discreet, subdued rustle; Lisa remained standing in her place motionless; from the concentrated expression of her face it could be seen that she was praying steadfastly and fervently. When she bowed to the cross at the end of the service, she also kissed the large red hand of the priest. Marya Dmitrievna invited the latter to have some tea; he took off his vestment, assumed a somewhat more worldly air, and passed into the drawing-room with the ladies. Conversation – not too lively – began. The priest drank four cups of tea, incessantly wiping his bald head with his handkerchief; he related among other things that the merchant Avoshnikov was subscribing seven hundred roubles to gilding the '*cumpola*' of the church, and informed them of a sure remedy against freckles. Lavretsky tried to sit near Lisa, but her manner was severe, almost stern, and she did not once glance at him. She appeared intentionally not to observe him; a kind of cold, grave enthusiasm seemed to have taken possession of her. Lavretsky for some reason or other tried to smile and to say something amusing; but there was perplexity in his heart, and he went away at last in secret bewilderment. . . . He felt there was something in Lisa to which he could never penetrate.

Another time Lavretsky was sitting in the drawing-room listening to the sly but tedious gossip of Gedeonovsky, when suddenly, without himself knowing why, he turned round and caught a profound, attentive questioning look in Lisa's eyes. . . . It was bent on him, this enigmatic look. Lavretsky thought of it the whole night long. His love was not like a boy's; sighs and agonies were not in his line, and Lisa herself did not inspire a passion of that kind; but for every age love has its tortures – and he was spared none of them.

XXXIII

ONE DAY LAVRETSKY, according to his habit, was at the Kalitins'. After an exhaustingly hot day, such a lovely evening had set in that Marya Dmitrievna, in spite of her aversion to a draught, ordered all the windows and doors into the garden to be thrown open, and declared that she would not play cards, that it was a sin to play cards in such weather, and one ought to enjoy nature. Panshin was the only guest. He was stimulated by the beauty of the evening, and conscious of a flood of artistic sensations, but he did not care to sing before Lavretsky, so he fell to reading poetry; he read aloud well, but too self-consciously and with unnecessary refinements, a few poems of Lermontov (Pushkin had not then come into fashion again). Then suddenly, as though ashamed of his enthusiasm, began, *à propos* of the well-known poem, 'A Reverie,' to attack and fall foul of the younger generation. While doing so he did not lose the opportunity of expounding how he would change everything after his own fashion, if the power were in his hands. 'Russia,' he said, 'has fallen behind Europe; we must catch her up. It is maintained that we are young – that's nonsense. Moreover we have no inventiveness: Homakov himself admits that we have not even invented mouse-traps. Consequently, whether we will or no, we must borrow from others. We are sick, Lermontov says – I agree with him. But we are sick from having only half become Europeans, we must take a hair of the dog that bit us' ('*le cadastre*,' thought Lavretsky). 'The best heads, *les meilleures têtes*,' he continued, 'among us have long been convinced of it. All peoples are essentially alike; only introduce among them good institutions, and the thing is done. Of course there may be adaptation to the existing national life; that is our affair – the affair of the official' (he almost said 'governing') 'class. But in case of need don't be uneasy. The institutions will transform the life itself.' Marya Dmitrievna most feelingly assented to all Panshin said. 'What a clever man,' she thought, 'is talking in my drawing-room!' Lisa sat in silence leaning back against the window; Lavretsky too was silent. Marfa Timofyevna, playing cards with her old friend in the corner, muttered something to herself. Panshin walked up and down the room, and spoke eloquently, but with secret exasperation. It seemed as if he were abusing not a whole generation but a few people known to him. In a great lilac-bush in the Kalitins' garden a nightingale had built its nest; its first evening notes filled the pauses of the eloquent speech; the first stars were beginning to shine in the rosy sky over the motionless tops of the limes. Lavretsky got up and began to answer Panshin; an argument sprang up. Lavretsky championed the youth and the independence of Russia; he was ready to throw over himself and his generation, but he stood up for the new men, their convictions and desires. Panshin answered sharply and irritably. He maintained that the intelligent people ought to change everything, and was at last even brought to the point of forgetting his position as a *kammerjunker*, and his career as an official, and calling Lavretsky an antiquated conservative, even hinting – very remotely it is true – at his dubious position in society. Lavretsky did not lose his temper. He did not raise his voice (he recollected that Mihalevitch too had called him antiquated but an antiquated Voltairean), and calmly proceeded to refute Panshin at all points. He proved to him the impracticability of sudden leaps and reforms from above, founded neither on knowledge of the mother-country, nor on any genuine faith in any ideal, even a negative one. He brought forward his own education as an example, and demanded before all things a recognition of the true spirit of the people and submission to it, without which even a courageous combat against error is impossible. Finally he admitted the reproach – well-deserved as he thought – of reckless waste of time and strength.

'That is all very fine!' cried Panshin at last, getting angry. 'You now have just returned to Russia, what do you intend to do?'

'Cultivate the soil,' answered Lavretsky, 'and try to cultivate it as well as possible.'

'That is very praiseworthy, no doubt,' rejoined Panshin, 'and I have been told that you have already had great success in that line; but you must allow that not every one is fit for pursuits of that kind.'

'*Une nature poétique*,' observed Marya Dmitrievna, 'cannot, to be sure, cultivate ... *et puis*, it is your vocation, Vladimir Nikolaitch, to do everything *en grand*.'

This was too much even for Panshin: he grew confused, and changed the conversation. He tried to turn it upon the beauty of the starlit sky, the music of Schubert; nothing was successful. He ended by proposing to Marya Dmitrievna a game of picquet. 'What! on such an evening?' she replied feebly. She ordered the cards to be brought in, however. Panshin tore open a new pack of cards with a loud crash, and Lisa and Lavretsky both got up as if by agreement, and went and placed themselves near Marfa Timofyevna. They both felt all at once so happy that they were even a little afraid of remaining alone together, and at the same time they both felt that the embarrassment they had been conscious of for the last few days had vanished, and would return no more. The old lady stealthily patted Lavretsky on the cheek, slyly screwed up her eyes, and shook her head once or twice, adding in a whisper, 'You have shut up our clever friend, many thanks.' Everything was hushed in the room; the only sound was the faint crackling of the wax-candles, and sometimes the tap of a hand on the table, and an exclamation or reckoning of points; and the rich torrent of the nightingale's song, powerful, piercingly sweet, poured in at the window, together with the dewy freshness of the night.

XXXIV

LISA HAD NOT uttered one word in the course of the dispute between Lavretsky and Panshin, but she had followed it attentively and was completely on Lavretsky's side. Politics interested her very little; but the supercilious tone of the worldly official (he had never delivered himself in that way before) repelled her; his contempt for Russia wounded her. It had never occurred to Lisa that she was a patriot; but her heart was with the Russian people; the Russian turn of mind delighted her; she would talk for hours together without ceremony to the peasant-overseer of her mother's property when he came to the town, and she talked to him as to an equal, without any of the condescension of a superior. Lavretsky felt all this; he would not have troubled himself to answer Panshin by himself; he had spoken only for Lisa's sake. They had said nothing to one another, their eyes even had seldom met. But they both knew that they had grown closer that evening, they knew that they liked and disliked the same things. On one point only were they divided; but Lisa secretly hoped to bring him to God. They sat near Marfa Timofyevna, and appeared to be following her play; indeed, they were really following it, but meanwhile their hearts were full, and nothing was lost on them; for them the nightingale sang, and the stars shone, and the trees gently murmured, lulled to sleep by the summer warmth and softness. Lavretsky was completely carried away, and surrendered himself wholly to his passion – and rejoiced in it. But no word can express what was passing in the pure heart of the young girl. It was a mystery for herself. Let it remain a mystery for all. No one knows, no one has seen, nor will ever see, how the grain, destined to life and growth, swells and ripens in the bosom of the earth.

Ten o'clock struck. Marfa Timofyevna went off up-stairs to her own apartments with Nastasya Karpovna. Lavretsky and Lisa walked across the room, stopped at the open door into the garden, looked into the darkness in the distance and then at one another, and smiled. They could have taken each other's hands, it seemed, and talked to their hearts' content. They returned to Marya Dmitrievna and Panshin, where a game of picquet was still dragging on. The last king was called at last, and the lady of the house rose, sighing and groaning from her well-cushioned easy-chair. Panshin took his hat, kissed Marya Dmitrievna's hand, remarking that nothing hindered some happy people now from sleeping, but that he had to sit up over stupid papers till morning, and departed, bowing coldly to Lisa (he had not expected that she would ask him to wait so long for an answer to his offer, and he was cross with her for it). Lavretsky followed him. They parted at the gate. Panshin waked his coachman by poking him in the neck with the end of his stick, took his seat in the carriage and rolled away. Lavretsky did not want to go home. He walked away from the town into the open country. The night was still and clear, though there was no moon. Lavretsky rambled a long time over the dewy grass. He came across a little narrow path; and went along it. It led him up to a long fence, and to a little gate; he tried, not knowing why, to push it open. With a faint creak the gate opened, as though it had been awaiting the touch of his hand. Lavretsky went into the garden. After a few paces along a walk of lime-trees he stopped short in amazement; he recognised the Kalitins' garden.

He moved at once into a black patch of shade thrown by a thick clump of hazels, and stood a long while without moving, shrugging his shoulders in astonishment.

'This cannot be for nothing,' he thought.

All was hushed around. From the direction of the house not a sound reached him. He went cautiously forward. At the bend of an avenue suddenly the whole house confronted him with its dark face; in two upstair-windows only a light was shining. In Lisa's room behind the white curtain a candle was burning, and in Marfa Timofyevna's bedroom a lamp shone with red-fire before the holy picture, and was reflected with equal brilliance on the gold frame. Below, the door on to the balcony gaped wide open. Lavretsky sat down on a wooden garden-seat, leaned on his elbows, and began to watch this door and Lisa's window. In the town it struck midnight; a little clock in the house shrilly clanged out twelve; the watchman beat it with jerky strokes upon his board. Lavretsky had no thought, no expectation; it was sweet to him to feel himself near Lisa, to sit in her garden on the seat where she herself had sat more than once.

The light in Lisa's room vanished.

'Sleep well, my sweet girl,' whispered Lavretsky, still sitting motionless, his eyes fixed on the darkened window.

Suddenly the light appeared in one of the windows of the ground-floor, then changed into another, and a third.... Some one was walking through the rooms with a candle. 'Can it be Lisa? It cannot be.' Lavretsky got up.... He caught a glimpse of a well-known face – Lisa came into the drawing-room. In a white gown, her plaits hanging loose on her shoulders, she went quietly up to the table, bent over it, put down the candle, and began looking for something. Then turning round facing the garden, she drew near the open door, and stood on the threshold, a light slender figure all in white. A shiver passed over Lavretsky.

'Lisa!' broke hardly audibly from his lips.

She started and began to gaze into the darkness.

'Lisa!' Lavretsky repeated louder, and he came out of the shadow of the avenue.

Lisa raised her head in alarm, and shrank back. She had recognised him. He called to her a third time, and stretched out his hands to her. She came away from the door and stepped into the garden.

'Is it you?' she said. 'You here?'

'I – I – listen to me,' whispered Lavretsky, and seizing her hand he led her to the seat.

She followed him without resistance, her pale face, her fixed eyes, and all her gestures expressed an unutterable bewilderment. Lavretsky made her sit down and stood before her.

'I did not mean to come here,' he began. 'Something brought me. . . . I – I love you,' he uttered in involuntary terror.

Lisa slowly looked at him. It seemed as though she only at that instant knew where she was and what was happening. She tried to get up, she could not, and she covered her face with her hands.

'Lisa,' murmured Lavretsky. 'Lisa,' he repeated, and fell at her feet.

Her shoulders began to heave slightly; the fingers of her pale hands were pressed more closely to her face.

'What is it?' Lavretsky urged, and he heard a subdued sob. His heart stood still. . . . He knew the meaning of those tears. 'Can it be that you love me?' he whispered, and caressed her knees.

'Get up,' he heard her voice, 'get up, Fedor Ivanitch. What are we doing?'

He got up and sat beside her on the seat. She was not weeping now, and she looked at him steadfastly with her wet eyes.

'It frightens me: what are we doing?' she repeated.

'I love you,' he said again. 'I am ready to devote my whole life to you.'

She shuddered again, as though something had stung her, and lifted her eyes towards heaven.

'All that is in God's hands,' she said.

'But you love me, Lisa? We shall be happy.' She dropped her eyes; he softly drew her to him, and her head sank on to his shoulder. ... He bent his head a little and touched her pale lips.

Half an hour later Lavretsky was standing before the little garden gate. He found it locked and was obliged to get over the fence. He returned to the town and walked along the slumbering streets. A sense of immense, unhoped-for happiness filled his soul; all his doubts had died away. 'Away, dark phantom of the past,' he thought. 'She loves me, she will be mine.' Suddenly it seemed to him that in the air over his head were floating strains of divine triumphant music. He stood still. The music resounded in still greater magnificence; a mighty flood of melody – and all his bliss seemed speaking and singing in its strains. He looked about him; the music floated down from two upper windows of a small house.

'Lemm?' cried Lavretsky as he ran to the house. 'Lemm! Lemm!' he repeated aloud.

The sounds died away and the figure of the old man in a dressing-gown, with his throat bare and his hair dishevelled, appeared at the window.

'Aha!' he said with dignity, 'is it you?'

'Christopher Fedoritch, what marvellous music! for mercy's sake, let me in.'

Without uttering a word, the old man with a majestic flourish of the arm dropped the key of the street door from the window.

Lavretsky hastened up-stairs, went into the room and was about to rush up to Lemm; but the latter imperiously motioned him to a seat, saying abruptly in Russian, 'Sit down and listen,' sat down himself to the piano, and looking proudly and severely about him, he began to play. It was long since Lavretsky had listened to anything like it. The sweet passionate melody went to his heart from the first note; it was glowing and languishing with inspiration, happiness and beauty; it swelled and melted away; it touched on all that is precious, mysterious, and holy on earth. It breathed of deathless sorrow and mounted dying away to the heavens. Lavretsky drew himself up, and rose cold and pale with ecstasy. This music seemed to clutch his very soul, so lately shaken by the rapture of love, the music was glowing with love too. 'Again!' he whispered as the last chord sounded. The old man threw him an eagle glance, struck his hand on his chest and saying deliberately in his own tongue, 'This is my work, I am a great musician,' he played again his marvellous composition. There was no candle in the room; the light of the rising moon fell aslant on the window; the soft air was vibrating with sound; the poor little room seemed a holy place, and the old man's head stood out noble and inspired in the silvery half light. Lavretsky went up to him and embraced him. At first Lemm did not respond to his embrace, and even pushed him away with his elbow. For a long while without moving in any limb he kept the same severe, almost morose expression, and only growled out twice, 'aha.' At last his face relaxed, changed, and grew calmer, and in response to Lavretsky's warm congratulations he smiled a little at first, then burst into tears, and sobbed weakly like a child.

'It is wonderful,' he said, 'that you have come just at this moment; but I know all, I know all.'

'You know all?' Lavretsky repeated in amazement.

'You have heard me,' replied Lemm, 'did you not understand that I knew all?'

Till daybreak Lavretsky could not sleep, all night he was sitting on his bed. And Lisa too did not sleep; she was praying.

XXXV

THE READER KNOWS how Lavretsky grew up and developed. Let us say a few words about Lisa's education. She was in her tenth year when her father died; but he had not troubled himself much about her. Weighed down with business cares, for ever anxious for the increase of his property, bilious, sharp and impatient, he gave money unsparingly for the teachers, tutors, dress and other necessities of his children; but he could not endure, as he expressed it, 'to be dandling his squallers,' and indeed he had no time to dandle them. He worked, took no rest from business, slept little, rarely played cards, and worked again. He compared himself to a horse harnessed to a threshing-machine. 'My life has soon come to an end,' was his comment on his death-bed, with a bitter smile on his parched lips. Marya Dmitrievna did not in reality trouble herself about Lisa any more than her husband, though she had boasted to Lavretsky that she alone had educated her children. She dressed her up like a doll, stroked her on the head before visitors and called her a clever child and a darling to her face, and that was all. Any kind of continuous care was too exhausting for the indolent lady. During her father's lifetime, Lisa was in the hands of a governess, Mademoiselle Moreau from Paris; after his death she passed into the charge of Marfa Timofyevna. Marfa Timofyevna the reader knows already; Mademoiselle Moreau was a tiny wrinkled creature with little bird-like ways and a bird's intellect. In her youth she had led a very dissipated life, but in old age she had only two passions left – gluttony and cards. When she had eaten her fill, and was neither playing cards nor chattering, her face assumed an expression almost death-like. She was sitting, looking, breathing – yet it was clear that there was not an idea in her head. One could not even call her good-natured. Birds are not good-natured. Either as a result of her frivolous youth or of the air of Paris, which she had breathed from childhood, a kind of cheap universal scepticism had found its way into her, usually expressed by the words: *tout ça c'est des bêtises*. She spoke ungrammatically, but in a pure Parisian jargon, did not talk scandal and had no caprices – what more can one desire in a governess? Over Lisa she had little influence; all the stronger was the influence on her of her nurse, Agafya Vlasyevna.

This woman's story was remarkable. She came of a peasant family. She was married at sixteen to a peasant; but she was strikingly different from her peasant sisters. Her father had been twenty years starosta, and had made a good deal of money, and he spoiled her. She was exceptionally beautiful, the best-dressed girl in the whole district, clever, ready with her tongue, and daring. Her master Dmitri Pestov, Marya Dmitrievna's father, a man of modest and gentle character, saw her one day at the threshing-floor, talked to her and fell passionately in love with her. She was soon left a widow; Pestov, though he was a married man, took her into his house and dressed her like a lady. Agafya at once adapted herself to her new position, just as if she had never lived differently all her life. She grew fairer and plumper; her arms grew as 'floury white' under her muslin-sleeves as a merchant's lady's; the samovar never left her table; she would wear nothing except silk or velvet, and slept on well-stuffed feather-beds. This blissful existence lasted for five years, but Dmitri Pestov died; his widow, a kind-hearted woman, out of regard for the memory of the deceased, did not wish to treat her rival unfairly, all the more because Agafya had never forgotten herself in her presence. She married her, however, to a shepherd, and sent her a long way off. Three years passed. It happened one hot summer day that her mistress in driving past stopped at the cattle-yard. Agafya regaled her with such delicious cool cream, behaved so modestly, and was so neat, so bright, and so contented with everything that her mistress signified her forgiveness to her and allowed her to return to the house. Within six months she had become so much attached to her that she raised her to be housekeeper, and intrusted the whole household management to her. Agafya again returned to power, and again grew plump and fair; her mistress put the most complete confidence in her. So passed five years more. Misfortune again overtook Agafya. Her husband, whom she had promoted to be a footman, began to drink, took to vanishing from the house, and ended by stealing six of the mistress's silver spoons and hiding them till a favourable moment in his wife's box. It was opened. He was sent to be a shepherd again, and Agafya fell into disgrace. She was not turned out of the house, but was degraded from housekeeper to being a sewing-woman and was ordered to wear a kerchief on her head instead of a cap. To the astonishment of every one, Agafya accepted with humble resignation the blow that had fallen upon her. She was at that time about thirty, all her children were dead and her husband did not live much longer. The time had come for her to reflect. And she did reflect. She became very silent and devout, never missed a single matin's service nor a single mass, and gave away all her fine clothes. She spent fifteen years quietly, peacefully, and soberly, never quarrelling with any one and giving way to every one. If any one scolded her, she only bowed to them and thanked them for the admonition. Her mistress had long ago forgiven her, raised her out of disgrace, and had made her a present of a cap of her own. But she was herself unwilling to give up the kerchief and always wore a dark dress. After her mistress's death she became still more quiet and humble. A Russian readily feels fear, and affection; but it is hard to gain his respect: it is not soon given, nor to every one. For Agafya every one in the house had great respect; no one even remembered her previous sins, as though they had been buried with the old master.

When Kalitin became Marya Dmitrievna's husband, he wanted to intrust the care of the house to Agafya. But she refused 'on account of temptation'; he scolded her, but she bowed humbly and left the room. Kalitin was clever in understanding men; he understood Agafya and did not forget her. When he moved to the town, he gave her, with her consent, the place of nurse to Lisa, who was only just five years old.

Lisa was at first frightened by the austere and serious face of her new nurse; but she soon grew used to her and began to love her. She was herself a serious child. Her features recalled Kalitin's decided and regular profile, only her eyes were not her father's; they were lighted up by a gentle attentiveness and goodness, rare in children. She did not care to play with dolls, never laughed loudly or for long, and behaved with great decorum. She was not often thoughtful, but when she was, it was almost always with some reason. After a short silence, she usually turned to some grown-up person with a question which showed that her brain had been at work upon some new impression. She very early got over childish lispings, and by the time she was four years old spoke perfectly plainly. She was afraid of her father; her feeling towards her mother was undefinable, she was not afraid of her, nor was she demonstrative to her; but she was not demonstrative even towards Agafya, though she was the only person she loved. Agafya never left her. It was curious to see them together. Agafya, all in black, with a dark handkerchief on her head, her face thin and transparent as wax, but still beautiful and expressive, would be sitting upright, knitting a stocking; Lisa would sit at her feet in a little arm-chair, also busied over some kind of work, and seriously raising her clear eyes, listening to what Agafya was relating to her. And Agafya did not tell her stories; but in even measured accents she would narrate the life of the Holy Virgin, the lives of hermits, saints, and holy men. She would tell Lisa how the holy men lived in deserts, how they were saved, how they suffered hunger and want, and did not fear kings, but confessed Christ; how fowls of the air brought them food and wild beasts listened to them, and flowers sprang up on the spots where their blood had been spilt. 'Wall-flowers?' asked Lisa one day, she was very fond of flowers. . . . Agafya spoke to Lisa gravely and meekly, as though she felt herself to be unworthy to utter such high and holy words. Lisa listened to her, and the image of the all-seeing, all-knowing God penetrated with a kind of sweet power into her very soul, filling it with pure and reverent awe; but Christ became for her something near, well-known, almost familiar. Agafya taught her to pray also. Sometimes she wakened Lisa early at daybreak, dressed her hurriedly, and took her in secret to matins. Lisa followed her on tip-toe, almost holding her breath. The cold and twilight of the early morning, the freshness and emptiness of the church, the very secrecy of these unexpected expeditions, the cautious return home and to her little bed, all these mingled impressions of the forbidden, strange, and holy agitated the little girl and penetrated to the very innermost depths of her nature. Agafya never censured any one, and never scolded Lisa for being naughty. When she was displeased at anything, she only kept silence. And Lisa understood this silence; with a child's quick-sightedness she knew very well, too, when Agafya was displeased with other people, Marya Dmitrievna or Kalitin himself. For a little over three years Agafya waited on Lisa, then Mademoiselle Moreau replaced her; but the frivolous Frenchwoman, with her cold ways and exclamation, *tout ça c'est des bêtises*, could never dislodge her dear nurse from Lisa's heart; the seeds that had been dropped into it had become too deeply rooted. Besides, though Agafya no longer waited on Lisa, she was still in the house and often saw her charge, who believed in her as before.

Agafya did not, however, get on well with Marfa Timofyevna, when she came to live in the Kalitins' house. Such gravity and dignity on the part of one who had once worn the motley skirt of a peasant wench displeased the impatient and self-willed old lady. Agafya asked leave to go on a pilgrimage and she never came back. There were dark rumours that she had gone off to a retreat of sectaries. But the impression she had left in Lisa's soul was never obliterated. She went as before to the mass as to a festival, she prayed with rapture, with a kind of restrained and shamefaced transport, at which Marya Dmitrievna secretly marvelled not a little, and even Marfa Timofyevna, though she did not restrain Lisa in any way, tried to temper her zeal, and would not let her make too many prostrations to the earth in her prayers; it was not a lady-like habit, she would say. In her studies Lisa worked well, that is to say perseveringly; she was not gifted with specially brilliant abilities, or great intellect; she could not succeed in anything without labour. She played the piano well, but only Lemm knew what it had cost her. She had read little; she had not 'words of her own,' but she had her own ideas, and she went her own way. It was not only on the surface that she took after her father; he, too, had never asked other people what was to be done. So she had grown up tranquilly and restfully till she had reached the age of nineteen. She was very charming, without being aware of it herself. Her every movement was full of spontaneous, somewhat awkward gracefulness; her voice had the silvery ring of untouched youth, the least feeling of pleasure called forth an enchanting smile on her lips, and added a deep light and a kind of mystic sweetness to her kindling eyes. Penetrated through and through by a sense of duty, by the dread of hurting any one whatever, with a kind and tender heart, she had loved all men, and no one in particular; God only she had loved passionately, timidly, and tenderly. Lavretsky was the first to break in upon her peaceful inner life.

Such was Lisa.

XXXVI

ON THE FOLLOWING day at twelve o'clock, Lavretsky set off to the Kalitins'. On the way he met Panshin, who galloped past him on horseback, his hat pulled down to his very eyebrows. At the Kalitins', Lavretsky was not admitted for the first time since he had been acquainted with them. Marya Dmitrievna was 'resting,' so the footman informed him; her excellency had a headache. Marfa Timofyevna and Lisaveta Mihalovna were not at home. Lavretsky walked round the garden in the faint hope of meeting Lisa, but he saw no one. He came back two hours later and received the same answer, accompanied by a rather dubious look from the footman. Lavretsky thought it would be unseemly to call for a third time the same day, and he decided to drive over to Vassilyevskoe, where he had business moreover. On the road he made various plans for the future, each better than the last; but he was overtaken by a melancholy mood when he reached his aunt's little village. He fell into conversation with Anton; the old man, as if purposely, seemed full of cheerless fancies. He told Lavretsky how, at her death, Glafira Petrovna had bitten her own arm, and after a brief pause, added with a sigh: 'Every man, dear master, is destined to devour himself.' It was late when Lavretsky set off on the way back. He was haunted by the music of the day before, and Lisa's image returned to him in all its sweet distinctness; he mused with melting tenderness over the thought that she loved him, and reached his little house in the town, soothed and happy.

The first thing that struck him as he went into the entrance hall was a scent of patchouli, always distasteful to him; there were some high travelling-trunks standing there. The face of his groom, who ran out to meet him, seemed strange to him. Not stopping to analyse his impressions, he crossed the threshold of the drawing-room. . . . On his entrance there rose from the sofa a lady in a black silk dress with flounces, who, raising a cambric handkerchief to her pale face, made a few paces forward, bent her carefully dressed, perfumed head, and fell at his feet. . . . Then, only, he recognised her: this lady was his wife!

He caught his breath. . . . He leaned against the wall.

'*Théodore*, do not repulse me!' she said in French, and her voice cut to his heart like a knife.

He looked at her senselessly, and yet he noticed involuntarily at once that she had grown both whiter and fatter.

'*Théodore!*' she went on, from time to time lifting her eyes and discreetly wringing her marvellously-beautiful fingers with their rosy, polished nails. '*Théodore*, I have wronged you, deeply wronged you; I will say more, I have sinned; but hear me; I am tortured by remorse, I have grown hateful to myself, I could endure my position no longer; how many times have I thought of turning to you, but I feared your anger; I resolved to break every tie with the past.... *Puis, j'ai été si malade....* I have been so ill,' she added, and passed her hand over her brow and cheek. 'I took advantage of the widely-spread rumour of my death, I gave up everything; without resting day or night I hastened hither; I hesitated long to appear before you, my judge ... *paraître devant vous, mon juge*; but I resolved at last, remembering your constant goodness, to come to you; I found your address at Moscow. Believe me,' she went on, slowly getting up from the floor and sitting on the very edge of an arm-chair, 'I have often thought of death, and I should have found courage enough to take my life ... ah! life is a burden unbearable for me now! ... but the thought of my daughter, my little Ada, stopped me. She is here, she is asleep in the next room, the poor child! She is tired – you shall see her; she at least has done you no wrong, and I am so unhappy, so unhappy!' cried Madame Lavretsky, and she melted into tears.

Lavretsky came to himself at last; he moved away from the wall and turned towards the door.

'You are going?' cried his wife in a voice of despair. 'Oh, this is cruel! Without uttering one word to me, not even a reproach. This contempt will kill me, it is terrible!'

Lavretsky stood still.

'What do you want to hear from me?' he articulated in an expressionless voice.

'Nothing, nothing,' she rejoined quickly, 'I know I have no right to expect anything; I am not mad, believe me; I do not hope, I do not dare to hope for your forgiveness; I only venture to entreat you to command me what I am to do, where I am to live. Like a slave I will fulfil your commands whatever they may be.'

'I have no commands to give you,' replied Lavretsky in the same colourless voice; 'you know, all is over between us . . . and now more than ever; you can live where you like; and if your allowance is too little—'

'Ah, don't say such dreadful things,' Varvara Pavlovna interrupted him, 'spare me, if only . . . if only for the sake of this angel.' And as she uttered these words, Varvara Pavlovna ran impulsively into the next room, and returned at once with a small and very elegantly dressed little girl in her arms. Thick flaxen curls fell over her pretty rosy little face, and on to her large sleepy black eyes; she smiled and blinked her eyes at the light and laid a chubby little hand on her mother's neck.

'*Ada, vois, c'est ton père,*' said Varvara Pavlovna, pushing the curls back from her eyes and kissing her vigorously, '*prie le avec moi.*'

'*C'est ça, papa?*' stammered the little girl lisping.

'*Oui, mon enfant, n'est-ce pas que tu l'aimes?*'

But this was more than Lavretsky could stand.

'In such a melodrama must there really be a scene like this?' he muttered, and went out of the room.

Varvara Pavlovna stood still for some time in the same place, slightly shrugged her shoulders, carried the little girl off into the next room, undressed her and put her to bed. Then she took up a book and sat down near the lamp, and after staying up for an hour she went to bed herself.

'*Eh bien, madame?*' queried her maid, a Frenchwoman whom she had brought from Paris, as she unlaced her corset.

'*Eh bien, Justine,*' she replied, 'he is a good deal older, but I fancy he is just the same good-natured fellow. Give me my gloves for the night, and get out my grey high-necked dress for to-morrow, and don't forget the mutton cutlets for Ada. . . . I daresay it will be difficult to get them here; but we must try.'

'*A la guerre comme à la guerre*,' replied Justine, as she put out the candle.

XXXVII

FOR MORE THAN two hours Lavretsky wandered about the streets of the town. The night he had spent in the outskirts of Paris returned to his mind. His heart was bursting and his head, dull and stunned, was filled again with the same dark senseless angry thoughts, constantly recurring. 'She is alive, she is here,' he muttered, with ever fresh amazement. He felt that he had lost Lisa. His wrath choked him; this blow had fallen too suddenly upon him. How could he so readily have believed in the nonsensical gossip of a journal, a wretched scrap of paper? 'Well, if I had not believed it,' he thought, 'what difference would it have made? I should not have known that Lisa loved me; she would not have known it herself.' He could not rid himself of the image, the voice, the eyes of his wife . . . and he cursed himself, he cursed everything in the world.

Wearied out he went towards morning to Lemm's. For a long while he could make no one hear; at last at a window the old man's head appeared in a nightcap, sour, wrinkled, and utterly unlike the inspired austere visage which twenty-four hours before had looked down imperiously upon Lavretsky in all the dignity of artistic grandeur.

'What do you want?' queried Lemm. 'I can't play to you every night, I have taken a decoction for a cold.' But Lavretsky's face, apparently, struck him as strange; the old man made a shade for his eyes with his hand, took a look at his belated visitor, and let him in.

Lavretsky went into the room and sank into a chair. The old man stood still before him, wrapping the skirts of his shabby striped dressing-gown around him, shrinking together and gnawing his lips.

'My wife is here,' Lavretsky brought out. He raised his head and suddenly broke into involuntary laughter.

Lemm's face expressed bewilderment, but he did not even smile, only wrapped himself closer in his dressing-gown.

'Of course, you don't know,' Lavretsky went on, 'I had imagined . . . I read in a paper that she was dead.'

'O – oh, did you read that lately?' asked Lemm.

'Yes, lately.'

'O – oh,' repeated the old man, raising his eyebrows. 'And she is here?'

'Yes. She is at my house now; and I . . . I am an unlucky fellow.'

And he laughed again.

'You are an unlucky fellow,' Lemm repeated slowly.

'Christopher Fedoritch,' began Lavretsky, 'would you undertake to carry a note for me?'

'H'm. May I know to whom?'

'Lisavet—'

'Ah . . . yes, yes, I understand. Very good. And when must the letter be received?'

'To-morrow, as early as possible.'

'H'm. I can send Katrine, my cook. No, I will go myself.'

'And you will bring me an answer?'

'Yes, I will bring an answer.'

Lemm sighed.

'Yes, my poor young friend; you are certainly an unlucky young man.'

Lavretsky wrote a few words to Lisa. He told her of his wife's arrival, begged her to appoint a meeting with him, – then he flung himself on the narrow sofa, with his face to the wall; and the old man lay down on the bed, and kept muttering a long while, coughing and drinking off his decoction by gulps.

The morning came; they both got up. With strange eyes they looked at one another. At that moment Lavretsky longed to kill himself. The cook, Katrine, brought them some villainous coffee. It struck eight. Lemm put on his hat, and saying that he was going to give a lesson at the Kalitins' at ten, but he could find a suitable pretext for going there now, he set off. Lavretsky flung himself again on the little sofa, and once more the same bitter laugh stirred in the depth of his soul. He thought of how his wife had driven him out of his house; he imagined Lisa's position, covered his eyes and clasped his hands behind his head. At last Lemm came back and brought him a scrap of paper, on which Lisa had scribbled in pencil the following words: 'We cannot meet to-day; perhaps, to-morrow evening. Good-bye.' Lavretsky thanked Lemm briefly and indifferently, and went home.

He found his wife at breakfast; Ada, in curl-papers, in a little white frock with blue ribbons, was eating her mutton cutlet. Varvara Pavlovna rose at once directly Lavretsky entered the room, and went to meet him with humility in her face. He asked her to follow him into the study, shut the door after them, and began to walk up and down; she sat down, modestly laying one hand over the other, and began to follow his movements with her eyes, which were still beautiful, though they were pencilled lightly under their lids.

For some time Lavretsky could not speak; he felt that he could not master himself, he saw clearly that Varvara Pavlovna was not in the least afraid of him, but was assuming an appearance of being ready to faint away in another instant.

'Listen, madam,' he began at last, breathing with difficulty and at moments setting his teeth: 'it is useless for us to make pretences with one another; I don't believe in your penitence; and even if it were sincere, to be with you again, to live with you, would be impossible for me.'

Varvara Pavlovna bit her lips and half-closed her eyes. 'It is aversion,' she thought; 'all is over; in his eyes I am not even a woman.'

'Impossible,' repeated Lavretsky, fastening the top buttons

of his coat. 'I don't know what induced you to come here; I suppose you have come to the end of your money.'

'Ah! you hurt me!' whispered Varvara Pavlovna.

'However that may be – you are, any way, my wife, unhappily. I cannot drive you away . . . and this is the proposal I make you. You may to-day, if you like, set off to Lavriky, and live there; there is, as you know, a good house there; you will have everything you need in addition to your allowance . . . Do you agree?' – Varvara Pavlovna raised an embroidered handkerchief to her face.

'I have told you already,' she said, her lips twitching nervously, 'that I will consent to whatever you think fit to do with me; at present it only remains for me to beg of you – will you allow me at least to thank you for your magnanimity?'

'No thanks, I beg – it is better without that,' Lavretsky said hurriedly. 'So then,' he pursued, approaching the door, 'I may reckon on—'

'To-morrow I will be at Lavriky,' Varvara Pavlovna declared, rising respectfully from her place. 'But Fedor Ivanitch—' (She no longer called him '*Théodore*.')

'What do you want?'

'I know, I have not yet gained any right to forgiveness; may I hope at least that with time—'

'Ah, Varvara Pavlovna,' Lavretsky broke in, 'you are a clever woman, but I too am not a fool; I know that you don't want forgiveness in the least. And I have forgiven you long ago; but there was always a great gulf between us.'

'I know how to submit,' rejoined Varvara Pavlovna, bowing her head. 'I have not forgotten my sin; I should not have been surprised if I had learnt that you even rejoiced at the news of my death,' she added softly, slightly pointing with her hand to the copy of the journal which was lying forgotten by Lavretsky on the table.

Fedor Ivanitch started; the paper had been marked in pencil. Varvara Pavlovna gazed at him with still greater humility. She was superb at that moment. Her grey Parisian gown clung gracefully round her supple, almost girlish figure; her slender, soft neck, encircled by a white collar, her bosom gently stirred by her even breathing, her hands innocent of bracelets and rings – her whole figure, from her shining hair to the tip of her just visible little shoe, was so artistic . . .

Lavretsky took her in with a glance of hatred; scarcely could he refrain from crying: 'Bravo!' scarcely could he refrain from felling her with a blow of his fist on her shapely head – and he turned on his heel. An hour later he had started for Vassily-evskoe, and two hours later Varvara Pavlovna had bespoken the best carriage in the town, had put on a simple straw hat with a black veil, and a modest mantle, given Ada into the charge of Justine, and set off to the Kalitins'. From the inquiries she had made among the servants, she had learnt that her husband went to see them every day.

XXXVIII

THE DAY OF the arrival of Lavretsky's wife at the town of O———, a sorrowful day for him, had been also a day of misery for Lisa. She had not had time to go down-stairs and say good-morning to her mother, when the tramp of hoofs was heard under the window, and with secret dismay she saw Panshin riding into the courtyard. 'He has come so early for a final explanation,' she thought, and she was not mistaken. After a turn in the drawing-room, he suggested that she should go with him into the garden, and then asked her for the decision of his fate. Lisa summoned up all her courage and told him that she could not be his wife. He heard her to the end, standing on one side of her and pulling his hat down over his forehead; courteously, but in a changed voice, he asked her, 'Was this her last word, and had he given her any ground for such a change in her views?' – then pressed his hand to his eyes, sighed softly and abruptly, and took his hand away from his face again.

'I did not want to go along the beaten track,' he said huskily. 'I wanted to choose a wife according to the dictates of my heart; but it seems this was not to be. Farewell, fond dream!' He made Lisa a profound bow, and went back into the house.

She hoped that he would go away at once; but he went into Marya Dmitrievna's room and remained nearly an hour with her. As he came out, he said to Lisa: '*Votre mère vous appelle; adieu à jamais,*' . . . mounted his horse, and set off at full trot from the very steps. Lisa went in to Marya Dmitrievna and found her in tears; Panshin had informed her of his ill-luck.

'Do you want to be the death of me? Do you want to be the death of me?' was how the disconsolate widow began her lamentations. 'Whom do you want? Wasn't he good enough for you? A *kammerjunker*! not interesting! He might have married any Maid of Honour he liked in Petersburg. And I – I had so hoped for it! Is it long that you have changed towards him? How has this misfortune come on us, – it cannot have come of itself! Is it that dolt of a cousin's doing? A nice person you have picked up to advise you!'

'And he, poor darling,' Marya Dmitrievna went on, 'how respectful he is, how attentive even in his sorrow! He has promised not to desert me. Ah, I can never bear that! Ah, my head aches fit to split! Send me Palashka. You will be the death of me, if you don't think better of it, – do you hear?' And, calling her twice an ungrateful girl, Marya Dmitrievna dismissed her.

She went to her own room. But she had not had time to recover from her interviews with Panshin and her mother before another storm broke over her head, and this time from a quarter from which she would least have expected it. Marfa Timofyevna came into her room, and at once slammed the door after her. The old lady's face was pale, her cap was awry, her eyes were flashing, and her hands and lips were trembling. Lisa was astonished; she had never before seen her sensible and reasonable aunt in such a condition.

'A pretty thing, miss,' Marfa Timofyevna began in a shaking

and broken whisper, 'a pretty thing! Who taught you such ways, I should like to know, miss? . . . Give me some water; I can't speak.'

'Calm yourself, auntie, what is the matter?' said Lisa, giving her a glass of water. 'Why, I thought you did not think much of Mr. Panshin yourself.'

Marfa Timofyevna pushed away the glass.

'I can't drink; I shall knock my last teeth out if I try to. What's Panshin to do with it? Why bring Panshin in? You had better tell me who has taught you to make appointments at night – eh? miss?'

Lisa turned pale.

'Now, please, don't try to deny it,' pursued Marfa Timofyevna; 'Shurotchka herself saw it all and told me. I have had to forbid her chattering, but she is not a liar.'

'I don't deny it, auntie,' Lisa uttered scarcely audibly.

'Ah, ah! That's it, is it, miss; you made an appointment with him, that old sinner, who seems so meek?'

'No.'

'How then?'

'I went down into the drawing-room for a book; he was in the garden – and he called me.'

'And you went? A pretty thing! So you love him, eh?'

'I love him,' answered Lisa softly.

'Merciful Heavens! She loves him!' Marfa Timofyevna snatched off her cap. 'She loves a married man! Ah! she loves him.'

'He told me' . . . began Lisa.

'What has he told you, the scoundrel, eh?'

'He told me that his wife was dead.'

Marfa Timofyevna crossed herself. 'Peace be with her,' she muttered; 'she was a vain hussy, God forgive her. So, then, he's a widower, I suppose. And he's losing no time, I see. He has buried one wife and now he's after another. He's a nice person: only let me tell you one thing, niece; in my day, when I was young, harm came to young girls from such goings on. Don't be angry with me, my girl, only fools are angry at the truth. I have given orders not to admit him to-day. I love him, but I shall never forgive him for this. Upon my word, a widower! Give me some water. But as for your sending Panshin about his business, I think you're a first-rate girl for that. Only don't you go sitting of nights with any animals of that sort; don't break my old heart, or else you'll see I'm not all fondness – I can bite too . . . a widower!'

Marfa Timofyevna went off, and Lisa sat down in a corner and began to cry. There was bitterness in her soul. She had not deserved such humiliation. Love had proved no happiness to her: she was weeping for a second time since yesterday evening. This new unexpected feeling had only just arisen in her heart, and already what a heavy price she had paid for it, how coarsely had strange hands touched her sacred secret. She felt ashamed, and bitter, and sick; but she had no doubt and no dread – and Lavretsky was dearer to her than ever. She had hesitated while she did not understand herself; but after that meeting, after that kiss – she could hesitate no more: she knew that she loved, and now she loved honestly and seriously, she was bound firmly for all her life, and she did not fear reproaches. She felt that by no violence could they break that bond.

XXXIX

MARYA DMITRIEVNA WAS much agitated when she received the announcement of the arrival of Varvara Pavlovna Lavretsky, she did not even know whether to receive her; she was afraid of giving offence to Fedor Ivanitch. At last curiosity prevailed. 'Why,' she reflected, 'she too is a relation,' and, taking up her position in an arm-chair, she said to the footman, 'Show her in.' A few moments passed; the door opened; Varvara Pavlovna, swiftly and with scarcely audible steps, approached Marya

Dmitrievna, and not allowing her to rise from her chair, bent almost on her knees before her.

'I thank you, dear aunt,' she began in a soft voice full of emotion, speaking Russian; 'I thank you; I did not hope for such condescension on your part; you are an angel of goodness.'

As she uttered these words Varvara Pavlovna quite unexpectedly took possession of one of Marya Dmitrievna's hands, and pressing it lightly in her pale lavender gloves, she raised it in a fawning way to her full rosy lips. Marya Dmitrievna quite lost her head, seeing such a handsome and charmingly dressed woman almost at her feet. She did not know where she was. And she tried to withdraw her hand, while, at the same time, she was inclined to make her sit down, and to say something affectionate to her. She ended by raising Varvara Pavlovna and kissing her on her smooth perfumed brow. Varvara Pavlovna was completely overcome by this kiss.

'How do you do, *bonjour*,' said Marya Dmitrievna. 'Of course I did not expect . . . but, of course, I am glad to see you. You understand, my dear, it's not for me to judge between man and wife' . . .

'My husband is in the right in everything,' Varvara Pavlovna interposed; 'I alone am to blame.'

'That is a very praiseworthy feeling,' rejoined Marya Dmitrievna, 'very. Have you been here long? Have you seen him? But sit down, please.'

'I arrived yesterday,' answered Varvara Pavlovna, sitting down meekly. 'I have seen Fedor Ivanitch; I have talked with him.'

'Ah! Well, and how was he?'

'I was afraid my sudden arrival would provoke his anger,' continued Varvara Pavlovna, 'but he did not refuse to see me.'

'That is to say, he did not . . . Yes, yes, I understand,' commented Marya Dmitrievna. 'He is only a little rough on the surface, but his heart is soft.'

'Fedor Ivanitch has not forgiven me; he would not hear

me. But he was so good as to assign me Lavriky as a place of residence.'

'Ah! a splendid estate!'

'I am setting off there to-morrow in fulfilment of his wish; but I esteemed it a duty to visit you first.'

'I am very, very much obliged to you, my dear. Relations ought never to forget one another. And do you know I am surprised how well you speak Russian. *C'est étonnant.*'

Varvara Pavlovna sighed.

'I have been too long abroad, Marya Dmitrievna, I know that; but my heart has always been Russian and I have not forgotten my country.'

'Ah, ah; that is good. Fedor Ivanitch did not, however, expect you at all. Yes; you may trust my experience, *la patrie avant tout*. Ah, show me, if you please – what a charming mantle you have.'

'Do you like it?' Varvara Pavlovna slipped it quickly off her shoulders; 'it is a very simple little thing from Madame Baudran.'

'One can see it at once. From Madame Baudran? How sweet, and what taste! I am sure you have brought a number of fascinating things with you. If I could only see them.'

'All my things are at your service, dearest auntie. If you permit, I can show some patterns to your maid. I have a woman with me from Paris – a wonderfully clever dressmaker.'

'You are very good, my dear. But, really, I am ashamed.' . . .

'Ashamed!' repeated Varvara Pavlovna reproachfully. 'If you want to make me happy, dispose of me as if I were your property.'

Marya Dmitrievna was completely melted.

'*Vous êtes charmante,*' she said. 'But why don't you take off your hat and gloves?'

'What? you will allow me?' asked Varvara Pavlovna, and slightly, as though with emotion, clasped her hands.

'Of course, you will dine with us, I hope. I – I will introduce you to my daughter.' Marya Dmitrievna was a little confused. 'Well! we are in for it! here goes!' she thought. 'She is not very well to-day.'

'*O ma tante*, how good you are!' cried Varvara Pavlovna, and she raised her handkerchief to her eyes.

A page announced the arrival of Gedeonovsky. The old gossip came in bowing and smiling. Marya Dmitrievna presented him to her visitor. He was thrown into confusion for the first moment; but Varvara Pavlovna behaved with such coquettish respectfulness to him, that his ears began to tingle, and gossip, slander, and civility dropped like honey from his lips. Varvara Pavlovna listened to him with a restrained smile and began by degrees to talk herself. She spoke modestly of Paris, of her travels, of Baden; twice she made Marya Dmitrievna laugh, and each time she sighed a little afterwards, and seemed to be inwardly reproaching herself for misplaced levity. She obtained permission to bring Ada; taking off her gloves, with her smooth hands, redolent of soap *à la guimauve*, she showed how and where flounces were worn and ruches and lace and rosettes. She promised to bring a bottle of the new English scent, Victoria Essence; and was as happy as a child when Marya Dmitrievna consented to accept it as a gift. She was moved to tears over the recollection of the emotion she experienced, when, for the first time, she heard the Russian bells. 'They went so deeply to my heart,' she explained.

At that instant Lisa came in.

Ever since the morning, from the very instant when, chill with horror, she had read Lavretsky's note, Lisa had been preparing herself for the meeting with his wife. She had a presentiment that she would see her. She resolved not to avoid her, as a punishment of her, as she called them, sinful hopes. The sudden crisis in her destiny had shaken her to the foundations. In some two hours her face seemed to have grown thin. But she did not shed a single tear. 'It's what I deserve!' she said to herself, repressing with difficulty and dismay some bitter impulses of hatred which frightened her in her soul. 'Well, I must go down!' she thought directly she heard of Madame Lavretsky's arrival, and she went down. . . . She stood a long while at the drawing-room door before she could summon up courage to open it. With the thought, 'I have done her wrong,' she crossed the threshold and forced herself to look at her, forced herself to smile. Varvara Pavlovna went to meet her directly she caught sight of her, and bowed to her slightly, but still respectfully. 'Allow me to introduce myself,' she began in an insinuating voice, 'your *maman* is so indulgent to me that I hope that you too will be . . . good to me.' The expression of Varvara Pavlovna, when she uttered these last words, cold and at the same time soft, her hypocritical smile, the action of her hands, and her shoulders, her very dress, her whole being aroused such a feeling of repulsion in Lisa that she could make no reply to her, and only held out her hand with an effort. 'This young lady disdains me,' thought Varvara Pavlovna, warmly pressing Lisa's cold fingers, and turning to Marya Dmitrievna, she observed in an undertone, '*mais elle est délicieuse!*' Lisa faintly flushed; she heard ridicule, insult in this exclamation. But she resolved not to trust her impressions, and sat down by the window at her embroidery-frame. Even here Varvara Pavlovna did not leave her in peace. She began to admire her taste, her skill. . . . Lisa's heart beat violently and painfully. She could scarcely control herself, she could scarcely sit in her place. It seemed to her that Varvara Pavlovna knew all, and was mocking at her in secret triumph. To her relief, Gedeonovsky began to talk to Varvara Pavlovna, and drew off her attention. Lisa bent over her frame, and secretly watched her. 'That woman,' she thought, 'was loved by *him*.' But she at once drove away the very thought of Lavretsky; she was afraid of losing her control over herself, she felt that her head was going round. Marya Dmitrievna began to talk of music.

'I have heard, my dear,' she began, 'that you are a wonderful performer.'

'It is long since I have played,' replied Varvara Pavlovna,

seating herself without delay at the piano, and running her fingers smartly over the keys. 'Do you wish it?'

'If you will be so kind.'

Varvara Pavlovna played a brilliant and difficult *étude* by Hertz very correctly. She had great power and execution.

'*Sylphide!*' cried Gedeonovsky.

'Marvellous!' Marya Dmitrievna chimed in. 'Well, Varvara Pavlovna, I confess,' she observed, for the first time calling her by her name, 'you have astonished me; you might give concerts. We have a musician here, an old German, a queer fellow, but a very clever musician. He gives Lisa lessons. He will be simply crazy over you.'

'Lisaveta Mihalovna is also musical?' asked Varvara Pavlovna, turning her head slightly towards her.

'Yes, she plays fairly, and is fond of music; but what is that beside you? But there is one young man here too – with whom we must make you acquainted. He is an artist in soul, and composes very charmingly. He alone will be able to appreciate you fully.'

'A young man?' said Varvara Pavlovna: 'Who is he? Some poor man?'

'Oh dear no, our chief beau, and not only among us – *et à Petersbourg*. A *kammerjunker*, and received in the best society. You must have heard of him: Panshin, Vladimir Nikolaitch. He is here on a government commission . . . a future minister, I daresay!'

'And an artist?'

'An artist at heart, and so well-bred. You shall see him. He has been here very often of late: I invited him for this evening; I *hope* he will come,' added Marya Dmitrievna with a gentle sigh, and an oblique smile of bitterness.

Lisa knew the meaning of this smile, but it was nothing to her now.

'And young?' repeated Varvara Pavlovna, lightly modulating from tone to tone.

'Twenty-eight, and of the most prepossessing appearance. *Un jeune homme accompli*, indeed.'

'An exemplary young man, one may say,' observed Gedeonovsky.

Varvara Pavlovna began suddenly playing a noisy waltz of Strauss, opening with such a loud and rapid trill that Gedeonovsky was quite startled. In the very middle of the waltz she suddenly passed into a pathetic motive, and finished up with an air from 'Lucia' *Fra poco*. . . . She reflected that lively music was not in keeping with her position. The air from 'Lucia,' with emphasis on the sentimental passages, moved Marya Dmitrievna greatly.

'What soul!' she observed in an undertone to Gedeonovsky.

'A *sylphide!*' repeated Gedeonovsky, raising his eyes towards heaven.

The dinner hour arrived. Marfa Timofyevna came down from up-stairs, when the soup was already on the table. She treated Varvara Pavlovna very drily, replied in half-sentences to her civilities, and did not look at her. Varvara Pavlovna soon realised that there was nothing to be got out of this old lady, and gave up trying to talk to her. To make up for this, Marya Dmitrievna became still more cordial to her guest; her aunt's discourtesy irritated her. Marfa Timofyevna, however, did not only avoid looking at Varvara Pavlovna; she did not look at Lisa either, though her eyes seemed literally blazing. She sat as though she were of stone, yellow and pale, her lips compressed, and ate nothing. Lisa seemed calm; and in reality, her heart was more at rest; a strange apathy, the apathy of the condemned had come upon her. At dinner Varvara Pavlovna spoke little; she seemed to have grown timid again, and her countenance was overspread with an expression of modest melancholy. Gedeonovsky alone enlivened the conversation with his tales, though he constantly looked timorously towards Marfa Timofyevna and coughed – he was always overtaken by a fit of coughing when he was going to tell a lie in her presence

– but she did not hinder him by any interruption. After dinner it seemed that Varvara Pavlovna was quite devoted to preference; at this Marya Dmitrievna was so delighted that she felt quite overcome, and thought to herself, 'Really what a fool Fedor Ivanitch must be; not able to appreciate a woman like this!'

She sat down to play cards together with her and Gedeonovsky, and Marfa Timofyevna led Lisa away up-stairs with her, saying that she looked shocking, and that she must certainly have a headache.

'Yes, she has an awful headache,' observed Marya Dmitrievna, turning to Varvara Pavlovna and rolling her eyes, 'I myself have often just such sick headaches.'

'Really!' rejoined Varvara Pavlovna.

Lisa went into her aunt's room, and sank powerless into a chair. Marfa Timofyevna gazed long at her in silence, slowly she knelt down before her – and began still in the same silence to kiss her hands alternately. Lisa bent forward, crimsoning – and began to weep, but she did not make Marfa Timofyevna get up, she did not take away her hands; she felt that she had not the right to take them away, that she had not the right to hinder the old lady from expressing her penitence, and her sympathy, from begging forgiveness for what had passed the day before. And Marfa Timofyevna could not kiss enough those poor, pale, powerless hands, and silent tears flowed from her eyes and from Lisa's; while the cat Matross purred in the wide arm-chair among the knitting wool, and the long flame of the little lamp faintly stirred and flickered before the holy picture. In the next room, behind the door, stood Nastasya Karpovna, and she too was furtively wiping her eyes with her check pocket-handkerchief rolled up in a ball.

XL

MEANWHILE, DOWN-STAIRS, preference was going on merrily in the drawing-room; Marya Dmitrievna was winning, and was in high good-humour. A servant came in and announced that Panshin was below.

Marya Dmitrievna dropped her cards and moved restlessly in her arm-chair; Varvara Pavlovna looked at her with a half-smile, then turned her eyes towards the door. Panshin made his appearance in a black frock-coat buttoned up to the throat, and a high English collar. 'It was hard for me to obey; but you see I have come,' this was what was expressed by his unsmiling, freshly shaven countenance.

'Well, *Woldemar*,' cried Marya Dmitrievna, 'you used to come in unannounced!'

Panshin only replied to Marya Dmitrievna by a single glance. He bowed courteously to her, but did not kiss her hand. She presented him to Varvara Pavlovna; he stepped back a pace, bowed to her with the same courtesy, but with still greater elegance and respect, and took a seat near the card-table. The game of preference was soon over. Panshin inquired after Lisaveta Mihalovna, learnt that she was not quite well, and expressed his regret. Then he began to talk to Varvara Pavlovna, diplomatically weighing each word and giving it its full value, and politely hearing her answers to the end. But the dignity of his diplomatic tone did not impress Varvara Pavlovna, and she did not adopt it. On the contrary, she looked him in the face with light-hearted attention and talked easily, while her delicate nostrils were quivering as though with suppressed laughter. Marya Dmitrievna began to enlarge on her talent; Panshin courteously inclined his head, so far as his collar would permit him, declared that, 'he felt sure of it beforehand,' and almost turned the conversation to the diplomatic topic of Metternich himself. Varvara Pavlovna, with an expressive look in her velvety eyes, said in a low voice, 'Why, but you too are an artist, *un confrère*,' adding still lower, '*venez!*' with a nod towards the piano. The single word *venez* thrown at him, instantly, as though by magic, effected a complete transformation in Panshin's whole appearance. His care-worn air disappeared; he smiled and grew lively, unbuttoned his coat, and repeating 'a poor artist, alas! Now you, I have heard, are a real artist'; he followed Varvara Pavlovna to the piano....

'Make him sing his song, "How the Moon Floats,"' cried Marya Dmitrievna.

'Do you sing?' said Varvara Pavlovna, enfolding him in a rapid radiant look. 'Sit down.'

Panshin began to cry off.

'Sit down,' she repeated insistently, tapping on a chair behind him.

He sat down, coughed, tugged at his collar, and sang his song.

'*Charmant*,' pronounced Varvara Pavlovna, 'you sing very well, *vous avez du style*, again.'

She walked round the piano and stood just opposite Panshin. He sang it again, increasing the melodramatic tremor in his voice. Varvara Pavlovna stared steadily at him, leaning her elbows on the piano and holding her white hands on a level with her lips. Panshin finished the song.

'*Charmant, charmante idée*,' she said with the calm self-confidence of a connoisseur. 'Tell me, have you composed anything for a woman's voice, for a mezzo-soprano?'

'I hardly compose at all,' replied Panshin. 'That was only thrown off in the intervals of business . . . but do you sing?'

'Yes.'

'Oh! sing us something,' urged Marya Dmitrievna.

Varvara Pavlovna pushed her hair back off her glowing cheeks and gave her head a little shake.

'Our voices ought to go well together,' she observed, turning to Panshin; 'let us sing a duet. Do you know *Son geloso*, or *La ci darem*, or *Mira la bianca luna*?'

'I used to sing *Mira la bianca luna*, once,' replied Panshin, 'but long ago; I have forgotten it.'

'Never mind, we will rehearse it in a low voice. Allow me.'

Varvara Pavlovna sat down at the piano, Panshin stood by her. They sang through the duet in an undertone, and Varvara Pavlovna corrected him several times as they did so, then they sang it aloud, and then twice repeated the performance of *Mira la bianca lu-u-una*. Varvara Pavlovna's voice had lost its freshness, but she managed it with great skill. Panshin at first was hesitating, and a little out of tune, then he warmed up, and if his singing was not quite beyond criticism, at least he shrugged his shoulders, swayed his whole person, and lifted his hand from time to time in the most genuine style. Varvara Pavlovna played two or three little things of Thalberg's, and coquettishly rendered a little French ballad. Marya Dmitrievna did not know how to express her delight; she several times tried to send for Lisa. Gedeonovsky, too, was at a loss for words, and could only nod his head, but all at once he gave an unexpected yawn, and hardly had time to cover his mouth with his hand. This yawn did not escape Varvara Pavlovna; she at once turned her back on the piano, observing, '*Assez de musique comme ça;* let us talk,' and she folded her arms. '*Oui, assez de musique,*' repeated Panshin gaily, and at once he dropped into a chat, alert, light, and in French. 'Precisely as in the best Parisian salon,' thought Marya Dmitrievna, as she listened to their fluent and quick-witted sentences. Panshin had a sense of complete satisfaction; his eyes shone, and he smiled. At first he passed his hand across his face, contracted his brows, and sighed spasmodically whenever he chanced to encounter Marya Dmitrievna's eyes. But later on he forgot her altogether, and gave himself up entirely to the enjoyment of a half-worldly, half-artistic chat. Varvara Pavlovna proved to be a great philosopher; she had a ready answer for everything;

she never hesitated, never doubted about anything; one could see that she had conversed much with clever men of all kinds. All her ideas, all her feelings revolved round Paris. Panshin turned the conversation upon literature; it seemed that, like himself, she read only French books. George Sand drove her to exasperation, Balzac she respected, but he wearied her; in Sue aud Scribe she saw great knowledge of human nature, Dumas and Féval she adored. In her heart she preferred Paul de Kock to all of them, but of course she did not even mention his name. To tell the truth, literature had no great interest for her. Varvara Pavlovna very skilfully avoided all that could even remotely recall her position; there was no reference to love in her remarks; on the contrary, they were rather expressive of austerity in regard to the allurements of passion, of disillusionment and resignation. Panshin disputed with her; she did not agree with him ... but, strange to say! ... at the very time when words of censure – often of severe censure – were coming from her lips, these words had a soft caressing sound, and her eyes spoke ... precisely what those lovely eyes spoke, it was hard to say; but at least their utterances were anything but severe, and were full of undefined sweetness.

Panshin tried to interpret their secret meaning, he tried to make his own eyes speak, but he felt he was not successful; he was conscious that Varvara Pavlovna, in the character of a real lioness from abroad, stood high above him, and consequently was not completely master of himself. Varvara Pavlovna had a habit in conversation of lightly touching the sleeve of the person she was talking to; these momentary contacts had a most disquieting influence on Vladimir Nikolaitch. Varvara Pavlovna possessed the faculty of getting on easily with every one; before two hours had passed it seemed to Panshin that he had known her for an age, and Lisa, the same Lisa whom, at any rate, he had loved, to whom he had the evening before offered his hand, had vanished as it were into a mist. Tea was brought in; the conversation became still more unconstrained.

Marya Dmitrievna rang for the page and gave orders to ask Lisa to come down if her head were better. Panshin, hearing Lisa's name, fell to discussing self-sacrifice and the question which was more capable of sacrifice – man or woman. Marya Dmitrievna at once became excited, began to maintain that woman is the more ready for sacrifice, declared that she would prove it in a couple of words, got confused and finished up by a rather unfortunate comparison. Varvara Pavlovna took up a music-book and half-hiding behind it and bending towards Panshin, she observed in a whisper, as she nibbled a biscuit, with a serene smile on her lips and in her eyes, '*Elle n'a pas inventé la poudre, la bonne dame.*' Panshin was a little taken aback and amazed at Varvara Pavlovna's audacity; but he did not realise how much contempt for himself was concealed in this unexpected outbreak, and forgetting Marya Dmitrievna's kindness and devotion, forgetting all the dinners she had given him, and the money she had lent him, he replied (luckless mortal!) with the same smile and in the same tone, '*je crois bien*,' and not even, *je crois bien*, but *j'crois ben!*

Varvara Pavlovna flung him a friendly glance and got up. Lisa came in: Marfa Timofyevna had tried in vain to hinder her; she was resolved to go through with her sufferings to the end. Varvara Pavlovna went to meet her together with Panshin, on whose face the former diplomatic expression had reappeared.

'How are you?' he asked Lisa.

'I am better now, thank you,' she replied.

'We have been having a little music here; it's a pity you did not hear Varvara Palovna, she sings superbly, *en artiste consommée.*'

'Come here, my dear,' sounded Marya Dmitrievna's voice.

Varvara Pavlovna went to her at once with the submissiveness of a child, and sat down on a little stool at her feet. Marya Dmitrievna had called her so as to leave her daughter, at least for a moment, alone with Panshin; she was still secretly hoping that she would come round. Besides, an idea had entered her head, to which she was anxious to give expression at once.

'Do you know,' she whispered to Varvara Pavlovna, 'I want to endeavour to reconcile you and your husband; I won't answer for my success, but I will make an effort. He has, you know, a great respect for me.'

Varvara Pavlovna slowly raised her eyes to Marya Dmitrievna, and eloquently clasped her hands.

'You would be my saviour, *ma tante*,' she said in a mournful voice: 'I don't know how to thank you for all your kindness; but I have been too guilty towards Fedor Ivanitch; he can not forgive me.'

'But did you – in reality—' Marya Dmitrievna was beginning inquisitively.

'Don't question me,' Varvara Pavlovna interrupted her, and she cast down her eyes. 'I was young, frivolous. But I don't want to justify myself.'

'Well, anyway, why not try? Don't despair,' rejoined Marya Dmitrievna, and she was on the point of patting her on the cheek, but after a glance at her she had not the courage. 'She is humble, very humble,' she thought, 'but still she is a lioness.'

'Are you ill?' Panshin was saying to Lisa meanwhile.

'Yes, I am not well.'

'I understand you,' he brought out after a rather protracted silence. 'Yes, I understand you.'

'What?'

'I understand you,' Panshin repeated significantly; he simply did not know what to say.

Lisa felt embarrassed, and then 'so be it!' she thought. Panshin assumed a mysterious air and kept silent, looking severely away.

'I fancy though it's struck eleven,' remarked Marya Dmitrievna.

Her guests took the hint and began to say good-bye. Varvara Pavlovna had to promise that she would come to dinner the following day and bring Ada. Gedeonovsky, who had all but fallen asleep sitting in his corner, offered to escort her home. Panshin took leave solemnly of all, but at the steps as he put Varvara Pavlovna into her carriage he pressed her hand, and cried after her, '*au revoir*!' Gedeonovsky sat beside her all the way home. She amused herself by pressing the tip of her little foot as though accidentally on his foot; he was thrown into confusion and began paying her compliments. She tittered and made eyes at him when the light of a street lamp fell into the carriage. The waltz she had played was ringing in her head, and exciting her; whatever position she might find herself in, she had only to imagine lights, a ballroom, rapid whirling to the strains of music – and her blood was on fire, her eyes glittered strangely, a smile strayed about her lips, and something of bacchanalian grace was visible over her whole frame. When she reached home, Varvara Pavlovna bounded lightly out of the carriage – only real lionesses know how to bound like that – and turning round to Gedeonovsky she burst suddenly into a ringing laugh right in his face.

'An attractive person,' thought the counsellor of state as he made his way to his lodgings, where his servant was awaiting him with a glass of opodeldoc: 'It's well I'm a steady fellow – only, what was she laughing at?'

Marfa Timofyevna spent the whole night sitting beside Lisa's bed.

XLI

LAVRETSKY SPENT A day and a half at Vassilyevskoe, and employed almost all the time in wandering about the neighbourhood. He could not stop long in one place: he was devoured by anguish; he was torn unceasingly by impotent violent impulses. He remembered the feeling which had taken possession of him the day after his arrival in the country; he remembered his plans then and was intensely exasperated with himself. What had been able to tear him away from what he recognised as his duty – as the one task set before him in the future? The thirst for happiness – again the same thirst for happiness.

'It seems Mihalevitch was right,' he thought; 'you wanted a second time to taste happiness in life,' he said to himself, 'you forgot that it is a luxury, an undeserved bliss, if it even comes once to a man. It was not complete, it was not genuine, you say; but prove your right to full, genuine happiness! Look round and see who is happy, who enjoys life about you? Look at that peasant going to the mowing; is he contented with his fate? . . . What! would you care to change places with him? Remember your mother; how infinitely little she asked of life, and what a life fell to her lot. You were only bragging it seems when you said to Panshin that you had come back to Russia to cultivate the soil; you have come back to dangle after young girls in your old age. Directly the news of your freedom came, you threw up everything, forgot everything; you ran like a boy after a butterfly.' . . .

The image of Lisa continually presented itself in the midst of his broodings. He drove it away with an effort together with another importunate figure, other serenely wily, beautiful, hated features. Old Anton noticed that the master was not himself: after sighing several times outside the door and several times in the doorway, he made up his mind to go up to him, and advised him to take a hot drink of something. Lavretsky swore at him; ordered him out; afterwards he begged his pardon, but that only made Anton still more sorrowful. Lavretsky could not stay in the drawing-room; it seemed to him that his great-grandfather Andrey was looking contemptuously from the canvas at his feeble descendant. 'Bah: you swim in shallow water,' the distorted lips seemed to be saying. 'Is it possible,' he thought, 'that I cannot master myself, that I am going to give in to this . . . nonsense?' (Those who are badly wounded in war always call their wounds 'nonsense.' If man did not deceive himself, he could not live on earth.) 'Am I really a boy? Ah, well; I saw quite close, I almost held in my hands the possibility of happiness for my whole life; yes, in the lottery too – turn the wheel a little and the beggar perhaps would be a rich man. If it does not happen, then it does not – and it's all over. I will set to work, with my teeth clenched, and make myself be quiet; it's as well, it's not the first time I have had to hold myself in. And why have I run away, why am I stopping here sticking my head in a bush, like an ostrich? A fearful thing to face trouble . . . nonsense! Anton,' he called aloud, 'order the coach to be brought round at once. Yes,' he thought again, 'I must grin and bear it, I must keep myself well in hand.'

With such reasonings Lavretsky tried to ease his pain; but it was deep and intense; and even Apraxya who had outlived all emotion as well as intelligence shook her head and followed him mournfully with her eyes, as he took his seat in the coach to drive to the town. The horses galloped away; he sat upright and motionless, and looked fixedly at the road before him.

XLII

LISA HAD WRITTEN to Lavretsky the day before, to tell him to come in the evening; but he first went home to his lodgings. He found neither his wife nor his daughter at home; from the servants he learned that she had gone with the child to the Kalitins'. This information astounded and maddened him. 'Varvara Pavlovna has made up her mind not to let me live at all, it seems,' he thought with a passion of hatred in his heart. He began to walk up and down, and his hands and feet were constantly knocking up against child's toys, books and feminine belongings; he called Justine and told her to clear away all this 'litter.' '*Oui, monsieur,*' she said with a grimace, and began to set the room in order, stooping gracefully, and letting Lavretsky feel in every movement that she regarded him as an unpolished bear. He looked with aversion at her faded, but still 'piquante,' ironical, Parisian face, at her white elbow-sleeves, her silk apron, and little light cap. He sent her away at last, and after long hesitation (as Varvara Pavlovna still did not return) he decided to go to the Kalitins' – not to see Marya Dmitrievna (he would not for anything in the world have gone into that drawing-room, the room where his wife was), but to go up to Marfa Timofyevna's. He remembered that the back staircase from the servants' entrance led straight to her apartment. He acted on this plan; fortune favoured him; he met Shurotchka in the courtyard; she conducted him up to Marfa Timofyevna's. He found her, contrary to her usual habit, alone; she was sitting without a cap in a corner, bent, and her arms crossed over her breast. The old lady was much upset on seeing Lavretsky, she got up quickly and began to move to and fro in the room as if she were looking for her cap.

'Ah, it's you,' she began, fidgeting about and avoiding meeting his eyes, 'well, how do you do? Well, well, what's to be done! Where were you yesterday? Well, she has come, so there, there! Well, it must . . . one way or another.'

Lavretsky dropped into a chair.

'Well, sit down, sit down,' the old lady went on. 'Did you come straight up-stairs? Well, there, of course. So . . . you came to see me? Thanks.'

The old lady was silent for a little; Lavretsky did not know what to say to her; but she understood him.

'Lisa . . . yes, Lisa was here just now,' pursued Marfa Timofyevna, tying and untying the tassels of her reticule. 'She was not quite well. Shurotchka, where are you? Come here, my girl; why can't you sit still a little? My head aches too. It must be the effect of the singing and music.'

'What singing, auntie?'

'Why, we have been having those – upon my word, what do you call them – duets here. And all in Italian: chi-chi – and cha-cha – like magpies for all the world with their long drawn-out notes as if they'd pull your very soul out. That's Panshin, and your wife too. And how quickly everything was settled; just as though it were all among relations, without ceremony. However, one may well say, even a dog will try to find a home; and won't be lost so long as folks don't drive it out.'

'Still, I confess I did not expect this,' rejoined Lavretsky; 'there must be great effrontery to do this.'

'No, my darling, it's not effrontery, it's calculation, God forgive her! They say you are sending her off to Lavriky; is it true?'

'Yes, I am giving up that property to Varvara Pavlovna.'

'Has she asked you for money?'

'Not yet.'

'Well, that won't be long in coming. But I have only now got a look at you. Are you quite well?'

'Yes.'

'Shurotchka!' cried Marfa Timofyevna suddenly, 'run and tell Lisaveta Mihalovna, – at least, no, ask her . . . is she down-stairs?'

'Yes.'

'Well, then; ask her where she put my book? she will know.'

'Very well.'

The old lady grew fidgety again and began opening a drawer in the chest. Lavretsky sat still without stirring in his place.

All at once light footsteps were heard on the stairs – and Lisa came in.

Lavretsky stood up and bowed; Lisa remained at the door.

'Lisa, Lisa, darling,' began Marfa Timofyevna eagerly, 'where is my book? where did you put my book?'

'What book, auntie?'

'Why, goodness me, that book! But I didn't call you though . . . There, it doesn't matter. What are you doing down-stairs? Here Fedor Ivanitch has come. How is your head?'

'It's nothing.'

'You keep saying it's nothing. What have you going on down-stairs – music?'

'No – they are playing cards.'

'Well, she's ready for anything. Shurotchka, I see you want a run in the garden – run along.'

'Oh, no, Marfa Timofyevna.'

'Don't argue, if you please, run along. Nastasya Karpovna has gone out into the garden all by herself; you keep her company. You must treat the old with respect.' – Shurotchka departed – 'But where is my cap? Where has it got to?'

'Let me look for it,' said Lisa.

'Sit down, sit down; I have still the use of my legs. It must be inside in my bedroom.'

And flinging a sidelong glance in Lavretsky's direction, Marfa Timofyevna went out. She left the door open; but suddenly she came back to it and shut it.

Lisa leant back against her chair and quietly covered her face with her hands; Lavretsky remained where he was.

'This is how we were to meet again!' he brought out at last.

Lisa took her hands from her face.

'Yes,' she said faintly: 'we were quickly punished.'

'Punished,' said Lavretsky. . . . 'What had you done to be punished?'

Lisa raised her eyes to him. There was neither sorrow nor disquiet expressed in them: they seemed smaller and dimmer. Her face was pale; and pale too her slightly parted lips.

Lavretsky's heart shuddered for pity and love.

'You wrote to me; all is over,' he whispered, 'yes, all is over – before it had begun.'

'We must forget all that,' Lisa brought out; 'I am glad that you have come; I wanted to write to you, but it is better so. Only we must take advantage quickly of these minutes. It is left for both of us to do our duty. You, Fedor Ivanitch, must be reconciled with your wife.'

'Lisa!'

'I beg you to do so; by that alone can we expiate . . . all that has happened. You will think about it – and will not refuse me.'

'Lisa, for God's sake, – you are asking what is impossible. I am ready to do everything you tell me; but to be reconciled to her *now*! . . . I consent to everything, I have forgotten everything; but I cannot force my heart. . . . Indeed, this is cruel!'

'I do not even ask of you, . . . what you say; do not live with her, if you cannot; but be reconciled,' replied Lisa, and again she hid her eyes in her hand. – 'Remember your little girl; do it for my sake.'

'Very well,' Lavretsky muttered between his teeth: 'I will do that, I suppose in that I shall fulfil my duty. But you – what does your duty consist in?'

'That I know myself.'

Lavretsky started suddenly.

'You cannot be making up your mind to marry Panshin?' he said.

Lisa gave an almost imperceptible smile.

'Oh, no!' she said.

'Ah, Lisa, Lisa!' cried Lavretsky, 'how happy you might have been!'

Lisa looked at him again.

'Now you see yourself, Fedor Ivanitch, that happiness does not depend on us, but on God.'

'Yes, because you—'

The door from the adjoining room opened quickly and Marfa Timofyevna came in with her cap in her hand.

'I have found it at last,' she said, standing between Lavretsky and Lisa; 'I had laid it down myself. That's what age does for one, alack! – though youth's not much better.'

'Well, and are you going to Lavriky yourself with your wife?' she added, turning to Lavretsky.

'To Lavriky with her? I don't know,' he said, after a moment's hesitation.

'You are not going down-stairs.'

'To-day, – no, I'm not.'

'Well, well, you know best; but you, Lisa, I think, ought to go down. Ah, merciful powers, I have forgotten to feed my bullfinch. There, stop a minute, I'll soon—' And Marfa Timofyevna ran off without putting on her cap.

Lavretsky walked quickly up to Lisa.

'Lisa,' he began in a voice of entreaty, 'we are parting for ever, my heart is torn, – give me your hand at parting.'

Lisa raised her head, her wearied eyes, their light almost extinct, rested upon him. . . . 'No,' she uttered, and she drew back the hand she was holding out. 'No, Lavretsky (it was the first time she had used this name), I will not give you my hand. What is the good? Go away, I beseech you. You know I love you . . . yes, I love you,' she added with an effort; 'but no . . . no.'

She pressed her handkerchief to her lips.

'Give me, at least, that handkerchief.'

The door creaked . . . the handkerchief slid on to Lisa's lap. Lavretsky snatched it before it had time to fall to the floor, thrust it quickly into a side pocket, and turning round met Marfa Timofyevna's eyes.

'Lisa, darling, I fancy your mother is calling you,' the old lady declared.

Lisa at once got up and went away.

Marfa Timofyevna sat down again in her corner. Lavretsky began to take leave of her.

'Fedor,' she said suddenly.

'What is it?'

'Are you an honest man?'

'What?'

'I ask you, are you an honest man?'

'I hope so.'

'H'm. But give me your word of honour that you will be an honest man.'

'Certainly. But why?'

'I know why. And you too, my dear friend, if you think well, you're no fool – will understand why I ask it of you. And now, good-bye, my dear. Thanks for your visit; and remember you have given your word, Fedya, and kiss me. Oh, my dear, it's hard for you, I know; but there, it's not easy for any one. Once I used to envy the flies; I thought, it's for them it's good to be alive, but one night I heard a fly complaining in a spider's web – no, I think, they too have their troubles. There's no help, Fedya; but remember your promise all the same. Good-bye.'

Lavretsky went down the back staircase, and had reached the gates when a man-servant overtook him.

'Marya Dmitrievna told me to ask you to go in to her,' he commenced to Lavretsky.

'Tell her, my boy, that just now I can't—' Fedor Ivanitch was beginning.

'Her excellency told me to ask you very particularly,' continued the servant. 'She gave orders to say she was at home.'

'Have the visitors gone?' asked Lavretsky.

'Certainly, sir,' replied the servant with a grin.

Lavretsky shrugged his shoulders and followed him.

XLIII

MARYA DMITRIEVNA WAS sitting alone in her boudoir in an easy-chair, sniffing *eau de cologne*; a glass of orange-flower-water was standing on a little table near her. She was agitated and seemed nervous.

Lavretsky came in.

'You wanted to see me,' he said, bowing coldly.

'Yes,' replied Marya Dmitrievna, and she sipped a little water: 'I heard that you had gone straight up to my aunt; I gave orders that you should be asked to come in; I wanted to have a little talk with you. Sit down, please,' Marya Dmitrievna took breath. 'You know,' she went on, 'your wife has come.'

'I was aware of that,' remarked Lavretsky.

'Well, then, that is, I wanted to say, she came to me, and I received her; that is what I wanted to explain to you, Fedor Ivanitch. Thank God I have, I may say, gained universal respect, and for no consideration in the world would I do anything improper. Though I foresaw that it would be disagreeable to you, still I could not make up my mind to deny myself to her, Fedor Ivanitch; she is a relation of mine – through you; put yourself in my position, what right had I to shut my doors on her – you will agree with me?'

'You are exciting yourself needlessly, Marya Dmitrievna,' replied Lavretsky; 'you acted very well, I am not angry. I have not the least intention of depriving Varvara Pavlovna of the opportunity of seeing her friends; I did not come in to you to-day simply because I did not care to meet her – that was all.'

'Ah, how glad I am to hear you say that, Fedor Ivanitch,' cried Marya Dmitrievna, 'but I always expected it of your noble sentiments. And as for my being excited – that's not to be wondered at; I am a woman and a mother. And your wife . . . of course I cannot judge between you and her – as I said to her herself; but she is such a delightful woman that she can produce nothing but a pleasant impression.'

Lavretsky gave a laugh and played with his hat.

'And this is what I wanted to say to you besides, Fedor Ivanitch,' continued Marya Dmitrievna, moving slightly nearer up to him, 'if you had seen the modesty of her behaviour, how respectful she is! Really, it is quite touching. And if you had heard how she spoke of you! I have been to blame towards him, she said, altogether; I did not know how to appreciate him, she said; he is an angel, she said, and not a man. Really, that is what she said – an angel. Her penitence is such . . . Ah, upon my word, I have never seen such penitence!'

'Well, Marya Dmitrievna,' observed Lavretsky, 'if I may be inquisitive: I am told that Varvara Pavlovna has been singing in your drawing-room; did she sing during the time of her penitence, or how was it?'

'Ah, I wonder you are not ashamed to talk like that! She sang and played the piano only to do me a kindness, because I positively entreated, almost commanded her to do so. I saw that she was sad, so sad; I thought how to distract her mind – and I had heard that she had such marvellous talent! I assure you, Fedor Ivanitch, she is utterly crushed, ask Sergei Petrovitch even; a heart-broken woman, *tout à fait*: what do you say?'

Lavretsky only shrugged his shoulders.

'And then what a little angel is that Adotchka of yours, what a darling! How sweet she is, what a clever little thing; how she speaks French; and understands Russian too – she called me "auntie" in Russian. And you know that as for shyness – almost all children at her age are shy – there's not a trace of it. She's so like you, Fedor Ivanitch, it's amazing. The eyes, the forehead – well, it's you over again, precisely you. I am not particularly fond of little children, I must own; but I simply lost my heart to your little girl.'

'Marya Dmitrievna,' Lavretsky blurted out suddenly, 'allow me to ask you what is your object in talking to me like this?'

'What object?' Marya Dmitrievna sniffed her *eau de cologne* again, and took a sip of water. 'Why, I am speaking to you, Fedor Ivanitch, because – I am a relation of yours, you know, I take the warmest interest in you – I know your heart is of the best. Listen to me, *mon cousin*. I am at any rate a woman of experience, and I shall not talk at random: forgive her, forgive your wife.' Marya Dmitrievna's eyes suddenly filled with tears. 'Only think: her youth, her inexperience . . . and who knows, perhaps, bad example; she had not a mother who could bring her up in the right way. Forgive her, Fedor Ivanitch, she has been punished enough.'

The tears were trickling down Marya Dmitrievna's cheeks: she did not wipe them away; she was fond of weeping. Lavretsky sat as if on thorns. 'Good God,' he thought, 'what torture, what a day I have had to-day!'

'You make no reply,' Marya Dmitrievna began again. 'How am I to understand you? Can you really be so cruel? No, I will not believe it. I feel that my words have influenced you, Fedor Ivanitch. God reward you for your goodness, and now receive your wife from my hands.'

Involuntarily Lavretsky jumped up from his chair; Marya Dmitrievna also rose and running quickly behind a screen, she led forth Varvara Pavlovna. Pale, almost lifeless, with downcast eyes, she seemed to have renounced all thought, all will of her own, and to have surrendered herself completely to Marya Dmitrievna.

Lavretsky stepped back a pace.

'You have been here all the time!' he cried.

'Do not blame her,' explained Marya Dmitrievna; 'she was most unwilling to stay, but I forced her to remain. I put her behind the screen. She assured me that this would only anger you more; I would not even listen to her; I know you better than she does. Take your wife back from my hands; come, Varya, do not fear, fall at your husband's feet (she gave a pull at her arm) and my blessing' . . .

'Stop a minute, Marya Dmitrievna,' said Lavretsky in a low but startlingly impressive voice. 'I dare say you are fond of affecting scenes' (Lavretsky was right, Marya Dmitrievna still retained her school-girl's passion for a little melodramatic effect), 'they amuse you; but they may be anything but pleasant for other people. But I am not going to talk to you; in *this* scene you are not the principal character. What do you want to get out of me, madam?' he added, turning to his wife. 'Haven't I done all I could for you? Don't tell me you did not contrive this interview; I shall not believe you – and you know that I cannot possibly believe you. What is it you want? You are clever – you do nothing without an object. You must realise, that as for living with you, as I once lived with you, that I cannot do;

not because I am angry with you, but because I have become a different man. I told you so the day after your return, and you yourself, at that moment, agreed with me in your heart. But you want to reinstate yourself in public opinion; it is not enough for you to live in my house, you want to live with me under the same roof – isn't that it?'

'I want your forgiveness,' pronounced Varvara Pavlovna, not raising her eyes.

'She wants your forgiveness,' repeated Marya Dmitrievna.

'And not for my own sake, but for Ada's,' murmured Varvara Pavlovna.

'And not for her own sake, but for your Ada's,' repeated Marya Dmitrievna.

'Very good. Is that what you want?' Lavretsky uttered with an effort. 'Certainly, I consent to that too.'

Varvara Pavlovna darted a swift glance at him, but Marya Dmitrievna cried: 'There, God be thanked!' and again drew Varvara Pavlovna forward by the arm. 'Take her now from my arms—'

'Stop a minute, I tell you,' Lavretsky interrupted her, 'I agree to live with you, Varvara Pavlovna,' he continued, 'that is to say, I will conduct you to Lavriky, and I will live there with you, as long as I can endure it, and then I will go away – and will come back again. You see, I do not want to deceive you; but do not demand anything more. You would laugh yourself if I were to carry out the desire of our respected cousin, were to press you to my breast, and to fall to assuring you that . . . that the past had not been; and the felled tree can bud again. But I see, I must submit. You will not understand these words . . . but that's no matter. I repeat, I will live with you . . . or no, I cannot promise that . . . I will be reconciled with you, I will regard you as my wife again.'

'Give her, at least, your hand on it,' observed Marya Dmitrievna, whose tears had long since dried up.

'I have never deceived Varvara Pavlovna hitherto,' returned

Lavretsky; 'she will believe me without that. I will take her to Lavriky; and remember, Varvara Pavlovna, our treaty is to be reckoned as broken directly you go away from Lavriky. And now allow me to take leave.'

He bowed to both the ladies, and hurriedly went away.

'Are you not going to take her with you!' Marya Dmitrievna cried after him. ... 'Leave him alone,' Varvara Pavlovna whispered to her. And at once she embraced her, and began thanking her, kissing her hands and calling her her saviour.

Marya Dmitrievna received her caresses indulgently; but at heart she was discontented with Lavretsky, with Varvara Pavlovna, and with the whole scene she had prepared. Very little sentimentality had come of it; Varvara Pavlovna, in her opinion, ought to have flung herself at her husband's feet.

'How was it you didn't understand me?' she commented: 'I kept saying "down."'

'It is better as it was, dear auntie; do not be uneasy – it was all for the best,' Varvara Pavlovna assured her.

'Well, any way, he's as cold as ice,' observed Marya Dmitrievna. 'You didn't weep, it is true, but I was in floods of tears before his eyes. He wants to shut you up at Lavriky. Why, won't you even be able to come and see me? All men are unfeeling,' she concluded, with a significant shake of the head.

'But then women can appreciate goodness and noble-heartedness,' said Varvara Pavlovna, and gently dropping on her knees before Marya Dmitrievna, she flung her arms about her round person, and pressed her face against it. That face wore a sly smile, but Marya Dmitrievna's tears began to flow again.

When Lavretsky returned home, he locked himself in his valet's room, and flung himself on a sofa; he lay like that till morning.

XLIV

THE FOLLOWING DAY was Sunday. The sound of bells ringing for early mass did not wake Lavretsky – he had not closed his eyes all night – but it reminded him of another Sunday, when at Lisa's desire he had gone to church. He got up hastily; some secret voice told him that he would see her there to-day. He went noiselessly out of the house, leaving a message for Varvara Pavlovna that he would be back to dinner, and with long strides he made his way in the direction in which the monotonously mournful bells were calling him. He arrived early; there was scarcely any one in the church; a deacon was reading the service in the choir; the measured drone of his voice – sometimes broken by a cough – fell and rose at even intervals. Lavretsky placed himself not far from the entrance. Worshippers came in one by one, stopped, crossed themselves, and bowed in all directions; their steps rang out in the empty, silent church, echoing back distinctly under the arched roof. An infirm poor little old woman in a worn-out cloak with a hood was on her knees near Lavretsky, praying assiduously; her toothless, yellow, wrinkled face expressed intense emotion; her red eyes were gazing fixedly upwards at the holy figures on the iconostasis; her bony hand was constantly coming out from under her cloak, and slowly and earnestly making a great sign of the cross. A peasant with a bushy beard and a surly face, dishevelled and unkempt, came into the church, and at once fell on both knees, and began directly crossing himself in haste, bending back his head with a shake after each prostration. Such bitter grief was expressed in his face, and in all his actions, that Lavretsky made up his mind to go up to him and ask him what was wrong. The peasant timidly and morosely started back, looked at him. ... 'My son is dead,' he articulated quickly, and again fell to bowing to the earth. 'What could replace the consolations of the Church to them?' thought Lavretsky; and he tried himself to pray, but his heart was hard and heavy, and his thoughts were far away. He kept expecting Lisa, but Lisa did not come. The church began to be full of people; but still she was not there. The service commenced, the deacon had already read the gospel, they began ringing for the last prayer; Lavretsky moved a little forward – and suddenly caught sight of Lisa. She had come before him, but he had not seen her; she was hidden in a recess between the wall and the choir, and neither moved nor looked round. Lavretsky did not take his eyes off her till the very end of the service; he was saying farewell to her. The people began to disperse, but she still remained; it seemed as though she were waiting for Lavretsky to go out. At last she crossed herself for the last time and went out – there was only a maid with her – not turning round. Lavretsky went out of the church after her and overtook her in the street; she was walking very quickly, with downcast head, and a veil over her face.

'Good-morning, Lisaveta Mihalovna,' he said aloud with assumed carelessness: 'may I accompany you?'

She made no reply; he walked beside her.

'Are you content with me?' he asked her, dropping his voice. 'Have you heard what happened yesterday?'

'Yes, yes,' she replied in a whisper, 'that was well.' And she went still more quickly.

'Are you content?'

Lisa only bent her head in assent.

'Fedor Ivanitch,' she began in a calm but faint voice, 'I wanted to beg you not to come to see us any more; go away as soon as possible, we may see each other again later – sometime – in a year. But now, do this for my sake; fulfil my request, for God's sake.'

'I am ready to obey you in everything Lisaveta Mihalovna; but are we really to part like this? will you not say one word to me?'

'Fedor Ivanitch, you are walking near me now. . . . But

already you are so far from me. And not only you, but—'

'Speak out, I entreat you!' cried Lavretsky, 'what do you mean?'

'You will hear, perhaps . . . but whatever it may be, forget . . . no, do not forget; remember me.'

'Me forget you—'

'That's enough, good-bye. Do not come after me.'

'Lisa!' Lavretsky was beginning.

'Good-bye, good-bye!' she repeated, pulling her veil still lower and almost running forward. Lavretsky looked after her, and with bowed head, turned back along the street. He stumbled up against Lemm, who was also walking along with his eyes on the ground, and his hat pulled down to his nose.

They looked at one another without speaking.

'Well, what have you to say?' Lavretsky brought out at last.

'What have I to say?' returned Lemm, grimly. 'I have nothing to say. All is dead, and we are dead (*Alles ist todt, und wir sind todt*). So you're going to the right, are you?'

'Yes.'

'And I to the left. Good-bye.'

The following morning Fedor Ivanitch set off with his wife for Lavriky. She drove in front in the carriage with Ada and Justine; he behind, in the coach. The pretty little girl did not move away from the window the whole journey; she was astonished at everything: the peasants, the women, the wells, the yokes over the horses' heads, the bells and the flocks of crows. Justine shared her wonder. Varvara Pavlovna laughed at their remarks and exclamations. She was in excellent spirits; before leaving the town, she had come to an explanation with her husband.

'I understand your position,' she said to him, and from the look in her subtle eyes, he was able to infer that she understood his position fully, 'but you must do me, at least, this justice, that I am easy to live with; I will not fetter you or hinder you; I wanted to secure Ada's future, I want nothing more.'

'Well, you have obtained your object,' observed Fedor Ivanitch.

'I only dream of one thing now: to hide myself for ever in obscurity. I shall remember your goodness always.'

'Enough of that,' he interrupted.

'And I shall know how to respect your independence and tranquillity,' she went on, completing the phrases she had prepared.

Lavretsky made her a low bow. Varvara Pavlovna then believed her husband was thanking her in his heart.

On the evening of the next day they reached Lavriky; a week later, Lavretsky set off for Moscow, leaving his wife five thousand roubles for her household expenses; and the day after Lavretsky's departure, Panshin made his appearance. Varvara Pavlovna had begged him not to forget her in her solitude. She gave him the best possible reception, and, till a late hour of the night, the lofty apartments of the house and even the garden re-echoed with the sound of music, singing, and lively French talk. For three days Varvara Pavlovna entertained Panshin; when he took leave of her, warmly pressing her lovely hands, he promised to come back very soon – and he kept his word.

XLV

LISA HAD A room to herself on the second storey of her mother's house, a clean bright little room with a little white bed, with pots of flowers in the corners and before the windows, a small writing-table, a book-stand, and a crucifix on the wall. It was always called the nursery; Lisa had been born in it. When she returned from the church where she had seen Lavretsky she set everything in her room in order more carefully than usual, dusted it everywhere, looked through and tied up with ribbon all her copybooks, and the letters of her girl-friends, shut up all the drawers, watered the flowers and caressed every blossom with her hand. All this she did without haste, noiselessly, with a kind of rapt and gentle solicitude on her face. She stopped at last in the middle of the room, slowly looked round, and going up to the table above which the crucifix was hanging, she fell on her knees, dropped her head on to her clasped hands and remained motionless.

Marfa Timofyevna came in and found her in this position. Lisa did not observe her entrance. The old lady stepped out on tip-toe and coughed loudly several times outside the door. Lisa rose quickly and wiped her eyes, which were bright with unshed tears.

'Ah! I see, you have been setting your cell to rights again,' observed Marfa Timofyevna, and she bent low over a young rose-tree in a pot; 'how nice it smells!'

Lisa looked thoughtfully at her aunt.

'How strange you should use that word!' she murmured.

'What word, eh?' the old lady returned quickly. 'What do you mean? This is horrible,' she began, suddenly flinging off her cap and sitting down on Lisa's little bed: 'it is more than I can bear! this is the fourth day now that I have been boiling over inside; I can't pretend not to notice any longer; I can't see you getting pale, and fading away, and weeping, I can't, I can't!'

'Why, what is the matter, auntie?' said Lisa, 'it's nothing.'

'Nothing!' cried Marfa Timofyevna; 'you may tell that to others but not to me. Nothing, who was on her knees just this minute? and whose eye-lashes are still wet with tears? Nothing, indeed! why, look at yourself, what have you done with your face, what has become of your eyes? – Nothing! do you suppose I don't know all?'

'It will pass off, auntie; give me time.'

'It will pass off, but when? Good God! Merciful Saviour! can you have loved him like this? why, he's an old man, Lisa, darling. There, I don't dispute he's a good fellow, no harm in him; but what of that? we are all good people, the world is not so small, there will be always plenty of that commodity.'

'I tell you, it will all pass away, it has all passed away already.'

'Listen, Lisa, darling, what I am going to say to you,' Marfa Timofyevna said suddenly, making Lisa sit beside her, and straightening her hair and her neckerchief. 'It seems to you now in the midst of the worst of it that nothing can ever heal your sorrow. Ah, my darling, the only thing that can't be cured is death. You only say to yourself now: "I won't give in to it – so there!" and you will be surprised yourself how soon, how easily it will pass off. Only have patience.'

'Auntie,' returned Lisa, 'it has passed off already, it is all over.'

'Passed! how has it passed? Why, your poor little nose has grown sharp already and you say it is over. A fine way of getting over it!'

'Yes, it is over, auntie, if you will only try to help me,' Lisa declared with sudden animation, and she flung herself on Marfa Timofyevna's neck. 'Dear auntie, be a friend to me, help me, don't be angry, understand me' . . .

'Why, what is it, what is it, my good girl? Don't terrify me, please; I shall scream directly; don't look at me like that; tell me quickly what is it?'

'I – I want,' Lisa hid her face on Marfa Timofyevna's bosom, 'I want to go into a convent,' she articulated faintly.

The old lady almost bounded off the bed.

'Cross yourself, my girl, Lisa, dear, think what you are saying; what are you thinking of? God have mercy on you!' she stammered at last. 'Lie down, my darling, sleep a little, all this comes from sleeplessness, my dearie.'

Lisa raised her head, her cheeks were glowing.

'No, auntie,' she said, 'don't speak like that; I have made up my mind, I prayed, I asked counsel of God; all is at an end, my life with you is at an end. Such a lesson was not for nothing; and it is not the first time that I have thought of it. Happiness was not for me; even when I had hopes of happiness, my heart was always heavy. I knew all my own sins and those of others, and how papa made our fortune; I know it all. For all that there must be expiation. I am sorry for you, sorry for mamma, for Lenotchka; but there is no help; I feel that there is no living here for me; I have taken leave of all, I have greeted everything in the house for the last time; something calls to me; I am sick at heart, I want to hide myself away for ever. Do not hinder me, do not dissuade me, help me, or else I must go away alone.'

Marfa Timofyevna listened to her niece with horror.

'She is ill, she is raving,' she thought: 'we must send for a doctor; but for which one? Gedeonovsky was praising one the other day; he always tells lies – but perhaps this time he spoke the truth.' But when she was convinced that Lisa was not ill, and was not raving, when she constantly made the same answer to all her expostulations, Marfa Timofyevna was alarmed and distressed in earnest. 'But you don't know, my darling,' she began to reason with her, 'what a life it is in those convents! Why, they would feed you, my own, on green hemp oil, and they would put you in the coarsest coarsest linen, and make you go about in the cold; you will never be able to bear all that, Lisa, darling. All this is Agafya's doing; she led you astray. But then you know she began by living and lived for her own pleasure; you must live too. At least, let me die in peace, and then do as you like. And who has ever heard of such a thing, for the sake of such a – for the sake of a goat's beard, God forgive us! – for the sake of a man – to go into a convent! Why, if you are so sick at heart, go on a pilgrimage, offer prayers to some saint, have a *Te Deum* sung, but don't put the black hood on your head, my dear creature, my good girl.'

And Marfa Timofyevna wept bitterly.

Lisa comforted her, wiped away her tears and wept herself, but remained unshaken. In her despair Marfa Timofyevna had recourse to threats: to tell her mother all about it . . . but that too was of no avail. Only at the old lady's most earnest entreaties Lisa agreed to put off carrying out her plan for six months. Marfa Timofyevna was obliged to promise in return that if, within six months, she did not change her mind, she would herself help her and would do all she could to gain Marya Dmitievna's consent.

In spite of her promise to bury herself in seclusion, at the first approach of cold weather, Varvara Pavlovna, having provided herself with funds, removed to Petersburg, where she took a modest but charming set of apartments, found for her by Panshin, who had left the O—— district a little before. During the later part of his residence in O—— he had completely lost Marya Dmitrievna's good graces; he had suddenly given up visiting her and scarcely stirred from Lavriky. Varvara Pavlovna had enslaved him, literally enslaved him, no other word can describe her boundless, irresistible, unquestioned sway over him.

Lavretsky spent the winter in Moscow; and in the spring of the following year the news reached him that Lisa had taken the veil in the B—— convent, in one of the remote parts of Russia.

EPILOGUE

EIGHT YEARS HAD passed by. Once more the spring had come.... But we will say a few words first of the fate of Mihalevitch, Panshin, and Madame Lavretsky – and then take leave of them. Mihalevitch, after long wanderings, has at last fallen in with exactly the right work for him; he has received the position of senior superintendent of a government school. He is very well content with his lot; his pupils adore him, though they mimick him too. Panshin has gained great advancement in rank, and already has a directorship in view; he walks with a slight stoop, caused doubtless by the weight round his neck of the Vladimir cross which has been conferred on him. The official in him has finally gained the ascendancy over the artist; his still youngish face has grown yellow, and his hair scanty; he now neither sings nor sketches, but applies himself in secret to literature; he has written a comedy, in the style of a 'proverb,' and as nowadays all writers have to draw a portrait of some one or something, he has drawn in it the portrait of a coquette, and he reads it privately to two or three ladies who look kindly upon him. He has, however, not entered upon matrimony, though many excellent opportunities of doing so have presented themselves. For this Varvara Pavlovna was responsible. As for her, she lives constantly at Paris, as in former days. Fedor Ivanitch has given her a promissory note for a large sum, and has so secured immunity from the possibility of her making a second sudden descent upon him. She has grown older and stouter, but is still charming and elegant. Every one has his ideal. Varvara Pavlovna found hers in the dramatic works of M. Dumas Fils. She diligently frequents the theatres, when consumptive and sentimental 'dames aux camélias' are brought on the stage; to be Madame Doche seems to her the height of human bliss; she once declared that she did not desire a better fate for her own daughter. It is to be hoped that fate will spare Mademoiselle Ada from such happiness; from a rosy-cheeked, chubby child she has turned into a weak-chested, pale girl; her nerves are already deranged. The number of Varvara Pavlovna's adorers has diminished, but she still has some; a few she will probably retain to the end of her days. The most ardent of them in these later days is a certain Zakurdalo-Skubirnikov, a retired guardsman, a full-bearded man of thirty-eight, of exceptionally vigorous physique. The French *habitués* of Madame Lavretsky's salon call him '*le gros taureau de l'Ukrāine*'; Varvara Pavlovna never invites him to her fashionable evening reunions, but he is in the fullest enjoyment of her favours.

And so – eight years have passed by. Once more the breezes of spring breathed brightness and rejoicing from the heavens; once more spring was smiling upon the earth and upon men; once more under her caresses everything was turning to blossom, to love, to song. The town of O——— had undergone little change in the course of these eight years; but Marfa Dmitrievna's house seemed to have grown younger; its freshly-painted walls gave a bright welcome, and the panes of its open windows were crimson, shining in the setting sun; from these windows the light merry sound of ringing young voices and continual laughter floated into the street; the whole house seemed astir with life and brimming over with gaiety. The lady of the house herself had long been in her tomb; Marya Dmitrievna had died two years after Lisa took the veil, and Marfa Timofyevna had not long survived her niece; they lay side by side in the cemetery of the town. Nastasya Karpovna too was no more; for several years the faithful old woman had gone every week to say a prayer over her friend's ashes. . . . Her time had come, and now her bones too lay in the damp earth. But Marya Dmitrievna's house had not passed into strangers' hands, it had not gone out of her family, the home had not been broken up. Lenotchka, transformed into a slim, beautiful young girl, and her betrothed lover – a fair-haired officer of hussars; Marya Dmitrievna's son, who had just been married in Petersburg and had come with his young wife for the spring to O———; his wife's sister, a school-girl of sixteen, with glowing cheeks and bright eyes; Shurotchka, grown up and also pretty, made up the youthful household, whose laughter and talk set the walls of the Kalitins' house resounding. Everything in the house was changed, everything was in keeping with its new inhabitants. Beardless servant lads, grinning and full of fun, had replaced the sober old servants of former days. Two setter dogs dashed wildly about and gambolled over the sofas, where the fat Roska had at one time waddled in solemn dignity. The stables were filled with slender racers, spirited carriage horses, fiery out-riders with plaited manes, and riding horses from the Don. The breakfast, dinner, and supper-hours were all in confusion and disorder; in the words of the neighbours, 'unheard-of arrangements' were made.

On the evening of which we are speaking, the inhabitants of

the Kalitins' house (the eldest of them, Lenotchka's betrothed, was only twenty-four) were engaged in a game, which, though not of a very complicated nature, was, to judge from their merry laughter, exceedingly entertaining to them; they were running about the rooms, chasing one another; the dogs, too, were running and barking, and the canaries, hanging in cages above the windows, were straining their throats in rivalry and adding to the general uproar by the shrill trilling of their piercing notes. At the very height of this deafening merry-making a mud-bespattered carriage stopped at the gate, and a man of five-and-forty, in a travelling dress, stepped out of it and stood still in amazement. He stood a little time without stirring, watching the house with attentive eyes; then went through the little gate in the courtyard, and slowly mounted the steps. In the hall he met no one; but the door of a room was suddenly flung open; and out of it rushed Shurotchka, flushed and hot, and instantly, with a ringing shout, all the young party in pursuit of her. They stopped short at once and were quiet at the sight of a stranger; but their clear eyes fixed on him wore the same friendly expression, and their fresh faces were still smiling as Marya Dmitrievna's son went up to the visitor and asked him cordially what he could do for him.

'I am Lavretsky,' replied the visitor.

He was answered by a shout of friendliness – and not because these young people were greatly delighted at the arrival of a distant, almost forgotten relation, but simply because they were ready to be delighted and make a noise at every opportunity. They surrounded Lavretsky at once; Lenotchka, as an old acquaintance, was the first to call him by his name, and assured him that in a little while she would have certainly recognised him. She presented him to the rest of the party, calling each, even her betrothed, by their pet names. They all trooped through the dining-room into the drawing-room. The walls of both rooms had been repapered; but the furniture remained the same. Lavretsky recognised the piano; even the embroidery-frame in the window was just the same, and in the same position, and it seemed with the same unfinished embroidery on it, as eight years ago. They made him sit down in a comfortable arm-chair; all sat down politely in a circle round him. Questions, exclamations, and anecdotes followed.

'It's a long time since we have seen you,' observed Lenotchka simply, 'and Varvara Pavlovna we have seen nothing of either.'

'Well, no wonder!' her brother hastened to interpose. 'I carried you off to Petersburg, and Fedor Ivanitch has been living all the time in the country.'

'Yes, and mamma died soon after then.'

'And Marfa Timofyevna,' observed Shurotchka.

'And Nastasya Karpovna,' added Lenotchka, 'and Monsieur Lemm.'

'What? is Lemm dead?' inquired Lavretsky.

'Yes,' replied young Kalitin, 'he left here for Odessa; they say some one enticed him there; and there he died.'

'You don't happen to know, . . . did he leave any music?'

'I don't know; not very likely.'

All were silent and looked about them. A slight cloud of melancholy flitted over all the young faces.

'But Matross is alive,' said Lenotchka suddenly.

'And Gedeonovsky,' added her brother.

At Gedeonovsky's name a merry laugh broke out at once.

'Yes, he is alive, and as great a liar as ever,' Marya Dmitrievna's son continued; 'and only fancy, yesterday this madcap' – pointing to the school-girl, his wife's sister – 'put some pepper in his snuff-box.'

'How he did sneeze!' cried Lenotchka, and again there was a burst of unrestrained laughter.

'We have had news of Lisa lately,' observed young Kalitin, and again a hush fell upon all; 'there was good news of her; she is recovering her health a little now.'

'She is still in the same convent?' Lavretsky asked, not without some effort.

'Yes, still in the same.'

'Does she write to you?'

'No, never; but we get news through other people.'

A sudden and profound silence followed. 'A good angel is passing over,' all were thinking.

'Wouldn't you like to go into the garden?' said Kalitin, turning to Lavretsky; 'it is very nice now, though we have let it run wild a little.'

Lavretsky went out into the garden, and the first thing that met his eyes was the very garden-seat on which he had once spent with Lisa those few blissful moments, never repeated; it had grown black and warped; but he recognised it, and his soul was filled with that emotion, unequalled for sweetness and for bitterness – the emotion of keen sorrow for vanished youth, for the happiness which has once been possessed. He walked along the avenues with the young people; the lime-trees looked hardly older or taller in the eight years, but their shade was thicker; on the other hand, all the bushes had sprung up, the raspberry bushes had grown strong, the hazels were a tangled thicket; and from all sides rose the fresh scent of the trees and grass and lilac.

'This would be a nice place for Puss-in-the-Corner,' cried Lenotchka suddenly, as they came upon a small green lawn, surrounded by lime-trees, 'and we are just five, too.'

'Have you forgotten Fedor Ivanitch?' replied her brother, . . . 'or didn't you count yourself?'

Lenotchka blushed slightly.

'But would Fedor Ivanitch, at his age—' she began.

'Please, play your games,' Lavretsky hastened to interpose; 'don't pay attention to me. I shall be happier myself, when I am sure I am not in your way. And there's no need for you to entertain me; we old fellows have an occupation which you know nothing of yet, and which no amusement can replace – our memories.'

The young people listened to Lavretsky with polite, but

rather ironical respect – as though a teacher were giving them a lesson – and suddenly they all dispersed, and ran to the lawn; four stood near trees, one in the middle, and the game began.

And Lavretsky went back into the house, went into the dining-room, drew near the piano and touched one of the keys; it gave out a faint but clear sound; on that note had begun the inspired melody with which long ago on that same happy night Lemm, the dead Lemm, had thrown him into such transports. Then Lavretsky went into the drawing-room, and for a long time he did not leave it; in that room where he had so often seen Lisa, her image rose most vividly before him; he seemed to feel the traces of her presence round him; but his grief for her was crushing, not easy to bear; it had none of the peace which comes with death. Lisa still lived somewhere, hidden and afar; he thought of her as of the living, but he did not recognise the girl he had once loved in that dim pale shadow, cloaked in a nun's dress and encircled in misty clouds of incense. Lavretsky would not have recognised himself, could he have looked at himself, as mentally he looked at Lisa. In the course of these eight years he had passed that turning-point in life, which many never pass, but without which no one can be a good man to the end; he had really ceased to think of his own happiness, of his personal aims. He had grown calm, and – why hide the truth? – he had grown old not only in face and in body, he had grown old in heart; to keep a young heart up to old age, as some say, is not only difficult, but almost ridiculous; he may well be content who has not lost his belief in goodness, his steadfast will, and his zeal for work. Lavretsky had good reason to be content; he had become actually an excellent farmer, he had really learnt to cultivate the land, and his labours were not only for himself; he had, to the best of his powers, secured on a firm basis the welfare of his peasants.

Lavretsky went out of the house into the garden, and sat down on the familiar garden-seat. And on this loved spot, facing the house where for the last time he had vainly stretched out his hand for the enchanted cup which frothed and sparkled with the golden wine of delight, he, a solitary homeless wanderer, looked back upon his life, while the joyous shouts of the younger generation who were already filling his place floated across the garden to him. His heart was sad, but not weighed down, nor bitter; much there was to regret, nothing to be ashamed of.

'Play away, be gay, grow strong, vigorous youth!' he thought, and there was no bitterness in his meditations; 'your life is before you, and for you life will be easier; you have not, as we had, to find out a path for yourselves, to struggle, to fall, and to rise again in the dark; we had enough to do to last out – and how many of us did not last out? – but you need only do your duty, work away, and the blessing of an old man be with you. For me, after to-day, after these emotions, there remains to take my leave at last, – and though sadly, without envy, without any dark feelings, to say, in sight of the end, in sight of God who awaits me: "Welcome, lonely old age! burn out, useless life!"'

Lavretsky quietly rose and quietly went away; no one noticed him, no one detained him; the joyous cries sounded more loudly in the garden behind the thick green wall of high lime-trees. He took his seat in the carriage and bade the coachman drive home and not hurry the horses.

'And the end?' perhaps the dissatisfied reader will inquire. 'What became of Lavretsky afterwards, and of Lisa?' But what is there to tell of people who, though still alive, have withdrawn from the battlefield of life? They say, Lavretsky visited that remote convent where Lisa had hidden herself – that he saw her. Crossing over from choir to choir, she walked close past him, moving with the even, hurried, but meek walk of a nun; and she did not glance at him; only the eye-lashes on the side towards him quivered a little, only she bent her emaciated face lower, and the fingers of her clasped hands, entwined with her rosary, were pressed still closer to one another. What were they both thinking, what were they feeling? Who can know? who can say? There are such moments in life, there are such feelings . . . One can but point to them – and pass them by.

VIRGIN SOIL

PART I

'Virgin Soil should be turned up not by a harrow skimming over the surface, but by a plough biting deep into the earth.'

From the Notebook of a Farmer.

I

AT ONE O'CLOCK on a spring day of 1868, in Petersburg, a man of twenty-seven, carelessly and shabbily dressed, was mounting the back stairs of a five-storeyed house in Officers' Street. Tramping heavily with his over-shoes trodden down at heel, and slowly rolling his bulky, ungainly person as he moved, this man at last reached the very top of the stairs. He stopped before a half-open door, hanging off its hinges, and without ringing the bell, merely giving a noisy sigh, he swung into a small anteroom.

'Is Nezhdanov at home?' he called in a deep and loud voice.

'He's not – I'm here, come in,' came from the next room another voice, a woman's, also rather gruff.

'Mashurina?' queried the new-comer.

'Yes, it's me. And you – Ostrodumov?'

'Pimen Ostrodumov,' he answered, and first carefully pulling off his rubber over-shoes, and then hanging his threadbare little old cloak on a nail, he went into the room from which the woman's voice had come.

This room, low-pitched and dirty, with its walls coloured a dingy green, was dimly lighted by two dusty windows. The only furniture in it was a small iron bedstead in the corner, a table in the middle, a few chairs, and a bookcase crammed with books. Near the table was sitting a woman of thirty, bareheaded, in a black woollen gown, smoking a cigarette. When she saw Ostrodumov come in, she held out her broad red hand to him without speaking. He shook it, also without speaking, and, sinking into a chair, he pulled a half-smoked cigar out of his side pocket. Mashurina gave him a light, he began smoking, and without saying a word, or even exchanging glances, they both set to puffing rings of bluish smoke into the close air, which was already saturated with tobacco fumes.

These two people had something in common, though in features they were not alike. About their slovenly figures, with coarse lips, and teeth, and noses (Ostrodumov was marked with smallpox too), there was an air of honesty and stoicism and industry.

'Have you seen Nezhdanov?' Ostrodumov inquired at last.

'Yes; he'll be here directly. He's gone to the library with the books.'

Ostrodumov turned aside and spat.

'How is it he's for ever gadding about now? There's no finding him.'

Mashurina took out another cigarette.

'He's bored,' she pronounced, carefully lighting it.

'Bored!' repeated Ostrodumov reproachfully. 'What self-indulgence! One would think we'd no work for him to do. Here are we praying we may get through all the work decently somehow, and he's bored!'

'Any letter come from Moscow?' inquired Mashurina, after a brief pause.

'Yes . . . the day before yesterday.'

'Have you read it?'

Ostrodumov merely nodded.

'Well . . . what's the news?'

'Oh – some one will have to go there soon.'

Mashurina took the cigarette out of her mouth.

'Why so? Everything's all right there, I'm told.'

'Yes, it's all right. Only one man's shown he's not to be depended on. So that . . . we must shift him, or else get rid of him altogether. Oh, and there are other things. They ask for you, too.'

'In the letter?'

'Yes.'

Mashurina shook back her heavy hair. Twisted up carelessly into a small knot behind, it fell in front over her forehead and eyebrows.

'Ah, well,' she declared; 'since the order's given, it's no use discussing it!'

'Of course not. Only it can't be done without money; and where are we to get the money?'

Mashurina pondered. 'Nezhdanov will have to produce it,' she said in an undertone, as though to herself.

'That's the very thing I've come about,' observed Ostrodumov.

'Have you got the letter with you?' Mashurina asked suddenly.

'Yes. Would you like to read it?'

'Yes, give it me . . . no, you needn't, though. We'll read it together . . . afterwards.'

'I tell the truth,' muttered Ostrodumov; 'you needn't doubt it.'

'Well, I don't doubt it.'

And both sank into silence again; and as before, only the rings of smoke floated from their silent lips, and coiling feebly rose above their dishevelled heads.

The thud of over-shoes was heard in the anteroom.

'Here he is!' whispered Mashurina.

The door was opened slightly, and in the crack was thrust a head — but not the head of Nezhdanov.

It was a little round head with rough black hair, a broad, wrinkled forehead, very keen, little brown eyes under bushy eyebrows, a nose pointing in the air like a duck's, and a tiny, rosy, comical mouth. This head took a look round, nodded, smiled — showing a number of tiny white teeth — and came into the room, accompanied by its rickety little body, short arms, and somewhat bandy and lame little legs. Directly Mashurina and Ostrodumov caught sight of this head, the faces of both expressed a sort of condescending contempt, as though each of them were inwardly saying, 'Oh! it's only he!' and they did not utter a single word, did not stir a muscle. However, the reception accorded him not only failed to embarrass the visitor, but apparently afforded him positive gratification.

'What's the meaning of this?' he said in a squeaky voice. 'A duet? Why not a trio? And where's the first tenor?'

'Do you mean to inquire after Nezhdanov, Mr. Paklin?' replied Ostrodumov with a serious face.

'Precisely so, Mr. Ostrodumov; I mean him.'

'He'll be here directly, most likely, Mr. Paklin.'

'It's very delightful to hear that, Mr. Ostrodumov.'

The little cripple turned to Mashurina. She sat scowling, and went on deliberately puffing at her cigarette.

'How are you, dear . . . dear . . . There, how annoying! I always forget your name and your father's.'

Mashurina shrugged her shoulders.

'And there's no need whatever to know them! You know my surname. What more do you want? And what a question: how are you! Can't you see I'm alive all right?'

'True, most true!' cried Paklin, his nostrils dilating and his eyebrows twitching; 'if you weren't alive, your humble servant would not have the pleasure of seeing you here and talking to you! Put my question down to a bad old-fashioned habit. But as for your name and your father's . . . You know it's rather awkward to say baldly, Mashurina! I'm aware, it's true, that you even sign your letters so: Bonaparte! – that's to say, Mashurina! But still, in conversation—'

'But who asks you to talk to me?'

Paklin laughed nervously, as though he were choking.

'There, that's enough, my dear creature – shake hands, don't be cross; don't I know you've the best heart in the world? and I've a good heart, too . . . Eh?'

Paklin held out his hand. . . . Mashurina looked at him darkly. She shook hands with him, however.

'If you positively must know my name,' she said, with the same gloomy face, 'by all means; my name's Fekla.'

'And mine, Pimen,' Ostrodumov added in his bass.

'Ah! that's very . . . very instructive! But that being so, tell me, O Fekla! and you, O Pimen! tell me why you behave with such unfriendliness, such persistent unfriendliness, to me, while I—'

'Mashurina thinks,' Ostrodumov interrupted, 'and she's not the only one who thinks it, that as you look at every subject from the ridiculous side, there's no relying upon you.'

Paklin turned sharply round on his heels.

'There she – that's the mistake people are continually making in criticising me, most honoured Pimen! In the first place, I'm not always laughing; and secondly, that would not in the least prevent your being able to rely upon me, which is proved, indeed, by the flattering confidence I've more than once enjoyed in your ranks! I'm an honest man, most reverend Pimen!'

Ostrodumov muttered something between his teeth, while Paklin shook his head and repeated, now without the faintest trace of a smile, 'No! I'm not always laughing! I'm anything but a light-hearted person! You need only look at me!'

Ostrodumov did look at him. And, in fact, when Paklin was not laughing, when he was silent, his face wore an expression almost of dejection, almost of terror; it became humorous and even malicious directly he opened his mouth. Ostrodumov said nothing, however.

Paklin again turned to Mashurina.

'Well, and how are your studies progressing? Are you successful in your truly philanthropic art? I should guess it's a difficult job helping the inexperienced citizen on his first entrance into the light of day?'

'No, not at all difficult, so long as he's not much bigger than you,' answered Mashurina, who had just taken her diploma as a midwife; and she smiled complacently. A year and a half before, she had left her own people, a family of poor nobles in South Russia, and had come to Petersburg with six roubles in her pocket; she had entered a lying-in institution, and by unceasing hard work had gained the coveted diploma. She was a single woman . . . and a very chaste single woman. Nothing wonderful in that, some sceptic will say, remembering what has been said of her exterior. Something wonderful and rare, let us be permitted to say.

Paklin laughed again when he heard her retort.

'You're a smart person, my dear!' he cried. 'You had me there nicely! I deserve it. Why did I stay such a shrimp! But what can have become of our host?'

Paklin purposely changed the subject. He had never been able to resign himself to his diminutive stature and his unsightly little person altogether. He felt it the more keenly as he was a passionate admirer of women. What would he not have given to attract them! The consciousness of his pitiful exterior was a much sorer wound to him than his humble origin, or his unenviable position in society. Paklin's father had been simply a tradesman, who, through shifty dodges of one sort and another, had risen to the rank of titular councillor. He had been a successful go-between in legal business, and a speculator and agent for houses and property. He had made a respectable fortune; but drank heavily towards the end of his life, and left nothing at his death. Young Paklin (he had been named Sila Samsonitch, that is, Strength, son of Samson, which he also regarded as a jeer at his expense) had been educated at a commercial school, where he learned German thoroughly. After various rather disagreeable experiences, he got at last into a private business house for a salary of about a hundred and fifty pounds a year. On that sum he kept himself, a sick aunt, and a humpbacked sister. At the time of our story he was just twenty-eight. Paklin was acquainted with a number of students, young men who liked him for his cynical wit, the light-hearted venom of his audacious talk, and his one-sided but genuine and unpedantic learning. Only occasionally he suffered at their hands. One day he was somehow late at a political gathering. . . . As he came in, he began at once hurriedly making excuses. . . .

'Poor Paklin was afeared!' sang out some one in a corner, and they all roared with laughter. Paklin at last laughed himself, though his heart was sore. 'He spoke the truth, the ruffian!' he thought to himself. He made Nezhdanov's acquaintance at a Greek eating-house, where he used to go and dine, and where he constantly expressed very free and bold opinions. He used to declare that the chief cause of his democratic frame of mind was the execrable Greek cookery, which upset his liver.

'Yes . . . really . . . what has become of our host?' repeated Paklin. 'I've noticed for some time past he's seemed out of spirits. Can he be in love? – Heaven forfend!'

Mashurina scowled.

'He's gone to the library for some books; he's no time to be in love and no one to be in love with.'

'How about you?' almost broke from Paklin's lips. 'I want to see him,' he uttered aloud, 'because I have to talk to him about an important affair.'

'What sort of affair?' put in Ostrodumov. 'Our affairs?'

'Perhaps yours . . . that is, our common affairs.'

Ostrodumov hummed. In his heart he was doubtful, but then he reflected, 'Who can tell? He's such a slippery eel!'

'Here he comes at last,' said Mashurina suddenly, and in her small unlovely eyes, that were fastened on the door of the anteroom, there was a flash of something warm and tender, a kind of deep inward spot of light. . . .

The door opened, and this time there entered a young man of three-and-twenty, a cap on his head and a bundle of books under his arm – Nezhdanov himself.

II

AT THE SIGHT of visitors in his room, he stopped short in the doorway, took them all in in a glance, flung off his cap, dropped the books straight on to the floor, and without a word went up to the bed and sat down on the edge of it. His handsome white face, which looked still whiter from the deep red of his wavy chestnut hair, expressed dissatisfaction and annoyance.

Mashurina turned slightly away, biting her lip; Ostrodumov growled: 'At last!'

Paklin was the first to approach Nezhdanov.

'What's wrong with you, Alexey Dmitrievitch, Hamlet of Russia? Has any one offended you? or is it a causeless melancholy?'

'Stop that, please, Mephistopheles of Russia,' answered Nezhdanov irritably. 'I'm not equal to a contest with you in dull smartness.'

Paklin laughed.

'You don't express yourself very accurately; if it's smart, it's not dull; if it's dull, it's not smart.'

'Very well, very well. . . . You're a witty fellow, we all know.'

'And you're in a highly nervous condition,' Paklin drawled; 'or has something really happened?'

'Nothing has happened in special; but what's happened is that one can't set one's foot into the street in this filthy town, in Petersburg, without coming across some meanness, idiocy, hideous injustice, rottenness! Life here's impossible any longer.'

'So that's why you've advertised in the paper for a place as tutor and are ready to go away,' Ostrodumov growled again.

'I should think so; I shall get away from here with all the pleasure in life! If only some fool can be found to give me a situation!'

'You must first do your duty *here*,' said Mashurina significantly, still looking away.

'And that is?' queried Nezhdanov, turning sharply round to her.

Mashurina pressed her lips tightly together. 'Ostrodumov will tell you.'

Nezhdanov turned to Ostrodumov. But the latter only cleared his throat and grunted: 'Wait a bit.'

'No, joking apart now, really,' interposed Paklin; 'you have heard something's gone wrong?'

Nezhdanov bounded up on the bed, as though some force were tossing him upwards.

'What more would you have going wrong?' he shouted, his voice suddenly growing loud. 'Half Russia's dying of hunger. The *Moscow Gazette*'s triumphant; they're going to introduce classicism; the students' benefit clubs are prohibited; everywhere there's spying, persecution, betrayal, lying, and treachery – we can't advance a step in any direction . . . and all that's not enough for him – he looks for something fresh to go wrong, he thinks I'm joking. . . . Basanov's arrested,' he added, dropping his voice a little; 'they told me at the library.'

Ostrodumov and Mashurina both at once raised their heads.

'My dear fellow, Alexey Dmitrievitch,' began Paklin, 'you are excited – no wonder. . . . But had you forgotten what an age and what a country we live in? Why, among us a drowning man has to make for himself the very straw he's to clutch at! What's the good of being sentimental over it? One must face the worst, my dear fellow, and not fly into a rage, like a baby—'

'Ah, don't, please!' Nezhdanov interrupted fretfully, and his face worked as if he were in pain. 'You, we all know, are a man of energy, you're afraid of nothing and nobody—'

'Me afraid of nobody—!' Paklin was beginning.

'Who could have betrayed Basanov?' Nezhdanov went on. 'I don't understand it!'

'Why, to be sure, a friend. They're grand hands at that – friends are. You must be on the look-out with them! I, for instance, had a friend, and a capital fellow he seemed; thought such a lot of me, of my reputation! One day he came to me. . . . "Fancy!" he cried, "the ridiculous slanders they've been spreading about you; they declare you poisoned your own uncle; that you were introduced into some house, and at once took a seat with your back to the lady of the house; and persisted in sitting so the whole evening! And that she fairly cried, yes, cried at the insult! What absurdity! what inanity! what fools can believe such a story?" And what followed? Why, a year later I quarrelled with that very friend. . . . And he writes in a letter of farewell: "You who killed your own uncle! You who were not ashamed to insult a respectable lady by sitting with your back to her! . . ." and so on, and so on. That's what friends are!'

Ostrodumov exchanged glances with Mashurina. 'Alexey Dmitrievitch!' he blurted in his heavy bass – he obviously wanted to cut short the useless eruption of words that was beginning – 'a letter has come from Vassily Nikolaevitch from Moscow.'

Nezhdanov gave a slight start and looked down.

'What does he write?' he asked at last.

'Well . . . they want me and her' – Ostrodumov indicated Mashurina – 'to go.'

'What? they ask for her too?'

'Yes.'

'Well, where's the difficulty?'

'Why, of course the difficulty's – money.'

Nezhdanov got up from the bed and went up to the window.

'Is a great deal wanted?'

'Fifty roubles . . . can't do with less.'

Nezhdanov was silent for a space.

'I haven't got it now,' he muttered at last, drumming on the pane with his finger-tips; 'but . . . I could get it. I will get it. Have you the letter?'

'The letter? It . . . that's to say . . . of course.'

'But why do you always keep things back from me?' cried Paklin. 'Haven't I deserved your confidence? Even if I didn't fully sympathise . . . with what you are undertaking, could you suppose me capable of turning traitor or chattering?'

'Unintentionally . . . perhaps!' Ostrodumov said in his deep notes.

'Neither intentionally nor unintentionally. There's Madame Mashurina looking at me with a smile . . . but I say—'

'I'm not smiling,' snapped Mashurina.

'But I say,' pursued Paklin, 'that you, gentlemen, have no intuition; that you don't know how to distinguish who are your real friends! If a man laughs, you think he's not serious . . .'

'To be sure!' Mashurina snapped again.

'Here, for instance,' Paklin hurried on with renewed vigour, this time not even replying to Mashurina, 'you are in want of money . . . and Nezhdanov hasn't it at the moment . . . well, I can let you have it.'

Nezhdanov turned quickly round from the window.

'No . . . no, . . . what for? I will get it . . . I will draw part of my allowance in advance. . . . They do owe me something, if I remember. But, I say, Ostrodumov; show the letter.'

Ostrodumov first remained for some time motionless; then he looked round, then he stood up, bent right down, and, tucking up his trouser, pulled out of the leg of his high boot a carefully folded ball of blue paper; having pulled this ball out, he, for some unknown reason, blew on it and gave it to Nezhdanov.

The latter took the paper, unfolded it, read it attentively, and handed it to Mashurina. . . . She first got up from her chair, then she too read it, and returned it to Nezhdanov, though Paklin was holding out his hand for it. Nezhdanov shrugged his shoulders and passed the mysterious letter to Paklin. Paklin, in his turn, ran his eyes over it, and, compressing his lips with great significance, he laid it in solemn silence on the table. Then Ostrodumov took it, lighted a large match, which diffused a strong smell of brimstone, and first raising the paper high above his head, as though he would show it to all present, he burned it up completely in the match, not sparing his fingers, and flung the ashes into the stove. No one uttered a single word, no one even moved, during this operation. The eyes of all were cast down. Ostrodumov had a concentrated and business-like air. Nezhdanov's face looked wrathful; there were signs in Paklin of being ill at ease; Mashurina might have been at a solemn mass.

So passed two minutes. . . . Then a slight awkwardness came over all of them. Paklin first felt the necessity of breaking the silence.

'Well, then,' he began, 'is my sacrifice on the altar of the fatherland accepted, or not? Am I permitted to contribute, if not fifty roubles, at least twenty-five or thirty, to the common cause?'

Nezhdanov all at once flew into a perfect fury. His irritability had been growing, it seemed. . . . The solemn burning of the letter had by no means allayed it; it was only waiting for an excuse to break out.

'I have told you already that it's not wanted, not wanted . . . not wanted! I won't allow it and I won't accept it. I'll get the money, I'll get it directly. I don't need help from any one!'

'All right, my dear fellow,' observed Paklin. 'I see, though you are a revolutionist, you're not a democrat!'

'Say at once that I'm an aristocrat!'

'Well, you are an aristocrat, really . . . to a certain degree.'

Nezhdanov gave a forced laugh.

'So you mean to hint at my being an illegitimate son. You needn't trouble, my kind friend. . . . Without your aid, I'm not likely to forget that.'

Paklin flung up his arms in despair.

'Alyosha, upon my word, what is the matter with you? How could you take my words like that! I don't know you to-day.' Nezhdanov made an impatient gesture of the head and shoulders. 'Basanov's arrest has upset you, but, you know, he used to behave so imprudently—'

'He used not to conceal his convictions,' Mashurina put in gloomily: 'it's not for us to find fault with him!'

'Of course; only he ought to have thought of others too, who may be compromised by him now.'

'Why do you suppose that of him?' . . . Ostrodumov boomed in his turn: 'Basanov's a man of strong will; he will never betray any one. As for prudence . . . let me tell you, we're not all equally able to be prudent, Mr. Paklin!'

Paklin was offended, and was about to retort, but Nezhdanov stopped him.

'Gentlemen,' he cried, 'be so good as to let politics alone for a time, please!'

A silence followed.

'I met Skoropihin to-day,' Paklin began at last, 'our great national critic and aesthetic enthusiast. What an intolerable creature! He's for ever boiling over and frothing, for all the world like a bottle of bad sour kvas. . . . The waiter, as he runs, holds it down with his finger instead of a cork, a fat raisin sticks in the neck – it goes on bubbling and hissing – and when once all the foam's flown out of it, all that's left at the bottom is a few drops of villainous sour stuff, which quenches no one's thirst, but only gives one a stomach-ache! . . . A most pernicious individual for young people to have to do with!'

The comparison Paklin had made, though true and apt, called up no smile on any one's face. Only Ostrodumov observed that young people who were capable of taking an interest in aesthetic criticism deserved no pity, even if Skoropihin did lead them astray.

'But really, one moment,' Paklin exclaimed with warmth – the less sympathy he met with, the hotter he got, – 'here we have a question, not political we admit, but important for all that. To listen to Skoropihin, every ancient work of art is no good, for the very reason that it is ancient. . . . If that's so, art is nothing but a fashion, and it's not worth while to talk seriously about it! If there is nothing stable, eternal in it – then away with it! In science, in mathematics, for instance, you don't regard Euler, Laplace, Hauss as antiquated imbeciles, do you? Are you prepared to reckon them as authorities, while Raphael and Mozart are fools? Does your pride revolt against their authority? The canons of art are more difficult to arrive at, than the laws of science . . . agreed; but they exist, and any one who doesn't see them, is blind; whether wilfully or not, makes no difference!'

Paklin ceased . . . and no one uttered a sound, as though all of them were holding water in their mouths, as though all were a little ashamed of him. Only Ostrodumov growled: 'And, all the same, I don't feel the least sorry for young men who are led astray by Skoropihin.'

'Oh, go to the devil with you!' thought Paklin. 'I'm off!'

He had come to see Nezhdanov with the object of communicating to him his views as to procuring the *Polar Star* from abroad (the *Bell* had already ceased to exist), but the conversation had taken such a turn, that it seemed better not even to raise this question. Paklin was already reaching after his hat, when suddenly, without any premonitory noise or knocking, there was heard in the anteroom a marvellously pleasant, manly, and mellow baritone, the very sound of which had somehow a suggestion of exceptional good breeding, good education, and even good perfume.

'Is Mr. Nezhdanov at home?'

They all looked at one another in amazement.

'Mr. Nezhdanov at home?' repeated the baritone.

'Yes,' answered Nezhdanov at last.

The door was opened discreetly and smoothly, and slowly removing his glossy hat from his comely short-cropped head, a man of about forty, tall, well-made, and dignified, came into the room. He was dressed in a very handsome cloth coat, with a superb beaver collar, though the month of April was drawing to its close. He struck all, Nezhdanov, Paklin, even Mashurina . . . even Ostrodumov! by the elegant self-possession of his carriage and the cordial ease of his address. They all instinctively rose on his entrance.

III

THE ELEGANTLY DRESSED man advanced to Nezhdanov, and, smiling benevolently, began: 'I have already had the pleasure of meeting you and even having some conversation with you, Mr. Nezhdanov, the day before yesterday, if you remember, at the theatre.' The visitor paused, as though waiting for something. Nezhdanov bent his head slightly, and flushed. 'Yes. . . . I have come to see you to-day in consequence of the advertisement you have put in the papers. I should be glad to have a few words with you, if only I'm not disturbing the lady and gentlemen present' – (the visitor bowed to Mashurina, and waved a hand wearing a grey Swedish glove in the direction of Paklin and Ostrodumov) – 'if I'm not interrupting them. . . .'

'No . . . why, . . .' Nezhdanov replied with some difficulty. 'My friends will excuse . . . Won't you sit down?'

The visitor gave his figure an affable bend, and politely taking hold of the back of a chair, drew it towards himself, but did not sit down – seeing that every one in the room was standing. He merely looked about him with his clear though half-closed eyes.

'Good-bye, Alexey Dmitritch,' Mashurina brought out abruptly; 'I'll come in later.'

'And I,' added Ostrodumov, 'I too'll come . . . later on.'

Passing by the visitor as though intentionally slighting him, Mashurina took Nezhdanov's hand, shook it vigorously and walked out, without saluting any one. Ostrodumov followed her, making a quite unnecessary amount of noise with his boots, and even snorting more than once, as though to say: 'So much for you with your beaver collar!'

The visitor followed them both with a civil but rather inquisitive glance; then he bent it upon Paklin, as though expecting that he too would follow the example of the two retreating guests. But Paklin, whose face had worn a peculiar forced smile from the moment of the stranger's appearance, edged away, and shrank into a corner. Then the visitor sank into the chair. Nezhdanov also took a seat.

'My surname's Sipyagin, – you have heard it, perhaps,' the stranger began with proud humility.

But first we must relate how Nezhdanov had met him at the theatre.

There had been a performance of Ostrovsky's drama, *Don't Sit in Another Man's Sledge*, on the occasion of a visit of Sadovsky from Moscow. The part of Rusakov was, as is well known, one of the famous actor's favourite parts. In the morning, Nezhdanov had gone to the box-office, where he found a good many people. He had intended to take a ticket for the pit, but at the very instant he went up to the desk, an officer, standing behind him, held out a three-rouble bill right across Nezhdanov, and shouted to the clerk: 'He' – (*i.e.* Nezhdanov) – 'is sure to want change, and I don't, so give me, please, a ticket for the front row, at once. . . . I'm in a hurry!'

'I beg your pardon,' Nezhdanov rejoined sharply, 'I, too, want a ticket for the front row,' and thereupon he flung into the little window three roubles – all the ready money he had. The clerk gave him a ticket, and in the evening Nezhdanov made his appearance in the aristocratic division of the Alexandrinsky Theatre.

He was shabbily dressed, had muddy boots and no gloves; he felt ill at ease and exasperated at himself for feeling so. Next him on the right was sitting a general, studded with stars; on the left the same elegantly dressed man, the privy councillor Sipyagin, whose visit two days later had so disturbed Mashurina and Ostrodumov. Every now and then the general took a passing look at Nezhdanov as though at something improper, unexpected, and even offensive; Sipyagin, on the other hand, cast upon him furtive but by no means hostile glances. All the persons surrounding Nezhdanov struck one, to begin with, rather as personages than persons; and then they were all intimately acquainted with one another, and exchanged brief remarks, or even simple exclamations and words of welcome – some of them speaking across Nezhdanov; while he sat motionless and awkward in his wide, comfortable arm-chair, like a kind of pariah. There were bitterness and shame and disgust in his soul; he did not gain much pleasure from Ostrovsky's comedy and Sadovsky's acting. And suddenly, marvellous to relate, during an *entr'acte*, his neighbour on the left, not the starred general, but the other, who wore no sign of distinction of any kind, addressed him softly and courteously, with a kind of ingratiating gentleness. He began speaking of Ostrovsky's play, wished to learn from Nezhdanov, as 'a representative of the younger generation,' what was his opinion of it? Astonished, almost scared, Nezhdanov at first answered abruptly and in monosyllables ... his heart was positively throbbing; but then he got angry with himself; what was he agitated for? wasn't he a man like all the rest? And he proceeded to lay down his opinions unconstrainedly, without reserve, and spoke in the end so loudly, with such enthusiasm, that he obviously annoyed his starred neighbour. Nezhdanov was a fervent admirer of Ostrovsky; but for all his appreciation of the talent shown by the author in the comedy, *Don't Sit in Another Man's Sledge*, he could not approve of the unmistakable intention to depreciate civilisation in the burlesqued character of Vihorev. His courteous neighbour listened to him with great attention and with sympathy, and in the next *entr'acte* began talking to him again, not this time of Ostrovsky's play, but of various general topics, of life, of science, and even of politics. He was obviously interested in the eloquent young man. Nezhdanov, far from being constrained even, as the phrase goes, let off steam a little, as much as to say, 'All right, if you want to know – here you are, then!' In his neighbour, the general, he roused more than simple discomfort – positive indignation and suspicion. At the close of the performance, Sipyagin took leave in a very cordial way of Nezhdanov, but did not seek to learn his surname, nor did he mention his own. While he was waiting on the stairs for his carriage, he jostled against a friend of his, an *aide-de-camp* of the Tsar, Prince G.

'I was looking at you from my box,' the prince said to him, grinning over his perfumed moustaches. 'Do you know whom you were talking to?'

'No, do you?'

'The lad's no fool, eh?'

'Far from it; who is he?'

Then the prince bent over to his ear and whispered in French, 'My brother – yes; he's my brother, a natural son of my father's . . . his name's Nezhdanov. I will tell you about it some day. . . . My father hadn't expected him; that's why he called him Nezhdanov – that is, unexpected. However, he provided for him. . . . *il lui a fait un sort.* . . . We let him have an allowance. He's a fellow with brains . . . he's had, thanks to my father again, a good education. But he's gone utterly crazy, a sort of republican. . . . We don't receive him. . . . *Il est impossible!* But good-bye, they're calling my carriage!' The prince departed, and the next day Sipyagin read in the paper the advertisement Nezhdanov had inserted, and he went to see him. . . .

'My surname's Sipyagin,' he told Nezhdanov, as he sat on a basket-chair facing him, and looked at him with his ingratiating eyes. 'I learned from the papers that you want a position as tutor, and I have come to you with this proposal. I am married; I have one son – nine years old, a boy – to speak frankly – of excellent abilities. We spend the greater part of the summer and autumn in the country, in the province of S———, four miles from the chief town of the province. Well, would you care to go there with us for the vacation, to teach my son the Russian language and history – the subjects you mentioned in your advertisement? I venture to think you will like me, my family, and the very situation of our place. There's a first-rate garden, streams, splendid air, a roomy house. . . . Will you consent? If so, I have only to inquire your terms, though I do not imagine,' added Sipyagin with a faint grimace, 'that any difficulties could arise between us on that score.'

All the while Sipyagin was speaking, Nezhdanov stared fixedly at him, at his small head, thrown a little back, at his low and narrow, but clever forehead, his delicate Roman nose, his pleasant eyes, his well-cut lips, from which the amiable words seemed to flow in an easy stream, at his long whiskers drooping after the English fashion – he stared and was puzzled. 'What does it mean?' he thought. 'Why does this man seem to be making up to me? He's an aristocrat – and I! How have we come together? And what brought him to me?'

He was so absorbed in his reflections that he did not open his mouth even when Sipyagin paused at the end of his speech, awaiting a reply. Sipyagin stole a glance at the corner where Paklin was ensconced, his eyes fixed as intently upon him as Nezhdanov's – was it the presence of this third person which prevented Nezhdanov from speaking out? Sipyagin raised his eyebrows high, as though submitting to the strangeness of the surroundings into which he had dropped, by his own act, however, and raising his voice also, he repeated his question.

Nezhdanov started.

'Of course,' he said rather hurriedly, 'I consent . . . gladly. . . . Though I must own . . . that I can't help feeling some astonishment . . . seeing that I have no recommendation . . . and indeed the opinions I expressed the day before yesterday at the theatre were rather calculated to dissuade you. . . .'

'There you are utterly mistaken, dear Alexey . . . Alexey Dmitritch! isn't that it?' declared Sipyagin smiling; 'I am, I venture to say, well known as a man of liberal, progressive ideas; on the contrary, your opinions, with the exception of all that is peculiar to youth, ever prone – don't be angry with me – to some exaggeration – those opinions of yours are in no way opposed to my own, and, indeed, I am delighted with their youthful enthusiasm!'

Sipyagin talked without the faintest hesitation; his even, rounded speech dropped 'smooth as honey upon oil.'

'My wife shares my way of thinking,' he went on; 'her views, very likely, approach yours even more closely; that's natural enough; she is younger! When, the day after our meeting, I read your name in the papers – you had published your name with your address, contrary, I may mention in passing, to the ordinary practice, though I had found out your name already at the theatre – well – that – that fact struck me. I saw in it – in this coincidence – the ... excuse the superstitious phrase ... so to say, the finger of fate! You referred to recommendations; but I need no recommendation. Your appearance, your personality attract me. That is enough for me. I am accustomed to believe my eyes. And so – may I reckon on it? You agree?'

'Yes ... of course ...' answered Nezhdanov, 'and I will try to justify your confidence; only let me mention one thing now: I am ready to teach your son, but not to look after him. I am not fit for that – and in fact I don't want to tie myself down, I don't want to lose my freedom.'

Sipyagin waved his hand lightly in the air as though driving away a fly.

'Don't be uneasy.... You're not made of that clay; and I don't want any one to look after him either – I am trying to find a teacher, and I have found him. Well, now, how about terms? financial considerations, filthy lucre?'

Nezhdanov was at a loss what to say....

'Come,' said Sipyagin, bending his whole person forward and affectionately touching Nezhdanov's knee with his finger-tips, 'between gentlemen such questions are settled in a couple of words. I offer you a hundred roubles a month; travelling expenses there and back are my affair, of course. You agree?'

Nezhdanov blushed again.

'That is far more than I meant to ask ... I—'

'Very good, very good ...' interposed Sipyagin ... 'I look on the matter as settled, then ... and on you as one of my household.' He got up from his chair and suddenly grew bright and expansive as though he had received a present. In all his gestures there appeared a certain affable familiarity, even playfulness. 'We will set off in a day or two,' he said in an easy tone; 'I like to meet the spring in the country, though by the nature of my occupations I'm a prosaic creature and chained to town. And so let us reckon your first month as beginning from to-day. My wife and son are already at Moscow. She started before me. We shall find them in the country, in the bosom of nature. We will travel together . . . as bachelors. . . . He, he!' Sipyagin gave a little affected nasal laugh, 'And now—'

He drew out of the pocket of his overcoat a black and silver pocket-book and took out of it a card.

'This is my address here. Come round . . . to-morrow. Yes . . . at twelve o'clock. We will have some more talk. I will develop some of my ideas on education . . . Oh – and we'll fix the day of our departure.' Sipyagin took Nezhdanov's hand. 'And do you know?' he added, his voice lowered and his head held aslant, 'if you need any advance . . . Please don't stand on ceremony! just a month in advance!'

Nezhdanov simply did not know what to reply, and with the same perplexity he gazed at the face so bright and cordial, and at the same time so alien to him, which was bent so close to him and smiling so kindly at him.

'You don't want it? eh?' whispered Sipyagin.

'If you'll allow me, I'll tell you that to-morrow,' Nezhdanov articulated at last.

'Excellent! And so – till we meet! Till to-morrow!'

Sipyagin dropped Nezhdanov's hand, and was about to go away. . . .

'Allow me to ask,' said Nezhdanov suddenly, 'you told me just now that you found out my name at the theatre? From whom did you learn it?'

'From whom? Oh, from a friend of yours, and I think a relation, Prince . . . Prince G.'

'The *aide-de-camp* of the Tsar?'

'Yes.'

Nezhdanov flushed more hotly than before, and opened his mouth . . . but he said nothing. Sipyagin again pressed his hand, but this time in silence, and bowing first to him, then to Paklin, he put on his hat just in the doorway and went out, still wearing his complacent smile on his face; in it could be discerned the consciousness of the profound impression which his visit must have produced.

IV

SIPYAGIN HAD SCARCELY crossed the threshold when Paklin leaped up from his chair, and, rushing up to Nezhdanov, began to congratulate him.

'Well, you have made a fine catch!' he declared, giggling and tapping with his feet. 'Why, do you know who that is? Sipyagin, every one knows him, a *kammerherr*, a pillar of society of a sort, a future minister!'

'I know absolutely nothing of him,' Nezhdanov declared sullenly.

Paklin threw up his arms in despair.

'That's just our misfortune, Alexey Dmitritch, that we know no one! We want to produce an effect, we want to turn the whole world upside down, but we live outside that world, we only have to do with two or three friends, and go revolving in a narrow little circle—'

'I beg your pardon,' interposed Nezhdanov: 'that's not true. We only don't care to consort with our enemies; but as for men of our own stamp, as for the people, we are continually entering into relations with them.'

'Stay, stay, stay, stay!' Paklin in his turn interposed. 'In the first place: as for enemies, let me remind you of Goethe's lines:

> *"Wer den Dichter will versteh'n*
> *Muss im Dichter's Lande gehn..."*

but I say:

> *"Wer die Feinde will versteh'n*
> *Muss im Feinde's Lande gehn..."*

To avoid one's enemies, not to know their manners and habits, is ridiculous! Ri ... di ... cu ... lous! ... Yes! yes! If I want to shoot a wolf in the forest I have to know all his holes! ... Secondly, you talked just now of entering into relations with the people.... My dear soul! In 1862 the Poles went "into the forest"; and we are going now into the same forest; that's to say, to the people, who are just as dark and obscure to us as any forest!'

'Then what's to be done, according to you?'

'The Hindoos fling themselves under the wheels of Juggernaut,' Paklin went on gloomily; 'it crushes them, and they die – in bliss. We too have our Juggernaut ... It crushes us indeed, but gives us no bliss.'

'Then what do you say's to be done?' Nezhdanov repeated almost with a shriek. 'Write novels with a "tendency," or what?'

Paklin flung wide his arms and bent his head towards his left shoulder.

'Novels, in any case, you could write, since you have a literary turn.... There, don't be angry, I won't! I know you don't like one to refer to it; besides, I agree with you: spinning out that sort of work with "padding" and all the new-fangled phrases too: – " 'Ah! I love you!' she bounded.... 'It's nothing to me,' he grated." It is anything but a lively job. That's why I repeat, form ties with all classes, from the highest downwards! We mustn't rest all our hopes on fellows like Ostrodumov! They're honest, excellent fellows, but then they're dense! dense! Just look at our worthy friend. Why, the very soles of his boots aren't what clever people wear! Why, what made him go away from here just now? He didn't like to remain in the same room, to breathe the same air, as an aristocrat!'

'I must ask you not to speak slightingly of Ostrodumov before me,' Nezhdanov interposed emphatically. 'He wears thick boots because they're cheaper.'

'I did not mean—' Paklin was beginning.

'If he doesn't care to remain in the same room with an aristocrat,' Nezhdanov continued, raising his voice, 'I applaud him for it; but the great thing is he knows how to sacrifice himself; he will face death, if need be, which you and I will never do!'

Paklin made a piteous little grimace, and pointed to his wasted, crippled little legs.

'Is fighting in my line, my friend Alexey Dmitritch? Good heavens! But never mind all that . . . I repeat, I'm heartily glad of your connection with Mr. Sipyagin, and I even foresee great advantages from that connection, for our cause. You will get into a higher circle! You will see those lionesses, those women of "velvet body worked by springs of steel," as it says in the *Letters from Spain*; study them, my dear boy, study them! If you were an epicurean, I should be positively afraid for you . . . upon my word, I should! But that's not your object in taking such an engagement, of course?'

'I am taking an engagement,' Nezhdanov caught him up, 'for the sake of bread and butter . . . And to get away from all of you for a time!' he added to himself.

'To be sure! to be sure! And so I say to you: study them! What a perfume that gentleman has left behind him!' Paklin sniffed with his nose in the air. 'It's the veritable *ambre* that the mayoress dreamed of in the *Revisor*!'

'He questioned Prince G. about me,' Nezhdanov muttered thickly, taking up his position again at the window: 'he probably knows my whole story now.'

'Not probably, but certainly! What of it? I'll bet you it was just that that gave him the idea of taking you as a tutor! Say what you like, you're an aristocrat yourself by blood, you know. And, of course, that means you're one of themselves! But I've stayed too long with you; it's time I was at the office, at the exploiter's! Good-bye for the present, my dear boy!'

Paklin was going towards the door, but he stopped and turned round.

'Listen, Alyosha,' he said in an ingratiating tone: 'you refused me just now; you will have money now, I know, but still allow me to make some sacrifice, however trifling, for the common cause! There's no other way I can help, so let me at least with my purse! Look; I put a ten-rouble bill on the table! Is it accepted?'

Nezhdanov made no answer, and did not stir.

'Silence gives consent! Thanks!' cried Paklin joyfully, and he disappeared.

Nezhdanov was left alone. . . . He went on staring through the window-pane into the dark, narrow court, into which no ray of sunshine fell even in summer, and dark too was his face.

Nezhdanov was the son, as we are already aware, of Prince G., a rich adjutant-general, and of his daughter's governess, a pretty 'institute-girl,' who had died on the day of his birth. Nezhdanov had received his early education at a boarding-school from an able and strict Swiss schoolmaster, and afterwards had gone to the university. He had himself wished to study law; but the general, his father, who detested the Nihilists, had made him enter 'in æsthetics,' as with a bitter smile Nezhdanov used to put it, that is, in the faculty of history and philosophy. Nezhdanov's father had been in the habit of seeing him only three or four times a year, but he took an interest in his welfare, and when he died bequeathed him, in memory of 'Nastenka' (his mother) a sum of 6000 roubles, the interest of which was paid him by way of a 'pension,' by his brothers, the Princes G. Paklin had not been wrong in describing him as an aristocrat; everything in him betrayed good birth: his little ears, hands and feet, the delicate but rather small features of his face, his soft skin, his fluffy hair, even his rather mincing but musical voice. He was terribly nervous, terribly self-conscious, impressionable, and even capricious; the false position in which he had been put from his very childhood had made him irritable and quick to take offence; but his inborn magnanimity had saved him from becoming suspicious and distrustful. This same false position of Nezhdanov's was the explanation of the contradictions to be met in his character. Daintily clean and fastidious to squeamishness, he forced himself to be cynical and coarse in his language; an idealist by nature, passionate and chaste, bold and timid at the same time, he was as ashamed of his timidity and of his purity as of some disgraceful vice, and made a point of jeering at ideals. His heart was soft and he shunned his fellows; he was easily enraged, and never harboured ill-feeling. He was indignant with his father for having made him study 'æsthetics'; ostensibly, as far as any one could see, he took interest only in political and social questions, and professed the most extreme views (in him they were more than a form of words!); secretly, he revelled in art, poetry, beauty in all its manifestations . . . he even wrote verses. He scrupulously concealed the book in which he scribbled them, and of all his friends in Petersburg, only Paklin – and that solely through the intuition peculiar to him – suspected its existence. Nothing so deeply offended, so outraged Nezhdanov as the faintest allusion to his poetical compositions – to that, as he considered, unpardonable weakness. Thanks to his Swiss schoolmaster, he knew a good many facts, and was not afraid of hard work; he even worked with positive fervour, though rather spasmodically and irregularly. His comrades loved him . . . they were attracted by his uprightness of character, his goodness and purity; but Nezhdanov had been born under no lucky star; life did not come easily to him. He was deeply conscious of this himself, and knew he was lonely in spite of the devotion of his friends.

He still stood at the window, thinking, thinking mournfully and drearily of the journey before him, of the new, unexpected turn in his life. He did not regret leaving Petersburg – he was leaving nothing in it specially precious to him; besides, he knew he would return in the autumn. And still a mood of dread and doubt came over him; he felt an involuntary dejection.

'A nice teacher I shall make!' crossed his mind, 'a fine sort of schoolmaster!' He was ready to reproach himself for having undertaken the task of education, and yet such a reproach would have been unjust. Nezhdanov possessed a fair amount of knowledge, and, in spite of his uneven temper, children were at ease with him, and he, too, readily grew fond of them. The depression which came upon Nezhdanov was that feeling preceding every change of place – that feeling known to all melancholy, all brooding natures. To people of a bold, sanguine character it is unknown: they are rather disposed to rejoice when the daily routine of life is broken up, when their habitual surroundings are changed. Nezhdanov became so deeply absorbed in his meditations that by degrees, almost unconsciously, he began translating them into words; the emotions passing over him were already ranging themselves into rhythmic cadences.

'Oof, the devil!' he cried aloud, 'I do believe I'm on the high road to a poem!'

He shook himself, turned away from the window. Catching sight of Paklin's ten-rouble note lying on the table, he thrust it in his pocket and set to walking up and down the room.

'I must take an advance,' he mused to himself; 'a good thing this gentleman offers it. A hundred roubles . . . and from my brothers – from their excellencies – a hundred roubles . . . fifty for debts, fifty or seventy for the journey . . . and the rest for Ostrodumov. And what Paklin gives – he can have too. And we shall have to get something from Merkulov too.'

Even while he was making these calculations in his head, the same cadences were again astir within him. He stopped, fell to dreaming . . . and, his eyes fixed on the distance, he stood rooted to the spot. Then his hands, gropingly, as it were, felt for and opened a drawer in the table and drew out from the very bottom of it a manuscript-book.

He sank on to a chair, his eyes still turned away, took up a pen, and humming to himself, at times shaking back his hair, with much blotting and scratching out, he set to tracing line after line.

The door into the anteroom was half opened, and Mashurina's head appeared. Nezhdanov did not notice her and went on with his work. Long and intently Mashurina gazed upon him, and, with a shake of her head to right and left, drew back. . . . But Nezhdanov all at once drew himself up, looked round, and exclaiming with vexation, 'Oh, you!' he flung the book into the table drawer.

Then Mashurina advanced with a firm step into the room.

'Ostrodumov sent me to you,' she observed jerkily, 'to find out when you can get the money. If you can let us have it to-day we will start this evening.'

'To-day I can't,' rejoined Nezhdanov, and he frowned; 'come to-morrow.'

'At what o'clock?'

'Two o'clock.'

'Very well.'

Mashurina was silent for a little. All at once she held out her hand to Nezhdanov.

'I think I interrupted you – forgive me; and besides . . . I'm just going away. Who knows whether we shall meet again? I wanted to say good-bye to you.'

Nezhdanov pressed her chilly red fingers.

'You saw that gentleman here?' he began; 'we came to terms. I am going to him as a tutor. His estate is in S—— province, near S—— itself.'

A rapturous smile flashed across Mashurina's face.

'Near S——! Then perhaps we shall see each other again. They may possibly send us there.' Mashurina sighed. 'Ah, Alexey Dmitritch. . . .'

'What?' inquired Nezhdanov.

Mashurina assumed a concentrated look.

'Never mind. Good-bye. Never mind.'

Once more she pressed Nezhdanov's hand and retreated.

'And in all Petersburg there is no one cares for me like that . . . queer creature!' was Nezhdanov's thought. 'But why need she have interrupted me? . . . It's all for the best, though!'

The following morning Nezhdanov betook himself to Sipyagin's town residence, and there, in a magnificent study, filled with furniture of a severe style, in full harmony with the dignity of a liberal politician and modern gentleman, he sat before a huge bureau, on which lay, in orderly arrangement, papers of no use to any one, beside gigantic ivory knives which never cut anything. For a whole hour he listened to the liberal-minded master of the house, and was immersed in the smooth flood of his clever, affable, condescending words. At last he received a hundred roubles in advance, and ten days later the same Nezhdanov, half-reclining on a velvet sofa in a reserved first-class compartment, beside this same clever liberal politician and modern gentleman, was being carried to Moscow on the jolting lines of the Nikolavsky railway.

V

IN THE DRAWING-ROOM of a large stone house, with columns and a Greek façade, built in the twenties of the present century by a landowner noted for devotion to agriculture and for the free use of his fists, the father of Sipyagin, his wife, Valentina Mihalovna, a very handsome woman, was from hour to hour expecting her husband's arrival, for which she had been prepared by a telegram. The decoration of the drawing-room bore the stamp of a modern, refined taste; everything in it was charming and attractive – everything, from the agreeably varied tints of the cretonne upholstery and draperies to the different lines of the china, bronze and glass knick-knacks, scattered about on the tables and *étagères*, – all fell into subdued harmony and blended together in the bright May sunshine which streamed freely in at the high, wide-open windows. The air of the room, heavy with the scent of lilies-of-the-valley (great nosegays of these exquisite spring flowers made patches of white here and there) was stirred from time to time by an inrush of the light breeze which was softly fluttering over the luxuriant leafage of the garden.

A charming picture! And the lady of the house, Valentina Mihalovna, completed the picture – lent it life and meaning. She was a tall woman of thirty, with dark brown hair, a dark but fresh face of one uniform tint, recalling the features of the Sistine Madonna, with marvellous deep, velvety eyes. Her lips were rather wide and colourless, her shoulders rather high, her hands rather large. . . . But, for all that, any one who had seen how freely and gracefully she moved about the drawing-room, at one time bending her slender, somewhat constricted figure over her flowers and sniffing them with a smile; at another moving some Chinese vase, then rapidly readjusting her glossy hair and half-closing her divine eyes before the glass – any one, we say, would certainly have exclaimed, to himself or aloud, that he had never met a more fascinating creature!

A pretty, curly-headed boy of nine, in a Scotch kilt, with bare legs, much pomaded and befrizzed, ran impetuously into the drawing-room, and stopped suddenly on seeing Valentina Mihalovna.

'What is it, Kolya?' she asked. Her voice was as soft and velvety as her eyes.

'Well, mamma,' the boy began in confusion, 'auntie sent me here. . . . She told me to bring her some lilies-of-the-valley . . . for her room. . . . She has none.'

Valentina Mihalovna took her little son by the chin and lifted his little pomaded head.

'Tell your auntie to send to the gardener for lilies; those

lilies are mine. . . . I don't want them touched. Tell her I don't like my arrangements disarranged. Can you repeat my words?'

'Yes, I can . . .' muttered the boy.

'Well, then, . . . say them.'

'I will say . . . I will say . . . you won't let her have them.'

Valentina Mihalovna laughed. Her laugh, too, was soft.

'I see it's no use giving you messages. Well, never mind; tell her anything you think of.'

The boy hurriedly kissed his mother's hand, which was completely covered with rings, and rushed headlong away.

Valentina Mihalovna followed him with her eyes, sighed, and went up to a cage of gold wire, on the walls of which a green parrot was clambering, warily hooking on by his beak and his claws; she teased him with her finger-tip; then sank into a low lounge, and, taking from a carved round table the last number of the *Revue des Deux Mondes*, she began to skim its pages.

A respectful cough made her look round. In the doorway stood a handsome footman in livery and a white cravat.

'What is it, Agafon?' inquired Valentina Mihalovna, still in the same soft voice.

'Semyon Petrovitch Kallomyetsev is here. Shall I show him up?'

'Ask him up, of course. And send word to Marianna Vikentyevna to come down to the drawing-room.'

Valentina Mihalovna flung the *Revue des Deux Mondes* on a little table, and, leaning back on the lounge, she turned her eyes upwards and looked thoughtful, which suited her extremely.

From the very way Semyon Petrovitch Kallomyetsev, a young man of two-and-thirty, entered the room, easily, carelessly, and languidly, from the way he suddenly beamed politely, bowed a little on one side, and drew himself up like elastic afterwards, from the way he spoke, half-condescendingly, half-affectedly, respectfully took Valentina Mihalovna's hand, and effusively kissed it – from all this one might judge that the visitor was not an inhabitant of the province, a mere casual country neighbour, even one of the richest, but a real Petersburg swell of the highest fashion. He was dressed, too, in the best English style: the coloured border of his white cambric handkerchief peeped in a tiny triangle out of the flat side pocket of his tweed jacket; a single eye-glass dangled on a rather wide black ribbon; the pale dull tint of his Suède gloves corresponded with the pale grey of his check trousers. Close shorn was Mr. Kallomyetsev, and smoothly shaven; his rather feminine face with its small eyes set close together, its thin depressed nose, and its full red lips, was expressive of the agreeable ease of a well-bred nobleman. It was all affability ... and it very easily turned vindictive, even coarse; some one or something had but to vex Semyon Petrovitch, to jar on his conservative, patriotic, and religious principles – oh! then he became pitiless! All his elegance evaporated instantly; his soft eyes glowed with an evil light; his little pretty mouth gave forth ugly words – and appealed, with piteous whines appealed, to the strong arm of the government!

Semyon Petrovitch's family had sprung from simple market-gardeners. His great-grandfather had been known in the parts from which he came as Kolomentsov. ... But his grandfather even had changed his name to Kollometsov; his father wrote it Kallometsev, finally Semyon Petrovitch had inserted the *y*, and quite seriously regarded himself as an aristocrat of the purest blood; he even hinted at his family's being descended from the Barons von Gallenmeier, one of whom had been the Austrian field-marshal in the Thirty Years' War. Semyon Petrovitch was in the ministry of the Court, he had the title of a *kammer-yunker*. He was prevented by his patriotism from entering the diplomatic service, for which he seemed destined by everything, his education, his knowledge of the world, his popularity with women, and his very appearance ... *mais quitter la Russie! jamais!* Kallomyetsev had a fine property, and had connections; he had the reputation of a trustworthy and devoted man – *un peu trop féodal dans ses opinions* – as the distinguished Prince B———, one of the leading lights of the Petersburg official world, had said of him. Kallomyetsev had come to S——— province on a two months' leave to look after his property, that is to say, 'to scare some and squeeze others.' Of course, there's no doing anything without that.

'I expected to find Boris Andreitch here by now,' he began, politely swaying from one foot to the other, and with a sudden sidelong look in imitation of a very important personage.

Valentina Mihilovna made a faint grimace.

'Or you would not have come?'

Kallomyetsev all but fell backwards, so unjust, so inconsistent with the facts did Valentina Mihalovna's question seem to him.

'Valentina Mihalovna!' he cried, 'heavens! could you suppose . . .'

'Well, well, sit down. Boris Andreitch will be here directly. I have sent the carriage to the station for him. Wait a little. . . . You will see him. What time is it now?'

'Half-past two,' replied Kallomyetsev, pulling out of his waistcoat pocket a big gold watch decorated with enamel. He showed it to Madame Sipyagin. 'Have you seen my watch? It was a present from Mihail, you know, the Servian prince . . . Obrenovitch. Here's his crest, look. We are great friends. We used to go hunting together. A capital fellow! And a hand of iron, as a ruler should have! Oh, he won't stand any nonsense! No-o-o!'

Kallomyetsev sank into an easy-chair, crossed his legs, and began in a leisurely way to draw off his left glove.

'If only we had some one like Mihail here in our province!'

'Why? Are you discontented with anything?'

Kallomyetsev puckered up his nose.

'Yes, always that provincial council! That provincial council! What good is it? It simply weakens the administration and arouses . . . superfluous ideas. . . .' (Kallomyetsev waved his bare left hand, freed from the compression of the glove) '... and impossible expectations.' (Kallomyetsev breathed on his hand.) 'I have talked of this at Petersburg ... *mais bah!* The wind's not in that quarter now. Even your husband ... imagine! But of course he's a well-known liberal!'

Madame Sipyagin drew herself up on the little lounge.

'What? You, M'sieu Kallomyetsev, you in opposition to the government!'

'I? In opposition? Never! On no account! *Mais j'ai mon franc parler*, I sometimes criticise, but I always submit!'

'And I do just the opposite; I don't criticise and I don't submit.'

'*Ah! mais c'est un mot!* I will, if you will allow me, repeat your remark to my friend, *Ladislas – vous savez –* he is writing a society novel, and has already read me some chapters. It will be magnificent! *Nous aurons enfin le grand monde russe peint par lui-même.*'

'Where is it to appear?'

'In the *Russian Messenger*, of course. It is our *Revue des Deux Mondes*. I see you are reading that.'

'Yes; but do you know, it is getting very dull?'

'Perhaps ... perhaps. ... And the *Russian Messenger*, perhaps, for some time past – to speak in the language of the day – has been just a wee bit groggy.'

Kallomyetsev laughed heartily; he thought it very amusing to say 'groggy,' and even 'a wee bit.'

'*Mais c'est un journal qui se respecte*,' he went on. 'And that's the chief thing. I, I must admit, take very little interest in Russian literature; such plebeians are always figuring in it nowadays. It's positively come to the heroine of a novel being a cook, a plain cook, *parole d'honneur!* But Ladislas's novel I shall certainly read. *Il y aura le petit mot pour rire* ... and the tendency! the tendency! The nihilists will be exposed. I can answer for Ladislas's way of thinking on that subject, *qui est très correct*.'

'More than one can say for his past,' remarked Madame Sipyagin.

'*Ah! jetons un voile sur les erreurs de sa jeunesse!*' cried Kallomyetsev, and he pulled off his right glove.

Again Valentina Mihalovna faintly fluttered her eyelids. She was in the habit of making rather free use of her marvellous eyes.

'Semyon Petrovitch,' she observed, 'may I ask you why it is that in speaking Russian you use so many French words? I fancy . . . excuse my saying so . . . that's gone out of fashion.'

'Why? why? Every one has not such a perfect mastery of our mother-tongue as you, for instance. As for me, I recognise the Russian language as the language of imperial decrees, of government regulations; I prize its purity. I do homage to Karamzin! . . . But the Russian, so to say, everyday language . . . does it really exist? How, for instance, could you translate my exclamation *de tout à l'heure? C'est un mot!* It's a word! . . . Fancy!'

'I should say: that's a clever saying.'

Kallomyetsev laughed.

'A clever saying! Valentina Mihalovna! But don't you feel there's . . . something scholastic directly. . . . All the raciness has gone. . . .'

'Well, you won't convince me. But what is Marianna doing?' She rang the bell; a page appeared.

'I gave orders to ask Marianna Vikentyevna to come down to the drawing-room. Hasn't my message been taken to her?'

Before the page had time to answer, there was seen in the doorway behind him a young girl in a loose dark blouse, with her hair cropped short, Marianna Vikentyevna, Sipyagin's niece.

VI

'I BEG YOUR PARDON, Valentina Mihalovna,' she said, going towards Madame Sipyagin; 'I was busy and I lingered.'

Then she bowed to Kallomyetsev, and, moving a little aside, seated herself on a small ottoman near the parrot, who had begun flapping his wings and craning towards her directly he caught sight of her.

'Why are you sitting so far away, Marianna?' observed Madame Sipyagin, following her with her eyes to the ottoman. 'Do you want to be close to your little friend? Only fancy, Semyon Petrovitch,' she turned to Kallomyetsev, 'that parrot's simply in love with dear Marianna.'

'That does not astonish me!'

'And me he can't endure.'

'Well, that is astonishing! You tease him, I suppose?'

'Never; quite the contrary. I give him sugar. But he will take nothing from me. No . . . it's a case of sympathy . . . and antipathy.'

Marianna glanced up from under her eyelids at Madame Sipyagin . . . and Madame Sipyagin glanced at her.

These two women did not like each other. In comparison with her aunt, Marianna might almost have been called 'a plain little thing.' She had a round face, a large hawk nose, grey eyes, also large and very clear, thin eyebrows, thin lips. She had cropped her thick dark-brown hair, and she looked unsociable. But about her whole personality there was something vigorous and bold, something stirring and passionate. Her feet and hands were tiny; her strongly knit, supple little body recalled the Florentine statuettes of the sixteenth century; she moved lightly and gracefully.

Marianna's position in the Sipyagins' household was a rather difficult one. Her father, a very clever and energetic man of half-Polish extraction, gained the rank of a general, but was suddenly ruined by being detected in a gigantic fraud on the government; he was brought to trial ... condemned, deprived of his rank and his nobility, and sent to Siberia. Afterwards he was pardoned ... and brought back; but he did not succeed in climbing up again, and died in extreme poverty. His wife, Sipyagin's sister, the mother of Marianna (she had no other children), could not endure the blow which had demolished all her prosperity, and died soon after her husband. Sipyagin gave his niece a home in his own house; but she was sick of a life of dependence; she strove towards freedom with all the force of her uncompromising nature, and between her and her aunt there raged a constant though hidden warfare. Madame Sipyagin considered her a nihilist and an atheist; Marianna, for her part, hated Madame Sipyagin, as her unconscious oppressor. Her uncle she held aloof from, as she did, indeed, from every one else. She simply held aloof from them; she was not afraid of them; she had not a timid temper.

'Antipathy,' repeated Kallomyetsev; 'yes, that's a strange thing. Every one is aware, for instance, that I'm a deeply religious man, orthodox in the fullest sense of the word; but a priest's flowing locks – his mane – I can't look at with equanimity; I have a sensation of positive nausea.'

And Kallomyetsev, with a reiterated wave of his clenched fist, tried to express his sensations of nausea.

'Hair in general seems rather to worry you, Semyon Petrovitch,' observed Marianna; 'I am sure you can't look at any one with equanimity whose hair is cropped like mine.'

Madame Sipyagin slowly raised her eyebrows and bent her head, as though amazed at the free and easy way in which young girls nowadays enter into conversation; while Kallomyetsev gave a condescending simper.

'Of course,' he replied, 'I cannot but feel regret for lovely curls like yours, Marianna Vikentyevna, which have fallen beneath the remorseless scissors; but I have no feeling of antipathy; and, in any case, . . . your example would have . . . would have . . . *proselytised* me!'

Kallomyetsev could not find the Russian word, and did not want to speak French after his hostess's observations.

'Thank goodness, dear Marianna does not wear spectacles yet,' put in Madame Sipyagin, 'and has not parted with cuffs and collars, though she does study natural science, to my sincere regret; and is interested in the woman question too . . . Aren't you, Marianna?'

This was all said with the object of embarrassing Marianna; but she was not embarrassed.

'Yes, auntie,' she answered, 'I read everything that's written about it; I try to understand exactly what the question is.'

'That's what it is to be young!' – Madame Sipyagin turned to Kallomyetsev; 'you and I don't care about these things now – eh?'

Kallomyetsev smiled sympathetically; he was bound to bear with the lady's jesting humour.

'Marianna Vikentyevna,' he began, 'is filled with the idealism . . . the romanticism of youth . . . which in time . . .'

'But I am slandering myself,' Madame Sipyagin interrupted: 'I take an interest in such questions too. I'm not quite elderly yet, you know.'

'And I take an interest in all such subjects,' Kallomyetsev exclaimed hurriedly; 'only I would forbid talking about it.'

'You would forbid talking about it?' Marianna repeated inquiringly.

'Yes! I would say to the public: I don't hinder your taking an interest . . . but as for talking . . . hush!' – he put his finger to his lips – 'any way, talking *in print* – I would prohibit – unconditionally!'

Madame Sipyagin laughed.

'What? You would have a commission appointed in some department to decide the question, wouldn't you?'

'And why not a commission? Do you think we should decide

the question worse than all the hungry penny-a-liners, who can never see beyond their noses, and fancy they are . . . geniuses of the first rank? We would appoint Boris Andreevitch president.'

Madame Sipyagin laughed more than ever.

'You must take care; Boris Andreevitch is sometimes such a Jacobin—'

'Jackó, jackó, jackó,' called the parrot.

Valentina Mihalovna shook her handkerchief at him.

'Don't prevent sensible people from talking! . . . Marianna, quiet him.'

Marianna turned to the cage and began scratching the parrot's neck, which he offered her at once.

'Yes,' Madame Sipyagin continued, 'Boris Andreevitch sometimes astonishes me. He has something . . . something . . . of the tribune in him.'

'*C'est parce qu'il est orateur!*' Kallomyetsev interposed hotly in French. 'Your husband has the gift of words, as no one else has; he's accustomed to success, too . . . *ses propres paroles le grisent* . . . add to that a liking for popularity . . . But he's a little off all that, isn't he? *Il boude?* – eh?'

Madame Sipyagin glanced towards Marianna.

'I have not noticed it,' she replied after a brief silence.

'Yes,' Kallomyetsev pursued in a pensive tone; 'he has been overlooked a little.'

Madame Sipyagin again indicated Marianna with a significant glance.

Kallomyetsev smiled and grimaced, as much as to say, 'I understand.'

'Marianna Vikentyevna!' he exclaimed suddenly, in a voice unnecessarily loud, 'are you intending to give lessons in the school again this year?'

Marianna turned round from the cage.

'And does that, too, interest you, Semyon Petrovitch?'

'To be sure; indeed it interests me very much.'

'You would not prohibit that?'

'I would prohibit Nihilists from even thinking about schools; but, under clerical guidance, and with supervision of the clergy, I would found schools myself!'

'Really, now? Well, I don't know what I am going to do this year. Everything turned out so badly last year. Besides, there's no school in summer-time.'

When Marianna talked, her colour gradually deepened as though her words cost her an effort, as though she were forcing herself to go on. There was still a great deal of self-consciousness about her.

'You are not sufficiently prepared?' inquired Madame Sipyagin with a quiver of irony in her voice.

'Perhaps not.'

'What?' Kallomyetsev exclaimed again. 'What do I hear? Merciful heavens! is preparation needed to teach the little peasant wenches their A B C?'

But at that instant Kolya ran into the drawing-room shouting: 'Mamma! mamma! papa is coming!' and after him there came rolling in on her fat little feet a grey-haired lady in a cap and yellow shawl, and she too announced that dear Boris would be here directly! This lady was Sipyagin's aunt, Anna Zaharovna by name. All the persons who were in the drawing-room jumped up from their places and rushed into the anteroom, and from there down the stairs out to the principal entrance. A long avenue of lopped fir-trees led from the highroad straight to this entrance; already a carriage was dashing along it, harnessed with four horses. Valentina Mihalovna, standing in front of all, waved her handkerchief, Kolya uttered a piercing shout; the coachman deftly drew up the heated horses, the groom flew headlong from the box and almost tore the carriage door off, lock, hinges, and all; and, with an amiable smile on his lips, in his eyes, over his whole face, Boris Andreevitch alighted, flinging his cloak off with a single easy gesture. Quickly and gracefully Valentina Mihalovna flung both arms about his neck, and kissed him three times. Kolya was stamping and tugging at his father's coat-tails behind . . . but he first kissed Anna Zaharovna, taking off his very uncomfortable and hideous Scotch travelling cap as a preliminary; then he exchanged greetings with Marianna and Kallomyetsev, who had also come out on the doorstep – (he gave Kallomyetsev a vigorous English '*shake-hands*,' working his arm up and down, as though he were tugging at a bell-rope) – and only then turned to his son; he took him under his arms, lifted him up, and drew him close to his face.

While all this was taking place, Nezhdanov crept stealthily with a guilty air out of the carriage and stood near the front wheel, keeping his cap on and looking up from under his brows. . . . Valentina Mihalovna, as she embraced her husband, glanced sharply over his shoulder at this new figure; Sipyagin had told her beforehand that he was bringing a tutor along with him.

The whole party, still exchanging welcomes and shaking hands with the newly arrived master, moved up the steps, along both sides of which were ranged the principal men- and maid-servants. They did not kiss his hand – that 'Asiaticism' had long been abandoned – but merely bowed respectfully; and Sipyagin responded to their salutations with a motion more of the nose and brows than of the head.

Nezhdanov too moved slowly up the broad steps. Directly he entered the anteroom, Sipyagin, who had been already on the look-out for him, presented him to his wife, Anna Zaharovna and Marianna; while to Kolya he said, 'This is your tutor, mind you obey him! give him your hand!' Kolya timidly stretched out his hand to Nezhdanov, then stared at him; but apparently finding nothing in him striking or attractive, clung again to his 'papa.' Nezhdanov felt ill at ease just as he had that time at the theatre. He had on an old, rather ugly great-coat; his face and hands were covered with the dust of the road. Valentina Mihalovna said something affable to him; but he did not quite catch her words and made no response; he only noticed that she gazed with peculiar brightness and affection at her husband and kept close to his side. He did not like Kolya's befrizzed, pomaded head of hair; at the sight of Kallomyetsev he thought, 'What a smug little phiz!' and to the others he paid no attention whatever. Sipyagin twice turned his head with dignity as though looking round at his household gods, a position which threw his long hanging whiskers and rather round little head into striking relief. Then he called to one of the footmen in his powerful resonant voice, which showed no trace of the fatigues of the journey: 'Ivan! take this gentleman to the green room and carry his trunk up there,' and informed Nezhdanov that he could rest now, unpack, and set himself to rights, and dinner would be ready at five o'clock precisely. Nezhdanov bowed, and followed Ivan into the 'green room,' which was on the second storey.

The whole party passed into the drawing-room. There words of welcome were repeated once more; a half-blind old nurse came in with a courtesy. From regard for her years, she was allowed by Sipyagin to kiss his hand, and then, with apologies to Kallomyetsev, he retired to his own room, escorted by his wife.

VII

THE SPACIOUS AND comfortable room to which the servant conducted Nezhdanov looked out on the garden. Its windows were open and a light breeze was faintly fluttering the white blinds; they swelled out like sails, rose and fell again. Gleams of golden light glided slowly over the ceiling; the whole room was full of a fresh, rather moist fragrance of spring. Nezhdanov began by dismissing the servant, unpacking his trunk, washing and changing his clothes. The journey had utterly exhausted him; the constant presence for two whole days of a stranger, with whom he had had much varied and aimless talk, had worked upon his nerves; something bitter, not quite weariness nor quite anger, was secretly astir in the very bottom of his soul; he raged against his faint-heartedness, and still his heart sank.

He went up to the window and began looking at the garden. It was an old-world garden, of rich black soil, such a garden as one does not see this side of Moscow. It was laid out on a long, sloping hill-side, and consisted of four clearly marked divisions. In front of the house for two hundred paces stretched the flower-garden, with straight little sandy paths, groups of acacias and lilacs, and round flower-beds; on the left, past the stable-yard, right down to the threshing-floor, lay the fruit-garden closely planted with apple, pear, and plum trees, currants and raspberries; just opposite the house rose intersecting avenues of limes forming a great close quadrangle. The view on the right was bounded by the road, shut in by a double row of silver poplars; behind a clump of weeping birches could be seen the round roof of a green-house. The whole garden was in the tender green of its first spring foliage; there was no sound yet of the loud summer buzz of insects; the young leaves twittered, and chaffinches were singing somewhere, and two doves cooed continually in the same tree, and a solitary cuckoo called, shifting her place at each note; and from the distance beyond the mill-pond came the caw in chorus of the rooks, like the creaking of innumerable cart-wheels. And over all this fresh, secluded, peaceful life the white clouds floated softly, with swelling bosoms like great, lazy birds. Nezhdanov gazed, listened, drank in the air through parted chilling lips.

And his heart grew lighter; a sense of peace came upon him too.

Meanwhile, in the bedroom downstairs, there was talk about him. Sipyagin was telling his wife how he had made his acquaintance, and what Prince G. had told him, and what discussions they had had on the journey.

'A good brain!' he repeated, 'and plenty of information; it's true, he's a red republican, but, as you know, that's nothing to me; these fellows have ambition, any way. And besides, Kolya's too young to pick up any nonsense from him.'

Valentina Mihalovna listened to her husband with an affectionate though ironical smile, as though he had been confessing a rather strange, but amusing prank; it was positively agreeable to her that her *seigneur et maître*, so solid a man, so important an official, was still as capable of perpetrating some sudden mischievous freak as a boy of twenty. Standing before the looking-glass in a snow-white shirt and blue silk braces, Sipyagin set to brushing his hair in the English fashion with two brushes, while Valentina Mihalovna, tucking up her little shoes under her on a low Turkish lounge, began to tell him various pieces of news about the estate, about the paper factory, which — sad to say — was not doing as well as it should, about the cook, whom they would have to get rid of, about the church, off which the stucco was peeling, about Marianna, about Kallomyetsev. . . .

Between the husband and wife there existed a genuine harmony and confidence; they did really live 'in love and good counsel,' as they used to say in old times; and when Sipyagin, on completing his toilet, asked Valentina Mihalovna in chivalrous fashion for 'her little hand,' when she gave him both, and with tender pride watched him kissing them alternately, the feeling expressed in both faces was a fine and genuine feeling, though in her it was reflected in eyes worthy of a Raphael, in him in the commonplace 'peepers' of a civilian general.

Precisely at five o'clock Nezhdanov went down to dinner, which was announced not even by a bell, but the prolonged boom of a Chinese *gong*. The whole party were already assembled in the dining-room. Sipyagin, from above his high cravat, greeted him cordially once more, and assigned him a place at the table between Anna Zaharovna and Kolya. Anna Zaharovna was an old maid, the sister of Sipyagin's deceased father; she smelt of camphor, like stored-up clothes, and had an anxious and dejected air. Her position in the household was that of Kolya's nurse or governess; her wrinkled face expressed her displeasure when Nezhdanov was seated between her and her little charge. Kolya stole sidelong glances at his new neighbour; the sharp child soon guessed that his tutor was ill at ease, that he was embarrassed; he did not raise his eyes, and scarcely ate anything. Kolya was pleased at this; till then he had been afraid his tutor might turn out to be cross and severe. Valentina Mihalovna too glanced at Nezhdanov.

'He looks like a student,' was her thought, 'and he's not seen much of the world; but his face is interesting and the colour of his hair's original, like that apostle whom the old Italian masters always depict as red-haired; and his hands are clean.' Every one at the table indeed glanced at Nezhdanov and, as it were, had pity on him, leaving him in peace for the present; he was conscious of this and was glad of it, and at the same time, for some reason or other, irritated. The conversation at table was kept up by Kallomyetsev and Sipyagin. They talked about the provincial council, the governor, the highway-rates, the terms of redemption, their common acquaintances in Petersburg and Moscow, of Mr. Katkov's school then just beginning to become influential, the difficulty of getting workmen, fines and damage caused by cattle, but also of Bismarck, of the war of 1866, and of Napoleon III., whom Kallomyetsev dubbed a capital fellow. The young *kammerjunker* gave expression to the most retrograde opinions; he went so far at last as to propose – ostensibly as a joke, it's true – the toast given by a gentleman, a friend of his, at a certain birthday banquet: 'I drink to the only principles I acknowledge,' the ardent landowner had exclaimed, 'to the knout and to Roederer!'

Valentina Mihalovna frowned, and observed that this quotation was *de très mauvais goût*. Sipyagin, on the contrary, expressed the most liberal opinions; amicably, and rather carelessly, he opposed Kallomyetsev; he even jeered at him a little.

'Your apprehensions in regard to the emancipation, my

dear Semyon Petrovitch,' he said to him, among other things, 'remind me of a memorial drawn up by our respected and excellent friend Alexey Ivanitch Tveritinov in 1860, and read by him everywhere in the Petersburg drawing-rooms. There was one particularly nice sentence describing how the liberated peasant would infallibly go, torch in hand, over the face of the whole country. You should have seen dear good Alexey Ivanitch, with distended cheeks and round eyes, bringing out of his infantine mouth, "T-t-torch! t-t-torch! he will go about t-torch in hand!" Well, the emancipation is an accomplished fact. . . . Where is the peasant with the torch?'

'Tveritinov,' Kallomyetsev answered in a gloomy tone, 'was only so far wrong that it's not peasants but other people who are going about with torches.'

At those words Nezhdanov, who till that instant had hardly noticed Marianna – she was sitting at the further diagonal corner – suddenly exchanged glances with her and at once felt that they – that sullen girl and he – were of the same faith, of the same camp. She had made no impression of any kind on him when Sipyagin had introduced him to her; why was it her eye he caught at this moment? He put the question to himself at that point: Wasn't it shameful, wasn't it disgraceful to sit and listen to such opinions without protesting, giving grounds by his silence for believing that he shared them? A second time Nezhdanov glanced at Marianna, and he fancied that he read the answer to his question in her eyes: 'Wait a little,' they seemed to say, 'it's not time now . . . it's not worth while . . . later on; there's always time. . . .'

It was pleasant to him to think that she understood him. He listened again to the conversation. . . . Valentina Mihalovna had taken her husband's place and was speaking out even more freely, even more radically than he. She could not comprehend, 'positively could not com-pre-hend,' how a man of education, still young, could adhere to old-fashioned conventionalism like that!

'I am sure, though,' she added, 'that you only say so for the sake of a paradox! As for you, Alexey Dmitritch,' she turned with a cordial smile to Nezhdanov (he was inwardly amazed that she knew his name and his father's), 'I know you don't share Semyon Petrovitch's apprehensions; Boris described to me your talks with him on the journey.'

Nezhdanov flushed, bent over his plate, and muttered something unintelligible; he was not so much shy as unaccustomed to exchange remarks with such distinguished personages. Madame Sipyagin still smiled upon him; her husband supported her patronisingly. ... But Kallomyetsev deliberately stuck his round eye-glass between his nose and his eyebrow, and stared at the student who dared not to share his 'apprehensions.' But to confuse Nezhdanov in *that* way was a difficult task; on the contrary, he drew himself up at once, and stared in his turn at the fashionable official; and just as suddenly as he had felt a comrade in Marianna, he felt a foe in Kallomyetsev! And Kallomyetsev was conscious of it; he dropped his eye-glass, turned away, and tried to laugh ... but unsuccessfully; only Anna Zaharovna, who secretly adored him, inwardly took his part, and was still more indignant at the uninvited neighbour who was separating her from Kolya.

Shortly afterwards the dinner came to an end. The party moved on to the terrace to drink coffee; Sipyagin and Kallomyetsev lighted cigars. Sipyagin offered Nezhdanov a genuine regalia, but he refused it.

'Ah! to be sure!' cried Sipyagin; 'I'd forgotten; you only smoke your cigarettes!'

'Curious taste,' Kallomyetsev observed, between his teeth.

Nezhdanov almost exploded. 'I know the difference between a regalia and a cigarette well enough, but I don't care to be under obligations,' almost broke from his lips. ... He restrained himself; but at once scored this second piece of insolence as a 'debt' to pay back against his enemy.

'Marianna!' Madame Sipyagin observed all at once, in a

loud voice, 'you need not stand on ceremony before a stranger . . . you may smoke your cigarette, and welcome. Besides,' she added, turning towards Nezhdanov, 'I have heard that in your set all the young ladies smoke?'

'Quite so,' Nezhdanov answered drily. It was the first word he had spoken to Madame Sipyagin.

'Well, I don't smoke,' she went on, with an ingratiating light in her velvety eyes. . . . 'I am behind the age.'

In a leisurely, circumspect fashion, as though in defiance of her aunt, Marianna drew out a cigarette and a box of matches, and began smoking. Nezhdanov, too, smoked a cigarette, lighting it from Marianna's.

It was an exquisite evening. Kolya and Anna Zaharovna went off into the garden; the rest of the party remained about an hour longer on the terrace, enjoying the air. The conversation became rather lively. . . . Kallomyetsev attacked literature; Sipyagin on that point, too, showed himself a liberal, championed the independence of literature, pointed out its utility, and even referred to Chateaubriand and the fact that the Emperor Alexander Pavlovitch had bestowed on him the order of St. Andrei the First-Called! Nezhdanov did not take part in this discussion; Madame Sipyagin looked at him with an expression which seemed on one hand to approve of his discreet reserve, and on the other, to be a little surprised at it.

Every one went back to the drawing-room for tea.

'We have a very bad habit, Alexey Dmitritch,' said Sipyagin to Nezhdanov; 'we play cards every evening, and what's more, a prohibited game . . . think of that! I won't invite you to join us . . . but Marianna will be so good as to play us something on the piano. You're fond of music, I hope, eh?' And without waiting for an answer, Sipyagin picked up a pack of cards. Marianna sat down to the piano, and played neither well nor ill a few of Mendelssohn's 'Songs without Words.' '*Charmant! charmant! quel toucher!*' Kallomyetsev, from a distance, shrieked as though he had been scalded; but this ejaculation was vociferated rather from politeness; and Nezhdanov too, in spite of the hope expressed by Sipyagin, had no passion for music.

Meanwhile Sipyagin and his wife, Kallomyetsev and Anna Zaharovna, had sat down to cards. ... Kolya came to say good-night, and after receiving a blessing from his parents and a large glass of milk instead of tea, he went off to bed; his father shouted after him that to-morrow he would begin his lessons with Alexey Dmitritch. Soon afterwards, seeing that Nezhdanov was hanging aimlessly about in the middle of the room, turning over the leaves of a photograph album with an embarrassed air, Sipyagin told him not to stand on ceremony, but to go and rest, as he must certainly be tired after the journey; that the great principle of his house was freedom.

Nezhdanov availed himself of this permission, and, saying good-night to every one, went away; in the doorway he stumbled against Marianna, and, again looking into her eyes, was again convinced that he should find a comrade in her, though she did not smile, but positively frowned upon him.

He found his room all filled with fragrant freshness; the windows had stood open the whole day. In the garden just opposite his windows, the nightingale was trilling its soft, melodious lay; there was a warm, dull glow in the night sky above the rounded tree-tops; it was the moon making ready to float upwards. Nezhdanov lighted a candle; the grey night-moths flew in from the garden in showers, and went towards the light, while the wind blew them back and set the candle's bluish-yellow light flickering.

'Strange!' thought Nezhdanov, as he lay in his bed. ... 'They seem good people, liberal, positively human ... but I feel so sick at heart. The *kammerherr* ... *kammerjunker*. ... Well, morning brings good counsel. ... It's no good sentimentalising.'

But at that instant, in the garden a watchman knocked loudly and persistently on his board, and a long drawn-out shout was heard:

'Li-isten there-re!'

'Ri-i-ight!' answered another lugubrious voice.

'Ugh! mercy on us! – it's like being in prison!'

VIII

NEZHDANOV WOKE UP early, and without waiting for a servant to make his appearance he dressed and went out into the garden. It was very large and beautiful, this garden, and was kept in splendid order; hired labourers were scraping the paths with spades; among the intense green of the bushes peeped the red kerchiefs of peasant-girls armed with rakes. Nezhdanov made his way to the lake: the fog of early morning had already disappeared from it, but the mist still clung about in parts, in shady nooks in the banks. The sun, not yet high in the sky, beat with rosy light over the broad, silky, leaden-hued surface. Some carpenters were busily at work near the washing-platform; a new, freshly painted boat lay there, feebly rocking from side to side, stirring a faint eddy in the water about it. The men's voices were heard seldom, and in reserved fashion: about everything there was a feeling of morning, of the peace and rapid progress of morning work, a feeling of order and regularity of life. And behold, at a bend of the avenue Nezhdanov saw before him the very personification of order and regularity – Sipyagin.

He wore an overcoat of a pea-green colour, made like a dressing-gown, and a striped cap; he leaned on an English bamboo cane, and his freshly shaven face was beaming with satisfaction; he had come out to look round his estate. Sipyagin greeted Nezhdanov cordially.

'Aha!' he cried, 'I see you're one of the young and early!' (He probably meant by this not very appropriate saying to express his approval of the fact that Nezhdanov had, like himself, not stayed late in bed.) 'We drink tea all together in the dining-room at eight, and lunch at twelve; at ten you will give Kolya your first lesson in Russian, and at two the history lesson. To-morrow, the 9th of May, is his name-day, and there will be no lessons; but I should like you to begin to-day.'

Nezhdanov bowed, while Sipyagin parted from him in the French fashion, raising his hand several times in rapid succession to his lips and nose, and walked on, smartly swinging his cane and whistling, not at all like an important official or dignitary, but like a good-natured Russian *country gentleman*.

Till eight o'clock Nezhdanov stayed in the garden enjoying the shade of the old trees, the freshness of the air, the song of the birds; the booming of the gong summoned him to the house, and he found the whole party in the dining-room. Valentina Mihalovna behaved very affably to him; in her morning dress she struck him as perfectly beautiful. Marianna's face wore its usual absorbed and sullen expression. At ten o'clock exactly the first lesson took place in the presence of Valentina Mihalovna; she had first inquired of Nezhdanov whether she would be in his way, and she behaved the whole time very discreetly. Kolya turned out to be an intelligent boy; after the first inevitable awkwardness and hesitation, the lesson went off satisfactorily. Valentina Mihalovna was left apparently well content with Nezhdanov; and several times she addressed him in an ingratiating manner. He held off ... but not too much so. Valentina Mihalovna was present also at the second lesson, on Russian history. She declared with a smile that on that subject she needed a teacher no less than Kolya himself, and behaved as quietly and sedately as during the first lesson. From three till five o'clock, Nezhdanov sat in his own room, wrote letters to Petersburg, and felt neither well nor ill: he was free from boredom and from depression; his overwrought nerves were gradually being soothed. They were unhinged again at dinner-time, though Kallomyetsev was absent, and the ingratiating friendliness of his hostess was unchanged; but that very friendliness rather irritated Nezhdanov. Moreover, his neighbour, the old maiden lady Anna Zaharovna, was obviously sulky and antagonistic, while Marianna was still serious, and Kolya even kicked him rather too unceremoniously. Sipyagin, too, seemed out of spirits. He was very much dissatisfied with the overseer of his paper-mill, a German whom he had engaged at a high salary. Sipyagin began abusing Germans in general, declaring that he was, to a certain extent, a Slavophil, though not a fanatic, and mentioned a young Russian, a certain Solomin, who, it was rumoured, had brought a neighbouring merchant's factory into excellent working order; he had a great desire to make the acquaintance of this Solomin. Towards evening Kallomyetsev, whose property was only eight miles from Arzhano, Sipyagin's village, arrived. There arrived, too, a Mediator, one of those landowners so aptly described by Lermontov in two famous lines:

'A cravat to the ears, and a coat to the heels,
A moustache and a squeak, and eyes muddy and thick.'

There came, too, another neighbour with a dejected, toothless countenance, but exceedingly sprucely dressed; and the district practitioner, a very ignorant doctor, who liked to show off with learned terms; he asserted, for instance, that he preferred Kukolnik to Pushkin because there was so much 'protoplasm' in Kukolnik. They sat down to play cards. Nezhdanov withdrew to his own room and read and wrote till after midnight.

The following day, the 9th of May, was Kolya's patron saint's day. The whole family in three open carriages, with grooms on foot-boards up behind, drove to church, though it was not a quarter of a mile off. Everything was done in grand and pompous style. Sipyagin had put on the ribbon of his order; Valentina Mihalovna was dressed in a charming Parisian gown of a pale lilac colour, and in church, during the service, she said her prayers over a tiny prayer-book bound in crimson velvet; this little book completely dumbfounded several old men, one of whom could not resist asking his neighbour: 'Is it a witch's charm, God forgive her, she's using, or what, eh?' The scent of the flowers that filled the church was blended with the powerful odour of new peasants' coats smelling of sulphur, tarred boots, and bast shoes, and above these and other smells rose the overwhelming sweetness of the incense. The deacons and choristers sang with astounding conscientiousness with the aid of some factory hands who had joined them; they even made an effort at part-singing! There was a moment when every one present felt ... something like dismay. The tenor voice (it belonged to a factory hand, Klima, a man in a galloping consumption), all alone and unsupported, broke into a chromatic series of flat minor notes; they were terrible, those notes, but if they had been cut out the whole concert would promptly have gone to pieces. ... However, the thing was got through somehow. Father Ciprian, a priest of the most respectable appearance, in full vestments, delivered a very edifying discourse from a manuscript-book; unfortunately, the conscientious father had thought it necessary to introduce the names of some wise Assyrian kings, the pronunciation of which cost him great pains, and though he succeeded in proving some degree of erudition, he was hot and perspiring from the exertion. Nezhdanov, who had not been at church for a long while, hid himself in a corner among the peasant-women; they scarcely glanced at him, crossing themselves persistently, bowing low, and discreetly wiping their babies' noses; but the little peasant-girls in new coats, and strings of glass drops on their foreheads, and the boys in belted smocks, with embroidered shoulder-straps and red gussets, stared intently at the new worshipper, turning right round facing him. ... And Nezhdanov looked at them, and various were his thoughts.

After the service, which lasted a very long while – for the thanksgiving of St. Nikolai the Wonder-worker, as is well known, is almost the most lengthy of all the services of the Orthodox Church – all the clergy, at Sipyagin's invitation, moved across to the manor-house. After performing a few more rites proper to the occasion – even sprinkling the rooms with holy water – they were regaled with a copious lunch, during which the edifying but rather exhausting conversation usual at such times was maintained. Both the master and the mistress of the house, though they never lunched at that time of the day, ate and drank a little. Sipyagin went so far as to tell an anecdote, thoroughly proper, but mirth-moving, and this, in face of his red ribbon and his dignity, produced an impression which might be described as comforting, and moved Father Ciprian to a sense of gratitude and amazement. In return, and also to show that he too on occasion could impart some piece of information, Father Ciprian described a conversation he had had with the bishop, when the latter made a tour of his diocese, and summoned all the priests of the district to see him at the monastery in the town. 'He was severe, very severe with us,' Father Ciprian declared; 'first he cross-questioned us about our parish, our arrangements, and then he began an examination. . . . He turned to me: "What's your church's dedication-day?" "The Transfiguration of our Saviour," said I. "And do you know the anthem for that day?" "I should hope so, indeed!" "Sing it!" Well, I began at once: "Thou wert transfigured on the mountain, O Christ our Lord. . . ." "Stop! what is the Transfiguration, and how must we understand it?" "In one word," said I, "Christ wished to show Himself to His disciples in His glory!" "Good," said he, "here's a little image for you to wear in memory of me." I fell at his feet. "I thank your Reverence!" . . . So he did not send me empty away.'

'I have the honour of his Reverence's personal acquaintance,' Sipyagin observed majestically. 'A most worthy pastor!'

'Most worthy indeed!' Father Ciprian re-echoed. 'Though he makes a mistake in putting too much trust in the diocesan superintendents. . . .'

Valentina Mihalovna mentioned the peasant school, referring to Marianna as the future schoolmistress; the deacon (the supervision of the school was intrusted to his charge), a man of Titanic build, with long waving hair vaguely recalling the combed tail of an Orlov horse, tried to express his approval; but not reckoning on the strength of his lungs, brought out such a deep note that he intimidated himself and alarmed the others. Soon after this the clergy retired.

Kolya in his new short jacket with gold buttons was the hero of the day; he received presents and congratulations; his hands were kissed on the front stairs and the back stairs, by factory hands, house-servants, old women and young women, and peasants – the latter, just as in the old serf days, were buzzing round tables laid out before the house with pies and pots of vodka. Kolya was abashed, and delighted, and proud, and shy, all at once; he caressed his parents and ran out of the room; but at dinner Sipyagin ordered up champagne, and before drinking to his son's health he made a speech. He spoke of the significance of 'serving one's country,' and the way he would wish his Nikolai (so he dubbed him) to go . . . and what was due from him: first, to his family; secondly, to his class, to society; thirdly, to the people, – yes, gentlemen, to the people; and fourthly, to the government! Gradually warming up, Sipyagin rose at last to genuine eloquence, while, like Robert Peel, he thrust one hand into a fold of his frock-coat; he became impressive at the word 'science,' and ended his speech by the Latin exclamation *laboremus*, which he at once translated into Russian. Kolya, with a glass in his hand, had to go the length of the table to thank his father, and be kissed by every one. Again it happened to Nezhdanov to exchange a look with Marianna. . . . They were both, probably, feeling the same thing. . . . But they did not speak to one another.

Everything he saw struck Nezhdanov, however, more as amusing and even interesting than as vexatious and distasteful, while the courteous lady of the house, Valentina Mihalovna, impressed him as a clever woman who knew she was playing a part and was at the same time secretly glad that there was another person clever and penetrating enough to comprehend her. . . . Nezhdanov probably did not suspect how greatly his vanity was flattered by her attitude to him.

The next day lessons began again, and daily life moved on its accustomed way.

A week passed by imperceptibly. . . . What were Nezhdanov's experiences and reflections can best be understood by an extract from a letter to Silin, his best friend, who had been a schoolfellow of his at the gymnasium. Silin did not live in Petersburg, but in a remote provincial town, with a well-to-do relative, on whom he was utterly dependent. His position was such that it was no good for him even to dream of getting away from there; he was a weakly, timid, and limited man, but of a singularly pure nature. He took no interest in politics, had read some few middling books, played on the flute to while away the time, and was afraid of young ladies. Silin loved Nezhdanov passionately – he was in general fervent in his attachments. To no one did Nezhdanov reveal himself so unreservedly as to Vladimir Silin; when he wrote to him he always felt as if he were in communion with some dear and intimate being inhabiting another world, or with his own conscience. Nezhdanov could not even imagine the possibility of living with Silin again as a comrade in the same town. . . . He would most likely have grown colder to him at once, they had so little in common; but he wrote a great deal to him with eagerness and complete openness. With others – on paper at least – he was always, as it were, showing off or artificial; with Silin – never! Silin, who was a poor hand with his pen, answered very little, in short awkward sentences; nor did Nezhdanov need voluminous replies; he knew without that that his friend drank in every word of his, as the dust in the road drinks in a drop of rain, kept his secrets as a holy thing, and, buried in a dreary solitude from which he would never emerge, simply lived in his friend's life. To no one in the world had Nezhdanov spoken of his relations with him; they were very precious to him.

'Well, dear friend – my pure Vladimir,' so he wrote to him

– he always called him pure, and with good reason – 'congratulate me: I have fallen into a snug berth, and can now rest and rally my forces. I am living as a tutor in the house of a rich swell, Sipyagin. I'm teaching his little son, feeding sumptuously (I have never been so well fed in my life!), sleeping soundly, walking to my heart's content in lovely country, and, what is the chief thing, I have escaped for a time from the care of my Petersburg friends; and though at first I was devoured by the most savage *ennui*, now I feel somehow better. Soon I must set to the work you know of (as the proverb has it: If you call yourself a mushroom you must go into the basket), and that's just what they let me come here for; but meanwhile I can lead a delicious animal existence, grow fat, and perhaps write verses, if the fit takes me. Impressions of the country, as they call it, I put off for another time. The estate seems well managed, though the factory, perhaps, is in rather a bad way. As for the peasants, some seem rather unapproachable; and the hired servants have all such decorous faces. But we will go into all that later on. The people of the house are cultivated, liberal; Sipyagin is always so condescending – oh! so condescending; and then all of a sudden he flies off into eloquence – a most highly cultivated person! The lady of the house is a perfect beauty – a sly puss, I should fancy; she fairly watches over one; and oh, isn't she soft! – not a bone in her body! I am afraid of her; you know what my manners are like with ladies! There are neighbours – wretched creatures – and one old lady who worries me. . . . But I am most interested in a girl – whether she is a relation or a companion, goodness knows; I have hardly spoken two words to her, but I feel she's made of the same clay as myself. . . .'

Here followed a description of Marianna's appearance and all her ways; then he went on:

'That she's unhappy, proud, self-conscious, reserved, and, most of all, unhappy, I feel no doubt about. Why she's unhappy, so far I don't know. That she's honest is clear to me: whether she is good-natured is still a question. Are there, in fact, any good-natured women who are not stupid? And is it necessary there should be? However, I know little enough of women in general. The lady of the house does not like her . . . and she reciprocates. . . . But which of them is in the right I don't know. I should suppose that it's rather the lady who is in the wrong . . . seeing that she's so very polite to her, while the girl's very eyebrows twitch with nervousness when she speaks to her patroness. Yes, she's a very nervous creature; in that, too, she's like me. And she's *out of joint* like me, though probably not in just the same way.

'When all this is a little clearer I will write to you. . . .

'She scarcely ever speaks to me, as I said just now; but in the few words she has addressed to me (always suddenly and unexpectedly) there is a sort of rough frankness. . . . I like it.

'By the way, is your relation still keeping you on short commons? Isn't he beginning to think of his end?

'Have you read the article in the *Messenger of Europe* on the last pretenders in the province of Orenburg? That happened in 1834, my dear boy! I don't care for that journal, and the author's a Conservative; but it's an interesting thing, and sets one thinking. . . .'

IX

MAY HAD ALREADY passed into its second half. The first hot days of summer had come.

At the end of his history lesson one day Nezhdanov went out into the garden, and from the garden into a birchwood which adjoined it on one side. Part of this wood had been cut down by timber merchants fifteen years before, but all the clearings were overgrown with thick young birch-trees. The trunks of the trees stood close like columns of soft dull silver, striped with greyish rings; the tiny leaves were of a uniform shining green, as though some one had washed them and put varnish on them; the spring grass pushed up in little sharp tongues through the dark even layer of last year's fallen leaves. Little narrow paths ran up and down all over the wood; yellow-beaked blackbirds, with a sudden cry, as though in alarm, fluttered across the paths, low down, close to the earth, and dashed like mad into the bushes. After walking for half an hour, Nezhdanov sat down at last on a felled stump, surrounded by grey, ancient chips; they lay in little heaps as they had fallen, struck off by the axe. Many times had the winter snow covered them and melted from off them in the spring, and no one had touched them. Nezhdanov sat with his back to a thick hedge of young birches, in the dense, soft shade. He thought of nothing; he gave himself up utterly to that peculiar sensation of the spring in which, for young and old alike, there is always an element of pain . . . the restless pain of expectation in the young . . . the settled pain of regret in the old. . . .

Suddenly Nezhdanov heard the sound of approaching footsteps.

It was not one person coming, and not a peasant in shoes or heavy boots, nor a barefoot peasant-woman. It seemed as though two persons were walking at a slow, even pace. . . . There was the light rustle of a woman's dress. . . .

Suddenly there came the sound of a hollow voice – the voice of a man: 'And so that is your last word? – never?'

'Never!' repeated another voice – a woman's – which seemed to Nezhdanov familiar, and an instant later, at a turn in the path, which at that point skirted the young birches, Marianna stepped out, escorted by a dark, black-eyed man, whom Nezhdanov had never seen till that instant.

Both stopped, as if they had been shot, at the sight of Nezhdanov, while he was so astounded that he did not even get up from the stump on which he was sitting. . . . Marianna blushed up to the roots of her hair, but at once smiled contemptuously. For whom was the smile meant – for herself for having blushed, or for Nezhdanov? . . . Her companion knitted his bushy brows, and there was a gleam in the yellowish whites of his uneasy eyes. Then he looked at Marianna, and both of them, turning their backs on Nezhdanov, walked away in silence, at the same slow pace, while he followed them with a stare of amazement.

Half an hour later he went home and to his room, and when, summoned by the booming of the gong, he went into the drawing-room, he saw in it the same swarthy stranger who had come upon him in the copse. Sipyagin led Nezhdanov up to him and introduced him as his *beau-frère*, the brother of Valentina Mihalovna – Sergei Mihalovitch Markelov.

'I hope you will be good friends, gentlemen!' cried Sipyagin, with the majestically affable though absent-minded smile characteristic of him.

Markelov performed a silent bow; Nezhdanov responded in a similar manner . . . while Sipyagin, with a slight toss of his little head and a shrug of his shoulders, moved away, as much as to say, 'I have done my duty by you . . . and whether you really do become friends is a matter of no importance to me!'

Then Valentina Mihalovna approached the couple, who stood immovable, and again presented them to one another, and with the peculiar caressing brightness which she seemed able at will to shed over her marvellous eyes, she addressed her brother:

'How is it, *cher Serge*, you've quite forgotten us? you did not even come for Kolya's name-day. Or have you had such piles of work? He's introducing new arrangements with his peasants,' she turned to Nezhdanov – 'very original ones too; three-quarters of everything for them, and one quarter for himself; and even then he thinks he gets too much.'

'My sister's fond of joking,' Markelov in his turn addressed himself to Nezhdanov; 'but I'm prepared to agree with her that for *one* man to take a quarter of what belongs to a *hundred* at least, is certainly too much.'

'And have you, Alexey Dmitrievitch, noticed that I'm fond

of joking?' inquired Madame Sipyagin, still with the same caressing softness both of eyes and voice.

Nezhdanov found no reply; and at that moment Kallomyetsev was announced. The lady of the house went to meet him, and a few moments later the butler appeared and in a sing-song voice announced that dinner was on the table.

At dinner Nezhdanov could not help watching Marianna and Markelov. They sat side by side, both with eyes downcast, and lips compressed, with a severe, gloomy, almost exasperated expression. Nezhdanov kept wondering too how Markelov could be Madame Sipyagin's brother. There was so little resemblance to be discerned between them. One thing, perhaps – both were of dark complexion; but in Valentina Mihalovna the uniform tint of her face, arms, and shoulders constituted one of her charms ... while in her brother it attained that degree of swarthiness which polite people describe as 'bronzed,' but which, to the Russian eye, inevitably suggests a leather gaiter. Markelov had curly hair, a rather hooked nose, full lips, sunken cheeks, a contracted chest, and sinewy hands. He was sinewy and dry all over; and he spoke in a harsh, abrupt, metallic voice. His eyes were sleepy, his face surly, a regular dyspeptic! He ate little, and busied himself in rolling up little pellets of bread, only occasionally casting a glance at Kallomyetsev, who had just returned from the town, where he had seen the governor, upon a matter rather unpleasant for him, Kallomyetsev. Upon this point he was studiously silent, though on other subjects he launched out freely.

Sipyagin, as before, pulled him up when he went too far. He laughed a great deal at his anecdotes, his *bons mots*, though he thought, '*qu'il est un affreux réactionnaire.*' Kallomyetsev declared among the rest that he had been thrown into perfect raptures over the name the peasants – *oui, oui! les simples moujiks!* – give to the lawyers – '*Loiars! loiars!*' he repeated in ecstasy: '*ce peuple russe est délicieux.*' Then he related how once when visiting a peasant-school he had put to the pupils the question: 'What is an ornithorhincus?' And as no one was able to answer, not even the teacher, then he, Kallomyetsev, put them another question: 'What is a wendaru?' quoting the line of Hemnitsev: 'The senseless wendaru that apes the other beasts.' And no one had answered that either. So much for your peasant-schools!

'But excuse me,' remarked Valentina Mihalovna, 'I don't know myself what those animals are.'

'Madam!' cried Kallomyetsev, 'there's not the slightest necessity for you to know.'

'And what need is there for the peasants to know?'

'Why, because it's better for them to know of an ornithorhincus or a wendaru than of Proudhon – or even Adam Smith!'

But at this point Sipyagin again pulled him up, maintaining that Adam Smith was one of the leading lights of human thought, and that it would be a good thing if all were to imbibe his principles . . . (he poured himself out a glass of Château d'Yquem . . .) with their mothers' (he held it to his nose and sniffed at the wine) milk! . . . He emptied the glass; Kallomyetsev drank too, and praised the wine.

Markelov paid no special attention to the flights of the Petersburg *kammerjunker*, but twice he looked inquiringly at Nezhdanov, and, tossing up a pellet of bread, all but flung it straight at the loquacious visitor's nose. . . .

Sipyagin let his brother-in-law alone; Valentina Mihalovna, too, did not address him; it was clear that both husband and wife were in the habit of regarding Markelov as an unaccountable creature, whom it was better not to provoke.

After dinner, Markelov went off to the billiard-room to smoke a pipe, and Nezhdanov went to his own room. In the corridor he came upon Marianna. He was about to pass her . . . she stopped him with an abrupt gesture.

'Mr. Nezhdanov,' she began in a not quite steady voice, 'it ought really to be just the same to me what you think about me; but all the same I consider . . . I consider . . .' (she was at a loss for a word . . .) 'I consider it fitting to tell you, that when you met me to-day in the copse with Mr. Markelov . . . Tell me, no doubt you wondered why it was we were both confused, and why we had come there, as though by appointment?'

'It certainly did strike me as a little strange,' Nezhdanov began.

'Mr. Markelov,' Marianna broke in, 'made me an offer, and I refused him. That's all I had to say to you; so – good-night. You can think of me what you choose.'

She turned swiftly away and walked with rapid steps along the corridor.

Nezhdanov went to his room, sat down at his window and pondered. 'What a strange girl! and why this wild freak, this uninvited confidence? What is it – a desire to be original, or simply affectation, or pride? Most likely pride. She can't put up with the smallest suspicion . . . She can't endure the idea that any one should judge her falsely. A strange girl!'

So mused Nezhdanov; and on the terrace below there was a conversation about him; and he heard it all very clearly.

'I know by instinct,' Kallomyetsev was asserting, 'that that's a red republican. While I was serving on special commission under the governor-general of Moscow, *avec Ladislas*, I got a quick scent for these gentlemen – the reds – and for dissenters too. I've a wonderfully keen nose, at times.' At this point Kallomyetsev described incidentally how he had once, in the environs of Moscow, caught by the heel an old dissenter, whom he had dropped in upon with the police, and who had all but jumped out of his cottage window. . . . 'And there he had been sitting as quiet as could be, till that minute, the rascal!'

Kallomyetsev forgot to add that the same old man, when shut up in prison, had refused all food, and starved himself to death.

'And your new tutor,' continued the zealous *kammerjunker*, 'is a red, not a doubt of it! Have you noticed that he never bows first?'

'And why should he bow first?' observed Madame Sipyagin; 'quite the contrary – I like that in him.'

'I am a guest in the house in which he is employed,' cried Kallomyetsev – 'yes, yes employed for money, *comme un salarié.* ... Consequently I am his superior, and he *ought* to bow first.'

'You are very exacting, Kallomyetsev,' interposed Sipyagin, with especial stress on the *y* in his name; 'all that, if you'll excuse my saying so, strikes one as rather out of date. I have purchased his services, his work, but he remains a free man.'

'He does not feel the curb,' continued Kallomyetsev, 'the curb, *le frein!* All these reds are like that. I tell you I've a wonderfully sharp nose for them! Ladislas might perhaps compare with me in that respect. If he fell into my hands, that tutor, I'd straighten him up a bit! Wouldn't I make him sit up! He'd sing a very different tune; and shouldn't he touch his hat to me! ... it would be sweet to see him!'

'Rotten drivel, little blustering idiot!' Nezhdanov was almost shouting from above. ... But at that instant the door of his room opened, and into it, to the considerable astonishment of Nezhdanov, walked Markelov.

X

NEZHDANOV ROSE FROM his place to meet him, while Markelov went straight up to him, and, without a bow or a smile, asked him, 'Was he Alexey Dmitriev Nezhdanov, student of the Petersburg University?'

'Yes ... certainly,' answered Nezhdanov.

Markelov pulled an open letter out of his side pocket. 'In that case, read this. From Vassily Nikolaevitch,' he added, dropping his voice significantly.

Nezhdanov unfolded and read the letter. It was something of the nature of a half-official circular, in which the bearer, Sergei Markelov, was recommended as one of 'us,' fully deserving of confidence; there followed, further, an exhortation concerning the urgent necessity of concerted action, and the propaganda of certain principles. The circular was addressed to Nezhdanov among others, also as being a trustworthy person.

Nezhdanov held out his hand to Markelov, asked him to sit down, and himself dropped into a chair. Markelov began, without a word, by lighting a cigarette. Nezhdanov followed his example.

'Have you had time yet to make friends with the peasants here?' Markelov asked at last.

'No; I've not had time yet.'

'You've not been here long, then?'

'I shall soon have been here a fortnight.'

'Been very busy?'

'Not very.'

Markelov coughed grimly.

'H'm! The peasants here are rather a wretched lot,' he resumed; 'an ignorant lot. They want teaching. There's great poverty, but no one to explain to them what their poverty comes from.'

'Those who were your brother-in-law's serfs, as far as I can judge, aren't poor,' remarked Nezhdanov.

'My brother-in-law's a humbug; he knows how to hoodwink people. The peasants about here are no good, certainly; but he has a factory. That's where one must make an effort. One need only stick the spade in there and the whole ant-heap will be on the move directly. Have you any books with you?'

'Yes . . . but not many.'

'I'll let you have some. But how is it you haven't?'

Nezhdanov made no answer. Markelov, too, was silent, and only blew the smoke out of his nostrils.

'What a beast that Kallomyetsev is, though!' he observed suddenly. 'At dinner I was thinking of getting up, going up to that worthy, and pounding that impudent face of his to atoms, for an example to others. But no! There's business of more importance just now than slaying *kammerjunkers*. Now's not the time to lose one's temper with fools for saying stupid things; it's time to prevent them doing stupid things.'

Nezhdanov nodded his head in confirmation, while Markelov again puffed away at his cigarette.

'Here, among all the servants, there's one sensible fellow,' he began again; 'not your servant Ivan . . . he's a dull fish, but another one . . . his name's Kirill, he waits at the sideboard' – (this Kirill had the character of being a sad drunkard) – 'you notice him. A drunken brute . . . but we can't afford to be squeamish, you know. And what have you to say of my sister?' he added suddenly, raising his head and fixing his yellow eyes on Nezhdanov. 'She's even more of a humbug than my brother-in-law. What do you think of her?'

'I think she's a very agreeable and amiable lady . . . and, moreover, she's very beautiful.'

'H'm! With what delicate precision you gentlemen from Petersburg express yourselves! . . . I can only admire it! Well . . . and as regards . . .' he began, but suddenly he scowled, his face darkened, and he did not complete his sentence. 'I see we must talk things over thoroughly,' he began again. 'We can't do it here. Who the devil can tell? They're listening at the door, I daresay. Do you know what I would suggest? To-day's Saturday; to-morrow, I suppose, you won't give my nephew any lessons? Will you?'

'I have a rehearsal of the week's work with him at three to-morrow.'

'A rehearsal! As if you were on the stage! It must be my sister who invents those expressions. Well, it's all the same. Would you care to come to me at once? My place is only eight miles from here. I have good horses: they fly like the wind – you shall stay the night, and spend the morning – and I'll bring you back to-morrow by three o'clock. Do you agree?'

'By all means,' said Nezhdanov. Ever since Markelov's entrance he had been in a state of excitement and embarrassment.

His sudden intimacy with him confused him; at the same time he felt drawn to him. He felt, he realised, that there was before him a person, dull, very likely, but unmistakably honest and strong. And then that strange meeting in the copse, Marianna's unexpected explanation. . . .

'Well, that's capital!' cried Markelov. 'You get ready meanwhile, and I'll go and order the coach to be put to. You needn't ask any questions of the heads of the house here, I hope?'

'I will mention it to them. I imagine I couldn't absent myself without.'

'I'll tell them,' said Markelov. 'Don't you be uneasy. They'll be frowning over their cards now; they won't notice your absence. My brother-in-law aims at becoming a political personage, but all he has to back him is that he plays cards splendidly. After all, though, men have made their fortunes that way! . . . So you get ready. I will make arrangements at once.'

Markelov went away; and an hour later Nezhdanov was sitting beside him on a broad leather cushion, in a wide, roomy, very old, and very comfortable coach; the squat little coachman on the box-seat whistled incessantly a wonderfully sweet bird's note; the three piebald horses, with black plaited manes and tails, galloped swiftly along the even road; and, already swathed in the first shadows of night (it struck ten just as they started), trees, bushes, fields, plains, and ravines, advancing and retreating again, glided smoothly by.

Markelov's small property (it consisted of about four hundred and fifty acres, and yielded about seven hundred roubles of revenue – it was called Borzyonkovo) was two miles from the provincial town, while Sipyagin's property was six miles from it. To reach Borzyonkovo they had to drive through the town. The new friends had not had time to exchange half a hundred words before they caught glimpses of the wretched little artisans' huts in the outskirts, with tumble-down, wooden roofs, with dim patches of light in the warped windows, and then under their wheels they heard the scrunch of the stone pavements of the town; the coach rocked, swaying from side to side, and, shaken at every jolt, they were carried past the dull stone houses of merchants, with two storeys and façades, churches with columns, taverns. . . . It was Saturday night; there were no people in the streets, but the taverns were still crowded. Hoarse voices broke from them, drunken songs, and the nasal notes of the concertina; from doors suddenly opened streamed the filthy, warm, acrid smell of alcohol, the red glare of lights. Before almost every tavern were standing little peasant carts, harnessed to shaggy, pot-bellied nags; they stood with their unkempt heads hanging down submissively, and seemed asleep; a ragged, unbelted peasant in a big winter cap, which hung in a bag over his neck, would come out of a tavern, and, his breast propped against the shafts, stay motionless, feebly fumbling and moving his hands as though looking for something; or a wasted factory hand, his cap awry, and his cotton shirt flying open, would take a few irresolute steps, barefoot – his boots having remained in the tavern – stop short, scratch his spine, and, with a sudden groan, go back again.

'The Russian's a slave to drink!' observed Markelov gloomily.

'It's sorrow drives him to it, Sergei Mihalovitch!' pronounced the coachman without turning round. Before each tavern he ceased whistling, and seemed to sink into deep thought.

'Get on! get on!' responded Markelov, with a savage tug at his own coat collar. The coach crossed a wide market-place, positively stinking of rush-mats and cabbage, passed the governor's house with striped sentry-boxes at the gates, a private house with a turret, a promenade set with trees, recently planted and already dying, a bazaar, filled with the barking of dogs and the clanking of chains, and, gradually reaching the boundaries of the town, and overtaking a long, long train of wagons, which had set off so late for the sake of the cool of the night, again emerged into the fresh air of the open country, on to the highroad planted with willows, and again moved on more smoothly and swiftly.

Markelov – a few words must be said about him – was six years older than his sister, Madame Sipyagin. He had been educated in an artillery school, which he left as an ensign; but just after attaining the rank of a lieutenant he had to retire, through a misunderstanding with the commander – a German. From that time forth he hated Germans, particularly Russian Germans. His resignation embroiled him with his father, whom he scarcely saw again till the day of his death; he inherited the little property from him, and settled in it. In Petersburg he had associated frequently with various intellectual and advanced people, whom he had positively adored; they completely formed his way of thinking. Markelov had read little – and chiefly books relating to the cause – Herzen in especial. He had retained his military habits; he lived like a Spartan and a monk. A few years before he had fallen passionately in love with a girl; but she had jilted him in the most unceremonious fashion, and had married an adjutant – also a German. Markelov began hating adjutants too. He used to try to write articles on the defects of our artillery, but he had not the slightest faculty of exposition; not a single article could he ever work out to the end, and yet he continued to cover large sheets of grey paper with his sprawling, illegible, childish handwriting. Markelov was a man, obstinate and dauntless to desperation, who could neither forgive nor forget, for ever resenting his own wrongs and the wrongs of all the oppressed, and ready for anything. His limited intellect went for one point only; what he did not understand, for him did not exist; but he scorned and hated treachery and falseness. With people of the higher class, with the 'reacs,' as he expressed it, he was short, and even rude; with the poor he was simple; with a peasant as friendly as with a brother. He managed his estate fairly well; his head was in a whirl of socialistic plans, which he could no more carry out than he could finish his articles on the defects of the artillery.

As a rule, he did not succeed – at any time, or in anything; in the regiment he had been nicknamed 'the unsuccessful.' Sincere, upright, a passionate and unhappy nature, he was capable at any moment of appearing merciless, bloodthirsty, of deserving to be called a monster, and was equally capable of sacrificing himself, without hesitation and without return.

The coach, at the second mile from the town, suddenly plunged into the soft gloom of an aspen wood, with the whisper and rustle of unseen leaves, with the fresh, keen forest fragrance, with vague patches of light overhead and tangled shadows below. The moon had already risen on the horizon, red and broad, like a copper shield. Darting out from under the trees, the coach faced a small manor-house. Three lighted-up windows stood out like shining squares on the face of the low-pitched house, which hid the moon's disc. The gates stood wide open and seemed as though they were never shut. In the courtyard in the half-dark could be seen a high trap with two white, hired horses fastened on behind. Two puppies, also white, ran out from somewhere and gave vent to piercing but not savage barks. People were moving about in the house. The coach rolled up to the steps, and with some difficulty getting out, and feeling with his foot for the iron carriage-step, put, as is usually the case, by the local blacksmith in the most inconvenient position, Markelov said to Nezhdanov: 'Here we are at home; and you will find guests here whom you know very well but don't at all expect to meet. Please come in.'

XI

THESE GUESTS TURNED out to be our old friends, Ostrodumov and Mashurina. They were both sitting in the small and very poorly furnished drawing-room of Markelov's house, drinking beer and smoking by the light of a kerosene lamp. They were not surprised at Nezhdanov's arrival; they knew

Markelov intended to bring him with him; but Nezhdanov was much surprised at seeing them. When he came in, Ostrodumov observed, 'How are you, brother?' and that was all. Mashurina first turned crimson all over, then held out her hand. Markelov explained to Nezhdanov that Ostrodumov and Mashurina had been sent down 'on the cause,' which was bound shortly now to take practical shape; that they had come from Petersburg a week ago; that Ostrodumov was remaining in S——— province for propaganda purposes, while Mashurina was going to K——— to see a certain person there.

Markelov suddenly grew hot, though no one had contradicted him. He gnawed his moustache, and with flashing eyes began to speak in a hoarse, agitated, but distinct voice of hideous acts of injustice that had been committed, of the necessity for immediate action, maintaining that practically everything was ready, and none but cowards could procrastinate; that some violence was as essential as the lancet's prick to the abscess, however ready to break the abscess might be! He repeated this simile of the lancet several times; it obviously pleased him; he had not invented it, but had read it in some book. It seemed that, having lost all hope of Marianna's reciprocating his feelings, he felt he had nothing now to lose, and only thought how to set to work as soon as might be 'for the cause.' His words came like the blows of an axe, with absolute directness, sharply, simply, and vindictively; monotonous and weighty, they fell one after another from his blanched lips, recalling the sharp, abrupt bark of a grim old watchdog. He said he knew the peasants of the neighbourhood and the factory hands well, and that there were capable people among them – Eremey of Goloplyok, for instance – who would be ready for anything you like any minute. The name of Eremey from the village of Goloplyok was constantly on his tongue. At every tenth word he struck the table with his right hand, not with the palm, but with the edge of his hand, while he thrust his left into the air, with the first finger held apart from the rest;

and those hairy, sinewy hands, that finger, the droning voice, and the blazing eyes, produced a powerful impression. On the road Markelov had said little to Nezhdanov; his anger had been rising . . . but now it broke out. Mashurina and Ostrodumov applauded him with a smile, a glance, sometimes a brief exclamation, but in Nezhdanov something strange was taking place. First he tried to reply; he referred to the harm done by haste, by premature, ill-considered action; above all, he was surprised to find it all so decided, that no doubt was felt, and no consciousness of the necessity of examining into the circumstances of the place, nor even of trying to find out precisely what the people wanted. . . . But afterwards his nerves were wrought upon and quivering like harp-strings, and in a sort of desperation, almost with tears of rage in his eyes, his voice breaking into a scream, he began speaking in the same spirit as Markelov, going further even than he had done. What impulse was working in him it would be hard to say. Was it remorse for having been, as it were, lukewarm of late? was it vexation with himself or with others, or the longing to stifle some worm gnawing within? or indeed was it a desire to show off before the comrades he was meeting again? . . . or had Markelov's words really influenced him – fired his blood? Till the very dawn the conversation continued; Ostrodumov and Mashurina did not stir from their seat, while Markelov and Nezhdanov did not sit down. Markelov stood on the same spot, for all the world like a sentinel, while Nezhdanov kept walking up and down the room with unequal steps, now slowly, now hurriedly. They talked of the measures and means to be employed, of the part each ought to take on himself; they examined and tied up in parcels various tracts and leaflets; they referred to a merchant, a dissenter, one Golushkin, a very trustworthy though uneducated man; to the young propagandist, Kislyakov, who was, they said, very able, though over hasty, and had too high an opinion of his own talents; the name of Solomin, too, was mentioned. . . .

'Is that the man who manages a cotton factory?' inquired Nezhdanov, remembering what had been said of him at the Sipyagins' table.

'Yes, that is he,' answered Markelov; 'you must get to know him. We have not tested him thoroughly yet, but he's a capable, very capable, fellow.'

Eremey of Goloplyok again figured in the conversation; to him were added the Sipyagins' Kirill and a certain Mendeley, also nicknamed the Sulker; only it was difficult to reckon on the Sulker – he was bold as a lion when sober, but a coward when he was drunk, and he almost always was drunk.

'And your own people, now,' Nezhdanov inquired of Markelov, 'are there any you can rely on?'

Markelov replied that there were some. He did not mention one of them by name, however, but went off into a discourse upon the artisans of the towns and the seminarists, who would be the more useful from their great bodily strength, and, if only it came to fighting with fists, would do great things! Nezhdanov made inquiries about the nobility. Markelov answered that there were five or six young noblemen; one of them, to be sure, was a German, and he the most radical of the lot, but, of course, there was no reckoning on a German . . . he might turn sulky or betray them any moment. But there, they must wait to see what news Kislyakov would send them. Nezhdanov inquired too about the army. At that Markelov hesitated, tugged at his long whiskers, and explained at last that there was nothing, so far, decisive. . . . Perhaps Kislyakov would have something to disclose.

'And who is this Kislyakov?' cried Nezhdanov impatiently.

Markelov smiled significantly, and said that he was a man . . . such a man. . . .

'I know him very little, though,' he added; 'I have only seen him twice altogether. But the letters that man writes! – such letters!! I will show you them. . . . You will be astonished. Such fire! And his activity! Five or six times he has raced right across

Russia and back ... and from every station a letter of ten – twelve pages!'

Nezhdanov looked inquiringly at Ostrodumov, but he sat like a statue, not an eyebrow twitching, while Mashurina's lips were compressed in a bitter smile, but she, too, was dumb as a fish. Nezhdanov tried to question Markelov about his reforms in a socialistic direction on his estate ... but at this Ostrodumov interposed.

'What's the good of discussing that now?' he observed. 'It makes no difference; everything must be transformed afterwards.'

The conversation turned again into a political channel. Nezhdanov was still devoured by a secret worm gnawing within; but the keener the inward torture, the more loudly and positively he spoke. He had drunk only one glass of beer, but from time to time it struck him that he was completely drunk; his head was in a whirl, and his heart throbbed painfully. When at last, at four o'clock in the morning, the discussion ceased, and, stepping over a little page asleep in the anteroom, they separated and went to their respective rooms, Nezhdanov, before he lay down, stood a long time motionless, his eyes fixed on the floor before him. He mused upon the continual, heart-rending note of bitterness in all Markelov had uttered. The man's pride could not but be wounded; he was bound to be suffering, his hopes of personal happiness were shattered, and yet how he forgot himself – how utterly he gave himself up to what he held for the truth! 'A limited nature,' was Nezhdanov's thought. ... 'But isn't it a hundred times better to be such a limited nature than such ... such as I, for instance, feel myself to be?'

But at once he struggled against his own self-depreciation.

'Why so? Am not I, too, capable of sacrificing myself? Wait a bit, my friends. ... And you, Paklin, shall be convinced in time that though I am an æsthetic, though I do write verses ...'

He pushed his hair back angrily, ground his teeth, and, hurriedly pulling off his clothes, flung himself into the damp, chill bed.

'Sleep well!' Mashurina's voice called through the door. 'I am next door to you.'

'Good-night,' answered Nezhdanov, and then it came into his mind that she had not taken her eyes off him all the evening.

'What does she want?' he muttered, and at once felt ashamed of himself. 'Ah, to sleep as soon as maybe!'

But it was hard to master his overwrought nerves . . . and the sun stood high in the sky when at last he fell into a heavy, comfortles sleep.

The next morning he got up late with a headache. He dressed, went to the window of his attic room, and saw that Markelov had practically no farm at all. His little box of a house stood on a ravine not far from a wood. A little granary, a stable, a cellar, a little hut with a half tumble-down thatch-roof, on one side; on the other, a diminutive lake, a patch of kitchen-garden, a hemp-field, another little hut with a similar roof; in the distance an outhouse, a barn, and an empty threshing-floor – this was all the wealth that could be seen. It all seemed poor, decaying, and not exactly neglected or run wild, but as though it had never thrived, like a tree that has not taken root well. Nezhdanov went downstairs. Mashurina was sitting behind the tea-urn in the dining-room, evidently waiting for him. He learned from her that Ostrodumov had gone off, on the cause, and would not be back for a fortnight; and Markelov had gone to see after his labourers. As May was drawing to a close and there was no pressing work to be done, Markelov had a plan for felling a small birch copse without outside help, and had set off there early in the morning.

Nezhdanov felt a strange weariness at heart. So much had been said overnight of the impossibility of delaying longer, it had so often been repeated that the only thing left to do was 'to act.' But how act? in what direction, and how without delay?

It was useless to question Mashurina; she knew no hesitation, she had no doubts as to what she had to do; it was to go to K———. Beyond that she did not look. Nezhdanov did not know what to say to her; and after drinking some tea, he put on his cap and went off in the direction of the birch copse. On the way he fell in with some peasants carting manure, formerly serfs of Markelov's. He began to talk to them . . . but did not get much out of them. They too seemed weary, but with an ordinary physical weariness, not at all like the feeling he was experiencing. Their former master, according to them, was a good-natured, simple gentleman, but queerish; they predicted his ruin, because 'he didn't understand how things should be done, and wanted to do things his own way, not as his fathers did before. And he's too wise, too – you can't make him out, do what you will; but a good-hearted gentleman, if ever there was one.' Nezhdanov went on further and came upon Markelov himself.

He was walking surrounded by a whole crowd of workmen; from a distance it could be seen that he was talking and explaining something to them; then he gave a despairing wave of the hand, as though he gave it up! Beside him was his bailiff, a dull-eyed young man, with no trace of authority in his bearing. This bailiff continually repeated, 'That shall be as you please, sir,' to the intense annoyance of his master, who looked for more independence from him. Nezhdanov went up to Markelov, and on his face he saw traces of the same spiritual weariness he was feeling himself. They exchanged greetings; Markelov began speaking at once, briefly though, of the questions discussed overnight, of the impending revolution; but the expression of weariness did not leave his face. He was all over dust and perspiration; shavings of wood, green strands of moss were clinging to his clothes; his voice was hoarse. . . . The men standing round him were silent; they were half scared, half amused. . . . Nezhdanov looked at Markelov, and Ostrodumov's words re-echoed again in his head: 'What's the good?

It makes no difference; it will all have to be transformed afterwards!' One labourer who had been in fault somehow began entreating Markelov to let him off the fine for his mistake. . . . Markelov at first flew into a rage, and shouted furiously at him, but afterwards he forgave him. . . . 'It makes no difference . . . it will all have to be changed later on. . . .' Nezhdanov asked him for horses and a conveyance to return home; Markelov seemed surprised at his wish, but answered that everything should be ready directly.

He went back to the house with Nezhdanov. . . . He was staggering as he walked, from exhaustion.

'What's the matter with you?' asked Nezhdanov.

'I am worn out!' said Markelov savagely. 'However you talk to these people, they can't understand anything, and they won't carry out instructions. . . . They positively don't understand Russian. The word "part" they know well enough . . . but "participation." . . . What is participation? They can't understand. And yet it's a Russian word, too, damn it! They imagine I want to make them a present of part of the land!' Markelov had conceived the idea of explaining to the peasants the principles of co-operation, and introducing it on his estate, but they resisted. One of them had gone so far as to say in this connection, 'There was a pit deep enough before, but now there's no seeing the bottom of it' . . . while the other peasants had with one accord given vent to a profound sigh which had crushed Markelov utterly.

On reaching the house he dismissed his attendant retinue, and began to see about the carriage and horses, and about lunch. His household consisted only of a little page, a cook, a coachman, and a very aged man with hairy ears, in a long-skirted cotton coat, who had been his grandfather's valet. This old man was for ever gazing with profound dejection at his master; he did nothing, however, and was scarcely perhaps fit to do anything; but he was always there, crouched up on the doorsill.

After a lunch of hard-boiled eggs, anchovies, and cold hash – the page handed the mustard in an old pomatum pot and vinegar in an eau-de-cologne bottle – Nezhdanov took his seat in the same coach in which he had come overnight; but instead of three horses they only harnessed two; the third had been shod and lamed. During lunch Markelov had said little, eaten nothing, and had drawn his breath painfully.... He had uttered two or three bitter words about his property, and again waved his hand as though to say ... 'It makes no difference, it will all have to be changed afterwards.' Mashurina asked Nezhdanov to take her as far as the town; she wanted to go there to do some shopping. 'I can walk back, or else get a lift in some peasant's cart.' Markelov escorted them both to the steps, and said vaguely that he should shortly come for Nezhdanov again; and then ... then – (he shook himself and plucked up his spirits again) – they must come to a definite arrangement; that Solomin should come too; that he, Markelov, was only waiting for news from Vassily Nikolaevitch, and then it only remained to 'act' promptly – since the peasants (the same peasants who did not understand the word 'participation') would not consent to wait longer!

'Oh, you were going to show me the letters of that – what's his name – Kislyakov?' said Nezhdanov.

'Later ...' Markelov replied hurriedly.... 'Then we will do everything – altogether.'

The carriage started.

'Be in readiness!' Markelov's voice was heard for the last time. He was standing on the steps, and beside him, with the same unchanged dejection on his face, straightening his bent back, clasping his hands behind him, diffusing an odour of ryebread and cotton fustian, and hearing nothing, stood the model servant, the decrepit old valet.

All the way to the town Mashurina was silent; she only smoked a cigarette. As they drew near the barrier she suddenly gave a loud sigh.

'I'm sorry for Sergei Mihalovitch,' she observed, and her face darkened.

'He's quite knocked up with worry,' remarked Nezhdanov; 'I think his land's in a poor way.'

'That's not why I'm sorry for him.'

'Why, then?'

'He's an unhappy man, unlucky! Where could one find a better fellow? But no – no one wants him anywhere.'

Nezhdanov looked at his companion.

'Do you know something about him, then?'

'I know nothing . . . but one sees it for oneself. Good-bye, Alexey Dmitritch.'

Mashurina got out of the coach, and an hour later Nezhdanov was driving into the courtyard of the Sipyagins' house. He did not feel very well. . . . He had spent a night without sleep . . . and then all the discussions . . . the talk. . . .

A beautiful face peeped out of a window and smiled graciously to him. . . . It was Madame Sipyagin welcoming him on his return.

'What eyes she has!' was his thought.

XII

A GREAT MANY people had come to dinner, and after dinner Nezhdanov profited by the general bustle to slip away to his own room. He wanted to be by himself if only to review the impressions he carried away from his expedition. At table Valentina Mihalovna had looked at him several times attentively, but apparently had not got a chance of speaking to him; Marianna, since that unexpected avowal which had so astounded him, seemed ashamed of herself and avoided him. Nezhdanov took up a pen; he felt a desire to converse on paper with his friend Silin; but he could not think what to say even to his friend; or perhaps, so many contradictory thoughts and sensations were clashing together in his head that he did not attempt to disentangle them, and put it all off to another day. Among the party at dinner had been Mr. Kallomyetsev too; never had he shown more arrogance and gentlemanly superciliousness; but his free and easy remarks had had no effect on Nezhdanov: he did not notice them. He seemed shut in by a sort of cloud; it stood like a veil of half-darkness between him and the rest of the world – and, strange to say, across this veil he could discern only three faces, and all three women's faces, and all three had their eyes persistently fastened upon him. They were: Madame Sipyagin, Mashurina, and Marianna. What did it mean? And why precisely these three? What had they in common? And what did they want with him?

He went early to bed, but could not get to sleep. He was haunted by thoughts, gloomy, though not exactly painful . . . thoughts of the inevitable end, of death. They were familiar thoughts. For long he was turning them this way and that, at one time shuddering at the probability of annihilation, then welcoming it, almost rejoicing in it. He felt at last the peculiar excitement he knew so well. . . . He got up, sat down to his writing-table, and, after thinking a little, almost without correction, wrote the following verses in his secret book:

> 'My dear one, when I come
> To die – this is my will:
> Heap up and burn my writings all,
> That they may die in the same hour!
> With flowers then deck me all about
> And let the sun shine in my room;
> Musicians place about my doors,
> And let them play no mournful dirge!
> But as in hours of revelry,
> Let the gay fiddles shrilly twang
> A rollicking, seductive waltz!
> Then, as upon my dying ear

> That reckless music dies away,
> I too would die, dropping asleep,
> And mar not with a useless moan
> The peace that comes with coming death.
> I'd pass away to other worlds,
> Rocked to my sleep by the light strains
> Of the light pleasures of our earth!'

When he wrote the words 'my dear one,' he was thinking of Silin. He declaimed his verses in an undertone to himself, and was surprised at what had come from his pen. This scepticism, this indifference, this light-minded lack of faith, how did it all agree with his principles? with what he had said at Markelov's? He flung the book in the table drawer, and went back to his bed. But he only fell asleep at dawn when the first larks were trilling in the paling sky.

The next day he had just finished his lesson, and was sitting in the billiard-room. Madame Sipyagin came in, looked round, and, going up to him with a smile, asked him to come to her room. She was wearing a light barege dress, very simple, and very charming; the sleeves ended in a frill at the elbow; a wide ribbon clasped her waist, her hair fell in thick curls on her neck. Everything about her seemed overflowing with kindness and sympathetic tenderness, a restrained, emboldening tenderness – everything: the subdued brilliance of her half-closed eyes, the soft languor of her voice, her gestures, her very gait. Madame Sipyagin conducted Nezhdanov to her boudoir, a bright, charming room, filled with the scent of flowers and perfumes, the pure freshness of a woman's garments, a woman's constant presence; she made him sit down in an easy-chair, seated herself near him, and began to question him about his journey, about Markelov's doings, with such tact, such gentleness, such sweetness! She showed sincere interest in her brother, whom, till then, she had not once mentioned in Nezhdanov's hearing; from some of her words it could be gathered that the feeling

Marianna had inspired in him had not escaped her; her tone was slightly mournful ... whether because his feeling was not reciprocated by Marianna, or because her brother's choice had fallen on a girl he really knew nothing of, was left undefined. But what was principally clear: she was obviously trying to win Nezhdanov, to arouse his confidence in her, to make him cease to be shy. Valentina Mihalovna went so far as to reproach him a little for having a false idea of her.

Nezhdanov listened to her, looked at her arms and her shoulders, at times glanced at her rosy lips, the faintly waving coils of her hair. At first his answers were very short; he felt a slight tightening in his throat and his chest ... but gradually this sensation was replaced by another, disturbing enough too, but not devoid of a certain sweetness: he had never expected such a distinguished and beautiful lady, such an aristocrat, would be capable of taking an interest in him, a mere student; and she was not simply taking an interest in him, she seemed to be flirting a little with him. Nezhdanov asked himself why she was doing all this? and he found no answer; nor, indeed, was he very anxious to find one. Madame Sipyagin talked of Kolya; she even began by assuring Nezhdanov that it was simply with the object of talking seriously about her son, to learn his views on the education of Russian children in general, that she wished to get to know him better. The suddenness with which this wish had sprung up might have struck any one as curious. But the root of the matter did not lie in what Valentina Mihalovna had just said, but in the fact that she had been overtaken by something like a wave of sensuality; a craving to conquer, to bring to her feet this stubborn creature, had asserted itself. ...

But at this point we must go back a little. Valentina Mihalovna was the daughter of a very stupid and unenergetic general, with only one star and a buckle to show for fifty years' service, and a very shy and intriguing Little Russian, endowed, like many of her countrywomen, with an exceedingly simple, and even foolish, exterior, from which she knew how to extract the maximum of advantage. Valentina Mihalovna's parents were not well-to-do people; she got into the Smolny Convent, however, and there, though she was regarded as a republican, she stood high in favour because she studied industriously, and behaved sedately. On leaving the Smolny Convent, she lived with her mother (her brother had gone into the country, her father, the general with the star and the buckle, was dead) in a clean, but very chilly flat; when people talked in their rooms, the breath could be seen coming in steam from their mouths; Valentina Mihalovna used to laugh and declare it was 'like being in church.' She was plucky in bearing all the discomforts of a poor, cramped style of living: she had a wonderfully good temper. With her mother's aid, she succeeded in keeping up and forming acquaintances and connections: every one talked about her, even in the highest circles, as a very charming, very cultivated girl, of the very best breeding. Valentina Mihalovna had several suitors; she had picked out Sipyagin from all the rest, and had very simply, rapidly, and adroitly made him in love with her. . . . Though, indeed, he soon recognised himself that a better wife for him could not have been found. She was clever, not ill-natured . . . rather good-natured of the two, fundamentally cold and indifferent . . . and she could not tolerate the thought of any one remaining indifferent to her. Valentina Mihalovna was full of that special charm which is peculiar to attractive egoists; in that charm there is no poetry nor true sensibility, but there is softness, there is sympathy, there is even tenderness. Only, these charming egoists must not be thwarted: they are fond of power, and will not tolerate independence in others. Women like Sipyagina excite and work upon inexperienced and passionate natures; for themselves they like regularity and a peaceful life. Virtue comes easy to them, they are inwardly unmoved, but the constant desire to sway, to attract, and to please, lends them mobility and brilliance: their will is strong, and their very fascination often depends on this strength of will. Hard it is for a man to hold his ground when for an instant gleams of secret softness pass unconsciously, as it seems, over a bright, pure creature like this; he waits, expecting that the time is come, and now the ice will melt; but the clear ice only reflects the play of the light, it does not melt, and never will he see its brightness troubled!

Flirtation cost Sipyagina little; she was well aware that there was no danger for her, and never could be. And meantime, to make another's eyes grow dim and then sparkle again, to set another's cheeks flushing with desire and dread, another's voice quivering and breaking, to trouble another soul – oh, how sweet that was to her soul! How pleasant it was late at night, as she lay down to untroubled slumbers in her pure, fresh nest, to recall those restless words and looks and sighs! With what a happy smile she retired into herself, into the consciousness of her inaccessibility, her impregnable virtue, and with what gracious condescension she submitted to the lawful embraces of her well-bred spouse! Such reflections were so soothing that she was often positively touched and ready to do some deed of mercy, to succour a fellow-creature. . . . Once she had founded a tiny alms-house after a secretary of legation, madly in love with her, had tried to cut his throat! She had prayed most sincerely for him, though the sentiment of religion had been feeble in her from her earliest years.

And so she talked to Nezhdanov, and tried in every way to bring him to her feet. She admitted him to her confidence, she, as it were, revealed herself to him, and with sweet curiosity, with half-maternal tenderness, watched this very nice-looking, interesting, and severe young radical slowly and awkwardly beginning to respond to her. In a day, an hour, a minute – all this would disappear, leaving no trace; but meanwhile she found it pleasant, rather amusing, rather pathetic, and even rather touching. Forgetting his origin, and knowing how such interest is appreciated by people who are lonely and among strangers, Valentina Mihalovna began questioning Nezhdanov about his youth, his family. . . . But guessing instantly by his confused and short replies that she had made a blunder, Valentina Mihalovna tried to smooth over her mistake, and opened her heart even more ingenuously to him. ... As in the languid heat of noonday a full-blown rose opens its fragrant petals, which are soon folded up close again by the bracing coolness of night.

She did not succeed, however, in fully effacing her mistake. Nezhdanov, touched on a sore spot, could not feel confiding as before. The bitter feeling he had always with him, always rankling at the bottom of his heart, was astir again; his democratic suspicion and self-reproach were awakened. 'This wasn't what I came here for,' he thought; Paklin's sarcastic advice recurred to him ... and he took advantage of the first instant of silence to get up, make a curt bow, and go out 'looking very foolish,' as he could not help whispering to himself.

His embarrassment did not escape Valentina Mihalovna ... but to judge from the little smile with which she watched him go out, she interpreted this embarrassment in a manner flattering to herself.

In the billiard-room Nezhdanov came upon Marianna. She was standing with her back to the window, not far from the door of the boudoir, her hands clasped tightly. Her face happened to be in almost black shadow; but her fearless eyes were looking so inquiringly, so fixedly at Nezhdanov, such scorn, such insulting pity were visible on her tightly closed lips, that he stood still in perplexity....

'You have something to say to me?' he said involuntarily.

Marianna did not at once answer. 'No ... or rather yes; I have. But not now.'

'When, then?'

'Wait a little. Perhaps – to-morrow; perhaps – never. You see, I know very little – of what you are really like.'

'Still,' began Nezhdanov, 'it has sometimes struck me ... that we have—'

'And you don't know me at all,' Marianna interrupted. 'But

there, wait a little. To-morrow, perhaps. Now I have to go to my . . . mistress. Good-bye till to-morrow.'

Nezhdanov took two steps forward, but suddenly turned back. 'Oh, by the way, Marianna Vikentyevna . . . I have been continually meaning to ask you: won't you let me go to the school with you – to see what you do there – before it's shut?'

'Certainly. . . . But it's not of the school that I wanted to talk to you.'

'What, then?'

'To-morrow,' repeated Marianna.

But she did not put it off till the next day; a conversation between her and Nezhdanov took place the same evening in one of the avenues of limes, not far from the terrace.

XIII

SHE WENT UP to him first.

'Mr. Nezhdanov,' she began in a hurried voice, 'you are, I fancy, completely fascinated by Valentina Mihalovna?'

She turned without waiting for an answer, and walked along the avenue; and he walked beside her.

'What makes you think that?' he asked after a brief pause.

'Isn't it so? If not, she has played her cards badly to-day. I can fancy how carefully she has been at work, how she has laid her little nets.'

Nezhdanov uttered not a word; he only stared from one side at his strange companion.

'Listen,' she continued; 'I'm not going to pretend; I don't like Valentina Mihalovna – and you know that well enough. I may strike you as unjust . . . but you should first consider . . .'

Marianna's voice broke. She was flushed and moved. . . . Emotion with her almost always took the form of seeming angry. 'You are probably asking yourself,' she began again, 'why is this young lady telling me all this? You must have thought the same, I suppose, when I told you something . . . about Mr. Markelov?'

She suddenly stooped down, picked a small mushroom, broke it in half and flung it away.

'You are wrong, Marianna Vikentyevna,' observed Nezhdanov; 'on the contrary, I thought I had inspired you with confidence – and that idea was a very pleasant one.'

Nezhdanov was not telling quite the truth; this idea had only just entered his head.

Marianna glanced at him instantly. Up till then she had looked away persistently.

'It's not so much that you inspire confidence,' she said as though reflecting; 'you are completely a stranger, you see. But your position – and mine – are very much alike. We are both alike unhappy; that's a bond between us.'

'Are you unhappy?' inquired Nezhdanov.

'And you – aren't you?' answered Marianna.

He said nothing.

'Do you know my story?' she began quickly; 'the story of my father? his exile? – no? well, then, let me tell you that he was brought up, tried, found guilty, deprived of his rank . . . and everything – and sent to Siberia. Then he died . . . my mother died too. My uncle, Mr. Sipyagin, my mother's brother, took care of me; I live at his expense; he's my benefactor and Valentina Mihalovna's my benefactress – and I repay them with the blackest ingratitude, because, I suppose, I have a hard heart – and the bread of charity is bitter – and I'm not good at bearing insulting condescension – and I can't put up with patronage . . . and I'm not good at hiding things; and when I'm for ever being hurt with little pin pricks, I only keep from crying out because I'm too proud.'

As she uttered these disconnected sentences, Marianna walked more and more rapidly. All at once she stood still.

'Do you know that my aunt – simply to get me off her hands – means to marry me . . . to that loathsome Kallomyetsev? Of course she knows my ideas – why, in her eyes, I'm a Nihilist! – while he, I'm not attractive to him, of course – I'm not pretty, you see; but I might be sold. That would be another act of charity, you know.'

'Why then didn't you . . .' Nezhdanov began, and he hesitated.

Marianna glanced at him for a moment. 'Why didn't I accept Mr. Markelov's offer, do you mean? Isn't that it? Well, but what could I do? He's a good man. But it's not my fault; I don't love him.'

Marianna again walked on in front as though she wished to save her companion from any obligation to reply to this unexpected confession.

They both reached the end of the avenue. Marianna turned quickly into a narrow path that ran through the densely planted firs, and walked along it. Nezhdanov followed Marianna. He was conscious of a twofold perplexity; it was amazing that this shy girl could suddenly be so open with him, and he wondered still more that her openness did not strike him as strange, that he felt it natural.

Marianna turned round suddenly and stood still in the middle of the path, so that it came to pass that her face was about a yard from Nezhdanov's and her eyes were fixed straight upon his.

'Alexey Dmitritch,' she said, 'don't suppose my aunt is ill-natured. . . . No! she is all deceit, she's an actress, she poses, she wants every one to adore her as a beauty, and to worship her as a saint! She makes a sympathetic phrase, says it to one person, and then repeats the phrase to a second and a third, and always with the same air of only just having thought of it, and that's just when she uses her wonderful eyes! She understands herself very well; she knows she's like a Madonna, and she cares for no one! She pretends she's always worrying over Kolya, but all she does is to talk about him with intellectual people. She wishes no harm to any one. . . . She's all benevolence! But they may break every bone in your body in her presence . . . it's nothing to her! She wouldn't stir a finger to save you; while if it were necessary or useful to her . . . then . . . oh, then!'

Marianna ceased; her wrath was choking her. She resolved to give it vent – she could not restrain herself; but speech failed her in spite of herself. Marianna belonged to a special class of unhappy persons (in Russia one may come across them pretty often). . . . Justice satisfies but does not rejoice them, while injustice, which they are terribly keen in detecting, revolts them to the very depths of their being. While she was talking, Nezhdanov was looking at her intently; her flushed face, with her short hair slightly dishevelled, and the tremulous twitching of her thin lips, impressed him as menacing, and significant, and beautiful. The sunlight, broken up by the thick network of twigs, fell on her brow in a slanting patch of gold; and this tongue of fire seemed in keeping with the excited expression of her whole face, her wide-open, fixed, and flashing eyes, the thrilling sound of her voice.

'Tell me,' Nezhdanov asked her at last, 'why did you call me unhappy? Is it possible you know about my past?'

Marianna nodded her head.

'Yes.'

'That is . . . how did you know of it? Some one talked to you about me?'

'I know . . . your origin.'

'You know. Who told you?'

'Why, the very Valentina Mihalovna whom you're so fascinated by! She didn't fail to mention in my presence, passing over it lightly, as her way is, but plainly – not with sympathy, but as a liberal who is superior to all prejudices – that there was, to be sure, a fact of interest in the life of our new tutor! Don't be surprised, please: Valentina Mihalovna, in the same incidental way, and with commiseration, informs almost every visitor that there is, to be sure, in her niece's life a . . . fact of interest: her father was sent to Siberia for embezzlement! She may fancy herself an aristocrat – she's simply backbiting and posing, your Sistine Madonna!'

'Excuse me,' remarked Nezhdanov, 'why is she "mine"?'

Marianna turned away, and again walked along the path.

'You had such a long conversation with her,' she uttered thickly.

'I hardly said a single word,' answered Nezhdanov; 'she was talking all the while alone.'

Marianna walked on in silence; but at this point the path turned aside, the pines, as it were, made way, and a small lawn stretched before them, with a hollow weeping birch in the middle and a round seat encircling the trunk of the old tree. Marianna sat down on this seat; Nezhdanov placed himself beside her; the long hanging branches, covered with tiny green leaves, swayed above both their heads. Around them lilies-of-the-valley peeped out white in the fine grass, and from the whole clearing rose the fresh scent of the young herbage, sweetly refreshing after the oppressive resinous odour of the pines.

'You want to come with me to look at the school here,' began Marianna. 'Well, then, let us go. . . . Only . . . I don't know. It will not be much pleasure to you. You've heard – our principal teacher is the deacon. He's a good-natured man, but you can't imagine what he talks about to his pupils! There is one boy among them. . . . His name is Garasei. He's an orphan, ten years old, and fancy, he learns faster than any of them!'

In suddenly changing the subject of conversation, Marianna herself seemed transformed. She grew rather pale and quiet . . . and her face expressed confusion; as though she began to be ashamed of all she had been saying. She apparently wanted to get Nezhdanov upon a question of some sort – the schools or the peasantry – anything, if only they might not continue in the same tone as before. But at that minute he was in no humour for 'questions.'

'Marianna Vikentyevna,' he began, 'I will speak to you

openly. I did not at all anticipate all that . . . has just passed between us.' (At the word 'passed' she turned away a little.) 'I think we have suddenly become very . . . very intimate. And it was bound to be so. We have long been getting closer to one another, but we did not put it into words. And so I, too, will speak to you without reserve. You are wretched and miserable in this house, but your uncle, though he's limited, still, so far as I can judge, he's a humane man, isn't he? Won't he understand your position and stand by you?'

'My uncle? To begin with, he's not a man at all: he's an official – a senator or a minister . . . I don't know. And secondly . . . I don't want to complain and slander people for nothing. I'm not wretched at all here; that's to say, I'm not oppressed in any way; my aunt's tiny pin-pricks are really nothing to me. . . . I'm absolutely free.'

Nezhdanov looked in bewilderment at Marianna.

'In that case . . . all you told me just now . . . '

'You are at liberty to laugh at me,' she said quickly; 'but if I am unhappy – it's not for my own unhappiness. It sometimes seems to me that I suffer for all the oppressed, the poor, the wretched in Russia . . . No, I don't suffer, but I am indignant – I am in revolt for them . . . that I'm ready for them . . . to lay down my life. I am unhappy because I'm a young lady – a hanger-on, because I can do nothing – am fit for nothing! When my father was in Siberia, while I was left with mother in Moscow – ah! how I longed to go to him! not that I had any great love or respect for him – but I so much wanted to know for myself, to see with my own eyes, how convicts and how prisoners live. . . . And what disgust I felt for myself and all those easy-going, prosperous, well-fed people! . . . And afterwards, when he came back, broken down, crushed, and began humiliating himself, fretting and trying to get on . . . ah, . . . that was hard! How well he did to die . . . and mother, too! But, you see, I was left behind. . . . For what? To feel that I've a bad nature, that I'm ungrateful, that nothing is right with me, and that I can do nothing – nothing for anything or anybody!'

Marianna turned away. Her hand had slid on to the garden-seat. Nezhdanov felt very sorry for her; he stroked the hand . . . but Marianna at once pulled it away, not because Nezhdanov's action struck her as unsuitable, but that he might not – God forbid! – imagine she was asking for his sympathy.

Through the branches of the pines there was a glimpse of a woman's dress.

Marianna drew herself up. 'Look, your Madonna has sent her spy out. That maid has to keep watch on me and report to her mistress where I am and with whom. My aunt most likely supposed that I was with you, and thinks it improper, especially after the sentimental scene she has been rehearsing with you. And, indeed, it's time to go back. Come along.'

Marianna got up; Nezhdanov, too, rose from his seat. She glanced at him over her shoulder, and suddenly there passed over her face an expression almost childish, charming, a little embarrassed.

'You're not angry with me? You don't think I, too, have been showing off to you? No, you don't think that,' she went on, before Nezhdanov could answer her in any way. 'You see, you are, like me, unhappy, and your nature, too, is . . . bad, like mine. To-morrow we will go to the school together, for we are friends now, you know.'

As Marianna and Nezhdanov approached the house, Valentina Mihalovna watched them with a spy-glass from the balcony, and with her usual sweet smile she slowly shook her head; then returning through the open glass door into the drawing-room, where Sipyagin was already seated at preference with the toothless neighbour, who had dropped in for tea, she observed in a loud, drawling tone, each syllable distinct: 'How damp the night air is! it's dangerous!'

Marianna glanced at Nezhdanov, while Sipyagin, who had just taken a point from his partner, cast a truly ministerial glance, sidelong and upwards, upon his wife, and then transferred this same cool, sleepy, but penetrating look to the young couple coming in from the dark garden.

XIV

A FORTNIGHT MORE PASSED. Everything went its accustomed way. Sipyagin arranged the duties of the day, if not like a minister, at least like the director of a department, and maintained the same lofty, humane, and somewhat fastidious deportment; Kolya had his lessons; Anna Zaharovna fretted in continual, suppressed anger; visitors came, talked, skirmished at cards, and apparently were not bored; Valentina Mihalovna continued to amuse herself with Nezhdanov, though a shade of something like good-natured irony was blended with her amenities. With Marianna, Nezhdanov grew unmistakably intimate, and to his surprise found that her temper was even enough, and that he could talk to her about anything without coming into violent opposition. In her company he twice visited the school, though at his first visit he was convinced that he could do nothing there. The reverend deacon was in full possession of it with Sipyagin's consent, and, indeed, by his wish. The worthy father taught reading and writing fairly, though on an old-fashioned method; but at examinations he propounded questions decidedly ridiculous; for instance, he one day asked Garasei, 'How would he explain the expression, "the waters in the firmament"?' to which Garasei, by the instruction of the same worthy father, was to reply, 'That is inexplicable.'

Moreover, the school, such as it was, was closed soon after – for the summer months – till autumn. Remembering the exhortation of Paklin and of others, Nezhdanov tried, too, to make friends with the peasants; but soon he realised that he was simply, so far as his powers of observation enabled him, studying them, not doing propaganda work at all. He had spent almost the whole of his life in town, and between him and the country people there was a gulf over which he could not cross. Nezhdanov succeeded in exchanging a few words with the drunkard Kirill, and even with Mendeley; but, strange to say, he was, as it were, afraid of them, and, except some very brief abuse of things in general, he got nothing out of them. Another peasant, called Fityuev, nonplussed him utterly. This peasant had a face of exceptional energy, almost that of some brigand chief. . . . 'Come, he's sure to be some use,' Nezhdanov thought. . . . But Fityuev turned out to be a wretched outcast; the mir had taken his land away from him, because he – a healthy and positively powerful man – *could not* work.

'I can't!' Fityuev would sob, with deep inward groans, and with a long-drawn sigh; 'I can't work! kill me! or I shall lay hands on myself!' And he would end by begging alms – a halfpenny for a crust of bread. And a face out of a canvas of Rinaldo Rinaldini!

The factory folk, too, were no good to Nezhdanov; all these fellows were either terribly lively or terribly gloomy . . . and Nezhdanov could not get on at all with them. He wrote a long letter on this subject to his friend Silin, complaining bitterly of his own incapacity, and ascribing it to his wretched education and disgusting artistic temperament! He suddenly came to the conclusion that his vocation, in propaganda work, was with the written, not the spoken, living word; but the pamphlets he planned did not work out. Everything he tried to put on paper made on him the same impression of something false, farfetched, artificial in tone and language, and twice – oh horror! he caught himself unconsciously wandering off into verse or into a sceptical, personal effusion. He positively brought himself – an extraordinary sign of confidence and intimacy! – to speak of this to Marianna . . . and was again surprised by finding a fellow-feeling in her, of course not with his literary bent, but with the moral malady which he was suffering from, and with which she, too, was familiar. Marianna was quite as much up in arms against all things artistic as he was; yet the reason she had not loved and married Markelov was in reality just that there was not a trace of the artistic nature in him! Marianna, of course, had not the courage to recognise this even to herself; but we know that it is what remains a half-suspected secret for ourselves that is strongest in us.

So the days went by slowly, unequally, but not drearily.

Something curious was taking place in Nezhdanov. He was discontented with himself, with his activity, or rather his inactivity; his words almost constantly had a ring of bitter and biting self-reproach; but in his soul – somewhere very deep within it – there was a kind of happiness, a sense of a certain peace. Whether it was the result of the country quiet, the fresh air, the summer, the good food, and the easy life, or whether it came from the fact that he was now, for the first time in his life, tasting the sweetness of close contact with a woman's soul – it would be hard to say; but, in fact, his heart was light, even though he complained – and sincerely – to his friend Silin.

This frame of mind was, however, suddenly and violently destroyed in a single day.

On the morning of that day he received a note from Vassily Nikolaevitch, in which he was directed in conjunction with Markelov, while awaiting further instructions, at once to make friends with and come to an understanding with the aforementioned Solomin, and a certain merchant, Golushkin, an Old Believer, living in S———. This note threw Nezhdanov into violent agitation; he could read reproach for his inactivity in it. The bitterness, that had all this time only raged in words, was stirred up again from the bottom of his heart.

Kallomyetsev came to dinner greatly perturbed and exasperated. 'Imagine,' he cried in a voice almost lachrymose, 'what a horrible thing I have just read in the paper: my friend, my dear Mihail, the Servian prince, has been murdered by some miscreants in Belgrade! This is what these Jacobins and revolutionists come to, if we don't put a firm stop to them!' Sipyagin 'begged leave to remark' that this revolting murder was probably not the work of Jacobins, 'whose existence can hardly be supposed in Servia,' but of men of the party of Karageorgievitch, the enemies of Obrenovitch. . . . But Kallomyetsev would hear nothing, and, in the same lachrymose voice, began again describing how the murdered prince had loved him, what a splendid gun he had given him! . . . Gradually branching off and getting more and more indignant, Kallomyetsev turned from foreign Jacobins to home-bred Nihilists and Socialists, and at last broke into a perfect philippic. Clutching a large, white roll with both hands, and breaking it in half over his soup-plate, quite in the style of real Parisians at the 'Café Riche,' he expressed his longing to crush, to grind to powder, all who were in opposition to any one or anything whatever! That was precisely his expression. 'It is high time,' he declared, lifting his spoon to his mouth, 'it's high time!' he repeated, as he gave his glass to the servant for sherry. He referred reverentially to the great Moscow journalists – and *Ladislas, notre bon et cher Ladislas* – was continually on his lips. And all through this he kept his eyes on Nezhdanov as though to transfix him with them. 'There, that's for you!' he seemed to say. 'Take that! I mean it for you! And there's more like it!' At last Nezhdanov could endure it no longer, and he began to retort. His voice, it is true, was a little uncertain and hoarse – not from fear, of course; he began to champion the hopes, the principles, the ideals of the younger generation. Kallomyetsev at once answered in a high pipe – indignation in him was always expressed by falsetto – and began to be abusive.

Sipyagin majestically took Nezhdanov's part; Valentina Mihalovna, too, agreed with her husband; Anna Zaharovna tried to distract Kolya's attention, and cast looks of fury in all directions from under her cap; Marianna sat as though turned to stone.

But suddenly, on hearing the name of *Ladislas* uttered for the twentieth time, Nezhdanov fired up, and with a blow on the table he cried: 'A fine authority! As though we didn't know what kind of a creature this *Ladislas* is! He, a hired puppet from his birth up, and nothing more!'

'Ah – a – a – so that – that's,' whined Kallomyetsev, stuttering with fury. . . . 'Is that how you allow yourself to refer to a man who enjoys the respect of persons of position like Count Blazenkrampf and Prince Kovrizhkin!'

Nezhdanov shrugged his shoulders. 'A great recommendation truly; Prince Kovrizhkin, the flunkey enthusiast—'

'*Ladislas* is my friend,' shrieked Kallomyetsev; 'he's my comrade . . . and I—'

'So much the worse for you,' interrupted Nezhdanov; 'it implies that you share his way of thinking, and my remarks apply to you as well.'

Kallomyetsev was livid with wrath.

'Wh-what! You l-laugh! You – you ought – instantly – be—'

'What are you pleased to do with me *instantly?*' Nezhdanov interrupted a second time with ironical politeness.

There is no knowing how this scuffle between the two enemies would have ended, if Sipyagin had not cut it short at the very commencement. Raising his voice and assuming an air in which it was hard to say which was the predominant element – the solemn authority of the statesman, or the dignity of the master of the house – he declared with calm insistence that he did not wish to hear any such intemperate expressions at his table; that he had long ago made it his rule (he corrected himself – his sacred rule) to respect every sort of conviction, but only on the understanding (here he raised his forefinger, adorned with an heraldic ring) that they were maintained within the limits of decorum and good breeding; that though on the one hand he could not but censure a certain intemperance in the language of Mr. Nezhdanov, pardonable, however, at his years, on the other hand he could not approve of the severity of Mr. Kallomyetsev's attacks on persons of the opposite camp, a severity to be attributed, however, to his zeal for the public welfare.

'Under my roof,' so he concluded, 'under the roof of the Sipyagins, there are neither Jacobins nor puppets, there are only well-meaning people, who, when once they understand one another, are bound to end by shaking hands!'

Nezhdanov and Kallomyetsev both held their peace, but they did not shake hands; apparently the hour of mutual comprehension had not come for them. Quite the contrary; they had never felt such intense mutual hatred. The dinner was concluded in unpleasant and awkward silence; Sipyagin tried to relate a diplomatic anecdote, but fairly gave it up in despair half-way through. Marianna stared doggedly at her plate. She did not care to show the sympathy aroused in her by Nezhdanov's remarks – not from cowardice, oh no! but she felt bound before everything not to betray herself to Madame Sipyagin. She felt her penetrating, persistent eyes fixed on her. And Madame Sipyagin did actually keep her eyes fixed on her, on her and Nezhdanov. His unexpected outburst at first astounded the sharp-witted lady; then all of a sudden she saw, as it were, a light upon it, so much so that involuntarily she murmured. Ah! . . . she suddenly divined that Nezhdanov was drifting away from her – Nezhdanov, who had so lately been in her grasp. Then something must have happened. . . . Could it be Marianna? Yes, of course it was Marianna . . . He attracted her . . . yes, and he . . .

'Steps must be taken,' was how she concluded her reflections, and meanwhile Kallomyetsev was choking with indignation. Even when playing preference, two hours later, he uttered the words, 'Pass!' or 'I buy!' with an aching heart, and in his voice could be heard a hoarse tremolo of wounded feeling, though he put on an appearance of 'being above it'! Sipyagin alone was in reality positively pleased with the whole scene. He had had a chance to show the power of his eloquence, to still the rising storm. . . . He knew Latin, and Virgil's *Quos ego!* was familiar to him. He did not consciously compare himself to Neptune quelling the tempest; but he thought of him with a sort of sympathy.

XV

DIRECTLY IT SEEMED possible, Nezhdanov went away to his room and locked himself in. He did not want to see any one, any one except Marianna. Her room was at the very end of the long corridor which intersected the whole top storey. Nezhdanov had only once, and then only for a few instants, been to her room; but it struck him that she would not be angry if he knocked at her door, that she even wished to have a talk with him. It was rather late, about ten o'clock; the Sipyagins, after the scene at dinner, had not thought it necessary to disturb him, and were still playing cards with Kallomyetsev. Valentina Mihalovna had twice inquired after Marianna, as she too had vanished soon after dinner.

'Where is Marianna Vikentyevna?' she asked first in Russian, then in French, not addressing herself to any one in particular, but rather to the walls, as people are wont to do when they are greatly astonished; but soon she too was absorbed in the game.

Nezhdanov walked once or twice up and down his room, then he went along the corridor to Marianna's door and softly knocked. There was no answer. He knocked once more, tried the door.... It appeared to be locked. But he had hardly got back to his own room, and sat down to the table, when his own door gave a faint creak and he heard Marianna's voice:

'Alexey Dmitritch, was that *you* came to me?'

He jumped up at once and ran into the corridor; Marianna was standing at his door, a candle in her hand, pale and motionless.

'Yes ... I ...' he whispered.

'Come along,' she answered, and walked along the corridor,

but before she got to the end she stopped and pushed open a low door with her hand. Nezhdanov saw a small, almost empty room. 'We had better go in here, Alexey Dmitritch, here no one will disturb us.' Nezhdanov obeyed. Marianna set the candle down on the window-sill and turned round to Nezhdanov.

'I understand why it was that you wanted to see me,' she began; 'it is very wretched for you living in this house, and so it is for me too.'

'Yes; I wanted to see you, Marianna Vikentyevna,' answered Nezhdanov, 'but it isn't wretched for me here since I have come to know you.'

Marianna smiled thoughtfully.

'Thanks, Alexey Dmitritch; but tell me, can you intend to stay here after all this hideous business?'

'I don't suppose they'll let me stay here, they'll dismiss me!'

'Wouldn't you dismiss yourself?'

'Of my own accord? . . . No.'

'Why?'

'You want to know the truth? because *you* are here.'

Marianna bent her head and moved a little further away into the room.

'And besides,' Nezhdanov went on, 'I am *bound* to stay here. You know nothing – but I want, I feel I ought, to tell you everything.'

He stepped up to Marianna and seized her by the hand. She did not take it away, but only looked into his face. 'Listen!' he cried on a sudden powerful impulse, 'listen to me!' And at once, without sitting down, though there were two or three chairs in the room, still standing in front of Marianna and keeping hold of her hand, with impulsive heat, with an eloquence unexpected by himself, Nezhdanov told her of his plans, his intentions, the reasons that had made him accept Sipyagin's offer, of all his ties, his acquaintances, his past, all that he had always concealed, that he had never spoken openly of to any one! He told her of the letters he received, of

Vassily Nikolaevitch, of everything – even of Silin! He spoke hurriedly, without reluctance, or the faintest hesitation, as though he were reproaching himself for not having initiated Marianna into all his secrets before, as though he were seeking her pardon. She heard him attentively, greedily; for the first minute she was bewildered. . . . But that feeling vanished at once. Gratitude, pride, devotion, resolution, that was what her soul was overflowing with. Her face, her eyes were bright; she laid her other hand on Nezhdanov's hand, her lips were parted in rapture. . . . She had suddenly grown marvellously beautiful!

He stopped at last, looked at her, and as it were for the first time saw *that* face, which seemed at the same time so dear and so familiar to him.

He gave a deep, long sigh. . . .

'Ah! I have done well to tell you everything!' – his lips were hardly able to utter the words.

'Yes, oh, so well, so well!' she repeated, also in a whisper. She unconsciously imitated him, and, indeed, her voice failed her too. 'And it means, you know,' she went on, 'that I am at your disposal, that I want too to be of use to your cause, that I am ready to do anything that is wanted, to go where I am ordered, that I have always, with my whole soul, yearned for the thing that you . . .'

She too was silent. Another word, and tears of emotion would have fallen in floods. All her strong nature was suddenly soft as wax. The thirst for activity, for sacrifice, immediate sacrifice – that was what mastered her.

The steps of some one in the corridor could be heard – cautious, rapid, light steps.

Marianna suddenly drew herself up, freed her hands; she was at once transformed and alert. Something scornful, something audacious came over her face.

'I know who is spying on us at this minute,' she said, so loudly that each of her words resounded distinctly in the corridor. 'Madame Sipyagin is spying on us . . . but I don't care a bit for that.'

The sound of steps ceased.

'What then?' Marianna said, turning to Nezhdanov, 'what am I to do? how am I to help you? Tell me . . . tell me soon! What's to be done?'

'What?' said Nezhdanov; 'I don't know yet . . . I got a letter from Markelov.'

'When? when?'

'This evening. I must go with him to-morrow to the factory to see Solomin.'

'Yes . . . yes. . . . That's a splendid man, now, Markelov. He's a real friend.'

'Like me?'

Marianna looked Nezhdanov straight in the face.

'No . . . not like you.'

'How? . . .'

She turned suddenly away.

'Ah! don't you understand what you have become to me, and what I am feeling at this moment? . . .'

Nezhdanov's heart beat violently; involuntarily he looked down. This girl, who loved him – him, a poor homeless devil – who believed in him, who was ready to follow him, to go with him towards the same aim – this exquisite girl – Marianna, at that instant, was to Nezhdanov the incarnation of everything good and true on earth – the incarnation of all the love of mother, sister, wife, that he had known nothing of – the incarnation of fatherland, happiness, struggle, freedom!

He raised his head, and saw her eyes again bent upon him. . . .

Oh, how that clear, noble glance sank into his soul!

'And so,' he began in an unsteady voice, 'I am going to-morrow. . . . And when I come back, Marianna Vikentyevna' – (he suddenly found it awkward to use this formal address) – 'I will tell you what I find out, what is decided. Henceforth everything I do, everything I think, everything, you shall be the first to know . . . Marianna.'

'Oh, my friend!' cried Marianna, and again she clasped his hand, 'and I make the same promise to you, dear.'

This last word came as easily and simply from her as though it could not be otherwise, as though it were the 'dear' of long, intimate companionship.

'Can I see the letter?'

'Here it is, here.'

Marianna skimmed through the letter, and almost with reverence she raised her eyes upon him.

'Do they intrust such important commissions to you, Alexey?'

He smiled at her in answer, and put the letter in his pocket.

'Strange,' he said, 'why, we have made known our love to each other – we love one another – and there has not been a word said about it between us!'

'What need?' whispered Marianna, and suddenly she flung herself on his neck, pressed her head to his shoulder. . . . But they did not even kiss – they would have felt it ordinary and somehow dreadful – and at once they separated, after tightly clasping each other's hands again.

Marianna turned away to get the candle, which she had put on the window-sill of the empty room, and only then something like embarrassment came over her. She extinguished it, and, gliding quickly along the corridor in the black darkness, she returned to her room, undressed and went to bed, still in the darkness – she felt it somehow comforting.

XVI

THE NEXT MORNING when Nezhdanov woke up he felt no embarrassment at the recollection of what had happened overnight; on the contrary, he was filled with a kind of serene and sober happiness, as though he had done something which ought really to have been done long before. Asking for two days' leave from Sipyagin, who consented at once, though stiffly, to his absence, Nezhdanov went to Markelov's. Before starting he succeeded in getting an interview with Marianna. She, too, was not at all ashamed or embarrassed; she looked calmly and resolutely at him, and calmly addressed him by his Christian name. She was only excited about what he would learn at Markelov's, and begged him to tell her everything.

'That's a matter of course,' answered Nezhdanov.

'And after all,' he reflected, 'why should we be disturbed? In our friendship, personal feeling has played . . . a secondary part – though we are united for ever. In the name of the cause? Yes, in the name of the cause!'

So fancied Nezhdanov, and he did not suspect how much of truth, and how much of falsehood, there was in his fancies.

He found Markelov in the same weary and morose frame of mind. They dined after a fashion, and then set off in the same old coach (they hired from a peasant a second trace-horse, a colt, who had never been in harness before – Markelov's horse was still lame) to the merchant Faleyev's big cotton factory, where Solomin lived. Nezhdanov's curiosity was aroused; he felt eager to make a closer acquaintance with a man of whom he had heard so much of late. Solomin was prepared for their visit; directly the two travellers stopped at the gates of the factory and gave their names, they were promptly conducted into the unsightly little lodge occupied by the 'superintendent of the machinery.' He was himself in the chief wing of the building; while one of the workmen ran to fetch him, Nezhdanov and Markelov had time to go to the window and look about them. The factory was apparently in a flourishing condition and over-burdened with work; from every side came the brisk, noisy hum of unceasing activity, the snorting and rattling of machines, the creaking of looms, the hum of wheels, the flapping of straps, while trolleys, barrels, and loaded carts moved in and out; there was the sound of loudly shouted instructions, bells and whistles; workmen in smocks with belts round the waist, their hair bound round with a strap, work-girls in print dresses hurrying by; horses were led by in harness. . . . There was the busy hum of the labour of thousands of human beings strained to their utmost. Everything moved in regular, rational fashion, at full speed; but not only was there no attempt at style or neatness, there was not even any trace of cleanliness to be observed in anything anywhere; on the contrary, on all sides one was impressed by neglect, filth, grime. Here a window was broken and there the plaster was peeling off, the boards were loose, a door yawned wide open; a great, black puddle, covered with an iridescent film of slime, stood in the middle of the principal courtyard; further on lay some discarded bricks; bits of matting and sailcloth, boxes, scraps of rope lay wallowing in the mud; shaggy and lean dogs crept about, not even barking; in a corner under a fence sat a pot-bellied, dishevelled little boy of four, crusted from head to foot with filth, crying hopelessly as though he had been deserted by the whole world; beside him, bespattered with the same filth, a sow, surrounded by a litter of spotted sucking-pigs, was inspecting some cabbage stalks; ragged linen was fluttering on a line; and what an odour, what a stench everywhere! A Russian mill, in fact; not a German or a French factory.

Nezhdanov glanced at Markelov.

'I have heard so much talked about Solomin's great abilities,' he began, 'that, I confess, all this disorder rather surprises me; I didn't expect it.'

'It isn't disorder,' answered Markelov grimly, 'it's the Russian sluttishness. For all that, it's turning over millions! And he has to adapt himself to the old ways, and to practical needs, and to the owner himself. Have you any notion what Faleyev's like?'

'Not the slightest.'

'The greatest skinflint in Moscow. A bourgeois – that's the word for him!'

At that instant Solomin came into the room. Again Nezhdanov was fated to be disappointed in him, as in the factory. At first sight Solomin gave one the impression of being a Finn or, still more, a Swede. He was tall, lean, broad-shouldered, with light eyebrows and eye-lashes; he had a long yellow face, a short broad nose, very small greenish eyes, a placid expression, large prominent lips, white teeth, also large, and a cleft chin covered with a faint down. He was dressed as a mechanic or stoker; an old pea-jacket with baggy pockets on his body, a crumpled oilskin cap on his head, a woollen comforter round his neck, and tarred boots on his feet. He was accompanied by a man about forty, in a rough peasant coat, with an exceedingly mobile gipsy face and keen jet-black eyes, with which he at once scanned Nezhdanov, directly he came into the room. . . . Markelov he knew already. His name was Pavel; he was said to be Solomin's right hand.

Solomin approached his two visitors without haste, pressed the hand of each of them in his horny, bony hand, without a word, took a sealed packet out of the table drawer and handed it, also without a word, to Pavel, who at once went out of the room. Then he stretched, and cleared his throat; flinging his cap off his head with one wave of his hand, he sat down on a wooden, painted stool, and, motioning Markelov and Nezhdanov to a similar sofa, he said, 'Please sit down.'

Markelov first introduced Solomin to Nezhdanov; he again shook hands with him. Then Markelov began talking of the 'cause,' and mentioned Vassily Nikolaevitch's letter. Nezhdanov handed the letter to Solomin. While he read it, attentively and deliberately, his eyes moving on from line to line, Nezhdanov watched him. Solomin was sitting near the window; the sun, now low in the sky, threw a glaring light on his tanned, slightly perspiring face and his light, dusty hair, showing up a number of golden threads among them. His nostrils quivered as his breath came and went while he read, and his lips moved as though he were forming each word; he held the letter with a strong grip, rather high up with both hands. All this, for some unknown reason, pleased Nezhdanov. Solomin gave the letter back to Nezhdanov, smiled at him, and again began listening to Markelov. The latter talked and talked, but at last he ceased.

'Do you know what,' began Solomin, and his voice, rather hoarse, but young and powerful, pleased Nezhdanov too, 'it's not quite convenient here at my place; let us go to your house, it's not more than five miles to you. I suppose you came in the coach?'

'Yes.'

'Well . . . then there will be room for me. In an hour my work is over and I am at liberty. We will have a talk. Are you at liberty too?' – he addressed Nezhdanov.

'Till the day after to-morrow.'

'That's capital. We will stay the night with Mr. Markelov. Can we do that, Sergei Mihalitch?'

'What a question! Of course you can.'

'Well, I'll be ready directly. Only let me clean myself up a bit.'

'And how are things going with you at the factory?' Markelov inquired significantly.

Solomin looked away.

'We will have a talk,' he said a second time. 'Wait a little. . . . I'll be back directly. . . . I've forgotten something.'

He went out. If it had not been for the good impression he had made on Nezhdanov, the latter would probably have thought, and perhaps even have said to Markelov, 'Isn't he shuffling out of it?' But no question of the sort even entered his head.

An hour later, at the time when from every floor of the vast building, on every staircase, and at every door the noisy crowd of factory hands were streaming out, the coach, in which were seated Markelov, Nezhdanov, and Solomin, drove out of the gates on to the road.

'Vassily Fedotitch! is it to be done?' Pavel, who had escorted Solomin to the gate, shouted after him.

'No; wait a little' . . . answered Solomin. 'That refers to a night operation,' he explained to his companion.

They reached Borzyonkovo; and had supper, rather for the sake of manners. Then cigars were lighted and the talk began, one of those interminable, midnight, Russian talks, which of the same form and on the same scale are hardly to be found in any other people. Here too, though, Solomin did not fulfil Nezhdanov's expectations. He spoke noticeably little . . . so little, that one might say he was almost continually silent; but he listened intently, and if he uttered any criticism or remark, then it was sensible, weighty, and very brief. It turned out that Solomin did not believe that a revolution was at hand in Russia; but not wishing to force his opinions on others, he did not try to prevent them from making an attempt, and looked on at them, not from a distance, but as a comrade by their side. He was very intimate with the Petersburg revolutionists, and was to a certain extent in sympathy with them, since he was himself one of the people; but he realised the instinctive aloofness from the movement of the people, without whom 'you can do nothing,' and who need a long preparation, and that not in the manner nor by the means of these men. And so he stood aside, not in a hypocritical or shifty way, but like a man of sense who doesn't care to ruin himself or others for nothing. But as for listening . . . why not listen, and learn too, if one can? Solomin was the only son of a deacon; he had five sisters, all married to village priests or deacons; but with the consent of his father, a steady, sober man, he had given up the seminary, had begun to study mathematics, and had devoted himself with special ardour to mechanics; he had entered the business of an Englishman, who had come to love him like a father, and had given him the means of going to Manchester, where he spent two years and learned English. He had lately come into the Moscow merchant's factory, and though he was exacting with subordinates, because that was the way of doing things he had learned in England, he was in high favour with them; 'he's one of ourselves,' they used to say. His father was much pleased with him; he used to call him 'a very steady-going chap,' and his only complaint was that his son didn't want to get married.

During the midnight conversation at Markelov's, Solomin was, as we have said already, almost completely silent; but when Markelov began discussing the expectations he had formed of the factory hands, Solomin, with his habitual brevity, observed that with us in Russia, factory workers are not what they are abroad – they're the meekest set of people.

'And the peasants?' inquired Markelov.

'The peasants? There are pretty many of the close-fisted, money-lending sort among them now, and every year there'll be more; but they only know their own interest; the rest are sheep, blind and ignorant.'

'Then where are we to look?'

Solomin smiled.

'Seek and ye shall find.'

He was almost constantly smiling, and the smile, like the man himself, was peculiarly guileless, but not meaningless. To Nezhdanov he behaved in quite a special way; the young student had awakened a feeling of interest, almost of tenderness, in him.

During this same midnight discussion, Nezhdanov suddenly got flushed and hot, and broke into an outburst; Solomin softly got up, and, moving across the room with his large tread, he closed a window that stood open behind Nezhdanov's head. . . .

'You mustn't get cold,' he remarked naïvely in reply to the orator's puzzled look.

Nezhdanov began questioning him as to what socialistic ideas he was trying to introduce into the factory in his charge, and whether he intended to arrange for the workpeople to have a share of the profits.

'My dear soul!' answered Solomin, 'we have set up a school and a tiny hospital, and to be sure our master struggled against that like a bear!'

Once only Solomin lost his temper in earnest, and struck the table such a blow with his powerful fist that everything shook upon it, not excepting a forty-pound weight that lay near the inkstand. He had been told of some legal injustice, the oppressive treatment of a workmen's guild. . . .

When Nezhdanov and Markelov started discussing how 'to act,' how to put their plans into execution, Solomin still listened with curiosity, even with respect; but he did not himself utter a single word. This conversation lasted till four o'clock. And what, what did they not discuss? Markelov, among other things, alluded mysteriously to the indefatigable traveller Kislyakov, to his letters, which were becoming more and more interesting; he promised to show Nezhdanov some of them, and even to let him take them home, since they were very lengthy, and not written in a very legible hand; and over and above this there was a great deal of erudition in them, and there were verses too, not only frivolous ones, but of a socialistic tendency! From Kislyakov, Markelov passed to soldiers, adjutants, Germans; he got at last to his articles on the artillery; Nezhdanov talked of the antagonism between Heine and Börne, of Proudhon, of realism in art; while Solomin listened, listened and pondered and smoked, and, still smiling and not saying a single smart thing, he seemed to understand better than any one what lay at the root of the matter.

It struck four. . . . Nezhdanov and Markelov were almost dropping with fatigue, while Solomin had not turned a hair. The friends separated, but first it was mutually agreed to go the next day to the town to see the merchant Golushkin on propaganda business. Golushkin himself was very zealous, and moreover he promised proselytes! Solomin expressed a doubt whether it was worth while to visit Golushkin. However, he agreed later that it was worth while.

XVII

MARKELOV'S GUESTS WERE still asleep when a messenger came to him with a letter from his sister, Madame Sipyagin. In the letter Valentina Mihalovna wrote to him of various trifling domestic details, asked him to send her back a book he had borrowed – and incidentally, in the postscript, told him of an 'amusing' piece of news: that his former flame, Marianna, was in love with the tutor, Nezhdanov – and the tutor with her; that she, Valentina Mihalovna, was not repeating gossip – she had seen it all with her own eyes, and heard it with her own ears. Markelov's face grew dark as night . . . but he did not utter one word; he gave orders to give the book to the messenger, and when he saw Nezhdanov coming downstairs he said, 'Good morning' to him, just as usual – even gave him the promised packet of Kislyakov's epistles; he did not stop with him, though, but went out 'to see after things.' Nezhdanov went back to his room, and looked through the letters. The young propagandist talked incessantly of himself, of his feverish activity; according to his own statement, he had during the last month journeyed through eleven districts, been in nine towns, twenty-nine villages, fifty-three hamlets, one farm, and eight factories; sixteen nights he had passed in hay-lofts, one in a stable, one even in a cow-shed (he mentioned, in a parenthetical note, that fleas did not affect him); he had got into mud-huts, into workmen's barracks; everywhere he had taught, preached, distributed pamphlets, and collected information by the way; some facts he had noted on the spot, others he carried in his memory on the latest system of mnemonics; he had written fourteen long letters, twenty-seven short ones, and eighteen notes, four of which were written in pencil, one in blood, one in soot and water; and all this he had managed to do because he had mastered the systematic disposition of his time, taking as his models Quintin Johnson, Karrelius, Sverlitsky, and other writers and statisticians. Then he talked again of himself, his lucky star; and how and with what additions he had completed Fourier's theory of the passions; declared that he was the first to reach the 'bed-rock,' that he should 'not pass from the world without leaving a trace behind,' that he himself wondered that he, a boy of two-and-twenty, should already have solved all the problems of life and of science, and that he should turn Russia upside down, that he would 'give her a shaking!' *Dixi!!* he added at the end of the line. This word, *Dixi*, occurred frequently in Kislyakov's effusions, and always with two exclamation marks. In one of the letters there was a socialistic poem, addressed to a girl, and beginning with the words:

'Love not me, but the idea!'

Nezhdanov marvelled inwardly, not so much at Mr. Kislyakov's self-conceit as at Markelov's honest simplicity . . . but then came the thought, 'Good taste be hanged! Mr. Kislyakov even may be of use.'

The three friends all met in the dining-room for morning tea, but the previous night's discussion was not renewed between them. Not one of them was disposed to talk, but only Solomin was placidly silent; both Nezhdanov and Markelov were inwardly perturbed.

After tea they set off to the town; Markelov's old servant, sitting on his locker, followed his former owner with his habitual dejected glance.

The merchant, Golushkin, with whom Nezhdanov was to make acquaintance, was the son of a wealthy merchant in the wholesale drug business – an Old Believer of the Fedosian sect. He had not increased his father's fortune by his own efforts, as he was, as it is called by the Russians, a *joueur*, an Epicurean of the Russian stamp, and had no sort of aptitude for business. He was a man of forty, rather stout, and ugly, pockmarked, with small pig's eyes; he talked in a great hurry, stumbling, as it were, over his words, gesticulating with his hands, swinging his legs, and going off into giggles ... and in general making the impression of a blockhead and a coxcomb of extraordinary vanity. He considered himself a man of culture, because he wore German clothes, and was hospitable, though he lived in filth and disorder, had rich acquaintances, and used to go to the theatre and 'protect' low music-hall actresses, with whom he communicated in an extraordinary would-be French jargon. The thirst for popularity was his ruling passion; for the name of Golushkin to be thundering through the world! As once Suvarov or Potemkin, why not now Kapiton Golushkin? It was just this passion, overcoming even his innate meanness, which had flung him, as he with some self-complacency expressed it, into the *opposition* (he had at first pronounced this foreign word simply *position*, but afterwards he had learned better), and brought him into connection with the nihilists; he uttered freely the most extreme views, laughed at his own Old Believers' faith, ate meat in Lent, played cards, and drank champagne like water. And he never got into trouble, because, he used to say, 'I have every authority bribed just where it's needed, every hole is sewn up, all mouths are shut, all ears are deaf.' He was a widower and childless; his sister's sons hung about him with timorous servility ... but he used to call them unenlightened clowns and barbarians, and would hardly look at them. He lived in a large stone house, rather sluttishly kept; in some rooms the furniture was all of foreign make – in others there was nothing but painted chairs and an American-leather sofa. Pictures were hung everywhere, and all of them were wretched daubs – red landscapes, pink marine views, Moller's 'Kiss,' and fat, naked women, with red knees and elbows. Though Golushkin had no family, there were a great many servants and dependants of different kinds under his roof; it was not from generosity that he kept them, but, again, from desire for power, so as to have a public of some sort at his command to show off before. 'My clients,' he used to call them when he was in a bragging mood;

he never read a book, but he had a capital memory for learned expressions.

The young men found Golushkin in his study. Dressed in a long coat, with a cigar in his mouth, he was pretending to read the newspaper. On seeing them, he at once jumped up, and fussed about, turning red, shouting for some refreshment to be brought immediately, asking questions, laughing – all at the same time. Markelov and Solomin he knew; Nezhdanov was a stranger to him. Hearing that he was a student, Golushkin laughed again, shook his hand a second time, and said: 'Capital! capital! our forces are growing. . . . Learning is light, ignorance is darkness. I've not a ha'porth of learning myself, but I've insight – that's how I've got on!'

It struck Nezhdanov that Mr. Golushkin was nervous and ill at ease . . . and that was actually the fact. 'Look out, brother Kapitov! mind you don't come a cropper in the mud!' was his first thought at the sight of any new person. Soon, however, he recovered himself, and in the same hurried, lisping, muddled language began talking of Vassily Nikolaevitch, of his character, of the necessity of pro-pa-gan-da (he had that word very pat, but he articulated it slowly); of how he, Golushkin, had discovered a capital new recruit, most trustworthy; of how it seemed now that the time was at hand, was ready for . . . for the lancet (at this he glanced at Markelov, who did not, however, stir a muscle); then, turning to Nezhdanov, he started singing his own praises, with as much zest as the great correspondent, Kislyakov, himself. He said that he had long left the ranks of the benighted, that he knew well the rights of the proletariat (that word, too, he had a firm hold of), that though he had actually given up commerce and taken to banking operations – to increase his capital – that was only that the aforesaid capital might be ready at any moment to serve . . . the good of the common movement, the good, so to speak, of the people; and that he, Golushkin, had in reality the greatest contempt for money! At this point a servant came in with refreshments, and

Golushkin cleared his throat expressively, and asked wouldn't he begin with a little glass of something? and set the example by gulping down a wineglass of pepper-brandy.

The visitors partook of the refreshments. Golushkin thrust some huge morsels of caviar in his mouth, and drank with unflagging punctuality, saying, 'Come, gentlemen, a glass of good Maçon now.'

Addressing himself again to Nezhdanov, he asked where he had come from, and how long and where he was staying; and learning that he was living at Sipyagin's, he cried: 'I know that gentleman. No good!' and then proceeded to abuse all the landowners of the province of S————, on the grounds, not only of their having no public spirit, but of their not even understanding their own interests. . . . Only, strange to say, though his language was strong, his eyes strayed restlessly about, and a look of uneasiness could be detected in them. Nezhdanov could not quite make out what sort of a person he was, and in what way he was of use to them. Solomin was silent, as usual; and Markelov had such a gloomy face, that Nezhdanov asked him at last, what was wrong with him? To which Markelov replied that there was nothing wrong with him, in the tone in which people commonly answer when they mean to give you to understand that there is something, but not for you to know. Golushkin again started abusing some one or other, then he passed to praise of the younger generation: 'such talented fellows,' he declared, 'are appearing among us nowadays! such talent! Ah! . . .'

Solomin cut him short with the question, who was the trustworthy young man he had spoken of, and where had he picked him up? Golushkin giggled, repeated twice; 'Ah, you shall see, you shall see,' and began cross-questioning him about his factory, and its 'shark' of an owner, to which Solomin replied in monosyllables. Then Golushkin poured out champagne for all; and, bending down to Nezhdanov's ear, he whispered, 'To the republic!' and drank off his glass at a gulp. Nezhdanov sipped his; Solomin remarked that he didn't drink wine in the morning; Markelov angrily and resolutely drained his glass to the last drop. He seemed devoured by impatience; 'here we are wasting our time,' he seemed to say, 'and not coming to the real matter to be discussed.' . . . He struck a blow on the table, exclaimed sternly, 'Gentlemen!' and was about to speak . . .

But at that instant there came into the room a sleek man with a foxy face and a consumptive appearance, in a merchant's dress of nankeen, with both hands outstretched like wings. Bowing to the party collectively, the man communicated something to Golushkin in a whisper: 'I'll come directly,' the latter replied hurriedly. 'Gentlemen,' he added, 'I must beg you to excuse me . . . Vasya here, my clerk, has told me of a *leetle* affair' (Golushkin pronounced it thus purposely, by way of being jocose) 'which absolutely necessitates my absenting myself for a while; but I hope, gentlemen, that you will consent to take a meal with me to-day at three o'clock; and then we shall be much more at liberty!'

Neither Solomin nor Nezhdanov knew what answer to make; but Markelov answered at once with the same sternness in his face and voice: 'Of course we will; it would be rather too much of a farce if we didn't.'

'I am greatly obliged,' said Golushkin hastily, and bending to Markelov, he added: 'A thousand roubles I devote to the cause in any case . . . have no doubt about that!'

And so saying he waved his right hand three times, with the thumb and little finger sticking out, as a sign of his good faith.

He escorted his guests to the door, and standing in the doorway, shouted, 'I shall expect you at three!'

'You may expect us!' Markelov alone responded.

'Well, my friends,' observed Solomin, directly they were all three in the street, 'I'm going to take a cab and go back to the factory. What are we to do till dinner-time? Waste our time idling about? And, indeed, our worthy merchant . . . it strikes me ... is like the goat in the fable, neither good for wool nor for milk.'

'Oh, there shall be some wool,' observed Markelov grimly. 'He was just promising some money. Or isn't he nice enough for you? We can't be particular. We're not so much courted that we can afford to be squeamish.'

'I'm not squeamish!' said Solomin calmly; 'I'm only asking myself what good my presence can do. However,' he added with a glance at Nezhdanov, and a smile, 'I will stay, by all means. Even death, as they say, is sweet in good company.'

Markelov raised his head.

'Let's go, meanwhile, to the public gardens; it's a lovely day. We can look at the people.'

'Very well.'

They went, Markelov and Solomin in front, Nezhdanov behind them.

XVIII

STRANGE WAS THE state of his mind. In the last two days so many new sensations, new faces.... For the first time in his life he had come close to a girl, whom, in all probability, he loved; he was present at the beginning of the thing to which, in all probability, all his energies were consecrated.... Well? was he rejoicing? No. Was he wavering, afraid, confused? Oh, certainly not. Was he, at least, feeling that tension of his whole being, that impulse forward into the front ranks of the battle, to be expected as the struggle grew near? No again. Did he believe, then, in this cause? Did he believe in his own love? 'Oh, damned artistic temperament! sceptic!' his lips murmured inaudibly. Why this weariness, this disinclination to speak even, without shrieking and raving? What inner voice did he want to stifle with those ravings? But Marianna, that noble, faithful comrade, that pure, passionate nature, that exquisite girl, did not she love him? Was not that an immense happiness, to have met her, to have gained her friendship, her love? And these two walking in front of him at this moment, this Markelov, this Solomin, whom he knew so little as yet, but to whom he felt so drawn, were they not fine types of the Russian nature, of Russian life, and was not it a happiness, too, to know them, to be friends with them? Then why this undefined, vague, gnawing sensation? How and why this dejection? 'If you're a brooding pessimist,' his lips murmured again, 'a damned fine revolutionist you'll make! You ought to be writing rhymes, and sulking and nursing your own petty thoughts and sensations, and busying yourself with psychological fancies and subtleties of all sorts, but at least don't mistake your sickly, nervous whims and irritability for manly indignation, for the honest anger of a man of convictions! O Hamlet, Hamlet, how to escape from the shadow of your spirit! How cease to follow you in everything, even in the loathsome enjoyment of one's own self-depreciation!'

'Alexey! Friend! Hamlet of Russia!' he heard suddenly, like the echo of these reflections, in a familiar squeaky voice. 'Is it you I see before me?'

Nezhdanov raised his eyes, and with amazement beheld Paklin! – Paklin, in quite an Arcadian get-up, a summer suit of flesh-colour, with no cravat round his neck, a large straw hat with a blue ribbon pushed on to the back of his head, and in varnished shoes!

He at once limped up to Nezhdanov and grasped his hands.

'First of all,' he began, 'though we are in a public garden, I must, for old custom's sake, embrace . . . and kiss you . . . Once, twice, thrice! Secondly, you must know that if I had not met you to-day, you would certainly have seen me to-morrow, as I knew your abode, and am, indeed, in this town with that object . . . how I got here, we will talk of hereafter; and thirdly, introduce me to your companions. Tell me briefly who they are, and them who I am, and then let's proceed to enjoy ourselves!'

Nezhdanov acted on his friend's request, named him, Markelov and Solomin, and told what each of them was, where he lived, what he did, and so on.

'Capital!' cried Paklin; 'and now let me lead you all far from the madding crowd, though there's not much of it here, certainly, to a secluded seat, where I sit, at moments of contemplation, to enjoy the beauties of nature. There's a wonderful view: the governor's house, two striped sentry-boxes, three policemen, and not one dog! Don't be too much surprised at the remarks with which I'm so perseveringly trying to amuse you! I'm the representative, in my friend's opinion, of Russian wit . . . no doubt that's why I'm lame.'

Paklin led the friends to the 'secluded seat,' and made them sit down on it, after dislodging two beggar women as a preliminary. The young men proceeded to 'exchange ideas,' generally a rather tedious process, especially at a first meeting, and a particularly unprofitable occupation at all times.

'Stay!' Paklin cried suddenly, turning to Nezhdanov. 'I must explain to you how it is I'm here. You know I always take my sister away somewhere every summer; when I found out that you had gone off into the neighbourhood of this town, I remembered that there were two wonderful creatures living in this very town, a husband and wife, who are connections of ours . . . on my mother's side. My father was a tradesman' – (Nezhdanov was aware of the fact, but Paklin mentioned it for the benefit of the other two) – 'but my mother was of noble family. And for ages they've been inviting us to come and see them! There! thought I . . . the very thing. They're the kindest people, it'll do my sister any amount of good – what could be better? Well, and so here we are. And it was just as I thought! I can't tell you how nice it is for us here! But what types! what types! you really must make their acquaintance! What are you doing here? Where are you going to dine? And why is it you were here, of all places?'

'We are going to dinner with a man called Golushkin . . . a merchant here,' answered Nezhdanov.

'At what o'clock?'

'Three.'

'And you are seeing him upon . . . upon . . .' Paklin took a comprehensive look at Solomin, who was smiling, and Markelov, whose face grew darker and darker. . . .

'Come, Alyosha, tell them . . . make some sort of Masonic sign, do . . . tell them they needn't be on their guard with me . . . I'm one of you . . . of your party. . . .'

'Golushkin, too, is one of us,' observed Nezhdanov.

'Now, I've a brilliant idea! There's a long while yet to three o'clock. Listen, let's go and see my relations!'

'Why, you're crazy! How could we? . . .'

'Don't worry yourself about that! I'll take all that on myself. Imagine: it's an oasis! Not a glimpse of politics, nor literature, nor anything modern has penetrated into it. A queer podgy sort of little house, such as you never see anywhere now; the very smell in it's antique; the people antique, the atmosphere antique . . . take it how you will, it's all antique, Catherine the Second, powder, hoops, eighteenth century! Just fancy a husband and wife, both very old, the same age, and without a wrinkle; round, chubby, spruce little things, a perfect pair of little poll-parrots; and good-natured to stupidity, to saintliness, no bounds to it! They tell me "boundless" good-nature often goes with an absence of moral feeling. . . . But I can't enter into such subtleties; I only know that my little old dears are the very soul of good-nature! Never had any children. The blessed innocents! That's what they call them in the town: blessed innocents. Both dressed alike in sort of striped gowns, and such good stuff: you can never see anything like that either nowadays. They're awfully like each other, only one has a mob-cap on her head, and the other a skull-cap, though that has the same sort of frilling as the mob-cap, only no strings. If it weren't for that difference, you wouldn't know which was which; especially as the husband has no beard. Their names are Fomushka and Fimushka. I tell you people ought to pay at the door to look at them, as curiosities. They love one another in the most impossible way; but if any one comes to visit them, it's "Delighted, so good of you!" And such hospitable creatures! they show off all their little tricks at once to amuse you. There's only one thing: one mustn't smoke; not that they're dissenters, but tobacco upsets them. . . . You see, no one smoked in their day. However, they can't stand canaries either, because that bird was very rarely seen in their day too. . . . And that's a great blessing, you'll admit! Well? will you come?'

'Really, I don't know,' began Nezhdanov.

'Stay; I haven't told you everything yet; their voices are just alike: with your eyes shut you wouldn't know which was speaking. Only Fomushka speaks just a little more expressively. Come, my friends, you are now on the brink of a great undertaking – perhaps, a terrible conflict. . . . Why shouldn't you, before flinging yourselves into those stormy deeps, try a dip. . . .'

'In stagnant water?' Markelov put in.

'And what if so? Stagnant it is, certainly; but fresh and pure. There are ponds in the steppes which never get putrid, though there's no stream through them, because they are fed by springs from the bottom. And my old dears have such springs too in the bottom of their hearts, and pure as can be. It all comes to this, would you like to know how people lived a century, a century and a half ago, make haste then and follow me. Or soon a day and hour will come – it's bound to be the same hour for both – and my poll-parrots will be knocked off their perches, and all that's antique will end with them, and the podgy little house will fall down, and the place of it will be overgrown with what, my grandmother used to tell me, always grows over the place where man's handiwork has been – that's to say – nettles, burdock, thistles, wormwood, dock leaves; the very street will cease to be, and men will come and go and never see anything like this again in all the ages!'

'Well!' cried Nezhdanov, 'let's be off directly!'

'I'm ready, with the greatest pleasure, indeed,' observed Solomin. 'It's not in my line, but it's interesting; and if Mr. Paklin can really guarantee that we should not be putting any one out by our visit, then . . . why . . .'

'Don't worry yourself!' Paklin cried in his turn; 'they'll be simply transported – that's all. No need of ceremony in this case! I tell you, they're blessed innocents; we'll make them sing to us. And you, too, Mr. Markelov, do you agree?'

Markelov shrugged his shoulders angrily.

'I'm not going to stay here alone! lead the way, if you please.'

The young men got up from the seat.

'You've a formidable gentleman there,' Paklin whispered to Nezhdanov, indicating Markelov, 'the very image of John the Baptist eating locusts . . . the locusts without the honey! But he,' he added with a nod in Solomin's direction, 'is delightful! What a jolly smile! I've noticed the only people who smile like that are those who're superior to other people – without being aware of it.'

'Are there ever people like that?' asked Nezhdanov.

'Not often; but there are some,' answered Paklin.

XIX

FOMUSHKA AND FIMUSHKA, otherwise Foma Lavrentyevitch and Evfimiya Pavlovna Subotchev, both belonged to the same family of pure Russian descent, and were considered to be almost the oldest inhabitants of the town of S———. They had been married very early, and a very long time ago had installed themselves in the wooden house of their ancestors on the outskirts of the town, had never moved from there, and had never changed their mode of life or their habits in any respect. Time seemed to have stood still for them; no 'novelty' had crossed the boundary of their 'oasis.' Their fortune was not large; but their peasants sent them up livestock and provisions several times a year, just as in the old days before the emancipation. At a fixed date the village elder appeared with the rents and a brace of woodcocks, supposed to be shot on the manorial forest domains, though the latter had in reality long ceased to exist. They used to regale him with tea at the drawing-room door, present him with a sheepskin cap and a pair of green wash-leather mittens, and bid him God-speed. The Subotchevs' house was filled with house-serfs, as in the old serf days. The old man-servant Kalliopitch, clothed in a jerkin of extraordinarily stout cloth with a stand-up collar and tiny steel buttons, announced in a sing-song chant that 'dinner is on the table,' and dozed standing behind his mistress's chair, all quite in the old style. The sideboard was in his charge; he had the care of 'the various spices, cardamums and lemons,' and to the question, 'Hadn't he heard that all serfs had received their freedom?' he always responded, 'To be sure, folks would for ever be talking some such idle nonsense; that like enough there was freedom among the Turks, but he, thank God, had escaped all that.' A girl, Pufka, a dwarf, was kept for entertainment, and an old nurse, Vassilyevna, used to come in during dinner with a large dark kerchief on her head, and talk in a thick voice of all the news – of Napoleon, of the year 1812, of Antichrist, and white niggers; or else, her chin propped in her hand, in an attitude of woe, she would tell what she had dreamed and what it portended, and what fortune she had got from the cards. The Subotchevs' house itself was quite different from all the other houses in the town; it was entirely built of oak and had windows exactly square. The double windows for winter were never taken out all the year round! And there were in it all kinds of little anterooms and passages, lumber-rooms and store-closets, and raised landings with balustrades and alcoves raised on rounded posts, and all sorts of little back premises and cellars. In front was a little palisade, and behind a garden, and in the garden outbuildings of every sort, granaries, cellars, ice-houses . . . a perfect nest of them! And it was not that there were many goods stored in all these outhouses; some, indeed, were tumbling down; but it had all been so arranged in old days, and so it had remained. The Subotchevs had only two horses, ancient, grey, and shaggy; one was covered with white patches from age; they called it the Immovable. They were – at most once a month – harnessed to an extraordinary equipage, known to the whole town, and presenting a resemblance to a terrestrial globe with one quarter cut out in front, lined within with foreign yellow material, closely dotted with big spots like warts. The last yard of that stuff had been woven in Utrecht or Lyons in the time of the Empress Elizabeth! The Subotchevs' coachman, too, was an exceedingly aged man, redolent of train-oil and pitch; his beard began just under his eyes, while his eyebrows fell in little cascades to meet his beard. He was so deliberate in all his movements that it took him five minutes to take a pinch of snuff, two minutes to stick his whip in his belt, and more than two hours to harness the Immovable alone. His name was Perfishka. If, when the Subotchevs were driving, their carriage had to go ever so little uphill, they were invariably alarmed (they were as frightened, however, going downhill), hung on to the straps of the carriage, and both repeated aloud: 'God grant the horses – the horses . . . the strength of Samuel, and make us . . . us light as a feather, light as a feather! . . .'

The Subotchevs were regarded by everyone in the town as eccentric, almost as mad; and indeed they were conscious themselves that they were not in touch with the life of the day . . . but they did not trouble themselves very much about that: the manner of life to which they had been born and bred and married they adhered to. Only one peculiarity of that manner of life had not clung to them: from their birth up they had never punished any one, never had any one flogged. If any servant of theirs proved to be an irreclaimable thief or drunkard, first they were patient and bore with him a long while, just as they would have put up with bad weather; and at last tried to get rid of him, to pass him on to other masters: let others, they would say, take their turn of them for a little. But such a disaster rarely befell them, so rarely that it made an epoch in their lives, and they would say, for instance, 'That was very long ago, it happened when we had that rascal Aldoshka,' or, 'when we had grandfather's fur cap with the fox's tail stolen.' The Subotchevs still had such caps. Another distinguishing trait of the old world was, however, not noticeable in them: neither Fimushka nor Fomushka was very religious. Fomushka went so far as to profess some of Voltaire's views; while Fimushka had a mortal dread of ecclesiastical personages; they had, according to her experience, the evil eye. 'The priest comes in to call on me,' she used to say, 'and then I look round and the cream's turned sour!' They rarely went to church, and fasted in the Catholic fashion, that's to say, ate eggs, butter, and milk. This was known in the town, and of course did not improve their reputation. But their goodness carried everything before it; and though the queer Subotchevs were laughed at and regarded as lunatics and innocents, they were all the same, in fact, respected. Yes; they were respected ... but no one visited them. This, however, was no great affliction to them. They were never bored when they were together, and therefore they were never apart and desired no other company. Neither Fomushka nor Fimushka had once been ill; and if either of them ever contracted some slight ailment, then they both drank lime-flower water, rubbed warm oil on their stomachs, or dropped hot tallow on the soles of their feet, and it was very soon over. They always spent the day in the same way. They got up late, drank chocolate in the morning in tiny cups of the shape of mortars; 'tea,' they used to declare, 'came into fashion after our time.' They sat down opposite to one another, and either talked (and they always found something to talk about!) or read something out of *Agreeable Recreations*, *The Mirror of the World*, or *Aonides*, or looked at a little old album bound in red morocco with gold edges, which once belonged, as an inscription recorded, to one Mme. Barbe de Kabyline. How and when this album had got into their hands they did not know themselves. In it were several French and many Russian poems and prose extracts, after the fashion, for example, of the following short meditations on Cicero: 'In what disposition Cicero entered upon the office of quæstor, he explains as follows: Invoking the gods to testify to the purity of his sentiments in every position with which he had hitherto been honoured, he deemed himself by the most sacred bonds bound to the worthy fulfilment thereof, and to that intent he, Cicero, not only suffered himself not the indulgence of the pleasures forbidden by law, but refrained even from those lighter distractions which are held to be indispensable by all.' Below stood the inscription: 'Composed in Siberia in hunger and cold.' A good specimen, too, was a poem entitled 'Tirsis,' where these lines were to be met:

> 'A settled peace is over all,
> The dew's asparkle in the sun,
> Nature it soothes, with freshness cool,
> Giving new life to the day begun!
> Tirsis alone, with soul dismayed,
> Sorrows, pines, so lone and so sad.
> His darling Aneta is far away,
> And what can then make Tirsis glad?'

and the impromptu composition of a captain who had come on a visit in 1790, dated 'May 6th':

> 'Never shall I forget
> Thee, lovely hamlet!
> For ever shall I recall
> How sweetly the time passed!
> What kindness I received

In thy noble owner's hall!
Five memorable happy days,
In a circle worthy of all praise!
With old and young ladies, not a few,
And other int'resting people too.'

On the last page of the album, instead of verses there were recipes for remedies against stomach-ache, spasms, and worms. The Subotchevs dined at twelve o'clock punctually, and always upon old-fashioned dishes: curd fritters, sour cucumber soups, salt cabbage pickles, hasty pudding, jelly puddings, syrups, jugged poultry, with saffron and custards, made with honey. After dinner they took a nap for just one hour and no longer, waked up, again sat opposite one another, and drank cranberry syrup and sometimes an effervescent drink called 'forty winks,' which, however, almost all popped out of the bottle, and afforded the old people great amusement and Kalliopitch great annoyance; he had to wipe up 'all over the place,' and he kept up a long grumble at the butler and the cook, whom he regarded as responsible for the invention of this beverage . . . 'What sort of good is there in it? it only spoils the furniture!' Then the Subotchevs again read something, or laughed at the pranks of the dwarf Pufka, or sang duets of old-fashioned songs (their voices were exactly alike, high, feeble, rather quavering, and hoarse – especially just after their nap, – but not without charm), or they played cards, always the same old games, cribbage, piquet, or even boston with double dummy! Then the samovar made its appearance; they drank tea in the evening. . . . This concession they did make to the spirit of the age, though they always thought it a weakness, and that the people were growing noticeably feebler through this 'Chinese herb.' As a rule, however, they refrained from criticising modern times or exalting the old days; they had never lived in any other way from their birth up; but that other people might live differently, better even, they readily admitted so long as they were not required to change their ways. At seven o'clock Kalliopitch served the supper, with the inevitable cold, sour hash; and at nine o'clock the high striped feather-beds had already taken into their soft embraces the plump little persons of Fomushka and Fimushka, and untroubled sleep was not slow in descending upon their eyelids; and everything was hushed in the old house; the lamp glowed, amid the fragrance of musk; the cricket chirped; and the kind-hearted, absurd, innocent old couple slept sound.

To these eccentrics, or, as Paklin expressed it, 'poll-parrots,' who were taking care of his sister, he now conducted his friends.

His sister was a clever girl, and not bad-looking. Her eyes were magnificent, but her unfortunate deformity had crushed her, deprived her of all self-confidence and joyousness, made her distrustful and even ill-tempered. And her name was very unfortunate, Snanduliya! Paklin had tried to make her change it to Sofya, but she clung obstinately to her queer name, saying that that was just what a hunchback ought to be called – Snanduliya. She was a good musician, and played the piano well: 'Thanks to my long fingers,' she observed with some bitterness; 'hunchbacks always have fingers like that.'

The visitors came upon Fomushka and Fimushka at the very minute when they had waked up from their after-dinner nap and were drinking cranberry water.

'We are stepping into the eighteenth century,' cried Paklin, directly they crossed the threshold of the Subotchevs' house.

And they were, in fact, confronted by the eighteenth century in the very hall, in the shape of low bluish screens covered with black cut-out silhouettes of powdered cavaliers and ladies. Silhouettes, introduced by Lavater, were much in vogue in Russia in the eighties of last century. The sudden appearance of so large a number of visitors – no less than four – produced quite a sensation in the secluded house. They heard a stampede of feet, both shod and naked; more than one woman's face was thrust out for an instant and then vanished again; some one was shut out, some one groaned, some one giggled, some one whispered convulsively, 'Get along with you, do!'

At last Kalliopitch made his appearance in his shabby jerkin, and, opening the door into the 'salon,' he cried in a loud voice:

'Your honour, Sila Samsonitch with some other gentlemen!'

The old people were far less fluttered than their servants. The irruption of four full-sized men in their drawing-room, comfortably large as it was, did indeed bewilder them a little, but Paklin promptly reassured them by presenting, with various odd phrases, Nezhdanov, Solomin, and Markelov to them in turn as good quiet fellows and not 'crown people.' Fomushka and Fimushka had a special dislike for 'crown' – that is, official – people.

Snanduliya, who appeared at her brother's summons, was far more agitated and ceremonious than the old Subotchevs. They asked their visitors, both together, and in exactly the same phrases, to sit down, and begged to know what they would take – tea, chocolate, or an effervescent beverage with jam? When they heard that their guests wanted nothing, since they had not long before lunched at the merchant Golushkin's and would shortly dine there, then they did not press them, and, folding their little hands across their little persons in precisely the same manner, they entered upon conversation.

At first the conversation flagged rather, but soon it grew livelier. Paklin diverted the old people hugely with Gogol's well-known story of the mayor who succeeded in getting into a church when it was full, and of the pie that was equally successful in getting into the mayor; they laughed till the tears ran down their cheeks. They laughed, too, in exactly the same way, with sudden shrieks, ending in a cough, with their whole faces flushed and heated. Paklin had noticed that, as a rule, quotations from Gogol have a very powerful and, as it were, convulsive effect upon people like the Subotchevs, but, as he was not so much anxious to amuse them as to show them off to his friends, he changed his tactics, and managed so that the old people were soon quite at ease and animated. Fomushka brought out and showed the visitors his favourite carved wood snuff-box, on which it had once been possible to distinguish thirty-six figures in various attitudes; they had long ago been effaced, but Fomushka saw them, saw them still, and could distinguish them and point them out. 'See,' he said, 'there's one looking out of window; do you see, he's put his head out . . .' and the spot to which he pointed with his chubby finger with its raised nail was just as smooth as all the rest of the snuff-box lid. Then he drew the attention of his guests to a picture hanging above his head, painted in oils; it represented a hunter in profile galloping full speed on a pale bay-coloured steed, also in profile, over a plain of snow. The hunter wore a tall white sheepskin cap with a blue streamer, a tunic of camel's hair, with a velvet border and a belt of wrought gold; a glove embroidered in silk was tucked into the belt, and a dagger, mounted in silver and black, hung from it. In one hand the hunter, who was very youthful and plump in appearance, held a huge horn, decked with red tassels, and in the other the reins and whip. All the four legs of the horse were suspended in the air, and on each of them the artist had conscientiously portrayed a horseshoe, and even put in the nails. 'And observe,' said Fomushka, pointing with the same chubby finger to four semi-circular marks in the white ground behind the horse's legs, 'the prints in the snow – even these he has put in!' Why it was that there were only four of these prints – not one was to be seen further back – on that point Fomushka was silent.

'And you know that it is I,' he added after a brief pause, with a modest smile.

'What!' exclaimed Nezhdanov, 'did you hunt?'

'I did . . . but not for long. Once the horse threw me at full gallop, and I injured my "kurpy," so Fimushka was frightened . . . and so she wouldn't let me. I have given it up ever since.'

'What did you injure?' inquired Nezhdanov.

'The *kurpy*,' repeated Fomushka, dropping his voice.

His guests looked at one another. No one knew what sort of thing a *kurpy* might be; at least, Markelov knew that the shaggy tuft on a Cossack or Circassian cap is called a *kurpy*, but surely Fomushka could not have injured that! But to ask him exactly what he understood by the word was more than any one could make up his mind to do.

'Well, now, since you've shown off,' Fimushka observed suddenly, 'I will show off, too.'

Out of a diminutive 'bonheur du jour,' as they used to call the old-fashioned bureau on tiny crooked legs, with a convex lid which folded up into the back of the bureau, she took a water-colour miniature in an oval bronze frame, representing a perfectly naked child of four years old, with a quiver on her shoulder and a blue ribbon round her breast, trying the points of the arrows with the end of her little finger. The child was very curly and smiling, and had a slight squint. Fimushka showed the miniature to her visitors.

'That was I!' she observed.

'You?'

'Yes, I. In my childhood. There was an artist, a Frenchman, who used to come and see my father – a splendid artist! And so he painted a picture of me for my father's birthday. And what a nice Frenchman he was! He came to see us afterwards, too. He would come in, scraping his foot as he bowed, and then giving it a little shake in the air, and would kiss your hand, and when he went away he would kiss his own finger and bow to right and to left, and before and behind! He was a delightful Frenchman!'

They praised his work; Paklin even professed to discern a certain likeness.

Then Fomushka began talking of the French of to-day, and expressed the opinion that they must all be very wicked!

'Why so, Foma Lavrentyevitch?'

'Why, only see what names they have now!'

'What, for instance?'

'Why, such as Nozhan-Tsent-Lorran (Nogent Saint Lorraine), a regular bandit's name!'

Fomushka inquired incidentally, 'Who was the sovereign now in Paris?'

They told him 'Napoleon,' and that seemed to surprise and pain him.

'Why so?'

'Why, he must be such an old man,' he began, and stopped, looking round him in confusion.

Fomushka knew very little French, and read Voltaire in a translation (in a secret box under the head of his bed he kept a manuscript translation of *Candide*), but he occasionally dropped expressions like 'That, my dear sir, is *fausse parquet*' (in the sense of 'suspicious,' 'untrue'), at which many people laughed till a learned Frenchman explained that it was an old parliamentary expression used in his country until the year 1789.

Seeing that the conversation had turned on France and the French, Fimushka screwed up her courage to inquire about one thing which was very much on her mind. She first thought of applying to Markelov, but he looked very ill-tempered; she might have asked Solomin . . . but no! she thought, 'he's a plain sort of person; he's sure not to know French.' So she addressed herself to Nezhdanov.

'There's something, my dear sir, I should like to learn from you,' she began, 'excuse me! My cousin, Sila Samsonitch, you must know, makes fun of an old woman like me, and my old-fashioned ignorance.'

'How so?'

'Why, if any one wants to put the question, "What is it?" in the French dialect, ought he to say, "Ke-se-ke-se-ke-se-là?"'

'Yes.'

'And can he also say, "Ke-se-ke-se-là?"'

'Yes, he can.'

'And simply, "Ke-se-là?"'

'Yes, he could say that too.'
'And all that would be the same?'
'Yes.'
Fimushka pondered deeply, and threw up her hands.
'Well, Silushka,' she said at last, 'I was wrong and you were right. But these Frenchmen! Poor things!'

Paklin began begging the old people to sing them some little ballad. . . . They both laughed and wondered how such an idea could occur to him; they soon consented, however, but only on the condition that Snanduliya sat down to the harpsichord and accompanied them – she would know what. In one corner of the drawing-room there turned out to be a diminutive piano, which not one of them had noticed at the beginning. Snanduliya sat down to this 'harpsichord,' struck a few chords. . . . Such toothless, acid, wizened, crazy notes Nezhdanov had never heard before in his life; but the old people began singing promptly:

> 'Is it to feel the smart,'

began Fomushka,

> 'That's hid in love,
> The gods gave us a heart
> Attuned to love?'

> 'Was there a love-sick heart,'

responded Fimushka,

> 'In the world ever,
> Quite free from woe and smart?'

> 'Never! never!'

put in Fomushka.

'Never! never!'

repeated Fimushka.

'Pain is of love a part
Ever! ever!'

they both say together.

'Ever! ever!'

Fomushka warbled alone.

'Bravo!' cried Paklin; 'that's the first verse; now the second.'
'Certainly,' answered Fomushka; 'only, Snanduliya Samsonovna, how about the shake? There ought to be a shake after my verse.'

'To be sure,' replied Snanduliya, 'you shall have your shake.'
Fomushka began again:

'Has ever lover loved
And known not grief and pain?
What lover has not sighed
And wept and sighed again?'

And then Fimushka:

'The heart is rocked in grief
As a ship floats on the main,
Why was it given, then?'

'For pain! for pain! for pain!'

cried Fomushka, and he waited to give Snanduliya time for the shake.

Snanduliya performed the shake.

'For pain! for pain! for pain!'

repeated Fomushka.

And then both together:

'Take, gods, my heart away,
  Again! again! again!
  Again! again! again!'

And the song wound up with another shake.

'Bravo! bravo!' they all shouted, with the exception of Markelov, and they even clapped their hands.

'And do they feel,' thought Nezhdanov directly the applause ceased, 'they are performing like some sort of buffoons? Perhaps they don't, and perhaps they do feel it and think "Where's the harm? no one's the worse for it; we amuse others, in fact!" And if you look at it properly, they're right, a thousand times right!'

Under the influence of these reflections, he began suddenly paying them compliments, in acknowledgement of which they merely made a sort of slight courtesy, without leaving their chairs. ... But at that instant, out of the adjoining room, probably a bedroom or maids'-room, where a great whispering and bustle had been audible a long while, appeared the dwarf, Pufka, escorted by the old nurse, Vassilyevna. Pufka proceeded to squeal and play antics, while the nurse one minute quieted her, and the next egged her on.

Markelov, who had long shown signs of impatience (as for Solomin, he simply wore a broader smile than usual) turned sharply upon Fomushka.

'I shouldn't have thought you,' he began in his abrupt fashion, 'with your enlightened intellect (you're a follower of Voltaire, aren't you?) could be amused by what ought to be a subject for compassion – I mean deformity.' Then he remembered Paklin's sister, and could have bitten his tongue off; while Fomushka turned red, murmuring, 'Why – why, I didn't . . . she herself—'

And then Pufka fairly flew at Markelov.

'What put that idea into your head,' she squeaked in her lisping voice, 'to insult our masters? They protect a poor wretch like me, take me in, give me meat and drink, and you must grudge it me. You envy another's luck, I suppose. Where do you spring from, you black-faced, worthless wretch, with moustaches like a beetle's?' Here Pufka showed with her thick, short finger what his moustaches were like. Vassilyevna's toothless gums were shaking with laughter, and her mirth was echoed in the next room.

'Of course I can't presume to judge you,' Markelov addressed Fomushka; 'to protect the poor and the crippled is a good action. But allow me to observe, to live in luxury, wallowing in ease and plenty, even without injuring others, but not to lift a finger to aid your fellow-creatures, doesn't imply much virtue; I, for one, to tell the truth, attach no value to that sort of goodness!'

Here Pufka gave a deafening howl; she had not understood a word of all Markelov said; but the 'black-browed fellow' was scolding . . . how dared he! Vassilyevna, too, muttered something indistinct, while Fomushka folded his little hands across his breast, and turning towards his wife, 'Fimushka, my darling,' he said, all but sobbing, 'do you hear what the gentleman says? You and I are sinners, miscreants, Pharisees . . . we're wallowing in luxury, oh! oh! . . . we ought to be turned into the streets . . . and have a broom put in our hands to work for our living. Oh, ho! ho!' Hearing these mournful words, Pufka howled louder than ever. Fimushka's eyes puckered up, the corners of her mouth dropped, she was just drawing in a deep breath so as to give full vent to her emotions.

There's no knowing how it would have ended if Paklin had not intervened.

'What's the meaning of this? upon my word,' he began with a wave of the hand and a loud laugh, 'I wonder you're not ashamed of yourselves. Mr. Markelov meant to make a little joke, but as he has such a very solemn face, it sounded rather alarming, and you were taken in by it! That's enough! Evfimiya Pavlovna, there's a dear, we've got to go in a minute, so, do you know what? you must tell all our fortunes before parting . . . you're a great hand at that. Sister! get the cards!'

Fimushka glanced at her husband, and he was sitting quiet, completely reassured; she, too, was reassured.

'The cards,' she said; 'but I've quite forgotten, my dear sir, it's long since I had them in my hand.'

But of her own accord she took out of Snanduliya's hands a pack of aged, queer ombre cards.

'Whose fortune shall I tell?'

'Oh, every one's,' said Paklin; while to himself he said, 'What a mobile old thing! you can turn her any way you like . . . she's a perfect darling! Every one's, granny, every one's,' he went on aloud; 'tell us our fate, our character, our future . . . tell us everything!'

Fimushka began shuffling the cards, but suddenly she threw down the whole pack.

'I don't need to use the cards!' she cried; 'I know the character of each of you without that. And as the character is, so is the fate. He, now' (she pointed to Solomin) 'is a cool man, constant; he, now' (she shook her finger at Markelov) 'is a hot, dangerous man . . .' (Pufka put out her tongue at him); 'as for you' (she looked at Paklin), 'there's no need to tell you; you know yourself – a weathercock! As for this gentleman' (she indicated Nezhdanov, and hesitated).

'What is it?' he said; 'tell me, please; what sort of man am I?'

'What sort of man are you? . . .' said Fimushka slowly, 'you're to be pitied — that's all.'

Nezhdanov shuddered.

'To be pitied? why so?'

'Oh! I pity you — that's all.'

'But why?'

'Oh, for reasons! My eye tells me so. Do you think I'm a fool? Oh, I'm cleverer than you, for all your red hair. . . . I pity you . . . that's your fortune!'

All were silent . . . they looked at one another, and were still silent.

'Well, good-bye, dear friends,' Paklin cried, 'we've stayed too long and tired you, I'm afraid. It's time these gentlemen were off . . . and I'll see them on their way. Good-bye; thanks for your kind reception.'

'Good-bye, good-bye, come again, don't stand on ceremony,' Fomushka and Fimushka cried with one voice. . . . Then Fomushka struck up suddenly like a refrain:

'Many, many years of life.'

'Many, many years,' Kalliopitch chimed in quite unexpectedly in the bass, as he opened the door to the young men.

And all four of them suddenly emerged into the street before the podgy little house; while at the window they heard Pufka's squeaky voice: 'Fools . . .' she shouted, 'fools! . . .'

Paklin laughed aloud; but no one responded. Markelov scanned each in turn as though he expected to hear some word of indignation. . . .

Solomin alone smiled his ordinary smile.

XX

'WELL, NOW,' PAKLIN was the first to begin, 'we have been in the eighteenth century; now lead the way full trot to the twentieth. . . . Golushkin's such an advanced man that it wouldn't do to reckon him in the nineteenth.'

'Why, do you know him?' inquired Nezhdanov.

'The earth is full of his glory; and I said, "lead the way," because I meant to come with you.'

'How's that? why, you don't know him, do you?'

'Get along! Did you know my poll-parrots?'

'But you introduced us!'

'Well, and do you introduce me. You can have no secrets from me, and Golushkin's an open heart. You'll see he'll be delighted to see some one new. And we don't stand on ceremony here in S———!'

'Yes,' muttered Markelov, 'people seem unceremonious here certainly.'

Paklin shook his head.

'That's, perhaps, meant for me. . . . So be it! I've deserved the reproach. But I say, my new acquaintance, defer for a time the gloomy reflections your bilious temperament inspires in you! And most of all—'

'And you, sir, my new acquaintance,' Markelov interrupted emphatically, 'let me tell you . . . by way of a word of warning, I never have the faintest taste for joking at any time, and especially not to-day! And what do you know about my temperament? It strikes me that we've not long – that it's the first time we've set eyes on each other.'

'There, there, don't be cross, and don't swear. I'll believe you without that,' said Paklin, and turning to Solomin: 'Oh, you,' he exclaimed, 'you whom the keen-sighted Fimushka herself called a cool man – and there certainly is something refreshing about you – say, had I the slightest intention of doing anything unpleasant to any one, or of joking unseasonably? I only suggested going with you to Golushkin; and besides, I'm an inoffensive creature. It's not my fault that Mr. Markelov has a bilious complexion.'

Solomin shrugged up first one shoulder, then the other; it was a habit of his when he could not make up his mind at once what to answer.

'There's no mistake,' he said at last, 'you couldn't give offence to any one, Mr. Paklin, and you don't want to; and why shouldn't you go to Mr. Golushkin's? We shall, I should fancy, spend our time just as pleasantly there as at your cousin's, and just as profitably.'

Paklin shook his finger at him.

'Oh! I see there's malice in you too! But you're going to Golushkin's yourself, aren't you?'

'To be sure I'm going. To-day's a day lost, any way.'

'Well then, *en avant, marchons*, to the twentieth century! to the twentieth century! Nezhdanov, you're an advanced man, lead the way!'

'All right, come along; only, don't repeat the same jokes too often, for fear of our thinking you're running out of your stock.'

'There'll always be plenty at your service,' retorted Paklin gaily, and he hurried, advancing, as he said, not by leaps and bounds, but by limps and bounds.

'An amusing chap, very,' Solomin remarked as he walked behind him arm-in-arm with Nezhdanov; 'if – which God forbid – they send us all to Siberia, there'll be some one to amuse us!'

Markelov walked in silence behind the rest.

Meanwhile in the house of the merchant Golushkin every measure was being taken to provide a 'chic' dinner. A fish-soup, very greasy and very disagreeable, was concocted; various *pâtés chauds* and *fricassées* were prepared (Golushkin, as a man on the pinnacle of European culture, though an Old Believer, went in for French cookery, and had taken a cook from a club, where he had been discharged for dirtiness); and, what was most important, several bottles of champagne had been got out and put in ice.

The host himself met the young men with the awkward tricks peculiar to him, a hurried manner and much giggling. He was, as Paklin had predicted, overjoyed to see him; he inquired about him: 'I suppose he's one of us?' and without waiting for an answer, cried, 'There, of course he's bound to be!' Then he told them that he had just come from that 'queer fish' of a governor, who was always worrying him on behalf of some – deuce knows what! – benevolent institution. . . . And it was absolutely impossible to say whether Golushkin was more pleased at having been received at the governor's, or at having succeeded in abusing him in the presence of advanced young men. Then he introduced them to the proselyte he had promised. And this proselyte turned out to be none other than the sleek, sickly little man with the foxy face who had come in with a message in the morning, and whom Golushkin addressed as Vasya, his clerk. 'He's not much of a talker,' Golushkin declared, pointing to him with all five fingers at once, 'but devoted heart and soul to our cause.' Vasya confined himself to bowing, blushing, blinking, and smirking so effectually, that again it was impossible to say whether he was a vulgar blockhead or a consummate knave and scoundrel.

'But to dinner, gentlemen, to dinner.'

After partaking freely of the preliminary appetisers on the sideboard, they sat down to the table. Immediately after the soup, Golushkin ordered up the champagne. In frozen flakes and lumps it dropped from the neck of the bottle into the glasses. 'To our . . . our enterprise!' cried Golushkin, with a wink and a nod in the direction of the servants, as though to give them to understand that in the presence of outsiders they must be on their guard! The proselyte Vasya still continued silent, and though he sat on the extreme edge of his chair and conducted himself in general with a servility utterly out of keeping with the convictions to which, in the words of his patron, he was devoted heart and soul, he drank away at the wine with desperate eagerness! ... The others, however, talked; that is to say, their host talked – and Paklin; Paklin especially. Nezhdanov was inwardly fretting; Markelov was angry and indignant, just as indignant, though in a different way, as at the Subotchevs'; Solomin was looking on, observant.

Paklin was enjoying himself! With his smart speeches he greatly delighted Golushkin, who had not the faintest suspicion that the 'little lame chap' kept whispering to Nezhdanov, who was sitting beside him, the cruellest remarks at his, Golushkin's, expense! He positively imagined that he was something of a simpleton, who might be patronised ... and that was partly why he liked him. Had Paklin been sitting next him, he would have poked him in the ribs with his finger or slapped him on the shoulder; as it was, he winked at him across the table and nodded his head in his direction ... but between him and Nezhdanov was seated first Markelov, like a storm-cloud, and then Solomin. However, Golushkin laughed convulsively at every word Paklin uttered, and even laughed on trust in advance, slapping himself on the stomach, and showing his bluish gums. Paklin soon saw what was required of him, and began abusing everything (it was a congenial task for him) – everything and everybody; conservatives, liberals, officials, barristers, judges, landowners, district councils, local assemblies, Moscow and Petersburg!

'Yes, yes, yes, yes,' put in Golushkin; 'to be sure, to be sure! Our mayor here, for instance, is a perfect ass! A hopeless noodle! I tell him one thing and another ... but he doesn't understand a word; he's just such another as our governor!'

'Is your governor a fool?' inquired Paklin.

'I tell you he's an ass!'

'Have you ever noticed, does he grunt or snuffle?'

'What?' asked Golushkin in some bewilderment.

'Why, don't you know? In Russia our great civilians grunt;

and our great army men talk through their noses; and it's only the very highest dignitaries who both grunt and snuffle at once.'

Golushkin roared with laughter till the tears ran down.

'Yes, yes,' he stuttered, 'he snuffles. . . . He's an army man!'

'Ugh, you booby!' Paklin was thinking to himself.

'Everything's rotten with us, go where you will,' bawled Golushkin, a little later. 'Everything's rotten, everything!'

'Most honoured Kapiton Andreitch,' Paklin observed sympathetically – (he had just been whispering to Nezhdanov, 'What makes him keep moving his arms about, as if his coat were too tight in the armholes?') – 'Most honoured Kapiton Andreitch, trust me, half-measures are no use now!'

'Half-measures!' screamed Golushkin, suddenly ceasing to laugh, and assuming a ferocious expression, 'there's only one thing now: to tear it all up from the roots! Vasya, drink, you dirty dog you, drink!'

'And so I am drinking, Kapiton Andreitch,' responded the clerk, emptying his glass down his throat.

Golushkin, too, tossed off a glassful.

'How is it he doesn't burst?' Paklin whispered to Nezhdanov.

'It's practice does it!' rejoined Nezhdanov.

But the clerk was not the only one who drank. By degrees the wine affected them all. Nezhdanov, Markelov, even Solomin, gradually took part in the conversation.

At first in a sort of disdain, in a sort of vexation with himself for not keeping up his character, for doing nothing, Nezhdanov began to maintain that the time had come to cease to play with mere words, the time had come to 'act,' – he even alluded to the 'bed-rock having been reached!' And then, without noticing that he was contradicting himself, he began to ask them to point out what real existing elements they could rely on – to declare that he couldn't see any. No sympathy in society, no understanding in the people.

He got no answer, of course; not because there was no answer to be given, but that every one was by now talking on his own account. Markelov kept up a monotonous, insistent drone with his dull, angry voice ('for all the world as if he were chopping cabbage,' remarked Paklin). Precisely what he was talking of, was not quite clear; the word 'artillery' could be distinguished in a momentary lull . . . he was probably referring to the defects he had discovered in its organisation. Germans and adjutants seemed also to be coming in for their share. Even Solomin observed that there were two ways of waiting: waiting and doing nothing, and waiting while pushing things forward.

'Progressives are no good to us,' said Markelov gloomily.

'Progressives have hitherto worked from above,' observed Solomin; 'we are going to try working from below.'

'No use, go to the devil, no use in it!' Golushkin cut in furiously; 'we must act at once, at once!'

'In fact, you want to jump out of window?'

'I'll jump out!' clamoured Golushkin. 'I will! and so'll Vasya! If I tell him, he'll jump out! Eh, Vasya? You'd jump, wouldn't you?'

The clerk drank off a glass of champagne.

'Where you lead, Kapiton Andreitch, there I follow. I shouldn't dare think twice about it.'

'You'd better not! I'd twist you into a ram's horn.'

Before long there followed what in the language of drunkards is known as a 'regular Babel.' A mighty clamour and uproar arose.

Like the first flakes of snow, swiftly whirling, crossing and recrossing in the still mild air of autumn, words began flying, tumbling, jostling against one another in the heated atmosphere of Golushkin's dining-room – words of all sorts – progress, government, literature; the taxation question, the church question, the woman question, the law-court question; classicism, realism, nihilism, communism; international, clerical, liberal, capital; administration, organisation, association, and even crystallisation! It was just this uproar which seemed to rouse Golushkin to enthusiasm; the real gist of the matter seemed to consist in this, for him. . . . He was triumphant! 'Here we are! Out of the way or I'll kill you! . . . Kapiton Golushkin's coming!' The clerk Vasya at last reached such a point of tipsiness, that he began snorting and talking to his plate, and suddenly shouted like one possessed: 'What the devil's the meaning of a *pro*gymnasium?'

Golushkin all at once got up, and throwing back his crimson face, in which an expression of coarse brutality and swagger was curiously mingled with the expression of another feeling, like a secret misgiving, even trepidation, he bawled, 'I will sacrifice another thousand! Vasya, out with it!' to which Vasya responded in an undertone, 'He's going it!'

Paklin, pale and perspiring (for the last quarter of an hour he had vied with the clerk in drinking), Paklin, jumping up from his place, and lifting both hands high above his head, cried brokenly, 'Sacrifice! he said, sacrifice! Oh, degradation of that sacred word! Sacrifice! No one dares to rise to thee, no one has the strength to fulfil the duties thou enjoinest, at least no one of us here present – and this lout, this vile money-bag, gloats over his swollen gains, scatters a handful of roubles, and shouts of sacrifice! And asks for gratitude; expects a wreath of laurel – the mean scoundrel!' Golushkin either did not hear, or did not understand what Paklin said, or possibly took his words for a joke, for he vociferated once more, 'Yes! a thousand roubles! Kapiton Andreitch's word is sacred!' He suddenly thrust his hand into his side pocket. 'Here it is, here's the cash! There, pocket it; and remember Kapiton!' As soon as he reached a certain pitch of excitement, he used to talk of himself in the third person, like a little child. Nezhdanov picked up the notes flung on the wine-stained cloth. Since there was nothing to stay for after this, and it was now late, they all got up, took their caps, and went away.

In the open air they all felt giddy, especially Paklin.

'Well? where are we going now?' he managed to articulate with some difficulty.

'I don't know where you're going,' answered Solomin; 'I'm going home.'

'To your factory?'

'Yes.'

'Now, in the middle of the night, on foot?'

'What of it? there are neither wolves nor brigands here, and I'm quite well and able to walk. It's cooler walking at night.'

'But, I say, it's three miles!'

'Well, what if it were four? Good-bye, my friends!'

Solomin buttoned up his coat, pulled his cap over his forehead, lighted a cigar, and set off with long strides up the street.

'And where are you going?' said Paklin, turning to Nezhdanov.

'I'm going to his place.' He indicated Markelov, who was standing stock-still, his arms folded across his breast. 'We have horses here and a carriage.'

'Oh, that's capital . . . and I, my dear boy, am going to the oasis, to Fomushka and Fimushka. And do you know what I would say to you, my dear boy? There's madness there and madness here . . . only that madness, the eighteenth-century madness, is closer to the heart of Russia than the twentieth-century. Good-bye, gentlemen; I'm drunk, don't be angry with me. Just let me say one thing! There's not a kinder and a better woman on earth than my sister, Snanduliya; and you see what she is – a hunchback, and her name's Snanduliya! That's how it always is in this world! Though it's quite right that should be her name. Do you know who Saint Snanduliya was? A virtuous woman, who visited the prisons and healed the wounds of the prisoners and the sick. Well, good-bye! good-bye, Alexey – man to be pitied! And you call yourself an officer . . . ugh! misanthrope! good-bye!'

He trailed away, limping and swaying from side to side, towards the oasis, while Markelov and Nezhdanov sought out the posting station where they had left their coach, ordered the horses to be put to, and half an hour later they were driving along the highroad.

XXI

THE SKY WAS overcast with low clouds, and although it was not perfectly dark, and in front the cart-ruts could be distinguished standing out on the road, to right and left, everything was in shadow, and the outlines of separate objects fell together into big confused patches of darkness. It was a dim, treacherous night; the wind blew in gusty, damp squalls, bringing with it the scent of rain and of broad fields of wheat. When they had passed the oak bushes which served as a landmark, and had to turn off into the by-road, driving was still more difficult; the narrow track was quite lost at times. . . . The coachman drove more slowly.

'I hope we're not going to lose our way,' observed Nezhdanov, who had been silent till then.

'No; we shan't lose our way!' answered Markelov. 'Two misfortunes don't come in one day.'

'Why, what was the first misfortune?'

'What? why, we've wasted our day for nothing – don't you reckon that as anything?'

'Yes . . . of course. . . . That awful Golushkin! We oughtn't to have drunk so much wine. My head aches now . . . fearfully.'

'I wasn't speaking of Golushkin; he at any rate gave us some money, so that was at least something gained by our visit!'

'Surely you don't regret Paklin's having taken us to his . . . what was it he called them – poll-parrots?'

'There's nothing to regret in it . . . and there's nothing to rejoice at either. I'm not one of those who take interest in such trifles. . . . I was not referring to that misfortune.'

'What, then?'

Markelov made no reply, he simply turned a little in his corner, as though he were wrapping himself up. Nezhdanov could not quite make out his face; only his moustaches stood out in a black transverse line; but ever since the morning he had been conscious of something in Markelov it was better not to touch upon – some obscure, secret irritation.

'Tell me, Sergei Mihalovitch,' he began after a long pause, 'are you in earnest in admiring Mr. Kislyakov's letters, that you gave me to read this morning? You know – excuse the crudity of the expression – it's all perfect rubbish!'

Markelov drew himself up.

'In the first place,' he began in a wrathful voice, 'I don't at all share your opinion about those letters. I think them very remarkable ... and conscientious! And secondly, Kislyakov toils and slaves, and, what's more, he *believes*; he believes in our cause, he believes in revolution! I must tell you one thing, Alexey Dmitrievitch, I notice that *you* – you are very lukewarm in our cause; you don't believe in it!'

'What makes you think that?' Nezhdanov articulated slowly.

'What? Why, every word you say, your whole behaviour! To-day at Golushkin's, who was it said he didn't see what elements we could depend on? You! Who asked us to point to any? You! And when that friend of yours, that grinning ape and buffoon, Mr. Paklin, began declaring, with eyes upturned to heaven, that not one of us was capable of sacrifice, who was it backed him up, who was it nodded his head in approval? Wasn't that you? Say what you please of yourself, and think of yourself what you know ... that's your affair ... but I know of people who are capable of renouncing everything that makes life sweet, even the bliss of love, to be true to their convictions, not to betray them! Oh, to-day, *you* are not capable of that, of course!'

'To-day? And why to-day?'

'Come, no humbug, for God's sake, you happy Don Juan, you myrtle-crowned lover!' shouted Markelov, totally oblivious of the coachman, who, though he did not turn round on the box, could hear everything perfectly distinctly. It is true the coachman was at that instant far more interested in the road than in any wrangling on the part of the gentlemen sitting behind him, and he cautiously and rather timorously urged on the centre horse, who shook his head and backed, letting the coach slide down a sort of rocky prominence, which certainly ought not to have been there at all.

'Excuse me, I don't quite understand you,' said Nezhdanov.

Markelov gave a forced, vindictive chuckle.

'You don't understand me! Ha! ha! ha! I know all about it, my fine gentleman! I know whom you had a love-scene with yesterday; I know who it is you've fascinated with your good looks and your fine talk; I know who lets you into her room . . . after ten o'clock at night!'

'Master!' the coachman suddenly addressed Markelov, 'take the reins . . . I'll get down and have a look. . . . I think we've got off the road. . . . There seems a sort of ravine here, or something. . . .'

The coach was, in fact, all on one side. Markelov clutched the reins handed him by the coachman, and went on as loudly as ever: 'I don't blame you, Alexey Dmitritch! You profited . . . of course. You were right. I only say that I don't wonder at your lukewarmness over our cause; you'd something else, I say again, in your heart. And I say, too, for my own part, what man can guess beforehand what will take girls' hearts, or understand what it is they want! . . .'

'I understand you now,' Nezhdanov began, 'I understand your mortification, guess who has spied on us and lost no time in telling you. . . .'

'It's not merit in this case,' Markelov went on, affecting not to hear Nezhdanov, and intentionally dwelling on and prolonging each word, 'not any extraordinary qualities of mind or body. . . . No! It's simply . . . the cursed luck of all illegitimate children, . . . of all . . . bastards!'

The last phrase Markelov uttered abruptly and rapidly, and at once was still as death.

Nezhdanov felt himself grow pale all over in the darkness,

and spasms passed over his face. He could scarcely restrain himself from flying at Markelov, seizing him by the throat . . . 'This insult must be washed out in blood, in blood. . . .'

'I've found the road!' cried the coachman, making his appearance at the right front wheel. 'I made a little mistake, kept too much to the left . . . it's no matter now! We'll be there in no time; there's not a mile before us. Be pleased to sit still!'

He clambered on to the box, took the reins from Markelov, turned the shaft horse's head. . . . The coach, after two violent jolts, rolled along more easily and evenly, the darkness seemed to part and to lift, there was a smell of smoke, in front rose a sort of hillock. Then a light twinkled . . . and vanished. . . . Another glimmered. . . . A dog barked. . . .

'Our huts,' said the coachman; 'ah, get along, my pretty pussies!'

The lights came more and more often to meet them.

'After that insult,' Nezhdanov began at last, 'you will readily understand, Sergei Mihalovitch, that I cannot spend a night under your roof; I am therefore, unpleasant as it is to me, forced to ask you to lend me your coach, when you reach home, so that I may return to the town; to-morrow I will find means of getting home; and then you shall receive from me the communication you doubtless expect.'

Markelov did not at once reply.

'Nezhdanov,' he said all at once in a low, but despairing voice, 'Nezhdanov! For God's sake come into my house, if only to let me beg on my knees for your forgiveness! Nezhdanov! Forget . . . Alexey! forget, forget my senseless words! Oh, if any one could feel how miserable I am!' Markelov struck himself on the breast with his fist, and it seemed to give forth a hollow groan. 'Alexey! be magnanimous! Give me your hand! . . . Don't refuse to forgive me!'

Nezhdanov held out his hand – irresolutely – still he held it out. Markelov squeezed it so that he almost cried out.

The coachman stopped at the steps of Markelov's house.

'Listen, Alexey,' Markelov was saying to him a quarter of an hour after in his room, . . . 'dear brother,' he kept addressing him by this familiar, endearing term; and in this affectionate familiarity to the man in whom he had discovered a successful rival, to whom he had only just offered a deadly insult, whom he had been ready to kill, to tear to pieces, there was the expression of irrevocable renunciation, and humble, bitter supplication, and a sort of claim too. . . . Nezhdanov recognised this claim by beginning to address Markelov in the same familiar way.

'Listen, Alexey! I said just now I had refused the happiness of love, renounced it so as to be wholly at the service of my convictions. . . . That was nonsense, bragging! I have never been offered anything of that sort, I have had nothing to renounce! I was born without gifts, and so I have remained. . . . And perhaps it was right it should be so. Since I can't attain to that, I have to do something else! Since you can combine both . . . can love and be loved . . . and at the same time serve the cause . . . well, you're a fine fellow! I envy you . . . but it is not so with me. I can't. You are happy! You are happy! I can't.'

Markelov said all this in a subdued voice, sitting on a low chair, his head bent and his arms hanging loose at his sides. Nezhdanov stood before him, plunged in a sort of dreamy attention, and though Markelov called him happy, he neither looked nor felt happy.

'I was deceived in my youth,' . . . Markelov went on; 'she was an exquisite girl, and yet she jilted me . . . and for whom? For a German! for an adjutant! while Marianna—'

He stopped. . . . For the first time he had uttered her name, and it seemed to burn his lips.

'Marianna did not deceive me; she told me plainly that she didn't care for me. . . . And how should she care for me? Well, she has given herself to you . . . Well, what of that? was she not free?'

'Oh, stay, stay!' cried Nezhdanov, 'what is it you are saying?

Given herself? I don't know what your sister has written to you; but I swear to you—'

'I don't say physically; but morally she has given herself, in heart, in soul,' interposed Markelov, who was obviously comforted for some reason or other by Nezhdanov's exclamation. 'And she has done well. As for my sister . . . Of course she had no intention of wounding. . . . At least, she didn't care about it one way or another; but she must hate you, and Marianna too. She was not lying . . . but there, enough of her!'

'Yes,' thought Nezhdanov to himself: 'she hates us.'

'Everything is for the best,' Markelov continued without changing his position. 'Now the last ways of retreat are cut off for me, now there is nothing to hinder me! Never mind Golushkin's being a blockhead; that's of no consequence. And Kislyakov's letters . . . they're absurd, perhaps . . . but we must look to the principal thing. According to him, everything's ready everywhere. You don't believe that, perhaps?'

Nezhdanov made no answer.

'You are right, perhaps; but you know if we wait for the moment when everything, absolutely everything, is ready, we shall never begin. If one weighs *all* the consequences beforehand, it's certain there will be some evil ones. For instance: when our predecessors organised the emancipation of the peasants, could they foresee that one result of this emancipation would be the rise of a whole class of money-lending landowners, who would lend the peasant a quarter of mouldy rye for six roubles, and extort from him' (here Markelov crooked one finger) 'first the full six roubles in labour, and besides that' (Markelov crooked another finger) 'a whole quarter of good rye, and then' (Markelov crooked a third) 'interest on the top of that? – in fact, they squeeze the peasant to the last drop! Our emancipators couldn't have foreseen that, you must admit! And yet, even if they had foreseen it, they'd have done right to free the peasants, and not to weigh all the consequences! And so, I have made up my mind!'

Nezhdanov looked questioningly, in perplexity, at Markelov; but the latter looked away into the corner. His brows were contracted and hid his eyes; he bit his lips and gnawed his moustache.

'Yes, I have made up my mind!' he repeated with a swing of his arm down on his knee. 'I'm an obstinate man, you know . . . I'm not half a Little-Russian for nothing.'

Then he got up, and, staggering as though his legs were failing him, he went into his bedroom, and brought out from there a small portrait of Marianna framed under glass.

'Take it,' he said in a mournful but steady voice; 'I did it once. I draw very badly; but look, I think it's like.' (The sketch, a pencil drawing taken in profile, was really like.) 'Take it, brother; it's my last bequest. Together with this portrait I give up to you all my right . . . I never had any . . . but you know, Alexey, everything! I give you everything, Alexey . . . and her, dear brother; she's a good . . .'

Markelov was silent; the heaving of his breast was visible.

'Take it. You're not angry with me, Alexey? Then take it. I have nothing now . . . I don't want that.' Nezhdanov took the portrait; but a strange sensation oppressed his heart. It seemed to him that he had no right to accept this gift; that if Markelov had known what was in his, Nezhdanov's, heart, he would not, perhaps, have given him the portrait. He held in his hand the little round piece of paper carefully set in its black frame with a mount of gold paper, and he did not know what to do with it. 'Here is a man's whole life in my hand,' was the thought that occurred to him. He realised what a sacrifice Markelov was making, but why, why was it to him? Should he give back the portrait? No! That would be a still crueller affront. . . . And after all, wasn't that face dear to him? didn't he love her?

Nezhdanov with some inward misgiving turned his eyes upon Markelov . . . wasn't he looking at him, trying to read his thoughts? But Markelov was again staring into the corner and gnawing his moustache.

The old servant came into the room with a candle in his hand.

Markelov started.

'It's time for bed, dear Alexey!' he cried. 'Morning brings better counsel. I will give you horses, you will drive home, and good-bye, brother.'

'And good-bye to you, too, old fellow!' he added suddenly, turning to the servant and slapping him on the shoulder. 'Think of me kindly!'

The old man was so astounded that he all but dropped the candle, and his eyes, bent on his master, expressed something other – and more – than his habitual dejection.

Nezhdanov went to his room. He was miserable. His head was still aching from the wine he had drunk, there were noises in his ears, and lights dazzling before his eyes, even though he shut them. Golushkin, the clerk Vasya, Fomushka, Fimushka, kept revolving before him; in the distance, Marianna's image seemed distrustful, would not come near. Everything he had said or done himself struck him as such lying and affectation, such superfluous and humbugging nonsense . . . and the thing that ought to be done, the aim that ought to be striven for, was not to be found anywhere, unattainable under lock and bar, buried in the bottomless pit. . . .

And he was beset with the unceasing desire to get up, go to Markelov, and say to him, 'Take back your present, take it back!'

'Ugh! what a loathsome thing life is!' he cried at last.

The next morning he went off early. Markelov was already on the steps, surrounded by peasants. Whether he had called them together, or they had come of themselves, Nezhdanov could not make out; Markelov said good-bye to him, very briefly and drily . . . but he seemed to be about to make some important communication to the peasants. The old servant was hanging about the steps with his unvarying expression.

The coach quickly passed through the town, and moved

at a furious pace directly the open country was reached. The horses were the same, but the coachman, either because Nezhdanov was living in a grand house, or for some other reason, was reckoning on something handsome 'for vodka' . . . and we all know that when a coachman has had vodka, or is confidently expecting it, the horses trot their best. It was fine weather, though fresh; lofty clouds were gambolling over the sky, there was a strong, steady breeze; the road, after the previous day's rain, was not dusty; the willows rustled, gleamed, and rippled, everything was moving, fluttering; the peewit's cry came whistling from the distant slopes, across the green ravines, just as though the cry had wings and was flying on them; the crows were glossing themselves in the sun; something like black fleas was moving across the straight line of the bare horizon – it was the peasants ploughing their fallow land a second time.

But Nezhdanov let it all pass by unseen; he did not even notice that he was driving into Sipyagin's property; he was overcome by his brooding thoughts.

He started, though, when he saw the roof of the house, the upper storey, Marianna's window. 'Yes,' he said to himself, and there was a glow of warmth about his heart; '*he* was right, she's a good girl, and I love her.'

XXII

HE HURRIEDLY CHANGED his clothes and went to give Kolya his lesson. Sipyagin, whom he met in the dining-room, bowed to him with chilly politeness, and muttering through his teeth, 'Had a pleasant visit?' went on to his study. The statesman had already decided in his diplomatic mind that directly the vacation was over he would promptly pack this tutor off to Petersburg, as he was 'positively too red,' and meanwhile he would keep an eye on him . . . '*Je n'ai pas eu la main heureuse cette fois-ci*,' he thought to himself; however, '*j'aurais pu tomber pire.*' Valentina Mihalovna's sentiments towards Nezhdanov were far more energetic and defined. She could not endure him now. . . . He – this little scrub of a boy! – had affronted her. Marianna had not been mistaken; it was she, Valentina Mihalovna, who had been spying on her and Nezhdanov in the corridor. . . . The distinguished lady was not above such a proceeding. In the course of the two days his absence had lasted, though she had said nothing to her 'thoughtless' niece, she had repeatedly given her to understand that she was aware of everything; that she would have been indignant, had she not been half-contemptuous, half-compassionate. . . . Her face was filled with restrained, inward contempt, her eyebrows were raised with something of irony and, at the same time, of pity whenever she looked at or spoke to Marianna; her superb eyes rested with tender perplexity, with mournful disgust, on the self-willed girl who, after all her 'fancies and eccentricities,' had come to . . . to . . . to kissing . . . in dark rooms . . . with a paltry little undergraduate!

Poor Marianna! Her stern, proud lips knew nothing as yet of any man's kisses.

Valentina Mihalovna had, however, given her husband no hint of the discovery she had made; she contented herself by accompanying a few words addressed to Marianna in his presence by a significant smile, in no way relevant to their apparent meaning. Valentina Mihalovna felt positively rather remorseful for having written the letter to her brother . . . but, all things considered, she preferred to repent and have done it, than be spared her penitence at the price of the letter not having been written.

Of Marianna, Nezhdanov had a glimpse in the dining-room at lunch. He thought her looking thin and yellow; she was not at all pretty that day; but the rapid glance she flung at him the instant he came into the room went straight to his heart. On the other hand, Valentina Mihalovna looked at him as though she were continually repeating inwardly, 'I congratulate you!

Well done! Very smart!' and at the same time she wanted to discover from his face whether Markelov had shown him the letter or not. She decided at last that he had shown it.

Sipyagin, hearing that Nezhdanov had been to the factory of which Solomin was the manager, began cross-questioning him about 'that manufacturing enterprise which presents so many striking points of interest'; but being shortly convinced from the young man's answers that he had really seen nothing there, he relapsed into majestic silence, with the air of reproaching himself for having expected any valuable information from such an undeveloped person! As they left the dining-room, Marianna managed to whisper to Nezhdanov, 'Wait for me in the old birch copse, Alexey; I will come directly I can get away.' Nezhdanov thought, 'She, too, calls me Alexey, just as he did.' And how sweet that familiarity was to him, though rather terrible too! and how strange, and how incredible, if she had suddenly begun addressing him as Mr. Nezhdanov again, if she had been more distant to him! He felt that that would be misery to him. Whether he was in love with her he could not be sure yet; but that she was precious to him, and near, and necessary – yes, above all, necessary, – that he felt to the very depths of his being.

The copse to which Marianna had sent him consisted of some hundreds of old birch-trees, mostly of the weeping variety. The wind had not dropped; the long bundles of twigs nodded and tossed like loosened tresses in the breeze; the clouds, as before, flew fast and high up in the sky, and when one of them floated across the sun, everything grew – not dark – but of one uniform tint. Then it floated past, and suddenly glaring patches of light were waving everywhere again, in tangled, medley riot, mingled with patches of shade . . . the rustle and movement were the same; but a kind of festive delight was added. With just such joyous violence, passion makes its way into a heart distraught and darkened by trouble. . . . And just such was the heart Nezhdanov carried within his breast.

He leaned against the trunk of a birch-tree, and began waiting. He did not really know what he was feeling, and indeed he did not want to know; he felt at once more disturbed and more light of heart than at Markelov's. He longed before all things to see her, to speak to her; the chain which so suddenly binds two living creatures together had him fast just then. Nezhdanov bethought himself of the rope flung to the quay when the ship is ready to be made fast. . . . Now it is twisted tight about a post, and the ship is at rest.

In harbour! God be thanked!

Suddenly he trembled. There was a glimpse of a woman's dress on the path in the distance. It was she. But whether she was coming towards him, or going away from him, he could not be sure, until he saw that the patches of light and shadow glided *from below upwards* over her figure . . . so she was approaching. They would have moved *from above downwards* if she had been walking away. A few instants more and she was standing near him, before him, with a bright face of greeting, a tender light in her eyes, a faint but gay smile on her lips. He snatched her out-stretched hands, but at first could not utter a word; she, too, said nothing. She had walked very quickly and was a little out of breath; but it could be seen she was immensely overjoyed that he was overjoyed to see her.

She was the first to speak.

'Well,' she began, 'tell me quickly what you've decided on!'

Nezhdanov was surprised.

'Decided! . . . why, were we to have decided on anything just now?'

'Oh, you know what I mean! Tell me what you talked about. Whom did you see? Have you made friends with Solomin? Tell me everything, everything! Stay a minute – let's go over there, further. I know a place . . . that's not so visible.'

She drew him after her. He followed her obediently right through the tall, scanty, dry grass.

She led him to the place she meant. There lay a great

birch-tree that had fallen in a storm. They sat down on the trunk.

'Come, tell me!' she repeated, but she went on herself at once: 'Ah, how glad I am to see you, dear! I thought these two days would never pass. You know, Alexey, I'm certain now that Valentina Mihalovna overheard us.'

'She wrote to Markelov about it,' said Nezhdanov.

'To Markelov!'

Marianna did not speak for a minute, and gradually crimsoned all over, not from shame, but from another stronger passion.

'Wicked, malicious woman!' she murmured slowly; 'she had no right to do that. . . . Well, never mind! Tell me, tell me everything.'

Nezhdanov began talking. . . . Marianna listened to him with a sort of stony attention, and only interrupted him when she noticed that he was hurrying things over, slurring over incidents. All the details of his visits were not however of equal interest to her; she laughed over Fomushka and Fimushka, but they did not interest her. Their life was too remote from her.

'It's just as if you were telling me about Nebuchadnezzar,' was her comment.

But what Markelov said, what Golushkin even thought (though she soon realised what sort of a creature he was), and, above all, what were Solomin's ideas, and what he was like – these were the points she wanted to hear about, and took to heart. 'When? when?' – that was the question that was continually in her head and on her lips when Nezhdanov was talking, while he seemed to avoid everything which could give a positive answer to that question. He began to notice himself that he laid stress precisely on those incidents which were of least interest to Marianna . . . and was constantly returning to them. Humorous descriptions made her impatient; a sceptical or dejected tone wounded her. . . . He had constantly to come to the 'cause,' the 'question.' Then on that subject no amount of talk wearied her. Nezhdanov was reminded of a summer he had spent with some old friends in the country before he was a student, when he used to tell stories to the children, and they, too, did not appreciate descriptions nor expressions of personal, individual sensation . . . they, too, had demanded action, facts! Marianna was not a child, but in the directness and simplicity of her feelings she was like one.

Nezhdanov praised Markelov with warmth and sincerity, and spoke with special appreciation of Solomin. Speaking almost in enthusiastic terms about him, he asked himself, what precisely was it gave him such a high opinion of that man? He had uttered nothing specially brilliant; some of his sayings seemed indeed directly opposed to his, Nezhdanov's, convictions. . . . 'He's a well-balanced character,' was his conclusion; 'that's it, business-like, cool, as Fimushka said, a solid fellow; calm, strong force; he knows what he wants, and has confidence in himself, and arouses confidence in others; there's no excitement . . . and balance! balance! . . . That's the great thing; just what I haven't got.' Nezhdanov was silent, absorbed in reflection. Suddenly he felt a caressing hand on his shoulder.

He raised his head; Marianna was looking at him with anxious, tender eyes.

'My dear! What is it?' she asked.

He took her hand from his shoulder, and for the first time kissed that strong little hand. Marianna gave a slight smile as though wondering how such a polite attention could occur to him. Then she in her turn grew thoughtful.

'Did Markelov show you Valentina Mihalovna's letter?' she asked at last.

'Yes.'

'Well . . . how was he?'

'He? He's the noblest, most unselfish fellow! He . . .' Nezhdanov was on the point of telling Marianna about the portrait – but he checked himself, and only repeated, 'the noblest fellow.'

'Oh, yes, yes!'

Marianna again fell to musing, and suddenly turning round towards Nezhdanov on the trunk which served them both for a seat, she said with vivid interest:

'Well, then, what did you decide?'

Nezhdanov shrugged his shoulders.

'Why, I've told you . . . nothing . . . as yet; we shall have to wait a little longer.'

'Wait longer? . . . What for?'

'Final instructions.' ('Of course that's a fib,' Nezhdanov thought.)

'From whom?'

'From . . . you know . . . Vassily Nikolaevitch. And, oh yes, we must wait too till Ostrodumov comes back.'

Marianna looked inquiringly at Nezhdanov.

'Tell me, did you ever see Vassily Nikolaevitch?'

'I have seen him twice . . . just a glimpse, that was all.'

'What is he? . . . a remarkable man?'

'How shall I tell you? He's the head now, and controls everything. We couldn't do without discipline in our work; obedience is essential.' ('And that's all rot,' was his inward comment.)

'What's he like to look at?'

'Oh, stumpy, heavy, dark. . . . High cheekbones, like a Kalmik . . . a coarse face. Only he has very keen, bright eyes.'

'And how does he talk?'

'He does not talk, so much as command.'

'Why was he made head?'

'Oh, he's a man of character. He wouldn't stick at anything. If necessary he'd kill any one. And so he's feared.'

'And what's Solomin like?' inquired Marianna, after a short pause.

'Solomin's not handsome either; only he has a nice, simple, honest face. You see faces like that among divinity students – the good ones.'

Nezhdanov described Solomin in detail. Marianna gazed a long . . . long time at Nezhdanov; then she said as though to herself: 'You have a good face too, I think; life would be sweet with you, Alexey.'

That saying touched Nezhdanov; he took her hand again, and was lifting it to his lips . . .

'Defer your civilities,' said Marianna smiling – she always smiled when her hand was kissed; 'you don't know; I've a sin to confess to you.'

'What have you done?'

'Why, in your absence I went into your room, and there on your table I saw a manuscript book of verses . . .' – (Nezhdanov started; he remembered that he had forgotten the book and left it on the table in his room) – 'and I must confess, I couldn't overcome my curiosity, and I read it. They are your verses, aren't they?'

'Yes; and do you know, Marianna, the best possible proof of how devoted I am to you and how I trust you, is that I'm hardly angry with you.'

'Hardly? Then, however little, you are angry? By the way, you call me Marianna – that's right; I can't call you Nezhdanov, I must call you Alexey. And the poem beginning: "My dear one, when I come to die," is that yours too?'

'Yes . . . yes. But please leave off. . . . Don't torment me.'

Marianna shook her head.

'It's very melancholy – that poem. . . . I hope you wrote it before you knew me. But it's real poetry so far as I can judge. It seems to me you might have been an author, only I know *for certain* that you have a better, higher vocation than literature. It was all very well to be busy with that – before, when nothing else was possible.'

Nezhdanov bent a rapid glance upon her.

'You think so? Yes, I agree with you. Better failure in this than success in the other.'

Marianna rose impulsively.

'Yes, my dearest, you are right!' she cried, and her whole face was radiant, glowing with the fire and light of rapture, with the softening of generous emotion: 'you are right, Alexey! But perhaps we shall not fail at once; we shall succeed, you will see – we shall be useful, our life shall not be spent in vain, we will go and live among the people. . . . Do you know any trade? No? well, never mind, we will work, we will devote to them, our brothers, all we know. I will cook, and sew, and wash, if need be. . . . You shall see, you shall see. . . . And there'll be no merit in it – but happiness, happiness. . . .' Marianna broke off; but her eyes – fixed eagerly on the distant horizon, not that which spread out before her, but another unseen, unknown horizon perceived by her – her eyes glowed. . . .

Nezhdanov bent down before her.

'O Marianna!' he whispered, 'I'm not worthy of you!'

She suddenly shook herself.

'It's time to go home, high time!' she said, 'or they'll be looking for us again directly. Though Valentina Mihalovna, I think, has given me up. In her eyes I'm ruined!'

Marianna uttered this word with such a bright and happy face, that Nezhdanov could not help smiling too as he looked at her, and repeated, 'Ruined!'

'But she's terribly offended,' Marianna went on, 'that you're not at her feet. But that's all of no consequence, there's something I must talk of. . . . You see, it will be impossible for me to stay here. . . . I shall have to run away.'

'Run away?' repeated Nezhdanov.

'Yes, run away. . . . You're not going to stay, are you? We will go together – we must work together. . . . You'll come with me, won't you?'

'To the ends of the earth!' cried Nezhdanov, and there was a sudden ring of emotion and a kind of impetuous gratitude in his voice. 'To the ends of the earth!' At that instant he would certainly have gone with her wherever she wished, without looking back.

Marianna understood him, and gave a short blissful sigh.

'Then take my hand, Alexey, only don't kiss it; and hold it tight, like a comrade, like a friend – there, so!'

They walked together to the house, pensive, blissful; the young grass caressed their feet, the young leaves stirred about them; patches of light and shade flittered swiftly over their garments; and they both smiled at the restless frolic of the light, and the merry bluster of the wind, and the fresh glitter of the leaves, and at their own youth and one another.

PART II

XXIII

DAWN WAS ALREADY beginning in the sky on the night after Golushkin's dinner, when Solomin, after about four miles of brisk walking, knocked at the gate in the high fence surrounding the factory. The watchman let him in at once, and, followed by three house-dogs, vigorously wagging their shaggy tails, he led him with respectful solicitude to his little lodge. He was obviously delighted at his chief's successful return home.

'How is it you're here to-night, Vassily Fedotitch? we didn't expect you till to-morrow.'

'Oh, it's all right, Gavrila; it's nice walking at night.' Excellent, though rather exceptional, relations existed between Solomin and his workpeople; they respected him as a superior and behaved with him as an equal, as one of themselves; only in their eyes he was a wonderful scholar! 'What Vassily Fedotitch says,' they used to repeat, 'is always right! for there's no sort of study he hasn't been through, and there isn't an Anglisher he's not a match for!' Some distinguished English manufacturer had once, as a fact, visited the factory; and either because Solomin spoke English to him, or that he really was impressed by his knowledge of his business, he kept clapping him on the shoulder, and laughing, and inviting him to come to Liverpool to see him; and he declared to the workpeople in his broken Russian, 'Oh, she's very good man, yours here! Oh! very good!' at which the workpeople in their turn laughed heartily, but with some pride; feeling, 'So our man's all that! One of us!'

And he really was one of them, and theirs.

Early the next morning Solomin's favourite, Pavel, came into his room; waked him, poured him water to wash with, told him some piece of news, and asked him some question. Then they had some tea together hurriedly, and Solomin, pulling on his greasy, grey working pea-jacket, went into the factory, and his life began to turn round again, like a huge fly-wheel.

But a fresh break was in store for it.

Five days after Solomin's return to his work, a handsome little phaeton, with four splendid horses harnessed abreast, drove into the factory yard, and a groom in pale pea-green livery was conducted by Pavel to the lodge, and solemnly handed Solomin a letter, sealed with an armorial crest, from 'His Excellency Boris Andreevitch Sipyagin.' In this letter, which was redolent, not of scent, oh, no! but of a sort of peculiarly distinguished and disgusting English odour, and was written in the third person, not by a secretary but by his Excellency himself, the enlightened owner of the Arzhano estate first apologised for addressing a person with whom he was not personally acquainted, but of whom he, Sipyagin, had heard such flattering accounts. Then he 'ventured' to invite Mr. Solomin to his country seat, as his advice might be of the utmost service to him, Sipyagin, in an industrial undertaking of some magnitude; and in the hope of Mr. Solomin's kindly consenting to do so, he, Sipyagin, was sending his carriage for him. In case it should be impossible for Mr. Solomin to get away that day, he, Sipyagin, most earnestly begged Mr. Solomin to appoint him any other day convenient to him, and he, Sipyagin, would gladly place the same carriage at his, Mr. Solomin's, disposal. There followed the usual civilities, and at the end of the letter was a postscript in the first person, 'I hope you will not refuse to dine with me *quite simply* – not evening dress.' (The words 'quite simply' were underlined.) Together with this letter the pea-green footman, with a certain show of embarrassment, gave Solomin a simple note, simply stuck up without a seal, from Nezhdanov, which contained only a few words, 'Please come, you are greatly needed here and may be of great service; I need hardly say, not to Mr. Sipyagin.'

On reading Sipyagin's letter, Solomin thought: 'Quite simply! how else should I go? I never had an evening suit in my life.... And why the devil should I go trailing out there? ... it's simple waste of time!' but after a glance at Nezhdanov's note, he scratched his head, and walked to the window, irresolute.

'What answer are you graciously pleased to send?' the pea-green footman questioned sedately.

Solomin stood a moment longer at the window, and at last, shaking back his hair and passing his hand over his forehead, he said, 'I will come. Let me have time to dress.'

The footman with well-bred discretion withdrew, and Solomin sent for Pavel, had some talk with him, ran over once more to the factory, and, putting on a black coat with a very long waist, made him by a provincial tailor, and a rather rusty top-hat, which at once gave a wooden expression to his face, he seated himself in the phaeton, then suddenly remembered he had taken no gloves, and called the ubiquitous Pavel, who brought him a pair of white chamois-leather gloves, recently washed, every finger of which had stretched at the tip and looked like a finger-biscuit. Solomin stuffed the gloves into his pocket, and said they could drive on. Then the footman with a sudden, quite unnecessary swiftness leaped on to the box, the well-trained coachman gave a shrill whistle, and the horses went off at a trot.

While they were gradually carrying Solomin to Sipyagin's estate, that statesman was sitting in his drawing-room with a half-cut political pamphlet on his knee, talking about him to his wife. He confided to her that he had really written to him with the object of trying whether he couldn't entice him away from the merchant's factory to his own, as it was in a very bad way indeed, and radical reforms were needed! The idea that Solomin would refuse to come, or even fix another day, Sipyagin could not entertain for an instant; though he had himself offered Solomin a choice of days in his letter.

'But ours are paper-mills, not cotton-spinning, you know,' observed Valentina Mihalovna.

'It's all the same, my love; there's machinery in the one and machinery in the other . . . and he's a mechanician.'

'But perhaps he's a specialist, you know!'

'My love – in the first place, there are no specialists in Russia; and, secondly, I repeat he's a mechanician!'

Valentina Mihalovna smiled.

'Take care, my dear; you've been unlucky once already with young men; mind you don't make a second mistake!'

'You mean Nezhdanov? But I consider I attained my object any way; he's an excellent teacher for Kolya. And besides, you know, *non bis in idem!* Pardon my pedantry, please. . . . That means, facts don't repeat themselves.'

'You think not? But I think everything in the world repeats itself . . . especially what's in the nature of things . . . and especially with young people.'

'*Que voulez-vous dire?*' asked Sipyagin, flinging the pamphlet on the table with a graceful gesture.

'*Ouvrez les yeux, et vous verrez!*' Madame Sipyagin answered him; they spoke French, of course, to one another.

'H'm!' commented Sipyagin. 'Are you alluding to the student fellow?'

'To *Monsieur le* student – yes.'

'H'm! has he got . . .' (he moved his hand about his forehead . . .) 'anything afoot here? Eh?'

'Open your eyes!'

'Marianna? Eh?' (The second 'eh?' was decidedly more nasal than the first.)

'Open your eyes, I tell you!'

Sipyagin frowned.

'Well, we will go into all that later on. Just now I only wanted to say one thing. . . . This fellow will probably be rather uncomfortable . . . of course, that's natural enough, he's not used to society. So we shall have to be rather friendly with him . . . so as not to alarm him. I don't mean that for you; you're a perfect treasure, and you can captivate any one in no time, if you choose to. *J'en sais quelque chose, Madame!* I mention it in regard to other people; for instance, our friend there.'

He pointed to a fashionable grey hat lying on a whatnot; the hat belonged to Mr. Kallomyetsev, who happened to be at Arzhano early that morning.

'*Il est très cassant*, you know; he has such an intense contempt for the people, a thing of which I deeply disapprove! I've noticed in him, too, for some time past, a certain irritability and quarrelsomeness. . . . Is his little affair in that quarter' (Sipyagin nodded his head in some undefined direction, but his wife understood him) 'not getting on well? Eh?'

'Open your eyes! I tell you again.'

Sipyagin got up.

'Eh?' (This 'eh?' was of an utterly different character, and in a different tone . . . much lower.) 'You don't say so! I may open them too wide; they'd better be careful.'

'That's for you to say; but as to your new young man, if only he comes to-day you needn't worry yourself – every precaution shall be taken.'

And after all, it turned out that no precaution was at all needed. Solomin was not in the least uncomfortable or alarmed. When the servant announced his arrival, Sipyagin at once got up, called out loudly so that it could be heard in the hall, 'Ask him up, of course, ask him up!' went to the drawing-room door and stood right in front of it. Solomin was scarcely through the doorway when Sipyagin, whom he almost knocked up against, held out both hands to him, and, smiling affably and nodding his head, said cordially, 'This is indeed good . . . on your part! . . . how grateful I am!' and led him up to Valentina Mihalovna.

'This is my good wife,' he said, softly pressing his hand against Solomin's back, and, as it were, impelling him towards Valentina Mihalovna; 'here, my dear, is our leading mechanician and manufacturer, Vassily . . . Fedosyevitch Solomin.'

Madame Sipyagin rose and, with a beautiful upward quiver of her exquisite eye-lashes, first smiled to him – simply – as to a friend; then held out her little hand, palm uppermost, her elbow pressed against her waist, and her head bent in the direction of her hand . . . in the attitude of a suppliant. Solomin let both husband and wife play off their little tricks upon him, shook hands with both, and took a seat at the first invitation to do so. Sipyagin began to fuss about him: 'Wouldn't he take something?' But Solomin replied that he did not want anything, wasn't in the least fatigued with the journey, and was completely at his disposal.

'You mean I may ask you to visit the factory?' cried Sipyagin, as though quite overcome, and not daring to believe in such condescension on the part of his guest.

'At once,' answered Solomin.

'Ah, how good you are! Shall I order the carriage? or perhaps you would prefer to walk? . . .'

'Why, it's not far from here, I suppose, your factory?'

'Half a mile, not more.'

'Then why order the carriage?'

'Ah, that's delightful, then! Boy, my hat, my stick, at once! And you, little missis, bestir yourself, and have a good dinner ready for us. My hat!'

Sipyagin was far more perturbed than his visitor. Repeating once more, 'But where's my hat?' he, the great dignitary, bustled out of the room like a frolicsome schoolboy. While he was talking to Solomin, Valentina Mihalovna was looking stealthily but intently at this 'new young man.' He was sitting calmly in his easy-chair, with his bare hands (he had not, after all, put on the gloves) lying on his knees, and calmly, though with curiosity, looking about at the furniture and the pictures. 'How is it?' she thought; 'he is a plebeian . . . an unmistakable plebeian . . . but how naturally he behaves!'

Solomin did certainly behave very naturally, and not as some do, who are simple indeed, but with a sort of intensity, as though to say, 'Look at me, understand what sort of a man I am,' but like a man whose feelings and ideas are strong without being complex. Madam Sipyagin wanted to enter into conversation with him, but, to her amazement, could not at once find anything suitable to say.

'Good heavens!' she thought, 'can I be impressed by this workman?'

'Boris Andreitch ought to be very grateful to you,' she said at last, 'for consenting to devote part of your valuable time to him. . . .'

'It's not so valuable as all that, madam,' answered Solomin; 'and I'm not come to you for very long.'

'*Voilà où l'ours a montré sa patte*,' she thought in French, but at that instant her husband appeared in the open doorway, with his hat on and his stick in his hand.

Turning half round, he cried with a free and easy air: 'Vassily Fedosyevitch! Ready to start?'

Solomin got up, bowed to Valentina Mihalovna, and walked out behind Sipyagin.

'Follow me, this way, this way, Vassily Fedosyevitch!' Sipyagin called, just as though he were going through a forest and Solomin needed a guide. 'This way! there are steps here, Vassily Fedosyevitch.'

'When you are pleased to call me by my father's name,' Solomin observed deliberately, . . . 'I'm not Fedosyevitch, but Fedotitch.'

Sipyagin looked back at him over his shoulder, almost in affright.

'Ah! I beg your pardon, indeed, Vassily Fedotitch.'

'Not at all; no occasion.'

They went into the courtyard. They happened to meet Kallomyetsev.

'Where are you off to?' he inquired, looking askance at Solomin; 'to the factory? *C'est là l'individu en question?*'

Sipyagin opened his eyes wide and slightly shook his head by way of warning.

'Yes, to the factory . . . to show my sins and transgressions to this gentleman – the mechanician. Let me introduce you: Mr. Kallomyetsev, our neighbour here; Mr. Solomin. . . .'

Kallomyetsev nodded his head twice, hardly perceptibly, not at all in Solomin's direction, without looking at him. But he looked at Kallomyetsev, and there was a gleam of something in his half-closed eyes.

'May I join you?' asked Kallomyetsev. 'You know I like instruction.'

'Of course you may.'

They went out of the courtyard into the road, and had not gone twenty steps when they saw the parish priest in a cassock, hitched up into the belt, making his way home to the so-called 'pope's quarter.' Kallomyetsev promptly left his two companions, and with long, resolute strides approached the priest, who was not at all expecting this and was rather disconcerted, asked his blessing, deposited a sounding kiss on his moist red hand, and, turning to Solomin, flung him a challenging glance. He obviously knew 'a fact or two' about him, and wanted to show off and to display his contempt for this learned rascal.

'*C'est une manifestation, mon cher?*' Sipyagin muttered through his teeth.

Kallomyetsev gave a snort.

'*Oui, mon cher, une manifestation nécessaire par le temps qui court!*'

They went into the factory. They were met by a Little Russian with an immense beard and false teeth, who had succeeded the former superintendent, the German, when Sipyagin finally dismissed him. This Little Russian was a temporary substitute; he obviously knew nothing of the business, and could do nothing but sigh and incessantly repeat 'Maybe' . . . and 'Just so.'

The inspection of the establishment began. Some of the factory hands knew Solomin by sight and bowed to him . . . and to one of them he even said, 'Hullo, Grigory! you here?'

He soon saw that the business was badly managed. Money had been laid out profusely but injudiciously. The machines turned out to be of poor quality; many were unnecessary and useless; many that were needed were lacking. Sipyagin kept constantly looking at Solomin's face to guess his opinion, put some timid questions, wished to know if he were pleased, at any rate, with the discipline.

'The system's all right,' answered Solomin, 'but can it give any return? I doubt it.'

Not Sipyagin only, but even Kallomyetsev, felt that Solomin was, as it were, at home in the factory, that everything in it was thoroughly familiar to him and understood to the smallest detail – that here he was master. He laid his hand on a machine as a driver lays his hand on a horse's neck; he poked his fingers into a wheel and it stopped moving or began going round; he scooped up in his hand out of the vat a little of the pulp of which the paper was made, and at once it revealed all its defects. Solomin said little, and did not even look at the Little Russian at all; in silence, too, he walked out of the factory. Sipyagin and Kallomyetsev followed him.

Sipyagin did not tell any one to accompany him . . . he positively stamped and gnashed his teeth. He was very much disturbed.

'I see by your face,' he said, addressing Solomin, 'that you're not pleased with my factory, and I know myself that it's in an unsatisfactory state and unprofitable; however, . . . please don't scruple to speak out . . . what are really its most important shortcomings? And what is to be done to improve it?'

'Paper-making's not in my line,' answered Solomin, 'but one thing I can tell you – industrial undertakings aren't the thing for gentlemen.'

'You regard such pursuits as degrading for gentlemen?' interposed Kallomyetsev.

Solomin smiled his broad smile.

'Oh, no! What an idea! What is there degrading about it?

And even if there were, the gentry aren't squeamish as to that, you know.'

'Eh? What's that?'

'I only meant,' Solomin resumed tranquilly, 'that gentlemen aren't used to that sort of business. Commercial foresight is needed for that; everything has to be put on a different footing; you need training for it. The gentry don't understand that. We see them right and left founding cloth factories, wool factories, and all sorts, but in the long-run all these factories fall into the hands of merchants. It's a pity, for the merchant's just as much of a blood-sucker; but there's no help for it.'

'To listen to you,' cried Kallomyetsev, 'one would suppose financial questions were beyond our nobility!'

'Oh, quite the contrary! the gentry are first-rate hands at that. For getting concessions for railroads, founding banks, begging some tax-exemption for themselves, or anything of that sort, none are a match for the gentry. They accumulate great capitals. I hinted at that just now, when you were pleased to take offence at it. But I was thinking of regular industrial enterprises. I say *regular*, because founding private taverns and petty truck-shops and lending the peasants wheat or money at a hundred and a hundred and fifty per cent., as so many of our landowning gentry are doing now – operations like that I can't regard as genuine commercial business.'

Kallomyetsev made no reply. He belonged to just that new species of money-lending landowner whom Markelov had referred to in his last talk with Nezhdanov, and he was the more inhuman in his extortions that he never had any personal dealings with the peasants; he did not admit them into his perfumed European study, but did business with them through an agent. As he listened to Solomin's deliberate, as it were, impartial speech, he was raging inwardly . . . but he was silent this time, and only the working of the muscles of his face betrayed what was passing within him.

'But, Vassily Fedotitch, allow me – allow me,' began

Sipyagin. 'All that you are expressing was a perfectly just criticism in former days, when the nobility enjoyed . . . totally different privileges, and were altogether in another position. But nowadays, after all the beneficial reforms . . . in our industrial age, why cannot the nobility turn their energies and abilities into such enterprises? Why should they be unable to understand what is understood by the simple, often unlettered, merchant? They don't suffer from lack of education, and one may even claim with confidence that they are in some sense the representatives of enlightenment and progress.'

Boris Andreevitch spoke very well; his fluency would have had great effect in Petersburg – in his department – or even in higher quarters, but on Solomin it produced no impression whatever.

'The gentry cannot manage these things,' he repeated.

'And why not? why?' Kallomyetsev almost shouted.

'Because they will always remain mere officials.'

'Officials?' Kallomyetsev laughed malignantly. 'You don't quite realise what you are saying, I fancy, Mr. Solomin.' Solomin still smiled as before.

'What makes you fancy that, Mr. Kolomentsev?' (Kallomyetsev positively shuddered at such a 'mutilation' of his surname.) 'No, I always fully realise what I am saying.'

'Then explain what you meant by your last expression.'

'Certainly; in my idea, every official is an outsider, and has always been so, and the gentry have now *become* outsiders.'

Kallomyetsev laughed still more.

'I beg your pardon, my dear sir; that I can't make head or tail of!'

'So much the worse for you. Make a great effort . . . perhaps you will understand it.'

'Sir!'

'Gentlemen, gentlemen,' Sipyagin interposed hurriedly with an air of searching earnestly about him for some one. 'If you please, if you please . . . *Kallomyetsev, je vous prie de vous calmer.* And dinner will be ready soon, to be sure. Pray, gentlemen, follow me!'

'Valentina Mihalovna!' whined Kallomyetsev, running into her boudoir five minutes later, 'it's really beyond everything what your husband is doing! One Nihilist installed here among you already, and now he's bringing in another! And this one's the worst!'

'How so?'

'Upon my word, he's advocating the deuce knows what; and besides – observe one thing: he has been talking to your husband for a whole hour, and *never once, not once,* did he say, Your Excellency! *Le vagabond!*'

XXIV

BEFORE DINNER SIPYAGIN called his wife aside into the library. He wanted to have a talk with her alone. He seemed worried. He told her that the factory was distinctly coming to grief, that this man Solomin struck him as a very capable fellow, though a trifle ... abrupt, and that they must continue to be *aux petits soins* with him. 'Ah! if we could only persuade him to come, what a good thing it would be!' he repeated twice. Sipyagin was much irritated at Kallomyetsev's presence.... 'Damn the fellow! He sees Nihilists on every side, and thinks of nothing but suppressing them. He's welcome to suppress them at home. He positively can't hold his tongue!'

Valentina Mihalovna observed that she would be delighted to be *aux petits soins* with this new guest, only he seemed not to care for these *petits soins* and not to notice them; not that he was rude, but very cool in a sort of way, which was extremely remarkable in a man *du commun.*

'Never mind ... do your best!' Sipyagin besought her. Valentina Mihalovna promised to do her best, and she did do her best. She began by talking *en tête-à-tête* to Kallomyetsev.

There is no knowing what she said to him, but he came to table with the air of a man who has 'undertaken' to be discreet and submissive whatever he may have to listen to. This opportune 'resignation' gave his whole bearing a shade of slight melancholy; but what dignity . . . oh! what dignity there was in every one of his movements! Valentina Mihalovna introduced Solomin to all the family circle (he looked at Marianna with most attention), and made him sit beside her, on her right hand, at dinner. Kallomyetsev was seated on her left. As he unfolded his napkin, he pursed up his face with a smile that seemed to say, 'Come, now, let us go through our little farce!' Sipyagin sat facing him, and with some anxiety kept an eye on him. By Madame Sipyagin's rearrangement of the seats at table, Nezhdanov was placed not beside Marianna, but between Anna Zaharovna and Sipyagin. Marianna found her card (for the dinner was a ceremonious affair) on the dinner-napkin between Kallomyetsev and Kolya. The dinner was served in great style; there was even a *menu* – a decorated card lay beside each knife and fork. Immediately after the soup, Sipyagin turned the conversation again on his factory, and on manufacturing industry in Russia generally; Solomin, after his habit, answered very briefly. Directly he began to speak, Marianna's eyes were fastened upon him. Kallomyetsev, as he sat beside her, had begun by addressing various compliments to her (seeing that he had been specially begged 'not to provoke an argument'), but she was not listening to him; and indeed he uttered these civilities in a half-hearted fashion to satisfy his conscience: he realised that there was some barrier between the young girl and him that he could not get over.

As for Nezhdanov, something still worse had come into existence between him and the head of the house. . . . For Sipyagin, Nezhdanov had become simply a piece of furniture, or an empty space, which he utterly – it seemed utterly – failed to remark! These new relations had taken shape so quickly and unmistakably, that when Nezhdanov during dinner uttered a few words in reply to an observation of his neighbour, Anna Zaharovna, Sipyagin looked round wonderingly as though asking himself, 'Where does that sound come from?'

Obviously Sipyagin possessed some of the characteristics that distinguish Russians of the very highest position.

After the fish, Valentina Mihalovna – who for her part had been lavishing all her arts and graces on her right, that is, on Solomin – remarked in English to her husband across the table that 'our guest drinks no wine, perhaps he would like beer. . . .' Sipyagin called loudly for 'ale,' while Solomin turning quietly to Valentina Mihalovna said, 'You don't know, madam, I expect, that I spent over two years in England, and can understand and speak English; I tell you this in case you might want to speak of something private before me.' Valentina Mihalovna laughed and began to assure him this precaution was quite unnecessary, since he would hear nothing but good of himself; inwardly she thought Solomin's action rather queer, but delicate in its own way.

At this point Kallomyetsev broke out at last.

'So you have been in England,' he began, 'and probably you studied the manners and customs there. Allow me to inquire, did you think they were worth imitating?'

'Some, yes; some, no.'

'That's short, and not clear,' observed Kallomyetsev, trying not to notice the signs Sipyagin was making to him. 'But you were speaking this morning about the nobles. . . . You have doubtless had an opportunity of studying what's called in England the *landed gentry* on the spot?'

'No; I had no such opportunity: I moved in a totally different sphere, but I formed a notion of these gentlemen for myself.'

'Well, do you imagine that such a *landed gentry* is impossible among us, and that in any case we ought not to wish for it?'

'In the first place, I certainly do imagine it to be impossible, and, secondly, I think it's not worth while wishing for it either.'

'Why so, my dear sir?' said Kallomyetsev. The last three

words were by way of soothing Sipyagin, who was very uneasy and could not sit still in his chair.

'Because in twenty or thirty years your *landed gentry* will cease to exist any way.'

'But, really, why so, my dear sir?'

'Because by that time the land will have come into the hands of owners, without distinction of rank.'

'Merchants?'

'Probably merchants; mostly.'

'How will that be?'

'Why, by their buying it – the land, I mean.'

'Of the nobles?'

'Yes, the nobles.'

Kallomyetsev gave a condescending smirk. 'You said the very same thing before, I remember, of mills and factories, and now you say it of the whole of the land.'

'Yes, I say the same now of the whole of the land.'

'And you will be very glad of it, I suppose?'

'Not at all, as I have explained to you already; the people will be no better off for it.'

Kallomyetsev faintly raised one hand. 'What solicitude for the people's welfare, only fancy!'

'Vassily Fedotitch!' cried Sipyagin at the top of his voice. 'They have brought you some beer! *Voyons, Siméon!*' he added in an undertone.

But Kallomyetsev would not be quiet.

'You have not, I see,' he began again, addressing Solomin, 'an over-flattering opinion of the merchants; but they belong by extraction to the people, don't they?'

'And so?'

'I supposed that everything relating to the people or derived from the people would be good in your eyes.'

'Oh, no, sir! You were mistaken in supposing that. Our people are open to reproach in many ways, though they're not always in the wrong. The merchant among us so far is a brigand;

he uses his own private property for brigandage. . . . What's he to do? He's exploited and he exploits. As for the people—'

'The people?' queried Kallomyetsev in high falsetto.

'The people . . . are asleep.'

'And you would wake them?'

'That wouldn't be amiss.'

'Aha! aha! so that's what—'

'Excuse me, excuse me,' Sipyagin pronounced imperiously. He realised that the instant had come to draw the line, so to speak . . . to close the discussion. And he drew the line! He closed the discussion! With a wave of his right hand from the wrist, while his elbow remained propped on the table, he delivered a long and detailed speech. On one side he commended the conservatives, on the other approved of the liberals, awarding some preference to the latter, reckoning himself among their number; he extolled the people, but referred to some of their weak points; expressed complete confidence in the government, but asked himself whether *all* subordinate officials were fully carrying out its benevolent designs. He recognised the service and the dignity of literature, but declared that without the utmost caution it was inadmissible! He looked towards the east; first rejoiced, then was dubious: looked towards the west; first was apathetic, then suddenly waked up! Finally, he proposed a toast in honour of the trinity: 'Religion, Agriculture, and Industry!'

'Under the ægis of power!' Kallomyetsev added severely.

'Under the ægis of wise and indulgent authority,' Sipyagin amended.

The toast was drunk in silence. The empty space to the left of Sipyagin, known as Nezhdanov, did, it is true, give vent to some sound of disapprobation, but, evoking no notice, it relapsed into silence; and the dinner reached a satisfactory conclusion, undisturbed by any controversy.

Valentina Mihalovna, with the most charming smile, handed Solomin a cup of coffee; he drank it, and was already looking for his hat . . . but, softly taken by the arm by Sipyagin, was promptly drawn away into his study, and received first a most excellent cigar, and then a proposal that he should enter his, Sipyagin's factory, on the most advantageous terms! 'You shall be absolute master, Vassily Fedotitch, absolute master!' The cigar Solomin accepted; the proposal he refused. He positively stuck to his refusal, however much Sipyagin insisted.

'Don't say "No" straight off, dear Vassily Fedotitch. Say at least that you'll think it over till to-morrow!'

'But that would make no difference. I can't accept your offer.'

'Till to-morrow! Vassily Fedotitch! what harm will it do to defer your decision?'

Solomin admitted that it would certainly do him no harm . . . he left the study, however, and again went in search of his hat. But Nezhdanov, who had not till that instant succeeded in exchanging a single word with him, drew near and hurriedly whispered: 'For mercy's sake, don't go away, or it will be impossible for us to have a talk.'

Solomin left his hat alone, the more readily as Sipyagin observing his irresolute movements up and down the drawing-room, cried, 'You'll stay the night with us, of course?'

'I am at your disposal,' answered Solomin.

The grateful glance flung at him by Marianna – she was standing at the drawing-room window – set him musing.

XXV

MARIANNA HAD PICTURED Solomin to herself as utterly different, before his visit. At first sight he had struck her as somehow undefined, lacking in individuality. . . . She had seen plenty of fair-haired, sinewy, thin men like that, she told herself! But the more she watched him, the more she listened to what he said, the stronger grew her feeling of confidence in him – confidence was just what it was.

This calm, heavy, not to say clumsy man was not only incapable of lying or bragging; one might rely on him, like a stone wall. . . . He would not betray one; more than that, he would understand one and support one. Marianna even fancied that this was not only her feeling – that Solomin was producing the same effect on every one present. To what he said, she attached no special significance; all this talk of merchants and factories had little interest for her; but the way he talked, the way he looked and smiled as he talked, she liked immensely. . . .

A truthful man . . . that was the great thing! that was what touched her. It is a well-known fact, though by no means easy to understand, that Russians are the greatest liars on the face of the earth, and yet there is nothing they respect like truth – nothing attracts them so much. Besides, Solomin was of a quite especial stamp, in Marianna's eyes; on him rested the halo of a man recommended by Vassily Nikolaevitch himself to his followers. During dinner Marianna had several times exchanged glances with Nezhdanov in reference to him, and in the end she suddenly caught herself in an involuntary comparison of the two men, and not to Nezhdanov's advantage. Nezhdanov's features were undoubtedly far handsomer and more pleasing than Solomin's; but his face expressed a medley of distracting emotions; vexation, embarrassment, impatience . . . even despondency; he seemed sitting on thorns, tried to speak, and broke off, laughing nervously. . . . Solomin, on the other hand, produced the impression of being, very likely, a little bored, but, any way, quite at home; and of being, in what he did or felt, at all times utterly independent of what other people might do or feel. 'Decidedly, we must ask advice of this man,' was Marianna's thought; 'he will be sure to give us some good advice.' It was she who had sent Nezhdanov to him after dinner.

The evening passed rather drearily; luckily dinner was not over till late, and there was not much time to get through before night. Kallomyetsev was politely sulky and said nothing.

'What's the matter?' Madame Sipyagin asked him half-jeeringly. 'Have you lost something?'

'That's just it,' answered Kallomyetsev. 'They tell a story of one of our commanders of the guards that he used to complain that his soldiers had lost their socks. "Find me that sock!" And I say, find me the word "sir"! That word "sir" has gone astray, and all proper respect and reverence for rank have gone with it!'

Madame Sipyagin declared to Kallomyetsev that she was not prepared to assist him in his quest of it.

Emboldened by the success of his 'speech' at dinner, Sipyagin delivered a couple of other harangues, letting drop as he did so a few statesmanlike reflections on indispensable measures; he dropped also a few sayings – *des mots* – more weighty than witty, he had specially prepared for Petersburg. One of these sayings he even said over twice, prefixing the phrases, 'if I may be permitted so to express myself.' It was a criticism of one of the ministers of the day, of whom he said that he had a fickle and frivolous intellect bent on visionary aims. On the other hand Sipyagin, not forgetting that he had to deal with a Russian – one of the people – did not fail to knock off a few sayings, intended to prove that he was himself, not merely Russian in blood, but a real Russian bear, every inch of him, and in close touch with the very inmost essence of the national life! Thus, for example, upon Kallomyetsev observing that the rain might delay getting in the hay, he promptly rejoined, 'Let the hay be black, for then the buckwheat'll be white'; he used proverbial terms such as, 'A store masterless is a child fatherless'; 'Try on ten times, for once you cut out'; 'Where there is corn, you can always find a bushel'; 'If the leaves on the birch are big as farthings by St. Yegor's day, there'll be corn in the barn by the feast of Our Lady of Kazan.' It must be admitted that he sometimes got them wrong, and would say, for instance, 'Let the carpenter stick to his last!' or 'Fine houses make full bellies!' But the society in which these mishaps befell did not for the most part even suspect that '*notre bon Russe*' had blundered; and indeed, thanks to Prince Kovrizhkin, it is pretty well inured to such Russian malapropisms. And all these saws and sayings Sipyagin would enunciate in a peculiar hale and hearty, almost thick, voice, '*d'une voix rustique*.' Such idioms, dropped in due place and season at Petersburg, set influential ladies of the highest position exclaiming, '*Comme il connaît bien les mœurs de notre peuple!*' While equally influential dignitaries of equally high position would add, '*Les mœurs et les besoins!*'

Valentina Mihalovna did her very best with Solomin; but the obvious failure of her efforts disheartened her; and as she passed Kallomyetsev she could not resist mumuring in an undertone, '*Mon Dieu, que je me sens fatiguée!*'

To which the latter responded, with an ironical bow, '*Tu l'as voulu, Georges Dandin!*'

At last, after the usual flicker-up of politeness and affability, displayed on all the faces of a bored assembly at the moment of breaking up, after abrupt handshaking, smiles and amiable simpers, the weary guests and weary hosts separated.

Solomin, who was conducted to almost the best bedchamber on the second floor, with English toilet accessories and a bathroom attached, made his way to Nezhdanov.

The latter began by thanking him warmly for consenting to stay the night.

'I know . . . it's a sacrifice for you. . . .'

'Oh, nonsense!' Solomin responded in his deliberate tones; 'much of a sacrifice! Besides, I can't say no to you.'

'Why so?'

'Oh, because I like you.'

Nezhdanov was delighted and astounded while Solomin pressed his hand. Then he seated himself astride on a chair, lighted a cigar, and, with both elbows on the chair-back, he observed, 'Come, tell me what's the matter.'

Nezhdanov, too, seated himself astride on a chair facing Solomin, but he did not light a cigar.

'What's the matter, you ask? . . . The matter is that I want to run away from here.'

'That is, you want to leave this house? Well, what of it? Good luck to you!'

'Not to leave . . . but to run away.'

'Why? do they detain you? You . . . perhaps you've received some salary in advance? If so, you need only say the word. . . . I should be delighted.'

'You don't understand me, my dear Solomin. . . . I said, run away – not leave – because I'm not going away from here alone.'

Solomin raised his head.

'With whom?'

'With that girl you saw here to-day. . . .'

'That girl! She has a nice face. You love one another, eh? . . . Or is it simply, you have made up your minds to go away together from a house where you are both unhappy?'

'We love one another.'

'Ah!' Solomin was silent for a while. 'Is she a relation of the people here?'

'Yes. But she fully shares our convictions, and is ready to go forward.'

Solomin smiled.

'And are you ready, Nezhdanov?'

Nezhdanov frowned slightly.

'Why that question? I will prove my readiness in action.'

'I have no doubts of you, Nezhdanov. I only asked because I imagine there is no one ready besides you.'

'What of Markelov?'

'Yes, to be sure, there is Markelov; but he, I expect, was born ready.'

At that instant some one gave a light, rapid tap at the door, and, without waiting for an answer, opened it. It was Marianna. She went up at once to Solomin.

'I am sure,' she began, 'you will not be surprised at seeing me here at such an hour. . . . He' (Marianna indicated Nezhdanov) 'has told you everything, of course. Give me your hand, and, believe me, it is an honest girl standing before you.'

'Yes, I know that,' Solomin responded seriously. He had risen from his seat directly Marianna appeared. 'I was looking at you at dinner-time and thinking, "What honest eyes that young lady has!" Nezhdanov has been telling me, certainly, of your plan. But why do you mean to run away, exactly?'

'Why? The cause I have at heart . . . don't be surprised; Nezhdanov has kept nothing from me . . . that work is bound to begin in a few days . . . and am I to remain in this aristocratic house, where everything is deceit and lying? People I love will be exposed to danger, and am I—'

Solomin stopped her by a motion of his hand.

'Don't upset yourself. Sit down, and I'll sit down. You sit down, too, Nezhdanov. Let me tell you, if you have no other reason, then there's no need for you to run away from here as yet. That work isn't going to begin as soon as you suppose. A little more prudent consideration is needed in that matter. It's no good blundering forward at random. Believe me.'

Marianna sat down and wrapped herself up in a big plaid, which she flung over her shoulders.

'But I can't stay here any longer. I'm insulted by every one here. Only to-day that imbecile, Anna Zaharovna, said before Kolya, alluding to my father, that the apple never falls far from the apple-tree. Kolya even was surprised, and asked what that meant. Not to speak of Valentina Mihalovna!'

Solomin stopped her again, and this time with a smile. Marianna realised that he was laughing at her a little, but his smile could never have offended any one.

'What do you mean, dear lady? I don't know who that Anna Zaharovna may be, nor what apple-tree you are talking about . . . but come, now; some fool of a woman says something foolish to you, and can't you put up with it? How are you going to get through life? The whole world rests on fools. No, that's not a reason. Is there anything else?'

'I am convinced,' Nezhdanov interposed in a deep voice, 'that Mr. Sipyagin will turn me out of the house of himself in a day or two. He has certainly been told tales. He treats me . . . in the most contemptuous fashion.'

Solomin turned to Nezhdanov.

'Then what would you run away for, if you'll be turned away in any case?'

Nezhdanov did not at once find a reply.

'I was telling you before—' he began.

'He used that expression,' put in Marianna, 'because I am going with him.'

Solomin looked at her, and shook his head good-humouredly.

'Yes, yes, my dear young lady; but I tell you again, if you are meaning to leave this house just because you suppose the revolution is going to break out directly—'

'That's what we wrote for you to come for,' Marianna interrupted, 'to find out for certain what position things are in.'

'In that case,' pursued Solomin, 'I repeat, you can stop at home – a good bit longer. If you mean to run away because you love each other and you can't be united otherwise, then—'

'Well, what then?'

'Then it only remains for me to wish you, as the old-fashioned saying is, love and good counsel, and, if need be and can be, to give you any help in my power. Because, my dear young lady, you, and him too, I've loved from first sight as if you were my own brother and sister.'

Marianna and Nezhdanov both went up to him on the right and the left, and each clasped one of his hands.

'Only tell us what to do,' said Marianna. 'Supposing the revolution is still far off . . . there are preparatory steps to be taken, work to be done, impossible in this house, in these surroundings, to which we should go so eagerly together . . . you point them out to us, you only tell us where we are to go. . . . Send us! You will send us, won't you?'

'Where?'

'To the peasants. . . . Where should we go, if not to the people?'

'Into the forest,' thought Nezhdanov. . . . Paklin's saying recurred to his mind. Solomin looked intently at Marianna.

'You want to get to know the people?'

'Yes; that is, we don't only want to get to know the people, but to influence . . . to work for them.'

'Very good; I promise you, you shall get to know them. I will give you a chance of influencing them and working for them. And you, Nezhdanov, are ready to go . . . for her . . . and for them?'

'Of course I am ready,' he declared hurriedly. 'Juggernaut,' another saying of Paklin's, recurred to him; 'here it comes rolling along, the huge chariot . . . and I hear the crash and rumble of its wheels. . . .'

'Very good,' Solomin repeated thoughtfully. 'But when do you intend to run away?'

'Why not to-morrow?' cried Marianna.

'Very good – but where?'

'Sh . . . gently . . .' whispered Nezhdanov. 'Some one is coming along the corridor.'

They were all silent for a space.

'Where do you intend to go?' Solomin asked again, dropping his voice.

'We don't know,' answered Marianna.

Solomin turned his eyes upon Nezhdanov. The latter merely shook his head negatively.

Solomin stretched out his hand and carefully snuffed the candle.

'I tell you what, my children,' he said at last, 'come to my factory. It's nasty there . . . but very safe. I will hide you. I have a little room there. No one will find you out. You need only get there . . . and we won't give you up. You will say, "There are a lot of people at the factory." That's a very good thing. Where there are a lot of people it's easy to hide. Will that do, eh?'

'We can only thank you,' said Nezhdanov; while Marianna, who had at first been taken aback by the idea of the factory, added quickly: 'Of course, of course. How good you are! But you won't leave us there long, I suppose? You will send us on?'

'That will depend on you. . . . But in case you meant to get married, it would be very convenient for you at the factory. Close by I've a neighbour there – he's a cousin of mine – a parish priest, by name Zosim, very amenable. He would marry you with all the pleasure in life.'

Marianna smiled to herself, while Nezhdanov once more pressed Solomin's hand, and after a moment's pause inquired, 'But, I say, won't your employer, the owner of the factory, have anything to say about it? Won't he make it unpleasant for you?'

Solomin looked askance at Nezhdanov.

'Don't worry about me. . . . That's quite a waste of time. As long as the factory goes all right, it's all one to my employer. Neither you nor your dear young lady have any unpleasantness to fear from him. And the workmen will be no danger to you. Only let me know beforehand. About what time am I to expect you?'

Nezhdanov and Marianna looked at one another.

'The day after to-morrow, early in the morning, or the day after that,' Nezhdanov said at last. 'We can't put it off any longer. It's as likely as not they'll turn me out of the house to-morrow.'

'All right . . .' assented Solomin, and he got up from his chair. 'I will look out for you every morning. And, indeed, I shan't be away from home all the week. Every step shall be taken in due course.'

Marianna drew near him (she was on her way to the door). 'Good-bye, dear, kind Vassily Fedotitch . . . that is your name, isn't it?'

'Yes.'

'Good-bye . . . at least, till we meet, and thanks – thank you!'

'Good-bye. . . . Good night, dear child.'

'And good-bye, Nezhdanov, till to-morrow . . .' she added.

Marianna went out quickly.

Both the young men remained for some time without moving, and both were silent.

'Nezhdanov . . .' Solomin began at last, and he broke off. 'Nezhdanov,' he began again, 'tell me about this girl . . . what you can tell me. What has her life been up till now? . . . Who is she? . . . and how does she come to be here?'

Nezhdanov told Solomin briefly what he knew.

'Nezhdanov,' he began again at last . . . 'you ought to take care of that girl; for . . . if anything . . . were to happen . . . you would be very much to blame. Good-bye.'

He went away, and Nezhdanov stood still for a while in the middle of the room; then muttering, 'Ah! it's better not to think,' he flung himself face downwards on the bed.

When Marianna got back to her room, she found on the table a small note, which ran as follows: 'I am sorry for you. You are going to your ruin. Think what you are doing. Into what abyss are you flinging yourself with your eyes shut? – for whom, and for what? – V.'

There was a peculiar delicate fresh scent in the room; it was clear that Valentina Mihalovna had only just gone out of it. Marianna took a pen, and, writing underneath, 'Don't pity me. God knows which of us two is most in need of pity. I only know I would not be in your place. – M.,' she left the note on the table. She had no doubt that her answer would fall into Valentina Mihalovna's hands.

The next morning Solomin, after seeing Nezhdanov, and absolutely declining to undertake the management of Sipyagin's factory, set off homewards. He mused all the way home, a thing which very seldom occurred with him; the motion of the carriage usually lulled him into a light sleep. He thought of Marianna and also of Nezhdanov. He fancied that if he had been in love, he – Solomin – he would have had quite a different face, that he would have talked and looked quite differently. 'But,' he reflected, 'since that has never happened to me, I can't tell, of course, what I should look like if it did.' He remembered an Irish girl whom he had once seen in a shop behind the counter; he remembered what wonderful, almost black, hair she had, her blue eyes and thick lashes, and how she had looked sadly and wistfully at him, and how long afterwards he had walked up and down the street before her windows, how excited he had been, and how he had kept asking himself, should he make her acquaintance or not? He was then staying in London. His employer had sent him there with a sum of money to make purchases for him. Solomin had been on the point of stopping on in London, of sending the money back to his employer, so strong was the impression made on him by the lovely Polly.... (He had found out her name; one of the other shopgirls had addressed her by it.) He had mastered himself, however, and went back to his employer. Polly had been far more beautiful than Marianna, but this girl had the same sad, wistful look in her eyes ... and she was a Russian....

'But what am I thinking about?' said Solomin, half aloud, 'bothering my head about other men's sweethearts!' and he gave a shake to the collar of his coat as though wishing to shake off all unnecessary ideas; and just then he drove up to the factory and caught a glimpse of the figure of the faithful Pavel in the doorway of his little lodge.

XXVI

SOLOMIN'S REFUSAL GREATLY offended Sipyagin – so much so that he suddenly arrived at the opinion that this home-bred Stevenson was not such a remarkable mechanician after all, and that, though he might very likely not be a complete sham, he certainly gave himself airs like a regular plebeian. 'All these Russians, when they imagine they know a thing, are beyond everything. *Au fond* Kallomyetsev is right.' Under the influence of such irritated and malignant sensations, the statesman – *en herbe* – was even more unsympathetic and distant when he looked at Nezhdanov. He informed Kolya that he need not work with his tutor to-day – that he must form a habit of self-reliance. . . . He did not, however, give the tutor himself his dismissal, as the latter had expected; he continued to ignore him. But Valentina Mihalovna did not ignore Marianna. A terrible scene took place between them.

At about two o'clock they happened somehow to be suddenly left alone together in the drawing-room. Each of them was immediately aware that the moment of the inevitable conflict had come, and so, after a momentary hesitation, they gradually approached each other. Valentina Mihalovna was faintly smiling, Marianna's lips were compressed; they were both pale. As she moved across the room, Valentina Mihalovna looked to right and to left and picked a leaf of geranium . . . Marianna's eyes were fixed directly upon the smiling face approaching her.

Madame Sipyagin was the first to stop, and, drumming with her finger-tips on the back of the chair: 'Marianna Vikentyevna,' she said in a careless voice, 'we have, I think, entered upon a correspondence with one another. . . . Living under one roof as we do, that is rather odd, and you are aware that I am not fond of oddities of any sort.'

'It was not I began that correspondence, Valentina Mihalovna.'

'No. . . . You are right. I am to blame for the oddity this time; but I could find no other means to arouse in you a feeling of . . . how shall I say? . . . a feeling of—'

'Speak out, Valentina Mihalovna; don't mince matters – don't be afraid of offending me.'

'A feeling . . . of propriety.'

Valentina Mihalovna paused; nothing but the light tap of her fingers on the chair-back could be heard in the room.

'How do you consider I have been careless of propriety?' asked Marianna.

Valentina Mihalovna shrugged her shoulders.

'*Ma chère, vous n'êtes plus une enfant*, and you understand me perfectly. Can you suppose your behaviour could remain a secret to me, to Anna Zaharovna, to the whole household, in fact? Besides, you have not taken much pains to keep it a secret. You have simply acted in bravado. Boris Andreitch alone has, perhaps, not observed it. . . . He is absorbed in other matters of more interest and importance. But, except for him, your conduct is known to all – all!'

Marianna grew steadily paler and paler.

'I would ask you, Valentina Mihalovna, to be more definite in your expressions. With what precisely are you displeased?'

'*L'insolente!*' thought Madame Sipyagin. She still restrained herself, however.

'You wish to know what I am displeased about, Marianna? Certainly. I am displeased at your prolonged interviews with a young man who by birth, by education, and by social position is far beneath you. I am displeased . . . no! that word is not strong enough – I am revolted by your late . . . your midnight visits to that young man's room. And that under my roof! Do you suppose that that is quite as it should be, and that I am to be silent, and, as it were, screen your flightiness? As a virtuous woman of irreproachable character . . . *Oui, mademoiselle, je l'ai été, je le suis, et le serai toujours* – I cannot help feeling indignant.'

Valentina Mihalovna flung herself into an arm-chair as though crushed by the weight of her indignation.

Marianna smiled for the first time.

'I do not doubt your virtue, past, present, and future,' she began, 'and I say so quite sincerely; but your indignation is needless; I have brought no disgrace on your roof. The young man to whom you allude . . . yes, I certainly . . . have come to love him. . . .'

'You love Monsieur Nezhdanov?'

'Yes, I love him.'

Valentina Mihalovna sat up in her chair.

'Good gracious, Marianna! why, he's a student, of no birth, no family – why, he's younger than you are!' (There was a certain spiteful pleasure in the utterance of these words.) 'What can come of it? and what can you, with your intellect, find in him? He's simply a shallow boy.'

'That was not always your opinion of him, Valentina Mihalovna.'

'Oh, mercy on us, my dear, let me alone. . . . *Pas tant d'esprit que ça, je vous prie.* It is you we are discussing – you and your future. Fancy! what sort of a match is it for you?'

'I must confess, Valentina Mihalovna, I had not thought of it in that light.'

'Eh? What? What am I to understand by that? You have followed the dictates of your heart, we are to suppose. . . . But all that is bound to end in marriage, isn't it?'

'I don't know. . . . I have not thought about that.'

'You have not thought about that? Why, you must be mad!'

Marianna turned slightly away.

'Let us make an end of this conversation, Valentina Mihalovna. It can lead to nothing. We shall never understand one another.'

Valentina Mihalovna got up impulsively.

'I cannot, I ought not to make an end of this conversation! It is too important. . . . I have to answer for you to . . .' Valentina Mihalovna had meant to say 'to God,' but she faltered, and said, 'to the whole world. I cannot be silent when I hear such senselessness! And why cannot I understand you? The insufferable conceit of these young people! No! . . . I understand you very well; I can see that you are infected with these new ideas which will inevitably lead you to your ruin! but then it will be too late.'

'Perhaps; but you may rest assured of one thing: even in my ruin, I shall never hold out a finger to you for aid.'

'Conceit again, this awful conceit! Come, listen to me,

Marianna, listen to me,' she went on, suddenly changing her tone. . . . She was on the point of drawing Marianna to her, but Marianna stepped back a pace, '*Écoutez-moi, je vous en conjure.* After all, you know I am not so old and not so stupid that it's impossible for us to understand each other. *Je ne suis pas une encroutée.* I was even regarded as a republican in my young days . . . just as you are. Listen to me. I will not affect what I don't feel. I have never felt a mother's tenderness for you, and it's not in your character to complain of that . . . but I have recognised and I do recognise that I have duties in regard to you, and I have always tried to perform them. Perhaps the match I dreamed of for you, and for which Boris Andreitch and I, both of us, would have been ready to make any sacrifices . . . that suitor did not fully answer to your ideas . . . but from the bottom of my heart—'

Marianna looked at Valentina Mihalovna, at the wonderful eyes, at the pink, faintly touched-up lips, at the white hands, with the slightly parted fingers adorned with rings, which the elegant lady was pressing so expressively to the bodice of her silk gown, – and suddenly she cut her short.

'A match, do you say, Valentina Mihalovna? Do you mean by a "match" that heartless, vulgar friend of yours, Mr. Kallomyetsev?'

Valentina Mihalovna took her fingers from her bodice.

'Yes, Marianna Vikentyevna, I mean Mr. Kallomyetsev – that cultivated, excellent young man, who will certainly make a wife happy, and whom no one but a madwoman could refuse – no one but a madwoman!'

'What's to be done, *ma tante*? It would seem I am one.'

'But what fault – what serious fault – do you find with him?'

'Oh, none at all. I despise him . . . that's all.'

Valentina Mihalovna shook her head from side to side impatiently, and again sank into an arm-chair.

'Let him be. *Retournons à nos moutons.* And so you love Mr. Nezhdanov?'

'Yes.'

'And you intend to continue . . . your interviews with him?'

'Yes, I intend to.'

'Well . . . and if I forbid you to?'

'I sha'n't listen to you.'

Valentina Mihalovna bounded up in her chair.

'Oh, you won't listen to me! Oh, indeed! And that's said to me by the girl I have loaded with benefits, whom I have cared for in my own house – that is what's said to me . . . is said to me . . .'

'By the daughter of a disgraced father,' Marianna put in gloomily. 'Go on; don't mince matters.'

'*Ce n'est pas moi qui vous le fais dire, mademoiselle*; but, any way, there's nothing to be proud of *in that*. A girl who lives at my expense—'

'Don't taunt me with that, Valentina Mihalovna! It would cost you more to keep a French governess for Kolya. . . . You know I give him French lessons.'

Valentina Mihalovna raised a hand holding a cambric handkerchief scented with ylang-ylang and embroidered with a huge white monogram in one corner, and tried to make some retort, but Marianna went on vehemently:

'You would have every right a thousand times over, every right to speak if, instead of all you have just been reckoning up, instead of all these pretended benefits and sacrifices, you were in a position to say, "the girl I have loved." . . . But you are too honest to tell such a lie as that.' Marianna was shaking as if she were in a fever. 'You have always hated me. At this very moment, at the bottom of your heart, as you said just now, you are glad – yes, glad – that I am justifying your constant predictions, that I am covering myself with scandal, with disgrace; all that you mind is that part of the disgrace may fall on your aristocratic, *virtuous* household.'

'You are insulting me,' faltered Valentina Mihalovna. 'Kindly leave the room.'

But Marianna could not control herself.

'Your household, you say, all your household and Anna Zaharovna and all know of my conduct! and they are all horrified and indignant. . . . But do you suppose I ask anything of you, or them, or any of these people? Do you suppose I prize their good opinion? Do you think the living at your expense, as you call it, has been sweet? I would prefer any poverty to this luxury. Don't you see that between your household and me there's a perfect gulf, a gulf that nothing can conceal? Can you – you're a clever woman, too – fail to realise that? And if you feel hatred for me, can't you understand the feeling I must have for you, which I don't particularise, simply because it is too obvious?'

'*Sortez, sortez, vous dis-je!* . . .' repeated Valentina Mihalovna, and she stamped with her pretty, slender little foot.

Marianna took a step in the direction of the door.

'I will rid you of my presence directly; but do you know what, Valentina Mihalovna? They say that even in Rachel's mouth in Racine's *Bajazet* that "*Sortez!*" was not effective, and you are far behind her! And something more, what was it you said? "*Je suis une honnête femme, je l'ai été, et le serai toujours.*" Only fancy, I am convinced I'm a great deal honester than you! Good-bye!'

Marianna went out hurriedly, while Valentina Mihalovna leaped up from her chair; she wanted to shriek, she wanted to cry. . . . But what to shriek she did not know; and tears did not come at her bidding.

She had to be content with fanning herself with her handkerchief; but the scent with which it was saturated affected her nerves still more. She felt unhappy, insulted. She was conscious of a grain of truth in what she had just heard. But how could any one judge her so unjustly? 'Can I be such a spiteful creature?' she thought, and she looked at herself in the looking-glass, which happened to be straight before her between two windows. The looking-glass reflected a charming face, somewhat discomposed, with patches of red coming out upon it, but still a fascinating face, exquisite, soft, velvety eyes. . . . 'I? I spiteful?' she thought again. . . . 'With eyes like those?'

But at that instant her husband came in, and she hid her face in her handkerchief again.

'What is wrong with you?' he inquired anxiously. 'What is it, Valya?' (He had invented that pet name, though he never allowed himself to use it except in absolute *tête-à-tête*, by preference in the country.)

At first she was reticent, declared there was nothing wrong, but ended by turning round in her chair, in a very graceful and touching way, and flinging her arms round his shoulders (he was standing bending over her), hiding her face in the open front of his waistcoat, and telling him everything; without any hypocrisy or hidden motive, she tried, if not to excuse, at least to some extent to justify Marianna; she threw all the blame on her youth, her passionate temperament, and the defects of her early education; she also, to some extent, and also with no double motive, blamed herself. 'With my daughter, this would never have happened! I should have looked after her very differently!' Sipyagin heard her out with indulgence, sympathy, and serenity; he kept his stooping posture since she did not take her arms from his shoulders, and did not remove her head; he called her an angel, kissed her on the forehead, announced that he saw now the course of action dictated to him by his position, the position of the head of the house, and withdrew with the gait of a man of humane but energetic character, who has to make up his mind to perform an unpleasant but inevitable duty.

About eight o'clock, after dinner, Nezhdanov was sitting in his room writing to his friend Silin: 'Dear Vladimir, I am writing to you at the moment of a vital change in my existence. I have been dismissed from this house. I am going away. But that would be nothing. I am going from here not alone. The girl I have written to you about accompanies me. We are bound together by the similarity of our fate in life, the identity of our views and efforts, by our mutual feeling too. We love each other; at least, I believe I am not capable of feeling the passion of love in any other form than that in which it presents itself to me now. But I should be lying to you if I said I had no secret feeling of terror, even a sort of strange sinking at heart. The future is all dark, and we are pushing forward together into this darkness. I need not explain to you what it is we are going into, and what work we have chosen. Marianna and I are not in search of happiness; we don't want to enjoy ourselves, but to struggle on together, side by side, supporting each other. Our aim is clear to us; but what ways will lead up to it, we do not know. Shall we find, if not sympathy and help, at least freedom to work? Marianna is a splendid, honest girl; if it is decreed that we perish, I shall not reproach myself for having led her to ruin, for there is no other life possible to her now. But Vladimir, Vladimir! my heart is heavy. I am tortured by doubt, not of my feeling for her, of course, but . . . I don't know. Anyhow, it's too late to turn back. Stretch out a hand to us both from afar, and wish us patience, power of self-sacrifice, and love . . . more love. And ye, unknown of us, but loved by us with all our being, every drop of our heart's blood, Russian people, receive us not too coldly, and teach us what we are to expect from you! Farewell, Vladimir, farewell!'

After writing these few lines, Nezhdanov set off to the village. The next night, the dawn was hardly breaking in the sky when he stood on the outskirts of the birch wood at no great distance from Sipyagin's garden. A little behind him, a little peasant's cart, harnessed to a pair of unbridled horses, could be seen behind the tangled green of a broad hazel-bush; in the cart, under the seat of plaited cord, a little grey-headed old peasant lay asleep on a bundle of hay, with his head on a patched overcoat. Nezhdanov kept incessantly looking towards the road, towards the clump of willows at the garden's edge; the grey stillness of night still hung over everything, the tiny stars strove feebly to outshine each other, lost in the waste depths of the sky. Along the rounded lower edges of the stretching clouds ran a pale flush from the east; thence too came the first chill breath of early morning. Suddenly Nezhdanov started and was all alert; somewhere near at hand there was first the shrill creak, then the thump of a gate; a little feminine figure wrapped in a shawl, with a bundle in its bare hand, stepped with a deliberate movement out of the still shadows of the willows on to the soft dust of the road, and crossing it in a slanting direction, apparently on tip-toe, turned towards the copse. Nezhdanov rushed up to it.

'Marianna?' he whispered.

'It's I!' came a soft reply from under the overhanging shawl.

'This way, follow me,' responded Nezhdanov, clutching her awkwardly by the bare hand that held the bundle.

She shrank up as if she felt chilled by the frost. He led her to the cart, and waked up the peasant. The latter jumped up quickly, clambered promptly on to the driver's seat, slipped the great-coat on to his sleeves, and caught up the cords that served for reins. The horses shook themselves; he cautiously encouraged them in a voice still hoarse from his heavy sleep. Nezhdanov made Marianna sit down on the cord seat of the cart, first spreading his cloak on it; he wrapped her feet in a rug – the hay at the bottom of the cart was damp – placed himself beside her, and, bending over to the peasant, said softly, 'Drive on you know where.' The peasant gave a tug to the reins, the horses came out of the thicket, snorting and shaking themselves; and, rattling and jolting on its narrow old wheels, the cart rolled along the road. Nezhdanov put one arm round Marianna's waist to support her; she lifted the shawl a little with her cold fingers, and turning and facing him with a smile, she said, 'How deliciously fresh it is, Alyosha!'

'Yes,' answered the peasant, 'there'll be a heavy dew!'

There was already such a heavy dew that the axles of the cart-wheels, as they caught in the tops of the tall weeds along the roadside, shook off whole showers of delicate drops of water, and the green of the grass looked bluish-grey.

Again Marianna shivered from the cold.

'How fresh, how fresh!' she repeated in a light-hearted voice. 'And freedom, Alyosha, freedom!'

XXVII

SOLOMIN RAN OUT to the gates of the factory directly they hurried to tell him that a gentleman and lady had arrived in a little cart, and were asking for him. Without saying good-morning to his visitors, simply nodding his head several times to them, he at once told the peasant to drive into the yard, and, directing him straight up to his little lodge, he helped Marianna out of the cart. Nezhdanov leaped out after her. Solomin led them both along a little, long, dark passage, and up a narrow winding little staircase, in the back part of the lodge, to the second storey. There he opened a low door, and they all three went into a small, fairly clean room with two windows.

'Welcome!' said Solomin, with his never-failing smile, which seemed broader and brighter than ever to-day.

'Here are your quarters, this room, and see here, another next to it. Not much to look at, but that's no matter; one can live in them, and there'll be no one here to spy on you. Here under the window you have what the landlord calls a flower-garden, but I should call it a kitchen-garden; it lies right up against the wall, and hedges to right and left. A quiet little nook it is! Well, welcome a second time, dear young lady, and you too, Nezhdanov, welcome!'

He shook hands with them both. They stood motionless, not taking off their wraps, and with silent, half-bewildered, half-delighted emotion they looked straight before them.

'Well, what now?' Solomin began again. 'Take off your things! What baggage have you got?'

Marianna showed the bundle which she was still holding in her hand.

'This is all I have.'

'And my trunk and bag are still in the cart. But I'll go and get them directly.'

'Stand still, stand still.' Solomin opened the door. 'Pavel!' he shouted into the darkness of the staircase, 'run out, mate. There are some things in the cart . . . bring them up.'

'Directly,' they heard the voice of the ubiquitous Pavel.

Solomin turned to Marianna, who had flung off her shawl and was beginning to unbutton her cloak.

'And did everything go off successfully?' he inquired.

'Everything . . . no one saw us. I left a letter for Mr. Sipyagin. I didn't take any dresses or clothes with me, Vassily Fedotitch, because as you are going to send us . . .' (Marianna for some reason could not make up her mind to add 'to the people'), 'well, any way, they'd have been of no use. But I have money to buy what is necessary.'

'We'll arrange all that later . . . and here,' said Solomin, pointing to Pavel, who came in with Nezhdanov's things, 'I commend to you my best friend here; you can rely on him fully . . . as you would on me. Did you speak to Tatyana about the samovar?' he added in an undertone.

'It'll be here directly,' answered Pavel; 'and the cream and everything.'

'Tatyana is his wife,' Solomin went on, 'and she is just as trustworthy as he is. Until you . . . well . . . are a bit used to it, she will wait on you, my dear young lady.'

Marianna flung her cloak on a little leather sofa that stood in the corner. 'Call me Marianna, Vassily Fedotitch – I don't want to be a young lady. And I don't want any one to wait on me. . . . I didn't come here to have servants. Don't look at my dress; I had – over there – nothing else. All that must be changed.'

The dress, of fine cinnamon-coloured cloth, was very simple; but cut by a Petersburg dressmaker, it fell in elegant folds about Marianna's waist and shoulders, and had altogether a fashionable air.

'Well, not servant, but a help, perhaps, in the American fashion. And you must have tea, any way. It's early days yet, and you must both be tired. I am going off now to see after things in the factory; we shall meet again later. Tell Pavel or Tatyana whatever you want.'

Marianna held out both hands quickly to him.

'How can we thank you, Vassily Fedotitch?' She looked at him quite moved.

Solomin softly stroked one of her hands. 'I should say, it's not worth thanking for . . . but that wouldn't be true. I'd better say that your thanks give me immense pleasure. So we're quits. Good-bye for the present! Pavel, come along.'

Marianna and Nezhdanov were left alone.

She rushed up to him, and, looking at him with just the same expression as she had looked at Solomin, only with even more delight, more emotion and gladness, 'Oh, my dear!' she said . . . 'We are beginning a new life. . . . At last! at last! You wouldn't believe how charming and delightful this poor little lodging where we are only to spend a few days seems to me compared with that loathsome mansion! Tell me are you glad, dear?'

Nezhdanov took her hands and pressed them to his heart.

'I am happy, Marianna, that I am beginning this new life with you! You will be my guiding star, dear, my support, my strength. . . .'

'Dearest Alyosha! But stay. I want to wash a little and make myself tidy. I'll go to my own room . . . and you, stay here. One minute. . . .'

Marianna went off into the other room, shut herself in, and a minute later half-opened the door, put her head in, and said, 'And oh! isn't Solomin nice!' Then she shut the door again, and the key clicked in the lock.

Nezhdanov went up to the window, and looked out into the

little garden . . . one old, very old apple-tree for some reason riveted his attention especially. He shook himself, stretched, began opening his trunk, and took nothing out of it; he fell to musing. . . .

In a quarter of an hour Marianna returned with a beaming, freshly washed face, all gaiety and alertness; and a few instants later Pavel's wife, Tatyana, appeared with the samovar, the tea-tray, rolls and cream.

In striking contrast to her gipsylike husband, she was a typical Russian woman, stout, with a flaxen head, with a big knob of hair tightly twisted round a horn comb, and no cap, with thick but pleasant features, and very good-natured grey eyes. She was dressed in a tidy though faded chintz gown; her hands were clean and well-shaped, though large; she bowed tranquilly, and with a firm, precise intonation, without any sort of affectation, she articulated, 'A very good health to you,' and set to work to lay the samovar and the tea things.

Marianna went up to her.

'Let me help you, Tatyana. Only give me a napkin.'

'No need, miss, we're used to it. Vassily Fedotitch has talked to me. If anything's wanted, kindly ask for it; we will do what we can with all the pleasure in life.'

'Tatyana, please don't call me miss. . . . I'm dressed like a lady, but still I'm . . . I'm quite . . .'

The steady gaze of Tatyana's keen eyes disconcerted Marianna; she broke off.

'And what then is it you will be?' Tatyana asked in her composed voice.

'I am certainly, if you like . . . I am a lady by birth; only I want to get rid of all that, and to become like all . . . like all simple women.'

'Ah, so that's it! Well, now I understand. You're one of them, I suppose, that want to be simplified. There are a good few of them about nowadays.'

'What did you say, Tatyana? To be simplified?'

'Yes . . . that's the word that's come up among us now. To be on a level with simple folks, it means – simplification. To be sure, it is a good work – to teach the peasants good sense. Only it's a difficult job! Oy, oy, di-ifficult! God give you good speed!'

'Simplification!' repeated Marianna. 'Do you hear, Alyosha? you and I are simplified creatures now!'

Nezhdanov laughed, and even repeated:

'Simplified creatures!'

'And what will he be to you – your good man or your brother?' asked Tatyana, carefully washing the cups with her large deft hands, as she looked with a kindly smile from Nezhdanov to Marianna.

'No,' answered Marianna, 'he's not my husband and not my brother.'

Tatyana raised her head.

'Then I suppose you are living in free grace. Nowadays that too is pretty often to be met with. It used to be more the way among the dissenters, but nowadays it's found among other folks too. Where there's God's blessing, one may live in peace! And there's no need of the parson for that. In our factory there are some live like that too. Not the worst chaps either.'

'What nice things you say, Tatyana! . . . "In free grace." . . . I like that very much. I'll tell you what I want to ask of you, Tatyana. I want to make myself, or to buy, a dress like yours, or rather commoner perhaps. And shoes and stockings and a kerchief, everything just as you have. I have money enough to get them.'

'To be sure, miss, we can manage all that. . . . There, I won't, don't be cross. I won't call you miss. Only what am I to call you?'

'Marianna.'

'And what are you named from your father?'

'But why do you want my father's name? Call me simply Marianna. The same as I call you Tatyana.'

'That's the same, and not the same. You'd better tell me.'

'Very well, then. My father's name was Vikent; and what was your father's?'

'Mine was Osip.'

'Well, then, I shall call you Tatyana Osipovna.'

'And I'll call you Marianna Vikentyevna. That will be capital!'

'Won't you drink a cup of tea with us, Tatyana Osipovna?'

'At this first acquaintance I might, Marianna Vikentyevna. I'll treat myself to a small cup, though Yegoritch will scold.'

'Who's Yegoritch?'

'Pavel, my husband.'

'Sit down, Tatyana Osipovna.'

'Indeed and I will, Marianna Vikentyevna.'

Tatyana seated herself on a chair and began to sip her tea through a piece of sugar. She continually turned the lump of sugar round in her fingers, screwing up her eye on the side on which she was nibbling the sugar. Marianna got into conversation with her. Tatyana answered without obsequiousness, and asked her questions and told her various things of her own accord. Solomin she almost worshipped, but her husband she put only second to Vassily Fedotitch. She was sick of factory life, though.

'You've neither the town here nor the country ... if it weren't for Vassily Fedotitch I wouldn't stay another hour.'

Marianna listened attentively to her talk. Nezhdanov, sitting a little on one side, watched his girl-friend, and was not surprised at her interest; for Marianna, it was all a novelty, but it seemed to him that he had seen hundreds of similar Tatyanas, and had talked to them hundreds of times.

'Do you know, Tatyana Osipovna,' said Marianna at last, 'you think we want to teach the people; no, we want to serve them.'

'How serve them? Teach them; that's the best service you can do them. Take me, for example. When I was married to Yegoritch, neither read nor write could I; but now I've learned, thanks to Vassily Fedotitch. He didn't teach me himself, but he paid an old man to. And he taught me. You see I'm young still, for all I'm a woman grown.'

Marianna was silent for a little.

'I should like, Tatyana Osipovna,' she began again, 'to learn some trade . . . we must have a talk about that. I sew very badly; if I were to learn to cook, I might become a cook.'

Tatyana pondered.

'Why be a cook? Cooks are in rich men's houses, or merchants'; poor people do their own cooking. And to cook for a union, for workmen. Well, that's quite the last thing!'

'But I might live in a rich man's house though, and make friends with poor people. Or how am I to get to know them? I sha'n't always have such luck as with you.'

Tatyana turned her empty cup upside down in the saucer.

'It's a difficult business,' she observed at last with a sigh, 'it can't be settled off-hand. I'll show you all I know, but I'm not clever at much. We must talk it over with Yegoritch. He's such a man! He reads books of all sorts, and he can see through anything in the twinkling of an eye.' Here she glanced at Marianna, who was rolling up a cigarette. . . .

'And there's something I would say to you, Marianna Vikentyevna, if you'll excuse me; but if you really want to be simplified, you'll have to give that up.' She pointed to the cigarette. 'For in such callings as a cook's, for instance, that would never pass; and every one would see at once that you're a young lady. Yes.'

Marianna flung the cigarette out of the window.

'I won't smoke . . . it's easy to get out of the way of it. Women of the people don't smoke, so I ought not to smoke.'

'That's a true word you've said, Marianna Vikentyevna. The male sex treat themselves to it even among us; but the female – no. . . . Ah! and here's Vassily Fedotitch himself coming up. That's his step. You ask him; he'll settle everything for you in the best way!'

She was right; Solomin's voice was heard at the door.

'May I come in?'

'Come in, come in,' called Marianna.

'That's an English habit of mine,' said Solomin as he came in. 'Well, how do you feel? You aren't dull yet? I see you're having tea here with Tatyana. You listen to her; she's a sensible person. . . . But my employer has turned up to see me to-day . . . when he's not wanted at all! And he'll stay to dinner. There's no help for it! He's the master.'

'What sort of man is he?' asked Nezhdanov, coming out of his corner.

'Oh, he's all right. . . . He has his eyes about him. One of the newer generation. Very affable, and wears cuffs, but pries into everything not a bit less than the old sort. He'd skin a flint with his own hands and say, "Turn a bit to this side, if you'll be so good; there's still a living spot here . . . I must give it a scouring!" Well, with me he's as soft as silk; I'm necessary to him! Only I've come to tell you that I'm not likely to manage to see you to-day. They will bring you your dinner. And don't show yourselves in the yard. What do you think, Marianna – will the Sipyagins search for you? will they make a hunt?'

'I think they won't,' answered Marianna.

'But I am sure they will,' said Nezhdanov.

'Well, any way,' pursued Solomin, 'you must be careful at first. Later on you can do as you like.'

'Yes; only there's one thing,' observed Nezhdanov: 'Markelov must know of my whereabouts; he must be told.'

'Why?'

'It can't be helped; for the cause. He has always to know where I am. It's a promise. But he won't blab!'

'Very well. We'll send Pavel.'

'And will there be a dress ready for me?' asked Nezhdanov.

'Your get-up, you mean? to be sure . . . to be sure. It's quite a masquerade. Not an expensive one, thank goodness. Good-bye; you must have a rest. Tatyana, come along.'

Marianna and Nezhdanov were again left alone.

XXVIII

FIRST THEY CLASPED each other's hands again; then Marianna cried, 'Come, I'll help you arrange your room,' and she began unpacking his things from the trunk and the bag. Nezhdanov would have helped her, but she declared she was going to do it all alone.

'Because I must get used to making myself useful.' And she did in fact hang up his coat on nails which she found in the table drawer, and knocked into the wall, unaided, with the back of a brush for want of a hammer; the linen she laid in a little old chest which stood between the windows.

'What's this?' she asked suddenly; 'a revolver? Is it loaded? What do you want with it?'

'It's not loaded ... but give it here, though. You ask what I want with it? How is one to get on without a revolver in our calling?'

She laughed and went on with her task, shaking out each thing separately and beating it with her hand; she even set two pairs of boots under the sofa; while the few books, a bundle of papers, and the little manuscript-book of verses she arranged in triumph on a three-legged corner-table, saying it was to be the writing- and work-table, while the other round table she called the dinner- and tea-table. Then taking the book of verses in both hands, she raised it to a level with her face, and looking over its edge at Nezhdanov, she said with a smile, 'We'll read all this through together some time when we're not busy, won't we? – eh?'

'Give me that book! I'll burn it!' cried Nezhdanov. 'It's worth nothing better.'

'Why did you bring it with you, if so? No, no, I'm not going to give it you to be burnt. Though they say authors always make that threat, but never do burn their things. But any way, I'd better carry it off!'

Nezhdanov tried to protest, but Marianna ran into the next room with the manuscript-book and returned without it.

She sat down close to Nezhdanov, and instantly got up again. 'You haven't been . . . in my room yet. Would you like to see it? It's as nice as yours. Come, I'll show you.'

Nezhdanov got up too and followed Marianna. *Her* room, as she called it, was a little smaller than *his* room; but the furniture in it seemed rather newer and cleaner; in the window stood a glass vase of flowers, and in the corner a little iron bedstead.

'See how sweet of Solomin!' cried Marianna; 'only one mustn't let oneself be too much spoilt; we shan't often meet with such quarters. And what I think is, what would be nice would be to arrange things so that whatever place we have to go to we could go both together, without parting. It will be difficult,' she added after a short pause; 'well, we'll think of it. Any way, I suppose you won't go back to Petersburg?'

'What should I do in Petersburg? Go to the university and give lessons? That would be of no use now.'

'We'll see what Solomin says,' observed Marianna; 'he'll best decide how and what to do.'

They went back to the first room and again sat down beside each other. They spoke with praise of Solomin, Tatyana, and Pavel; they mentioned Sipyagin, and said how their old life seemed suddenly so far away from them, it seemed lost in a cloud; then they pressed each other's hands again, and exchanged glances of delight; then they talked of what sort of people they ought to try to do propaganda among, and how they must behave not to be suspected.

Nezhdanov maintained that the less they thought about that, the more simply they behaved, the better.

'Of course!' cried Marianna. 'Why, we want to be simplified, as Tatyana says.'

'I didn't mean in that sense,' Nezhdanov was beginning. 'I meant to say that we ought not to be constrained—'

Suddenly Marianna laughed.

'I remembered, Alyosha, how I called us both "simplified creatures"!'

Nezhdanov smiled too, repeated 'simplified,' and then sank into thought.

Marianna, too, was thoughtful.

'Alyosha!' she said.

'What?'

'I think we both feel a little awkward. Young people, *des nouveaux mariés*,' she explained, 'the first day of their honeymoon must feel something of the sort. They are happy . . . they are very content, and a little awkward.'

Nezhdanov smiled – a forced smile.

'You know very well, Marianna, that we are not a young couple in that sense.'

Marianna got up and stood directly facing Nezhdanov.

'That depends on you.'

'How?'

'Alyosha, you know that when you tell me as an honest man – and I shall believe you, for you really are an honest man – when you tell me that you love me with that love . . . well, that love that gives one a right to another person's life, – when you tell me that, I am yours.'

Nezhdanov blushed and turned a little away.

'When I tell you that . . .'

'Yes, then! But you see yourself you do not tell me so now. . . . Oh, yes, Alyosha, you certainly are an honest man. There, let us talk of matters of more importance.'

'But you know I love you, Marianna!'

'I don't doubt that . . . and I shall wait. There, I've not quite put your writing-table to rights yet. Here's something still wrapped up, something stiff.'

Nezhdanov jumped up from his chair.

'Let that be, Marianna. . . . Please . . . leave that alone.'

Marianna turned her head over her shoulder to look at him, and raised her eyebrows in amazement.

'Is it a mystery? A secret? You have a secret?'

'Yes . . . yes,' said Nezhdanov, and greatly disconcerted he added, by way of explanation, 'It's . . . a portrait.'

This word fell from him unconsciously. In the paper Marianna held in her hands there was wrapped up, in reality, her portrait, given to Nezhdanov by Markelov.

'A portrait?' she articulated in a voice of surprise. . . . 'A woman's?'

She gave him the little parcel, but he took it awkwardly; it almost slipped out of his hands and fell open.

'Why, it's . . . my portrait!' cried Marianna quickly. 'Well, I've a right to take my own portrait.' She took it from Nezhdanov.

'Did you sketch this?'

'No . . . not I.'

'Who, then? Markelov?'

'You've guessed. . . . It was he.'

'How did you come by it?'

'He gave it to me.'

'When?'

Nezhdanov told her how and when it had been given. Whilst he was speaking, Marianna glanced first at him and then at the portrait . . . and the same thought flashed through the heads of both: 'If *he* were in this room, he would have the right to ask.' . . . But neither Marianna nor Nezhdanov uttered this thought aloud . . . possibly because each of them was conscious of the thought in the other.

Marianna softly wrapped the portrait in the paper again, and laid it on the table.

'He's a good man!' she murmured. . . . 'Where is he now?'

'Where? . . . At home. I am going to see him to-morrow or next day to get books and pamphlets. He meant to give them to me, but I suppose he forgot it when I was leaving.'

'And do you think, Alyosha, that in giving you the portrait he renounced everything . . . absolutely everything?'

'I thought so.'

'And you hope to find him at home?'

'Of course.'

'Ah!' – Marianna lowered her eyes and dropped her hands. 'And here's Tatyana bringing us our dinner,' she cried suddenly. 'What a splendid woman she is!'

Tatyana appeared with knives and forks, table-napkins, and plates and dishes. While she was laying the table she told them what had been passing in the factory.

'The master came from Moscow by rail, and he set to running from floor to floor like one possessed; to be sure, he knows nothing about things, he only does like that for show, to keep up appearances. But Vassily Fedotitch treats him like a babe in arms. The master thought he'd say something nasty to him, so Vassily Fedotitch suppressed him at once: "I'll throw it all up directly," says he, so our gentleman pretty soon changed his tune. Now they're dining together; and the master brought a companion with him. . . . And he does nought else but admire everything. And a moneyed man he must be, this companion, to judge from the way he holds his tongue and shakes his head. And he's stout too, very stout! A regular Moscow swell! Ah, it's a true saying: "It's downhill to Moscow from all parts of Russia; everything rolls down to her."'

'How you do notice everything!' cried Marianna.

'Yes, I'm pretty observant,' replied Tatyana. 'Come, your dinner's ready. And may it do you good. I'll sit here a little bit, and watch you.'

Marianna and Nezhdanov sat down to dinner; Tatyana leaned against the window-sill and rested her cheek in her hand.

'I watch you,' she repeated . . . 'and what poor young tender things you both are! . . . It's so pleasant to see you that it quite makes my heart ache! Ah, my dears! you're taking up a burden beyond your strength! It's such as you that the inspectors of the Tsar are ever eager to clap in custody!'

'Nonsense, my good soul, don't frighten us,' observed Nezhdanov. 'You know the saying: "If you choose to be a mushroom, you must go in the basket with the rest."'

'I know . . . I know; but the baskets nowadays are so narrow and hard to creep out of!'

'Have you any children?' Marianna asked, to change the conversation.

'Yes; a son. He begins to go to school. I had a little girl too; but she's no more, poor darling! She met with an accident; fell under a wheel. And if only it had killed her at once! But no, she lingered in suffering a long while. Since then I've grown tender-hearted; before then I was as hard as a tree!'

'Why, what of your man Pavel Yegoritch? didn't you love him?'

'Eh! that was a different matter; the feeling of a girl. And how about you, now – do you love your man?'

'Yes.'

'Very much?'

'Yes.'

'Yes? . . .' Tatyana looked at Nezhdanov, then at Marianna, and said no more.

It was again Marianna's lot to change the conversation. She told Tatyana she had given up smoking; the latter approved of her resolution. Then Marianna asked her again about clothes; and reminded her she had promised to show her how to cook. . . .

'Oh, and one thing more: could you get me some stout, coarse yarn? I'm going to knit myself some stockings . . . plain ones.'

Tatyana answered that everything should be done in due course, and, clearing the table, she went out of the room with her calm, resolute gait.

'Well, what shall we do now?' Marianna said, turning to Nezhdanov; and without letting him answer, 'What do you say? since our real work only begins to-morrow, shall we devote this evening to literature? Let's read your poems! I shall be a severe critic.'

For a long while Nezhdanov would not consent.... He ended, however, by giving in, and began to read out of his manuscript-book. Marianna sat close beside him, and watched his face while he was reading. She had spoken truly; she turned out to be a severe critic. Few of the verses pleased her; she preferred the purely lyrical, short ones, that were, as she expressed it, non-didactic. Nezhdanov did not read quite well; he had not the courage to attempt elocution, and at the same time was unwilling to fall into quite a colourless tone; the result was neither one thing nor the other. Marianna suddenly interrupted him with the question, Did he know a wonderful poem of Dobrolyubov's beginning, 'Let me die – small cause for grief'?*
and thereupon read it to him – also not very well – in a rather childish manner.

Nezhdanov observed that it was bitter and painful to the last degree, and then added that he, Nezhdanov, could never have written such a poem, because he had no reason to be afraid of tears over his grave ... there would be none.

---

* And let me die – small cause for grief;
One thought alone frets my sick mind;
That death may chance to play
An unkind jest with me.

I dread lest over my cold corpse
The scalding tears should flow;
And lest some one with stupid zeal
Lay flowers upon my bier;

Lest flocking round in unfeigned grief,
My friends walk after it to the grave;
Lest as I lie under the earth,
I may become one loved and prized;

Lest all so eagerly desired,
And so in vain by me – in life,
May smile on me consolingly
Above the stone that marks my grave.

DOBR., *Works*, vol. iv. p. 615.

'There will be, if I outlive you,' Marianna articulated slowly; and raising her eyes to the ceiling, after a brief silence, in an undertone as though speaking to herself, she queried, 'How ever did he draw a portrait of me? From memory?'

Nezhdanov turned quickly to her. . . .

'Yes, from memory.'

Marianna was amazed at his answering. It seemed to her that she had merely thought the question.

'It is astonishing . . .' she went on in the same subdued voice; 'why, he has no talent for drawing. What was I going to say?' she resumed aloud; 'oh, about Dobrolyubov's poem. One ought to write poems like Pushkin's, or such as that one of Dobrolyubov's: this is not poetry . . . though it's something as good.'

'And poems like mine,' said Nezhdanov, 'ought not to be written at all? Eh?'

'Poems like yours please your friends not because they are very fine, but because you are a fine person, and they are like you.'

Nezhdanov smiled.

'You have buried them, and me with them!'

Marianna gave him a slap on his hand and told him he was too bad. . . . Soon after she announced that she was tired and was going to bed.

'By the way, do you know,' she added, shaking her short, thick curls, 'I've got one hundred and thirty-seven roubles; what have you?'

'Ninety-eight.'

'Oh! but we're rich . . . for simplified creatures. Well, good-bye till to-morrow!'

She went out; but a few instants later her door was slightly opened, and through the narrow crack he heard first, 'Good-bye!' then more softly, 'Good-bye!' and the key clicked in the lock.

Nezhdanov sank on to the sofa and covered his eyes with

his hand. . . . Then he got up quickly, went up to the door, and knocked.

'What is it?' came from within.

'Not till to-morrow, Marianna . . . but to-morrow!'

'To-morrow,' responded a gentle voice.

XXIX

THE NEXT DAY early in the morning Nezhdanov again knocked at Marianna's door.

'It's I,' he said in answer to her 'Who's there?' 'Can you come out to me?'

'Wait a minute . . . directly.'

She came out, and uttered a cry of astonishment. For the first minute she did not recognise him. He had on a long full-skirted coat of threadbare, yellowish nankin, with tiny buttons and a high waist; he had combed his hair in the Russian style, with a straight parting in the middle; his neck was wrapped in a blue kerchief; in his hand he held a cap with a broken peak; on his feet were unpolished high boots of calf leather.

'Good gracious!' cried Marianna; 'how . . . horrid you look!' and thereupon she gave him a rapid embrace, and a still more rapid kiss. 'But why are you dressed like that? You look like a poor sort of shopkeeper . . . or a pedlar, or a discharged house-serf. Why that coat with skirts, and not simply a peasant's smock?'

'That's just it,' began Nezhdanov who in his get-up did really resemble a pedlar, and he was conscious of this himself, and was full of vexation and embarrassment at heart; he was so much embarrassed that he kept striking himself on the breast with the outspread fingers of both hands, as though he were brushing himself.

'In a smock I should have been recognised at once, so Pavel declared; and this costume . . . in his words . . . looked as though I'd never had any other dress cut for me in my life! Not very flattering to my vanity, I may remark in parenthesis.'

'Do you really mean to go out at once . . . to begin?' Marianna inquired with keen interest.

'Yes; I shall try, though . . . in reality . . .'

'Happy fellow!' interrupted Marianna.

'This Pavel is really a wonderful man,' Nezhdanov went on; 'he knows everything, directly he sets eyes on you; and then all of a sudden he purses up his face, as though he were outside it all, – and wouldn't meddle in anything! He serves the cause himself – and makes fun of it all the while. He brought me the pamphlets from Markelov; he knows him and speaks of him as Sergei Mihalovitch. But for Solomin he'd go through fire and water.'

'And so would Tatyana,' observed Marianna. 'Why is it people are so devoted to him?'

Nezhdanov did not answer.

'What sort of pamphlets did Pavel bring you?' asked Marianna.

'Oh! the usual things. "The Tale of Four Brothers," . . . and others too . . . the ordinary well-known things. However, those are best.'

Marianna looked round anxiously.

'But what of Tatyana? She promised to come so early.'

'Here she is,' said Tatyana, coming into the room with a small bundle in her hand. She was standing at the door, and had heard Marianna's exclamation.

'You need not be in a hurry; it's not such a treat as all that.'

Marianna fairly flew to meet her.

'You have brought it!'

Tatyana patted the bundle.

'Everything's here . . . fully prepared. . . . You've only got to put the things on . . . and go out in your finery for folks to admire you.'

'Ah, come along, come along, Tatyana Osipovna, dear. . . .'

Marianna drew her into her room.

Left alone, Nezhdanov paced twice up and down with a peculiar stealthy gait. . . . (he imagined for some reason that that was just how small shopkeepers walked); he sniffed cautiously at his own sleeve, and the lining of his cap – and frowned; he looked at himself in a little looking-glass hanging on the wall near the window, and shook his head; he certainly looked very unattractive. 'All the better, though,' he thought. Then he took up a few pamphlets, stuffed them in his skirt pocket, and murmured a few words to himself in the accent of a small shopkeeper. 'I fancy that's like it,' he thought again; 'but after all, what need of acting? my get-up will answer for me.' And at that point Nezhdanov recollected a German convict, who had had to run away right across Russia, and he spoke Russian badly, too; but thanks to a merchant's cap edged with cat's-skin, which he had bought in a provincial town, he was taken everywhere for a merchant, and had successfully made his way over the frontier.

At that instant Solomin came in.

'Aha! brother Alexey,' he cried; 'you're studying your part! Excuse me, brother; in that disguise one can't address you respectfully.'

'Oh, please do. . . . I'd meant to ask you to call me so.'

'Only it's awfully early yet; but, there, I suppose you want to get used to it. Well, then, all right. But you'll have to wait a bit; the master's not gone yet. He's asleep.'

'I'll go out later on,' answered Nezhdanov. 'I'm going to walk about the neighbourhood till I get instructions of some sort.'

'That's right! Only I tell you what, brother Alexey . . . I may call you Alexey, then?'

' 'Lexey, if you like,' said Nezhdanov, smiling.

'No; we mustn't overdo it. Listen! good counsel is better than money, as they say. I see you have pamphlets there; you can give them to whom you please – only not in the factory!'

'Why not?'

'Because, in the first place, it would be risky for you; secondly, I have pledged myself to the owner that there shall be nothing of the sort going on – after all, the factory's his, you know; and thirdly, we have something started there – schools and so on. And – well – you might ruin all that. Act as you please, as best you may – I will not hinder you; but don't touch my factory hands.'

'Caution never comes amiss . . . hey?' Nezhdanov remarked with a malignant half-smile.

Solomin smiled his own broad smile.

'Just so, brother Alexey; it never comes amiss. But who is this I see? Where are we?'

These last exclamations referred to Marianna, who appeared in the doorway of her room in a sprigged chintz gown, that had seen many washings, with a yellow 'kerchief on her shoulders and a red one on her head. Tatyana was peeping out from behind her back, in simple and kindly admiration of her. Marianna looked both fresher and younger in her simple costume; it suited her far better than the long full-skirted coat suited Nezhdanov.

'Vassily Fedotitch, please don't laugh,' Marianna entreated, and she flushed the colour of a poppy.

'What a pretty pair!' Tatyana was exclaiming, meanwhile clapping her hands. 'Only you, my dear laddie, don't be angry, you're nice, very nice – but beside my little lass here you cut no figure at all.'

'And, really, she's exquisite,' thought Nezhdanov; 'oh! how I love her!'

'And look-ee,' went on Tatyana, 'she's changed rings with me. She's given me her gold one and taken my silver one.'

'Girls of the people don't wear gold rings,' said Marianna.

Tatyana sighed.

'I'll take care of it for you, dearie, never fear.'

'Well, sit down; sit down, both of you,' began Solomin, who had been all the time watching Marianna, with his head a little bent; 'in old days you remember folks always used to sit down together for a bit when they were setting off on their road. And you've both a long, hard road before you.'

Marianna, still rosy red, sat down; Nezhdanov too sat down; Solomin sat down; and last of all Tatyana too sat down on a thick log of wood standing on end.

Solomin looked at all of them in turn:

> 'Step back a bit
> And look at it,
> How nicely here we all do sit . . .'

he said, slightly screwing up his eyes; and all of a sudden he burst out laughing, but so nicely that, far from feeling offended, they were all delighted.

But Nezhdanov suddenly got up.

'I'm off,' he said, 'this minute; though this is all very delightful – only a trifle like a farce with dressing-up in it. Don't be uneasy,' he turned to Solomin; 'I won't touch your factory hands. I will do a little talking about the suburbs, and come back, and I'll tell you all my adventures, Marianna, if only there's anything to tell. Give me your hand for good luck!'

'A cup of tea'd be as well first,' observed Tatyana.

'No! tea-drinking indeed! If I want anything I'll go to a tavern or simply a gin-shop.'

Tatyana shook her head.

'Those taverns swarm along our highroads nowadays like fleas in a sheepskin. The villages are all so big – why, Balmasovo . . .'

'Good-bye, till we meet . . . may I leave good luck with you!' Nezhdanov added, correcting himself and entering into his part as a small shopkeeper. But before he had reached the door, Pavel poked his head in from the corridor under his very nose, and handing him a long thin staff, peeled, with a strip of bark running round it like a screw, he said: 'Please take it, Alexey Dmitritch; lean on it as you walk; and the further you hold the stick away from you the better effect it will have.'

Nezhdanov took the staff without speaking and went off; Pavel followed him. Tatyana was about to go away too; Marianna got up and stopped her.

'Wait a little, Tatyana Osipovna; I want you.'

'But I'll be back in a minute with the samovar. Your comrade went off without any tea, – he was in such a desperate hurry. . . . But why should you deny yourself? Later on things'll be clearer.'

Tatyana went out; Solomin too rose. Marianna was standing with her back to him, and when she did at last turn round to him – seeing that for a very long time he had not uttered a single word – she caught in his face, in his eyes which were fastened upon her, an expression she had never seen in him before, an expression of inquiry, of anxiety, almost of curiosity. She was disconcerted and blushed again. And Solomin seemed ashamed of what she had caught sight of in his face, and he began talking louder than usual:

'Well, well, Marianna . . . here you've made a beginning.'

'A fine beginning, Vassily Fedotitch! How can one call it a beginning? I feel somehow very stupid all of a sudden. Alexey was right; we are really acting a sort of farce.'

Solomin sat down again on his chair.

'But, Marianna, let me say . . . How did you picture it to yourself – the beginning? It's not a matter of building barricades with a flag over them, and shouting hurrah! for the republic! And that's not a woman's work either. But you now to-day will start training some Lukerya in something good, and it'll be a hard task for you, as Lukerya won't be over quick of understanding, and she'll be shy of you, and will fancy too that what you're trying to teach her won't be of the least use to her; and in a fortnight or three weeks you'll be struggling with some other Lukerya, and meanwhile you'll be washing a child or teaching him his A B C, or giving medicine to a sick man . . . that will be your beginning.'

'But the sisters of mercy do all that, you know, Vassily Fedotitch! What need, then . . . of all this?' Marianna pointed to herself and round about her with a vague gesture. 'I dreamt of something else.'

'You wanted to sacrifice yourself?'

Marianna's eyes glistened.

'Yes . . . yes . . . yes!'

'And Nezhdanov?'

Marianna shrugged her shoulders.

'What of Nezhdanov! We will go forward together . . . or I will go alone.'

Solomin looked intently at Marianna.

'Do you know what, Marianna . . . you will excuse the unpleasantness of the expression . . . but to my idea, combing the scurfy head of a dirty urchin is a sacrifice, and a great sacrifice, of which not many people are capable.'

'But I would not refuse to do that, Vassily Fedotitch.'

'I know you wouldn't! Yes, you are capable of that. And that's what you will be doing for a time; and afterwards, maybe – something else too.'

'But to do that I must learn from Tatyana!'

'By all means . . . get her to show you. You will scour pots, and pluck chickens. . . . And so, who knows, maybe you will save your country!'

'You are laughing at me, Vassily Fedotitch.'

Solomin shook his head slowly.

'O my sweet Marianna! believe me, I am not laughing at you; and my words are the simple truth. You now, all of you, Russian women, are more capable, and loftier too, than we men.'

Marianna raised her downcast eyes.

'I should like to justify your expectations, Solomin . . . and then – I'm ready to die!'

Solomin got up.

'No, live . . . live! That's the great thing. By the way, don't you want to find out what is taking place in your home now, as regards your flight? Won't they take steps of some sort? We need only drop a word to Pavel – he'll reconnoitre in no time.'

Marianna was surprised.

'What an extraordinary man he is!'

'Yes . . . he's rather a wonderful fellow. For instance, when you want to celebrate your marriage with Alexey – he'll arrange that too with Zosim. . . . You remember I told you there was a priest. . . . But I suppose there's no need of him for a while? No?'

'No.'

'No, then.' Solomin went up to the door that separated the two rooms – Nezhdanov's and Marianna's – and bent down over the lock.

'What are you looking at there?' asked Marianna.

'Does it lock?'

'Yes,' whispered Marianna.

Solomin turned to her. She did not raise her eyes.

'Then, there's no need to find out what are Sipyagin's intentions?' he observed cheerfully; 'no need, eh?'

Solomin was about to go away.

'Vassily Fedotitch . . .'

'What is it?'

'Tell me, please, why is it you, who are always so silent, are so talkative with me? You don't know how much it pleases me.'

'Why is it?' – Solomin took both her little soft hands in his big rough ones – 'Why? – Well, it must be because I like you so much. Good-bye.'

He went out . . . Marianna stood a little, looked after him, thought a little, and went off to Tatyana, who had not yet brought in the samovar, and with whom she did – it is true – drink tea, but she also scoured pots, and plucked chickens, and even combed out the tangled mane of a small boy.

About dinner-time she returned to her little apartments. . . . She had not long to wait for Nezhdanov.

He returned, weary and covered with dust, and almost fell on to the sofa. She at once sat down beside him. 'Well? well? Tell me!'

'You remember those two lines,' he answered in a weak voice:

> ' "It would all have been so comic
> If it had not been so sad"?

Do you remember?'

'Of course I do.'

'Well, those lines apply precisely to my first expedition. But no! There was positively more of the comic in it. In the first place, I'm convinced that nothing's easier than to play a part; no one dreamt of suspecting me. But there was one thing I had not thought of – one wants to make up some sort of story beforehand . . . they keep asking one – where you're from, and what you're doing – and you have nothing ready. However, even that's hardly necessary. One's only to propose a dram of vodka at the gin-shop, and lie away as one pleases.'

'And you . . . did tell lies?' asked Marianna.

'I lied . . . the best I could. The second point is: all, absolutely all the people I talked to are discontented; and no one even cares to know how to remedy this discontent! But at propaganda I seem to be a very poor hand; two pamphlets I simply left secretly in a room – one I thrust into a cart. . . . What'll come of them the Lord only knows! I offered pamphlets to four men. One asked was it a religious book, and did not take it; another said he could not read, and took it for his children as there was a woodcut on the cover: a third began by agreeing with me. "To be sure, to be sure . . ." then all of a sudden fell to swearing at me in the most unexpected way, and he too did not take one; the fourth at last took one, and thanked me very much for it, but I fancy he couldn't make head or tail of what I said to him. Besides that, a dog bit my leg; a peasant woman brandished a fire-shovel at me from the door of her hut, shouting, "Ugh! you beast! You Moscow loafers! Will nothing drown you?" And a soldier on furlough, too, kept shouting after me, "Wait a minute, we'll put a bullet through you, my friend"; and he'd got drunk on my money!'

'Anything more?'

'Anything more? I've rubbed a blister on my heel; one of my boots is awfully big. And now I'm hungry, and my head's splitting from the vodka.'

'Have you drunk much, then?'

'No, not much – only to set the example; but I've been in five gin-shops. But I can't stand that filth – vodka – a bit. And how our peasant can drink it passes my understanding! If one must drink vodka to be simplified, I'd rather be excused.'

'And so no one suspected you?'

'No one. An innkeeper, a stout, pale man with whitish eyes, was the only person who looked at me suspiciously. I heard him tell his wife to "keep an eye on that red-haired chap . . . with the squint." (I never knew till then that I squinted.) "He's a sharper. Do you see how ponderously he drinks?" What ponderously means in that context I didn't understand; but it could hardly be a compliment. Something after the style of Gogol's "movy-ton" in the *Revising Inspector*; do you remember? Perhaps because I tried to pour my vodka under the table on the sly. Ugh! it's hard, it's hard for an æsthetic creature to be brought into contact with real life!'

'Better luck next time,' Marianna consoled Nezhdanov. 'But I'm glad that you look at your first attempt from a humorous point of view. . . . You weren't bored really?'

'No, I wasn't bored; in fact, I was amused. But I know for a certainty I shall begin to think over it now, and I shall feel so sick and so sad.'

'No, no! I won't let you think. I'm going to tell you what

I've been doing. Dinner'll be brought us in directly; by the way, I must tell you I've scoured out most thoroughly the pot Tatyana's cooked the soup in. . . . And I shall tell you . . . everything over every spoonful.'

And so she did. Nezhdanov listened to her chat, and looked and looked at her . . . so that several times she stopped to let him tell her why he was looking at her like that. . . . But he was silent.

After dinner she offered to read aloud to him some of Spielhagen. But before she had finished the first page, he got up impulsively, and, going up to her, fell at her feet. She stood up, he flung both his arms round her knees, and began to utter passionate words – disconnected and despairing words! 'He would like to die, he knew he would soon die. . . .' She did not stir, did not resist; she calmly submitted to his abrupt embrace, calmly, even caressingly, looked down at him. She laid both hands on his head, that was shaking convulsively in the folds of her dress. But her very calmness had a more powerful effect on him than if she had repulsed him. He got up, murmured: 'Forgive me, Marianna, for what has passed to-day and yesterday; tell me again that you are ready to wait till I am worthy of your love, and forgive me.'

'I have given you my word . . . and I can't change.'

'Thank you; good-bye.'

Nezhdanov went out; Marianna locked herself in her room.

XXX

A FORTNIGHT LATER, in the same place, this was what Nezhdanov was writing to his friend Silin, as he bent over his little three-legged table, on which a tallow candle gave a dim and niggardly light. (It was long after midnight. On the sofa and on the floor lay mud-stained garments, hurriedly flung off; a fine, incessant rain was pattering on the window-panes, and a strong, warm wind breathed in great sighs about the roof.)

'DEAR VLADIMIR, – I am writing to you without putting an address, and this letter will even be sent by a messenger to a distant posting station, because my presence here is a secret; and to tell it you might mean the ruin not of myself alone. It will be enough for you to know that I have been living at a large factory, together with Marianna, for the last fortnight. We ran away from the Sipyagins' the very day I wrote to you last. We were given a home here by a friend. I will call him Vassily. He is the chief person here – a splendid fellow. Our stay in this factory is only temporary. We are here till the time comes for action – though, to judge by what has happened so far, this time is hardly likely ever to come! Vladimir, my heart is heavy, heavy. First of all, I must tell you that though Marianna and I have run away together, we are so far as brother and sister. She loves me . . . and has told me she will be mine if . . . I feel I have the right to ask it of her.

'Vladimir, I don't feel I have the right! She believes in me, in my honesty – I'm not going to deceive her. I know I have never loved any one and never shall love (that's pretty certain!) any one more than her. But, for all that, how can I unite her fate for ever to mine? A living being – to a corpse? Well, not a corpse – to a half-dead creature! Where would one's conscience be? You will say, if there were a strong passion – conscience would have nothing to say. That's the very point: that I am a corpse; an honest, well-meaning corpse, if you like. Please don't cry out that I always exaggerate. . . . All I am telling you is the truth! the truth! Marianna is a very concentrated nature, and now she is all absorbed in her activity, in which she believes. . . . While I?

'Well, enough of love and personal happiness, and everything of that sort. For the last fortnight now I have been "going to the people," and alack and alack! anything more absurd you cannot imagine. Of course, there the fault lies in me, and not in the work itself. Granted, I'm not a Slavophil; I'm not one of those who find their panacea in the people, in contact with them; I don't lay the people on my aching stomach like a flannel bandage . . . I want to have an influence on them myself; but how? How accomplish that? It appears when I am with the people that I am always only stooping to them, and listening; and when it does happen that I say anything, it's below contempt! I feel myself I'm no good. It's like a bad actor in the wrong part. Conscientiousness is quite out of place in this, and so is scepticism, and even a sort of pitiful humour directed against myself. . . . It's all not worth a brass farthing! It's positively sickening to remember; sickening to look at the rags I drag about on me, at this masquerade, as Vassily expresses it! They maintain one ought first to study the people's talk, learn their character and habits. . . . Rubbish! rubbish! rubbish! One must *believe* in what one says, and then one may say what one likes. I once chanced to hear something like a sermon from a sectarian prophet. There's no saying what rot he talked; it was a sort of hotch-potch of ecclesiastical and bookish language, with simple peasant idioms, and that not Russian, but White Russian of some sort. . . . And you know he kept pounding away at the same thing, like a plover calling! "The spirit has dee-scended, the spirit has dee-scended!" But then his eyes were ablaze, his voice firm and hoarse, his fists clenched – he was like iron all over! The listeners did not understand, but they revered him! And they followed him! While I start speaking like a criminal – I'm begging pardon all the while. I ought to go to the sectarians, really; their art is not great . . . but there's the place to get faith, faith! Marianna there has faith. She's at work from early morning, busy with Tatyana, a peasant-woman here, good-natured and not a fool; by the way, she says of us that we want simplification, and calls us simplified folks; – well, Marianna busies herself with this woman, and never sits down a minute; she's a regular ant! She's delighted that her hands are getting red and rough; and looks forward to some day, if necessary, the scaffold! While awaiting the scaffold, she has even tried giving up shoes; she went somewhere barefoot, and came back barefoot. I heard her afterwards washing her feet a long while; I see she walks cautiously on them – they're sore from not being used to it; but she looks as joyful, as radiant, as though she had found a treasure, as though the sun were shining on her. Yes, Marianna's first-rate! And when I try to talk to her of my feelings, to begin with, I feel somehow ashamed, as though I were laying hands on what's not mine; and then that look . . . oh, that awful, devoted, unresisting look. . . . . "Take me," it seems to say . . . "*but remember!* And what need of all this? Isn't there something better, higher upon earth?" That is, in other words, "Put on your stinking overcoat, and go out to the people." . . . And so, you see, I go out to the people. . . .

'Oh, how I curse at such times my nervousness, delicacy, sensitiveness, squeamishness, all I have inherited from my aristocratic father! What right had he to shove me into life, supplying me with organs utterly unfit for the surroundings in which I must move? To hatch a chicken and shove it into the water! An artist in the mud! a democrat, a lover of the people, whom the mere smell of that loathsome vodka, "the green wine," turns ill and nearly sick?

'See what I've worked myself up to – abusing my father! And, indeed, I became a democrat of myself; he'd no hand in that.

'Yes, Vladimir, I'm in a bad way. I have begun to be haunted by some grey, ugly thoughts! Can it be, you will ask me, that I have not even during this fortnight come across anything consolatory, any good, live person, however ignorant? What shall I say? I have met something of the sort . . . I've even come across one very fine, splendid, plucky chap. But turn it which way I will, I'm no use to him with my pamphlets, and that's all about it! Pavel – a man in the factory here – (he's Vassily's right hand, a very clever, very sharp fellow, a future "head" . . . I fancy

I wrote to you about him) – he has a friend, a peasant, Elizar is his name . . . a clear brain, too, and a free spirit, untrammelled in every way; but directly we meet, it's as though there's a wall between us! his face is nothing but a "No!" And again another fellow I met with . . . he was one of the hot-tempered sort, though. "Now then, sir," says he, "no soft soap, please, but say straight out, are you giving up all your land, as it is, or not?" "What do you mean?" I answered; "I'm not a gentleman!" (and I even added, I remember, "Lord bless you!"). "But if you're a common man," says he, "what sort of sense is there in you? Do me the favour to let me alone!"

'And another thing. I've noticed if any one listens to you very readily, takes pamphlets at once, you may be sure he's one of the wrong sort, a featherhead; or you'll come on a fine talker, an educated fellow, who can do nothing but keep repeating some favourite expression. One, for instance, simply drove me distracted; everything with him was "product." Whatever you say to him, he keeps on, "To be sure, a product!" Ugh, to the devil with him! One remark more. . . . Do you remember at one time, a long while ago, there used to be a great deal of talk about "superfluous" people – Hamlets? Fancy, such "superfluous" people are to be found now among the peasants! with a special tone of their own, of course. . . . Moreover, they're for the most part of consumptive build. Interesting types, and they come to us readily; but for the cause they're no good – just like the Hamlets of former days. Come, what is one to do, then? Found a secret printing-press? Why, there are books enough as it is, both of the sort, "Cross yourself and take up the hatchet," and the sort that say, "Take up the hatchet" simply. Write novels of peasant life, filled out with padding? They wouldn't get printed, most likely. Or first take up the hatchet? . . . But against whom, with whom, what for? So that the national soldier may shoot you down with the national rifle! Well, that's a sort of complex suicide! It would be better to make an end of myself. At least I shall know when and how, and shall choose myself what part to aim at. . . . Really, I fancy if there were a war of independence going on now anywhere, I would set off there, not to liberate anybody whatever (the idea of liberating others when one's own people are not free!), but to make an end of myself.

'Our friend Vassily, the man who has taken us in here, is a happy man; he is of our camp, and a quiet fellow in a way. He's not in a hurry. Another man I should abuse for that . . . but him I can't. And it seems as though the whole basis of it doesn't lie in convictions, but in character. Vassily has a character you can't pick holes in. Well, to be sure he's right. He sits a great deal with us, with Marianna. And here's a curious fact. I love her and she loves me (I can see you smiling at that phrase, but, by God, it's so!); and we have hardly anything to say to one another. But she argues and discusses with him, and listens to him. I'm not jealous of him; he's taking steps for getting her into some place, at least she asks him about it; only my heart aches when I look at them. And yet imagine: if I were to falter out a word about marriage, she'd agree at once, and the priest, Zosim, would put in an appearance: "Esaias, be exalted," and all the rest in due order. Only, it would make it no better for me, and *nothing would be changed.* . . . There's no way out of it! Life's cut me on the cross, dear Vladimir, as you remember our friend the drunken tailor used to complain of his wife.

'I feel, though, that it won't last long, I feel that something is preparing. . . .

'Haven't I demanded and proved that we ought to "act"? Well, now we are going to act.

'I don't remember whether I wrote to you of another friend of mine, a dark fellow, a relation of the Sipyagins. He may, very likely, cook a kettle of fish that won't be swallowed too easily.

'I quite meant to finish this letter before, but there! Though I do nothing, nothing at all, I scribble verses. I don't read them to Marianna, she doesn't much care for them, but you . . . sometimes even praise them; and what's of most importance, you won't talk about them to any one. I have been struck by one universal phenomenon in Russia. Any way, here they are – the verses:

'SLEEP

'A long while I had not been in my own land. . . .
But I found in it no change to notice –
Everywhere the same deathlike, senseless stagnation,
Houses without roofs, walls tumbling down,
And the same filth and stench and poverty and boredom!
And the same slavish glance, now insolent, now abject!
Our people were made free; and the free arm
Hangs as before like a whip unused.
All, all is as before. . . . And in one thing alone
Europe, Asia, the whole world we have outstripped!
No! never yet have my dear countrymen
Sunk into a sleep so terrible!

'Everything is asleep; everywhere, in village and in town,
In cart, in sledge, by day, by night, sitting and standing . . .
The merchant, the official sleeps; the sentinel at his post
Stands asleep in the cold of the snow and in the burning heat!
And the prisoner sleeps; and the judge snores;
Dead asleep are the peasants; asleep, they reap and plough;
They thresh asleep; the father sleeps, the mother and children
All are asleep! He that flogs is asleep, and he too that is flogged!
Only the Tsar's gin-shop never closes an eye;
And grasping tight her pot of gin,
Her brow on the Pole and her heels on the Caucasus,
Lies in interminable sleep our country, holy Russia!

'Please forgive me: I didn't want to send you such a melancholy letter without giving you a little amusement at the end (you'll certainly notice some halting lines ... but what of it!). When shall I write to you again? Shall I write again? Whatever becomes of me, I am sure you will not forget your faithful friend,

'A.N.

'*P.S.* – Yes, our people is asleep. . . . But I fancy if anything ever does wake it, it won't be what *we* are thinking of. . . .'

After writing the last line Nezhdanov flung down the pen, and saying to himself, 'Well, now try to sleep and forget all this rot, rhymester', he lay down on the bed ... but it was long before sleep visited his eyes.

Next morning Marianna waked him, passing through his room to Tatyana; but he had only just had time to dress when she came back again. Her face expressed delight and agitation; she seemed excited.

'Do you know, Alyosha, they say that in the T——— district, not far from here, it has begun already!'

'Eh? what has begun? who says so?'

'Pavel. They say the peasants are rising, refusing to pay taxes, collecting in mobs.'

'You heard that yourself?'

'Tatyana told me. But here's Pavel himself. Ask him.'

Pavel came in and confirmed Marianna's tale.

'There's disturbance in T——— district, that's true!' he said, shaking his beard and screwing up his flashing black eyes. 'It's Sergei Mihalovitch's work, one must suppose. It's five days now he's not been at home.'

Nezhdanov snatched up his cap.

'Where are you going?' asked Marianna.

'Where? ... there,' he answered, scowling, and not raising his eyes; 'to T——— district.'

'Then I'll go with you. You'll take me, won't you? Only let me put a big kerchief over my head.'

'It's not a woman's work,' said Nezhdanov sullenly, as before looking down as though irritated.

'No! . . . no! . . . You do right to go; or Markelov would think you a coward. . . . And I will go with you.'

'I'm not a coward,' said Nezhdanov in the same sullen voice.

'I meant to say he would take us both for cowards. I'm coming with you.'

Marianna went into her room for the kerchief, while Pavel uttered in a sort of stealthy inward whistle, 'Ah-ha, aha!' and promptly vanished. He ran to warn Solomin.

Marianna had not reappeared when Solomin came into Nezhdanov's room. He was standing with his face to the window, his forehead resting on his arm, and his arm on the window-pane. Solomin touched him on the shoulder. He turned quickly round. Dishevelled and unwashed, Nezhdanov had a wild and strange look. Though indeed Solomin too had changed of late. He had grown yellow, his face looked drawn, his upper teeth were slightly visible. . . . He too seemed unhinged, so far as his 'well-balanced' nature could be.

'So Markelov could not control himself,' he began; 'this may turn out badly, for him chiefly . . . and for others too.'

'I want to go and see what's going on . . .' observed Nezhdanov.

'And I too,' added Marianna, making her appearance in the doorway.

Solomin turned slowly to her.

'I would not advise you to, Marianna. You might betray yourself and us; without meaning to and utterly needlessly. Let Nezhdanov go and see what's in the air a little, if he likes . . . and the less of that the better! – but why should you?'

'I don't like to stay behind when he goes.'

'You will hamper him.'

Marianna glanced at Nezhdanov. He stood immovable, with an immovable, sullen face.

'But if there's danger?' she said.

Solomin smiled.

'Don't be afraid . . . when there's danger, I'll let you go.'

Marianna silently took the kerchief off her head and sat down.

Then Solomin turned to Nezhdanov.

'And do you, brother, really look about a little. Perhaps it's all exaggerated. Only, please, be careful. Some one shall go with you, though. And come back as quick as possible. You promise? Nezhdanov, do you promise?'

'Yes.'

'Yes, for certain?'

'Since every one obeys you here, Marianna and all.'

Nezhdanov went out into the passage without saying good-bye. Pavel popped up out of the darkness and ran down the staircase before him, his iron-shod boots ringing as he went. Was *he* then to accompany Nezhdanov?

Solomin sat down by Marianna.

'You heard Nezhdanov's last words?'

'Yes; he's vexed that I listen to you more than to him. And indeed it's the truth. I love *him*, but I obey *you*. He's dearer to me . . . but you're nearer.'

Solomin cautiously stroked her hand with his.

'This . . . is a most unpleasant affair,' he observed at last. 'If Markelov's mixed up in it – he's lost.'

Marianna shuddered.

'Lost?'

'Yes. . . . He does nothing by halves, and he won't hide behind others.'

'Lost!' murmured Marianna again, and the tears ran down her face. 'O Vassily Fedotitch! I am very sorry for him. But why can't he be victorious? Why must he inevitably be lost?'

'Because in such undertakings, Marianna, the first always

perish, even if they succeed. . . . And in the work *he*'s plotting for, not only the first and the second, but even the tenth . . . and the twentieth.'

'Then we shall never live to see it?'

'What you are dreaming of? Never. With our eyes we shall never look upon it; with these living eyes. In the spirit . . . to be sure, that's a different matter. We may gratify ourselves by the sight of it that way now, at once. There's no restriction there.'

'Then how is it you, Solomin—'

'What?'

'How is it you are going along the same way?'

'Because there's no other; that is, speaking more correctly, my aim is the same as Markelov's; but our paths are different.'

'Poor Sergei Mihalovitch!' said Marianna mournfully. Solomin again gave her a discreet caress.

'Come, come; there's nothing certain yet. We shall see what news Pavel brings. In our . . . work one must be of good courage. The English say, "Never say die." A good proverb. Better than the Russian, "When trouble comes, open the gates wide." It's useless lamenting beforehand.'

Solomin got up from his seat.

'And the place you meant to get me?' asked Marianna suddenly. The tears were still glistening on her cheeks; but there was no sadness in her eyes.

Solomin sat down again.

'Do you want so much to get away from here as soon as possible?'

'Oh, no! but I should like to be of use.'

'Marianna, you are of great use even here. Don't forsake us, wait a little. What is it?' Solomin asked of Tatyana, who came in.

'Well, there's some sort of a female article asking for Alexey Dmitritch,' answered Tatyana, laughing and gesticulating. 'I was for saying that he wasn't here, not here at all. We don't know any such person, says I. But then it—'

'Who's – it?'

'Why, this same female article took and wrote her name on this slip of paper here, and says I'm to show it, and that'll admit her; and that if Alexey Dmitritch really isn't at home, then she can wait.'

On the paper stood in large letters, 'Mashurina.'

'Show her in,' said Solomin. 'You won't mind, Marianna, if she comes in here? She, too, is one of ours.'

'Oh, no! indeed!'

A few seconds later Mashurina appeared in the doorway, in the same dress in which we saw her at the beginning of the first chapter.

XXXI

'IS NEZHDANOV NOT AT HOME?' she asked; then, seeing Solomin, she went up to him, and gave him her hand. 'How are you, Solomin?' At Marianna she simply cast a sidelong glance.

'He will soon be back,' answered Solomin. 'But let me ask, from whom did you find out . . .?'

'From Markelov. Though indeed it's known in the town . . . to two or three people already.'

'Really?'

'Yes. Some one has blabbed. Besides, they say Nezhdanov himself has been recognised.'

'So much for this dressing-up business!' muttered Solomin. 'Let me introduce you,' he added aloud. 'Miss Sinetsky, Miss Mashurin! Pray sit down!'

Mashurina gave a slight nod and sat down.

'I have a letter for Nezhdanov; and for you, Solomin, a verbal message.'

'What sort of message? From whom?'

'From a person you know. . . . How are things with you? . . . is everything ready?'

'Nothing is ready.'

Mashurina opened her tiny little eyes as wide as she could.

'Nothing?'

'Nothing.'

'You mean absolutely nothing?'

'Absolutely nothing.'

'Is that what I'm to say?'

'That's what you must say.'

Mashurina pondered a minute, then she took a cigarette out of her pocket.

'A light – can you give me?'

'Here's a match.'

Mashurina lighted her cigarette.

'They expected something quite different,' she began. 'And all around – it's not as it is with you. However, that's your affair. I'm not here for long. Only to see Nezhdanov and to give him the letter.'

'Where are you going?'

'Oh, a long way from here.' (She was in fact going to Geneva, but she did not care to tell Solomin so. She did not regard him as altogether trustworthy; besides, there was an 'outsider' sitting there. Mashurina, who hardly knew a word of German, was being sent to Geneva in order to hand to a person there, utterly unknown to her, a torn scrap of cardboard with a vine-branch sketched on it, and two hundred and seventy-nine roubles.)

'Where's Ostrodumov? Is he with you?'

'No. He's near here . . . he got stuck on the way. But he'll come when he's wanted. Pimen's all right. No need to worry about him.'

'How did you come here?'

'In a cart . . . how else should I? Give me another match. . . .'

Solomin gave her a lighted match.

'Vassily Fedotitch!' a voice whispered all at once at the door. 'Please, sir!'

'Who's there? What do you want?'

'Please come,' the voice repeated with persuasive insistency. 'There's some strange workmen come here; they keep jawing away, and Pavel Yegoritch isn't here.'

Solomin excused himself, got up and went out.

Mashurina fell to staring at Marianna, and stared at her so long that the latter was quite out of countenance.

'Forgive me,' she said suddenly in her gruff, abrupt voice; 'I'm a rough sort, I don't know how to put things. Don't be angry; you needn't answer if you don't want to. Are you the girl that ran away from the Sipyagins'?'

Marianna was somewhat disconcerted; however, she said, 'Yes.'

'With Nezhdanov?'

'Well, yes.'

'If you please . . . give me your hand. Forgive me, please. You must be good, since he loves you.'

Marianna pressed her hand.

'Do you know Nezhdanov well?'

'Yes, I know him. I used to see him in Petersburg. That's what makes me say so. Sergei Mihalitch, too, told me. . . .'

'Ah, Markelov! You have seen him lately?'

'Yes. Now he's gone away.'

'Where?'

'Where he was ordered.'

Marianna sighed.

'Ah, Miss Mashurin, I fear for him.'

'To begin with, I'm not "Miss." You ought to cast off all such manners. And, secondly . . . you say, "I fear." That won't do either. You will come not to fear for yourself, and to give up fearing for others. Though indeed I'll tell you what strikes me: it's easy for me, Fekla Mashurina, to talk like that. I'm ugly. But of course . . . you're a beauty. That must make it all the harder for you.' (Marianna looked down and turned away.) 'Sergei Mihalovitch told me. . . . He knew I had a letter for

Nezhdanov. . . . "Don't go to the factory," he said to me, "don't take the letter; it will be the breaking-up of everything there. Stay away! They're both happy there. . . . So let them be! Don't meddle!" I should be glad not to meddle . . . but what was I to do about the letter?'

'You must give it without fail,' Marianna assented. 'But oh, how kind he is, Sergei Mihalitch! Can it be that he will be killed, Mashurina . . . or be sent to Siberia?'

'Well, what then? Don't people come back from Siberia? And as for losing one's life! Life's sweet to some, and to some it's bitter. His life is not made of refined sugar either.'

Mashurina again turned an intent and inquisitive gaze on Marianna.

'Yes, you are certainly beautiful,' she cried at last, 'a perfect little bird! I'm beginning to think Alexey's not coming. . . . Shouldn't I give you the letter? Why wait?'

'I will give it him, you may rest assured.'

Mashurina rested her cheek in her hand, and for a long, long time she did not speak.

'Tell me,' she began . . . 'excuse me . . . do you love him very much?'

'Yes.'

Mashurina shook her heavy head.

'Well, there's no need to inquire whether he loves you. I'm going, though, or perhaps I shall be too late. You tell him that I have been here . . . sent my greetings to him. Tell him Mashurina has been. You won't forget my name? No, Mashurina. And the letter. . . . Wait a bit, where have I put it to? . . .'

Mashurina stood up, turned away, making a pretence of rummaging in her pockets, but meanwhile she rapidly put into her mouth a little folded scrap of paper and swallowed it. 'Ah, my goodness! What a piece of idiocy! Can I have lost it? Lost it really is. What a misfortune! If any one were to find it! . . . No; it's nowhere. So it has turned out as Sergei Mihalitch wished, after all!'

'Look again,' whispered Marianna.

Mashurina waved her hand.

'No! What's the use? It's lost!'

Marianna went up to her.

'Well, kiss me, then!'

Mashurina suddenly took Marianna in her arms and pressed her to her bosom with more than a woman's force.

'I wouldn't have done that for anybody,' she said thickly, 'it's against my conscience . . . it's the first time! Tell him to be more careful. . . . And you too. Mind! It'll soon be a bad place for you here, very bad. Get away both of you, while . . . Good-bye!' she added in a loud sharp voice. 'But there's something else . . . tell him. . . . No, there's no need. It's no use.'

Mashurina went out, slamming the door, and Marianna was left pondering in the middle of the room.

'What does it all mean?' she said at last; 'why, that woman loves him more than I love him! And what was the meaning of her hints? And why did Solomin go out so suddenly and not come back?'

She began walking up and down. A strange sensation – a mixture of dismay and annoyance and bewilderment – took possession of her. Why had she not gone with Nezhdanov? Solomin had dissuaded her . . . and where was he himself? And what was going on all around her? Mashurina of course had not given her that fatal letter, out of sympathy for Nezhdanov. . . . But how could she bring herself to such an act of insubordination? Did she want to show her magnanimity? What right had she? And why had *she*, Marianna, been so much touched by that action? And was she really touched by it? An ugly woman was attracted by a young man. . . . After all, what was there out of the way in that? And why did Mashurina assume that Marianna's devotion to Nezhdanov was stronger than her sense of duty? Perhaps Marianna had not at all desired such a sacrifice! And what could have been contained in the letter? A call to immediate action? What then?

'And Markelov? He is in danger ... and are we doing anything?' she asked herself. 'Markelov spares us both, gives us the chance of being happy, won't separate us ... what is that? Magnanimity too ... or contempt?

'And did we run away from that detestable house only to be together, billing and cooing like doves?'

Such were Marianna's meditations. ... And stronger and stronger was the part played in her feelings by the same exasperated annoyance. However, her vanity had been wounded. Why had every one left her alone – *every one*?

This 'fat' woman had called her a beauty, a little bird ... why not a doll at once? And why was it Nezhdanov had not gone alone but with Pavel? As though he needed some one to look after him! And after all, what were Solomin's convictions really? He wasn't a revolutionist at all! And was it possible any one imagined that her attitude to it all was not a serious one?

Such were the thoughts that whirled chasing one another in confusion through Marianna's heated brain. Compressing her lips and folding her arms like a man, she sat down at last by the window, and again stayed immovable, not leaning back in her chair, all alertness and intensity, ready to spring up any minute. Go to Tatyana, work, she would not; she wanted to do one thing only; to wait! And she waited, obstinately, almost spitefully. From time to time her own mood struck her as strange and incomprehensible. ... But it made no difference! Once it even occurred to her to wonder whether jealousy was not at the root of all her feeling. But recalling the figure of poor Mashurina, she merely shrugged her shoulders and dismissed the idea with a mental wave of her hand.

Marianna had long to wait; at last she caught the sound of two persons' steps mounting the stairs. She turned her eyes on the door ... the steps drew nearer. The door opened and Nezhdanov, supported under Pavel's arm, appeared in the doorway. He was deadly pale, and without his cap; his dishevelled hair fell in moist tufts over his brow; his eyes were staring straight before him, seeing nothing. Pavel led him across the room (Nezhdanov's legs moved with an uncertain, feeble totter) and seated him on the sofa.

Marianna jumped up.

'What is it? What's wrong with him? Is he ill?'

But as he settled Nezhdanov, Pavel answered her with a smile, looking round over his shoulder.

'Don't worry yourself, miss, it'll soon pass off. . . . It's just from not being used to it.'

'But what is it?' Marianna queried insistently.

'He's a little tipsy. Been drinking on an empty stomach; that's all!'

Marianna bent over Nezhdanov. He was half-lying across the sofa; his head had sunk on to his breast, his eyes were glassy. . . . He smelt of spirits; he was drunk.

'Alexey!' broke from her lips.

He raised his heavy eyelids with an effort and tried to smile.

'Ah! Marianna!' he stammered, 'you always talked of sim-sim-plification; see now, I'm really simplified. For the people's always drunk, so—'

He broke off; then muttered something indistinct, closed his eyes and fell asleep. Pavel laid him carefully on the sofa.

'Don't be worried, Marianna Vikentyevna,' he repeated, 'he'll sleep a couple of hours and wake up as good as new.'

Marianna was on the point of asking how it had happened; but her questions would have detained Pavel; and she wanted to be alone . . . that is, she did not want Pavel to see him in such a disgraceful state before her longer than could be avoided. She turned away to the window, while Pavel, who had taken in the situation at a glance, carefully covered Nezhdanov's legs with the skirts of his long coat, put a pillow under his head, once more murmured, 'It's nothing!' and went out on tip-toe.

Marianna looked round. Nezhdanov's head sank heavily

into the pillow: on his white face could be seen a tense immobility, as on the face of a man mortally sick.

'How did it happen?' she thought.

XXXII

THIS WAS HOW it had happened.

On taking his seat in the cart with Pavel, Nezhdanov suddenly fell into a state of intense excitement; and directly they drove out of the factory yard and began rolling along the highroad towards T——— district, he began shouting, stopping the peasants that passed, and addressing them in brief, disconnected sentences. 'Eh, are you asleep?' he would say. 'Rise! the time has come! Down with the taxes! Down with the landowners!' Some peasants stared at him in amazement; others went on paying no attention to his shouts; they took him for a drunken man; one even said when he had got home that he had met a Frenchman shouting some stammering, incomprehensible stuff. Nezhdanov had enough sense to know how unutterably stupid and even meaningless what he was doing was; but he gradually worked himself up to such a point that he did not realise what was sense and what was nonsense. Pavel tried to quiet him, told him he couldn't really go on like that; that soon they would reach a large village, the first on the borders of T——— district, 'Lasses' Springs,' – that there they could reconnoitre. . . . But Nezhdanov did not listen . . . and at the same time his face was strangely sad, almost despairing. Their horse was a very plucky round little beast with a clipped mane on his scraggy neck; he plied his sturdy little legs very actively, and kept pulling at the reins, as though he were hastening to the scene of action and taking persons of importance there. Before they reached 'Lasses' Springs,' Nezhdanov noticed, just off the road, before an open corn barn, eight peasants; he sprang at once out of the cart, ran up to them with sudden shouts and backhanded gestures. The words, 'Freedom! forward! Shoulder to shoulder!' could be distinguished, hoarse and noisy, above a multitude of other words less comprehensible. The peasants, who had met before the granary to deliberate how it could be filled, if only in appearance (it was the commune granary, and consequently empty) stared at Nezhdanov and seemed to be listening to his address with great attention; but can hardly have understood much, as when at last he rushed away from them, shouting for the last time, 'Freedom!' one of them, the most acute, shook his head with an air of deep reflection, and commented, 'Wasn't he severe?' while another observed, 'Some captain, seemingly!' to which the acute peasant rejoined, 'To be sure – he wouldn't strain his throat for nothing. That's what they give us nowadays for our money!' Nezhdanov himself, as he clambered into the cart and sat beside Pavel, thought to himself, 'Lord! what idiocy! But there, not one of us knows just how one ought to stir up the people – isn't that it, perhaps? There's no time to analyse now. Tear along! Does your heart ache? Let it!'

They drove into the village street. In the very middle of it a good many peasants were crowding round a tavern. Pavel tried to restrain Nezhdanov; but he flew head over heels out of the cart, and with a wailing shout of 'Brothers!' he was in the crowd. . . . It parted a little; and Nezhdanov again fell to preaching, looking at no one, in a violent passion as it seemed, and almost weeping.

But here the result that followed was quite different. A gigantic fellow with a beardless but ferocious face, in a short greasy cape, high boots, and a sheepskin cap, went up to Nezhdanov, and clapping him on the shoulder with all his might, 'Bravo! you're a fine chap!' he bellowed in a voice of thunder; 'but stop a bit! don't you know, dry words scorch the mouth? Come this way! It's much handier talking here.' He dragged Nezhdanov into the tavern; the rest of the crowd trooped in after them. 'Miheitch!' bawled the young giant, 'look sharp!

two penn'orth! My favourite tap! I'm treating a friend! Who he is, what's his family, and where he's from, old Nick knows, but he's laying into the gentry pretty hot. Drink!' he said turning to Nezhdanov, and handing him a full heavy glass, moist all over the outside as though perspiring, 'drink – if you've really any feeling for the likes of us!' 'Drink!' rose a noisy chorus around. Nezhdanov grasped the pot (he was in a sort of nightmare), shouted, 'To your health, lads!' and emptied it at a gulp. Ugh! He drank it off with the same desperate heroism with which he would have flung himself on a storm of battery or a row of bayonets. . . . But what was happening in him? Something seemed to dart along his spine and down his legs, to set his throat, his chest, and his stomach on fire, to drive the tears into his eyes. . . . A shudder of nausea passed all over him, and with difficulty he kept it down. . . . He shouted at the top of his voice, if only to drown the throbbing in his head. The dark tavern room seemed suddenly hot, sticky, stifling, full of crowds of people! Nezhdanov began talking, talking endlessly, shouting wrathfully, malignantly, shaking broad, horny hands, kissing slobbery beards. . . . The young giant in the cape kissed him too, he almost crushed his ribs in. And he showed himself a perfect demon. 'I'll split his gullet for him!' he roared, 'I'll split his gullet for him! if any one's rude to our brother! or else I'll pound his skull into a jelly. . . . I'll make him squeak! I'm up to it, I am; I've been a butcher; I'm a good hand at that sort of job!' And he shook his huge freckled fist. . . . And then, good God! some one bellowed again, 'Drink!' and again Nezhdanov gulped down that loathsome poison. But this second time it was terrible! He seemed to be full of blunt hooks tearing him to pieces inside. His head was on fire, green circles were going round before his eyes. There was a loud roar, a ringing in his ears. . . . Oh, horror! A third pot. . . . Was it possible he had emptied it? Purple noses seemed to creep up close and hem him in, and dusty heads of hair, and tanned necks and throats ploughed over with networks of wrinkles. Rough hands caught hold of him. 'Hold on!' raging voices were bawling. 'Talk away! The day before yesterday another, a stranger, talked like that. Go on! . . .' The earth seemed reeling under Nezhdanov's feet. His own voice sounded strange to him, as if it came from a long way off. . . . Was it death, or what?

And all of a sudden . . . a sense of the fresh air on his face, and no more hubbub, no red faces, no stench of spirits, sheepskins, pitch and leather. . . . And again he was sitting in the cart with Pavel, at first struggling and shouting, 'Stop! Where are you off to? I'd not time to tell them anything, I must explain . . .' then adding, 'And you yourself, you sly devil, what are your views?' To which Pavel replied, 'It would be nice if there were no gentry, and the land was all ours – what could be better? but there's been no order to that effect so far'; while he stealthily turned his horse's head, and suddenly lashing him on the back with the reins, set off at full trot away from the din and clamour . . . to the factory. . . .

Nezhdanov dozed and was jolted about, but the wind blew sweetly in his face, and kept back gloomy thoughts.

Only he was vexed that he had not been allowed to explain himself fully. . . . And again the wind soothed his heated face.

And then the momentary vision of Marianna, a momentary burning sense of disgrace, and sleep, heavy, deathlike sleep. . . .

All this Pavel told afterwards to Solomin. He made no secret of the fact that he had not hindered Nezhdanov's getting drunk . . . he could not have got him away else. The others wouldn't have let him go.

'But there, when he was getting quite feeble, I begged them with many bows: "Honest gentlemen," says I, "let the poor boy go; see, he's quite young. . . ." And so they let him go. "Only give us half a rouble for ransom," says they. And so I gave it them.'

'Quite right,' said Solomin approvingly.

Nezhdanov slept; and Marianna sat at the window and looked into the little enclosure. And, strange to say, the angry, almost wicked thoughts and feelings that had been astir within her before Nezhdanov's arrival with Pavel left her all at once; Nezhdanov himself was far from being repulsive or disgusting to her; she pitied him. She knew very well that he was neither a rake nor a drunkard, and was already pondering what to say to him when he should wake up: something affectionate, that he might not be too much distressed and ashamed. 'I must manage so that he should tell of his own accord how this mishap befell him.'

She was not excited; but she felt sad . . . desperately sad. It was as if a breath had blown upon her from that real world which she had been struggling to reach . . . and she shuddered at its coarseness and darkness. What Moloch was this to which she was going to sacrifice herself?

But no! It could not be! This was nothing; it was a chance event, and would be over directly.

It was the impression of an instant, which had impressed her only because it was unexpected. She got up, went to the sofa, on which Nezhdanov was lying, passed a handkerchief over his pale brow, which was contracted with suffering even in his sleep, and pushed back his hair. . . .

Again she felt sorry for him, as a mother pities her sick child. But it made her heart ache a little to look at him, and she softly went away into her room, leaving the door ajar.

She did not take up any work, and sat down again, and again a mood of musing came upon her. She felt the time melting away, minute after minute flying past, and it was positively sweet to her to feel it, and her heart beat, and again she fell to waiting for something.

Where had Solomin got to?

The door creaked softly, and Tatyana came into the room.

'What do you want?' asked Marianna almost with annoyance.

'Marianna Vikentyevna,' began Tatyana in an undertone, 'look here. Don't you upset yourself, for it's a thing that will happen in life, and thank God too—'

'I'm not the least upset, Tatyana Osipovna,' Marianna cut her short. 'Alexey Dmitritch isn't quite well; it's of no great consequence! . . .'

'Well, now, that's first-rate! But here have I been thinking, my Marianna Vikentyevna doesn't come, what's wrong with her, thinks I? But for all that I wouldn't have come in to you, for in such cases the first rule is "mind your own business!" Only here's some one – I don't know who – come to the factory. A little man like this, and a bit lame; and nothing'll content him but to get at Alexey Dmitritch! It seems so queer; this morning that female came asking for him . . . and now here's this lame man. "And if," says he, "Alexey Dmitritch's not here," we're to let him see Vassily Fedotitch! "I won't go without," says he, "for," says he, "it's very important business." We try to pack him off like that female; tell him Vassily Fedotitch isn't here . . . has gone away, but this lame man keeps on, "I'm not going," says he, "if I've to wait till midnight. . . ." So he's walking in the yard. Here, come this way into the passage; you can see him from the window. . . . Can you tell me what sort of a fine gentleman he is?'

Marianna followed Tatyana – she had to pass close by Nezhdanov – and again she noticed his brow contracted painfully, and again she passed her handkerchief over it. Through the dusty window-pane she caught sight of the visitor, of whom Tatyana had been speaking. He was a stranger to her. But at that very instant Solomin came into sight round the corner of the house.

The little lame man went rapidly to him, and held out his hand. Solomin took it. He obviously knew the man. Both of them vanished. . . .

But now their steps could be heard on the stairs. . . . They were coming up. . . .

Marianna went back hurriedly into her room and stood still in the middle, hardly able to breathe. She felt dread . . . of what? She did not know.

Solomin's head appeared in the doorway.

'Marianna Vikentyevna, allow us to come in to you. I have brought a person whom it's absolutely necessary for you to see.'

Marianna merely nodded in reply, and behind Solomin in walked – Paklin.

XXXIII

'I'M A FRIEND of your husband's,' he said, bowing low to Marianna and trying, as it seemed, to conceal his scared and excited face; 'I'm a friend, too, of Vassily Fedotitch's. Alexey Dmitritch is asleep; he is, I hear, unwell; and I have unfortunately brought bad news, which I have already communicated in part to Vassily Fedotitch, and in consequence of which decisive measures must be taken.'

Paklin's voice broke continually, like that of a man who is parched and tortured by thirst. The news he brought was really very bad! Markelov had been seized by the peasants and carried off to the town. The stupid clerk had betrayed Golushkin; he had been arrested. He, in his turn, was betraying everything and every one, was eager to go over to orthodoxy, was offering to present the high school with the portrait of the bishop Filaret, and had already forwarded five thousand roubles for distribution among 'crippled soldiers.' There was not a shadow of doubt that he had betrayed Nezhdanov; the police might make a raid upon the factory any minute. Vassily Fedotitch, too, was in some danger. 'As far as I'm concerned,' added Paklin, 'I'm surprised really that I'm still walking about at liberty; though to be sure I have never taken any part precisely in politics and had no hand in any plans. I have taken advantage of this forgetfulness or oversight on the part of the police to warn you and consult you as to what means may be employed . . . to avert an unpleasantness.'

Marianna heard Paklin to the end. She was not frightened

– she even remained perfectly serene. . . . But to be sure, some steps would have to be taken! Her first action was to look to Solomin.

He, too, seemed composed; only the muscles were faintly twitching about his lips, with something unlike his habitual smile.

He understood what her look meant; she was waiting for him to say what steps were to be taken.

'It's rather a ticklish business, certainly,' he began; 'it would be as well, I imagine, for Nezhdanov to keep in hiding for a time. By the way, how did you learn that he was here, Mr. Paklin?'

Paklin waved his hand.

'An individual told me. He'd seen him wandering about the neighbourhood making propaganda. Well, he kept an eye on him, though with no evil intent. He is a sympathiser. Pardon me,' he added, turning to Marianna, 'but really, our friend Nezhdanov has been very . . . very indiscreet.'

'It's no use blaming him now,' Solomin began again. 'It's a pity we can't talk things over with him; but his indisposition will be over by to-morrow, and the police are not so rapid in their movements as you imagine. You, too, Marianna Vikentyevna, ought to go away with him, I suppose.'

'Undoubtedly,' Marianna replied, thickly but resolutely.

'Yes,' said Solomin. 'We shall have to think things over; we shall have to find ways and means.'

'Allow me to lay one idea before you,' began Paklin; 'the idea entered my head as I came in here. I hasten to observe that I dismissed the cabman from the town, a mile away.'

'What is your idea?' asked Solomin.

'I'll tell you. Let me have horses at once . . . and I will gallop off to the Sipyagins.'

'To the Sipyagins!' repeated Marianna. . . . 'What for?'

'You shall hear.'

'But do you know them?'

'Not in the least! But listen. Consider my proposition thoroughly. It seems to me simply a stroke of genius. You see, Markelov's Sipyagin's brother-in-law, his wife's brother. Isn't that so? Is it possible that gentleman will do nothing to save him? And moreover, Nezhdanov himself! Granting that Mr. Sipyagin is angry with him. . . . Still, you see, for all that, Nezhdanov has become a relation of his by marrying you. And the danger hanging over our friend's head—'

'I'm not married,' observed Marianna.

Paklin positively started.

'What? Not managed that all this time! Well, never mind,' he went on; 'one can fib a little. It's just the same thing; you're going to be married directly. Indeed, one can't devise any other plan! Take into consideration the fact that Sipyagin up till now has not gone so far as to persecute you. Consequently, he has a certain . . . magnanimity. I see that expression's not to your taste; let's say, a certain affectation of generosity. Why shouldn't we utilise it in the present case? Think of it!'

Marianna raised her head and passed her hand over her hair.

'You may utilise what you please for Markelov's benefit, Mr. Paklin . . . or for your own; but Alexey and I desire neither the protection nor the patronage of Mr. Sipyagin. We did not leave his house to go knocking at his door as beggars. We will owe nothing either to the magnanimity nor the affectation of generosity of Mr. Sipyagin or his wife!'

'Those are most praiseworthy sentiments,' responded Paklin (but, 'My! that's a nice wet blanket!' was his inward comment), 'though, on the other hand, if you come to reflect . . . However, I am ready to obey you. I will exert myself on Markelov's account, our dear, good Markelov only! I venture only to observe that he is not his blood relation, but only related to him through his wife, while you—'

'Mr. Paklin, I beg you!'

'Oh, yes . . . yes! But I can't refrain from expressing my regret, for Sipyagin is a man of great influence.'

'So you've no fears for yourself?' queried Solomin.

Paklin straightened his chest.

'At such moments one must not think of oneself,' he said proudly. And all the while, it was just of himself he was thinking. He wanted (poor, feeble little creature!) to be the first in the field, as the saying is. On the strength of the service rendered him, Sipyagin might, if need arose, speak a word for him. For as a fact, he too – say what he would – was implicated; he had listened . . . and even gone chattering about himself.

'I think your idea's not a bad one,' observed Solomin at last, 'though I put little confidence in its success. Any way, you can try. You will do no harm.'

'Of course not. Come, supposing the very worst; suppose they kick me out. . . . What harm will that do?'

'There'll certainly be no harm in that. . . .' ('*Merci!*' thought Paklin.) While Solomin went on: 'What o'clock is it? Five o'clock. No time to waste. You shall have the horses directly. Pavel!'

But instead of Pavel, on the threshold they saw Nezhdanov. He staggered, steadying himself on the doorpost, and opening his mouth feebly, stared with bewildered eyes, comprehending nothing.

Paklin was the first to approach him.

'Alyosha!' he cried, 'you know me, don't you?'

Nezhdanov gazed at him, blinking slowly.

'Paklin?' he said at last.

'Yes, yes; it's I. You are not well?'

'Yes . . . I'm not well. But . . . why are you here?'

'I'm here . . .' But at that instant Marianna stealthily touched Paklin on the elbow. He looked round, and saw she was making signs to him. . . . 'Ah, yes!' he muttered. 'Yes . . . to be sure! Well, do you see, Alyosha,' he added aloud, 'I've come on important business, and must go on further at once. . . . Solomin will tell you all about it – and Marianna . . . Marianna

Vikentyevna. They both fully approve of my plan – it's a matter that concerns us all: that is, no, no,' he interpolated hurriedly in response to a gesture and a glance from Marianna. . . . 'It's a matter concerning Markelov, our common friend Markelov; him alone. But now, good-bye! Every minute's precious – good-bye, friend. . . . We shall meet again. Vassily Fedotitch, will you come with me to give orders about the horses?'

'Certainly. Marianna, I'd meant to say to you, keep up your spirits! But there's no need. You're the real thing!'

'Oh, yes! oh, yes!' chimed in Paklin: 'you're a Roman woman of the time of Cato! Cato of Utica! But come along, Vassily Fedotitch, let us go!'

'You've plenty of time,' observed Solomin with a lazy smile. Nezhdanov moved a little aside to let them both pass. . . . But there was still the same uncomprehending look in his eyes. Then he took two steps, and slowly sat down on a chair facing Marianna.

'Alexey,' she said to him, 'everything is discovered; Markelov has been seized by the peasants he was trying to incite; he's under arrest in the town, and so is that merchant you dined with; most likely the police will soon be here after us. Paklin has gone to Sipyagin.'

'What for?' muttered Nezhdanov, hardly audibly. But his eyes grew clearer, his face regained its ordinary expression. The stupor had left him instantly.

'To try whether he will intercede.'

Nezhdanov drew himself up. . . . 'For us?'

'No; for Markelov. He wanted to beg for us too . . . but I would not let him. Did I do right, Alexey?'

'Right?' said Nezhdanov, and without getting up from his chair, he held out his hands to her. 'Right?' he repeated, and, drawing her close to him and hiding his face against her, he suddenly burst into tears.

'What is it, dear? what is it?' cried Marianna. Now, too, as on that day when he had fallen on his knees before her, faint and breathless with a sudden torrent of passion, she laid her two hands on his trembling head.

But what she felt now was not at all what she had felt then. Then she had given herself up to him. She had submitted, and simply waited for what he would say to her. Now she pitied him, and thought of nothing but how to comfort him.

'What is it, dear?' she said. 'What are you crying for? Surely not because you came home in rather . . . a strange state! That can't be! Or are you sorry for Markelov, and afraid for me and you? Or are you grieving for our shattered hopes? You didn't expect everything to run smoothly, you know!'

Nezhdanov suddenly raised his head.

'No, Marianna,' he said, gulping down his sobs, 'I'm not afraid for you nor for myself. . . . But yes . . . I am sorry—'

'For whom?'

'For you, Marianna! I'm sorry you have bound up your life with a man unworthy of it.'

'Why so?'

'Well, if only because he can be shedding tears at such a moment!'

'It's not you weeping; it's your nerves!'

'My nerves and I are all one! Come, Marianna, look me in the face: can you really say now that you don't regret . . .'

'What?'

'That you ran away with me?'

'No.'

'And will you go further with me? Everywhere?'

'Yes!'

'Yes? Marianna . . . Yes?'

'Yes. I have given you my word, and so long as you are the man I loved, I will not take it back.'

Nezhdanov went on sitting in his chair; Marianna stood before him. His arms lay about her waist; her hands rested on his shoulders. 'Yes, no,' thought Nezhdanov . . . 'but yet – before, when it was my lot to hold her in my arms, just as at this moment, her body was at least motionless; but now, I feel it gently and perhaps against her will shrink away from me!' He loosened his arms . . . Marianna did, in fact, scarcely perceptibly draw back.

'I tell you what!' he said aloud, 'if we must run away . . . before the police discover us . . . I suppose it would be as well for us to be married first. Most likely we shouldn't meet with such an accommodating priest as Zosim anywhere else!'

'I'm ready,' said Marianna.

Nezhdanov looked intently at her.

'Roman maiden!' he said with an evil half-smile. 'What a sense of duty!'

Marianna shrugged her shoulders.

'We must speak to Solomin.'

'Yes . . . Solomin . . .' Nezhdanov drawled. 'But he too, I suppose, is in some danger. The police will seize him too. It strikes me he has done more and known more about it than I.'

'I know nothing about that,' said Marianna. 'He never talks about himself.'

'Unlike me in that!' thought Nezhdanov. 'That was what she meant! Solomin . . . Solomin,' he repeated after a long silence. 'Do you know, Marianna, I should not pity you, if the man with whom you had linked your life for ever had been like Solomin . . . or had been Solomin himself.'

Marianna, in her turn, looked intently at Nezhdanov.

'You had no right to say that,' she said finally.

'I'd no right! How am I to understand those words? Do they mean that you love me? or that I ought not any way to touch on that question?'

'You had no right to say it,' repeated Marianna.

Nezhdanov's head drooped.

'Marianna!' he articulated in a somewhat changed voice.

'Well?'

'If I were now . . . if I put you that question – you know? . . . No, I ask nothing of you . . . good-bye.'

He got up and went out; Marianna did not try to keep him. Nezhdanov sat down on the sofa and hid his face in his hands. He was frightened by his own thoughts, and tried not to think. He had one feeling only, that a sort of dark, underground hand seemed to have clutched at the very root of his being, and would not let him go. He knew that that sweet, precious woman he had left in the next room would not come out to him; and he dared not go in to her. And what would be the use? What could he say?

Rapid, resolute footsteps made him open his eyes.

Solomin walked across his room, and, knocking at Marianna's door, went in.

'Make way for your betters!' muttered Nezhdanov in a bitter whisper.

XXXIV

IT WAS TEN O'CLOCK in the evening in the drawing-room of the mansion of Arzhano. Sipyagin, his wife, and Kallomyetsev were playing cards, when a footman came in and announced the arrival of a stranger, Mr. Paklin, who wanted to see Boris Andreitch on the most urgent and important business.

'So late!' wondered Valentina Mihalovna.

'Eh?' queried Boris Andreitch, wrinkling up his handsome nose. 'What did you say was the gentleman's name?'

'He said Paklin, sir.'

'Paklin!' cried Kallomyetsev. 'A truly rural name. Paklin' (*i.e.* stuffing) '... Solomin' (*i.e.* strawing) '... *De vrais noms ruraux, hein?*'

'And you say,' pursued Boris Andreitch, turning to the footman with the same expression of displeasure, 'that his business is important, urgent?'

'So the gentleman says, sir.'

'H'm ... some beggar or swindler' ('Or both together,' put

in Kallomyetsev). 'Quite likely. Ask him into my study.' Boris Andreitch got up. '*Pardon, ma bonne.* Have a game of écarté while I'm gone, or wait for me. I'll be back directly.'

'*Nous causerons . . . allez!*' said Kallomyetsev. When Sipyagin came into his study and saw Paklin's pitiful, feeble little figure meekly huddled against the wall between the fireplace and the door, he was seized with that truly ministerial sensation of lofty compassion and fastidious condescension so characteristic of the Petersburg higher official.

'Mercy on us! What a poor little plucked bird!' he thought, 'and I do believe he's lame too!'

'Be seated,' he said aloud, giving vent to the benevolent baritone notes of his voice, and affably throwing back his little head; and he took a seat before his visitor.

'You are tired from your journey, I presume; take a seat, and let me hear what is the important business that has brought you to me so late.'

'Your Excellency,' began Paklin, dropping discreetly into a chair, 'I have made bold to come to you—'

'Wait a bit, wait a bit,' Sipyagin interrupted him; 'I've seen you before. I never forget a face I have once met; I always recollect it. Eh . . . eh . . . eh . . . precisely . . . where have I met you?'

'You are right, your Excellency. . . . I had the honour of meeting you in Petersburg at a person's who . . . who . . . since then . . . has unfortunately . . . incurred your displeasure.'

Sipyagin got up quickly from his chair.

'At Mr. Nezhdanov's! I remember now. Surely you haven't come from him?'

'Oh, no, your Excellency; quite the contrary . . . I . . .'

Sipyagin sat down again.

'That's as well. For in that case I would promptly have asked you to leave the house. I can give no admittance to any mediator between me and Mr. Nezhdanov. Mr. Nezhdanov has shown me one of those affronts which are not forgotten. . . . I am above revenge, but I wish to know nothing of him, nor of the girl – more depraved in mind than in heart' (this phrase Sipyagin must have repeated thirty times since Marianna's flight) – 'who could bring herself to leave the home where she had been cared for to become the mistress of a base-born adventurer! It's enough for them that I consent to forget them!'

At this last word Sipyagin made a downward motion of his wrist away from him.

'I forget them, sir!'

'Your Excellency, I have already submitted to you that I have not come here from them, though I may nevertheless inform your Excellency, among other things, that they are already joined in the bonds of lawful matrimony.' . . . ('There, it's all one!' thought Paklin; 'I said I'd lie a bit here, and I'm lying. Here goes!')

Sipyagin moved his head restlessly to right and left against the back of his easy-chair.

'That is a matter of no interest to me, sir. One foolish marriage the more in the world, that's all. But what is this most urgent business to which I am indebted for the pleasure of your visit?'

'Ugh! the damned director of a department!' Paklin thought again. 'That's enough of your airs and graces, you ugly English monkey-face.'

'Your wife's brother,' he said aloud – 'Mr. Markelov – has been seized by the peasants he had meant to incite to insurrection, and is now in custody in the governor's house.'

Sipyagin jumped up a second time.

'What . . . what did you say?' he stammered, not at all in his ministerial baritone, but in a sort of piteous guttural.

'I said your brother-in-law had been seized and is in chains. Directly I learned this fact, I took horses and came to warn you. I imagined that I might be rendering a service both to you and to that unfortunate man whom you may be able to save!'

'I am much obliged to you,' said Sipyagin in the same feeble voice; and with a violent blow on a bell shaped like a mushroom, he filled the whole house with its clear, metallic ring. 'I am much obliged to you,' he repeated more sharply; 'though let me tell you, a man who has trampled underfoot every law, human and divine, were he a hundred times my kinsman, is in my eyes not to be pitied; he is a criminal!'

A footman darted into the room.

'Your orders, sir?'

'The coach! This minute the coach and four! I am driving to the town. Filip and Stepan to come with me!' The footman darted out. 'Yes, sir, my brother-in-law is a criminal; and I am driving to the town, not to save him! Oh, no!'

'But, your Excellency . . .'

'Such are my principles, sir; and I beg you not to trouble me with objections!'

Sipyagin fell to walking up and down the room, while Paklin's eyes grew round as saucers. 'Ugh, you devil!' he was thinking; 'and you call yourself a liberal! Why, you're a roaring lion!' The door opened, and with quick steps there entered first Valentina Mihalovna, and behind her Kallomyetsev.

'What is the meaning of this, Boris? you have ordered the coach out? you are going to the town? what has happened?'

Sipyagin went up to his wife, and took her by her arm, between the wrist and the elbow. '*Il faut vous armer de courage, ma chère.* Your brother is arrested.'

'My brother? Sergei? What for?'

'He has been preaching Socialistic theories to the peasants!' (Kallomyetsev gave vent to a faint whistle.) 'Yes! He has been preaching revolution! he has been making propaganda! They seized him, and gave him up. Now he's – in the town.'

'The madman! But who has told you this?'

'Mr. . . . Mr. . . . what's his name? Mr. Konopatin brought this news.'

Valentina Mihalovna glanced at Paklin. He gave a forlorn bow. 'My! what an elegant female!' was his thought. Even at such painful moments . . . alas, how susceptible was poor Paklin to feminine charms!

'And you mean to go to the town – so late?'

'I shall find the governor still up.'

'I always predicted that it must end so,' put in Kallomyetsev. 'It could not be otherwise! But what splendid chaps our Russian peasants are! Delightful! *Pardon, madame, c'est votre frère! Mais la vérité avant tout!*'

'Can you really mean to go, Boris?' asked Valentina Mihalovna.

'I'm convinced too,' continued Kallomyetsev, 'that that fellow too, that *tutor*, Mr. Nezhdanov, has had a hand in it. *J'en mettrais ma main au feu.* They're all in one boat! Has he been caught? You don't know?'

Again Sipyagin made a downward gesture from his wrist.

'I don't know, and I don't want to know! By the way,' he added, turning to his wife, '*il paraît qu'ils sont mariés*.'

'Who said so? The same gentleman?' Valentina Mihalovna again looked at Paklin, but this time she screwed up her eyes as she did so.

'Yes.'

'In that case,' put in Kallomyetsev, 'he knows where they are for a certainty. Do you know where they are? Do you know where they are? Eh? eh? eh? Do you know?' Kallomyetsev began pacing up and down before Paklin, as though to bar the way to him, though the latter showed not the faintest inclination to escape. 'Speak! Answer! Eh? Eh? Do you know? Do you know?'

'If I did know,' Paklin said with annoyance – his wrath was stirred at last and his little eyes flashed – 'if I did know, I should not tell you.'

'Oh . . . oh . . . oh!' muttered Kallomyetsev. 'You hear . . . you hear! Why, this fellow, too . . . this fellow, too, must be one of their gang!'

'The coach is ready!' a footman announced. Sipyagin seized his hat with a graceful, resolute gesture; but Valentina

Mihalovna begged him with such insistence to put off going till next morning – she laid before him such cogent reasons, the darkness on the road, and every one would be asleep in the town, and he would merely be upsetting his nerves and might catch cold – that Sipyagin at last was persuaded by her, and exclaiming, 'I obey!' with a gesture as graceful, but no longer resolute, he laid his hat on the table.

'Take out the horses!' he commanded the footman; 'but to-morrow at six in the morning precisely, let them be ready! Do you hear? You can go! Stop! The visitor ... the gentleman's conveyance can be dismissed! Pay the man! Eh? I fancy you spoke, Mr. Konopatin? I'll take you with me to-morrow, Mr. Konopatin! What do you say? I don't hear. ... You will take some vodka, I daresay? Some vodka for Mr. Konopatin! No! You don't drink it? In that case, Fyodor, show the gentleman to the green room! Good-night, Mr. Kono—'

Paklin lost all patience at last.

'Paklin!' he roared, 'my name is Paklin!'

'Yes, yes; well, that's much the same. It's not unlike, you know. But what a powerful voice you have for one of your build! Good-night, Mr. Paklin. ... I've got it right now, eh? *Siméon, vous viendrez avec nous?*'

'*Je crois bien!*'

And Paklin was led off to the green room. And he was even locked in there. As he got into bed, he heard the key turn in the ringing English lock. Violently he swore at himself for his 'stroke of genius,' and he slept very badly.

Early next morning, at half-past five, he was called. Coffee was handed him; while he drank it, a footman with embroidered shoulder-knots waited with the tray in his hands, and shifted from one leg to the other, as though he would say, 'Hurry up, you're keeping the gentlemen waiting!' Then he was conducted down-stairs. The coach was already standing before the house. There, too, was Kallomyetsev's open carriage. Sipyagin made his appearance on the steps in a camel's-hair cloak with a round collar. Such cloaks had not been worn for many years except by a certain very important dignitary whom Sipyagin was trying to please and to imitate. On important official occasions, therefore, he wore such a cloak.

Sipyagin greeted Paklin fairly affably, and with an energetic gesture motioned him to the coach and asked him to take his seat. 'Mr. Paklin, you will come with me, Mr. Paklin! Put Mr. Paklin's bag on the box! I am taking Mr. Paklin!' he said, with an emphasis on the word Paklin, and an accent on the letter *a*, as though he would say, 'You've a name like that and presume to feel insulted when people change it for you! There you are, then! Take plenty of it! I'll give you as much as you want! Mr. Paklin! Paklin!' The unlucky name kept resounding in the keen morning air. It was so keen as to set Kallomyetsev, who came out after Sipyagin, muttering several times in French, 'B-r-r-r! B-r-r-r! B-r-r-r!' and wrapping himself more closely in his cloak he seated himself in his elegant open carriage. (His poor friend the Servian prince, Mihal Obrenovitch, on seeing it had bought one exactly like it at Binder's ... *vous savez Binder, le grand carrossier des Champs-Élysées?*) From the half-open shutters of a bedroom Valentina Mihalovna peeped out 'in the trailing garments of the night,' as the poet has it.

Sipyagin took his seat and kissed his hand to her.

'Are you comfortable, Mr. Paklin? Drive on!'

'*Je vous recommande mon frère; épargnez-le!*' Valentina Mihalovna was heard to say.

'*Soyez tranquille!*' cried Kallomyetsev, glancing smartly up at her from under the edge of a travelling cap that he had designed himself, with a cockade in it.... '*C'est surtout l'autre qu'il faut pincer!*'

'Drive on!' repeated Sipyagin. 'Mr. Paklin, you're not cold? Drive on!'

The two carriages rolled away.

For the first ten minutes both Sipyagin and Paklin were silent. The luckless Sila in his shabby little suit and greasy cap seemed a still more pitiful figure against the dark-blue background of the rich silky material with which the inside of the coach was upholstered. In silence he looked round at the delicate, pale-blue blinds that ran up rapidly at a mere finger's touch on a button, and at the rug of soft white sheepskin at their feet, and the box of red wood fitted in in front, with a movable tray desk for letters, and even a shelf for books. (Boris Andreitch did not much care to work in his coach, but he wished to make people believe he liked to work on his journeys like Thiers.) Paklin felt intimidated. Sipyagin glanced at him twice over his glossily shaven cheek, and with majestic deliberation pulled out of his side pocket a silver cigar-case with a curly monogram on it in old Slavonic type, and offered him . . . positively offered him a cigar, balancing it between the second and third fingers of a hand in an English glove of yellow dogskin.

'I don't smoke,' muttered Paklin.

'Ah!' responded Sipyagin, and he himself lighted the cigar, which appeared to be a most choice regalia.

'I ought to tell you . . . dear Mr. Paklin,' he began, puffing affably at his cigar, and emitting delicate rings of fragrant smoke . . . 'that I . . . am in reality . . . very grateful . . . to you. . . . I may have seemed . . . somewhat short . . . to you yesterday . . . though that is not . . . a characteristic . . . of mine at all' (Sipyagin intentionally cut his sentence up meaningly), 'I venture to assure you of that. But, Mr. Paklin, put yourself in my . . . place' (Sipyagin rolled the cigar from one corner of his mouth to the other). 'The position I occupy makes me . . . so to say . . . conspicuous; and all of a sudden . . . my wife's brother . . . compromises himself . . . and me in this incredible manner! Eh! Mr. Paklin? You perhaps think that's of no great matter?'

'I don't think that, your Excellency.'

'You don't know for what precisely . . . and where exactly, he was arrested?'

'I heard it was in T——— district.'

'From whom did you hear that?'

'From . . . from a man.'

'Well, it would hardly be from a bird. But what man?'

'From . . . from an assistant of the director of the business of the governor's office.'

'What's his name?'

'The director?'

'No, the assistant.'

'His . . . his name is Ulyashevitch. He's a very good public servant, your Excellency. When I heard of that occurrence, I hurried at once to you.'

'To be sure, to be sure! And I repeat that I am very grateful to you. But what madness! Isn't it madness? eh? Mr. Paklin? eh?'

'Perfect madness!' cried Paklin, and the perspiration zigzagged in a hot rivulet down his back. 'It comes,' he went on, 'of not in the least understanding the Russian peasant. Mr. Markelov, so far as I know him, has a very kind and generous heart; but he has never understood the Russian peasant' (Paklin glanced at Sipyagin, who, turning slightly towards him, was scanning him with a chilly but not hostile expression). 'The Russian peasant cannot ever be induced to revolt except by taking advantage of his devotion to a higher authority, some sort of Tsar. Some sort of legend must be invented – you remember the false Demetrius – some sort of regal insignia, branded in burnt patches on the breast.'

'Yes, yes, like Pugatchev,' interrupted Sipyagin in a tone that seemed to say, 'I've not forgotten my history . . . you needn't enlarge!' and adding, 'It's madness! madness!' he turned to the contemplation of the swift coil of smoke rising from the end of his cigar.

'Your Excellency!' observed Paklin, gathering courage, 'I told you just now I didn't smoke . . . but that's not quite accurate. I do smoke at times; and your cigar smells so delicious. . . .'

'Eh? what? what's that?' said Sipyagin, as though waking up; and without letting Paklin repeat what he had said, he proved in the most unmistakable manner that he had heard him, and had uttered his reiterated questions solely for the sake of his dignity, by offering him his open cigar-case.

Paklin discreetly and gratefully lighted a cigar.

'Now, I fancy, is a good moment,' he thought; but Sipyagin anticipated him.

'You spoke to me, too, do you remember?' he said carelessly, interrupting himself to look at his cigar, and to jog his hat forwards on to his forehead, 'you spoke . . . eh? you spoke of . . . that friend of yours who has married my . . . relation. Do you see them? They are settled not far from here?'

'Aha!' thought Paklin, 'Sila, look out!'

'I have seen them only once, your Excellency! they are living, as a fact . . . at no great distance from here.'

'You understand, of course,' Sipyagin went on in the same manner, 'that I have no further serious interest, as I explained to you, either in that frivolous girl or in your friend. Good heavens! I've no prejudices, but you will agree with me, this is beyond everything. It's folly, you know. Though I imagine they have been more drawn together by political sympathies' ('Politics!' he repeated with a shrug of his shoulders) 'than by any other feeling.'

'Indeed I imagine so, your Excellency!'

'Yes, Mr. Nezhdanov was a red-hot republican. I must do him the justice to admit that he made no secret of his opinions.'

'Nezhdanov,' Paklin hazarded, 'has been led away, perhaps, but his heart—'

'Is good,' put in Sipyagin: 'to be sure . . . to be sure, like Markelov's. They all have good hearts. Probably he too has taken part – and will be too . . . We shall have to protect him too.'

Paklin clasped his hands before his breast.

'Ah, yes, yes, your Excellency! Extend your protection to him! Indeed . . . he deserves . . . deserves your sympathy.'

'H'm,' said Sipyagin; 'you think so?'

'If not for his own sake, at least . . . for your niece's; for his wife's!' ('O Lord! O Lord!' Paklin was thinking, 'what lies I'm telling!')

Sipyagin puckered up his eyes.

'You are, I see, a very devoted friend. That's excellent; that's very praiseworthy, young man. And so, you say, they're living near here?'

'Yes, your Excellency; at a large establishment . . .' Paklin bit his tongue.

'Tut . . . tut-tut . . . at Solomin's! so they're there! I was aware of that – indeed, I'd been told so, I'd been informed. . . . Yes.' (Mr. Sipyagin was not in the least aware of it, and no one had told him so; but recollecting Solomin's visit, and their midnight interview, he dropped this bait . . . And Paklin rose to it at once.)

'Since you know that,' he began, and a second time he bit his tongue. . . . But it was too late. . . . From the mere glance flung at him by Sipyagin he realised that he had been playing with him all the while, as a cat plays with a mouse.

'I must tell your Excellency, though,' the luckless wretch faltered, 'that I really know nothing. . . .'

'And I ask you no questions, upon my word! What do you mean? What do you take me, and yourself, for?' said Sipyagin haughtily, and he promptly withdrew into his ministerial heights.

And again Paklin felt himself a wretched little, entrapped creature. . . . Till that instant he kept his cigar in the corner of his mouth, remote from Sipyagin, and had stealthily puffed the smoke on one side; now he took it out of his mouth altogether, and ceased smoking.

'Good Lord!' he groaned inwardly – and the sweat trickled over his shoulders more plentifully than before. 'What have I done! I have betrayed everything and every one! . . . I've been fooled, bought with a good cigar! . . . I'm an informer . . . and what can be done to undo the harm now? Lord!'

There was nothing to be done. Sipyagin began to doze with the same dignified, solemn ministerial air, wrapped up in his camel's-hair cloak. . . . And before another quarter of an hour had passed, both the carriages stopped in front of the governor's house.

XXXV

THE GOVERNOR OF the town of S———— was one of those good-natured, careless, worldly generals, those generals endowed with an exquisitely well-washed white body, and an almost equally pure soul, those well-born, well-bred generals, kneaded, so to speak, of the most finely sifted flour, who, though they never lay themselves out to be 'shepherds of the people,' do nevertheless give proof of very tolerable administrative abilities; and doing very little work, for ever sighing for Petersburg and dangling after pretty provincial ladies, are of the most unmistakable service to their province and leave pleasant memories behind them. He had only just got out of bed, and, sitting in a silk dressing-gown and a loose night-shirt before his looking-glass, he was dabbing his face and neck with eau-de-cologne, after taking off a perfect collection of little amulets and relics as a preliminary, – when he was informed of the arrival of Sipyagin and Kallomyetsev on important and urgent business. With Sipyagin he was very intimate, called him by his Christian name, had known him from his youth up, was continually meeting him in Petersburg drawing-rooms, and of late he had begun, every time his name occurred to him, to ejaculate mentally a respectful 'Ah!' as on hearing the name of a future statesman. Kallomyetsev he knew rather less and respected much less, seeing that for some time past 'unpleasant' complaints had begun to be made against him; he regarded him, however, as a man – *qui fera chemin* – one way or another.

He gave orders that the visitors should be asked into his

study, and promptly came into it in the same silk dressing-gown, and without even an apology for receiving them in such an unofficial attire; and he shook hands cordially with them. Only Sipyagin and Kallomyetsev had, however, been conducted to the governor's study; Paklin had been left in the drawing-room. As he crawled out of the coach, he had tried to sneak off, muttering that he had business at home; but Sipyagin with courteous firmness had detained him (Kallomyetsev had skipped up and whispered in Sipyagin's ear: *'Ne le lâchez pas! Tonnerre de tonnerre!'*) and taken him in along with him. To the study, however, he had not led him, but had requested him, still with the same courteous firmness, to wait in the drawing-room till he should be sent for. Paklin even here hoped to slink off . . . but, at a hint from Kallomyetsev, a stalwart gendarme showed himself at the door. . . . Paklin remained.

'You guess, no doubt, what has brought me to you, *Voldemar*?' began Sipyagin.

'No, dear boy, I can't guess,' answered the amiable epicurean, while a smile of welcome curved his rosy cheeks and showed a glimpse of his shining teeth, half hidden by silky moustaches. . . .

'What? . . . Don't you know about Markelov?'

'What do you mean? – Markelov?' the governor repeated with the same expression. He had, to begin with, no clear recollection that the man arrested the day before was called Markelov; and he had besides utterly forgotten that Sipyagin's wife had a brother of that surname. 'But why are you standing, Boris? sit down; won't you have some tea?'

But Sipyagin was in no mood for tea.

When he explained at last what was the matter and for what reason he and Kallomyetsev had made their appearance, the governor uttered a pained exclamation, and slapped himself on the forehead, while his face assumed an expression of grief.

'Yes . . . yes . . . yes!' he repeated; 'what a misfortune! And he's here now – to-day – for a while; you know we never keep *that sort* with us longer than one night; but the commander of police is out of the town, so your brother-in-law's been detained. . . . But to-morrow they will forward him. Dear me! how very unfortunate! How distressed your wife must be! What is it you wish?'

'I should have liked to have an interview with him, here – if it's not contrary to law.'

'My dear fellow! laws are not made for men like you. I *do* feel for you! . . . *C'est affreux, tu sais!*'

He gave a peculiar ring. An adjutant appeared.

'My dear baron, if you please – some arrangements here.' He told him what he wanted. The baron vanished. 'Only fancy, *mon cher ami*, you know they all but murdered him. They tied his hands behind him, clapped him in a cart, and off they went with him! And he – fancy! isn't in the least angry with them – not a bit indignant – dear, dear! He's so composed altogether. . . . I was astonished! but there, you will see for yourself. *C'est un fanatique tranquille.*'

'*Ce sont les pires*,' Kallomyetsev pronounced sententiously.

The governor gave him a dubious look.

'By the way, I must have a word with you, Semyon Petrovitch.'

'Why, what is it?'

'Oh, something's amiss.'

'And what?'

'Well, I must tell you; your debtor, that peasant who came to me with a complaint—'

'Well?'

'He's hanged himself, you know.'

'When?'

'It's of no consequence when: but it's a bad business.'

Kallomyetsev shrugged his shoulders, and with a dandified swing of his elegant person moved away to the window. At that instant the adjutant brought in Markelov.

The governor had spoken truly about him; he was unnaturally

calm. Even his habitual moroseness had vanished from his face and was replaced by an expression of a sort of indifferent weariness. It did not change when he saw his brother-in-law, and only in the glance he flung at the German adjutant escorting him there was a momentary flash of his old hatred for that class of persons. His coat had been torn in two places and hurriedly sewn up with coarse thread; on his forehead, over one eyebrow, and on the bridge of his nose could be seen small scars covered with clotted blood. He had not washed, but had combed his hair. Stuffing both hands up to the wrists into his sleeves, he stood not far from the door. His breathing was quite even.

'Sergei Mihalovitch!' Sipyagin began in an agitated voice, going two steps towards him, and stretching out his right hand so that it might touch him or stop him if he were to make a forward movement. 'Sergei Mihalovitch! I am not here to express to you our amazement, our deep distress – that you cannot doubt! You have yourself *willed* your own ruin! And you have ruined yourself! But I desired to see you so as to say to you . . . er . . . er . . . to render . . . to give you the chance of hearing the voice of common sense, honour, and friendship! You may still mitigate your lot; and, believe me, I will, for my part, do all that lies in my power, and the honoured head of this province will support me in this.' Here Sipyagin raised his voice: 'Unfeigned penitence for your errors, and a full confession without reserve, which shall be duly represented in the proper quarters . . .'

'Your Excellency,' Markelov began all at once, addressing the governor, and the very sound of his voice was quiet, though a little hoarse, 'I imagined it was your pleasure to see me to make a further examination of me or something. . . . But if you have summoned me only at the desire of Mr. Sipyagin, give orders, please, for me to be taken back; we can't understand one another. All he says . . . is so much Greek to me.'

'Greek . . . indeed!' Kallomyetsev intervened in a haughty treble; 'but it's not Greek to you to set peasants rioting! That's not Greek, is it? Eh?'

'What have you here, your Excellency? some sub in the secret police, eh? So zealous in his work?' queried Markelov, and a faint smile of pleasure quivered on his pale lips.

Kallomyetsev, with a hiss of anger, was stamping . . . But the governor stopped him.

'It's your own fault, Semyon Petrovitch. Why do you interfere in what's not your business?'

'Not my business! . . . I should say it's the public business . . . of all us noblemen! . . .'

Markelov scanned Kallomyetsev with a cold, prolonged gaze, as though it were for the last time, and turned a little towards Sipyagin. 'And since you, brother-in-law, want me to explain my views to you, here you are. I recognise that the peasants had the right to arrest me and give me up if they didn't like what I said to them. They were free to do that. *I* had come to them; not they to me. And the government, if it sends me to Siberia . . . I'm not going to grumble – though I don't regard myself as guilty. It's doing its own work, for it's guarding itself. Is that enough for you?'

Sipyagin flung up his hands.

'Enough! What a thing to say! That's not the question, and it's not for us to criticise the action of the government; what I want to know is, do you feel . . . do you, dear Sergei, feel' – (Sipyagin resolved to try an appeal to the feelings) – 'the senselessness, the madness of your attempt? are you prepared to prove your *repentance* in act? and can I answer, to a certain extent answer, for you, Sergei?'

Markelov knitted his bushy brows.

'I have said my say . . . and I don't want to repeat it.'

'But repentance! What of your repentance?'

Suddenly Markelov grew restive.

'Ah, let me alone with your "repentance"! Do you want to crawl inside my soul? Leave that at least to me.'

Sipyagin shrugged his shoulders.

'There, you are always like that; you will never listen to the voice of reason! You have still a possibility of extricating yourself without scandal or dishonour.'

'Without scandal or dishonour . . .' Markelov repeated grimly. 'We know those phrases! They are always used to suggest a man's doing something scoundrelly. That's what they mean!'

'We sympathise with you,' Sipyagin continued to exhort Markelov, 'and you hate us.'

'A nice sort of sympathy! You pack us off to Siberia to hard labour; that's how you show your sympathy for us! Ah, let me alone . . . let me alone, for mercy's sake!'

And Markelov's head sank on his breast. There was great confusion in his soul, quiet as he was outwardly. More than all he was fretted and tortured by the thought that he had been betrayed by none other than Eremey of Goloplyok! Eremey in whom he had believed so blindly! That Mendely, the Sulker, had not followed him had not really surprised him. . . . Mendely had been drunk and was frightened. But Eremey! To Markelov, Eremey was a sort of personification of the Russian peasantry. . . . And he had deceived him. Then, was all Markelov had been toiling for, was it all wrong, a mistake? And was Kislyakov a liar, and were Vassily Nikolaevitch's orders folly, and were all the articles and books, works of socialists and thinkers, every letter of which had seemed to him something beyond doubt, beyond attack – was all that too rubbish? Could it be? And that splendid simile of the swollen abscess, ready for the stroke of the lancet, was that too a mere phrase? 'No! no!' he murmured to himself, and over his bronzed cheeks flitted a faint tinge of brickdust colour; 'no; it's all true; all . . . it is *I* am to blame, I didn't understand, I didn't say the right thing, I didn't go the right way to work! I ought simply to have given orders, and if any one had tried to hinder or resist, put a bullet through his head! what's the use of explanations here? Any one not with us has no right to live . . . spies are killed like dogs, worse than dogs!'

And all the details of his capture passed before Markelov's mind. . . . First the silence, the leers, the shouts at the back of the crowd. Then one fellow comes up sideways as if to salute him. Then that sudden rush! And how they had flung him down! . . . 'Lads . . . lads! . . . what are you about?' And they, 'Give us a belt here! Tie him!' . . . The shaking of his bones . . . and helpless wrath . . . and the stinking dust in his mouth, in his nostrils. . . . 'Toss him . . . toss him into the cart.' Some one guffawing thickly . . . ugh!

'I didn't go the right way – the right way to work!' That was just what fretted and tormented him; that he himself had fallen under the wheel was his personal misfortune: it had no bearing on the cause in general; that he could bear . . . but Eremey! Eremey!

While Markelov stood, his head sunk on his breast, Sipyagin drew the governor aside and began talking to him in undertones, with slight gesticulations and a shake of two fingers on his forehead, as though he would suggest that the poor fellow was not quite right in that region, and would try altogether to arouse, if not sympathy, at least indulgence for the crazy creature. And the governor shrugged his shoulders, turned up and then half-closed his eyes, regretted his own helplessness in the matter, but gave some vague promises. . . . *'Tous les égards . . . certainement, tous les égards,'* . . . the delicately lisped words were heard softly uttered through his scented moustaches. . . . 'But you know, dear boy, the law!' 'Of course – the law!' Sipyagin assented with a sort of stoical submissiveness.

While they were conversing in this way in the corner, Kallomyetsev simply could not stand still; he moved up and down, cleared his throat, hummed and hawed, exhibiting every sign of impatience. At last he went up to Sipyagin, and hurriedly remarked: *'Vous oubliez l'autre!'*

'Ah, yes!' said Sipyagin aloud. *'Merci de me l'avoir rappelé.* I must lay the following fact before your Excellency,' he said, turning to the governor. . . . (He used this formal address to his dear Voldemar intentionally, not to compromise the prestige of authority before a revolutionist.) 'I have good grounds for supposing that my *beau-frère*'s mad attempt has certain ramifications; and that one of those branches, that is, one of the suspected persons, is at no great distance from this town. Send,' he added, in an undertone, 'for the man . . . there, in your drawing-room. . . . I brought him with me.'

The governor glanced at Sipyagin, thought with reverence, 'What a fellow!' and gave the necessary order. A minute later, the 'servant of God,' Sila Paklin, stood before him.

Sila Paklin was beginning to make a low bow to the governor; but catching sight of Markelov he did not complete his salutation – he remained as he was, bent in half, twisting his cap about in his hands. Markelov cast a heedless glance in his direction, but can hardly have recognised him; for he sank again into thought.

'Is this – the branch?' queried the governor, pointing at Paklin with a large white finger adorned with a turquoise.

'Oh, no!' responded Sipyagin with a half-smile. 'However,' he added, after a moment's thought, 'here, your Excellency,' he began again aloud, 'before you is one Mr. Paklin. He is, to the best of my belief, a resident in Petersburg, and an intimate friend of a certain person who filled the position of tutor in my family, and left my house, taking with him – I blush to add – a young girl, a relative of my own.'

'*Ah! oui, oui*,' muttered the governor, and he flung up his head; 'I had heard something . . . the Countess was telling me . . .'

Sipyagin raised his voice.

'That person is a certain Mr. Nezhdanov, strongly suspected by me of perverted ideas and theories . . .'

'*Un rouge à tous crins*,' put in Kallomyetsev.

'Of perverted ideas and theories,' repeated Sipyagin still more distinctly, 'and is certainly not without a share in all this propaganda; he is . . . in hiding, as I have been informed by Mr. Paklin, in the factory of the merchant Faleyev . . .'

At the words 'I have been informed,' Markelov glanced a second time at Paklin, but only smiled, slowly and indifferently.

'Excuse me, excuse me, your Excellency,' cried Paklin, 'and you, Mr. Sipyagin; I never . . . never. . . .'

'You say the merchant Faleyev?' said the governor, addressing Sipyagin, and merely twirling his fingers in Paklin's direction, as much as to say, 'Silence there, my good man.' 'What's coming to them, our respectable bearded shopkeepers? Yesterday they caught another one about the same business. You may have heard his name – Golushkin, a rich man. But there, he'll never make a revolution. He's grovelling on his knees now.'

'The merchant Faleyev does not come into the affair,' Sipyagin struck off; 'I know nothing of his views; I am speaking only of his factory, in which, according to Mr. Paklin's story, Mr. Nezhdanov may be found at this moment.'

'I didn't say so!' Paklin wailed again. 'It was *you* said so!'

'Excuse me, Mr. Paklin,' Sipyagin went on, uttering every word with the same relentless distinctness. 'I respect the sentiment of friendship which inspires your denial.' ('Why – he's a regular Guizot!' the governor was thinking to himself.) 'But I will venture to put myself before you as an example. Do you suppose the sentiment of kinship is less strong in me than your feeling of friendship? But there is another feeling, sir, which is stronger still, and which ought to be our guide in all our deeds and actions – the feeling of duty!'

'*Le sentiment du devoir*,' Kallomyetsev explained.

Markelov scanned both the speakers.

'Mr. Governor,' he observed, 'I repeat my request: order me, if you please, to be removed from these chatterers.'

But here the governor lost patience a little.

'Mr. Markelov!' he exclaimed, 'I should advise you, in your position, to show more restraint in your language, and more respect for your superiors . . . especially when they are expressing patriotic sentiments such as you have just heard from the lips of your *beau-frère*. I shall be very happy, my dear Boris,' added the governor, turning to Sipyagin, 'to bring your noble action before the notice of the minister. But where precisely is this Mr. Nezhdanov to be found – in this factory?'

Sipyagin knit his brows.

'He is with a certain Mr. Solomin, the overseer of the machinery there – so this Mr. Paklin has informed me.'

It seemed to afford Sipyagin a peculiar satisfaction to torment poor Sila; he was making him pay now for the cigar he had given him in the carriage, and the familiarity of his behaviour, and even some little flattery wasted on him.

'And this Solomin,' put in Kallomyetsev, 'is an unmistakable radical and republican, and it would be quite as well for your Excellency to turn your attention to him too.'

'Do you know these people . . . Solomin . . . and what's his name – Nezhdanov?' the governor questioned Markelov in a rather authoritative nasal.

Markelov's nostrils dilated vindictively.

'And do you, your Excellency, know Confucius and Livy?'

The governor turned away.

'*Il n'y a pas moyen de causer avec cet homme*,' he observed, shrugging his shoulders. 'Baron, here, please!'

The adjutant darted up to him; and Paklin, seizing the opportunity, limped hobbling up to Sipyagin.

'What are you doing?' he whispered; 'do you want to ruin your own niece? Why, she's with him, with Nezhdanov! . . .'

'I am ruining no one, sir,' Sipyagin responded aloud; 'I am obeying the dictates of my conscience, and—'

'And your wife, my sister, who keeps you under her thumb?' Markelov put in quite as loudly.

Sipyagin, at the phrase, did not turn a hair. . . . It was too much beneath him!

'Listen,' Paklin continued, whispering – his whole body was shaking with excitement and possibly with fear – and his eyes glittered with hate and the tears made a lump in his throat; tears of pity for *the others*, and anger with himself; 'listen, I told you she was married – that's not true – I told you a lie! – but this marriage must take place now – and if you prevent this, if the police make a raid on them, there will be a stain on your conscience which nothing can wipe off, and you—'

'The fact you have communicated,' Sipyagin interrupted still louder, 'if only it is true, which I have good reason to doubt, can only hasten the measure I should think it necessary to take; and as to the purity of my conscience, sir, I will ask you not to concern yourself about it.'

'It's polished, brother,' Markelov put in again; 'there's a coat of Petersburg varnish laid on it; nothing will touch it! Ah, Mr. Paklin, you may whisper as you will, you'll never whisper your way out of this business, no fear!'

The governor thought it needful to cut short these recriminations.

'I presume,' he began, 'that you have said all you need to, gentlemen; and so, my dear baron, you may remove Mr. Markelov. *N'est-ce pas*, Boris, you have no further need . . . ?'

Sipyagin made a deprecating gesture.

'I have said all I could!'

'Very well. . . . My dear baron . . .'

The adjutant approached Markelov, clinked his spurs, made a horizontal motion with his arm. . . . 'If you please!' Markelov turned and went out. Paklin – only in imagination, it must be owned, but with bitter sympathy and pity – shook his hand.

'And we'll send our fellows to the factory,' pursued the governor. 'Only there's one thing, Boris; I fancy – this gentleman' – (he indicated Paklin with a turn of his chin) – 'gave you some information about your young relation. . . . Possibly she is there, in the factory. . . . If so . . .'

'She could not be arrested in any case,' observed Sipyagin profoundly; 'possibly she will come to her senses and return. If you will permit it, I will write her a little note.'

'I shall be obliged if you will. And, of course, you may rest assured. . . . *Nous coffrerons le quidam . . . mais nous sommes galants avec les dames . . . et avec celle-là donc!*'

'But you are taking no measures with regard to that Solomin!' Kallomyetsev exclaimed, plaintively. He had been all the while on the alert trying to catch the governor's remarks a little aside to Sipyagin. 'I assure you, he's the ringleader! I've an instinct in these things . . . a perfect instinct!'

'*Pas trop de zèle*, dear Semyon Petrovitch,' observed the governor with a smirk. 'Remember Talleyrand! If there's anything amiss, he won't escape us either. You'd much better devote your thoughts to your . . .' The governor made a gesture suggesting a noose round the neck. . . . 'And by the way,' he turned again to Sipyagin – '*et ce gaillard-là*' (he again indicated Paklin by a turn of his chin), '*qu'en ferons-nous?* He doesn't look formidable.'

'Let him go,' said Sipyagin softly, and he added in German: '*Lass den Lumpen laufen!*'

He imagined, for some unknown reason, that he was making a quotation from Goethe, from *Götz von Berlichingen*.

'You can go, sir!' observed the governor aloud. 'We have no further need of you! Good-bye, till we meet again.'

Paklin made a general bow and went out into the street, utterly crushed and humiliated. Good God! this contempt annihilated him!

'What am I?' he thought in unutterable despair; 'both coward and informer? Oh, no . . . no; I'm an honest man, gentlemen, and I'm not quite devoid of all manliness!'

But what was this familiar figure standing on the steps of the governor's house, gazing at him with dejected eyes, full of reproach? Why, it was Markelov's old servant. He had, seemingly, come to the town after his master, and would not move away from his prison. . . . But why did he look like that at Paklin? It was not he who had betrayed Markelov!

'And what induced me to go poking my nose where I was

no manner of use?' he thought again in desperation. 'Why couldn't I have kept quiet and minded my own business? And now they'll talk, and most likely write: "A certain Mr. Paklin has told of everything, he has betrayed them . . . his friends, betrayed them to the enemy!"' He recalled at this point the glance Markelov had flung at him, he recalled his last words: 'You'll never whisper your way out, no fear!' – and then those aged, dejected, despairing eyes! And as it is written in the scriptures, 'he wept bitterly,' and made his way to the oasis, to Fomushka and Fimushka, to Snanduliya. . . .

XXXVI

WHEN MARIANNA, THE same morning, came out of her room, she saw Nezhdanov dressed and sitting on the sofa. In one hand he held his head, the other lay weak and motionless on his knees. She went up to him.

'Good morning, Alexey. . . . You've not undressed? you've not slept? How pale you are!'

His heavy eyelids rose slowly.

'No, I didn't undress, I've not been asleep.'

'Are you ill, or is it the result of yesterday?'

Nezhdanov shook his head.

'I couldn't sleep after Solomin went into your room.'

'When?'

'Yesterday evening.'

'Alexey, are you jealous? Well, that's something new! And what a time you've chosen to be jealous! He only stayed with me a quarter of an hour. . . . And we were talking about his cousin, the priest, and how to arrange our marriage.'

'I know he only stayed a quarter of an hour; I saw when he came out. And I'm not jealous, oh, no! But still, I couldn't get to sleep, after that.'

'Why?'

Nezhdanov did not speak.

'I kept thinking . . . thinking . . . thinking!'

'What about?'

'You . . . and him . . . and myself.'

'And what conclusion did you come to?'

'Must I tell you, Marianna?'

'Yes, tell me.'

'I thought that I'm in your way . . . and his . . . and my own.'

'Mine? his? I can fancy what you mean by that, though you do declare you're not jealous. But your own?'

'Marianna, there are two men in me, and one won't let the other live. So that I suppose in fact it would be better for both to cease to live.'

'Come, hush, Alexey, please! What makes you want to torture yourself and me? We ought to be considering now what steps we must take. . . . They won't leave us in peace, you know.'

Nezhdanov took her hand affectionately.

'Sit beside me, Marianna, and let us talk a little, like friends. While there is still time. Give me your hand. I think it would be as well for us to explain ourselves, though, they do say, explanations of all sorts only lead to greater confusion. But you are kind and wise; you will understand it all, and what I don't say out, you will think for yourself. Sit down.'

Nezhdanov's voice was very soft, and a peculiar affectionate tenderness was apparent in his eyes, which were fixed intently on Marianna.

She sat down readily at once beside him and took his hand.

'Thank you, dear one. Now listen. I won't keep you long. I've gone over all I want to say, in my head, during the night. Well, don't think that what happened yesterday has upset me unduly; I was certainly very ridiculous and even a little disgusting; but you thought nothing base or low of me, I know . . . you know me. I said that what happened hasn't upset me; that's not true, it's nonsense . . . it has upset me, not because

I was brought home drunk, but because it has been the final proof to me of my failure! And not only because I can't drink as Russians drink, but in everything! everything! Marianna, I'm bound to tell you that I have no faith now in the cause which brought us together; for which we left that house together; to tell the truth, I had grown lukewarm when your enthusiasm warmed me and set me on fire again. I don't believe in it! I don't believe in it!'

He laid the hand that was free over his eyes and was silent for an instant. Marianna too uttered not a word and looked down. . . . She felt that he had told her nothing new.

'I used to think,' Nezhdanov went on, taking his hand away from his eyes, but not looking again at Marianna, 'that I did believe in the cause itself, and only doubted of myself, my own power, my own fitness; my abilities, I thought, do not correspond with my convictions. . . . But it seems these two things can't be separated, and what's the object of deceiving oneself? No, I don't believe in the *cause itself*. And you do believe in it, Marianna?'

Marianna sat up and raised her head.

'Yes, Alexey, I do believe in it. I believe in it with all the strength of my soul, and I will devote all my life to this cause! To my last breath!'

Nezhdanov turned towards her and scanned her from head to foot in a touched and envious glance.

'Yes, yes; I expected that answer. So you see that there is nothing for us to do in common; you have severed our tie yourself at one blow.'

Marianna did not speak.

'Now Solomin,' began Nezhdanov again, 'though he does not believe . . .'

'What?'

'No! He does not believe . . . but he does not need to; he moves calmly forward. A man going along a road to a town doesn't ask himself whether the town has a real existence.

He goes on and on. That's like Solomin. And nothing more's needed. But I . . . can't go forward; I don't want to go back; standing still I'm sick of. Whom could I presume to ask to be my companion? You know the proverb, "One at each end of the pole and the burden is borne easily"; but if one cannot hold up his end, what becomes of the other?'

'Alexey,' Marianna ventured uncertainly, 'I think you are exaggerating. We love one another, don't we?'

Nezhdanov gave a heavy sigh.

'Marianna . . . I revere you . . . and you pity me, and each of us trusts implicitly in the other's honesty; that's the real truth! But there's no love between us.'

'Stop, Alexey, what are you saying? Why, this very day, directly, there will be a search for us. . . . We must set off together, you know, and not part. . . .'

'Yes; and go to the priest Zosim to get him to marry us, as Solomin proposes. I know very well that in your eyes this marriage is nothing but a passport; a means of avoiding annoyance from the police . . . but, nevertheless, it does in a way pledge us . . . to life in common, side by side . . . or if it does not *pledge* us, at least it presupposes a desire to live together.'

'What do you mean, Alexey? Are you going to stay here?'

'Yes,' all but broke from Nezhdanov's lips, but he recollected himself and said:

'N . . . n . . . no.'

'Then you are going away from here, but not where I go?'

Nezhdanov warmly pressed the hand which still lay in his.

'To leave you without a protector, without a champion, would be a crime, and I won't do that, mean as I may be. You shall have a champion. . . . Do not doubt it!'

Marianna bent down towards Nezhdanov, and, putting her face close to his, tried anxiously to look into his eyes, into his soul – into his very soul.

'What is the matter with you, Alexey? What is in your heart? Tell me! You frighten me. Your words are so enigmatical, so strange. . . . And your face! I have never seen you with such a face!'

Nezhdanov gently turned her away, and gently kissed her hand. This time she did not resist, and did not laugh, and still looked at him with anxiety and alarm.

'Don't alarm yourself, please! There's nothing strange in it. The whole trouble is this: Markelov, they say, was beaten by the peasants; he felt their fists, they bruised his ribs. . . . I've not been beaten by the peasants – they even drank with me, drank my health . . . but they have bruised my soul worse than Markelov's ribs. I was born all out of joint. . . . I tried to set myself right, but only put myself more out of joint than ever. That's just what you see in my face.'

'Alexey,' said Marianna slowly, 'it would be very wrong of you not to be open with me.' He clasped her hands.

'Marianna, my whole being is before you, as it were in your hand; and whatever I do, I tell you beforehand, you will be surprised at nothing, nothing in reality!'

Marianna wanted to ask for an explanation of those words, but she did not ask for it . . . besides, at that instant Solomin came into the room.

His movements were sharper and more rapid than usual. His eyes were screwed up, his wide lips were drawn tight, his whole face looked as it were sharper, and wore a dry, hard, almost surly expression.

'My friends,' he began, 'I've come to tell you that delay's out of the question. Get ready. . . . It's time for you to go. You must be ready within an hour. You must go to your wedding. There's no news whatever from Paklin; his horses were first kept at Arzhano and then sent back. . . . He remained there. Probably they took him to the town. He wouldn't tell tales, of course, but there's no knowing, he might let something out, perhaps. Besides, they might find out from the horses. My cousin has been told to expect you. Pavel will go with you. He will be the witness.'

'And you, Solomin . . . Vassily?' asked Nezhdanov. 'Aren't you coming? I see you're dressed for a journey,' he added, glancing at the high boots Solomin was wearing.

'Oh, I put them on . . . it's muddy out of doors.'

'But aren't you going to answer for us, Vassily?'

'I don't suppose . . . any way, that's my affair. So in an hour's time. Marianna, Tatyana wants to see you. She has been preparing something out there.'

'Oh, yes! And I was meaning to go to her. . . .'

Marianna was moving to the door. . . .

Something strange, something akin to terror, misery, came out on Nezhdanov's face. . . .

'Marianna, are you going away, dear?' he said suddenly in a failing voice.

She stopped.

'I'll be back in half an hour. It won't take me long to pack.'

'Yes; but come to me. . . .'

'Certainly, what for?'

'I wanted to have one more look at you.' He took a long, slow look at her. 'Good-bye, good-bye, Marianna!'

She was bewildered.

'Why . . . what on earth am I talking about? I'm talking rubbish. Why, you'll be back in half an hour, won't you? Eh?'

'Of course.'

'To be sure. . . . Forgive me. My head's reeling from want of sleep. I too will . . . pack up directly.'

Marianna went out of the room. Solomin was about to follow her.

Nezhdanov stopped him.

'Vassily!'

'Well?'

'Give me your hand. I have to thank you, dear friend, for your hospitality.'

Solomin laughed.

'What an idea!' However, he gave him his hand.

'And something more,' Nezhdanov went on: 'if anything happens to me, may I rely on you, Vassily, not to leave Marianna?'

'Your wife that is to be?'

'Yes, Marianna!'

'To begin with, I'm sure nothing will happen to you; but you can set your mind at rest: Marianna is as precious to me as she is to you.'

'Oh! I know that . . . I know that! That's right, then. Thanks. In an hour, then?'

'Yes.'

'I will be ready. Good-bye!'

Solomin went out and overtook Marianna on the stairs. He had it in his mind to say something to her about Nezhdanov, but he was silent. And Marianna on her side was aware that Solomin had it in his mind to speak to her, and about Nezhdanov too, and that he was silent. And she was silent too.

XXXVII

DIRECTLY SOLOMIN WENT OUT, Nezhdanov jumped up from the sofa, walked twice from one corner to the other, then stood still for a minute in a sort of petrified stupefaction in the middle of the room; suddenly he shook himself, hurriedly flung off his 'masquerading' get-up, kicked it into a corner, took out and put on his own former attire. Then he went up to the three-legged table, took out of the drawer two sealed envelopes and another small article, which he thrust into his pocket; the envelopes he left on the table. Then he crouched down before the stove, and opened the little door. . . . In the stove lay a whole heap of ashes. This was all that was left of Nezhdanov's manuscripts, of his book of verse. . . . He had burned it all during the night. But there in the stove, on one side, sticking close against one wall, was Marianna's portrait, given him by Markelov.

It seemed he had not had the heart to burn the portrait too! Nezhdanov took it carefully out and laid it on the table beside the sealed envelopes. Then with a resolute gesture he clutched his cap and was making for the door . . . but he stopped short, turned back, and went into Marianna's room. There he stood a minute, looked round him, and, approaching her little narrow bed, bent down, and with one stifled sob pressed his lips, not to the pillow, but to the foot of the bed. . . . Then he got up at once, and, pulling his cap over his eyes, rushed out.

Meeting no one, either in the corridor, on the stairs, or below, Nezhdanov slipped out into the little enclosure. It was a grey day with a low-hanging sky, and a damp breeze that stirred the tops of the grasses and set the leaves on the trees shaking; the factory made less rattle and roar than at the same time on other days; from its yard came a smell of coal, tar, and tallow. Nezhdanov took a sharp, searching look round, and went straight up to the old apple-tree which had attracted his attention on the very day of his arrival, when he had first looked out of the window of his little room. The stem of this apple-tree was overgrown with dry moss; its rugged, bare branches, with reddish-green leaves hanging here and there upon them, rose crooked into the air, like old bent arms raised in supplication. Nezhdanov stood with firm tread on the dark earth about its roots, and took out of his pocket the small object that he had found in the table drawer. Then he looked attentively at the windows of the little lodge. . . . 'If any one catches sight of me this minute,' he thought, 'then, perhaps, I will put it off.' . . . But nowhere was there a sign of one human face . . . everything seemed dead, everything had turned away from him, gone for ever, left him to the mercy of fate. Only the factory thickly roared and hummed, and overhead fine keen drops of chilly rain began falling.

Then Nezhdanov, glancing through the crooked branches of the tree under which he was standing, at the low, grey, callously blind, damp sky, yawned, shrugged, thought, 'There's nothing else left – I'm not going back to Petersburg, to prison,' flung away his cap, and feeling already all over a sort of mawkish, heavy, overpowering languor, he put the revolver to his breast, pulled the trigger. . . .

Something seemed to strike him at once, not very violently even . . . but he was lying on his back, trying to understand what had happened to him, and how he had just seen Tatyana. . . . He even tried to call her, to say, 'Ah, I don't want . . .' but now he was numb all over, and there was a whirl of muddy green turning round and round over his face, in his eyes, on his head, in the marrow of his bones – and a sort of terrible flat weight seemed crushing him for ever to the earth.

Nezhdanov had really caught a glimpse of Tatyana at the very minute when he pulled the trigger of the revolver. She had gone up to one of the windows, and had caught sight of him under the apple-tree. She had hardly time to think, 'Whatever is he doing in this rain under the apple-tree without a hat on?' when he rolled over on his back like a sheaf of corn. She did not hear the shot – the report was very faint – but she at once saw something was wrong, and rushed in hot haste down into the garden. . . . She ran up to Nezhdanov. 'Alexey Dmitritch, what's the matter?' But already darkness had overtaken him. Tatyana bent over him, saw blood.

'Pavel!' she cried in a voice not her own – 'Pavel!'

In a few instants, Marianna, Solomin, Pavel, and two of the factory hands were in the enclosure. They lifted Nezhdanov up at once, carried him into the lodge, and laid him on the very sofa on which he had spent his last night.

He lay on his back with half-closed, fixed eyes, and face fast turning grey. He gave slow, heavy gasps, sometimes with a sob, as though he were choking. Life had not yet left him. Marianna and Solomin were standing one on each side of the sofa, both almost as pale as Nezhdanov himself. Shaken, agitated, stunned, they were both – especially Marianna – but not astounded. 'How was it we did not foresee this?' they were

thinking, and at the same time it seemed to them that they had
... yes, they had foreseen it. When he had said to Marianna,
'Whatever I do, I tell you beforehand, nothing will come as
a surprise to you,' and again when he had talked of the two
men within him who could not live together, had not something stirred within her akin to a vague presentiment? Why
had she not stopped at once and pondered on those words, on
that presentiment? Why was it she did not dare now to look
at Solomin, as though he were her accomplice ... as though
he too were feeling a sting of conscience? Why was it she was
feeling, not only boundless, despairing pity for Nezhdanov,
but a sort of horror and dread and shame? Could it be, it had
rested with her to save him? Why was it they had neither dared
utter a word? Scarcely dared breathe – and waited ... for what?
Merciful God!

Solomin sent for a doctor, though of course there was no
hope. On the small wound, now black and bloodless, Tatyana
laid a large sponge of cold water; she moistened his hair too
with cold water and vinegar. All at once Nezhdanov ceased
gasping and stirred a little.

'He is coming to himself,' whispered Solomin.

Marianna was on her knees near the sofa. . . .

Nezhdanov glanced at her ... up till then his eyes had had
the fixed look of the dying.

'Oh, I'm ... still alive,' he articulated, scarcely audibly.
'Failed again ... I'm keeping you.'

'Alyosha!' moaned Marianna.

'Oh, yes ... directly. . . . You remember, Marianna, in my
... poem ... "With flowers then deck me ..." where are the
flowers? But you're here instead. . . . There, in my letter. . . .'

He suddenly shivered all over.

'Ah, here she is. . . . Give each other ... both ... your hands
– before me. . . . Quick . . . take . . .'

Solomin grasped Marianna's hand. Her head lay on the
sofa, face downwards, close to the wound.

Solomin stood stern and upright, looking dark as night.

'Yes . . . good . . . yes . . .'

Nezhdanov began to sob again, but in a strange, unusual way. . . . His breast rose, his sides heaved. . . .

He obviously was trying to lay his hand on their clasped hands, but his hands were dead already.

'He is passing,' murmured Tatyana, who stood in the doorway, and she began crossing herself.

The sobbing gasps grew briefer, fewer. . . . He still sought Marianna with his eyes . . . but a sort of menacing, glassy whiteness was overspreading them. . . .

'Good . . .' was his last word.

He was no more . . . and the linked hands of Solomin and Marianna still lay on his breast.

This was what he had written in the two short letters he left. One was addressed to Silin, and consisted of only a few lines:

'Good-bye, brother, friend, good-bye! By the time you get this scrap of paper, I shall be dead. Don't ask how and why, and don't grieve; believe that I'm better off now. Take our immortal Pushkin and read the description of the death of Lensky in *Yevgeny Onyegin*. Do you remember? – "The windows are white-washed; the mistress has gone. . . ." That's all. It's no good my talking to you . . . because I should have too much to say, and there's no time to say it. But I could not go away without telling you; or you would have thought of me as living still, and I should be wronging our friendship. Good-bye; live, Your friend. – A.N.'

The other letter was somewhat longer. It was addressed to Solomin and Marianna. This was what it contained: 'My children!' (Immediately after these words there was a break; something had been erased, or rather smudged over as though tears had fallen on it.) 'You will think it strange, perhaps, that I address you in this way. I am almost a child myself, and you, Solomin, are older of course than I am. But I am dying, and standing at the end of life I regard myself as an old man. I am much to blame to both of you, especially you, Marianna, for causing you such grief (I know, Marianna, you will grieve) and having given you so much anxiety. But what could I do? I could find no other way out of it. I could not *simplify myself*; the only thing left was to blot myself out altogether. Marianna, I should have been a burden to myself and to you. You are great-hearted, you would have rejoiced in the burden, as another sacrifice . . . but I had no right to take such a sacrifice from you; you have better and greater work to do. My children, let me unite you, as it were, from the grave. . . . You will be happy together. Marianna, you will infallibly come to love Solomin; as for him . . . he has loved you ever since he first set eyes on you at the Sipyagins'. That was no secret to me though we did run away together a few days after. Ah, that morning! How glorious it was, how sweet and young! It comes to me now as a token, as a symbol of your life together – yours and his – and I was merely by accident in his place that day. But it's time to make an end; I don't want to work on your feelings. . . . I only want to justify myself. To-morrow you will have some very sorrowful moments. . . . But there's no help for it! There's no other way, is there? Good-bye, Marianna, my good, true girl! Good-bye, Solomin! I leave her in your care. Live happily – live to the good of others; and you, Marianna, think of me only when you are happy. Think of me as a man who was true and good too, but one for whom it was somehow more fitting to die than to live. Whether I really loved you, I don't know, my dear; but I know that I have never felt a feeling stronger, and that it would have been more terrible to me to die without that feeling to carry with me to the grave.

'Marianna! if you ever meet a girl called Mashurina – Solomin knows her, I fancy – by the way, you have seen her too – tell her I thought of her with gratitude not long before my death. . . . She will understand.

'But I must tear myself away. I looked out of window just

now; among the rapidly moving clouds there was one lovely star. However rapidly they moved, they had not been able to hide it. That star made me think of you, Marianna. At this instant you are sleeping in the next room, and suspecting nothing. . . . I went to your door, listened, and I fancied I caught your pure, calm breathing. . . . Good-bye, good-bye, my dear! good-bye, my children, my friends! – Your A.

'Fie! fie! How came I, in a last letter before death, to say nothing of our great cause? I suppose because one can't tell lies on the point of death. . . . Marianna, forgive me this postscript. . . . The falsehood's in me, not in what you have faith in!

'Oh! something more: you will think, perhaps, Marianna, "He was afraid of the prison where they would certainly have put him, and he thought of *this* expedient to escape it." No; imprisonment's nothing of any consequence; but to be in prison for a cause you don't believe in – that's really senseless. And I am putting an end to myself, not from dread of being in prison. Good-bye, Marianna! Good-bye, my pure, spotless girl!'

Marianna and Solomin read this letter in turn. After that she put her portrait and the two letters in her pocket, and stood motionless.

Then Solomin said to her:

'Everything is ready, Marianna; let us go. We must carry out his wishes.'

Marianna approached Nezhdanov, touched his chill brow with her lips, and turning to Solomin said, 'Let us go.'

He took her by the hand, and together they went out of the room.

When a few hours later the police made a descent on the factory, they found of course Nezhdanov – but a corpse. Tatyana had laid the body out decorously, put a white pillow under his head, crossed his arms, and even put a nosegay of flowers on the little table beside him. Pavel, who was primed with all needful instructions, received the police-officers with the profoundest obsequiousness and a sort of derision, so that the latter hardly knew whether to thank him or to arrest him too. He described circumstantially how the suicide had taken place, and regaled them with Gruyère cheese and Madeira; but professed perfect ignorance of the whereabouts at the moment of Vassily Fedotitch and the lady who had been staying there, and confined himself to assuring them that Vassily Fedotitch was never away long, on account of his work; that he'd be back to-day, or else to-morrow, and he would then, without losing a minute, give notice of the fact. He was the man for that – accurate!

So the worthy police-officers went away with nothing, leaving a guard in charge of the body and promising to send the coroner.

XXXVIII

TWO DAYS AFTER all these events, there drove into the courtyard of the 'accommodating' priest Zosim a little cart in which sat a man and a woman, already well known to the reader, and the day after their arrival they were legally married. Soon afterwards they disappeared, and the worthy Zosim never regretted what he had done. At the factory Solomin had left a letter addressed to the owner and delivered to him by Pavel; in it was given a full and exact account of the state of the business (it was doing splendidly), and a request was made for three months' leave of absence. This letter had been written two days before Nezhdanov's death, from which it may be concluded that Solomin even then thought it necessary to go away with him and Marianna and keep out of sight for a time. Nothing was revealed by the inquiry held over the suicide. The body was buried; Sipyagin cut short all further search for his niece.

Nine months later Markelov was tried. At the trial he behaved himself just as he had done before the governor, with composure, a certain dignity, and some weariness. His habitual sharpness was softened, but not by cowardice; there was another, nobler feeling at work. He made no defence, expressed no regret, blamed no one and mentioned no names; his emaciated face with its lustreless eyes preserved one expression – submission to his fate, and firmness; his mild but direct and truthful answers awakened in his very judges a sentiment akin to sympathy. Even the peasants who had seized him and gave witness against him – even they shared this feeling, and spoke of him as a 'simple,' good-hearted gentleman. But his guilt was too apparent; he could not possibly escape punishment, and it seemed as though he himself accepted this punishment as his due. Of his fellow-conspirators, few enough, Mashurina kept out of sight; Ostrodumov was killed by a shopkeeper whom he was inciting to revolt, and who gave him an 'awkward' blow; Golushkin, in consideration of his 'heartfelt penitence' (he almost went out of his senses with alarm and agitation), received a light sentence; Kislyakov was kept a month under arrest and then set free, and even allowed to 'gallop' about the provinces unchecked; Nezhdanov was set free by death; Solomin, through lack of evidence, was left undisturbed though under suspicion. (He did not, however, avoid trial, and made his appearance when wanted.) Of Marianna nothing ever was said; and Paklin completely evaded all difficulties – indeed, no notice was taken of him at all.

A year and a half had gone by, the winter of 1870 had come. In Petersburg – Petersburg where the privy councillor and chamberlain Sipyagin was beginning to take an important position, where his wife patronised the arts, gave musical evenings, and founded soup-kitchens, and where Mr. Kallomyetsev was regarded as one of the most promising secretaries of his department – along one of the streets of Vassily Ostrov walked, hobbling and limping, a little man in a shabby overcoat with a catskin collar. It was Paklin. He had changed a good deal of late; a few silver threads could be seen among the long tufts of hair that stuck out below his fur cap. There chanced to be coming towards him along the pavement a rather stout, tall lady, closely muffled in a thick cloth cloak. Paklin cast an indifferent glance in her direction, passed her by . . . then suddenly stood still; thought a minute, flung up his arms and quickly turning and overtaking her, he looked up under her hat at her face.

'Mashurina?' he said in a low voice.

The lady scanned him majestically, and without uttering a word walked on.

'Dear Mashurina, I recognise you,' Paklin went on, hobbling along beside her, 'only don't you, please, be afraid. I wouldn't betray you, I am too delighted to have met you! I'm Paklin, Sila Paklin, you know, Nezhdanov's friend. . . . Come and see me; I live only a step or two away. Please do!'

'*Io sono contessa Rocca di Santo Fiume!*' the lady answered in a low voice, but in a wonderfully pure Russian accent.

'Come, nonsense! . . . a fine contessa! . . . Come and see me. Let us have a chat. . . .'

'But where do you live?' the Italian countess asked suddenly in Russian. 'I've no time to lose.'

'I live here, in this street – that's my house, the grey one there, with three storeys. How kind it is of you not to persist in trying to mystify me! Give me your hand, come along. Have you been here long? And how are you a countess? Have you married some Italian count?'

Mashurina had not married an Italian count. She had been provided with a passport made out in the name of a certain Countess Rocca di Santo Fiume, who had died not long before, and with this she had with the utmost composure returned to Russia, though she did not know a word of Italian and had the most Russian of faces.

Paklin conducted her to his humble lodgings. The hunchbacked sister with whom he was living came to meet the visitor from behind the screen that separated the tiny kitchen from the equally tiny passage.

'Here, Snapotchka,' he said, 'I commend to you a great friend of mine; give us some tea as quick as you can.'

Mashurina, who would not have gone to Paklin's if he had not mentioned Nezhdanov's name, took off her hat, and, passing her masculine hand over her still cropped hair, bowed and sat down in silence. She was altogether unchanged, she was even wearing the very same dress that she had worn two years before; but in her eyes there was a sort of immovable grief, which added something touching to the habitually stern expression of her face.

Snanduliya went for the samovar, while Paklin placed himself opposite Mashurina, lightly patted her on the knee, and hung down his head; but when he tried to speak, he was obliged to clear his throat; his voice broke and tears glistened in his eyes. Mashurina sat stiff and motionless, without leaning back, in her chair, and looked morosely away.

'Yes, yes,' began Paklin, 'those were times! Looking at you, I remember . . . many things, and many people, dead and living; my poll-parrots too are dead . . . but you didn't know them, I fancy; and both on the same day, as I foretold. Nezhdanov . . . poor Nezhdanov! . . . you know, of course . . . ?'

'Yes, I know,' said Mashurina, still looking away.

'And do you know about Ostrodumov, too?' Mashurina merely nodded. She wanted him to go on talking of Nezhdanov, but she could not bring herself to ask him about him. He understood her without that.

'I was told that in the letter he left he mentioned you – was that true?'

Mashurina could not answer at once.

'It is true,' she brought out at last.

'He was a marvellous fellow! Only, he got out of his right track! He was about as good a revolutionist as I was. Do you know what he really was? The idealist of realism! Do you understand me?'

Mashurina flung a rapid glance at Paklin. She did not understand, and indeed she did not care to take the trouble to understand him. It struck her as strange and unsuitable that he should dare to compare himself with Nezhdanov; but she thought, 'Let him brag now.' (Though he was not bragging at all, but rather, to his own ideas, humbling himself.)

'A fellow called Silin found me out here,' Paklin continued. 'Nezhdanov had written to him too just before his death. And he, this Silin, was inquiring whether one couldn't get hold of any of his papers. But Alyosha's things had been put under seal . . . and besides, there were no papers among them; he burned everything, he burned his poems too. You didn't know perhaps that he wrote poetry? I am so sorry about them; I am sure some of them must have been very good. All that has vanished with him, all lost in the common vortex, and dead for ever! Nothing's left but the memories of his friends till they pass away in their turn!'

Paklin paused.

'The Sipyagins,' he went on again: 'do you remember those condescending, dignified, loathsome swells? They're at the tip-top of power and glory by now!'

Mashurina did not 'remember' the Sipyagins in the least; but Paklin hated them both, especially Mr. Sipyagin, to such a degree that he could not deny himself the pleasure of 'pulling them to pieces.' 'They say there's such a high tone in their house! they're always talking about virtue! But I've observed, whenever there's too much talk about virtue, it's for all the world like too much smell of scent in a sickroom; you may be sure there's some hidden nastiness to conceal! It's a suspicious sign! Poor Alexey! they were the ruin of him, those Sipyagins!'

'How's Solomin doing?' asked Mashurina. She had suddenly ceased to feel any inclination to hear anything about *him* from this man.

'Solomin!' cried Paklin. 'That's a first-rate fellow. He has got on splendidly. He threw up his old factory and carried off the best workmen with him. There was one chap there . . . a regular firebrand, they say! Pavel was his name . . . he took him along with him. Now they say he has a factory of his own, a small one, somewhere out Perm way, on co-operative principles. He's a man that'll stick to what he's about! He'll carry anything through! He's a sharp fellow, ay, and a strong one too. He's first-rate! And the great thing is: he's not trying to cure all the social diseases all in a minute. For we Russians are a queer lot, you know, we expect everything; some one or something is to come along one day and cure us all at once, heal all our wounds, extract all our diseases like an aching tooth. Who or what this panacea is to be – why, Darwinism, the village commune, Arhip Perepentyev, a foreign war, anything you please! Only, we must have our teeth pulled out for us! It's all sluggishness, apathy, shallow thinking! But Solomin's not like that – no, he's not a quack doctor, he's first-rate!'

Mashurina waved her hand as though she would say, 'He may be dismissed, then.'

'Well, and that girl,' she inquired – 'I've forgotten her name – who ran away with him, with Nezhdanov?'

'Marianna? Oh, she's that same Solomin's wife now. It's more than a year since she was married to him. At first it was only formal, but now they say she really is his wife. Yes, yes.'

Marianna waved her hand again. Once she had been jealous of Marianna for Nezhdanov's sake; now she felt indignant with her for being capable of infidelity to his memory. 'I daresay there's a baby by now,' she commented contemptuously.

'Very likely, I don't know. But where are you off to?' Paklin added, seeing that she was taking up her hat. 'Stay a little, Snapotchka will give us some tea directly.' It was not so much that he wanted to keep Mashurina particularly, as that he could not let slip an opportunity of giving utterance to all that had accumulated and was seething in his breast. Since Paklin had returned to Petersburg, he had seen very few people, especially of the younger generation. The Nezhdanov affair had scared him; he had grown very cautious and avoided society, and the younger men on their side looked very suspiciously upon him. One young man had even abused him to his face as an informer. With the elder generation he did not much care himself to consort; so that it had sometimes been his lot to be silent for weeks together. He did not speak out freely before his sister – not that he supposed her to be incapable of understanding him, oh no! He had the highest opinion of her intellect. . . . But with her he would have had to talk seriously and perfectly truthfully; directly he fell into 'playing trumps,' as they say, she would begin gazing at him with a peculiar intent and compassionate look; and he was ashamed. And how is a man to get on without a little 'trumping,' just a low 'trump' occasionally! And so life in Petersburg had begun to be a weariness of the flesh to Paklin, and he even thought about moving elsewhere, to Moscow perhaps. Reflections of all sorts, speculations, fancies, epigrams, and sarcasms, were stored up within him, like water in a closed mill. . . . The floodgates could not be raised; the water had grown stagnant and stale. Mashurina had turned up . . . so he lifted the floodgates and talked and talked. . . . He fell upon Petersburg, Petersburg life, and all Russia. No one and nothing was spared. Mashurina took a very limited interest in all this, but she did not contradict or interrupt him . . . and that was all he wanted.

'Yes, indeed,' he said, 'these are nice little times, I can assure you! In society the stagnation's absolute; every one bored to perdition! In literature a vacuum clean swept! In criticism . . . if an advanced young reviewer has to say that "it's characteristic of the hen to lay eggs," it takes him twenty whole pages to expound this mighty truth, and even then he doesn't quite manage it! They're as soft, these fellows, let me tell you, as feather-beds, as greasy as cold stew, and foaming at the mouth they utter commonplaces! In science . . . ha! ha! ha! we've a renowned *Kant* of our own indeed, if it's only the *Kant*' (*i.e.* braiding) 'on our engineers' collars! In art it's just the same! If you care to go to the concert to-day, you will hear the national singer Agremantsky. . . . He is having an immense success.

'... And if a stuffed bream, a *stuffed bream*, I tell you, were possessed of a voice, it would sing precisely like that worthy! And Skoropihin even – you know our time-honoured Aristarchus – praises him! It's something, he declares, quite unlike Western art! He praises our miserable painters too! He used once to rave, he says, over Europe, over the Italians; but he has heard Rossini and thought "Pooh, pooh!" he has seen Raphael – "Pooh, pooh!" And that "pooh" is quite enough for our young men; they repeat "pooh" after Skoropihin, and they're contented if you please! And meanwhile the people's poverty is fearful, they are utterly crushed by taxes, and the only reform that's been accomplished is that all peasants have taken to caps while their wives have given up coifs. . . . And the famine! The drunkenness! The usurers!'

But at this point Mashurina yawned, and Paklin saw he must change the subject.

'You have not yet told me,' he said to her, 'where you have been these two years, and whether you have been here long, and what you have been doing and how you came to be transformed into an Italian, and why—'

'There's no need for you to know all that,' Mashurina interrupted; 'what's the use? That's not in your line now.'

Paklin felt a pang, and to hide his confusion he laughed a short, forced little laugh.

'Well, that's as you please,' he rejoined. 'I know I'm regarded as out-of-date by the present generation; and to be sure, I can't reckon myself . . . among the ranks of those who . . .' He did not complete his sentence. 'Here is Snapotchka bringing us some tea. You must take a cup, and listen to me. . . . Perhaps in my words you may find something of interest to you.'

Mashurina took a cup and a small lump of sugar, and began to sip the tea and nibble at the sugar.

Paklin's laugh was genuine this time.

'It's as well there are no police here, or the Italian Countess . . . what is it?'

'Rocca di Santo Fiume,' said Mashurina, with imperturbable gravity, as she imbibed the scalding liquid.

'Rocca di Santo Fiume!' repeated Paklin, 'and she sips her tea through the sugar! That's too unlikely! The police would be on the alert in a minute.'

'Yes,' observed Mashurina, 'a fellow in uniform bothered me abroad; he kept asking me questions; I couldn't stand it at last. "Let me alone, do, for mercy's sake!" I said.'

'Did you say that in Italian?'

'No, in Russian.'

'And what did he do?'

'He? Why, walked off, to be sure.'

'Bravo!' cried Paklin. 'Hurrah for the Contessa! Another cup, do! Well, what I wanted to say to you was, you spoke rather coolly of Solomin. But do you know what I can assure you? Fellows like him – they are the real men. One doesn't understand them at first, but they're the real men, take my word for it; and the future's in their hands. They're not heroes; not even "the heroes of labour," about whom some queer fish – an American or an Englishman – wrote a book for the edification of us poor wretches; they're sturdy, rough, dull men of the people. But they're what's wanted now! Just look at Solomin; his brain's clear as daylight, and he's as healthy as a fish. . . . Isn't that a wonder! Why, hitherto with us in Russia it's always been the way that if you're a live man with feelings and a conscience, you're bound to be an invalid! But Solomin's heart, I daresay, aches at what makes ours ache, and he hates what we hate – but his nerves are calm, and his whole body responds as it ought . . . so that he's a splendid fellow! Yes, indeed, a man with an ideal, and no nonsense about him; educated – and from the people; simple – and a little shrewd. . . . What more do you want . . .?

'And never you mind,' pursued Paklin, working himself up more and more, and not noticing that Mashurina had long ceased to attend, and was once more gazing away into the distance; 'never mind if there are swarms of all sorts in Russia: Slavophils and officials and generals, plain and decorated, and Epicureans and imitators and queer fish of all sorts. (I used to know a lady called Havronya Prishtehov, who suddenly without rhyme or reason turned legitimist, and assured every one that when she died they need only open her body and they would find the name of Henri v. engraved in her heart . . . on the heart of Havronya Prishtehov!) Never mind all that, my dear madam, but let me tell you our only true way lies with the Solomins, coarse, plain, shrewd Solomins! Recollect *when* I am saying this to you, in the winter of 1870, when Germany is making ready to crush France – when—'

'Silushka,' Snanduliya's soft little voice was heard saying behind Paklin's back, 'I think in your speculations on the future you forget our religion and its influence. . . . And besides,' she added hurriedly, 'Madame Mashurina is not listening to you. . . . You had better offer her another cup of tea.'

Paklin pulled himself together.

'Ah, yes, dear lady – won't you really?'

But Mashurina stared, turned her gloomy eyes upon him, and said absently, 'I wanted to ask you, Paklin, haven't you any notes of Nezhdanov's or his photograph?'

'I have a photograph . . . yes; and I fancy rather a good one, in the table. I'll find it for you directly.'

He began rummaging in the drawer, while Snanduliya went up to Mashurina, and with a long, intent look of sympathy she clasped her hand like a comrade.

'Here it is! I have found it!' cried Paklin, and he gave her the photograph. Mashurina, with hardly a glance at it, and without a word of thanks, crimsoning all over, thrust it quickly into her pocket, put on her hat, and was making for the door.

'Are you going?' said Paklin. 'Tell us, at least, where you live?'

'As it happens.'

'I understand, you don't wish me to know, then! Well, tell

me, please, one thing any way: are you still working under the orders of Vassily Nikolaevitch?'

'What is that to you?'

'Or perhaps of some other – Sidor Sidoritch?'

Mashurina made no answer.

'Or does some one anonymous direct you?'

Mashurina was already across the threshold.

'Perhaps it is some one anonymous!'

She slammed the door behind her.

A long while Paklin remained standing before this closed door.

'Anonymous Russia!' he said at last.